*"I would like to ded[icate this book]
to my husband, Ken, th[e love of my life,]
and to my loving [fa]mily"*

Thanks also to my editor, Roy Robins, without whom I would not have been able to complete my novels.

A resounding Thank You to Toby Meyer for providing such stunning artwork for the covers of both of my books, and for being the first friend to read my novels and love them!

Sincere thanks to Nigel Dickson, who assisted me in uploading my novels to Amazon and with the design of the books.
His computer-savvy, knowledge, and patience were invaluable.

And finally, a heartfelt Thank You to my readers, each and every one of you. If one of the places or spaces described in my novel feels very different, or even at odds with, your personal experience of it, feel free to preserve your own experience of that place or space.

This novel is just that, a novel. Names, characters, business, events, and incidents are the products of my imagination.
Any resemblance to actual persons, living or dead, or actual events, is purely coincidental.

Copyright © 2023 Yvonne Spektor
Cover designs © 2023 Toby Meyer
Picture credits; Dreamstime, Shutterstock, Images by StockSnap from Pixabay, T.Schmidt and Toby Mayer
All rights reserved. Used with permission.

No part of this book may be reproduced or used in any manner without the prior written permission of the copyright owner, except for the use of brief quotations in a book review.

ISBN 978-1-7392966-0-5

Part 1

Introduction

Saffron Asher-James sat staring out of the window, pressed her intercom and spoke with her secretary. 'Can you organise a pot of tea for two, Lisa,' Safi said. 'Make sure I am not disturbed for the next few hours. And show Polly into my study as soon as she arrives. I will let you know when I want the car brought round to drive us back to the city.'

Sipping her favourite herbal tea, with a slight ache in her heart, Safi let go and thought once again of the past.

The past – how could she escape it? After all, it was hers just as much as this study, this window, this chair. And all the pain and joy and doubt and dread, that belonged to her, too. And yet she had tried – and failed – to escape the past for so long, and at such cost.

Polly being Polly had been characteristically persuasive; Safi had agreed to an in-depth article on her life to be written for one of the top glossy magazines. Dredging up those memories would hopefully be easier with an old acquaintance.

Polly arrived with her usual fanfare. Age had not dampened her eccentric style or her enthusiasm for a good story. Her normally coiffed hair, now silver-grey, was worn short and stylish. Her choice of dress had always been classical, but she knew how to accessorise to make any piece of clothing look expensive.

'My only sacrifice to age is comfortable shoes,' she had told Safi once. 'I no longer do heels; lucky for me my posture is good.'

Polly took out her recorder and set it on the table between them. 'Should we begin?'

Safi could still feel the thrill of that first flight into the unknown. Back then, she had craved excitement and adventure, a journey of self-discovery – well, she had certainly got more than she had bargained for.

Leaning back in her chair, cradling the warm cup in her hands, her thoughts travelled back to a younger Saffron, trusting and hungry for life. Her mind journeyed to foreign lands, each with its own strange set of rules, and to intrigue and betrayal way beyond her understanding. Indeed, she was still trying to explain her past to herself – perhaps this interview would help to set things straight: not only for Polly's readers, but for Safi herself as well.

Chapter 1

Jittery with nerves but madly excited, Safi boarded the plane that would take her away from a safe and comfortable life to one of the most exhilarating cities in the world. When she turned eighteen, Safi's father, Leonard, finally succumbed to her powers of persuasion, allowing her to defer a year of study. Fiona, her mum, insisted Safi stay with a relative until she found her feet. The most exciting part was Leonard's news: he had secured a temporary position for her with a Manhattan advertising agency for a year's work experience. The agency in question had on occasion worked with Leonard's agency on English accounts.

Safi's heart flip-flopped with fear and excitement as she sat back trying to enjoy the flight. She was familiar with advertising agencies, having spent many school breaks working at her father's one in Brighton. If all worked out with the job, she would be thrown in at the deep end to fend for herself. She suspected her parents hoped that such an experience would bring her running back home with her tail between her legs – well, she wasn't about to let that happen.

In the year leading up to her departure, Safi had determined not to allow her hopes and desires to disappear into thin air. Her Brighton friends had given her hunger for travel and adventure short shrift; her ideas were too radical for their tastes. Safi did not share their desire for a county lifestyle of horses, charity work, and domesticity. She kept her journal hidden from prying eyes.

On turning seventeen, her first major challenge had been to convince her parents to support her wish to live and work in a foreign country. Persuading them had not been easy. They were proud of her academic achievements; obtaining a place at Oxbridge, a pucker red brick university, was their idea of reaching the top of the educational pile, but Safi deferred reading English Literature for a year. Her parents were distraught, with her father convinced that she would never return to study.

Saying goodbye to her friends was hellishly difficult; more than she'd imagined. They had all formed a close bond over the years going through school. Not wanting to experience life away from home as an extended holiday, or to throw herself into extended study, the only alternative was time away from home on her own.

She was searching for something elusive, she could feel it in her gut. Whatever it was that she was searching for would surely find her. The excitement building up inside her was palpable. On opening her eyes after take-off, she had doubts: was she mad to do this on her own?

On arriving at JFK International Airport Safi felt exhilarated. The Big Apple was waiting to be explored. The taxi driver seemed to recognise the address in the lower East Side where she was staying with Daniel Asher, the cousin she had not yet met. Sitting in the cab Safi felt every bone in her body alive and alert. The traffic was lighter than she expected and the iconic yellow cab seemed to travel at an incredible speed on the Expressway. She opened her window slightly to feel and smell the New York air.

As they entered Manhattan, she became aware of the frenetic pace. The discordant noise was something she was going to have to get used to: honking horns, endless traffic jams, potholes the cab kept thumping over, and sirens from enormous red fire engines screaming past. Everyone appeared to be oblivious to the frenetic discordant cacophony around them, sipping their lattes at sidewalk cafés or speaking on their cell phones as they raced along the sidewalks.

The cab driver accelerated from intersection to intersection, eventually dropping her off in front of a building hemmed in on all sides by shops, coffee bars, grocery stores, flower sellers, restaurants, even laundromats. Safi found it all incredibly urban compared to Hove, a suburban area of Brighton, where she had spent all of her life. Making her own way from the airport, landing in the midst of this urban hustle and bustle, her head spun with excitement – she had arrived at last!

Her head promptly stopped spinning when she found that she had to drag her bags up five flights of stairs to her cousin's apartment's very top floor. Gasping for breath, she found a key hidden under a mat decorated with the face of a Bulldog, and let herself in. On entering, all Safi could do was gape. Canvasses were leaning on every wall, and covering a huge wooden refectory table off to the side of a vast space were tins of paint in every conceivable colour. Lining the walls were shelves stacked with tin cans filled with brushes and bottles of what appeared to be turpentine.

Just as Safi was about to investigate the apartment, she realised she was not alone. Observing her every move, the largest English Bulldog she had ever seen sat lazing on one of the sofas, which was part of the same cavernous expanse that seemed to go on forever. The Bulldog wore a black leather collar with studs and a stars-and-stripes scarf attached. Safi loved dogs, so having him around was going to be just fine.

The loft had a high-gloss, black open-planned kitchen: a stainless-steel island ran the length of the tall units, softened only by six upholstered high-backed chairs in natural linen, and opening onto what appeared to be living room, artist studio, and banks of windows. There were scattered shabby cowhide sofas, armchairs, an overflowing floor-to-ceiling bookcase, and more books lying in piles just about everywhere.

On investigating further, she found a large room off a passageway that seemed to mostly consist of a bed with an open-plan bathtub sitting in a bay window. The smaller room tucked away at the end of the corridor was more traditional, with shower-room attached. Safi lugged her bags in here, hoping it was the guest room meant for her.

A few minutes later and a mug of tea in hand, feeling a little more familiar with her surroundings, she allowed herself to look with a more critical eye. The loft had magnificent views of Manhattan. Opening one of the windows she found it led onto a roof terrace; climbing the few steps to the terrace she found an oasis of calm. Fully grown trees and lush plants in huge ceramic tubs bordered comfortable outdoor garden furniture that was shaded by a giant canvas umbrella and a hammock to lounge in. Safi felt overwhelmed. She could not wait to meet this cousin who had been kind enough to have her stay until she found her feet. She felt vindicated, staying in this unbelievable space owned by the artist cousin who on reflection could not be considered boring; her parents might have unwittingly done her a huge favour.

Back indoors, much too inquisitive not to peek behind the sheets covering the tall canvasses of various sizes, she found to her amazement paintings of voluptuous naked women in different poses. In each painting, sometimes half-hidden, a Bulldog lolled amongst the Rubenesque women posing for the artist who she presumed was her cousin. The models were all incredibly beautiful, with tattoos of animals or roses visible on parts of their body. Apart from the Bulldog, some of the women posed with exotic birds; once or twice Pugs were featured.

The bodies of the models appeared to glisten. Safi had to touch the surface of the canvas to make sure they were actually paintings and not photographs. The subject had a sophisticated air rather than a tacky one; Safi decided that this modern twist on the vast and richly painted baroque paintings were incredibly intriguing. Pulling off one of the covers, she sat back on the sofa with the dog to admire the work from a distance. She could not decide why they did not appear to be tacky; after all, she was sure most people would find them semi-pornographic.

Safi lay back and squinted at the languishing, voluptuous model staring directly at her out of the painting with an intense yet carefree expression. The model leaned over a bowl of apples, her outstretched hand rested on the Bulldog's head, a leopard was tattooed on her shoulder. Safi realised that it was the model's insouciance and completely relaxed pose that made the whole unrealistic scene look so natural. How did her cousin manage that? The effect was quite fantastic. He might even be a genius – no, she was being ridiculous … still, the thought of the next few days made her burn with anticipation. She could not wait to meet the artist, wishing he would arrive back soon. Perhaps she would get a taste of his life, which she hoped would be as fabulous as art.

Hearing the muffled hum of her cell phone, Safi scrambled in her travel bag. She expected it to be her parents, but found a message from her cousin instead. She had to read it several times to make sure she had not imagined what he had written. First of all, he signed off 'Dax.' She felt sure her folks had referred to him as Daniel.

Anyhow, the note informed her that Dax was not returning immediately as planned: he was Upstate on business, and was leaving Safi in charge of Bruno, who had to have at least one long walk a day. The doggie park was five minutes away. Bruno loved the terrace and had his patch up there. The rest Dax left to Safi to discover for herself. If she needed anything, Pete in the bar below would help.

Staring at Bruno for a few moments, she tried to ignore a growing feeling of anxiety. This was no time to start panicking, she was going to have to throw herself out there, it's what she had challenged herself to do – and now she had absolutely no excuse.

'Well, Bruno, baby,' Safi said, 'it's you and me for a while until your daddy decides to come home. I guess you need a lead, so let's go find one. I'm starving. Pete will have to be our friend for the time being.'

The dog seemed to understand every word, got off the couch, stretched his Victorian forelegs and then the back ones, and loped off to the front door, waiting for Safi to catch up. Grabbing her rucksack and Bruno's lead from a hook at the front door, she suddenly remembered the key. She charged back, leaving Bruno at the open door.

The door had shut when Safi returned. Bruno was almost on the third landing by the time she, totally out of breath, caught up with him, managing to put the lead onto his spiked collar; but Bruno was far too strong. Deciding that Bruno was definitely the boss if their relationship was going to work, she allowed him to take the lead, meekly following as he pulled her into Pete's Bar, where he was greeted like a long-lost pal, by, she presumed, Pete the barman.

Pete was a lovely, craggy-faced African American who Safi immediately warmed to. He indicated she take a seat at the bar, gave Bruno his bowl of treats and informed Safi that he was happy to be of help any time. He enquired whether she was hungry and kindly gave her the bar menu and told her to order anything she fancied. He recommended the house special and his best raspberry smoothie.

While waiting for her burger, Safi confided in Pete about not knowing a soul in Manhattan and how excited she was about exploring the city. Pete listened while serving other clients. When Safi's meal arrived he stood at a distance watching her, from time to time making little understanding noises while talking to Bruno; the noises put Safi at ease and she knew she would be spending a lot of time down here with Pete, her first friend in New York City!

Safi had lived in the apartment for almost two weeks with the Rubenesque ladies and Bruno the Victorian Bulldog; they were all very happy together. The canvasses were now all uncovered, giving Safi a wonderful warm feeling when waking in the mornings. She loved being surrounded by these wonderfully rounded womanly figures; she never felt lonely at all. Bruno was a pleasure to look after and had taken to sleeping with her at night.

Pete the Barman had suggested some great places for a newcomer in NYC to visit, and Safi followed his instructions to a tee. Her favourite haunts quickly became art galleries and museums; she loved the MOMA. Initially intimidated by the crowds of people she encountered wherever she went, she soon found herself speaking to anyone who looked interesting standing in line, waiting to enter wherever she happened to find herself on any particular day.

It was coming up to her second week in NYC and still she had not heard from Dax or knew when he would return. Safi had spoken with her folks in England, who were quite happy with her situation, telling her to take advantage of her free time to do as much sightseeing as she could before starting her job at the agency, which was another four weeks away, hoping Dax would return before then, wondering who would care for Bruno while she was away at work.

Safi returned with Bruno from their morning coffee and croissant at Pete's after their early morning stroll to the doggie park, where Bruno met his doggie pals every day and Safi quite a few of the owners. Sandy the Pug and Bruno were firm friends, and Safi was not averse to Sandy's walker, a very cool guy who Safi had learnt was a part-time law student at Columbia.

Unlike most law students she knew, Niles was interested in the arts. Safi found it easy to talk with him and looked forward to their meetings, making sure she and Bruno were at the doggie park more or less at the same time as Sandy and Niles. Safi hoped that Niles would ask her out but so far to her disappointment nothing had happened.

On returning to the apartment that morning, after their coffee and walk, Safi sensed that Bruno was restless. He raced to the top, snorting and panting. Reaching the door, he yelped to be let in. Lying in the middle of the entrance hall floor were piles of magazines and papers, a leather rucksack with a silk chemise scarf tied to the handle. Bruno had disappeared inside so Safi shyly shouted, 'Hello! Is anyone here?'

The main bedroom door was closed, but Safi could hear voices out on the roof terrace so she made her way up. As she reached the roof terrace what greeted her was not one person but several, and they were all deeply in animated conversation. Safi heard snippets of their conversation as she passed through the terrace door on her way up. She stood for what seemed ages, observing everyone, although it must have been only moments before they became aware of her. Bruno was happily sleeping in his special place under the hammock. Conversation stopped mid-sentence when they noticed her. Safi felt all eyes riveted in her direction. She had no idea which of the five men out on the terrace was her cousin, having looked at all the framed photos she still had not decided who Dax was.

A tall, immaculately dressed, attractive man came towards her and took both of her hands in his. He looked Safi up and down and gave a low whistle, saying, 'My, my, my, you are absolutely gorgeous! I am Daniel, your cousin. Welcome, Safi, and thank you so much for taking care of Bruno. Are you okay?'

Safi nodded shyly, suddenly feeling extremely out of place. Daniel took her hand and gently pulled her into the group sitting around on the terrace furniture. He introduced her to Dax, who Safi immediately recognised from the photos around the apartment.

'Dax is my partner,' Dan said softly but proudly. 'And he is the artist.'

Eager to find out what Safi thought of his work, he pulled her closer as she sat down next to him. Dax was taken with her right off, but did not want to overpower her with his extrovert personality, or too many questions, but as always, he just couldn't help himself. Safi had been living with his Rubenesque ladies, after all, and he just had to know what she thought of them.

Safi couldn't help noticing Dax's excitable, drawn-out vowels, and the way he sort of mashed his words together. By comparison, Daniel's accent seemed less pronounced and softer in tone. Later she learnt that Dax had grown up on Long Island, while Daniel was born and bred in Manhattan.

'We noticed that you have been living with the ladies,' Dax said. 'You removed the sheets. What did you think of them?'

Suddenly finding her voice, Safi told Dax the paintings were 'genius, I love them.'

This seemed to please everyone in the group. They sat Safi down and told her the canvasses were for Rubicov, a new Russian restaurant opening up in the Meatpacking District. Safi learnt that Daniel was an architect and designer and was responsible for the interior of Rubicov. Restaurants and hotels were his speciality. The friends on the terrace were all connected to Daniel's team. They fired questions at Safi about how she liked Manhattan.

'I did the usual touristy things,' Safi replied, mentioning Pete the barman having been a godsend who had made her feel secure right off.

Pleased to hear this, Daniel told Safi she was welcome to stay as long as she wished. Drawn to Safi's understated English charm, Dax took charge fussing about her hair and 'fresh-faced appearance' (as he called it), which she realised meant trainers, T-shirt, the skinny jeans she lived in, and the fact that she wore no makeup. He wanted to know whether this was her 'look.' Everyone, including Safi, laughed. Not having anything as definitive as a 'look,' she realised given half the chance Dax would be turning her into a Manhattan girl, for sure, looks-wise anyhow.

That morning, Dax joined Safi for Bruno's walk. Over breakfast at Pete's, Dax wanted to know about almost everything, making her realise she had fallen into a wonderful warm caring family of gorgeous gay guys she already absolutely adored.

Dax informed Safi that they were going to include her as a guest for the Rubicov opening party. Agreeing to Dax being in charge of her makeover for the event, she got ready for her shopping experience. She had not yet ventured into any of the boutiques or department stores; not knowing the ropes or having money, she thought anything amazing would cost more than she could afford. This information did not seem to faze Dax one iota. They walked the short distance to where he stored his Harley for use around the city; giving Safi a helmet, they sped off weaving through the traffic.

On entering Barneys, they were met by a beautifully groomed assistant who welcomed Safi like a long lost friend, whisking her off to various departments. Lauren was a buyer and personal shopper for VIPs; Dax had arranged for them to spend time together while he went off to do some business in the store. Lauren took Safi to look at various lines, introducing her to the latest designers who mattered in NYC.

Safi tried to take it all in but felt totally out of her depth. Everyone seemed so incredibly sophisticated, it all seemed to come so naturally to them. She began to doubt herself for the first time, feeling very dowdy and quite out of touch. Living in Brighton was not exactly the end of the world, but her friends, although fashion conscious, were more into the music scene than the fashion one. Dax had gone through Safi's wardrobe – what there was of it, at least – and had advised her to invest in some dresses, high heel pumps, and at least one fashionable purse, as they seemed to call handbags in the US. He had advised Safi to be more prepared than she was for work and also told her not to worry about money, they would sort it out, finding plenty for her to do to make up for any dollars spent on the clothing.

Over lunch, Lauren helped Safi understand that forging her own style was important. It would set her apart and give her confidence in her new environment, which, in turn, would help her fit into the Manhattan social scene. Safi's accent was superb, Lauren said, and she was obviously a hugely attractive girl, hiding the potential to be stunning. Lauren told Safi that her height was perfect; she was tall enough to look leggy in flats, but not too tall for Louboutins.

Louboutins! How on earth was Safi going to afford designer anything? Indeed, Safi had never before considered that she was old enough to worry herself about any of this stuff. Sensing Safi's discomfort, noticing her wonderful natural sparkle disappear, Lauren changed the subject, which allowed Safi to indulge in her favourite topic of the moment, Pete the barman, who she thought the most incredible person she had met so far, and Niles from the dog park, who she had completely fallen for, but who, apart from chatting about the arts, had not taken notice of her in any way that mattered, which Safi found disheartening.

Having to return to work, Lauren excused herself, but not before giving Dax a knowing look and leaving Safi with her business card, telling her that she would be more than happy to shop with her. Dax did not want to encourage Safi's relationship with Niles, who he considered to be a sexual chameleon. No one really got to know his preferences; he liked to throw his net out far and wide.

Chapter 2

Sunday brunch was a huge thing in Manhattan, and the two D's (as Safi now referred to them) took her for brunch. They sat out on the sidewalk, with Bruno neatly tucked under the table. Daniel and Dax introduced Safi to more people than she had met since her arrival in New York. She was getting used to the two D's way of life and loved the Village vibe, the informality and conviviality, the way people just spoke to you, no introductions necessary. So much less formal than back home in England, but not too familiar either; people just loved to chat freely to each other.

After brunch, Daniel, who Safi had hardly seen the whole week, invited Safi to his offices to see where he worked. She was completely blown away; it was a hive of creativity but also extremely organised, just like Daniel himself, who seemed to be all business, explaining what his staff did on a daily basis: keeping in touch with manufacturers in the interior business. It was also important to wine and dine everyone in the trade, he said. They had people who fired up contacts, and those who did the legwork, and others who worked on finding new materials. Safi having worked for her father in the ad agency understood the professionalism of Daniel's work; he ran his design company not unlike her father did his. She found that unlike Dax, Daniel was very intense and loved every angle of his profession, which kept him totally involved most of the time.

He sat Safi down. 'We should talk.'

His voice was unusually stern and she wondered whether she had done something to upset him, but Daniel softened and told Safi that his father and Safi's dad were first cousins. Although Daniel had never met Safi's dad, he knew that Leonard had been a very important person in his father's life, as they had grown up together in England. Daniel felt Safi was going to be his responsibility while she lived in Manhattan; he wanted her to feel completely safe and free to speak to him about anything that worried her. He realised that he was often away, but he hoped that he and Dax – who he loved more than life itself – could become Safi's second family.

'Now tell me what you thought of your trip to Barneys, where you met the wonderfully talented Lauren. You know, she dresses many celebrities, she has impeccable taste, and you would be in very safe hands with her. She helps everyone find his or her own style. You are almost twenty. Dax and I wondered, since you are starting work in a few weeks, it may help you fit right in at the agency if, with the help of Lauren's guidance, you present yourself indelibly. What do you think?'

Overwhelmed once again by their caring attitude, she felt it would be rude to decline their suggestions but worried about cost, knowing her father had told her that she was totally on her own regarding money. Safi decided to confide her concerns to Daniel and told him that her father was not bankrolling her on this adventure, she was totally on her own, apart from their help, so far.

Daniel seemed to absorb everything she said. 'Safi,' he began, 'I respect your father's sentiments about you fending for yourself, but you would do Dax and I a great honour if you would agree to accept our offer of help until you find your feet. With respect, I don't believe your dad realises New York life is very different from living in Brighton – which I am sure is fabulous, especially living near the water – but here image is important. It gives you confidence and it helps others understand, in a way, who they are dealing with. I know you are only just discovering who you are and who you want to be, but believe me when I tell you that finding your style is just as important as embarking on this adventure to find out what you want to be, right?'

She had to smile: Daniel was so intuitive and persuasive; no wonder everyone loved him and respected his advice. Besides, it was sort of cool learning this kind of stuff, especially from her cousin and his partner. Her first lesson in finding out who she wanted to be. Independence was important, but this kind of help she would never have imagined she needed, and accepting it had value.

She agreed with Daniel, but made him promise to allow her to work off the debt she owed to him and Dax. They did a high-five and Safi left Daniel at the office to do some last-moment tweaking for the opening of Rubicov, which Safi was now looking forward to.

She took herself off to a small coffee shop, opened her journal and started to pen down her feelings. Her feelings were so intense – she needed to get them down and out of her system. Safi felt she was losing her strong desire to find her own way, pragmatically she felt incredibly grateful to Daniel and Dax, yet at the same time, wondered whether their kindness would smother her strong need for independence, they were the safety net she was trying to avoid.

She sat with the pen poised just about to jot her answers down to her dilemma, when she heard a familiar voice saying hello. Safi slammed the journal shut and jumped up, dropping her journal on the pavement. As she bent down to pick it up, Niles and Safi bumped heads. Both laughing and rubbing their bruised foreheads, they started again. Niles took the empty seat at Safi's outdoor table and enquired about the journal she was so busy scribbling in. Safi explained that she was not an artist doing sketches. The journal was her therapy; it was helping her clear her mind of confused thoughts. Niles smiled, patted the journal, and told Safi journalling was a wise thing to do, as it was far cheaper than seeing a therapist, which most New Yorkers did at some stage.

Niles remained chatting for over an hour when he suddenly received a call. With a light peck on Safi's cheek, he said goodbye and was gone, leaving her flustered, feeling even more confused and low. She decided to continue penning her feelings; it was her only salvation. Two hours in and at least a dozen coffees later, she decided it was time to return to the apartment with a renewed sense of self.

Daniel remained at the office late into the night, doing his usual last-moment preparation for the latest opening of another prestigious restaurant in Manhattan. The team had successfully turned around a number of restaurants, hotels, and high-end clubs. Daniel enjoyed the variety. His team were becoming well-known; they had more work than they could handle, which was a blessing after all the hard work he and Dax had put in over the years, building up a successful architectural design company.

While happy with the end result for the restaurant, club, and apartments they had worked on for Rubicov, Dan found that the long hours away from Dax were taking its toll on them both. The two D's had been a successful team for five years, working on many projects together. They had met when studying at Cooper Union, and had now been a couple for ten years. Dax wanted them to seal their union with marriage. Daniel, on the other hand, opted for the traditional view of marriage as a contract between a man and a woman; although not religious, he valued conservative traditions. He agreed that a union would make their legal ramifications less complicated and that their life would be more secure if anything had to happen to either of them.

Daniel would, without hesitation, leave everything he owned to Dax. But Dax was less traditional: he wanted their love to be sealed with a religious union. Furthermore, Dax had also mentioned children, which scared the hell out of Daniel. They had many friends who had gone down the marriage route, after which they had either adopted or had surrogate babies. But Daniel wasn't remotely ready for such a life-changing decision.

Like his father, Rupert Asher, Daniel's mother had been of the Jewish faith. Neither of his parents had strong feelings about religion; his conservative opinions were entirely his own.

He hoped that Safi would be the distraction both he and Dax needed to give him breathing space, putting off discussing marriage for the foreseeable future. He would encourage Safi to become part of their lives. Dax had taken a shine to Safi and he hoped she would be a distraction, helping to bridge the gulf growing between them until he was ready to deal with the marriage issue that he knew would not go away for ever.

Dan was pinning his hopes on Safi in more ways than one. He had come to see her as a means to tackle a heart-breaking problem he found impossible to resolve. He realised he was grasping at straws, but he believed Safi could help moderate and soften Rupert's feelings of betrayal and his inflexible attitude to having a gay son.

Connecting with family, who Rupert had also become estranged from over the years, might be what Rupert needed more than he would ever admit. Dan's mother had died from cervical cancer in her early forties, which left his father traumatised and ill-equipped to bring up his only child on his own. Rupert, previously a charismatic, gregarious person, became neurotic and overprotective of Daniel, never allowing him the space to spread his wings.

When Daniel met Dax at college, his inhibited, conservative attitudes to being gay were challenged. Dax encouraged Daniel to come out, which had been life-changing for Daniel. He grew to value Dax and his family's relaxed liberal attitude to life, but it had irrevocably damaged his close relationship with his own father.

Rupert had spent his childhood in England. He and Safi's father, Leonard, were first cousins and had grown up together. Rupert's parents' decision to immigrate to the States when Rupert was a teenager put an end to the cousins' close friendship.

Rupert and Leonard's grandparents had built up a textile empire. Daniel's grandfather expanded that empire stateside, successfully branching out into other areas. When Daniel's mother passed away, Rupert felt it was best to sell his shares in the empire. Rupert lavished his love and attention on Daniel, and depended on his son to provide him with the family he never had. When Daniel revealed his sexual preference when coming out with Dax as his partner, Rupert could not accept his son's chosen lifestyle and rejected him out of hand. Daniel was as good as dead. Rupert refused all attempts at reconciliation throughout Daniel's ten years with Dax.

Leonard had always been his own man and had gone into advertising, the family textile empire her great grandfather and grandfather had built ended after her grandfather died. Safi's arrival in New York had rekindled memories long dormant for Daniel. The family connection jarred his emotions bringing into sharp focus his estranged relationship with his father. Ignorant of the important link she represented to lost family, Safi's connections now offered new opportunities to help re-ignite those familial emotions, Daniel hoped with Safi's help, in Rupert.

Rupert had not yet met Safi, and Daniel was hoping once she had settled down he could encourage a meeting between them. Daniel held onto the belief that family ties would help ignite all the old memories and soften his father's impasse, allowing him the opportunity to face his stubbornness without losing face, rekindle a bond between them and allow their rift to heal. Daniel needed his father's approval and his father needed his son's love; if Safi gave them an opening to re-establish contact it would fill the hole that was blocking so much in his otherwise successful life.

The office allowed him the space to think about his unresolved problematic issues, engineering a meeting between Safi and Rupert was grasping at straws, but all other attempts had failed. Maybe the time was right – after all, Rupert wasn't getting any younger, growing old alone couldn't be much fun.

Back at the apartment, Safi decided to pluck up courage, calling the number on Lauren's card, hoping that she would have the time to help her choose an outfit for Friday's opening of Rubicov. She also wanted to put her best foot forward at the advertising agency when she started. But above all she had an ulterior motive: Niles!

Somehow she was going to get him to notice that she was not the innocent little English rose he seemed to imagine she was. Safi found Dax at home with Bruno, both relaxing on the roof terrace, watching dusk transforming the New York City skyline into a glamorous backdrop of sparkling lights. Dax, drink in hand, with Bruno noisily munching a bone under the hammock (his favourite spot), patted the seat, inviting Safi to join him. He poured her a tall glass of Chardonnay. After clinking glasses, Dax enquired what she had in mind for her last few weeks of freedom, and how she felt about starting at the advertising agency.

Enjoying the cold bubbles as they trickled down her throat, Safi sat in thought for some time. She appreciated his genuine interest but felt her British reserve creeping up on her. She felt suddenly shy and, not sure how much she really wanted to share, smiled anxiously

'Oh,' she replied, 'you know, nervous but also excited.'

Dax already adored Safi but he did not want to push her to trust him, he wanted her to be able to do so when it suited her. So he changed tact and enquired whether she had given any more thought to contacting Lauren. She laughed, knowing how keen he was for Lauren to style her.

'I have just messaged her and was hoping she would have time next week to help me out,' Safi said. Just then her cell pinged and she gave it to Dax to see.

'Wow! She means business,' Dax said. 'You are really lucky, Safi. Lauren is going to take you with her to visit some young designers and I am sure you will find what you like.'

Safi tried to be casual but she was feeling incredibly excited about meeting Lauren, going to the designer workshops was just down her street: she much preferred to have clothes that were individual rather than off-the-rack, if she was going to find her style.

'I meet her first thing Monday morning at the Meatpacking District for an early breakfast,. Thank you, I really do appreciate everything you have done for me.'

Before Dax could reply, Daniel had joined them and Bruno was doing his usual excitable snorting and grunting at seeing his master. Shortly, both Dax and Daniel retired for the night, leaving Safi to watch the glamorous sparkling Manhattan skyline, with time to collect her thoughts.

Bruno had gone down with the two D's and Safi had lost her sleeping partner. It was time to retire with her journal. Safi's room was located at the end of the passage, where she had a corner space with floor-to-ceiling windows overlooking various billboards and the rooftops with their water tanks jutting out at odd angles, an urban landscape she had grown to love. The night view always excited her when she retired, comfortable against the large white pillows on the double bed, with the tall studded linen headboard. She surveyed the room appreciatively now that she had settled down. Small details she hadn't noticed before revealed themselves, like the bed linen: crisp, white, apart from the dark grey shabby chic armchair in the corner that had become her clothes horse now piled high with various jeans and tops.

Deciding to clean up, she set about folding her clothes away into her small walk-in closet. Catching sight of herself in the full-length mirror, she suddenly stopped. Had she put on weight, she wondered. Having had no exercise for over a month and eating whatever came her way she was sure had not helped her figure at all. Never having had a weight problem, she certainly did not want to start now and decided that it was time to get onto the scale, just to make sure.

Safi pulled her clothes off and examined her body in the mirror. She allowed her hands to follow the contour of her body; starting at her neck she allowed them to wander over her breasts to her thighs. Niles immediately flashed into her mind and she could not deny that even the thought of him gave her a warm feeling. Allowing her hands to lightly caress herself, she suddenly dropped onto the floor holding herself, not being able to let go the feelings of excitement coursing through her, Safi's fingers found their way into her wetness she touched herself tenderly becoming more passionate as she felt the electricity shoot through her body, leaving her gasping for breath, cupping herself tightly as the waves swept over her, putting her fingers into her mouth she stared into space.

Feelings of exhaustion suddenly taking hold, she slowly gathered her strength, deciding a warm shower would clear her mind, wondering whether it was Niles or the lack of sex that had caught her so off guard.

Graham, Safi's old boyfriend, had gone up to London to work in the City; at first they stayed in touch but it soon became obvious that work and the fast pace of life in the City was more appealing than his old girlfriend back home in the counties. New York had always been her intention and their relationship slowly petered out with no ill feelings on either side. Graham had grown up around Safi, they had gone to school together and even though he had gone to university they remained a couple. Once his job in London had materialised Safi realised it was time to follow her own dreams.

In bed with her journal, Safi re-read her wild dreams of a future she had wished for and written about so long ago. Did all those dreams still hold, were they her true reasons for leaving England for New York? Forcing herself to start at the beginning, she was aghast at her childish immature wild desire for excitement. My God, she was quite the saucy one; no one would call her reserved if they read the stuff she had penned.

She had tried to use her diary and her words to determine her identity. But that wasn't at all easy, and not least because she found that she was, in so many ways, a contradiction. For instance, she did not want to be a one-man woman, she wanted to explore her sexuality, she wanted to taste all life had to offer. The thought of following her sexual desires exhilarated her, but was she capable of being a free spirit? Was it her mom's memories of the sixties and seventies growing up in London, strolling around Carnaby Street that had influenced her feelings of free love and all that hippy stuff? She had always been pragmatic did she have it in her not to try to control everything?

But then she also wanted to have a happy marriage, like her folks. Would she want marriage if she followed her desire for excitement, or would it take her in another direction? Perhaps she would find the excitement she was seeking was not all she imagined.

Drugs did not excite her. She had tried various uppers with Graham; they always made her feel out of control, she wanted something she could experiment with in a less destructive way. Her natural instinct was to settle for the safe option, to be a free spirit, to go where opportunity took her.

What kind of excitement was she looking for: a sexual high, or to succeed independently? Both, she hoped, would materialise. She wanted to fly like a bird, to follow a path less travelled, landing where fate dictated, but not against her will. Her mom always said passion was the most important. She understood having passion would be the ultimate feeling for what she found her potential in. She had such conflicting desires, journalling them and reading them back to herself made Safi realise that she hadn't a clue where to start.

Understanding her confused feelings wasn't nearly as easy as penning down her thoughts. One did not necessary help with the other. It was giving her a tension headache, all of this trying to find herself. She was leaving little space for serendipity, which is what would happen if she just went with the flow, instead of trying to make things happen the way she imagined they would.

Shutting the curtains on the Manhattan night she was not part of yet, she resolved to allow herself to go with the flow, rather than becoming a slave to her inner thoughts. As her head hit the pillow, Safi's last thoughts were of Niles, she had never felt so intensely about anyone so quickly before, why wasn't he showing any interest in her? Maybe her makeover with Lauren would help.

She woke the following morning ready for her day with Lauren, the styled and groomed Manhattanite. They met at a café in the Upper East Side. Lauren looking relaxed in skinny blue jeans and a crisp white shirt finished off with tan flat pumps and LV shopper – or was that called a purse too? It was hard to comprehend that a purse was to keep money in, which Safi kept inside the fringed, battered so-called handbag hanging across her body.

There were so many different pronunciations to words she had already learnt: wader instead of water, faucet instead of tap, bathroom instead of loo. But Safi was taking note, and her folks had already noticed that her accent was changing. She certainly did not want to lose her Britishness: it was an asset, for sure. Everyone seemed to love her accent.

Lauren ordered egg whites and a green juice, all very healthy. Safi was starving, not having eaten the sushi Daniel had brought home the night before. She ordered a full American breakfast: her eggs sunny side up with hash browns, apple-smoked crispy bacon and bran muffin and coffee. Lauren could not help laughing and noted that she was envious of Safi's youth and lithe figure. Lauren was relaxed and Safi found her very easy to chat with, finding her knowledge of life in New York exhilarating and trying to absorb as much information as she could.

She admired Lauren's natural relaxed sophistication, her long chestnut locks worn below her shoulders, casually groomed and swept off her face, the expensive-looking delicate necklace casually hanging over the crisp white shirt. Safi imagined the necklace to be beyond her pocket; she had no idea what it was and was too shy to ask, but she loved the little pearl daisies surrounded by tiny sparkling diamonds and matching delicate bracelet round her wrist it – all added to the casual elegance she exuded.

They set off to various small workshops in rundown buildings. Once inside all the designers were professionally confident in their attitude to their work. They welcomed Safi and allowed her to try on as many of the samples as she wished from their past season. But when Lauren mentioned that she would be at the opening of Rubicov, their attitudes changed, out came the new season's line of dresses. They dressed her from top to toe with shoes and bags to match.

By the time Lauren and Safi had been to their fourth designer, Safi was loaded down with bags of clothes to choose from. She could not believe how generous all of the designers were. She wanted to return their beautiful things, but Lauren told her not to worry, she would be including them in her line of young designers at Barneys, so they were more than thrilled to have her wear their clothes.

Overwhelmed, feeling more than a little lightheaded with her new wardrobe, she kissed Lauren on both cheeks. Never in her life had she felt so spoilt; keeping her feet firmly on the ground could be a problem, if this overindulgence were to continue. She reminded herself this was a once-in-a-lifetime, short-lived opportunity. Grabbing a cab with all her bags safely in the trunk, she leaned back, exhilarated, hardly believing her luck since her feet touched down on New York soil. She knew Dax would expect a fashion show, and if he wanted to choose her outfit for Rubicov's opening evening, she was more than happy to comply.

Dax had been at Rubicov, helping to position and hang the heavily baroque gold-framed voluptuous ladies on the red plush fabric-covered walls.

The ground-floor restaurant space was furnished with plush seating in the centre and private banquettes down the sides, with oversized rough circular wooden light fittings hung low over the tables, filled with candles of every size, which added a distinctly gothic touch. The bar had a floor-to-ceiling tropical coral fish tank with a bar encircling it. A members club on the first floor had a bank of elevators leading to expensive apartments above.

The invitation for the opening said from 9.30pm. Dax had been working with Daniel and the design team starting at dawn. He felt done in, the last moment changes had taken forever. Daniel and some of the design team had fallen in love with the painting of Bruno for the circular staircase landing and the painting of the Pugs to be hung over the reception area. Everyone on the team agreed with Daniel, Dax reluctantly bowed to majority opinion. It was his first attempt at painting to a brief for a restaurant and he felt a certain sense of responsibility, hoping his ladies would be admired for their elegant and rich vibrant baroque overtones.

Daniel had approved of the baroque edge for this particular commission and he hoped they had delivered. It had been a particularly stressful time for Dax, having had to move out of his old studio halfway through the commission and having to store his work all over the apartment with a temporary workshop installed in their dining space. Now that his new studio was complete, he was moving in after the opening.

The new studio was in an old factory with floor-to-ceiling windows. After searching for a very long time, Daniel had found the space by accident in the Meatpacking District. It was ideal for Dax. The owners had been reluctant to have it torn down as it seemed to be the last bastion left in the fast-changing area. The lower floor had been sold off for an upmarket food emporium, which left the upper floor space ideal as an artist studio and gallery. Daniel had done work for the owner and he was happy to let Dax use the upper floor. If this commission was well received, it would make all the stress of moving worthwhile, and mean Dax would not have to push his new commissions to later and later dates.

He hated to disappoint clients; he had worked many years building up a reputation. Dax had done a degree in design and graphics at Cooper Union. After graduating he and Dan had often worked as a team: Dan as the interior architect steadily building up their contacts, Dax supplying the murals or art work for various spaces.

Dax's family lived on Long Island, where Dax had grown up and gone to school. His parents were considered well-heeled, and although Dax had never needed anything in life, his father had tried to encourage him to go into property (unlike his brothers who were accountants and lawyers). But Dax, being the youngest, had leaned towards the arts. His mother had always known that her youngest child was gay, and having two butch brothers helped his father accept that Dax was the girl his mother never had. They supported him through his difficult teenage years, and his brothers had always protected him from being teased or bullied for his ebullient, feminine personality. Nobody started with Ethan and Harley, who were football jocks playing all the sports Dax shunned from an early age.

Meeting Daniel soon after moving to Manhattan had been the best thing that had ever happened to Dax, as far as Dax was concerned. Daniel was everything Dax could never be: intellectual, well-read, and with an easy elegance and manner most found as charismatic as he did. Although Dan had not come out until he met Dax, no one ever thought of Daniel as gay, with his square jaw line and broad-shouldered, masculine looks.

Dax was unmistakably gay and had never tried to hide his love of all things feminine and arty; he was flamboyant in dress and leaned towards emotional extrovert behaviour. Unlike Daniel, he preferred to dress how he chose, often attracting attention. Daniel was his rock and his confidant, he had replaced Dax's brothers, who had always been all things to him while growing up.

Being with Daniel gave him credibility in the eyes of those who often dismissed his extrovert flamboyance as mere theatrics, overlooking his obvious talents. They complemented each other perfectly in personality. Daniel was more introverted and serious in all things, while he added lightness and fun to their relationship, Daniel succeeded in reigning in his excesses, helped him grow; with Daniel he felt safe to be Dax.

Dax's family accepted Daniel without question and he quickly became part of their lives. They felt devastated for Daniel, who had lost his only close family. They tried to make up for his loss, by including him in all their celebrations. Unlike Dax's family, Rupert could not accept his son having a same-sex partnership, which was unimaginable behaviour to Dax and his family. Dax had tried on many occasions, without Dan's knowledge, to approach Rupert, but had always been rebuffed, eventually giving up. He continued to hope that Dan's father would eventually come round, but it had been years and they were still estranged.

Back at the apartment, Safi laid all her new designer wardrobe out on the double bed with shoes and bags suggested for each out fit and sat excitedly on the terrace with Bruno waiting for Dax and Daniel to come home. Lauren had suggested a hair salon that Safi could just pop into and there were drop-in nail places all over, too. Safi looked at her watch deciding she had time to kill and may as well go and get herself groomed. On returning back to the apartment, with her hair washed and styled in a sharp long bob, her nails painted a dark red, she felt ready for her first special night out in Manhattan.

Chapter 3

Arriving at Rubicov with Daniel and Dax she felt like a movie star. The guys looked amazingly handsome in their tuxedoes. Dax had approved of Safi's choice and both thought her hair very chic. Safi had chosen to wear a red halterneck dress with a low cowl back and a fluted hemline that finished just above her knees. She wore silver skyscraper Louboutin crystal stiletto sandals with red signature sole with a silver mesh vintage clutch, which she held tightly to stop herself from fidgeting, this being her first magical night out in Manhattan.

On either side of the central revolving door were imposing tall pillar-box red high-gloss doors adorned with large circular gold disc handles. Muscle-bulging security men clasping guest lists stood like statues framing each door. Passing through into the inner sanctum, Safi gasped at the opulence of the reception area. Hanging over Italian marble flooring to match the Uffizi Gallery in Florence was a massive art-deco light. Beyond sparkled a dark reception desk, on the red wall behind the desk, hung Dax's magnificent naked lady, languishing in a tall-winged armchair eating blood-red cherries from a silver bowl with the two Pugs at her feet, on a floor not unlike the one they were standing on. The painting was truly magnificent and lent an exotic, dramatic yet sophisticated air to the entrance, the aura it created was definitely a showstopper.

Moving beyond the reception area, passing a thick triple-layered glass central table, hanging white orchards trailed from white birdcages over the edges of the table. There was so much to take in Safi wanted to linger in the opulent beauty. The circular bar to the side was packed with guests drinking champagne, the central coral fish tank hypnotic, which she appreciated as a diversion if she were to be left on her own during the evening.

They were met by the owner, and as Safi was introduced to Alexi Rubicov, she noticed him appraising her openly. Taking her hand in both of his saying 'Charming, let me introduce you to Sasha, my son, he will chaperone you.'

Wow! was all Safi could think when introduced. Sasha was definitely elegant, very tall, slim and beautifully dressed, more European, she guessed, with his skinny-fitting black jeans, a double breasted velvet fitted tux jacket, white shirt and a kerchief in his pocket, Safi could not help noticing his shoes, which were highly polished pointed lace-up brogues and when they sat at the bar she noted no socks. This guy knew how to dress and he was incredibly handsome in a Slavic way. Sasha had a mixed transatlantic accent and was charm personified. She found that she was quite at ease with Sasha and they launched into chatting about England, Italy and France, all of which she loved.

Sasha, she learnt, was born in St Petersburg but went to boarding school in England, and then onto an American university. Very cosmopolitan and suave, he spoke Russian, French, Italian and English fluently, too. Sipping her third champagne flute on an empty tummy was making her feel more outspoken than she usually allowed herself to be. When Sasha enquired how she was enjoying Manhattan, Safi replied honestly, telling him that this was her first real night out since she had arrived and that she had not yet met anyone to hang out with apart from Bruno the Bulldog. Throwing his head back, Sasha laughed at Safi's beguiling naïveté and honesty, finding it refreshing to have such a magnificent-looking girl with no airs or a hardened New York edge about her.

He took Safi's hand and looked into her huge black eyes in a very serious manner. 'If you will give me the honour of showing you about and introducing you to my New York City, I would be honoured and overjoyed,' he said. 'But honestly, I really do not think you will be lonely for too long. Do you see those chaps over there? Well, they have been eyeing you since you came in. Would you like to meet them? They are all chums, and if I hog you to myself for much longer, I will be truly slaughtered, they are glancing this way, so let's go over, should we.'

Safi thought Sasha charmingly old-fashioned, and she loved his friends: they were mostly Americans who made her feel very special. She was grateful for the trays of food passing by, her legs on such high heels were feeling like jelly after having had only champagne since she arrived.

Sasha whisked her off to show her the rest of the building. As they climbed the marbled staircase to the next floor, Safi had to stop to admire Dax's work hanging on the landing of the first flight of stairs. It was more imposing than the painting at the entrance. Staring up at the dark-eyed beauty staring down at them, Safi pointed to Bruno and said, 'By the way, that's Bruno, my only sleeping companion since I've been here.'

They both laughed, as Safi realised what she had just said. Sasha leant back to admire the work.

'Tell me,' he said, 'how do you relate to the rest of the painting, apart from Bruno your sleeping partner?'

There was a definite twinkle in his eyes. Looking up at Sasha, she felt aware of his sensual masculinity for the first time: he was incredibly sexy in a relaxed way; exciting her somewhere way down in her tummy were butterflies. She tried to be nonchalant and turned her answer into another question, not being sure her answer wouldn't betray her feelings.

'I have been living with these magnificent beauties for a few weeks in Daniel's apartment,' she said. 'They have been keeping Bruno and I company when we were alone and I have grown to admire their incredible feminine power, do they have any effect on you?'

Taken aback by Safi's reply and confident attitude, Sasha leaned over and kissed Safi on both cheeks, then lightly on her mouth. 'Safi,' he whispered, 'you are magnificent, do you know that?'

Safi felt her head swimming and suddenly felt renewed confidence flooding through her. She enjoyed being admired by this handsome foreigner, he was not scared of his feminine side, that was for sure, and it pleased her.

'I think they are the sexiest, most voluptuous modern images I have seen for a very long time,' he said. 'Quite brilliant, and I think they lend an air of aristocratic naughtiness to the whole establishment, which is exactly what we wanted. Come let me show you upstairs.'

They entered a vast room fashioned like the men's-only club Safi imagined they had all over London, but this room had a more modern feel and did not exclude the female sex. Dark ebony bookcases lined the walls, plush sofas and armchairs were arranged in groups creating a homely feel. There was a grand piano in high-gloss red with tall bevelled mirrors leaning against wood-panelled walls.

'This is a casual lounging area for the guests of our club to relax in from the busy madness out there in the streets,' Sasha said. 'We also have a function room for private parties and a smoking room.'

Safi approved and thought Daniel and his team were worth their reputation; they had interpreted the brief to a tee, capturing the Russian atmosphere without overstatement. Safi found herself surrounded by Sasha's friends who pointed out celebrities to her that she had not previously noticed, including what she surmised were oligarchs with their Russian girlfriends, who Safi couldn't take her eyes off, they were glamour personified, and some had the longest legs she had ever seen, high heels adding to their statuesque imposing image.

Only when the first course arrived did she realise how famished she was. Finally allowing the food and wonderful wine and conversation to buzz around her, she gathered her thoughts and wondered why she had been so nervous about meeting new people. After all, this is what she had dreamt of: one of her desires was to indulge in opportunities and encourage serendipitous adventures. She hoped that Sasha would return; she had felt something in her stir when he kissed her and she wanted to get to know him. Dax and Daniel were going to get grilled about Sasha and all the other people she had met. She hoped they would approve of Sasha if – a big if – he asked her out. A part of her wanted their approval.

As desert was about to be served, Sasha joined their table and Safi could not help her inner smile; it was butterflies all over again. He was charm personified, and she could not help wondering whether he was just being polite – surely someone with his connections would have a girlfriend? Or girlfriends … ?

When Sasha was not in earshot, she turned to one of his friends. 'I was wondering,' she said, not at all shyly, 'does Sasha have lots of girlfriends? Is he dating someone? He seems to flirt with everyone in an incredibly suggestive way.'

Before he could answer Sasha was right next to them. Taking Safi by the hand, he led her away from the table to meet someone he thought she would find helpful to know while she was in NYC.

Standing at the table covered in orchards was Lauren, looking her usual groomed self in a slim-fitting, double-breasted white tux open to her ribs. A huge diamond-studded cross lay between her breasts. The tux jacket had a low back, exposing her tan. Her hair was up in a messy chignon with tendrils hanging down. She looked effortlessly chic as she turned to greet Sasha. Safi caught sight of who Lauren had been chatting with. Holding her breath, she felt a little dazed as Niles turned to acknowledge her.

Looking up, noticing Safi, Lauren exclaimed, 'Saffron, my goodness, you look incredible. Where has that English rose gone? I love the new you, and the hair is tres chic. You are even more stunning now. Niles, meet my friend Safi.'

Niles smiled broadly and said, 'We already know each other. And Safi knows Sandy, too. Lauren is the friend whose dog I walk.'

'I had no idea you were Sandy's owner, Lauren,' Safi mumbled, feeling mortified that she had been going on about Niles when she had first met Lauren. She hoped Lauren had completely forgotten. 'Gosh, what a small world. Bruno and Sandy are crazy about one another. I would never have guessed that you two were friends when I mentioned the doggie park.'

Niles took Safi's hand and twirled her around. 'I like this new you,' he said. 'I can tell Lauren's impeccable taste has been at work.'

Sasha, standing by holding onto Safi's elbow, whispered in her ear. 'Come and meet the best gossip columnist in NYC. You never know, she may be of help to you; she knows just about everyone worth knowing.'

Polly Grant was a formidable, sharp-witted New Yorker. She took one look at Safi alongside Sasha and exclaimed, 'Sasha, who is this beautiful young creature? Do introduce.'

Polly was quite scary but her smile was disarming and she held Safi captivated. Finding out that Safi was Daniel's cousin seemed to bring out a softer side in the acerbic older woman. Polly asked Sasha to leave them, declaring that the two women needed to become better acquainted.

Before Safi could relate to Sasha that she preferred his company, he was gone.

'Saffron, I do love the name,' Polly said, as though this was an interview – and, in a way, perhaps it was. 'To start with, you must be aware that you are hanging on the arm of one of the most eligible bachelors in Manhattan. He is not only debonair and charming, he is marvellously Russian, of course. And oh-so-snare-able a cosmopolitan player. A prize indeed.'

Safi laughed nervously. 'Oh, I have just met him, Polly. I am sure he has absolutely no interest in me.'

'That answer is cute. Have you got an interest in him? Ah, I can tell by that expression that you do. Good luck, my dear, you are going to need it. I will be watching with interest.'

Not knowing how to relate or what to make of Polly, Safi was about to excuse herself when Niles appeared beside her.

'Niles, darling,' Polly exclaimed, 'how lovely to see you are you acquainted with our lovely Saffron.'

'I have come to save her from your clutches, Polly. Safi and I are old dog-walking friends.'

'Oh my, I see delicious complications ahead for our dear Saffron. Manhattan's two most eligible bachelors at her beck and call. I love it already.'

'Oh Polly, for heaven's sake, give the girl a break – she has just arrived and is still finding her feet.'

As she was about to leave with Niles, Sasha was back at her side, and both men escorted her away from Polly Grant.

'Well, what did you think of Polly?' inquired Sasha.

Safi smiled as they joined Daniel and Dax at the bar. But instead of answering Sasha's question, she told the two D's: 'Sasha has just introduced me to Polly, and Niles saved me from further interrogation.'

Daniel threw his head back and laughed, telling Safi not to be intimidated by Polly's overbearing manner, she was actually a wonderful woman who had helped many young girls new to New York. He advised her to keep Polly's business card in a safe place, she was a valuable asset and confidant. Thanking Sasha for looking after Safi, the two D's excused themselves, leaving her alone once again with Sasha and Niles.

Safi felt she needed to save the situation she found herself in. She did not want to alienate either Sasha or Niles: she was attracted to both, even though they were incredibly different. Niles was all-American, while Sasha was totally cosmopolitan, with a decidedly European dress sense and mannerisms. Lightheaded and at a loss for words, she enquired whether Niles and Sasha were acquainted.

Sasha shook Niles hand and explained that although he went to college in the States, he had been living in Moscow for the last couple of years and had just flown over for the opening of his family's new Rubicov restaurant. Hoping Sasha would once more be a New Yorker in the not-too-distant future, Safi found her heart sinking. She felt incredibly greedy; she wanted both these men in her life. She noticed Niles' upbeat attitude and realised that he was more than a little pleased with the fact that Sasha did not live here. She hoped that this was because Niles wanted Safi to himself.

Lauren suggested going on to a club. 'No need to worry,' she added, 'I will tell Daniel that we will be looking after you while showing off the seedier side of the city, as our guest.'

Chapter 4

Daniel's cell pinged and a frown crossed his brow, as he wondered who could be messaging at this hour. Dax was watching him closely, trying to figure out if it was about Safi: she had not yet arrived home from her evening with Lauren and her friends. Daniel shrugged and said, 'No, it wasn't from Safi. She is obviously having a good time, but I am concerned that she has not called. Am I being neurotic?'

Dax, feeling much the same, decided to make light of it. 'Well, she is in interesting company, but I don't think she has any idea that Lauren is gay and that Niles plays both ways. I know she was crazy about him when she first met him at the dog park with Lauren's dog Sandy, but both Lauren and I decided it best not to encourage her by telling her that we knew who Niles was – perhaps we were wrong?'

Not sure he was capable of doing the father thing, a new dimension in their lives suddenly having to worry about the wellbeing of a young girl, Daniel thought it might be more than he bargained for if they continued to go down this familial route.

By all accounts, the evening had proved a marketing success. Daniel was pleased the Rubicov's were happy with the final touches approving of Dax's work and Dax was thrilled with the response to his Rubenesque Ladies, everyone adored the ambience they lent to the overall décor.

After moving into his new studio, Dax hoped new commissions would arrive on the success of the Rubicov opening.

Before the text about Safi, they had been discussing a dinner party to introduce their new charge to friends, having the dining table back would make a welcome change from entertaining in Pete's Bar. Daniel wished he could tempt his dad to join them, if he mentioned Safi was staying, but he knew it was a hopeless sentimental thought until he managed to get the two of them together. His father had an apartment near Central Park where he could often be found playing chess on a Sunday; the plan he had in mind might just work…

But then his phone pinged again. The message wasn't from Safi, but it was about her. And it wasn't good.

Safi woke not knowing where she was. She allowed her eyes to roam around the room. Her mouth felt like blotting paper, her head like a wrecking ball she tried to lift off the pillow, but the room wouldn't stop spinning. Deciding to stay put a little longer, she began to recall the incredible evening at Rubicov. Then she remembered leaving with Niles, Sasha, and Lauren. But she drew a total blank about the rest of the night. Becoming aware of voices and clinking cups, she dragged herself out of the bed, found a wrap and slowly made her way towards a much needed cuppa.

In conversation at the kitchen counter were Lauren and a gorgeous creature Safi had not met before. Safi noted the intensity of their body language. Lauren had been stroking the gorgeous exotic creature's face with one hand, their free hands tightly interlinked. Not sure whether to intrude, Safi was about to tiptoe back to the room when Lauren called out to her before she had a chance to retrace her steps, inviting Safi to join them.

Bianca looked as if she'd been crying. 'Hi, I am Bianca, a friend of Lauren's from Brazil. Nice to meet you.'

Bianca moved over to allow Safi to join them at the breakfast bar, while Lauren busied herself pouring tea for Safi. Not trusting herself to ask the right questions until she had had something to fill the void in her stomach, Safi smiled self-consciously at Bianca and Lauren, hoping that she did not appear too out of it, which she definitely decided she was, not sure why as she was never much of a drinker.

Lauren was peering at Safi with concern, encouraging her to eat the toast and honey she put in front of her, and to drink as much liquid as she could. Not about to argue, Safi downed two glasses of orange juice and three slices of toast with honey together with lashings of marmalade jam (a combination she had taken a liking to since staying with Daniel).

Bianca excused herself. Staring at Lauren, her vision less blurred, Safi steadied herself on the stool. She decided to ask Lauren straight out why she could not remember anything about their evening together after leaving Rubicov.

'Lauren, I seem to have drawn a blank about our evening after Rubicov.'

Feeling more than a little guilty, Lauren moved round to Safi's side and took Safi's hand, hoping to set her mind at rest and to enlighten Safi about their evening without scaring her too much.

'Well, I really don't know how to tell you this, Safi,' Lauren began, 'so I am just going to spell it out, I hope you won't judge me harshly for not looking after you a lot better. I am still shaken about Dax and Daniel's reaction to what happened.'

Safi was feeling much better but completely at a loss and alarmed allowing Lauren to continue, a weird shiver ran up her spine as she noticed Lauren's discomfort and what did the two D's have to do with this?

Lauren tried to explain that they had found her totally out of it in the ladies' toilets, not knowing what had happened they tried to revive her, but could not get Safi to talk sense.

Niles had left her alone at the table while Sasha was at the bar and Lauren was catching up with Bianca, an old girlfriend. Safi, trying to remember what Lauren was trying to tell her, found bits and pieces falling into place, suddenly remembering an English guy chatting her up: he was pretty smashed and had become very fresh, sliding closer to Safi, whispering stuff into her ear. She had given him the brush-off, but when he left the table she had suddenly felt weird after finishing her champagne and found her way to the toilets.

He had obviously doctored her drink. Niles and Sasha had realised this and together they had managed to get her home to Lauren and to bed. Niles and Sasha had called incredibly worried about how she was.

Allowing Safi to digest the information, Lauren called Niles leaving him a message then Sasha to let them know Safi miraculously seemed to be doing a whole lot better than when they found her the night before.

Sasha insisted on speaking with Safi. 'Safi, please allow me to take you out this evening to apologise, that's if you'll ever trust me again.'

Feeling a prickle of excitement, she managed to accept his invitation, but not before teasing him about being a less then trusting date and hoped he would be more attentive when she saw him next. Giving Lauren the phone back, she had to stop herself from giggling, noticing Lauren's expression of relief and surprise at her ability to flirt when in such bad shape.

Safi could not help staring at Bianca's outfit: suede skinny jeans, thigh high boots, her never ending legs and shoulder length dark blonde hair scraped back into a ponytail, silk scarf not to mention the unbelievable Gucci rucksack slung casually over her shoulder, she had to be a model, even though her boots were flat, she towered over them.

Bianca was hugging Lauren, it appeared to be rather more than a casual friendly goodbye, although Lauren seemed less forthcoming there was definitely more going on between them, then met the eye.

Lauren and Bianca said their farewell in private at the elevator and left Safi wondering whether they might be a couple. On returning, Lauren smiled apologetically for Bianca's emotional state, explaining Bianca's lifestyle in graphic detail. She travelled most of the time, they were close, but it was impossible for her to have a proper relationship with anyone. Bianca was her family's sole breadwinner: she made a fortune modelling, and had photo-shoot assignments all over the globe and was always on the move.

Safi decided not to pry further, but tucked away her suspicions about Lauren's sexual preferences and decided to quiz Dax when she had a chance, finding it hard to believe that such incredibly feminine beautiful women would be gay. She was realising all relationships were pretty complicated and not always as straightforward as she imagined them to be.

At the apartment later that afternoon, Safi took the opportunity to have some alone time. She was definitely shaken by what had happened and decided she needed to hear her mother's voice. After catching up with news at home and calling to say hello to her dad at work, Safi started to feel less insecure about being so far away from home. She had no intention of sharing any of the details with her folks. They were missing her and discussed visiting over Christmas, staying for a week on route to warmer climes. Safi was delighted and realised how much she was missing her folks: even though she had not been away that long, it felt like months and she knew once work started at the agency her time would not be her own any longer, she hoped that Christmas would allow her some quality time with them.

Daniel and Dax repeatedly mentioned they were keen she remained with them until she found her feet and that's what she was going to do. Things were improving she had a date with the sophisticated sensual Sasha the thought sent a shiver up her spine. Not quite sure whether it was excitement or nervous exhaustion from the previous evening she collapsed onto the bed hoping a short rest would restore her confidence.

The cell pinged breaking her train of thought reaching into her purse noting three messages, a whole new feeling of being connected at last, thrilled she opened her messages, she had to answer them before resting.

Dax wanted to know if she was home and okay, she texted him back to put his mind at rest, feeling selfish for not thinking about doing so earlier. Daniel wanted to know if she had enjoyed the evening; he was worried, too. Safi replied in the only way she knew how to convey her feelings, typed 'WONDERFUL! Thank You!' and pressed send.

The final text was from Sasha: he was calling for her at 7.30: plenty of time to recharge her batteries before her first proper date in New York.

Aware of voices, Safi woke up shocked to find it was past 7.30; she had slept for hours. Jumping up smoothing down her hair, she peeked into the passage to see who was home. Standing at the kitchen counter wine glasses in hand were Daniel, Dax and Sasha! Suddenly feeling self-conscious and shy, trying to seem bright and apologetic as she ventured out making the most of a very embarrassing situation. She had hoped to be dressed and ready for Sasha when he arrived. Instead she was dishevelled, wearing an old tracksuit.

Greeting her in unison, they seemed at a loss for words. Then Daniel and Dax suddenly both pounced holding her close in a protective embrace wanting to know whether she was okay and how mortified they were about what had happened to her at the club the previous evening.

Dax appeared overwhelmed by the news of the night club fiasco and would not let go until she convinced them there was nothing a good rest and a glass of wine couldn't fix.

Sasha held out a glass to her and Safi smiled weakly at him in apology, but he was having none of it and seemed just as concerned as Dax and Daniel were.

Niles apparently had called and Lauren had been seeking their forgiveness all day long. On returning home, Safi learnt they had found her soundly asleep and had decided to leave her to rest. Since they had not received any replies to their many texts, Pete the barman had been notified to check up on Safi to see that she was home safely, when he arrived to take Bruno for his afternoon outing. He had reported back that she was out for the count under a fur throw with Bruno tucked up beside her.

Safi had to laugh; besides the embarrassment she felt, there was also a wonderful feeling of warmth that made her feel safe and cared for by all these fantastic new people in her life. Things were definitely looking up she could almost say she had a life! But she could not ignore the nagging realization had she been on her own she would be dealing with this alone, a sobering thought.

She recounted her memories of the evening after leaving Rubicov but besides waking up at Lauren had a very vague recollection of some witty English guy chatting her up when alone at the table for what seemed a very short time.

He had put his free arm around her distracting her by doing so because she tried to disengage herself by picking up her champagne glass after which she remembered excusing herself to go to the bathroom, mostly to rid herself of his unwanted attention.

Lauren had filled them in: apparently after returning to the table with Bianca to find Safi gone, not finding her on the dance floor, they decided to check the restroom, where they found the attendant bent over Safi, exclaiming in Spanish, 'Beautiful lady very white and collapse.'

It was all falling into place; suddenly, Safi found herself giggling madly and could not stop herself, realising that she was behaving like an idiot, still she was unable to stop and suddenly her giggling turned into tears.

When she finally stopped, she found herself being tightly held by Sasha, not knowing what to say. Wanting to defuse the embarrassing moment, Safi shyly smiled up at Sasha, and said, 'Where are you taking me for dinner? I'm famished.'

Dissolving into relieved nervous laughter, Dax dramatically exclaiming that he was beyond exhausted with nerves!! Sasha feeling the tension break and not wanting to take Safi away from her family suggested they all go down to Pete's Bar for dinner.

Together with Bruno they all trekked down the six flights straight into Pete's Bar where Safi received another major comforting hug from Pete the barman, fussing over her wellbeing, behaviour he normally reserved only for Bruno. Not minding the attention one bit she squashed up close to Sasha allowing the rest of the evening to wash over her, listening to animated conversation about Rubicov enjoying Pete's house burger and fries and while the others downed beers, she felt safer with Diet Coke, for the time being.

She fell into bed looking forward to a date alone with Sasha the following evening.

Bruno was waiting for her the next morning ready for his usual walk. On returning she found Dax had dismantled his temporary workspace ready for relocation to the new studio. He had received many calls and had secured a number of new projects on the back of his Rubenesque paintings for Rubicov.

Daniel was busier than ever but determined to be more social now that Safi was living with them. He had been threatening to organise a casual Sunday night dinner to introduce her to their friends, on returning later that afternoon she found that the refectory table was free of paintbrushes and in surprising good shape.

Daniel had wasted little time adding his sophisticated touch once more with objet d'art running along the length of the table from one end to the other. Large studded weathered leather winged chairs at either end, with low natural linen upholstered benches along the sides.

Safi admired Daniels easy elegance yet casual comfortable masculine approach to his home furnishing. The entrance, open planned kitchen and vast loft space beyond now took on a comforting ambience, she felt at home in.

Safi pulled the large wing chair out and seated herself at the head of the table with a pile of art books and mug of tea, but her mind was firmly on what she was going to wear for her date with Sasha.

Earlier that afternoon she had met Niles for coffee. He had been attentive and concerned about the unfortunate nightclub mishap but showed little interest beyond friendship.

Lauren, she learnt, was away on business and would call on her return to find out how she was holding up. Niles was keeping his distance and she had not figured out why, perhaps she had misread the signs oh well, for now Sasha was enough to keep her smiling. Her feelings about him she hoped would develop into more than friendship, a romantic interest in her life would do nicely even from a distance, it had been a long time since her last serious relationship with Graham in England.

Leaving the dining room making her way up to the roof terrace a little chilly with fall approaching, she noticed that Dan had thrown large soft mohair blankets over the outdoor furniture, was there anything he did not think of? She covered herself and Bruno with a soft blanket and together they dozed off waiting for Dan and Dax to return, there was so much she needed to ask them.

Her unfortunate drug incident had forged a closer bond between them – she felt Dan and Dax had become incredibly important in her life. If she was going to remain in New York for any length of time, it would be because she had them, they made her feel she belonged they were her new family. Perhaps they needed her, too. She liked to think so.

Chapter 5

Daniel had tried unsuccessfully to contact his father once more. He hoped that Rupert would soften his stance once he learnt of his cousin's daughter's arrival in New York, to say nothing of finding out that Safi was staying with Daniel and Dax.

Rupert's life was now a busy one: he had enough capital to live comfortably in retirement, but he retained his interest in the textile industry. When he was not on his travels, he could be found chilling at one of his Upstate homes or playing chess with his buddies in Central Park near his Fifth Avenue apartment.

On each past occasion Daniel would leave his father messages on various numbers, hoping that this time would be different, that he would finally receive a reply. All attempts remained unanswered; Daniel had not tried for a while, but he felt Safi's arrival in their lives might just coax his father into action, out of family duty to his cousin Leonard, Safi's father, if nothing else.

Putting concerns about Rupert aside, Daniel decided to invest more quality time in Dax and Safi. Their lives had become ever more entwined and complicated. Daniel set about inviting close friends to join them for casual Sunday brunches, now that their dining area was no longer an artist studio they could resume a normal lifestyle.

The appearance of Saffron had shifted their world in a good way, introducing a caring family atmosphere into their lives, something they had both come to enjoy. It allowed Dan's softer side to show which Dax loved, and Daniel had to admit that he felt his attitude to their old issues changing.

He still did not feel comfortable about marriage between same-sex couples, but he now felt less threatened and more inclined to discuss their differences of opinion, mostly the legal difficulties concerning a partnership.

Above all else, Daniel wanted to make Dax happy; if this meant putting his own unresolved ideas between them up for discussion it might help bring about a more balanced tone to the endless arguments and frustration he caused between himself and Dax. Daniel's reflex was to sidestep any discussions he found uncomfortable; this he knew made Dax feel insecure and unhappy.

Up until Safi's arrival in their lives they had kept themselves professionally occupied, or so they thought. Daniel now knew he was prepared to admit his inner feelings about marriage, were closer to Dax's than he ever imagined.

Trying to repair Daniel's estrangement from Rupert would become their single most important issue before any impending union between them could go ahead.

Daniel knew that having a family of their own would be the most important issue for Dax, and Daniel felt this happiness would be his ultimate gift of love to Dax.

He recognised the old issues that had been a bone of contention between them for many years had evaporated, and he felt a sudden thrill of excitement, a lightness of spirit he had not felt since they moved in together twelve years ago.

Instinctively optimistic, feeling Safi would be the one to help open Rupert's heart before it was too late, Daniel felt the need to share his change of heart with Dax.

Dax could tell by the rare urgency in Dan's voice during their conversation that Daniel had had some kind of epiphany, probably some new huge project in the offing, but instead Dan disclosed his plans about arranging various dinner parties at home over the festive season.

Not being able to constrain his feelings of excitement, Dan put down the phone, leaving Dax bewilderedly staring down at his cell phone, not knowing what to make of their conversation or Daniels out-of-character light-hearted behaviour.

Dax made short-shrift of incoming calls and called Daniel back, telling himself he had to stop jumping to conclusions and allowing his imagination to run wild.

Frustratingly Daniel's cell was endlessly busy. Throwing on a sweater over his work overalls, Dax issued orders for his assistants to lock up. If he did not return anything important was to be diverted to his messaging service.

The cab ride over to Dan's seemed to take for ever: there was endless traffic up ahead and still he could not get through to Dan. So his only option was to distract himself by calling Safi; she would keep him chatting about what she was going to wear for her date with the delectable Sasha.

He was about to ask Safi if she had told Dan anything he should know when the cab pulled up outside Dan's offices. Dax was mounting the steps to the building when Dan appeared at the entrance, looking more intense than ever. Together they walked off to their favourite small coffee place across the street. Settled in a booth with their lattes, they discussed the future, as Dan saw it unfolding.

Reaching over, Dax put his hand over Daniel's, encouraging him to take his time; he knew something important was on Dan's mind, something that might affect both their lives, so he gave Dan space to collect his thoughts and waited for him to start speaking in his own time. Whatever was on Dan's mind was obviously important, judging by his body language.

Looking Dax straight in the eyes, Dan said, 'Dax, when would you like to tie the knot?' A faint smile danced around his eyes.

But Dax became very quiet and pale, his hand in Dan's had become icy, finding his voice at last he whispered, 'Dan, you know I love you, for God's sake, tell me what's going on. Are you dying, why this change of heart so suddenly?'

Daniel realised it must be difficult to comprehend a sudden change of heart after his prolonged dogmatic stance against single-sex marriage; he owed Dax an explanation.

'No, I'm not dying, Dax! I was making all these social arrangements for the first time in years to introduce Safi to our friends when it suddenly hit me that having her in our lives had changed something inside me, suddenly I wanted more. I felt that we had both achieved our career goals and that we are now filling our lives with nothing but work and networking, it hasn't fulfilled me for quite some time. Safi needing us has made me see that our lives have been empty and I suddenly felt that you were right! Getting married would push our relationship forward it would open up so many other possibilities for us, that's if you still want me, after all these years of being pig-headed.'

Dax felt his heart leap with joy, blood was pounding in his ears; this was more than he could have wished for or imagined when Dan called earlier. Dan bent over and dusted off the tears running down Dax's cheeks with his pocket hanky and they sat in silence for some time enjoying a rare moment of contentment.

On entering the apartment, they were greeted by two glass bowls filled with mixed roses of every colour. Safi was in the kitchen getting her usual mug of tea. Initially excited by her gesture of gratitude to them, she was suddenly shy when they both stopped in their tracks on seeing the two-dozen roses she had tried to artfully but casually arrange in the clear glass bowls on the steel breakfast bar.

'Safi! Are these from you? They are absolutely wonderful. How did you know we love brightly coloured mixed roses?'

She had to own up to badgering Pete for some clues; she wanted to thank them for being so caring and for putting up with her for all this time. Dan and Dax, both still on a high about their decision to get married, each grabbed one of Safi's hands to show they loved the gesture.

'So, what are we waiting for, Safi? It's time to show us your glad rags for this evenings date with Sasha.'

Safi did not need any more encouragement and flew into her room to try on the choices she had discussed with Dax.

Sasha arrived to find Safi dressed and ready for their first evening alone. She looked more beautiful each time he saw her, nervously smiling as she sipped a cocktail with Dan and Dax.

Safi felt great her legs looked endlessly long in tight fitting black trousers with a floating pale pink sheer sleeveless top skimming her slim curvaceous body. She had decided with Dax's help to wear strappy black heels instead of boots and one of the incredible black pearl-chained Chanel jackets Lauren had given her.

She was pleased to notice Sasha had not taken his eyes off her. She had chosen a hairstyle he liked, wearing it loosely tied to the side with a heavy straight fringe. Dax noted that she could have come straight out of the pages of American Vogue.

The charming thing to the two D's was that Safi had no airs or graces; the newfound sophistication seemed to have no other affect than to give her confidence, giving her an alluringly bashful sexuality.

After drinks and chatting with Dan about Rubicov, Sasha decided that it was time to have Safi to himself. They hailed a cab and Sasha looped his arm through Safi's, holding her hand softly but with an air of possession that she liked. He had old-world manners that gave Safi a thrill: telling her to remain in the cab until he came around to open the door and help her out. He made her feel valued and desired, a woman instead of a nineteen-year-old girl, which, in turn, helped her behave more like one. This was a whole new experience that she loved.

On entering the restaurant, they were shown to a long bar where Sasha ordered her a peach Bellini that she enjoyed a little too much. After her third martini, she wasn't at all confident she would make it to the table without falling over in her Jimmy Choos. But Sasha was taking charge again, holding her firmly around the waist, making the trip to the table pretty uneventful.

The waiter pulled the chair out for her and, trying not to fall ungracefully into the chair, Safi confided to Sasha that she had not eaten for hours. Sasha helped her choose, ordering starters and mains, and leaving desert for them to decide on after the main course.

Safi tried to concentrate on Sasha and the incredible flavours of the dishes, but the restaurant was buzzing with young, elegantly dressed people; the noise level was incredibly high, every time either of them spoke, they had to lean in close to hear, making Safi realise that to be heard one had to use an animated voice that was at least an octave louder than a spoken voice. She found the whole scene funny and could not stop herself laughing, making Sasha laugh, too – and suddenly they could not stop. Sasha came over to Safi and stage-whispered in her ear,

'I think we skip next course, how about you coming to my place for a special Russian dessert.' Not even the Russian accent put her off; she did not need another invitation. Pulling her chair back, she took Sasha's hand while he discussed something with the maître d'.

She was dying to see his apartment, which was in the Rubicov building.

The building's façade was black granite; gold lettering reminded one it was a Rubicov building. Bronze sculptures were inlaid one either side of the façade into the black granite. The reception area was an opulent space with relaxed white Le Corbusier leather seating overhanging Arco floor lamps and gold-framed Russian Iconic paintings offset by a sleek wooden reception desk with art deco lighting at either end. The atmosphere was contemporary with Russian overtones but not morbidly so.

Sasha led her through the reception area to the bank of silver and black art deco elevators. As the elevator ascended, Safi felt weirdly self-conscious, aware of the overwhelming heightened tension between them. Sasha was every inch the gentleman, but lurking just below the surface she could sense growing fission between them.

On entering the apartment, the tension was diverted somewhat as she was met with a hard-edged modern interior; the only softness to the contemporary minimalist black marble flooring and abstract art was the plush red velvet sofas offset by rich Persian rugs, adding warmth to balance the high-gloss black units that lined the walls filled with objets d'art artfully mixed with contemporary and Russian pieces. Living with Dan and Dax had sharpened her appreciation of interior spaces; this space screamed 'No one really lives here!' – something she would love to change.

Safi's parents' home was comfortably furnished in original classic Bauhaus period-pieces and considered retro-modern, but was nothing compared to what she had been exposed to in Manhattan. On reflection, Safi deciding she did not feel uncomfortable in opulent surroundings and quite liked being surrounded by style and beauty.

Appreciative of her interest, Sasha delighted in showing her the rest of the three-bedroom apartment, ending up at a high-gloss black breakfast bar where he mixed two vodkas: one on the rocks, adding a generous amount of cranberry juice to Safi's (obviously her dessert).

Sipping their drinks in the occasional seating overlooking Manhattan by night, quietly enjoying each other's company, Sasha said, 'I feel so comfortable with you, Safi. I think you are a lovely person not only beautiful to look at, but to be with, too.'

She stared at Sasha, not quite knowing how to put her thoughts into action, acknowledging to herself that all she wanted was to end this amazing evening in his bed: but did she want to break this dreamlike spell of happiness; just being with Sasha was an aphrodisiac?

Feeling her desire, Sasha took her drink out of her hand, put it on the small table between the chairs, stood and pulled her towards him. Holding her very tightly, he bent down, pulled her chin up towards his lips, brushing her lips with his. Safi, feeling the same sensual excitement, leaned into Sasha, giving herself over completely, returning his kiss with her tongue, feeling his heart against her beating loudly.

She stretched her arms round his neck and pulled him in closer to her body. Sasha pushed the jacket off her shoulders, allowing it to drop, and lifted her top; not removing his eyes from hers, he undid her zip, pushed her gently into the armchair, and pulled her heels off. As she lifted herself, he pulled her trousers down.

Lifting her out of the chair he whistled appreciatively. Safi blushed but did not want to appear self-conscious; taking his hand, she led him to the bedroom, pushed him down on the bed and straddled him, undoing his shirt one button at a time, kissing his chest as she went down towards his fly button. Suddenly he flipped her around and undid his belt and as his trousers and boxers dropped to the floor, Safi felt her G-string disappear and Sasha on top of her kissing her deeply from behind, as his fingers stroked her. Safi gave a little gasp as she felt Sasha enter slowly, pulling her hard against him, she felt herself arch into Sasha, and before she could control it she was convulsing against him as he came inside her.

Sasha slowly lifted himself off Safi, and turned her back towards him. Kissing her softly he removed her bra, teasing her nipples with his teeth, she thought she would scream. Her body felt oversensitised but ripe with passion. She realised that she was ready for whatever Sasha had in mind. He moved down her body, kissing her gently. She thought she had died and gone to heaven. Never had she felt her body respond so freely and willingly to new sensations. It was more than she could take, and before her mind could catch up with the sensations she felt building in her body, she was lost in another release, her hands grabbing the soft bedding underneath her.

When at last she opened her eyes, Sasha was lying next to her, watching her with a huge smile on his lips. She put her hands through his thick dark hair and let it slip to his mouth; he softly kissed and sucked each finger, releasing the same sensation deep down inside her. Then Sasha told her to sleep, that he had something to take care of. Pulling the soft throw over her, she lay hugging the pillow, too tired to think about anything, thankful she had, had a contraceptive implant inserted before she left for the States.

Not wanting to upset Daniel, Sasha decided it better to take Safi back to their apartment. Safi reluctantly agreed it would be better to stay over another time when the two D's got used to the idea of her having a boyfriend. If, indeed, there was another time – she certainly hoped there would be, and that wasn't just a one-night thing for Sasha.

Sasha was so attentive and gentle with her; he fussed over her being warm enough and waited patiently while she tried to make herself look decent. In fact, she looked pretty ravished, a look she quite liked and it felt good too. Asking the cab to wait, Sasha walked her to the door, held her close, kissed her lightly on the nose, walking back to the cab, and called 'See you.'

Safi's heart sank; it was not what she wanted to hear at all. She stared after the cab as it sped off and climbed the steps feeling a little less light-hearted than before. On entering the apartment, she made straight for the kettle, wanting to settle on her bed with a hot mug of tea. She hated the American kettles, which whistled noisily when the steam escaped; she grabbed it not wanting to make too much noise. Too late! Someone had heard the kettle, damn; perhaps they had just gone to the bathroom. She froze as she waited, not ready yet to speak to anyone. But it was too late, both Dan and Dax had joined her in the kitchen, eager for news of the evening.

Not wanting to disappoint, Safi told them about the peach martinis; then, not able to hide her feelings, she blurted out that she was absolutely totally and utterly in love with Sasha!

'Then why are you looking so glum?' Dax wanted to know.

Not sure herself, Safi decided to recount his last words, 'See you,' when dropping her at the door.

Dax looked straight at Safi. 'Oh my God, you slept with him.'

Safi looked down at the floor, not knowing how to answer. She had never encountered such direct openness before, but Dax had the habit of allowing words to fall out of his mouth before thinking … and it was written all over her face.

'Let's sit down, Safi, let's talk. I can see you have conflicted emotions, and to be honest I can't speak for Sasha, but one thing I know is a girl in love.'

She followed them to the lounge and Dax enquired whether Sasha treated her well, seeing the shock on Safi's face, they both laughed. 'We don't want to hear the intimate details, just how he treated you?'

This she knew how to answer, and her face softened. 'He was amazing, he treated me so gently. I have never been treated with such care ever before by a guy; that's why I am so upset.'

Dan took Safi's hand. 'You know, I don't know Sasha well, but I prefer him to Niles, to be honest; if it were Niles I would be very concerned, but enough of that now.'

'Go to bed and try and sleep. By tomorrow it may all look quite differently; if not, we will go from there; how does that sound?'

Safi looked at her newfound confidants got up slowly, and gave them a hug. 'You know, I would never have confided any of this to my folks, or even my close friends back home. I feel so much better now, thank you for putting up with me. I know it must be odd for you, too, but I have never felt closer and more trusting of anyone in my life. I feel I can share anything with you both.' Safi knew they were choked up, suddenly feeling exhausted, she went to bed.

Dax had gone by the time Safi crawled out of bed, but Dan was waiting for her in the kitchen with a mug of hot tea. 'Are you hungry?' he asked.

'Starving.'

'Good, I got Dax to bring up some fresh bagels, cream cheese, and lox.'

Dan could not help smiling as Safi wolfed down her food; she was still girlish in many ways, yet he knew she had grown up a great deal since arriving in Manhattan, not sure if all of it was to her advantage. Dan took a seat in the leather swivel barstool next to Safi with his coffee.

'I have some news,' he said. 'I spoke with Sasha this morning. I thought you'd want to know.'

Aghast, Safi cried, 'Oh God! You did not call him, please say no–'

'No, actually he called me.'

With a pained expression she waited for Dan to tell her what Sasha had wanted. Not teasing her any longer, knowing how wound up she was last night, Dan said, 'Well,' failing to hide a smile, 'he is mad about you, too.'

Safi, now bursting with excitement, said, 'Really! Why did he call you? I don't understand. I guess you are right about him having old-fashioned European manners.'

Safi moved her shoulders in a resigned fashion, and Dan realised she had no idea that Sasha was that much older than her.

'He is eleven years older than you, I believe.'

'That's not a problem,' Safi replied, 'my dad is almost ten years older than my mom, and they have been happy, so far, as I recall.'

'I gathered that you enjoyed him taking charge from your enthusiastic description of your evening with him last night.'

Safi looked at Dan with an irritated expression, wanting him to hurry up and get to the point. 'Well,' she said, 'are you going to tell me what happened when you spoke?'

'Actually, I told him that it was your decision to make, Safi. I guess after what you told me about your folks' age gap it's not an issue.'

'Not for me, did he say anything else and how do you know he is mad about me?' Safi heard her cell and ran to the bedroom to pick up the call; she popped her head out to indicate to Dan that it was from Sasha, and with a nervous giggle dashed back into her room and flung herself onto the bed to take his call.

When Safi emerged from her room half an hour later, Dan was on a call. Seeing Safi's miserable face, he ended his call to find out what had happened.

Safi sat down on the arm of the armchair in a resigned manner, knowing Dan deserved an explanation for her demeanour. 'Sasha is leaving for Moscow in a week and does not know when he will be back.' Dan enquired whether that was it. 'No.'

Dan sat patiently, knowing that Dax would have been better at this than he was; still, he could not leave without knowing the full extent of their conversation, in case Safi needed some comforting that he was, in any case, not sure he was capable of giving. After a pause Safi blurted out the rest of the conversation with Sasha.

'Sasha told me that if I reciprocated his feelings and his age did not matter, he wanted to see me every night until he leaves. If after a week I was still mad about him he could possibly relocate to New York, but we would be apart for quite some time before he was able to leave Moscow.'

Dan felt at a loss as to how to respond. He decided that his best option was to gauge her feelings and help her wade through her emotions.

'So how do you feel now that he has declared his feelings for you? Do you really want him to relocate here for you? It's a huge ask, don't you think, after only one week?'

'I feel completely confused and happy all at the same time. I don't think I have ever felt this way before. Do you believe in love at first sight?'

Dan racked his brain for something reassuring to say. 'I guess all you can do is take one day at a time. A week together may make all the difference to knowing how, or if, you want to continue with this relationship.'

'I know,' Safi said. Suddenly she felt overwhelmed, not ready for such a full-on long-distance romance, and everything that, that entailed. She had only a week of freedom before her job at the agency started, and she had thought that her last week would be occupied with getting herself sorted out before she started another new phase in her life. Why did everything have to happen all at the same time? Her emotions were all over the place. Dan left Safi alone with her thoughts, knowing she had quite a day ahead of her.

Safi decided her best course of action was to take Bruno out for some fresh air; it might just clear her thoughts about seeing Sasha later that evening. Not concentrating on where Bruno was heading, she found herself in the dog park, found a bench, and watched Bruno playing with the other dogs. She was pleased Niles wasn't around with Sandy. How had sleeping with a guy become this complicated? School days were definitely behind her, since her break up with Graham and arriving in New York, her life had become layered with complication. Trying to take stock of her situation was pointless, her thoughts endlessly going round in conflicting circles about how she felt about a long-term relationship; tying herself down to an absent lover was not her idea of fun.

Bruno deposited back at home, Safi grabbed a cab and headed for Dax's studio: he wanted to show her something he was working on for a client. On arriving at the studio, Safi was told all of his assistants were out on work-related jobs; taking Safi by the hand with a flourish he propelled her up a spiral wrought-iron staircase.

At the top was a huge expanse of wooden flooring with bay windows along one side. Leaning on the white walls on the opposite side were five tall canvasses butted up together. Safi walked along the canvasses, looking at the thickly layered texture. She sat on the window ledge to take in the scene that unfolded. As her eyes swept over the canvasses she noticed the bold brush strokes and the muted earthy ochres. She became aware of images etched in blacks and browns with greens, reds and oranges overlapping. Abstract figures appeared in movement: some upright, others sitting, lying, or upside down; they were all larger than life but together their forms were given a serious yet playful dimension in a landscape of texture and colour.

Safi was speechless. 'I love it,' she finally said. 'How do you manage to bring such powerful authority to your work and at the same time it has a sense of humour?'

Dax stared at Safi. He was in awe of her ability to cut through everything, to the core. 'Safi, if you are able to critique my work with such clarity, I have every confidence that you will find your way through your present complications with Sasha, just follow your instincts and go with them. I can't see that you will go wrong.'

Safi suddenly looked mortified, hoping that she had not said anything out of place about Dax's work.

'I did not mean it to be a critique of your work,' she said. 'I'm so sorry I just got swept away by its impact. I know I am not qualified, it's just my opinion.'

'I know, Safi, and I appreciate it: your honesty is always refreshing. This work is for a hotel reception they have not yet seen it, but I am showing it to the creative director tomorrow and hoping that it has the same impact on him.'

Sasha collected her from the apartment and stayed for drinks with Dax and Dan while she collected a coat and stuffed a change of underwear into her bag just in case. She had decided with Dax that it might be a good idea to sleep over if things worked out between them; she had never stayed over with anyone before, and if Sasha was going to relocate, she wanted to experience what it was like to wake up with him, or was that her excuse? She knew she was being calculating, that it might be better if it just happened, but under the circumstances they did not seem to have that much time to allow things to just unfold.

The moment Sasha walked in all her doubts vanished, her tummy performed a hundred somersaults, turning her into a quivering mess. They took their leave of Dan and Dax, who behaved like two mother hens, handing over their chick. Sasha just smiled understandingly but made it pretty clear what his intentions were towards Safi in his masterful charming way, this made Safi feel she belonged: a feeling she liked after her previous feelings of insecurity about the sudden intensity of their relationship.

He had a car waiting outside with a driver, one of the black limos Safi had seen outside the Rubicov apartment block; they were upscale private cabs, she had learnt. The seats were soft grey leather, and as Safi relaxed into them and the cab took off, Sasha leant over and kissed her cheek, his hand holding the inside of her thigh tightly, making her feel warm and excited inside.

One minute passed happily holding Sasha's hand before she enquired where they were going. 'I am taking you to a very well-known London restaurant that has just opened here. I thought you might enjoy some well-cooked English food.'

Safi realised that even if he told her the name of the restaurant it would probably not be one she had ever been to, but when he mentioned La Caprice, she was relieved that it rang a bell. It was one of her mother's favourite places when they were in London, and Safi had been there for Sunday brunch with her folks.

'I have been to the one in London,' she said, but she did not mention her folks, not wanting to mention the difference between their ages, knowing that it was a point of contention for Sasha.

La Caprice was elegantly casual. Safi indulged in the fancy fish and chips and mushy peas followed by a plate of mixed frozen berries and hot white chocolate sauce, a favourite of her mother's. She felt sorry for the piano player with his back to the diners, mentioning this to Sasha he whispered in her ear that he thought La Caprice's days were numbered, he felt they did not have enough Brits to make it a viable concern, whereas Rubicov was not only packed every night with Russians and Eastern Europeans, it was also popular with the Americans.

Safi wanted to jump to La Caprice's defence; it just seemed unfair of Sasha to be so pompous about Rubicov. Or maybe he wasn't being pompous at all, maybe he just knew his stuff; she was prepared to give him the benefit of the doubt and let it slip from her mind, wondering where they were headed: she was not at all sure whether he would take her back to his apartment or drop her back home. She did not want to appear forward so waited for Sasha to give the driver the address then settled back into the soft leather seats, trying not to show her relief, there was a moment of doubt until she recognised his address.

'You did want to come back to my place, I hope, if not it's not a problem,' Sasha said softly. Not wanting him to think she was too eager, showing a moment's hesitation, Safi saw the disappointment on Sasha's face as he was about to redirect the driver; she quickly took his hand whispering in his ear, 'I wasn't at all sure after your conversation with Dan that you wanted to continue with this, but I do, so yes, I do want to come back to your place, not only to talk but to be with you, if you'll let me stay until you leave.'

Sasha looked surprised; he had not expected her to be so direct. He quickly overcame his initial shock, and suddenly they both laughed, realising they had much to find out about each other, Safi was definitely not a push over, underneath the English reserve there was perhaps an iron will, to be discovered.

'I think before the week is out you may just be a little sick of me, Safi, perhaps it's not such a good idea, from my point of view?' Safi giggled. 'Well that goes for me, too, but I am so excited, Sasha, I have never done anything like this before and I know it's the right thing for us to do, we hopefully will last longer than a week, if not I'm going to lose confidence in my judgement, and probably never trust it again!' They both burst out laughing: Sasha at Safi's honesty, and Safi at his expression, which was a mixture of terror and delight.

'I think I have opened Pandora's box, where has that naïve girl I met at Rubicov gone?'

'Corrupted by your charm,' Safi teased.

'I think we are in for a very interesting week, then,' Sasha said, teasing back.

Suddenly they both relaxed in each other's company, but Safi felt as if her life had just begun. She had never felt this crazy about anyone – it had to be for real. She prayed this was the man for her, but sensed a reluctance on Sasha's part; perhaps he regretted his initial declaration to Dan: she would just have to change his mind, that was all. She had no idea where all this sudden confidence on her part came from, but she felt emboldened in his company and determined to follow her instincts – isn't that what she had wanted when she embarked on this crazy adventure, to be free to grab opportunities when they presented themselves? To experience the world, in all of its chaos and colourfulness, its unpredictability.

The week passed in a lover's haze for Safi; she had never felt so blissfully happy in anyone's company before. Sasha was the perfect host, lover and companion. He spoilt her at every opportunity with affection and shared his interest in art and enthused about his fascination for antique objets d' art. She had absorbed more than she thought was possible about various ancient cultural objects.

They trawled the galleries one day, then markets the next. Sasha seemed to know instinctively when something was genuine and when it was not. He always bargained to secure what he felt was a good price, but for Safi it seemed outrageous to spend thousands of dollars on such small objects, even if they were made from antique ivory yellowed with age or gold or bronze, at times even precious stones were encrusted on the tiniest pieces, all beautifully crafted. They visited museums and spent hours at the Metropolitan. Sasha loved the history of the different cultures; he seemed to know a great deal about the history of many of the pieces they viewed.

He insisted on buying her a gift, something for her to remember him by when they were apart. Together they visited high-end stores on Fifth Avenue in the end they loved Chopard's Happy Hearts in white gold, small diamonds and agate, a green stone to match her eyes, a necklace of hearts which suited her best, and she felt less ostentatious in their jewellery; while it felt young and appropriate for her age, the price tag definitely did not!

Safi felt thoroughly spoilt and at the same time she felt there was something about Sasha's behaviour that sent a clear message that Safi got: it did not make her feel uncomfortable but it did give her a sense of his commitment to her and what that commitment meant, if they were going to embark further on this path together.

She understood in no uncertain terms that he was in charge and what he wanted from her was to show unquestionable devotion to him alone. She was not sure whether she was capable of pleasing him all of the time, but she was ready to try. He was an exciting person to be with. She loved this new feeling of belonging, the thrill of being with someone who took charge and had a totally different attitude to family, work and life.

Everything about his family was to do with their businesses. Safi had learnt the family were involved in many various concerns. He had an older brother, Mika, the trouble-shooter for the family, and a sister, Yvetta, who had opened art galleries in Moscow and was building up a very important client base at home and abroad. His parents were divorced and his mom, Anna, oversaw most of their Russian-based companies. Alexi, his dad, lived in London with his second wife. His father took care of their overseas enterprises, but mostly loved opening new restaurants and private clubs in Mayfair and abroad. Sasha was obviously very proud of his family and their achievements since Russia had opened up to the rest of the world. Yvetta, who he often spoke to in Russian, Safi gathered, was a feisty, complicated character and would be important to get along with, if life with her brother was going to happen at all.

Getting ready for Sasha to depart for JFK on their last Sunday morning together was more difficult than Safi envisaged. Sasha had briskly sent her off in a cab to return home to Dan and Dax. Sasha and Safi's farewell had been hesitant but passionate, yet when she left waving goodbye, she felt a distinct coldness on his part. She was not at all sure whether it was her insecurity or his pretence at casual light-heartedness about their separation, but she was sure something had changed. He did not radiate the same warmth, and as the cab sped off, Safi realised that keeping this relationship alive was going to be a tough call.

Safi was grateful that Dan and Dax were at home; she did not want to be alone. The two D's were trying hard not to show they were dying to find out how her week with the delectable Sasha had gone. They held off until she put her bags down. Together with Bruno, the three decided to go for brunch, at which Safi poured out her heart, not being able to stop herself from enthusing over everything Sasha did or said. A small part of her mind was aware that she was completely under his spell and that her days ahead were going to be lonely. She was starting her job at the ad agency, her father would expect her to be committed and alert enough to give a good impression on her first day.

That evening Safi spoke to her father and assured him that she was excited about starting and would call to let him know how things were after her first day.

Her father informed her that her parents had booked flights over, and together with her brother, Jake, would be arriving the first week before Christmas. Her dad was looking forward to visiting the agency and hoped the English account would be successful.

Chapter 6

Safi was up at dawn and nervously dressing for her first day at work. Not knowing what to expect, she opted for a trouser suit, crisp white shirt, kitten heels, and a sensible purse slung over her shoulder. Having to make two changes to reach her subway stop, feeling like any other New Yorker with coffee to go in hand, she walked into a glass tower building with hundreds of other employees going in different directions.

She found her way to the reception desk of the vast foyer where a groomed bespectacled women directed her to the correct bank of elevators, which would take her straight up to the ad agency. On entering she was met by a friendly, chaotic group of people, who introduced themselves as the team heading up the English account. They were directed to a room by an older woman who introduced herself as Kate, the creative director, who they would be answering to before any of their ideas were passed onto the client.

As they were introducing themselves, they were interrupted by a voice that sounded mildly familiar to Safi; on turning to see who it was, Safi recognised the voice as unmistakably Yorkshire. There was something else about it, though – she was sure they had met before.

Greg, she learnt, was heading up their team; as he spoke Safi tried to place his face, and noticed that he had a very casual individual style, with his red lace-up Converse boots over cargo pants and, slim fitting cord jacket with a kerchief, a bit like a dandy, if it wasn't for the black T-shirt worn underneath and, she noticed the look was carefully finished off by round clear framed gold trimmed glasses.

Everyone round the table was introducing themselves, and when it came to Safi's turn, she suddenly recalled with a shock of clarity where she knew Greg from; her blood ran cold, the colour draining from her face. She felt her fingers digging into the arms of her chair as she fought for some composure. Not wanting to seem odd, she chose to stare straight at Greg, letting him know that she recognised him.

Greg smiled disarmingly at Safi, acknowledging that he had worked at her father's agency in Brighton on occasion as a freelancer and that he had seen her when she worked there during her holidays from school. Noticing that Safi was struggling to find her voice, he continued to introduce her to the team, mentioning they were working jointly with Safi's father's Brighton agency on this particular account. Safi tried to smile and managed to introduce herself as the junior of the team, ready to learn from the masters. The others had all voiced their strengths and, with British modesty or a young person's naiveté, Safi found that difficult to do. She opted instead to use her inexperience as an advantage, adding that she would be able to contribute as they progressed and that she understood the brief was to appeal to Americans while retaining the history and integrity of the British product. When the meeting concluded, Greg asked Safi to stay behind while the others left for a coffee break.

Not at all sure what stance to take, Safi remained seated. Greg did not try to come over but stayed at the head of the table. They stared at one another for a while. When Greg lowered his eyes, Safi saw his hand trembling slightly. When he looked up she realised that he was as affected by seeing her as she was by seeing him.

'Firstly,' Greg began haltingly, 'let me say that I did not realise what had happened to you that evening until I saw you being helped out of the club by your friends.'

Totally confused, Safi felt she was lost for words once again: what was this guy talking about? Had he not drugged her drink?

'I know you will find this hard to believe,' he continued, 'but when I came over to chat you up, I put my drink down on the table next to yours. When I slipped my arm behind you, you were trying to spot your friends; not finding them, you picked up your glass, gulped it down and excused yourself from the table.'

Greg looked at Safi for confirmation. She had to acknowledge he was telling the truth, but what was he getting at? 'I believe you took my drink by mistake, we were both drinking the complimentary cocktail the club handed out as we entered.'

Safi sat back. She had been convinced, as had everyone else, that he had drugged her drink; now she learnt it was her own fault all this time.

'If that's what happened,' she said, 'may I ask why your drink was drugged?'

'Well, I have to admit that I popped some uppers into my drink. It does not affect me adversely, but unfortunately it did you, and, I'm truly sorry about that' Safi sat quietly for a while, taking this information in. She was pleased that Greg had not drugged her drink on purpose. She decided to believe his side of the story, there was nothing else she could do; they had to work together and he was going to be her project manager and team leader.

'We have to work together, Greg, and I am pleased that it was an accident – otherwise, things might have been very awkward for us both.' Safi took Greg's outstretched hand and they shook on starting over. On leaving for their coffee break, Greg commented that Safi had changed quite a lot since he saw her last as a school girl at the ad agency in Brighton. Blushing, Safi acknowledged his comment and, his side of the explanation then decided without hesitation to let Greg know that she had a boyfriend.

Laughing, Greg told Safi he never mixed business with pleasure. When recognising who she was, the kid from Brighton, he was as shocked as she was to come face-to-face with her at this morning's meeting. The rest of the day was uneventful, but Safi knew that it was going to take time to completely trust Greg. So far he had kept his distance from her, but she knew that they would both have to overcome their awkwardness if they were to work on the same team.

They agreed to keep quiet about their awkward meeting at the club; it would not bode well for the two British people on their team not to like or trust one another, and, after all, he had to report directly to Safi's father as team leader.

Safi had not heard from Sasha all day. She knew Moscow was seven hours ahead, but expected and hoped he would text when he touched down to let her know he had arrived safely.

On arriving back at the apartment, she was thrilled to find a long box containing a red rose with a message from Sasha, saying, 'Hope your first day at work was good missing you speak soon.' It was signed 'S x.'

Thrilled, she quickly checked her cell to see if she had missed any calls. She had received a call from Lauren, who had arrived back in town and wanted her to call to set up a date to meet. Everything always seemed to happen at once. Safi heard Dax and Dan return as her cell phone pinged. She popped her head out to let them know she was home and on a call. Closing the door, Safi lay back on her bed, cradling the cell while kicking off her shoes.

She loved hearing Sasha's voice, but suddenly felt shy, not knowing why they both seemed to struggle to make a connection; everything they said felt strained. Sasha tried to sound light-hearted but failed miserably. She longed just to be able to touch him and before she knew it she was giggling madly; finding her laughter infectious, he started laughing, too.

'You'll never guess what I am thinking of' she said in a husky whisper. Their conversation suddenly took on a very sexy tone, and before Safi knew it she was feeling hot and bothered, but not able to get any release. Sasha told her to tell him what she was doing. Shyly, she told Sasha she had just touched herself while pretending it was him. This set Safi off totally and before she could stop, she exploded with excitement. Hearing her fast breathing he asked Safi to tell him what she would do to him. She did not have any hesitation describing how she felt encouraged by the groaning on the other end of the line. Both were quiet and then started giggling.

'If this is how it's going to be, I want a FaceTime call so we can see each other,' Sasha said.

Safi sighed and whispered, 'I think I'm madly in love.'

'I hope with me, or else I'm sending over a bodyguard to keep an eye on you.'

Safi laughed softly as they reluctantly ended their call.

She had never done anything remotely like this before; she found the whole experience liberating and so hot. Since being in New York, her life seemed to have become both frustrating and exciting. She just never seemed to know what lay around the next corner and felt exhilarated by all her new experiences.

Dan decided his father and Safi should meet; it was time for her to become acquainted with the rest of her family. Also, his dad was missing out: Safi was such a delight, hopefully a reminder of the close relationship he used to have with Leonard when they were growing up in England.

All calls to Rupert had gone unanswered, as usual, but Dan kept in touch with some of the friends his dad hung out with: they were his link to knowing how his father was doing. Not knowing where his dad was at any particular time, he decided to call one of his closest friends for information and to check all was well.

Jack Levy was an old trusted family friend and Dan liked him a great deal. After chatting about their respective lives, Dan eventually got onto his usual questions inquiring about his father's wellbeing and where he was.

Learning that his dad had a new love interest in his life did not surprise Dan. A handsome man of means with enough charm to coax a wild animal to eat from his hand, Rupert had never become serious with any of his love interests.

He learnt that his dad had just returned from one of his many trips abroad and had a date with Jack to play chess in Central Park that Sunday. Dan decided to take Jack into his confidence and told him about the arrival of Safi, with whom, he said, he thought his dad would love to meet. Together Jack Levy and Dan devised a plan for that Sunday: the chess game took place most of the day outside their usual coffee shop in the park.

An invitation to dinner with one of Dax's clients to view his work in situ felt a good time to take this opportunity to tell Safi about their plans to get married. Dax knew she would love to see the work she had critiqued so eloquently at the hotel. Dan did not see it Dax's way and thought it better to have a casual evening at Pete's Bar, sharing their news with both Pete and Safi in an environment that they all felt comfortable in. Dax, on the other hand, felt doing it at Pete's Bar would make it general knowledge, and neither of them wanted that to happen before announcing it to their family and close friends.

Dan brooded for a while, but eventually agreed Dax had a point about Pete's Bar being too public to keep it under wraps. Pete would have to find out, with everyone else, at the party they were planning to hold in the month ahead to make their announcement public.

Having waded through their address books, they agreed to send out a blanket email invitation for a brunch on the last Sunday of October before it got too cold to use their roof terrace. They both had a busy schedule, but Dan had kept up his promise to himself to free up his workload and had made all his away dates for after the New Year.

Safi had started her job in the second week of September and Dan wanted the meeting with his father to go ahead for the coming weekend before Rupert took off on one of his many trips or decamped to his Upstate home with the new love in his life.

He hoped that his father would reconsider if he welcomed a relationship with his cousin's daughter. Safi, he believed, would soften his father's attitude, allowing him hopefully to put aside his stubborn pride and to join his family again. It was a long shot and more than Dan could hope for, but he was determined to try.

Although he had turned seventy, Rupert was young at heart, and Dan wouldn't be able to reconcile his guilt if he had not made every effort to become a family unit once more before his father's health failed. Dan knew that Dax supported him and had himself tried to persuade Rupert to reunite with Dan. Dax's parents had on many occasions tried to include Rupert in their Thanksgiving celebrations but he had always declined.

Dan felt this last push might be his final opportunity to make things right with his father. Feeling the need to share his news about himself and Dax, life for them all could change dramatically in the next year. Especially if they were to adopt or have children. His father would have the grandchildren he always desired, even if not in a conventional way.

This was something Dan felt he not only wanted to do for Dax, but for his father too now that he had become familiar and accustomed to the idea of marriage to Dax, having children wasn't a huge leap.

Safi's week at work had been pleasant enough and Greg had kept his end of their agreement. He had not excluded her from any project meetings on product design. They had to familiarise themselves with a collection of quintessentially British products, and one of those products was Marmite. It was a product so engrained in the British consciousness Safi found it hard to imagine how Americans would take to it, most people she knew hated it! The product had been around before Safi was born and she understood that it had an acquired taste: one either loved it or hated it. They were encouraged to show it in the British way, toast fingers with lashings of butter spreading the product on top.

At the first tasting the Americans on their team almost gagged, but on second attempts some of them actually liked the idea of marketing it as a rare British eccentricity acquiring a daring palette.

Everyone seemed to find this idea the way to go, with the teams splitting to work on product design and slogans to please the British manufacturer, if they were to successfully launch more of their products onto the US niche market; some of their other products were enjoying a quaint popularity.

Safi found herself on the slogan team, which was her preferred strength. She hoped to contribute in a small way. The girls had taken to Safi; she found going out after work for drinks was their way to bond and unwind.

The guys seemed to have better things to do, and only one or two had hung out with them after work. She was relieved not to be in Greg's company after work; they still maintained a healthy distance. and it seemed no one had noticed their discomfort around one another; the famous British reserve had its benefits.

The team met every morning for the first week to keep the product idea on line. If anyone objected strongly to any of the ideas, it would be noted; that way they would not waste time. The first meeting went without objection, but as the week progressed it became obvious that Greg had his own agenda, and the creative teams were struggling to come up with an image sharp enough to please the slogan team.

By the end of the first week, Safi felt Greg's guidance divisive rather than helpful to their teams, yet his dismissive attitude to their efforts brought the two teams closer together, which enabled them to pool their ideas into one strong message. Safi's initial conclusion about his attitude was way off, she now got it, Greg's talent was quite considerable; he managed to manipulate everyone into bringing their best talents to the fore in a less competitive manner enabling them to work against him, rather than one another. She had seen her father work this magic before and it always resulted in a united effort, making the product the object of importance rather than the egos on the team.

She was starting to get the measure of Greg as a master manipulator, someone who she needed to stay alert around for more reasons than one. He was obviously brilliant at his job, and she understood now why he had joined the team from the agency in England. Safi felt she could learn a great deal from watching him operate from a quiet distance, as long as they kept a respectful working relationship. She did not think their paths would ever cross again in a personal way – they both wanted to make sure of that. Safi started to relax. She found her team members to be affable and friendly, and none of them seemed to mind her hanging about to watch and learn from either team.

Sasha called her every evening and during the day he would text on occasion, always letting her know that he still desired and missed her madly. She kept him entertained with anecdotes from home and at work, but had not yet told him that she was working with Greg, the guy he had sworn to punish if ever he came across him.

She preferred not to invite trouble, deciding not to confide in Sasha about Greg. Instead, she told him Dan and Dax had concocted some hare-brained scheme for her to meet with uncle Rupert on the weekend. She promised to call as soon as she was free. Sasha told her that he felt for Dan and Dax, but that he also understood Rupert's attitude, knowing homosexuality was something his own family struggled to deal with. Yvetta tried the family's patience in more ways than one, often straying from the conventions they had been brought up in.

Safi absorbed this information, but did not question him further, making a mental note to enquire what he meant about Yvetta. She realised her and Sasha's cultures were profoundly different on many levels; this fact made him more rather than less attractive.

He always surprised her with his passionate interests, be it art or insight into Russian culture, he made everything more interesting when caught up in his orb, which was dangerously intoxicating and made one feel alive. She was still waiting for the right time to have FaceTime sex and determined to make it happen perhaps late one night when they were both more chilled.

Saturdays were dedicated to catching up with her chores; she had also arranged to meet up with Lauren for a quick lunch before popping into her local nail place for a manicure.

They met at the same brunch place where Safi had ordered a full American breakfast with all the trimmings, while Lauren picked at egg whites and confided her fear of indulging her food desires.

Lauren swept into the restaurant, looking every inch the fashionably sophisticated buyer Safi had first met with Dax all those weeks ago – accompanying her was the dreaded Polly, the gossip columnist she had met at the opening of Rubicov!

Polly wore oversized black sunglasses, a Birkin bag, and clothes only Polly could carry off with total panache. She greeted Safi like a long-lost friend, insisting on hearing every bit of her news and how the romance with the delectable Sasha was going.

Lauren drank her latte in silence while Polly held the floor. Then Polly suddenly air-kissed them both farewell, but not before giving Safi her parting advice.

'Insist Sasha come to the States,' Polly said, 'if you must continue this love affair. Never go to Moscow, dear, it's a very odd place.'

Then she was off to another table where a friend had arrived to lunch with her. Lauren giggled and Safi realised there was no controlling Polly, who had clearly joined them of her own accord: she was a law unto herself.

They spent the rest of the lunch catching up, with Lauren confiding she had stepped up her relationship with Bianca the Brazilian model:

they had moved in together. Bianca needed a secure nest when she returned from her travels, and the only person she felt happy and safe to share her life with was Lauren.

She wondered whether Lauren needed this arrangement, too, if she was now tired of living alone. As she walked in from work, Dan and Dax rushed her into the shower to dress for their evening out. Safi knew Dan was tense about her meeting Rupert the next day, but she noticed a certain excited urgency in their manner when they entered the restaurant.

She had not realised they were dining at the hotel where Dax recent large diptych had been hung. On passing the reception area both Dan and Safi stopped in their tracks. Dax's work hung behind the length of the endless reception desk: the muted colours were arresting, it was both powerful and playful with its energetic upside-down figures in the landscape.

Travelling up the escalators, they stood facing the reception, admiring Dax's work until it disappeared from sight.

The popular Fusion restaurant was packed with elegant diners; everyone wanted to try the new celebrity chef's culinary recipes. She had made an effort to wear a dress; she knew how the two D's loved to show her off and Safi certainly didn't mind in the least.

They were treated to the best the chef had to offer. Dishes appeared steaming, with one dish more delicious than the other. Chopsticks flying, they tucked into mouth-watering dumplings with delicious steaming vegetables. While waiting for the main dishes to arrive Dan announced that they had something very special to share with Safi. The two men were holding hands, an unusual display of public affection for Dan. More than that, she noticed that Dax was bristling with excitement. Before Dan could utter another word Dax blurted,

'Safi, we are going to get married!'

'Oh, Dax, we were going share this news together.'

They giggled at Dax's unbridled excitement, calming down in time to start their next course. Sharing their plans, they told Safi how her arrival in their lives had changed both their own outlook on life: she had filled their lives with more than work. It was something they both needed and had come to value, even with all of Safi's ups and downs.

Dan confessed her meeting with his dad was something he dreaded; if it failed they would continue their union without Rupert, but Dan had high hopes that Safi would soften his stubborn attitude and bring him back into their lives.

If meeting Safi did not help, Dan would then pin his hopes on Leonard

Usually optimistic, Safi was doubtful her meeting Rupert would help. She left the restaurant drunk on sake, hoping for her meeting with Rupert the next day to succeed.

They hardly ate a thing for breakfast. It was a beautiful fall day the trees were dressed in splendid fall colours, the sky was cobalt blue and the air was crisp and fresh, but Safi felt chilled to the bone and more than just a little apprehensive about approaching Rupert out of the blue, in the middle of his chess game. Her only comfort was having Dan and Dax camouflaged in sunglasses, beanies, muffled in scarves, huddled together on a bench in close proximity.

Safi recognised Rupert right off he was an attractive older man, especially his mane of silver hair kept under control with a red bandanna tied round his head. He resembled her grandfather quite a bit, which made her feel less apprehensive about approaching him. He was making a move on the board when Safi approached their table. She stood quietly behind Rupert, watching the game, until Jack Levy winked, letting her know he was aware of her. Dan had introduced them earlier at the restaurant before Jack and Rupert met for the game.

As planned, Jack knocked over his coffee, stopping play momentarily. Safi took her cue; it was now or never, if she did not open her mouth the moment would be lost and she would definitely get cold feet.

She leaned over, helping Jack to mop up, then kissed Rupert on the cheek, speaking rapidly. 'Hello, Uncle Rupert. Dan said I would find you here. I am Saffron, Leonard's daughter. I have been so looking forward to meeting you. Dad always talks about what terrors you two were growing up together in England.'

Rupert stared at Safi in alarm; aside from the endless chatter he recognised this beautiful young lady, she was the splitting image of her dad. Her disarming natural openness to his better judgement was hard to ignore. He hated his game interrupted or his concentration for that matter Jack had already done that by knocking the coffee all over the chessboard.

Collecting himself after a moment's hesitation, Rupert stood up, grabbed both of Safi's hands, and kissed her on both cheeks, holding her close in a warm bear hug.

'Jack, let's take this lovely young lady for coffee. We can play again – later. I want to find out how that cousin of mine is doing.'

Safi had not thought past introducing herself to Rupert, but understood that it was important to take up any invitation he might offer, for Dan's sake. Jack insisted on staying to pack up. Safi tried to see if Dan had seen them entering the café where the chess tables were set up together.

Rupert appeared at their booth with steaming coffee; she waited for Rupert to open the conversation, noticing that he was taking his time to collect his thoughts. Safi watched Rupert through the steam as she blew to cool her coffee. She wondered whether he was having second thoughts about welcoming her into his life; moments ticked by before Rupert spoke.

Once he began reminiscing about England, his childhood, and the wonderful times he had shared with his younger cousin, her father, Safi realised that Rupert missed the family connection more than he himself had realised. She encouraged him by asking leading questions, hoping he would fill in some of the gaps since breaking off relations with her father and with Dan.

She listened as Rupert explained about his family leaving England when he was in his early teens. His parents had left him in England for quite some time before they were able to settle in the States. Rupert had been put into an English boys' boarding school while his parents built up their contacts and business in America.

This had been a difficult period in Rupert's life, though he brushed off his boarding school experience with exaggerated nonchalance. Many children attended boarding school in England and Safi had heard some awful stories. For this reason, she decided not to question Rupert about his experiences. Instead, she encouraged him to talk about what seemed to interest him most. His time with her dad and their family. Rupert said he adored being part of a large family but that when they left for America everything changed.

Both families went their separate ways and the business was eventually sold. Rupert spoke fleetingly about his adored wife, mentioning that she had died unexpectedly, which resulted in his life changing: he felt his place was to look after Dan.

Safi found her opportunity: this was when she could tell Rupert how much she loved Daniel and what a wonderful person Rupert's son was, staying with him had turned out to be her anchor. He had made her so welcome in Manhattan. She had not mentioned Dax, not wanting to force the subject, but could tell that Rupert was going to allow her to talk so she decided to tell him as much as possible while having the chance.

She told him how incredible Daniel was, how she admired him about Rubicov and how Dan and Dax had made her feel secure and loved during her time with them. Living with the two D's was for her like living with her own family. Not wanting to overplay her hand about Dan and Dax, she changed tact and told Rupert about her job at the ad agency.

Jack, who Safi thought was a dead ringer for Woody Allen, joined them and the conversation became more general. Safi left Rupert with the news that her parents would be visiting in December and that she hoped they could all reunite over Christmas. Excited at her news, Rupert told Safi his travels always took him everywhere but England, and although he had meant to visit her father he had sadly never been back.

She promised to set up another meeting before Rupert went off to his Upstate home. She left Rupert in the coffee shop with hugs and literally ran all the way back to Daniel and Dax, who were two frozen ice blocks still on the bench in the park, where she had left them. On seeing Safi, Daniel almost fell off the bench with anticipation; running to meet her halfway, he grasped her hands in his, hugging her close. 'Safi, how is he?' he said excitedly. 'What did he say?'

Thank goodness for Dax, who diffused Dan's emotions by hugging them both, suggesting they go for lunch to warm up and allow Safi to tell all in her own time.

At lunch, Safi gave a blow-by-blow account, telling Dan that his dad had not stopped her once when she spoke about her time with them or how wonderful she thought Dan was, how she loved being in their lives, or when she enthused about their talents, or when she babbled on about their business success as a couple. Rupert had indulged her patiently, she informed them, listening to her with mild amusement, obviously knowing what she was trying to achieve. 'He didn't need to, Dan, so I believe he was genuinely interested.'

Dan was sure his dad already knew most of Safi's news about him and Dax, what Dan really wanted to gauge was his father's emotional reaction while she was effusing about them. Dan looked at Safi with apprehension. 'I truly felt that your dad was hungry for any news about you,' Safi said, 'and that even though he was being polite when I spoke of my time here, he showed far more interest when I spoke about you! I wasn't aware of any negative behaviour on his part, not even when I was mentioning Dax.'

The two D's found this to be the most interesting bit of information, and Daniel wondered whether his father was starting to soften, regretting their estrangement.

Safi decided to put her two pennies in for what it was worth, and told Daniel that she thought his dad had gone beyond knowing how to repair their relationship. She believed they should wait until her folks arrived: Rupert, she thought, was excited to reconnect with that side of his family again.

Safi believed her father was the person to bring them together. Leonard had a special gift with people, she had seen him heal rifts before and she felt that it would not take much for Daniel's dad to grab any link to bring them back together.

'I will contact Rupert before he goes away again,' Safi said, and inquired whether she could tell him about their plans to marry.

'I would have to give it a lot of thought,' Dan replied slowly, 'that would be too much too soon. I do not want to make it more difficult for him to accept us. Once we have reunited, we would perhaps tell him we are hoping he will be part of the family again when we get married.'

'Okay, but please can I share the news with Sasha when he calls?'

'Really, Safi, you are incorrigible – not another word until we break the news at the party, not even to Pete.'

Chapter 7

Sasha was calling in the evening and Safi was relieved she would be alone in the apartment. She was planning on seducing Sasha, even if it had to be on FaceTime, the computer was all the contact they had. When Dan and Dax left for their evening, Safi ran to her room to try on the sexy laced-up satin corset with suspenders and delicate lace bra she had bought for the occasion. She dressed herself in front of the mirror, checking to see whether the Victoria's Secret sheer knickers and pull-up hose looked good; she hoped it did not look tacky. She had purposely not bought black, thinking a soft pale pink would give a sophisticated feminine edge to the barely-there lingerie.

She sat on a stool, carefully pulling up the nude hose. Then, standing in front of the long mirror, she looked at her behind in the barely-there thong, turning to admire the bra, the lift just enough not to look ridiculous.

Pulling a tracksuit on, she waited excitedly for his call, having worked out how she was going to play this, knowing he would be disappointed to find her in a tracksuit. Her plan was this: as he voiced his disappointment, she was going to suggest that she remove the tracksuit and wow him with what was underneath; containing herself waiting for the call was like watching paint dry.

She decided to re-apply her makeup and brush her hair to make up time; there was at least another five minutes to wait. Oh shit, she needed the loo, she knew the cell would ring, but she couldn't wait, nature called.

She ran to get her phone, then back to the bathroom, starting to pull down her tracksuit bottoms she realised she had to be gentle with the delicate lace panties and suspenders. She pulled them down carefully, sighing with relief. As she reached for the loo paper her cell started vibrating on the floor next to the toilet.

Panicking, not knowing whether to pick up the phone first or to finish, she yanked up her lace panties and put her finger right through the hose. Flustered, she pulled up her tracksuit bottoms, stretched over to retrieve the now frantically dancing vibrating cell phone, slipped, and found herself lying flat on her stomach on the bathroom floor, bruising her knees and elbows as she hit the tile. The cell had slid even further out of reach, scrambling to reach the damn thing before it stopped.

What a klutz. She picked up the cell, hoping he would press redial before she felt the need to call back. Managing to stop herself from cracking up hysterically, she remained composed as the phone rang. With the sound of laughter in her voice, she faltered her hello.

'What's so funny… I haven't said a word yet?'

'Oh, nothing, I dropped the phone when you called the first time from nerves while I was in the bathroom, then slipped when I tried to retrieve it, and by then it had stopped ringing.'

Sasha tried to see the funny side, but Safi could tell that it had somehow spoilt his romantic mood. Thankfully, through the course of their conversation, she sensed his mood changing for the better. He was sounding more relaxed, remembering they were supposed to be having their FaceTime on the iPad. Sasha called back and Safi was ready this time when he popped up on the screen, handsome and larger than life.

Sasha immediately told Safi how he missed her and that she looked more beautiful than he remembered. 'What are you wearing?' he asked.

Safi nonchalantly said, 'A tracksuit. It's Sunday night, I'm in my chilling clothes.'

'You did not dress up for me in anything special?' Sasha asked.

Safi smiled, wickedly pulling off the tracksuit and stood on her knees so that Sasha could see her suspenders, panties, and laced-up corset; then she turned around slowly so he could see the back. There was an ominous silence, then she heard a low whistle and knew he loved it.

'I love it. Oh my God, this is torture, I can't touch you.'

Safi slowly moved her hand in a tantalizing downward spiral, first to her breasts, each one in turn, then down her tummy, unhooking the suspenders and letting them snap.

She could hear his groan.

Watching in fascination, wishing she could touch him, feeling odd about having iPad sex, she brushed her prudishness aside, not wanting to spoil the moment. Sasha's breathing heightened her excitement, and she fell forward onto the bed as she too shivered into an orgasm.

They lay on their separate beds, thousands of miles apart, spent but happy. Both started to giggle at the ridiculous way they were having sex.

Sasha told Safi he would try and fly over in December to meet with her parents and to spend Christmas and New Year with her. Ecstatic at the news and happier than she had been for a while, they air-kissed goodnight. She crawled into bed, hugging the pillow, counting the weeks until they would be back together. Lord knows, she did not know whether she could keep up the phone sex for too long.

The relaxed creative atmosphere at work kept her from missing Sasha every moment of every day. The weeks flew by. The ad campaign was spot-on; she felt confident that with refinement they would be able to show the client something special.

Greg kept his distance from the rest of the female staff, never including himself in after-work drinks. He had obviously been shaken by the events that overshadowed their first meeting as much as she was. She was beginning to believe his side of the story, but remained on guard, preferring to play it safe.

The team were lovely (especially Nicky Ray) and made her time at work socially fun and interesting; they met up for dinner or movies after work on odd evenings.

Nicky Ray hailed from Texas; Safi loved listening to her Texan drawl, her lazy easy relaxed manner. Nicky Ray's wicked sense of humour was a welcome relief, during long intense days at work, amongst so many self-serious, workaholic New Yorkers. She was a tall, horsey blonde with impeccable taste in clothes, always looking stylish rather than fashionable.

Safi tried to mimic Nicky Ray's effortless style, but it was harder work than she imagined; she just could not carry it off in the same nonchalant way. Nicky Ray endlessly teased Safi about her English ways and threatened to introduce her to hoedown Southern ways at a Texan bar in Manhattan where line-dancing was the thing. Safi found anything her newest girlfriend suggested was okay with her.

Nicky Ray had been to the best schools Southern money could buy and her Southern charms were captivating. Safi decided to introduce her to Lauren and Bianca; perhaps they would join them at the Texan bar. The image of Lauren with a beer bottle in hand was hilarious and, Safi felt sure, would appeal to Nicky Ray's sense of humour, too: to have an English rose and a typical New Yorker meet with her Southern friends.

Safi arranged a Friday evening at Pete's Bar to introduce Nicky Ray to Lauren and Bianca and the rest of her NY family, who, she hoped, would find her equally entertaining.

Sitting at a long wooden table in Pete's Bar waiting for Nicky Ray to arrive, Safi wondered whether they too would be beguiled by her new Texan friend when she made her entrance. Nicky Ray had charisma in spades; she was not exactly beautiful in the conventional sense, but when she walked into Pete's Bar swinging that thick, long blonde hair every head turned, even laidback Pete did a double take.

Nicky Ray made the most of her Southern roots; she seemed totally at home wearing her Texan-styled clothes in Manhattan.

That evening she wore endless blue jeans tucked into black Texan boots, a black leather belt with huge silver buckle and turquoise stones hung low on her hips, and a crisp white shirt covered with a long suede fringed gilet finished a look only Nicky Ray could get away with and not appear out of place. She was an extrovert but carried her style with a classic dramatic twist accompanied by a wide white beaming smile – a disarming combination that she knew got her the attention she obviously enjoyed.

Everyone introduced themselves to Nicky Ray, including Pete, bringing her a bottle of his best beer. She immediately had everyone eating out of her hand and Safi noticed that Lauren and Bianca were completely taken with her. Bianca, she noticed, had faded into the background, which was not easy for her to accomplish, being a Brazilian Victoria's Secret model.

Lauren and Nicky Ray immediately hit it off, much to Safi's surprise as they seemed polar opposites in every way; but to Nicky Ray's credit she effortlessly brought Bianca out of her shell. She seemed to have won everyone over with very little effort.

The evening ended with Nicky Ray being invited to Dan and Dax's upcoming bash the following Sunday.

Dax could not resist the intrigue developing between Lauren, Bianca and Nicky Ray, but Safi was adamant her friend was very far from gay. As they entered the apartment Safi's cell pinged. It was Lauren wanting Nicky Ray's cell number. Safi felt it was not her business to get involved in Lauren's affairs and passed on the number, then shot out to tell Dax and Dan.

She met with Rupert one Friday evening. This time, Jack Levine, his chess companion, was replaced with Samantha, his new love interest, as Dan liked to call her.

Safi was a little taken aback at how young Samantha appeared. Samantha was a Chinese-American, at least thirty years Rupert's junior, Safi supposed. Sam, as Rupert called her, was in her forties. Rupert took them to a wonderful Italian restaurant, where he was greeted as a longstanding regular. He introduced Safi as his cousin's daughter from England, and happened to add that she was living with his son, Daniel. She found this encouraging and couldn't wait to tell Dan.

Over dinner they spoke about Sam's work and how she had met Rupert at a cocktail party held by mutual friends.

'We have been going together for more than one year. I am looking forward to meeting your family, Rupert, so far I have only met your friends!'

The dinner went without incident; nothing further was said about family during the evening. Afterwards, however, standing on the sidewalk while waiting for a cab, Rupert pulled her aside.

'I miss family, to be honest. It pleases me you are staying with Daniel. I will be returning to my Park Avenue apartment for the festive season to see your father. Leonard and I have a hell of a lot to catch up on.' Safi found Rupert's deliberate theatrical switch from a transatlantic accent into a British one amusing, as if he wanted her to know that he was still a Brit at heart.

When Safi returned to the apartment Daniel was waiting, eager for any news about Rupert, no matter how small.

She filled Daniel in about the evening, trying to remember the smallest details and what his father had said on parting. The depth of Daniel's anguish over their long separation was taking its toll, as Daniel hungrily hung onto every word.

Usually the strong one, with more than a bit of English reserve, Daniel visibly crumbled with emotion at the slightest possibility of a reunion with his dad.

Safi felt at a loss, not knowing how to react or show she understood how important this direct contact with his father was, to Dan, this was the closest he had come to his father acknowledging he existed, since cutting off all ties several years ago.

Safi kneeled in front of Dan's seat, putting her head on his lap. Bruno was lying next to him too, and together she felt they managed to comfort him.

He stroked Safi's hair, then patted Bruno. Safi felt Dan relax, taking the opportunity to break the tenseness of the moment she jokingly pretended to tease Bruno.

'You better be careful or I will replace you as top dog!'

Dax returned, wanting to hear the gossip of the evening all over again. He was intrigued by Samantha and wanted to know everything about her: what she looked like, what she wore, and what Safi thought of her. All thought it was a good sign Safi liked her and that Rupert had been with her for more than one year.

'Well, at long last that old goat is seeing sense,' Dax said. 'Why would he want to grow old alone and miserable. Samantha won't hang around when Rupert is no longer attractive or of any use to her in the sack; she won't tie herself down to a doddering old man, that's for sure.'

'Hopefully, you are right, Dax, because I feel this may be my last chance to have my father in our lives before he is too old to enjoy our company or our family when we have one.'

Dax always became an emotional wreck whenever Daniel voiced his commitment to their future.

Safi felt involved in their struggle: she loved her parents dearly, but with Dan and Dax she had truly learnt how to show compassion for someone other than herself. She wasn't singing to her own song sheet, instead something far better was happening to her: she was growing up; she was still able to do as she damn well pleased without being completely self-absorbed.

Daniel and Dax had spent every spare moment happily arranging the Sunday evening party. Apart from Dan's father, they were thrilled everyone else on their list had accepted. Dax found it almost impossible not to share his happy news with his family before they announced it publicly, but on discussion with Dan they decided to keep shtum, not wanting it to seep out.

Pete organised the bar and their favourite Italian was catering. They wanted it to be a relaxed evening, nothing too formal, so Italian seemed the perfect option, knowing there would be an endless supply of delicious antipasto, with their signature dishes of the pasta everyone loved for mains, topped off with classic Italian desserts.

The guest list had grown from a cosy dozen to a surprisingly large one of twenty friends and family. Wanting Safi to feel included in their big day, Dax had added Nicky Ray to the mix.

Dax being Dax insisted on a shopping expedition that was mostly for himself, but he managed to persuade Dan and Safi to accompany him. Safi, who now never had retail therapy far from her mind, was thrilled to tag along.

Together they visited Lauren at Barneys, each having her undivided attention. Dan stuck with the designer who fitted his conservative minimal style with his usual choice of greys, blacks or navy blue. He always wore Italian leather shoes and belts.

Dax tried to encourage Dan to introduce colour and suggested a cashmere pullover sporting a small amount of purple. He was delighted that Dan approved of his choice. Dan, in turn, suggested choosing something less flamboyant for Dax to wear.

It took Dax a few moments of hesitation to agree.

Safi and Lauren spent the afternoon crying tears of laughter, watching both Dan and Dax model their crazy choices for one another before deciding what to buy. Lauren had chosen well for Safi, and by the time they left for home all agreed the shopping excursion had been a great decision, but it was definitely going to be a one-off, she couldn't imagine such a spontaneous togetherness over retail therapy would appeal to Dan's idea of a good time.

They spent the rest of the evening at Pete's Bar, with Safi giving her take on the two D's ridiculous choices for one another, and how both ended up with their original choices. Pete was wonderful at indulging Safi, and together with Dax and Dan they egged her on, helping to turn the whole buying episode into a comic farce, with only Bruno showing little interest.

Safi confided to Sasha that she was fearful that Rupert's stubbornness concerning Dan would doom Dan's dream of a Christmas reunion. At some point during their separation, Sasha had become bossy, wanting to know every detail to do with her social life. Safi regaled him with anecdotes, hoping not to bore him, but Sasha always questioned who everyone was and how they fitted into her lifestyle.

He seemed to disapprove of Nicky Ray, wanting to know who she hung out with after work. Safi preferred to block any worrying thoughts concerning his line of questioning by diverting his attention with their regular FaceTime sex sessions, which they seemed to have got down to a fine art, each knowing exactly what turned the other on.

Buying the sexiest underwear she could find, their role-playing with Sasha's direction had become something neither of them wanted to spoil with disagreements. Being so far apart it was easy, Safi thought, to be jealous, so she forgave his bad-tempered display of possessiveness.

She never displayed the same amount of interest in his lifestyle. She had given this thought and realised that not having been to Moscow for some unknown reason enabled her to feel less insecure about him straying.

She was content not to know more than he wished to tell her. This almost-indifference seemed to make Sasha want her more, and Safi further placated him with their role-playing, which she found madly exciting.

She still had not confided about Greg to Sasha, and time had run out on her mentioning it now. She feared giving Sasha a reason not to trust her – or, for that matter, not to trust Greg.

Sasha suggested she visit with him in Russia once her time at the ad agency was up; she would anyway have to leave once her work permit was up. She had no idea whether the agency would reemploy her. She did want to remain in New York, of course, but the agency would have no need of her once the account for the client was complete.

The thought of not being able to return to New York was more than she wanted to dwell on, she wasn't ready to leave.

Somehow, Sasha and Safi managed to chat and text, but it was almost always unsatisfactory. Sundays had become their only time to really connect. It was the glue that held them together. Sasha arriving at the same time as her family over the festive period made Safi excited and apprehensive about him being there, mostly about him meeting her parents; she was not sure they would approve of this older man in her life, they might feel she was out of her depth.

She pushed back the nagging thoughts popping into her consciousness, knowing the moment she spoke with Sasha they usually flew out of the window, replaced by desire but not only physical desire, Safi found on some deeper level they had a genuine need for each other. Safi knew in Sasha she had found excitement and, a challenging adventure.

Instead, she indulged in secret shopping sprees at Victoria's Secret on a weekly basis, filling her drawers to overflowing with flimsy underwear to show off over the festive season when they would be together.

The team had reached the final proposal on the ad campaign, tweaking some odds and ends to make it concise and clear in every aspect before presenting the work for final approval. Their team had formed a close working relationship and Safi found her skills as a team member on the creative side had greatly improved. She still lacked experience, but on the whole, she was delighted they found her to be a valuable member on the team.

Greg seemed to enjoy having another Limey to bounce ideas off; he encouraged her to voice her opinions as much as everyone else's. His contribution as the project manager forged a competitive yet cohesive environment, bringing the best out of everyone.

She had learnt to respect his abilities and had found him to be someone they could count on in a positive way, never allowing anyone to doubt their ability.

He deserved the benefit of the doubts she had harboured against him since their dramatic second meeting at the conference table on her first day at work.

She certainly could not fault his behaviour towards her at work, allowing her to benefit from everyone else's experience. He had earned her silence about their first unfortunate meeting. She was most certainly never going to mention it to her father. Greg was someone her father would want on his team if he ever returned to England and happened to work for her father's agency again.

Friday rolled around and, for the first time since the project started, everyone found they had free time to meet up in their usual bar across from the agency. Safi found herself in Greg's company socially once more. They both kept their distance, but she found herself quite at home in his company, both in and out of the office. He seemed to have changed, too; he was no longer the cocky, arrogant Limey know-it-all he displayed when she was in his company briefly at their last social meeting.

He did, though, remain quintessentially British and eccentric in his style of dress. Tight skinny pants, usually in a bright colour red, she noticed was the favoured colour worn with a white cotton T-shirt. Slim-fitting dark jacket with a flamboyant kerchief in the top pocket or around his neck. His shoes were always noticeably pointy, or he wore lace-up Converse boots with white laces. He wore his long wavy hair neatly swept off his face rounding off his look with elongated dark-framed glasses, a sort of Jarvis Cocker lookalike. Safi wondered whether Greg, like Nicky Ray. managed to throw his style together effortlessly, or had they both cultivated something, she thought unique.

Nicky Ray was holding court, regaling everyone with her Southern anecdotes. Greg, Safi noticed, hung on her every word. Safi wondered whether there was something more going on between them. Nicky Ray was definitely performing just for his benefit.

Greg had never come up in their conversations, Safi reflected. She wondered whether Nicky Ray was purposely cultivating their friendship due to her being British, like Greg. Her Southern charms were hard to ignore, or her charismatic personality. People were drawn to Nicky Ray's unworldly guile, but Safi found her pretty savvy about life in general.

After the evening ended, they all went their separate ways, with Nicky Ray adding, 'Just can't wait for Sunday to roll on by. I am just crazy for Lauren and gorgeous Bianca, aren't they a hoot?'

After whistling down a cab, Nicky Ray was gone, leaving Safi more intrigued than ever. She couldn't wait to chat to Dax about everything; he was always so good at ferreting information out of everyone, and she wanted him to do some serious snooping when he spoke with Lauren.

Chapter 8

When Safi arrived back at the loft she found the two D's fretting neurotically over everything, including the weather; hoping to use the roof terrace, they were hanging onto every weather report, visibly sighing when Sunday was declared a sunny cold clear day. Daniel had strategically placed heaters with more fitted under the canvas parasol to keep the guests warm. The garden furniture had mohair blankets thrown casually over them and new lighting had been installed for the occasion, with alternate trees covered in white twinkle lights creating a festive atmosphere. The hammock had Bulldog-faced cushions comfortably piled together at one end, with a large fringed blanket hanging over both sides at the other end. Flickering candles on the coffee table added a romantic flavour with snuggle-down comfort.

Indoors, the loft apartment had been swept clean and polished to the highest standard by Marita, the cleaning lady, who had been called in for extra duty; even the bathrooms fixtures reflected mirrored light, not a water spot to be seen. The kitchen had become Pete's domain, the breakfast bar covered in glasses for every occasion: champagne, wine and alcohol, including soft drinks.

The dining table had been cleared ready for the Italian feast to be laid out on. The D's excitement was palpable, and it had its effect on Safi; she wanted to be feel part of this momentous occasion. Not wanting to let the side down, she ran into her bedroom to check that it reflected the tidiness of Marita's efforts.

All journals and books had been artfully arranged on side tables; the last vestiges of Dax's art materials had been carted off to his new studios. Dan had taken this opportunity to fix anything that needed repair. Plumbers and painters had been through the apartment in the last week, and Safi had noticed that her (and Bruno's) favourite shabby winged arm chair had been carted off to reappear in tan and white cowhide with brass studs, looking very smart; even Bruno seemed to be ignoring it, in favour of the sofa.

Dax was fussing over when to announce their news: should it be before the meal or later in the evening. He decided it was best to announce it during the reception, after everyone had arrived and before the evening started. He wanted Dan to announce their engagement formally, having everyone charge their champagne glasses, having always adored the thought of being engaged.

Dan and Safi fell about giggling; neither could imagine Dax remaining or containing his excitement before the announcement, it was going to be impossible to keep him calm and not to give all away before Dan had a chance to utter a word.

Saturday was taken up with caterers, flowers arriving in magnificent glass vases to be strategically placed around the loft. Dan loved roses and dozens had been sent in pale colours adding, Safi thought, a soft sophisticated touch to the masculine comfortable furniture Dan preferred to live with. Saturday night was spent quietly in Pete's Bar. Safi felt they were all in a reflective mood, and the previous day's excitement had been replaced, she felt, by the finality of their decision and pledge to one another.

Not having easy access and having also to consider the stairs, the caterers opted for an early Sunday morning start. Dan wanted to give them free rein, not wanting anyone to get under their feet, they decided it best to take Bruno out of everyone's way.

He would be going for an early morning walk and off to the groomers while they went out for brunch to relax before the guests arrived. Dan wondered what their nuptials would entail if they were making such a fuss over the engagement announcement and confided in Safi about scribbling a few words.

Dax declaring, he adored every mad moment; this was their special time and he could not wait to tell the world, hoping for double madness when they prepared for the wedding. Dan calmly resigned himself to Dax's exuberance; Safi could tell he had accepted all the hoopla, enjoying Dax happiness.

They had thrown themselves wholeheartedly behind this decision to make their union official. Dax expected positive support from his family and those close enough to make a difference to their lives. It had therefore been a tremendous effort for Dax not to spill the beans to his family, but he wanted it to be a surprise for them, too, so he managed to avoid his brothers and his mother's questions when calling with a date for their diaries. He knew they would be the first through that door; they had all heard so much about Saffron and her effect on their lives.

Dax thought his mother would be the least shocked at their decision to marry.

She understood her son and his need for a legal union. She loved Daniel, he had been a wonderful calming influence, helping to channel Dax's energy into a constructive, successful career. The only person Dax and Daniel were concerned about was Rupert; they would have been overjoyed had he accepted their invitation, but as always, they had not received any reply to their written invite, which had been sent personally with Safi.

Safi had, on occasion, taken Bruno to the park, where she knew Rupert would be playing chess with his friends; she would sit and watch them contentedly for a while wanting Rupert to become accustomed to her presence in his life. Rupert, for his part, welcomed Safi and seemed to enjoy her and Bruno's company when they appeared unannounced on occasion.

Always grateful for any news about his father, Daniel thought having Safi deliver their invitation their best bet, though in truth they held very little hope of him showing up on their special day.

Dan was pinning his hopes on Safi's father's persuasive charms to work magic on Rupert's stubborn nature, hoping that reconnecting with his past life would bring him to his senses and give him an excuse to make up with his only son.

On returning to the apartment, they found organised chaos as the caterers and Pete were putting their finishing touches to both the bar and the table, which was now groaning with anti-pastas of every kind. The lasagnes and famous meatballs in tomato sauce were all lined up in the kitchen on warmers. Salads were heaped in large containers. The deserts had been stored in the built-in larder fridge.

Safi could not contain herself: the tiramisu, her favourite, and the oranges in syrup, plus the exotic platters of fruit, just had to be sampled, but Mario caught her red-handed as she was about to help herself to some of the fruit, barring anyone from the kitchen until the food was served, including Bruno, who looked adorable in his new red kerchief and smelling positively wonderful to everyone – everyone, that is, apart from Bruno who appeared to be disgusted with his cleanliness.

Dan busied himself reorganising some of the furniture, while Dax decided it was time to dress. Dax wanted to call Samantha, with whom he had made contact, hoping she might have some good news for him about Rupert. Samantha had given Safi her number and made it obvious to Safi that she would be very happy to be of any help in getting Rupert together with his son. Safi, in turn, had given Dax Samantha's number, which, unbeknownst to either Safi or Daniel, he had called.

Over coffee, they had decided she would encourage Rupert to attend their Sunday party, a way of breaking the ice, before his cousin, Leonard, arrived. He had not heard from Samantha and wondered whether she had had any success. Not having any luck contacting her, he left a message for her to call back. He was on the terrace when his cell pinged. Samantha had left a message: Rupert had not given her any indication one way or another about attending the party, but he had not declined either. She apologised for not being able to tie him down to any definite reply. She added that she had tried to encourage him, and that she thought Safi had a positive influence; if he were to change his mind, she would text him again.

The guests were invited for early evening. The weather for once seemed to be perfect, if cold; it was dry and crisp for those who favoured the terrace, and the heaters had been turned on, making it pleasantly cosy. Daniel made his way down to greet his first guests.

As he entered the loft through the glass doors, the colour drained from his face. Standing with champagne glass in hand, chatting to Safi, surrounded by Dax and his family, stood Rupert; with him stood an attractive young Chinese woman who Dan supposed was Samantha.

Rupert seemed perfectly calm, enjoying all the attention he was receiving from those around him. Steven, Dax's younger brother, spotted Dan and made his way over, realizing the impact of the situation on both father and son.

No one, including Dan, knew what to expect. Rupert, sensing Dan, turned to face him. Time seemed to freeze; all Dan could see were images of himself as a small boy, being loved and cared for by this man, who now seemed a total stranger, barely recognisable. Somehow, in spite of the estrangement and unfamiliarity, or perhaps because of it, almost instinctively, Dan found himself moving towards his father. All sound was blocked out of his consciousness; it was just the two of them, when Rupert stuck out his hand towards Dan as if to shake hands. It was too much for Dan; taking his father's hand, he pulled him into a bear hug that seemed to last forever.

Dax's family were walking towards the apartment when Ethan, Dax's younger brother, who had met Rupert, when accompanying Dax, in the early years of their relationship to soften Rupert's, attitude to their relationship, recognised him right off. Noticing Rupert sitting in his vintage Jaguar outside the apartment, realizing the delicate situation he bent down to greet Rupert nonchalantly inviting him to join them on their climb to Dan and Dax's loft for the party. Samantha took his hand gently and coaxed him out of the car to greet Dax's family. She joined them and introduced herself and together they made their way up the stairs. Dax dad, lagged behind, texting Dax to warn him of Rupert's arrival. Dax received the text as Daniel was making his way up to the terrace, having no time to warn him.

Dax composed himself to greet Rupert as his family burst through the door together with Rupert and Samantha, who introduced herself to Dax with a knowing smile. The shock of seeing Rupert momentarily had everyone talking at once. Dax signalled to Pete, who immediately calmed the hysteria by handing out champagne.

Rupert, surrounded by Dax's family, turned to see Daniel coming towards him. Not having time to overthink the situation, he did what all men of his generation do: he stuck out his hand to greet his son. But Daniel took his hand and pulled him in close, and Rupert felt himself let go of all the years of longing in that moment, having his son in his arms, the boy he had loved more than any other person after his wife had died.

When Dan and Rupert eventually parted, everyone, including Daniel, was crying. 'So sorry, my boy, I am a stubborn old man. It took these two wonderful women to help me come to my senses.' Rupert usually full of bluff and swagger, had a frog in his throat and, a visible shake as he withdrew, still holding onto his son's hand. Daniel having found his composure just grabbed his dad, holding him close.

'Dad, I have you back in my life now and that's all that matters to me. I love you.'

People were arriving and Pete tried to hold them back with champagne, in order to give Dan and his dad a chance to compose themselves before the party began.

'Let's celebrate, Rupert, this has been a long time coming,' Dax said, taking Safi by the hand and propelling them towards their guests to be introduced.

'Meet Rupert, Dan's father, and Saffron, Dan's cousin, our adopted daughter from England.'

This gave everyone, including Dan, a chance to recover their composure. Dax, literally shaking, sank into the closest armchair, asking his brother Harley to fetch him a vodka. Allowing the strong liquid to hit his gut, he felt his senses reel and the elation of the moment returned as he saw Dan's father happily charming one of his guests.

Dax had pulled himself together to welcome everyone as they arrived, while also trying to arrange his thoughts back into some semblance of coherence, remembering there was a reason for this party. That was when he suddenly had visions of Dan's father walking out of his life once more on hearing about the intended union between himself and his son.

Claude whispered in French to his Parisian partner 'I detect some Les liaisons dangereuses,' as they sipped their champagne, watching the interaction between the tall Texan beauty and stunning Brazilian amazon. As they mingled amongst the guests.

Daniel tried to entertain his guests and, tried to join in a conversation with his design team who had started up an interesting conversation with a documentary film maker about the sudden influx of Russian money that was floating around Manhattan, but his thoughts were a tumultuous jumble; he had to remove himself from the party to regain his equilibrium; He had too much to lose to make a mess of things now. Sitting on the edge of the bath in the bay window, Dan found that he had no idea what he was going to do; he did not want to take a chance of alienating his father again, but if the announcement did not go ahead, he would hurt Dax and he could not envisage a life without Dax.

Sitting with his head in his hands for what seemed ages, he became aware of Dax standing in front of him. As their eyes met, Dax immediately understood Daniel's fears were the same as his.

To his own astonishment, Dax felt a surge of uncontrolled jealousy surging through him. Before he disintegrated into a screaming harridan, he bristled instead and walked out, leaving Daniel in no doubt about what had to be done. Dan understood Dax's resentment: he did not deserve to be usurped by Rupert; his dad had deserted him for years while Dax had always been there for him.

Joining his guest on the terrace, Daniel made his way towards Samantha, who was chatting to Clarissa a diminutive power house in the financial world. Clarissa excused herself grabbing another flute of champagne she propelled herself down the stairs to mingle with Dax family to see if she could pick up some gossip about the party. Dan was hoping to seek out Samantha for some advice. Finding her a charming, open person and easy to talk to, he led her to a private area on the roof terrace, where there were relatively few guests, braving the crisp cold air.

Immediately aware of the urgency in his manner, she volunteered her assistance. Dan decided to confide their intention about the announcement and his concerns relating to his father's reaction. Understanding the predicament, she volunteered to leave with Rupert before they served the desert; she knew there was a football game he was keen on seeing. She said that she would solicit Jack Levine, who had been invited as Dan's only contact with Rupert in the now forgotten wilderness years. and, suggest departing the party to catch the game, leaving Dan free to make the announcement.

Feeling conflicted by Daniel's attitude to their union, Dax gave Daniel no indication about his feelings, but Daniel could tell that something was wrong. He would have to work hard to get Dax to forgive him., for having doubts about announcing their engagement, not wanting to alienate Rupert. Daniel was not good at showing his feelings at the best of times, but the occasion called for drastic action on his part.

Grabbing Dax by the hand, he propelled him up to the terrace, where he pushed him down onto one of the empty sofas. Still bristling with anger, Dax reluctantly turned to face Dan. He knew instantly by Dan's expression that everything would be okay; they were on the same page again; hugging Dan they made their way down to enjoy the rest of the party. As they parted Dan whispered, 'We announce the engagement before dessert.'

Dax, free to enjoy their guests without worrying about Rupert he floated off on a cloud caught by Polly Grant, who instantly tried to wheedle some salacious gossip out of him, about Bianca, but was stopped in her tracks, when she realised Dan's father had reunited with his son, that was all

Polly needed to keep her appetite for a good story satisfied. She winked at Dan, in a knowing way as she made her way over to engage Rupert in conversation, she would be able to kill two birds with one stone, as Bianca was chatting to, an extremely attractive older man, she had learnt was Dan's father Rupert.

Safi introduced Rupert to Nicky Ray and Lauren, but she could see it was Bianca who held his attention; she did look stunning in a short skirt with over-the-knee moleskin boots. Safi noted that Rupert had an eye for the girls; he seemed to flirt with everyone quite openly. It did not seem to bother Samantha, who laughed good-naturedly at his shenanigans.

Saying 'It makes him feel young, who am I to stop his overactive imagination?' Bianca for her part seemed to be enjoying Rupert's attention; but Lauren looked less than happy, turning her attention to Nicky Ray.

Safi noticed them cosying up on one of the sofas, whispering and giggling with one another. Dax, wise to a situation when he saw one developing, saved the day by plonking himself between them. Nothing passed him by, Safi thought; he had noticed Lauren's discomfort and probably wanted to avoid any scene from happening.

Daniel had disengaged Rupert to introduce him to friends. Safi found herself watching the party from the sidelines. She wished Sasha had been there to witness the reunion between Dan and his father, she could not wait to describe the heart-wrenching scene to him. Noticing Polly's dramatic costume jewellery as only Polly could wear, in contrast the other guests were casually underdressed. There was a palpable energy of excitement in the air, and she turned around to catch Pete's eye, wondering whether he felt it too.

As she made her way over to Pete, hoping to gauge his reaction to everything, Safi heard a yelp from Lauren as she watched Nicky Ray throw her wine in Bianca's face. There was a moment's suspended silence from everyone who noticed the incident, before Dax tried to separate them. But Nicky Ray was having none of it; her Southern pride took over as she grabbed Bianca by the hair.

Lauren looked mortified, her sophisticated veneer evaporated in an instant, replaced by a shocked screech as her hand flew over her mouth. Everyone watched in disbelief as the amazons – one from Brazil, the other from Texas – literally attacked one another.

Nicky Ray was accusing Bianca of calling her a 'Texan slut.'

'No one, especially not a stupid Brazilian Gringo is going to get away with calling me a slut.'

Bianca, true to her Brazilian street roots, punched Nicky Ray out cold. Cursing in Portuguese, she grabbed her purse and Lauren by the arm and made her way through the shocked guests and down the stairs, before anyone had time to say 'Yankee Doodle' from Harley Dax, brother who was standing next to Safi, and Ethan added the 'Dandy.' This left Pete to attend a dazed Nicky Ray, now completely embarrassed with tears welling up in an already swollen eye.

Daniel, Dax, and Safi stood watching the whole drama unfold in total disbelief. A moment before, everyone had just finished their delicious pasta dishes, laughing and chatting, standing around munching on the salads. The catfight had changed the mood, everyone was buzzing with chatter about the fight they had just witnessed.

Polly wickedly amused, turned to a friend, and quipped, 'No one could call this a dull afternoon.'

Pete managed to get Nicky Ray up off the floor, taking her into Safi's bedroom and signalling for Safi to remain with Nicky Ray until he returned with an icepack for her eye. Safi had no idea what to say to Nicky Ray, so she just sat and held her hand, hoping to calm her down. She realised that Nicky Ray saw herself as the innocent party; Safi, on the other hand, wasn't so sure, having witnessed her flirting with just about everyone, and quite blatantly with Lauren, obviously stirring up jealous feelings in Bianca's hot Latin blood.

What followed was clever manipulation on Pete's part. Pete's heroic and gentle doctoring and considerable skill managed to persuade Nicky Ray to see the whole incident as hilariously funny, forgetting all about her litigious mumbling of suing for assault. On hearing, her hysterical laughter Dax bravely showed his face encouraging her to join the party.

'Everyone can't wait to see that knockout punch,' Dax quipped.

Nicky Ray liked nothing more than being the centre of attention, and within half an hour was back to normal, leaving everyone else a bit bewildered by the afternoon's sudden turn of events with, of all things, a cat fight.

Jack Levine, Rupert's chess buddy and guest at the party, having had more than a little to do with Safi meeting Dan's dad, had no problem persuading Rupert to leave with him to watch the game. Rupert having flirted with Bianca thought egotistically that he might have caused the row, but Jack assured him it was probably more complicated; finding Daniel they bid everyone goodbye, Rupert promising to call.

The timing was perfect: not only would it help everyone focus on the real reason for the party, it was also time to relieve Dax from his animated suspension; so much had happened already, they needed to have their own shot at the limelight.

Mario, who had been as taken with events as the rest of the guests, got back to laying out the deserts, wondering what the next drama would be; it seemed each course brought on another round of entertainment. Daniel managed to indicate their moment had come and Dax joined him at the refectory table.

Pete was requested to fill everyone's champagne flute for a toast. Dan looked over at the expectant faces of his family and friends, wondering whether the next bombshell he was going to drop would, after all these years, come as a surprise to anyone?

'Before getting stuck into these incredible deserts, I would like to thank Mario for helping to make today a delicious one, and to Pete, a valued friend and part of our family, thank you for everything. Dax and I would like to add a little drama of our own: after many years of being together, and with Dax's endless love, patience, and support, I have come to realise our love would not be complete without hopefully a family and a legal union.'

Turning to Dax, Dan continued, 'Dax, I hope you will accept my proposal with this ring and continue to be by my side into old age.'

Dax, never a shrinking violet and knowing Dan hated displays of public affection, pulled Dan's chin towards him and kissed him passionately.

Everyone surged towards them, most agreeing that they never believed Dan would compromise his beliefs. Knowing how important this was for Dax, his family were overcome with shocked emotion, welcoming Dan into their family. Dax's mother, Rachel, demanded to know how long Dax had kept this happy secret from her. After everyone had calmed down, Dax announced he wanted to add a few words of his own.

'Safi, where are you? I would like to mentioned that without your darling presence in our lives, neither Dan nor I would have reached this moment in our relationship. More than that, without your generous intervention, we know that Rupert, Dan's father, might never have become part of our lives again. We love you, please stay part of our lives always.'

Safi, still reeling from the day's drama, suddenly felt quite inadequate; lost for words, she was grateful for Pete's strong arm around her shoulders. Embarrassed, she smiled weakly, hoping Nicky Ray and Bianca's behaviour had not spoilt their day, and wished Dax had not invited her.

As for the reunion, she was amazed at Dan's fortitude during the rest of the day, knowing how long he had waited for his father to become part of his life again. Suddenly she realised that Rupert had missed their announcement and a small part of her was relieved, not knowing how Rupert would have reacted. She wondered whether Dax had engineered his father-in-law-to-be's early departure? Happily, the rest of the evening went without incident; most of their friends departed after desert. The only people who remained were Dax's family, who wanted to recap the dramas of the day.

Nicky Ray had apologised for her bad behaviour and made Safi promise not to mention it at work; she would think of something to explain her black eye.

Safi's opinion of Nicky Ray, Lauren, and Bianca's behaviour made her feel, for the first time, ambivalent towards them. It would take her a while to process her thoughts; it occurred to her that she may have to reassess whether or not these women were decent people – or, at the very least, had Safi's best interests at heart. She excused herself from Dan and Dax and his family, knowing that Sasha would be waiting for her to call as soon as the party was over, to get all the gossip. Sitting on her bed with the iPad, ready to call Sasha, she found it was her parents she really wanted to talk to. She missed them, especially her mom.

Her father answered the call and Safi found herself pouring out the day's events, realising, perhaps for the first time, just how significant it was. Her father realised it, too, and put her on speaker phone, so her mother could listen too. Leonard was overjoyed to hear that Rupert had managed to come to terms with his demons and agreed with Safi that missing the announcement of Dan and Dax's engagement was a good thing, too much too soon could have tipped the scales in the wrong direction.

She put Dan and Dax on the phone so that her parents could congratulate them, too. After that, Safi still couldn't bring herself to ring off, although she noticed Sasha was trying to get through. She was feeling more than a little homesick after the day's excitement. Staying to chat to Dax family and then late into the night with the two D's, she found it was much too late to call him, remembering to charge her cell she found irate texts from Sasha, wanting to know where she was. She texted back 'tired speak 2 morrow Safi x.'

Falling into bed she felt strangely pleased with herself. It had been their first Sunday without speaking and she didn't feel at all guilty, admitting she did not always have the energy to be the fun person he expected or a sexy playmate, either.

They had an early start at the agency tomorrow; he would have to wait until she arrived back after work. Safi woke with an uneasy feeling in the pit of her stomach; she felt anxious about seeing Nicky Ray at work, not knowing how she would relate to her. The more she thought about it, the more she felt that Nicky Ray had engineered that jealous response from Bianca.

Sasha was bothering her, too: she suddenly felt their long-distance relationship was not fulfilling her; it left her feeling empty, lonely, and unloved most of the time. While her friends all had partners to keep them company, she had ended up with sexy underwear and iPad sex for company. Seeing the funny side, she giggled to herself, noticing couples all around her some, with their kids, others parting affectionately as they got off at their subway stop. For the first time, she became aware of a sadness enveloping her. It seemed everyone had a life, besides her; as Safi stepped off the train, she wondered whether she was feeling homesick for the first time since arriving in New York.

Chapter 9

Safi was relieved and not at all surprised when Nicky Ray called in ill. No one seemed bothered and the day progressed in a busy haze; the project had suddenly, finally, come together. The team had been given the go-ahead from the creative director to prepare for the clients to view the ad before they shut for the New Year.

If the ad campaign were successful, it would mean she would be without employment. Her work permit at its end, she would have to leave the States before re-entering, either as a tourist or on another work-related permit, if she could persuade the agency to re-employ her.

Her family would be visiting for the festive season and she now felt ambivalent about Sasha coming too. She would have to sort herself out before her life fell apart, leaving her with nothing to return to, one way or another.

Her friends back home had kept in touch with her infrequently; Safi was as much to blame as they were, too busy to keep up with any degree of consistency.

She had outgrown Brighton and would surely feel an outsider if she returned after her life in Manhattan; the thought alone was a depressing one. Her closest friends had moved to London, her long-term boyfriend, Graham, had been out of her life before she had left for her New York adventure.

Working for her father would be awkward and a backward step not to mention dull after the excitement of the New York agency plus the thought of returning to her home town filled her with dread. Moscow was an option for a short period before returning to New York, not if her romance with Sasha ended?

With all these thoughts milling around in her head on her ride home, she almost missed her stop. As she walked into her room the cell phone pinged. Hoping it was Sasha, she was surprised to see it was Bianca, who had never called her before. Judging from her quavering voice, Bianca was distraught.

Safi wondered how she would console Bianca when she herself was floundering. Bianca was at Pete's Bar and needed to talk, she said. Safi could hardly refuse to join her for a chat. She supposed it was flattering Lauren's partner had sought her out as a confidant. She threw on her slouchy torn jeans and flats, happy to be rid of her heels. Sensing she was about to go out again, Bruno was waiting at the door; since Pete's Bar was his favourite haunt (and since she didn't much feel up to going out alone), she happily took him along.

Bianca was sitting hunched at a corner booth nursing a coffee. Pete for once was not around. Safi joined Bianca while Bruno settled down in his personally named bed under the bar.

They had sat quietly for some time, both nursing their coffees, the steam rising into their faces not unpleasantly, when Bianca turned to Safi.

'You must understand I am from the favela in the Brazilian slums. I have fought hard to work my way out. I was at the right place at the right time, and, given a chance by a talent scout, took the opportunity and the rest is history.'

Safi realised Bianca did not want to dwell on her childhood, nor did she want pity, she was stating hard fast facts, Safi decided to listen without comment or question or judgement.

'I left home at sixteen and have never returned. My family are no longer living in the favela. I never knew my father. Violence thrives in the favela; they preyed on girls like me, we either became their women to do with as they wished, or we were used as drug mules.'

All of this tumbled out without Bianca taking a breath. Safi had gleaned much of this from Lauren: Bianca had had a tough beginning; she alone had helped her family to leave the slums of Rio.

'Here in New York I found safety,' Bianca continued, 'but I never felt safe with men. I work with them professionally, that's all. I met Lauren at a Go See for Barneys and we became firm friends. She has been my rock ever since we met. We have had an on-off relationship, I love Lauren and want to settle down with her, but I am not sure she has ever felt that way for me.

Living with her the last few months has been heavenly for me. I have never felt safer or more settled in my life. I reject jobs that keep me out of the country for more than a month at a time.

I thought we were going to go the distance, but now Lauren is not speaking to me; she blames me for spoiling Dan and Dax's party, their special day, she blames me for embarrassing her in front of everyone. I don't know how to fix this.'

Safi sat quietly, digesting Bianca's story, feeling slightly inadequate not knowing how she could help her. One thing she knew was that she did not think Bianca was to blame for what happened at the party.

She told Bianca how she saw the fiasco from her viewpoint, that far from being the blameworthy one, Bianca was in fact blameless. Hearing this lifted Bianca's spirits and lit up her beautiful features into a radiant smile that had been sadly missing in action for hours.

Grabbing Safi's hand, Bianca implored her to call Lauren.

'Please tell Lauren how you see this, how that awful Southern creature has caused this nasty incident and rift between us.'

Safi wasn't sure she wanted to get that involved.

'Safi, she was goading me from the start, playing me for a sucker, I had to fight my corner; it is not easy to feel safe around a monster like Nicky Ray. To her, everyone is fair game and exists for her own amusement. I was not going to stand for it, or be her plaything!

You did notice how that bitch flirted with all the older men beforehand, got bored and turned her feminine wiles on Lauren, blatantly ignoring me, while also obviously trying to get a rise out of me. How dare the bitch!'

Safi had witnessed Bianca's Latin temper; she needed to placate her somehow and also get Lauren on-side: that way, Bianca could restore her dignity and Lauren her anger.

'First off,' Bianca began, 'I have to say sorry to your cousins, Daniel and Dax, they are wonderful people, do you think they will want to talk to me again?'

Safi picked up her cell. She had five messages from Sasha; not having time to read them, she called Dan and Dax, asking if they wanted to join her at Pete's Bar.

'Well you will have the opportunity to speak to them personally,' she said to Bianca, 'in a few moments they are joining us.'

Dan had no idea how to relate to Bianca or her hot Latin temper. He accepted her apology, then left her in Dax's capable hands to help her sort out her love life with Lauren. It was just up his street; he loved nothing better than a love tryst. Safi and Dan moved to another table to order dinner and to wait for Pete to arrive, so they could recap the whole day, wanting to hear what he thought of Rupert turning up and also to gauge everyone's opinion about their announcement. Pete knew most of their close friends, of course, and had chatted to everyone while preparing the drinks.

 Dan had wasted little time contacting his dad the following morning. They had many years to make up, and he wanted Safi to join them for brunch with Rupert and Samantha the following Sunday. It was hard to believe but suddenly, finally, he had family of his own again; also, he needed to break their news to his dad. He did not want to begin this new relationship with any secrets, it was a chance he had to take.

Dan was meeting Rupert during the week; he could not believe things had turned around in such a short space of time: one moment it seemed an impossible dream, the next his father was back in his life again. Life had taken a turn he had only ever dreamed of, that is until the wonderful Safi had entered their lives. Dan wished he knew how to convey his and Dax's total unwavering admiration and love for what she had done for them They had to show their gratitude one way or another, how was the question?

Bianca was on her way out with Dax when Pete joined them at the table for dinner. Safi could not wait to hear what Dax said to Bianca, knowing how he disapproved of Lauren's fickle relationships. Daniel was interested but knew nothing would stop Dax dramatizing the blow-by-blow details, elated with his effort to bring Lauren and Bianca together.

Dax accompanied Bianca to meet with Lauren at a corner coffee shop. Bianca was a bag of nerves, so Dax volunteered to be there when they met. On spotting Lauren, he left Bianca in the coffee shop, nervously watching while he stood outside chatting to a very contrite Lauren on the pavement.

Bianca could see Lauren listening to Dax, noting she spent most of her time staring at her feet, wondering what Dax had been able to say to make her seem almost humble, something completely foreign to Lauren's personality.

When Lauren entered the coffee shop to confront Bianca, her attitude had undergone a complete transformation.

'Let's go home,' Lauren said.

Dax could tell the girls had no fight left as they left the coffee shop hand in hand.

Retelling the story back at the bar, Dax hastened to add that he had told Lauren a few home truths. By then, Lauren had already had second thoughts about her own behaviour in the matter, so there was little else to add. He could tell she had forgiven Bianca, and added that, to his mind, it was Bianca who should have forgiven Lauren for encouraging Nicky Ray. Everyone agreed on the Nicky Ray issue, there was little doubt she was an incorrigible flirt, with any sex.

Nicky Ray was a force to be reckoned with. Later that day, at the bar, Pete advised her to decline all invitations to be social, adding ' that girl's trouble for sure.' Safi couldn't argue with that.

Back in the apartment, Safi sat on her bed reading her texts from Sasha, none of which filled her with joy. She thought he was being a real bastard, selfish and petulant about her lack of contact. She was not in the mood for a confrontation, and when her Skype sprang to life she shut the lid and disconnected.

Turning up her music, she stepped into her shower. The hot water soothing her mood, she washed and dried her hair. Still feeling wretched, though, she climbed into bed and sobbed, not sure why she felt so sad. The first text from Sasha was upsetting enough: 'I don't take lightly to being ignored Safi.' The second text made everything worse: 'Why the hell are you ignoring all my calls.' And the third text was just plain awful: 'I'm not amused, Safi, Sundays are ours and why should I share you, it's our only time to connect!'

How dare he read her the riot act, she was sick of the whole debacle on the iPad. And that was to say nothing of the last text: 'Is there another man, you better tell me.'

She had lost trust in both Lauren and Nicky Ray, who had their own problems to sort out. For the first time, her excitement about being away from family and friends played on her mind; if she was going to return to live in New York she needed to sort out her life. Having always felt sure about what she wanted, being so insecure and uncertain was a feeling she did not like. It made her feel lonely and vulnerable; she was being a wimp and resolved to toughen up.

Safi woke the following morning to a soft knock at her door. Daniel entered tentatively with a cup of tea, seeing her red eyes he sat on the end of her bed, waiting for her to have the first few sips of the hot tea.

'I received a call from Sasha last night.'

Shit, this immediately brought on more tears. She handed Daniel her cell phone to read his nasty texts.

Dax by this time had joined them and was sitting next to Safi, with his arms around her shoulders, stroking her hair. They were both upset for her, hating to see her so low.

Daniel passed Dax the texts to read. Shaking his head he cursed softly at Sasha's selfish stupidity as he scrolled through a dozen texts, all of which were demanding and brutishly self-indulgent. 'Call me back straight away' ... 'If I don't hear from you in the next 5 min I WILL SPANK YOU OVER MY KNEE when I next see you!!!!' Was this guy being serious?

'What did he want?' Safi managed to ask, not really wanting to know. She was still angry and hurt. Dan suggested she hang out at home, but Safi thought it a bad idea. She needed to talk things through with them both, feeling very confused about her life.

It was Saturday and Dax had some paperwork and suggested Safi come into work with him for the day; he needed company as his staff were all out on various jobs.

Looking at Daniel, he tentatively told Safi, 'Sasha wanted to know if everything is okay. You have not been answering his calls or texts. He was worried he had angered you with his latest messages and I can now see why!'

Safi poured her heart out to the two D's about how low she was feeling, about Sasha and their long-distance relationship. How she felt about being away from home, not knowing whether she had a job to return to, or if she would be able to return.

'I feel disappointed in my girlfriends, I no longer know whether to continue my friendship with either of them – or with Sasha, for that matter. It seems I have reached a crossroad and have to make up my mind. You are the only stability in my otherwise pathetic life,' she said. 'Since the reunion with Rupert, your problems have been resolved perhaps it's time for me to move on. I don't want to outstay my welcome. I adore you, and love New York, but my lifestyle would have to change, I need to revaluate my needs, I've become too dependent on you both.'

Dan and Dax were mortified Safi felt she had no other option but to move on;, they understood her dilemma with Sasha, but did not necessarily agree with her about reaching a crossroad, although they certainly did not mean to invalidate how she felt in any way.

Dax said encouragingly, 'Don't make any drastic decisions until after Christmas, your folks will be here and, you will be able to discuss your options to stay.'

Safi shook her head.

Dan added, 'Let's give these issues some thought.'

Over lunch, Safi picked at her food, waiting to hear what they thought she should do. Mostly she was undecided about Sasha; she knew things could not continue as they were. She would have to speak to him to resolve their relationship one way or another, even if it was just to say goodbye.

The two D's managed to convince her to put aside her concerns about a job and returning to the States for the time being, until something could be worked out. All their suggestions made sense, yet it still depended on her being able to renew her travel and work permit when they expired. The uncertainty was enormous and unsettling.

Dan's suggestion she enrol as a student on her return would make it easier for her to remain in the States. She had deferred a year, perhaps she could apply for a bursary with her grades from the UK. Safi realised she was very quickly entering hard reality, after her initial introduction to New York, which had been a fairy tale existence she could not realistically hope to continue. And now, she told herself, the hard part begins for independence. Should she return to England, to take up her deferred degree in English Literature at Oxford, her parents would be thrilled, or try to find a way to remain in the States?

She was not averse to that idea, if she managed to get a place at a prestigious college in the States; it was her best option to remain in New York.

Dan and Dax returned to work and Safi made her way back to the apartment, gearing herself up to have it out with Sasha, on FaceTime.

The two D's suggested she follow her instincts where Sasha was concerned; putting off the inevitable, she popped into Pete's Bar before calling Sasha.

The first thing she saw when she entered was Pete, who was vigorously nodding his head, indicating she look over to the side seating area. Safi stood rooted to the spot; she recognised who it was straight away; Pete's face registered his surprise. She remained out of his eye-line, trying desperately to collect her thoughts before announcing her arrival.

Noting the wire leading from his ear to his cell lying on the table, the call becoming more animated, he suddenly jumped up. Turning around he saw Safi rooted to the spot, staring at him with a shocked expression. He pulled the wire out and ended his call. His face an unreadable mask as he came towards her, she felt her knees tremble as Sasha pulled her close to his chest and buried his face in her hair. Safi's heart was pounding in her ears, pressed up against Sasha's neck, enveloped by his cologne, the pent-up hurt and anger joined the dust on Pete's wooden floorboards.

Lifting her face, Sasha looked into her eyes, then kissed her gently. Safi felt herself responding and before she knew it they were locked in a passionate embrace; only Pete's wolf-whistle brought them back to earth.

Laughing, they walked hand in hand over to the bar, taking seats facing Pete, who took one look at their happy faces, poured two glasses of champagne and a beer for himself, clinked glasses and left them in charge of the bar until he returned with Bruno, who needed an outing.

No one else was in the bar, afternoons were quiet, most drifted in after work, staying on until after midnight. Pete usually had the bar to himself once the lunchtime rush was over. His cook and waiters were changing their shifts for the evening. Sasha and Safi found themselves alone. Neither knowing how to start the conversation, feeling self-conscious in one another's company, Sasha took Safi's hand and held it up to his lips, kissing it softly, beseeching her to forgive him with his eyes. For the first time since seeing him, Safi found herself feeling happy again, all her former angst gone; nothing mattered now he was here, in person.

Longing to be close to him more than anything, she had to remind herself why she had felt so wretched before he appeared out of nowhere to sweep her off her feet. She was flattered that he cared for her enough to fly all the way from Moscow to make things right between them, suddenly she dissolved into uncontrollable tears. Sasha momentarily sat rooted, not knowing how to react without making her feel patronised.

He pulled her in close against his chest until her tears subsided; lifting her chin he kissed her tenderly, wiping away remnants of her tears, while Safi collected herself, blowing her nose, mortified about not having more control over her emotions. Pete and Bruno came bounding into the bar, pretending not to notice Safi's tear-stained face gave them permission to skedaddle so Pete could get on with work. Fussing over Bruno, they left Safi asking Pete to let the two D's know she was with Sasha!

Hailing a cab, they made their way to Sasha's apartment in the Rubicov building. On entering she had forgotten how opulently luxurious it was with its rich red velvet sofas, objet d'art displayed on shelves especially made to show them off with down lighting. Safi was not sure she remembered it being this magnificent.

Safi stood, in awe, appreciating it all over again, noticing for the first time the Miro hanging on a red wall just off the entrance (had that been there before? she could not have been so infatuated not to have noticed a Miro, surely?).

Walking up to it she turned around to question Sasha, but before one word came out of her mouth, he smiled and said, 'No, you have not seen it before, this is Yvetta's, my sister's, apartment, the gallery owner.'

'Oh, why are we in her apartment?'

'The Miro is the reason it was installed today; she wanted me to be here when it was hung. Since I have missed them, I am pleased to see it looks brilliant, she will be thrilled. She would have been less than happy if she knew I was not here to oversee things. All is well, so let's go back to my apartment.'

Holding hands in the lift to Sasha's apartment, she couldn't help but wonder whether his sudden appearance was for the Miro's installation, not for her?

Before Safi could voice her doubts, Sasha cut her off by explaining the call he was on when he saw her at Pete's Bar. Apparently his sister was insisting Sasha go over to her apartment for the hanging, not knowing his reasons for being in New York. He was voicing his exasperation and cut her off, when noticing Safi.

'I have to call Yvetta back to let her know all is well, then we can relax and talk.'

Pretending they had a bad line, Sasha assured his sister that the Miro was perfection. Safi could hear Yvetta's excitement; she insisted on a photo immediately, so he returned to take one with his cell. Yvetta, Safi realised, was a very persistent woman.

While Sasha rushed back to take the photo, she made herself comfortable in one of the armchairs facing the city. She felt more than a little confused, not sure what she believed, her emotions all over the place. Half an hour ticked by before Safi realised Sasha hadn't returned from Yvetta's apartment, where he'd gone to photograph that Miro.

She was beginning to feel like a spare part; it made her feel foolish and angry, and she wondered whether she should leave. As she was wrestling with her emotions, Sasha returned and dropped down in an exasperated fashion in the seat next to her. Safi noticed a scowl across his face. He was clearly angry. She decided to put her own doubts aside and waited for him to explain.

'I told my secretary to inform everyone I would not be attending the meeting today. She is someone I pay a great deal; she messed up and I am fuming. My sister just told me everyone turned up for this meeting and when my secretary informed them of my absence, Yvetta tried to cover for me but she was furious that it happened. The whole thing put her – and us – in a terrible position. It's done now. I will deal with it on my return.'

She watched his demeanour, feeling slightly less doubtful and a tad more secure when Sasha suddenly exclaimed, 'Safi, I am starving, would you mind very much if we popped down to Rubicov for a meal before we talk? I am not sure I will be able to concentrate or give you the attention you deserve.'

Safi found herself being convinced by his sincerity and her reasons for being overwrought and depressed seemed to recede. The longer she found herself in his company, the less she doubted him – or herself. As he took charge, her concerns began to feel childish, especially since he was here to be with her.

Small talk was the order of the day. Sasha was ravenous and the staff plied them with masses of dishes that seemed to never stop arriving. Safi, who initially had no appetite, found herself having to sample dish after dish at the insistence of the waiters, encouragingly plying her with wine and champagne while Sasha had his vodka shots between each course. By the time they returned to the apartment, they were too tipsy and too tired to talk, and Safi texted the two D's to say she would be staying over.

She fell into bed alongside Sasha; a warm comforting feeling of belonging enveloped her as they curled up together. Neither bothered about making love; it would happen when they were ready. She fell into a trouble-free sleep for the first time in ages.

Waking at dawn, rested once again (for what felt like the first time in months, in fact), aware of being together, they lustfully attacked each other, driven by pent-up emotion and longing, devouring each hungrily.

Sasha rolled on top of her with an urgency and passion she responded to automatically. They both collapsed with joy at being together again, holding hands before they turned to one another, this time starting their lovemaking in a slow, deliberate fashion, with Safi opening up to Sasha physically in a way she had never experienced before finding her shy hesitant reluctance to completely give herself over disappear, as Sasha was now turning his full attention to her needs only, caressing her slowly to climax, she felt her body was satisfied but her emotions were not, she found she hungered for more, until they both had nothing left to give, falling into a sound sleep.

Safi woke to a winter sun streaming into their bedroom, watching Sasha sleep like a baby, she suddenly noticed the time. She grabbed her cell to text Greg.

'Not feeling well enough to make it in today.' She could not concentrate on work when Sasha was in town, who knew how long for?

She felt okay about it, not having missed a day since starting.

Turning round to see Sasha watching her, she smiled and crawled back onto the bed, playfully kissing him all over

'I am not going into work today,' she informed him. 'Hope that's okay with you.'

There was no need to reply; he grabbed Safi, pulling her back under the duvet.

Both starving, they showered together and left the apartment to find a place for breakfast, which was never a problem in Manhattan. Finding a small, cosy-looking table, they ordered the all-American breakfast of pancakes, maple syrup, eggs, hash browns, apple-smoked bacon with toast and jam. They drank endless amounts of refilled coffee as they giggled, realising the emotional charge of the last twelve hours had turned them into hungry, love-sick fools.

Sitting back, Sasha stared at Safi, a dark look crossing his face. Her elation was short-lived, she knew it meant that their time together was probably short-lived, too, and felt her buoyant mood ebbing away.

Words were required to break the silence, but they continued to stare at one another knowing, they could not put off the seriousness of the moment any longer.

She could no longer take the tension and began fidgeting, trying to find the words.

Safi began hesitantly trying to convey her feelings, telling Sasha how sad she had begun to feel. Realising how lonely she had become and that FaceTime sex no longer did it for her (it made her feel dirty and depressed; quite pathetic really), as she watched others around her in real-time relationships while hers was carried out in cyberspace with no one to touch.

She mentioned work fleetingly but not Greg. She continued by describing her concerns at work, not knowing whether she had a job to return to or, whether she would be able to return when her papers ran out.

Sasha sat back listening to Safi fill him in on everything that was happening in her life and realising being apart was never going to work if their relationship was going to last. He listened to Safi's needs and understood her frustration at not having anyone to share her daily life with.

They sat in silence for a long time and she began to wonder whether he had anything to say. Sasha looked at Safi intently he could see that she was expecting him to speak but he had to work things through pragmatically; he did not want to add to her problems, he wanted to find solutions to them before he ventured a response.

Not speaking, he held her hand tightly, shifting up for her to join him on his side of the wooden table, patting the cushion.

'Safi, I came because I knew things weren't working out. I am not sure how we are going to resolve our issue of being together unless ...'

'Unless what?'

'I want you with me in Russia until I have finished my present project in Moscow. I could start another project here in America. Would you consider coming to Moscow for an extended time until I am able to leave? That is our only solution pragmatically to be together. To be honest, I did not realise how awful you were feeling. Please accept my apology for making you so unhappy, it was never my intention. Those texts I sent were unacceptable, I know. My behaviour selfish, I had, had a little too much to drink, and I was jealous and thought I had lost you, stupid really to think behaving like a brute would get you back?'

Not knowing how to respond, Safi sat with Sasha, neither of them wanting their wonderful day to dissolve into one of frustrating sadness at their obvious logistical problems. For once, Safi was aware of her youth; had she been older it would be her decision alone to go to Moscow to be with Sasha, but she knew her parents would find it hard to give her their blessing without a fight.

She felt her happiness hung in the balance and was fast ebbing away. She would follow him wherever he went. She could admit it now, if only to herself: she was madly in love; her parents were going to be made to see it her way, even if Sasha was ten years her senior. After all her dad was much older than her mom.

Hiding her fears, she smiled, trying to put a brave face on it; they both understood the complications her age brought to an already unbearable situation. Safi could not keep the hopelessness out of her voice; the more she thought about him being so far away, the less she felt able to cope with the situation.

Trying not to dissolve into tears, she put her head on his shoulder. She had resigned herself to face another few months away from him until he came for the festive holidays. Not really wanting to know how long they had, she tried to remain upbeat when she enquired when he would be leaving.

By the way Sasha's shoulders drooped in resignation she understood there would be almost no time to get used to the idea of having him close, one, moment here and the next gone quite an unbearable thought.

'Tomorrow.'

By the strangled tone in his voice she could feel his pain.

'What time?'

'Late evening. Can we spend the day together? Do you think you can miss another day? I know it's asking a lot, but I can't let you go while I am only here another few hours.'

Safi did not even have to consider the question.

'I will go in on Friday; they won't mind. She did not want to give Sasha the impression that she was a slacker who did not have a work ethic. We have become a close team during the months we have worked on this project, which is almost complete. All there is for me to do is to be supportive, apart from the print department finalising the graphics, it's a waiting game for the team until the client arrives to view and hopefully approve what the team have proposed.'

Noticing the breakfast had been cleared and that it was almost lunch time, Sasha paid the bill and they made their way back to his apartment, feeling more than a little sorry for themselves; nothing had been resolved one way or another.

They had a night and day together; neither wanting to spoil the time left, they tried to discuss when Sasha would be back, counting the days made it seem less far away. He would arrive on Christmas day and would stay on until after New Year. Sasha was hoping he would be able to persuade Safi's parents to allow her to join him in Moscow for an extended time, until they could both return together. It was the most they could both hope for without causing a rift between Safi and her family.

The two D's had invited them for dinner. Dax was going to try his hand at making them a meal. He loved cooking – Safi, he declared, could vouch for his culinary skills. Some attempts, he had to admit, were less than perfect. His chef's hat was on and he was feeling confident about the chicken already prepared; all he had to do was pop it into the oven. They were on speakerphone with Dax, who had both Safi and Sasha laughing at his attempts to persuade them of his culinary abilities, promising not to poison them.

Sasha had the chef at Rubicov prepare them one of his Russian speciality deserts, called a Napoleon: layers of thin pastry filled with crème patisserie; they left with dessert, Russian vodka, Cristal champagne advised by the sommelier. On route, Sasha insisted on buying flowers; Safi's suggested mixed roses. They arrived with arms full of gifts, completely out of breath as they fell into the loft, almost tripping over themselves as Bruno excitedly ran in between their legs in greeting.

Dan met them at the entrance, ushering them into the kitchen, where Rupert and Samantha were already tasting Dax's attempts to impress them with his before-dinner snacks. For starters, he had prepared asparagus spears with vinaigrette or a choice of hot butter sauce. The table had been laid and looked incredible; the lights had been dimmed and Safi realised the significance of the meal.

Having Rupert and Samantha and herself with Sasha was for the two D's the beginning of domesticity, something neither had bothered with before Safi's (and now Rupert's) arrival in their lives.

Rupert was charm personified, fussing around Dan all evening. Samantha engaged Sasha in conversation, while Safi stayed with Dax in the kitchen, trying to calm his already frazzled nerves. Dax had been true to his word: the dishes were more than okay, they were delicious. Everyone tucked into the roast chicken, roast potatoes, and green salad. Dax was brimming with obvious pride over the success of the meal.

Rupert entertained them with jokes, some less than appropriate. The vodka helped relax the atmosphere. Dax tried to engage Rupert in conversation, but gave up when only receiving monosyllables in response. During the dessert, the attention shifted to Safi and Sasha, and questions mostly from Dan and Dax started flying in all directions. Being polite, Sasha tried to placate them when he announced that he and Safi had ironed out their logistical problems, announcing Safi was going to join him in Moscow when her visa was up, and they intended to return to the States together after his present project was completed.

Safi nodded in agreement, noticing everyone around the table staring at them in open-mouthed shock.

'Don't you think it's a good idea,' continued Safi, not perturbed by their obvious surprise.

Holding Sasha's hand, the lovers kissed, not aware of Dan's obvious concern and Dax's bristling disapproval.

Samantha tried to lighten the mood by asking Safi how long they had been seeing one another. Had her folks met Sasha, and had they been together long before Sasha had returned to Russia? The questions seemed to go on and on. Sasha could tell that Safi was uncomfortable, so he reassuringly squeezed her hand under the table. Then politely replied,

'Well, it's obvious in both our situations, don't you agree, that love can conquer and overcome most obstacles. Russia has changed, of course, and it won't be for ever. I have every intention of returning to America. Everyone is welcome to visit with us while Safi is in Moscow.'

He managed to change the subject with the perfect diversion, a toast to Dan and Dax, then to Dax's wonderful meal; he then turned to Rupert and made a toast to father and son.

Rupert and Samantha departed before coffee was served, leaving Safi and Sasha alone with Dan and Dax. Dan endeavoured to re-engage them in conversation about their plans, wishing them luck over the festive season with Safi's folks; it would, he believed, be a tall order getting her folks on side.

Safi looked at them beseechingly to take her side when the time came to broach the subject with her folks, even though they hadn't met they were family after all. The two D's tried their best to be supportive. Sasha could tell they, like everyone else, had reservations. He did not want Safi to go against their wishes, but was determined to put their minds at rest. Dan, he hoped, would be on-side; having worked for his family, he felt confident of their support.

Leaving the loft, having said their goodbyes, Safi and Sasha hit the sidewalk, feeling free and alone at last. Sasha suggested they walk the few blocks back to his apartment. He held Safi close; it was fresh out but not yet cold. On their way, they stopped off at a jazz bar, found a secluded table for two, cuddled into the corner sofa, ordered drinks, and watched as the bar started to fill up with people. The jazz was cool and mellow, relaxing them for the first time since Sasha's arrival.

The evening seemed to go on for ever. neither wanting it to end, knowing it was their last night together. Sasha ordered vodka on ice, while Safi chose white wine. The club was buzzing and the jazz band had been joined by a sultry-voiced female singer they both loved. The waiter made his way over, putting down a champagne stand filled with ice. He opened the bottle, filling two flutes and presenting them with a flourish; both puzzled, they politely tried to tell him that he probably had the wrong table. Safi saw the waiter pointing to another table; waving at them were Polly the gossip columnist together with Lauren, Bianca, and Niles. Waving back, Sasha and Safi held up their flutes; then Safi noticed Greg and her heart sank: how on earth was she going to explain her absence from work now?

Her only choice was to come clean about Sasha's surprise visit. She wondered how was it possible for her life to get any more complicated. Shit, shit, shit, how was she to explain Greg to Sasha? She hoped Sasha wouldn't recognise Greg; after all, the club incident was months ago. And Sasha had only seen him fleetingly at the club the night she inadvertently finished his drink with drugs. A huge mistake once more on her part, not having filled Sasha in. Neither had she told Sasha that Greg was her boss on the project at the agency. To make things worse, she had no idea why Greg was in Polly's company; it was all quite bizarre and freaking her out.

Sasha could tell Safi was feeling uncomfortable. Safi wondered how they were going to leave without saying hello. Her life was getting to be more complicated with every day that passed. They did not have long to wait before Polly made her way over to greet Sasha.

Calling for another champagne flute, she joined them. Safi liked Polly, but was wary of Polly's ability to see through everyone's armour. Polly, never one to waste time with small talk, immediately figured out that Safi was embarrassed.

'Well, you two love birds have managed to keep this long-distance affair going, how wonderful! I hope you are here to stay. Sasha, we can't have this beautiful girl spending all her time in Manhattan without a beau, pining her little heart out for you.'

This was the kind of old fashioned talk Polly enjoyed disarming her prey with, little did they know she was more up to date than most.

Sasha leaned over and kissed Polly on the cheek; playing her game, he gave her the answer she was looking for. 'Oh no. unfortunately I return tomorrow, but I will be back to fetch Safi to join me in Moscow when I return for Christmas; with her parents blessing, of course.'

Polly, unflappable as always, never one to show her hand, said, 'Well, good for you; and how do you feel about this, Safi, you will be joining Russian royalty, you know?'

Safi laughed nervously.

'I can't wait.'

'I will be calling, Safi. Of course, I am sure you were devastated to have missed the party of the season, Sasha?'

Safi smiled bravely, wondering what exactly she had heard, and from whom, about the 2 D's party after the catfight. Leaning over, Polly stage-whispered, 'Don't worry about Greg; he admires your talent and I am sure he is right.'

Getting up from the table in her usual dramatic fashion, she bid them goodnight, blowing a kiss as she made her way back to her table.

'Who is Greg?' Sasha inquired. Safi knew it was now or never but how much was she going to tell Sasha? 'Oh, he is the project manager of our account at the agency.'

'Ah, so you are in trouble?'

Safi tried to put a brave face on knowing Sasha could tell she was concerned at having been caught out; laughing. he leaned over and whispered in her ear, trying to make light of her situation, with a joke of his own, reminding her he had missed a meeting too.

'That makes two of us playing hooky. I was caught out by Yvetta!'

Not having thought of Sasha being answerable to his sister, she stared at him for a moment. Sasha took one look at her face, hugged her close, and burst out laughing. Seeing the funny side Safi realised he was teasing her, they both could not stop; tears were running down Safi's face as she fell back into Sasha's arms. Everyone around them started giggling with them, joining in with whatever they were finding so funny. When they eventually recovered themselves, Sasha noticed that Polly and her table had left. Feeling safe to leave without incident, they made their way back to the apartment. When she saw Greg her excuses would now be self-explanatory.

Safi and Sasha spent the night making love and talking into the early hours of the morning before they dropped off to sleep, waking up at noon. Feeling the pressure of Sasha's departure, they decided it was best to spend the rest of the afternoon lunching and mooching around the galleries.

Not wanting Safi to be alone when he left, they slowly made their way back to Pete's Bar where they spent the last few hours together. Sasha hung on as long as possible, then jumped up, kissed Safi warmly, said his goodbyes to Pete, and was gone.

Safi watched as he walked out of her life again, hoping that Christmas day would bring him back as planned.

Pete handed Safi Bruno's lead. 'Time for Bruno's walk.'

Pete's expression said it all get on with life and right now is a good a time as any.

It was getting dark out, and she closed her coat to the cold wind, pulled her hat low and with a heavy heart walked Bruno, stopping from time to time for him to sniff around. They kept walking until Bruno sat down, refusing to go another step. Safi realised her feet were like ice blocks. She bent down, rubbed Bruno, noticing how cold his coat felt and that his panting sounded more laboured than usual. Feeling guilty, she looked about to get her bearings; they weren't far from the groomer. She gently shoed him in, relieved when they recognised Bruno.

She bought Bruno a warm fleece-lined coat and after well-deserved snacks and a bowl of water, she managed to coax him out back onto the pavement, feeling guilty enough to hail a cab home instead of making Bruno walk.

She called the two D's to put their minds at rest, and found several messages, noticing her cell had been on silent. Checking the messages, Safi found three from Sasha, whose flight had been delayed; she sighed, feeling it probably less painful having not spoken with him. One of the messages was from Greg. Pressing 'call back,' he answered, 'Safi, you okay?'

She did not quite know how to reply, found herself stupidly nodding her head. When she did not answer, he continued. ' Look, I owe you one. Don't worry, I will see you tomorrow. Cheer up, old girl, love never runs smoothly.' Relieved, she sighed, 'Thanks, see you tomorrow.'

Bruno shot out of the cab as Safi opened the door, heading for Pete's Bar. Safi managed to retrieve Bruno as he manoeuvred between the legs of drinkers. Pete waved as Safi put his leash on, leading him back out. Obviously pleased to be back home, he wolfed down his food, drank his water, jumped onto his favourite chair, ignored everyone, and went to sleep snoring as only Bulldogs can.

They all stood around, watching Bruno, never having seen him so out of sorts. Looking resigned, Safi shook her shoulders.

'I guess he did not like our walk; too far and too cold,' she answered before they asked about his new fleece. 'Oh, and the groomers saved us by putting him in this beautiful fleece. He was frozen, we took a cab back.'

Dan sat next to Bruno, stroking him while he slept. 'I guess he isn't so young any longer. We will have to be gentler with him in future.'

Safi had no idea how old Bruno was. Feeling more than a little guilty, she was shocked to learn that he was eleven years old, not young in dog years.

'Now that Bruno is happily settled, how are things with you, Safi?' Dan asked.

'I am happy and miserable all at the same time, an odd feeling. The good news is Greg's been okay with me playing hooky.'

The two D's sat Safi down and chatted with her while Dax prepared them a quick pasta, making light of the past few days with Sasha. They could tell that Safi herself was conflicted about her love life and did not want to draw her out just yet, wanting Safi to feel comfortable enough with them not to feel she was being judged.

Chapter 10

Dan and Dax felt indebted and attached to Safi. Neither wanted to see her unhappy; her life was getting complicated just as theirs was reaching a plateau. They felt more relaxed and at peace now than they had ever been in the past. Daniel, having his father back in his life, felt a lightness of spirit he had not allowed himself to feel before. Rupert had kept to his word: he now called Dan every day to chat. At first the calls were curt and to the point, but over the weeks they relaxed into a more traditional father and son routine.

Rupert wanted to know more and more about Daniel's life and what he had missed out on. Daniel was delighted to fill in the gaps for his father. Daniel held no grudges, only sadness at the wasted years. He had no intention of delving into his father's psyche; he knew he had Safi and Samantha to thank for the sudden change; not least of which Dan believed was his pride at not losing face with his cousin Leonard when they met to reminisce.

Rupert was not only a stubborn man, but also a very proud one. Dan understood his father's idiosyncrasies. His dad had given up on life. His number one priority and his raison d'être was caring for Dan. Only after Dan moved out when going to college did Rupert reengage with his own life. Daniel had always felt indebted to his father for giving up so much and for providing him with the stability he needed when going through his school years. His father became outraged at any suggestion from others to send him away to a boarding school or employ a full-time housekeeper.

Rupert never spoke of his years in an English boarding school while his parents moved to the United States. Dan knew it wasn't a happy time for his father. Dan encouraged every opportunity to become closer with his dad; he too wanted to recapture their lost years. They knew their first few meetings alone would be difficult; to ease into a relationship again, to make things less awkward, both chose places with a buzz. Rupert, gaining confidence once more with his son, showed interest in his profession, allowing Dan for the first time in his professional life to feel a worth in his own achievements. He took his father on a Recce of his work: they visited skyscrapers, offices, restaurants, and hotels he had a hand in designing with his team, not forgetting to mention Dax's involvement in their success.

Rupert could not hide his pride. Daniel's gayness did not overshadow his own feelings of achievement in having a small hand in his son's success. Dan welcomed his father's pride; it never occurred to him he no longer needed his father's approval he still wanted it, needed it. Rupert found himself invited to Sunday brunches and Friday suppers, along with Samantha.

Both father and son were now hungry for each other's approval. They had not meant to exclude Safi, but she suddenly felt less important. Hating herself for feeling needy, she kept to herself, spending more time with Pete in the bar and taking a reluctant Bruno for shorter walks. Work was winding down; the project had been accepted by the clients and everyone seemed relaxed and happy.

For a week, Nicky Ray had floated into work wearing dark glasses, feigning an eye infection. Her Texan charm had lost its power over Safi;

they no longer met socially after work. Nicky Ray had wasted little time turning her Southern charms onto someone else in the office. Greg had wizened up to her character and wisely allowed her to lend her skills to another team. Interestingly, no one on their team seemed to be put out. Nicky Ray had obviously outlived her Southern charm.

After a week back at the agency, Greg invited Safi to join him for lunch. The restaurant across the street from the agency had large windows onto the street with an open, busy environment. They both ordered burgers and fries, made small talk while they were waiting for the food to arrive.

'Safi,' Greg began, 'I wanted you to know that Polly is related to me, and she has taken a real shine to you.'

Safi was aghast; the world was getting ever smaller, it seemed.

'How are you related?'

'She is my aunt. I had no idea that she knew you until the other evening. She is quite a character, don't you think?'

'Did you meet Niles and Lauren through Polly?' Safi asked.

Greg kept quiet for some time, then he smiled at Safi conspiratorially, leaned back in his chair, crossed his legs, put his hands behind his head, surveying her in a quizzical manner.

'Well, I believe you know the relationship between Lauren and Bianca quite well?'

Safi nodded, waiting for him to continue. 'Did you know that Niles is related to Lauren?'

'I found out at the Rubicov party, yes.'

'Ah, well, to be honest, I met Niles at the club that evening. He stayed on after you left with Lauren and Sasha.'

This shocked Safi; she had not realised that Niles had remained at the club.

'I can see that you are surprised.'

'Well yes, after what happened … you know?'

'Yes, I understand your confusion but it's quite simple, really. I guess Niles did not see the need to return home with everyone. Once he saw you all leave safely in the taxi, he returned to the club.'

Now Safi wanted to know more.

'Did Sasha return too?'

Greg shook his head. 'Not that I know of.'

Remembering Sasha's concern for her wellbeing the next day, Safi wanted to know whether Niles knew.

'Did Niles know what happened at the club between us that night?'

Greg stared at her with concern; he had not planned to discuss the incident with the drugs again. But he evidently had no control of the conversation now.

'Safi, this has nothing to do with the drugs, please believe me. Niles returned to the club; that is how I found out that you were okay. I hadn't figured out about the drinks yet when I met with him again, after that evening.'

'Oh.'

Safi was furiously trying to work out if Greg was being honest with her about Niles.

'Niles to this day does not know what happened. He believes that I had seen the incident and therefore inquired about it: that's all.'

She was not going to confide in Greg that she had a thing for Niles, but had petered out once she met Sasha, but something about Greg's behaviour made Safi wonder whether there was something else he had not yet told her.

'Niles and I have become close since we met,' Greg said. 'You could say we are seeing each other.'

This statement completely floored Safi; she had no idea Niles was gay. She had, after all, seen him with the woman. And what about Greg, whom she had watched Greg flirting with – well, he had flirted with her, for one. Confused, she opened her mouth, closed it again. Greg, saved her the trouble.

'I can see you are either shocked or confused – perhaps both?'

'Both, actually. I was sure Niles – and, for that matter, you – liked the opposite sex?' Greg smiled. Safi could tell he was laughing at her; she felt foolish. Greg looked closely at her, leaned in and playfully whispered, 'We like both.'

Now her confusion turned to embarrassment. She wasn't sure whether she felt angry at herself or with Greg. He seemed to be enjoying himself too much at her expense.

She picked at the cold fries, dipping them into the ketchup, trying to give herself time to think of something clever to say; but her mind drew a total blank. She could feel herself blushing, hating herself for showing her naivety.

Greg allowed her to stew; trying to catch her eye he smiled: had she overcome her shock at his confession? Safi feeling the need to reply, said, 'I honestly thought you had a thing going with Southern Charm?'

Greg almost fell off his chair.

'With that self-absorbed Texan drama-queen, you've got to be kidding; she flirts with anything that moves, as long as she's the centre of attention. The only love affairs she has is with herself.'

Feeling a little less foolish, Safi laughed in agreement with Greg.

'I heard all about her shenanigans at Dan's party,' Greg said. 'I wish I had been there to see Bianca slugging her one.'

Enjoying Greg's honesty, they both relaxed laughing at Nicky Ray's behaviour. Greg took Safi's hand. 'You know, if it weren't for Sasha, both Niles and I could fancy you. Oh, don't look so shocked, Safi; you are a stunningly beautiful girl, anyone in their right mind would fancy you. I just hope Sasha is worthy of your affections. He is Russian, after all, even if he has an English education.'

Safi wondered how she had suddenly become so familiar with him, or why he was ingratiating himself with her. She was not going to discuss her relationship with her boss, but she was curious about his comment. Still, she decided to push the conversation in a more professional direction.

'I was wondering whether any of you would be re-employed after this project is over?'

'I am going to confide in you, but you have to promise me that you will keep this under your hat, until it's made public.'

'Well, I have been in meetings with the creative director recently. The client has been happy with the way the product has been handled and has approved the campaign. If it is successful, they will use it again in other countries.'

'Where does that leave us when it's all wrapped up?'

'They have offered me other projects, but this is why I wanted to talk to you. The clients are connected to a new ad agency in Moscow, mostly to promote English products, and wanted to know whether I would consider heading up a team there for another product in the future. I thought it might appeal to you, if you are going to be living there for an extended time with Sasha?'

Visibly surprised, Safi opted for a measured response. 'Gosh, that's interesting, are you going to take it up then?'

'I probably will,' Greg said slowly. 'The experience here has been invaluable; I think Moscow would be even more so. Working in different countries is something I enjoy.'

'If I do remain there for an extended time, I would love to be involved, thank you for thinking of me.'

'Well, more than likely, it might not coincide with your plans; but if it does, Safi, I will be in touch.'

By the time Greg called for the check, Safi could no longer concentrate on Greg or the restaurant or anything else. Her mind was reeling with possibilities. She needed to think. Greg was networking; he was good at making useful contacts.

Sasha, she knew, would be a valuable contact for him if he relocated to Moscow; as for her, well everything was still undecided. Sasha had not met her family yet, she had that to overcome first before contemplating working in Moscow of all places.

Returning to the office, her mind still as busy as Times Square, she had to admit to herself that Greg had turned out to be okay. She could not help liking him; he had an infectious personality and he was undoubtedly very good at his job.

Sasha and Safi had spent many hours talking about how to solve their immediate logistical problem. After returning to Moscow, Sasha emailed and texted with Safi daily. Both felt closer since his recent visit and neither wanted to complicate the relationship with facetime sex, knowing it had messed with her head last time around, Sasha was playing it safe, but as one week of texting and emailing turned into two, they both realised how much they missed touching. Sasha was aching for Safi. As much as she hated the cybersex they had been having, a small part of her missed it, too.

Both were counting the days until Christmas, when Safi knew he would be back in her life again, but could they hold out until then? Sasha did not want Safi to suffer from the dislocated loneliness of an online relationship, and suggested they stop the cybersex and wait until they were together and could engage in the real thing. Safi had reluctantly agreed, teasing that she might have to find a fill-in during his absence. Sasha threatened to send a bodyguard to shadow her every step if she ever said anything like that again! Safi loved it when he took charge; it made her feel cared for, but she wasn't at all sure she'd appreciate having to go everywhere with a bodyguard. Laughing, she complied meekly to behave before she jumped anyone else's bones.

Sasha had returned to Moscow, determined to have Safi in his life on a permanent basis. Sasha and Safi had their work cut out for them, persuading her parents of his suitability. He had his own parents to convince that this love affair with Safi was genuine. Yvetta had humoured him about being in lust, as his older sister she had always felt in charge, though Sasha was the one his family relied on to keep his sister from her excesses. Both had attended English boarding schools from a very young age, travelling long distances from Russia for their education. After finishing their schooling in Britain, they had both completed their education in the States.

Yvetta had completed her education at Harvard, remaining on to work at Christies in New York and then in London. Sasha had followed suit, finishing his degree at Harvard Business School. The family business was waiting for his return to Moscow.

Alexi, his father, loved London, considering it the centre of the world. After the success of the London Rubicov restaurant, he expanded, opening his newest Rubicov restaurant with a club and apartments in Tribeca. The venture was going well and he was considering whether to open on the West Coast. Sasha knew his father would never live in America; he loved Europe too much.

Russia was more in Yvetta's and his mother's blood; Rubicov in Moscow had a strong team and his cousins were all working for their diverse family enterprises. One of them would be equally suitable to take over the running of Rubicov in Moscow. Rubicov had opened smaller coffee houses and bars in Moscow and St Petersburg, all now used only organic food for the restaurants all over the world. Organic farming was something they were cultivating with their Russian partners.

Yvetta had not shown interest in the family business, returning to Moscow with a business plan. She tried to persuade her family to invest in her passion for the arts. Yvetta hoped with her family's backing she would be able to open her own contemporary gallery in Moscow and St Petersburg. She was passionate about encouraging Russian artists and investing in Russian culture. She had made contacts in the art world, both in Europe and America, and was determined to use their expertise to build a prestigious gallery.

Sasha had never wanted any other profession; their family had come from nothing and built a successful empire. Stepping out of line for Sasha was not an option; his family, he knew, would not tolerate it.

His family had thrown him in at the deep end after finishing university. Sasha was groomed to run the Moscow restaurant while his father travelled, keeping an eye on his flagship restaurant in London and more recently the New York Rubicov.

Apart from restaurants, his family invested in property with portfolios in London, New York, and Europe. His father would expect a report on his recent trip to New York; nothing escaped his notice.

The family was expecting Alexi in Moscow for an annual board meeting. No business or personal affairs were ever discussed on the phone or online; he was hoping to sound his father out on his thoughts about Safi, joining him in Moscow for an extended time. Alexi was nothing but pragmatic, and Sasha felt he needed pragmatism where Safi was concerned.

The LA Rubicov was only in the pipeline; the property deal had taken longer than usual to complete but he hoped it was where they could transfer to once it had been completed.

London was where his father preferred to spend his time, believing it to be the most civilized city in the universe. To be successful in London meant one had arrived, he always said. He could stand shoulder to shoulder with other Russians, discussing their multibillion assets around the globe.

Sasha's parents had married when they were teenagers: his mother barely seventeen and his father only nineteen. They worked for the Communist regime. If one was connected politically, it helped the whole family. Alexi had always remained well connected, especially with the police in various cities.

The extended family stuck together, starting first one market stall until they had enough money to own another. In this way, they built up their small market-stall business into one that could sustain them. Sasha's mother, with the help from family, ran the market stalls while his uncles began working for restaurants in five-star European hotels in Moscow, honing their expertise from the ground up. When Western ways slowly became more acceptable, the family opened small Western-style cafés. Attracting a good clientele, he opened another larger coffee shop, and then another. With Alexi's investment in the gas industry after the communist era ended, the family suddenly enjoyed financial independence, expanding in many other enterprises.

His parents had split while both he and his sister were at boarding school in England. Assets were never an issue; his mother controlled many of the businesses and their family the produce side of the restaurants in Russia and Moscow.

Sasha managed the day-to-day running of Rubicov, while his cousins ran the smaller businesses. Everything was expected to run like clockwork; kitchens had to run to exact timing, serving staff had to be trained to the highest standards, maintenance of the interior and the building was all Sasha's domain. He managed everything that had to do with the running of Rubicov in Moscow.

It was a high-end restaurant attracting the movers and shakers in the city. They opened their doors to politicians and stars, oligarchs and industrialists, not to mention undesirables who Sasha remained on good terms with out of choice, never refusing them a table.

His father kept a close watch but had allowed Sasha to spread his wings. Alexi had remarried a young Russian ballerina, twenty years his junior, who had recently given him another daughter, Marina. Marina had become everyone's darling; the family adored her – even Anna, his mother, who had never wanted to marry again.

Most Russian families endured loss and tragedy through the communist era. During perestroika and after Gorbachev became president, Sasha's maternal grandfather was released from prison.

Anna's father had been a professor at one of the universities where he had been arrested for subversive literature, while Sasha's paternal grandfather had been sent to a Gulag in Siberia for crimes few understood. The inhumane treatment and conditions had taken his life before political prisoners were released.

The family had known starvation and hardship through the Cold War era, when no one trusted anyone, not even one's closest neighbour. Sasha's parents had kept them close, moving to the countryside where they managed to scavenge out an existence for their children in the early years through the market stalls. Even though private enterprise was not encouraged, they managed to remain below the radar, moving from place to place, salvaging meagre produce from the land.

Eventually, through favours and contacts in the right places with the right people (like the police) life became less restricted for them. Alexi made lucrative in-roads, quickly being considered a good Russian, the kind the new Russia needed, a Russian with the right credentials to do business with. His connections in the upper echelon helped when vouchers were handed out as shares to the vast industries. Having enough roubles to collect vouchers to buy shares in the gas industries made Alexi and his family one of the wealthiest oligarchs in Russia.

Sasha's parents worked day and night building up their considerable empire, believing in an education outside the country for their two younger children. His mother lost interest in travelling; she preferred to remain in Moscow, while his father enjoyed the high life. They respected one another's differences and parted amicably, remaining business partners. Both had considerable influence on their children; it was taken for granted all three children would join their family business.

Yvetta posed a problem as she was entering an area they had no knowledge of. After considerable investigation, Sasha's father brought her business under the family umbrella. Sasha hoped to be treated in the same considered way when stating his desire to move to the LA Rubicov.

He hoped his parents would welcome Safi into their family. Yvetta had remained single; she had many suitors, though Sasha doubted she would marry a Russian: she liked to be the boss, something Russian men did not take to very well. Lifestyles for the young had changed drastically over the years, although politics was still never far from anyone's mind. There were many changes ahead, and he believed his family would be safer if their businesses were outside the country.

Yvetta and Sasha had become part of the young Russian elite: educated outside the country like many other young Russians, they preferred to spread their wings. Some, like Sasha and Yvetta, had returned home, hoping to build their own futures free from their parents' historical baggage, they wished for a democratic future in Eastern Europe. Politics in Russia had never been without hardship for the Russian people; they had a long and weighty history. Some of the elderly generation preferred the old, pre-Soviet Russia, while most wished for a less corrupt and more open Russia: all of them felt a fierce loyalty to their roots.

Alexi preferred to remain in London, where he felt free to conduct his business in private. Russia had been a dangerous country to be successful in; success often meant dealing with corrupt elements in the government and police, including elements in the underworld.

Alexi had had his fair share of danger during his years spent labouring in the markets with his stalls. Enemies were easy to make, but he had powerful friends in the police and underworld, who had saved him on many occasions. Eventually he had been noticed and had secured an important position in the gas industry, which helped his family during the worst years under the Communists.

Alexi hoped his children would become part of the new Russia; as part of the educated elite, they would be free to travel, taking advantage of their status both at home and abroad. Sasha had been a constant worry for his family: a gentle, sickly child, he had grown up to be a studious, sensitive young man.

Both children had been sent to English boarding schools at a very young age. Yvetta had attended a ladies' college in Cheltenham, while Sasha had attended a boarding school in Scotland. Both only saw each other four times a year, when home from school on holidays. Their parents would on occasion fly them to the South of France, to holiday in their villa, where they would be encouraged to learn French and Italian. They spoke several languages with ease.

Yvetta felt at home in Europe: she would have preferred to have been sent to the Sorbonne in Paris, but her family had opted for both their children to complete their education in the United States. Although strong-willed, both children believed their parents knew best, and they almost never questioned the decisions made for them: it was not the way they had been brought up; respect was everything. Sasha found it difficult to go against his father's wishes, whereas his sister, he noticed, always used her femininity with great success, when it came to changing their father's mind for anything she wanted or did not want. Sasha, being the boy, was expected to toe the line.

Safi, he felt, was the one person in his life he wasn't prepared to compromise. His parents hoped he would marry and settle down with a Russian girl whose family they approved of. As it happened, English girls had always been Sasha's weakness; he was attracted to their reserved sophistication. American girls, he found, had mapped out their future, leaving little room for mystery or adventure.

Safi had come into his life when he most needed a diversion from hard work and hard play. She had the right mix of naïveté and beauty; he loved that she seemed ridiculously unspoilt. As he grew to know her, he found her wonderfully sensual, with an exciting adventurous spirit. She made him feel unselfish. With her, he found that he wanted more than just sex; he felt the need to be her protector, to shield her from life's harsh realities.

It seemed she was too willing to throw herself into unknown situations, revelling in what life seemed to throw her way, without considering the consequences. Enjoying the excitement of the moment, this also disturbed Sasha, who wondered whether her English eccentricity left her vulnerable. She was so beautiful, yet had a wild side he felt could easily turn into decadence: her determination to be independent at all costs ruining what he so admired about her natural, naïve beauty.

Sasha was pacing up and down, waiting to speak to his father in private. He had prepared his case, waiting for his father to conclude his meetings of the day. Sasha wanted to speak with him in his offices rather than at home, where everyone would have an opinion, weakening his case in his father's eyes. Whenever his father was in town, a family dinner would be organised: a celebration with vodka between each course, not a time for serious discussions but a time for fooling about. Sasha did not want his love life to be the topic of conversation, which it often was; most of his other cousins had settled down and he was the youngest and the only one not yet engaged or married.

Hearing his father's secretary rounding up his calls, Sasha knocked, on the ornately carved wooden doors, walked into the office where Alexi sat behind a French antique desk with gold inlay, offset by the glass and chrome coffee tables and white leather sofas, to lighten the heavy wood panelling, making his intentions clear by sitting down opposite his father at the desk – a marked difference from their usual casual chit-chat over drinks. He waited for his full attention before presenting his case. Known as the playboy in the family, Sasha had to be persuasive, his intentions had to be taken seriously. He knew that it was no small matter for Safi to live with him in Moscow, a city notoriously hard for foreigners, especially for a young innocent naïve, English girl.

Alexi, a balding rotund man with a ready smile and infectious charm, stared at Sasha for a while after hearing his son's desires to bring Saffron over to Moscow. He understood his son's attraction: Safi was a beauty, there was no doubt about that. He had no objection to an affair. The problem was a logistical one.

'Do you think Safi would like having a bodyguard follow her wherever she goes, because, Sasha, that is what she is going to have to put up with, if she comes to live here, with you.'

Sasha thought for a moment before replying. 'To be honest, I don't know the answer to that question. We have not discussed the logistics of her moving here in detail.'

'Well, I suggest you do when you are there for the festive season. I am sure her parents' attitude to your wishes will be a deciding factor, in her decision-making, too.' Sasha nodded, knowing his father was right about persuading her family. But, before he met with Safi's family, Sasha wanted to know he had his father's blessing to go ahead with their plans. Alexi rose, bear-hugged his son, and said,

'Well, I wish you luck. Let's go home and eat, I am starving.'

On returning to his apartment, Sasha immediately emailed Safi that they had to prepare something to present to her parents. He felt frustrated having to persuade both their families of something the couple believed was right for them. Christmas day was coming up faster than they both realised; it was literally only six weeks before they would be together. Both were pent-up with desire and excitement and anxious about the reception Sasha would receive from her parents. Safi knew her mother would be on their side; it was her father they would have to convince. In his eyes, at barely nineteen, Safi was still the baby of the family. Sasha was almost thirty.

Safi would have a tough job to prove her father's doubts wrong. Since his last visit, Safi and Sasha had spoken with one another on a daily basis. He did not want to jeopardise his chances with Safi. Three weeks of speaking with Sasha every day had brought them closer than ever. Safi now confided all her fears and hopes to Sasha. He found himself responding to her trust in him, which gave him the added determination to have her with him on a permanent basis. Their longing for one another had become unbearably painful and he wanted an end to it; he had realised that he no longer cared for anyone else in his life but Safi.

Safi had resigned herself to conversations with Sasha to break the loneliness she felt at not having him in her life. The added worry about her folks arriving worsened her anxiety about them meeting and liking him. She was now determined to spend her life with Sasha away from New York; she no longer wanted to return to England. She knew this would be the hardest sell she would ever have to make; it was not that she had to have her family's approval, but Sasha needed his, and, they both wanted to enter into their relationship without the added frustration of having both families in agreement about their love affair not working, a tall order for them to overcome.

Chapter 11

Safi and Greg had become friends, and had now met after work on numerous occasions. She had been out with Niles and Greg, and on occasion Lauren and Bianca had joined them. Apart from Bianca, they all knew Sasha, which made it easier for her to talk about him in their company. She was tired of having to continuously explain her situation, which she found she had to do with anyone new. Sasha had become a phantom boyfriend when disentangling from unwanted amorous situations, usually late at night. Socially, she appreciated being included in Greg's plans, it kept her busy and less lonely.

Greg had engineered for Safi to dine with Polly and himself one evening. She met with them at a restaurant of Polly's choice, which turned out to be the Opera Café, which neither had ever heard of. Half way through the evening, an opera singer who Safi recognised as the well-known Josh Groban casually started singing to their delight as he made his way around the tables. Josh chose to stop at their table. Polly bristled with charm, engaging him with her amusing, sophisticated chat. 'Now you see why I love this place, there is always someone to mention in my column.'

When there was no one else for Polly to charm, she plagued Safi about her affair with the delectable Sasha. Safi tried her best to give as little of her personal life away as possible. Greg fortunately kept diverting Polly's attention to diner's she may have more interest in and Safi managed to leave with most of her secrets intact, or so she believed. Polly had a way of making the least objectionable thing one said feel up for grabs. She had them howling with laughter most of the evening, with anecdotes of people she knew or recognised, Polly seemed to know intimate stories about almost everyone, most amusing rather than slanderous.

'Safi, darling, do you see that young couple over to your right? Well, my dear, he is Russian, too, and with a starlet from those madly popular vampire blockbusters. Perhaps you will meet all these interesting people when you are with Sasha. Promise you will keep me informed. Do you promise, darling, to regale me with some delightful titbits? I so love to keep up to speed with the love affairs of the young.'

Safi and Greg enjoyed Polly's company; it was hard not to be infected by her insatiable appetite for gossip.

While calling a cab for Safi, Greg thanked her. 'I owe you one for saving me from an evening out alone with Polly; she is more than I can handle on my own.'

Work for them had become a series of meetings with the creative director who knew Safi's father personally. The London agency had recommended Greg and they had accepted Safi as part of the team, a favour to her father. Safi appreciated the opportunity, but had not been aware that her father had known Stephanie, the creative director. Safi was relieved and grateful that it was not referred to while she worked on the account with Greg. Stephanie had informed them of her father's upcoming visit to the agency, when they would discuss further shared accounts on both sides of the Atlantic. It had been a successful venture for both agencies.

Greg had confided in Safi that he had not accepted the offer in Russia. He wanted to remain in the States and would be looking out for other possibilities. He was returning to London for Christmas to be with his family, remaining in Britain until he could secure another job in the States. A part of Safi felt disappointed; she had not realised she counted on having another Brit to lean on while in Moscow. Suddenly, the thought of being totally dependent on Sasha became a daunting prospect.

Daniel had travelled to the West Coast on business and Rupert had offered to accompany him. Daniel immediately accepted the offer, wanting to spend as much alone-time with his dad as he could. Dax encouraged Dan to be with his father, complaining only to Safi and Pete about Rupert's continued and deliberate dismissive attitude towards him.

Pete put it down to jealously; he believed having Dan back in his life made Rupert see Dax as an unwelcome intrusion to share his son with. Everyone agreed with Pete's assessment of the situation, but no one had any advice for Dax: it was a difficult problem that would have to sort itself out with time and patience. Dax was inclined to agree with them, though he was finding it more and more upsetting. The closer Dan became to Rupert, the harder Dax found it to keep quiet about Rupert's behaviour towards him, and his growing resentment.

Daniel was expected to return from the coast a week before Safi's parents would be arriving; not soon enough, as far as Dax was concerned. Special consideration had been taken for everything to go smoothly at the party. There were so many people to consider: Daniel had agreed to find opportunities for Rupert to spend time with Safi's parents, knowing how excited his father was about seeing Leonard.

Dax was getting more neurotic by the day; he needed Daniel at home. After all, they would be celebrating with three families for the festive holiday. Dax's family would be a handful on their own. Not to mention that Daniel's father, plus all of Safi's family, including Sasha, would be sitting at their table for the first time. Tensions would be high.

It was an anxious time for Safi, having her parents approve of Sasha, and Dax wanted to engage his own family in the excitement about their upcoming union. It was a milestone in their lives to have everyone together in their home: both men wanted it to be a joyous occasion, free from drama, which would perhaps be an impossible achievement, with so many personalities and problems looming.

Safi and Dax had gone through the menu umpteen times. Dax had ordered a stuffed turkey with all the trimmings, basted and ready to put in the oven. For those who were not into turkey, Dan had insisted on a leg of lamb, seasoned and herb-crusted. Almost all dishes had been ordered from their favourite deli, including potato roasted in duck fat with Brussel sprouts and chestnuts. Sugared carrots and candied sweet-potato dishes with cinnamon, mint jelly for the lamb and cranberry for the turkey. Five different repeat orders for all vegetable dishes. Mulled wine, including mince-pie delicacies, were to be enjoyed before everyone was seated. Desserts had been the most fun. Together they had chosen a huge mixed-cherry-brandy-and-date cake to be set alight as it was brought to the table, with brandy butter and ice cream and Eton Mess, which Safi insisted on.

Pete was invited to join them after his voluntary charity rounds were done. He helped at the local church soup kitchen every year, closing the bar during the day and opening in the evening for those who chose to ignore Christmas or to escape family. Unlike Thanksgiving, a quintessentially American holiday, Christmas was for the kids and the Europeans, to Pete's mind. He was happy for Dan and wanted to share in their special day; he had developed a soft spot for Rupert and wanted to see things work out for Safi and Sasha: they had a rough ride ahead for sure. He had promised to join the festivities for dessert, not being able to resist a good alcohol-soaked, candied fruitcake.

The table plan had been executed to the last detail by Dan, who had suggested himself and Dax at either end of the table. Dax would carve the turkey, while Dan would carve the lamb. Platters of food would be placed on the oversized ornate French console that doubled as a server for the festivities. Winged-angel silver candelabras, holding glass bowls with candles in them, were to be strategically placed at either end of the console for effect. Dax had splurged on luxurious crackers, ordering assorted arranged dried fruits, scented leaves and flowers to decorate the table, leaving nothing to chance for the festive lunch.

They had placed a garlanded reef with red berries and herbs on the front door above Bruno's welcome mat. Everything was boxed and ready to arrange for the day before Christmas. Everyone had been given strict instructions. Rupert was to arrive before noon, while Safi and Sasha had been ordered to entertain her family; only arriving with them at twelve sharp, not a minute earlier or later.

Dax's family, on the other hand, were ordered not to set foot on their threshold until half past twelve. Staggering everyone's arrival would allow Dan and Dax to welcome everyone individually before the next onslaught.

A Christmas tree had been ordered by Sasha to arrive a day before Christmas. He had called Daniel to request it be kept a secret from Safi.

The tree would be decorated by the department store he had ordered it from; on arrival they would only need to place their gifts below. Sasha had requested a guest list and had ordered all his gifts online from his favourite stores to be delivered wrapped and gift-tagged. With his mother and Yvetta's help, he decided on appropriate gifts for everyone. At first Dan had wanted to decline Sasha's offer, wanting the purchase and decoration of the tree to be a family affair, but he quickly reconsidered, realising Sasha's need to contribute and that Safi would want him to feel part of the family.

Rupert had arranged to spend some time with Leonard and to entertain Safi's family when they arrived. Safi knew that her father's first point of call would be to visit the advertising agency before they closed for the festive break.

It was a matter of days before her family arrived; she was anxious and excited about their arrival. She hoped that they would recognise (and applaud) her independence, needing their approval when finding out about her plans not to return to England, when her visa expired, but instead to accompany Sasha to Moscow.

She was determined to see her plans through with Sasha and prayed that her family would be won over by the couple's love for one another and commitment to be together.

Sasha and Safi tried to plan his arrival down to the last detail; he would arrive a day after her family, which gave her time to be with them. Safi had arranged to meet with her family at their hotel on arrival; she would remain with her mother and brother while her father made his way to the agency for his meeting.

The team had spent a fun time in a local bar, goodbyes were said and numbers were exchanged. Greg had already left for the UK. There was no real need for Safi to return to the agency; she preferred not to be there when her father was having meetings with her now former bosses, she felt it would be in bad taste and did not want to feel uncomfortable in their company.

Dan could not contain himself his relationship with his father had moved forward in leaps and bounds. Rupert had become, Dan felt, like a shadow, wanting to be included in everything his son did. Daniel felt his father's need to be close to him a blessing after their years apart. Neither felt the need to rehash the past; they seemed to move forward, allowing their union to blossom in the here and now. Daniel indulged his father's need to talk to him daily, sometimes several times a day. Dax found it to be claustrophobic and an intrusion into their lives, but felt he had no right to upset Dan, discussing his displeasure only with Pete and Safi.

When Rupert was not calling several times a day, he often dropped by unannounced to join Dan for lunch. Sometimes Dax or Safi joined them, too. Daniel could not help noticing his father's displeasure. Rupert now had little interest in Safi, or, for that matter, Dax.

Daniel humoured them: 'He'll soon tire of us all and move to his Upstate home with Sam.' Daniel knew how hurtful it was for Dax, and how he hated being ignored. If only his father was more accepting of Dax; his relationship with Rupert was so precious to both of them, he did not want to create a division between them, and was prepared to indulge his bad behaviour, but knew he had to keep Dax from blowing a gasket.

Dax was reaching the end of his tether: Rupert seemed to be dealing with their union by pretending it did not exist. Dan knew he would eventually have to deal with the situation, deciding to put it off until after Christmas. Hoping that his reunion with Leonard would be a welcome distraction, lessening his focus on Dan.

Rupert's relationship with Samantha had taken a backseat, too; since welcoming his son back into his life he had little time for any other distractions. Samantha was self-sufficient and independent of mind; she had plans to return to Hong Kong, which she had not yet shared with him.

Her company was relocating to England, and, she was keen to return to her roots for a while to absorb the changeover. Since Hong Kong became one with Mainland China on midnight of the third of September 2019, there had been some unrest, but ultimately the Two System rule had not made that much difference to Hong Kong yet. During her years in the United States much had changed. Before Rupert's reunion with Dan, she had played with the idea of having him join her, but understood that his situation had changed dramatically. She hoped to persuade him to visit for an extended period, instead.

Samantha had become closer to Dax; they discussed Rupert's newfound (or rekindled) obsession with his son. It was one of those situations Dax found hard to get his head around. Of course, he was happy; on the other hand, he was experiencing feelings of untold frustration, not knowing how to deal with the present situation. Samantha helped Dax to deal with Rupert's long-suffering absence and sudden overpowering return into their lives.

She had patiently listened to Dax's complaints about Rupert's intolerance towards him, how Rupert avoided reality by keeping him at arm's length. Dax noted that Dan, too, found his father's attitude to their union bizarre. They were of the opinion that past childhood experiences at an all-boys boarding school accounted for his attitude towards homos, as he insisted on calling them when off-guard. Yet he was positively charming when in Lauren or Bianca's company.

Dax confided he found being in Rupert's company distasteful, but did his best to hide his feelings from Dan, which was a first for him. Having always been open about everything, Dax was beginning to wonder whether Rupert's arrival mightn't now be destructive rather than the healing one he had imagined it would be.

Samantha, having her own problems where Rupert was concerned, placated Dax on the rare occasions they had a chance to unburden themselves over a drink about their frustration with Rupert's behaviour. They were hoping Leonard's influence would lessen his ingrained prejudices, though Dax selfishly hoped Rupert would follow Samantha to Hong Kong, leaving Dan and himself alone, able to breathe once more without his constant intrusion into their lives.

Greg had left with no fanfare; everyone had come to respect his leadership role during the project, hoping to work with him on others. Safi noticed that his English reserve was never far from the surface; he appeared flamboyant in his dress, but when it came to his profession he was totally committed to success, rather than encouraging familiarity with those he worked with; keeping his private life very much to himself. Apart from Safi, he did not socialise with anyone else outside of occasional, after-work drinks. Safi had learnt Greg had fallen out with Niles before leaving, which may have accounted for his quick and quiet departure. The team were expecting a full-on drinks party before he returned to England, and without Greg everyone drifted apart unceremoniously.

Over time, Safi had come to trust him; he had turned out to be a valued friend in Sasha's absence. Ludicrously, they had been thrown together after their shaky start: this had allowed them to bond in an odd way; it was their secret to keep, both preferring to put the drugs issue behind them as an unfortunate misunderstanding.

She arranged to meet Lauren at Barneys for a quick working lunch. Lauren gulped down the last dregs of her coffee, kissed Safi, made a call-me sign, and was gone. Safi sat by herself, watching the New Yorkers as they chatted and preened confidently. She almost felt at home now, though part of her still felt like a newcomer.

The bill paid, she made her way back to the apartment, wondering how she would manage in Moscow if, after all this time, she still felt like an outsider in Manhattan. But she would have Sasha in Moscow, surely that would make a difference? The thought was both exciting and nerve-wracking. So much relied on the next few days going smoothly; her heart lurched in her chest at the thought of what lay ahead, and all of the uncertainty.

Back at the apartment she was greeted by a whirlwind of activity. Dan had taken delivery of umpteen packages, containers filled with festive decorations. Food had been delivered to be stored in their larder fridge and freezer. Platters were being set out, cutlery was being cleaned, and the dishwasher was being filled with crockery that had not seen the light of day for quite some time.

The usually large refectory table was no longer a repository for Dan's African objet d'art, it was covered with a massive white tablecloth with alternate place settings in stunning gold, peach-patterned Versace Chargers.

The two centrepieces had been decorated to complement Dan's ornate platters, with green foliage and orange, peach, and pink blossoms, intertwined with perfectly wrapped crackers placed at intervals along the table; the result was stunning.

Safi stood in awe, staring at the transformation that had occurred in her short absence. The two D's came to join her at the table, admiring their handiwork and waiting for Safi to comment. She caught their eye in the cracked antique mirror above the console table. Holding their gaze, she conveyed her delight, then clapped her hands to show her approval, turned and bowed teasingly to show her total admiration for their talents. Both satisfied, they ordered her to the kitchen to unpack the third load in the dishwasher for the twenty place-settings.

Together they worked late into the night, laying the table and rearranging furniture for the Christmas lunch. True to his perfectionist nature, Dan wanted everything prepared. Leaving little to chance, he had arranged everything to the last detail. The Christmas tree was to be installed the following evening when Safi was with her parents and Rupert.

Sasha was arriving early on Christmas morning and he had arranged to meet Safi and her parents at their hotel for an early breakfast, before heading to Dan and Dax's apartment for the party. Not a single moment was left to chance, and this was the way Dan liked it.

Safi crawled into bed, too tired to worry about her parents or Sasha, knowing she had to be up at dawn to greet her parents and brother at their hotel.

Safi lay in bed, staring at the neon lights on the buildings, watching them fade as the skyscrapers appeared once more as the dawn light filtered through the sheer blinds on her windows. Her mind numb, swinging her legs over the end of the bed, she stretched, forcing herself to feel energised. Instead, she felt unexpectedly sick, ran to the bathroom, and retched into the toilet.

Sinking down onto the floor, she wondered what she had eaten to make her feel so queasy. Of course, she knew full well the cause of the nausea was anxiety about Sasha meeting her parents; she was a nervous wreck. As the shower pounded over her, she washed her hair, dressed in winter whites, pulling her flat black boots up over her knees, threw on her long black puffer coat with the black fur mufflers over her ears, and headed out of the door, hoping to pick up a coffee and croissant on the way.

Light snow was falling as she made her way to the Bowery Hotel, where she hoped to wait for her family as calmly as her nerves would allow. Safi reached the Bowery reception at 7am: confirming her parents' booking, she settled down to wait with a newspaper in front of a welcome fire burning in the grate. She could see the reception area from the armchair she had chosen. As she settled into the chair, her cell pinged; her parents were in a cab heading towards the hotel.

Not being able to sit still, she found her way to Jemma, the restaurant attached to the hotel, and booked a table for breakfast. Then she walked outside and found herself marching up and down in front of the hotel in the freezing cold. She watched a dog come out of the hotel for his walk, thinking momentarily of Bruno, while nervously gaping inside every cab as it pulled up to the curb.

Not being able to take the cold, she stepped inside to warm herself by the fire when she recognised her father's voice. Safi literally flew to the reception finding her parents being ushered in by the doorman, who was smiling broadly at her. Her nerves melted as she threw her arms around her dad, hugging him tightly, then her mom and brother joined in, all English reserve forgotten. She found her throat constricting, tears welling up with pent-up emotion. Her mom held her at arm's length and with a look of approval. She could see that her brother was impressed, too, but her father wanted to know where she was hiding the old Saffron he knew and loved? Laughing, they made their way to Jemma's for breakfast, while their room was being prepared.

Over breakfast, Safi caught up on their news and tried to edit her own news about her and Sasha, and joining him in Moscow, in order to spare them until Sasha's arrival the following day. Rupert had been given strict instructions to allow Safi to see her parents on her own before he descended on them. Leonard had made arrangements with the agency for a morning meeting and had arranged to meet Rupert for lunch nearby. Dan had arranged to meet everyone later that evening at Pete's Bar for dinner. The hectic seasonal schedule had begun in earnest.

Safi was helping her mother unpack when her brother popped in to ask if she wanted to explore the area with him. Seeing her mom was in need of catch-up sleep, she agreed. Jake was only eighteen months older than Safi and they had got on well as kids. Jake, unlike Safi, had been into sports and had taken a gap year in Australia, travelling through Southeast Asia. He had always wanted to settle in Australia and was determined to find a job there after completing his business and IT degree. The States had never held the same interest for him as they had for Safi.

They found a coffee shop, where they exchanged small talk about their past and present lives. Jake, trim and muscular with boyish looks, was a head taller than Safi. He confided that he had a steady girlfriend but that if he managed to secure the job he had applied for in Melbourne, he would be going on his own.

Safi told Jake about her life in NYC and how Dan and Dax had supported her in almost every way, helping her to find her feet. But, she added, she had complicated her life by falling in love with a Russian guy, who Jake would be meeting the following day. She tried to make light of her situation, but Jake encouraged her to talk to him. Safi found that she needed to tell someone besides Pete and Dan and Dax what she had in mind – someone in her family, someone who knew her family, someone close to her who always had her best interests at heart, and, Jake was a listener, he had always put up with her anxieties, about everything, as they got older. After hearing Safi's intentions, Jake whistled softly; she understood that this was an inference to their parent's reaction to the news. They discussed how best to break her intentions to go to Russia with Sasha to their folks. Jake had to admit that he could not see Leonard going for the Moscow bit. Jake's reference to their dad's reaction to Moscow had her tasting the breakfast, all over again.

Safi agreed, confiding that she was sick with nerves about them meeting Sasha and hoping that Sasha would somehow be able to persuade them with his considerable good manners and charm. They bundled up against the cold weather, making their way back to the hotel to collect their mother for an early dinner at Pete's Bar.

Chapter 12

On finishing his meeting at the agency, Leonard made his way across the street to meet Rupert. Bending into the bitterly cold December wind, he found his mind retracing their childhood growing up in England and wondered whether they would recognise one another; years had elapsed since they had seen each other. After his mother had passed away, Rupert had never returned to England with his father to see the family.

Leonard found a place at the long bar, ordered a drink and settled down to people watch, hoping Rupert and himself would recognise one another. Draining his drink, he turned to ask the barman for a refill when he noticed the man sitting alongside him at the bar. There was definitely something familiar about him. He hoped an English accent would give him a heads-up, so that he would not embarrass himself unnecessarily.

Leonard felt a hand over his. turning suddenly to face the man next to him, he found smiling, familiar eyes staring into his.

'Allow me get that, Leonard,' the man said. They stared at one another for what seemed ages; then hugged warmly before sitting down again and launching into familiar laughter, firing questions at one another.

Finding their table, they settled down to exchange past and present history, chatting endlessly until both noticed that it had become dark out. Jet lag and alcohol was catching up with Leonard, but he knew Safi would be bitterly disappointed if he did not make a show at Pete's Bar.

Fortunately, Rupert lived only a few blocks away. Leonard did not know whether he could face the brutally cold wind or, for that matter, a rush-hour subway ride. Noticing Leonard's exhaustion, Rupert called ahead for the concierge to bring his car to the front of his apartment block. Then he told Leonard to take forty winks in the passenger seat, while he fought his way through the traffic towards Pete's Bar.

Leonard relaxed in the warmth of the Lincoln, the soft leather headrest supporting his head as he dropped off to sleep. Rupert waited for his breathing to even out and dialled Dan and then Safi to let them know that they were on their way and would meet at Pete's. Leonard was still in dreamland when Rupert pulled the car up outside the bar. He tried to nudge Leonard awake, but was finding it difficult, Leonard now snoring his head off. Smiling to himself, Rupert hung on a while longer, hoping Leonard would wake on his own, but soon realised something drastic was called for. He wound down the windows on all four sides, allowing the bitterly cold wind into the car, switched off the engine, and waited to see whether the cold icy wind on Leonard's face would do the trick. He did not have long to wait before Leonard's eyes fluttered open; on seeing Rupert he shot up, hitting his head against the dashboard.

'Jesus, that hurt,' Leonard said, fully awake now. 'Where the hell are we? It's blowing a blizzard in here.'

'Outside Pete's Bar,' Rupert replied. 'They will be waiting inside and I am dying for you to meet that boy of mine.'

As the two old silver foxes, walked into the bar, Leonard found himself surrounded by not only Safi but also three handsome chaps, all leaning over eagerly to greet him. Rupert broke in to do the introductions. First he met Dan, then Dax, then Safi introduced what looked like an elegantly dressed male model, but Leonard could tell by their body language that this guy was something more to his daughter than just a pal. Sasha bent slightly at the waist. then offered Leonard his hand; shaking it firmly he introduced himself in transatlantic English with a tinge of an accent. After a short greeting of a few words, everyone crowded round, including Pete the barman, who Leonard took an immediate shine to, as he handed him a much-needed warm larger.

Dan found them a large circular booth, seated closely together apart from Safi and Sasha in chairs at the end of the table. The conversation seemed to take on a life of its own, with everyone chatting at once.

Sasha found himself sitting next to Leonard on one side, with Dan, next to Safi, on the other. Rupert was directing his attention to Dan, and Leonard found himself relating to Dan comfortably, but part of his attention was on this young handsome man with Safi; he could not tear his eyes away from their body language, which he found irritating, knowing full well that she obviously wanted them to accept Sasha, but he was finding it difficult to see his little girl all grown up with another man – and he appeared significantly older than Safi – not at all a boy, and obviously the centre of her world; the attraction between them was unmistakable.

The evening was a delight for all. Dan loved being with family, catching up on old stories and reminiscing easily. Rupert was on fine form, regaling them with hilarious anecdotes from their childhood in England. The Lincoln was fortunately large enough to transport Safi's family back to their hotel. Safi could tell her parents were being restrained; they put on a brave face, making arrangements to meet them for breakfast at the hotel, and waved them goodbye.

Sasha had found an earlier flight, unbeknown to Safi, surprising her on her return with her brother to the hotel. He was waiting for her in the lounge, where she introduced him to her mother and brother, who he had no trouble charming. Over tea, seated beside a log fire, Sasha became acquainted with one part of Safi's family, knowing that winning over her father would be his most challenging task, later that evening at Pete's Bar. The two D's were determined no one should see the Christmas tree until they arrived for the festivities. They wanted it to have an element of surprise. On waving goodbye to her family, they hugged Dan and Dax and made their way to Sasha's apartment.

Safi felt elated, all her former doubts dissipating now that Sasha was with her; his early arrival had taken the stress out of waiting and wondering. They were both in this together. She knew her mom and Jake had warmed to Sasha; now all they had to do was bring her dad around.

They clung to each other through the night, finding it hard to sleep after making love. Sasha had arranged with Safi to arrive a few moments after Safi, making it less obvious they had spent the night together. Safi woke to find a note from Sasha about a sudden business meeting at Rubicov with one of the chefs.

Finding herself alone, Safi showered, put on her winter whites, then found the most exquisite full-length puffer jacket with fur running the whole length of the front and hood. She loved the taupe colour and taupe fur; it fitted her like a dream. Feeling luxurious and toasty-warm, she made her way to meet her family for an early breakfast, hoping they would not fire too many questions at her before Sasha arrived to join them. Putting her hand in one of the coat pockets, she found a card: 'With all my love, Sasha.'

Promptly, as arranged, Sasha rang the bell at Dan's at six, carrying hot coffee and bagels, ready to help with the Christmas tree.

The tree had been stored on the roof terrace; Dan had not wanted the delivery men to prepare the tree so it was left for them to do.

Unpacking the three boxes, they figured out that it fitted together in parts, making it an impressive size: the silver tree looked spectacular against the floor-to-ceiling loft windows; it sparkled against the grey sky as the snowflakes blew against the windows, giving it a soft, fairy-tale glow. They worked like daemons hanging the white fairy lights, deftly suspending the rest of the spectacular decorations found in the boxes.

Standing back to admire the tree, Dax offered Sasha the stepladder to add the final touch to the top of the tree; opening the last container, they found a huge silver crystal star. Sasha placed his beautifully gold, gift-wrapped boxes with red or Scottish ribbons under the tree, adding to the festive atmosphere, but no one had time to mull over the finished product as, within minutes, Sasha found himself out on the street once more, hailing a cab to meet Safi and her family for the breakfast inquisition.

His time away from Safi had not dulled his feelings; in fact, it had done the opposite. It had intensified his love, making him more determined to win her folks over.

Nervous about his plan backfiring, he would have to wait for the right moment to present Safi with the gift he hoped would take the wind out of their sails.

He found them hugging hot mugs of coffee. Safi looked relieved to see him; he slipped in next to her, feeling her hand slip into his and squeezing it reassuringly. After initial greetings, they ordered breakfast while waiting for their food to arrive. Sasha was relieved when the conversation became light-hearted. Jake thankfully diverted everyone's thoughts with his teasing, not only of Safi but of his parents, too. Jake seemed to have an easy manner with everyone, capturing their idiosyncrasies with humorous accuracy, having them all laughing at themselves good-naturedly.

They were expected at Dan's for one pm, allowing them ample time to consume a decent breakfast before indulging in Christmas lunch, which they were all sure wouldn't start until after two.

By noon they were onto their coffee refills, discussing what to do until they were expected, Sasha invited them to join him at Rubicov for a tour of their latest building and restaurant. He hoped they would allow him to entertain them as his guests, before returning to Moscow. On their conducted tour around Rubicov, Sasha pointed out Dax paintings and Dan's architectural interior-design features. He touched on his family's life in Russia, explaining how their fortunes had improved with his father's determination to change their lives once the old Russia became open to the rest of the world.

Leonard started to enjoy his time with Sasha, finding conversation easy; they discussed the current political situation in Russia with Putin at the helm. Sasha happily encouraged Leonard to delve into his past and present. After all, he was a proud Russian, with a Western education; he shared the Russian passion for its history and culture, but wished for democratic change. The tour encompassed the restaurant, club, and their apartment block, but skipped showing them his apartment, instead showing them his sister's, on Safi's mother's request. Safi lagged behind, relieved at Sasha's choice; she would have felt mortified had he chosen his apartment: it would have seemed in bad taste, besides her stuff was everywhere and she was not remotely ready to share that side of their relationship with them. They were complimentary about Yvetta's exquisite taste, noticing her art collection, which, Sasha explained was her passion and her job.

The tour did not leave time for anything else and they made their way to Dan's, arriving together with Rupert on the dot at two. Rupert had been given strict instructions to give them time together before he descended on them.

'I know I am supposed to arrive at 2.30, but it's too bad. I am here now there; was very little traffic. We have exactly forty-five minutes before Dax's family descend on us with their wives and children, so we better make the most of Dan and Dax while we can – they have everything planned to military precision.'

On entering the apartment, Dan and Dax were there to greet them with champagne. After hugs all round, they were ushered into the lounge area to settle around the Christmas tree, everyone whooping in delight at the tree and all the gift packages.

Dax's family arrived while Safi was giving her parents a guided tour around the loft. On descending from the roof terrace, they exchanged greetings and introductions. The two D's, bursting with pride, watched everyone mixing happily; they arranged the final touches to the dining area and invited them to the table to be seated.

Finding their places, they pulled crackers; the kids, all at one end of the table, were delighted with the bendy toys flying out of their crackers. Everyone else was impressed with rings, cufflinks, and tie pins, bargaining for the one's they did not get, until someone cleverly noticed that the gold and silver was plated rather than precious metal, all declaring relief, having wondered the cost of such extravagant crackers.

The carving on either end of the table was cheered by all, making it a competition to see who could finish their carving first, Dan or Dax.

Safi and Sasha stood next to each, holding the serving platters ready as they sliced and placed them on the huge platters with great dexterity and speed.

Dan expertly cut the lamb to the bone, while Dax pulled and sliced the turkey. As they neared the end, Dan slowed down, to allow Dax to finish first, but no one would stand for it. A truce was declared, on condition the last few pieces were unceremoniously passed along the table for everyone to taste.

Free-flowing wine and champagne added to the frivolity around the table. Dan and Dax were overwrought with joy, seeing their respective families happily sharing a festive meal together. Groaning at the thought of dessert, the brandy pudding was put off until everyone had opened their gifts.

The collection under the tree was piled high with boxes; opening all those gifts would make an ample break before they returned to the table for pudding.

Dax noticed Rupert's attitude towards him appeared to be less dismissive; not wanting to discourage him, he welcomed this new warmth and tried to reciprocate.

Daniel thought his father unusually reserved; they decided Leonard's presence was the influencing factor, jokingly reminding themselves to thank him and not forget to cajole him to issue Rupert with an invite to England.

Dax's brothers were keeping his glass well-filled with wine, and were not surprised when he dozed off not long after they all started opening their gifts. Safi controlled the gift-giving; trying not to allow it to turn into a mad frenzy, they all wanted to share in the surprised delight or the suppressed disappointments.

The kids opened their gifts, greedily discarding sweaters, scarves, or hats with speed, when finding new computer games. The puzzles of London were greeted with amusement. The wrapping paper piling up disappeared into garbage bags as they hit the floor. Dax, incapable of abiding a mess, darted about ridding the floor of bunting, boxes, and gift wrapping.

A pile of gifts was building up in front of Rupert's chair, but no one bothered to wake him, leaving him to sleep his hangover off. Sasha had managed to buy everyone tasteful, small, inexpensive gifts, surprising everyone at his incredible thoughtfulness; they noted his Russian warmth as they delighted in his choices.

Safi had bought the same gift for everyone, and she jokingly apologised for her dire financial plight, pretending shocked hilarity as each received the same pair of tartan socks. 'I did find something different for Uncle Rupert, though,' she said, which brought more laughter as his snoring became louder by the minute.

After everyone besides Rupert had opened their gifts, Safi handed Sasha his, watching him open it nervously. Looking over at Dax, Safi noticed him watching Sasha with the same intensity. As the wrapping came off, Sasha held a square frame in his hands. He carefully removed the protective layer. Turning the frame round he gasped, staring at him out of the canvas was Safi: her beautiful brown eyes perfectly captured by Dax. He had found her innocence, yet there was a slight devilish smile playing around her full lips.

'What do you think?'

'I love it, Safi. It's the best gift I have ever received. And Dax, I am honoured to have one of your paintings, thank you!'

The painting was passed around, everyone commenting on its beauty and artfulness, all thinking it captured Safi perfectly.

Sasha took a box out of his pocket and tentatively handed it to Safi.

'I hope I made the right choice, Safi.'

He sat back, watching Safi pulling the ribbon loose on the gift packaging. Everyone was now quiet, watching to see what he had bought for her.

Safi looked up, catching her father's expression of admiration as he studied the painting Dax had painted of her. Then Leonard's eyes moved to Sasha, as his beloved daughter unwrapped the small package. Finding a red box, she opened it tentatively before gasping with shock. She stared up at Sasha, who took the box from her. Holding the square, two-carat diamond ring, he got down on one knee and held her hand, slipping the ring on her finger.

'Safi, will you marry me?'

Safi threw her arms around his neck, whispering, 'Yes, yes, yes,' with tears running down her cheeks. Apart from a few gasps at the scene in front of them, not a sound could be heard – until a sudden groan diverted everyone's attention towards Rupert, clasping his chest.

Suddenly there was mayhem. Everyone rallied round Rupert. While Dax lifted his arms above his head with difficulty, Dan grabbed his cell and called 911 emergency services. Leonard made everyone move aside to give Rupert some room. They put cold compresses on his face, leaving the ice on his forehead. Someone had him on the floor and was trying CPR on his chest. They took the children into another room to divert their attention from the drama unfolding in front of them. Was Rupert suffering a heart attack? No one could tell for sure until the paramedics arrived.

Arriving in record time, taking over before anyone could ask any questions, the paramedics stabilised Rupert before moving him to the ambulance, and then on to the hospital. Dan and Leonard drove behind the ambulance, while Dax and everyone else remained behind in shock. One of the paramedics assured them that Rupert would be fine, but that he had had a lucky escape, having been around people who probably saved his life!

Momentarily, everyone stood around in shock when Dax tried to bring some normality back to their day by offering dessert and coffee, which was now waiting on the table. The attention returned to Safi; exhilarated at the thought of being engaged, she showed off her ring. Her mother had responded kindly, hugging her tightly.

'I knew there was something about that young man. I have never seen you so taken with anyone before.'

Sasha hugged Fiona, promising to care for Safi with every fibre in his body when she joined him in Moscow. Fiona stared at Sasha, trying to take in what he had just said.

'Do you mean that you will be living in Moscow for the foreseeable future, once you are married?'

Sasha tried to make light of it, knowing that her mother would be finding it hard to come to terms with losing her daughter to another foreign city.

'Oh, for the time being, yes, until I am able to relocate to either Europe or the States. I was hoping to ask Leonard for Safi's hand in marriage the traditional way, but time and circumstances took care of that idea.'

Fiona smiled, weakly knowing her husband had not reacted well to the clever little drama, as he called it, being enacted in their midst. Leonard had his doubts about their motives, but before anyone could react to what was happening, they had to deal with Rupert. Leonard would have to deal with Safi and Sasha when he returned from the hospital the following day, right now she was keeping the peace for as long as she could.

Dax and the other guests swooned around Safi and Sasha, all admiring the ring and wishing them happiness and a great future. Safi and Sasha escaped to the roof terrace, where Sasha picked her off the ground, hugging her tightly. The surprise element had gone exactly as he had hoped. No one could have known that Rupert would fall ill: it was a shame, but Sasha was satisfied with the outcome.

Safi stared at him in disbelief. 'Sasha, what on earth has got into you? I had no idea you were going to spring that on me at all. Since when have you been planning this?'

For a moment, looking at her hesitantly, Sasha was not sure whether Safi was happy. 'Don't tell me you are having second thoughts, please?'

'Not at all, but I do want to know how and when you decided you wanted to marry me?'

'I knew your parents would not agree about you coming to Moscow. I love you, Safi, so the only way I could see this working out was if you agreed to marry me.'

'Well, I think it's a brilliant move. I cannot see how my father can say no now.'

'When were you thinking of me coming to Moscow to join you?'

'Is tomorrow too soon? Joking aside, the sooner the better as far as I'm concerned, but it's up to you, of course. Perhaps you want to spend time with your family before, now that we know it will happen.'

Safi sat for a while; not being able to think straight, she decided to sleep on it.

'I will make up my mind after we have spoken with my dad, then we can discuss the logistics, what do you say?'

They agreed and went down to join the others, who were toasting for a speedy recovery for Rupert. Pete had arrived to find out the sad news and was told about Safi and Sasha. He came straight up to congratulate them; with a knowing twinkle he shook Sasha's hand, congratulating him on a smart move.

The family were sitting around trying to keep busy, waiting for a call from either Dan or Leonard, when the doorbell sounded urgently. Waiting at the door, Dax greeted Leonard, who had a grim expression on his face. Once inside, he sat down on one of the bar stools in the kitchen. Pete offered him a whiskey, which he accepted. He drank a few sips, put it down, and gave everyone the up to date report on Rupert's health.

'The doctors have stabilised him. He is attached to machines, but they will really only be able to tell in twenty-four hours, when he has had a scan. The doctors feel Rupert may be lucky, having been treated almost immediately; he should make a full recovery but it's a warning. Dan wanted to remain with him a while longer. He was advised to return in the morning.'

The family slowly departed. Pete remained to keep Dax company until Dan returned.

Having not spoken with her father since her engagement, Safi noticed his exhaustion and understood that she would have to wait until everyone was ready to address her new status. Her parents hugged, said goodbye, and returned to their hotel.

Safi and Sasha arranged another breakfast meeting with her parents the following morning at the Bowery. Then the newly engaged couple, deciding fresh air would help calm their nerves and clear their minds, from the highly charged emotional day. They walked the ten blocks to Sasha's apartment. The wind was bitingly cold and Safi for the first time realised that she had not thanked Sasha for the beautiful fur-lined puffer coat; she loved it, it was perfect for the arctic weather they were experiencing. Sasha smiled and, not wanting to put Safi off, decided not to tell her that New York winters were warm compared with Moscow's below-zero temperatures.

Finding themselves alone for the first time in hours, Safi sat in the last of the day's winter sunshine, admiring her ring as the facets glistened in the sun, while Sasha, preparing soup with saltine crackers, watched her from the kitchen. She was without a doubt one of the most unspoilt girls he had ever met.

Showering her with gifts would make him happy, but he had to keep reminding himself not to overdo things, wanting her to remain who she was. Life in Moscow would be very different to the one she was used to in England, or New York, for that matter. They had not spoken about life in Russia; he hoped to avoid going into detailed explanations about curtailing her freedom to go wherever she pleased in Moscow. She would have security accompany her when she went out on her own. None of this mattered to Sasha; he knew once she was with him things would work out. Justifying this to her father, however, was a matter he didn't relish dealing with.

She watched him preparing a light supper. She could hardly contain her excitement; leaning forward, she touched Sasha's hand, bringing him towards her. Without a word, she climbed over the kitchen bar and flung her legs and arms around him. She just wanted to be close. He pulled her sweater off over her head, then her boots and jeans came off in one.

Lifting her he carried her into the shower, allowing the hot water to warm them after the cold walk home – to hell with the soup, it could wait. Right now he was hungry only for her.

Sasha held out a fluffy towelling gown for Safi as she stepped out of the shower. Fastening the belt tightly she snuggled up into the softness. Warm, satisfied, and cosy in the gowns, they sat at the kitchen bar, quietly eating thick minestrone soup, crumbling the saltines into the bowl, enjoying their moment of total togetherness.

Safi woke early, mentally ready to face her parents and their obvious concerns about her engagement to a man they knew next to nothing about. Trusting him with her care was understandably a major hurdle for her folks to overcome.

Sasha joined her at the window, watching the yellow cabs snaking their way through the white world below, snowflakes hitting hard against the frenetic wipers, creating visibility.

The snowploughs had obviously been busy during the night, pilling high mounds of snow on the sidewalks, leaving partly clear roads. The streets, momentarily deserted at such an early hour, would soon be busy; New Yorkers never missed their morning coffees or lattes, whatever the weather.

Safi's thoughts moved to Rupert and his sudden heart attack. Everyone was shocked but relieved that it had occurred while he was around family and friends. Dax's brothers had been amazing; the guests were all impressed with the first-aid they immediately administered to Rupert. The emergency services taking over expertly left no one in doubt that Rupert had been extremely fortunate.

Dan would remain at his bedside until he recovered – after which Safi wondered whether he would insist on Rupert coming to stay at the loft. She could not see that working out. it was a pity Samantha was out of town, she wondered if anyone had let her know. Safi and Sasha, filled with nervous energy and feeling the pressure of the day bearing down on them, decided to throw on their warmest clothes and make their way to the closest coffee shop as a diversion before meeting her parents for breakfast.

Sasha was not expecting an easy ride; it had not escaped his notice that Leonard was more than a little hostile towards him. Safi's mother had been less hostile, but he could tell that neither looked thrilled with the turn of events at the Christmas party. Alone time with Safi now was important; he did not want her to cave under the pressure of her parent's disapproval; at the same time, he did not want to cause a rift between them. Making a run for it through snow flurries, they found an open coffee shop close by, already filled with people drinking lattes, busy on their laptops.

Safi found a corner table for them to cosy up at while Sasha ordered coffee and croissants. Back at the table, they settled down with magazines and the Sunday papers for an hour before they made their way over to the Bowery. Waiting for a reasonable hour, Safi called Dan to get an update on Rupert. Dan was already at Rupert's beside and answered on the first ring.

He whispered to Safi as he made his way to the reception area to take her call. Rupert was still asleep; the tests and scans from the night before had shown that he had had a lucky escape. He was stable but would need a double stent to regulate his heartbeat. He would remain in hospital until it was fitted. She suddenly felt a lump forming in her throat. Rupert had been such a large part of all their lives before, and, after she arrived to live with Dan and Dax, who had become her surrogate parents; the thought of losing any one of them made her shiver.

'Safi are you still there,' he said, swallowing hard.

'Yes, sorry. Please give Rupert our love. Can we visit with him later today?'

'See how things go your end. Perhaps you can come with your dad when he visits. I will give him all the news and keep him entertained until he has had enough, which I am sure will be sooner rather than later.'

'Okay, but send love.'

She dialled Dax, hoping to find him awake – which he was. They fell into their old habit of chatting about everything: Dan, the party, Sasha and her parents. Dax kept her laughing throughout the conversation, having a word with Sasha as well, wishing them luck, and making them promise to call him as soon as the inquisition was over. Sasha nodded at Safi indicating that they had procrastinated long enough and it was time for them to face the music. Zipping into their warm coats, they braved the snow flurry and managed to catch a cab as they hit the sidewalk. Taking Sasha's hand, Safi squeezed it reassuringly. She understood his trepidation and felt it herself; neither of them knew what the next few hours would bring.

Leonard was waiting in the foyer of the hotel as they made their way through the doors. When he leaned down to kiss Safi, she noticed he was dressed for the outdoors, and didn't know whether he had just returned or was about to leave. This was cleared up, however, when he said to Sasha,

'Let's take a walk, we can find a place nearby to chat.'

Safi stared at Sasha helplessly. 'Dad, it's freezing out. Can't you stay here in the lounge and talk. Mom and I will be having breakfast in Jemma, so we won't disturb you.'

Sasha decided that she had a point, and he guided Leonard to the lounge where they found a secluded spot to settle down in. Safi relieved that her father (sometimes so stubborn) complied so easily, found her mother waiting for her in the restaurant. Her brother had obviously made himself scarce.

She hoped they would be able to discuss the engagement, too, once her father had grilled Sasha long enough. Safi knew it would not take long to get her mom on-side; she would get swept up in Safi's excitement and love for Sasha. Her dad, on the other hand, wasn't going to be a pushover. The couple's engagement and excitement with frivolous arrangements would be the least of his concerns.

Sasha and Leonard sat opposite one another in deep leather armchairs, a fire glowing in an iron grate in front of them. At this early hour the lounge was deserted, its usual dark atmosphere lending an ominous side to their meeting. Taking the initiative, Sasha sat forward in his seat, his eyes finding Leonard's. He reached out with one hand, took Leonard's hand in his, and put his other hand on top of Leonard's, hoping this intimate gesture would underscore the sincerity of his actions.

'I love Safi. I understand you are concerned about her welfare. I give you my word that I will care for her, with my life.' He let go of his hand and waited for Leonard to speak.

Leonard stared at Sasha, ignoring his declaration of love for his daughter. For a moment, he was silent. Then he started firing off questions.

'Firstly, what is your age?'

'Twenty-nine.'

'That is a ten-year gap!'

'With respect, is there not a large age-gap between Safi's mother and yourself?'

Momentarily taken aback, Leonard dismissed this out of hand.

'Secondly, what is Safi going to do while she is living with you out there? She has a promising career ahead of her in advertising; if she lets that slip now, and things do not work out between you, she won't have anything to fall back on.'

Sasha knew this would be an issue, one he understood only too well. After all, he worked for his own father; not going into the family business had never been an option. Sasha had been wracking his brain about handling just such a question, but kept coming up with no answer. He stared at Leonard, knowing he would have to give a satisfactory reply that showed he did not dismiss his daughter's wellbeing out of hand. Leonard would judge him on his reply.

'Well, to be honest, Safi and I have been discussing that very question, and we have not yet resolved the issue. There have been options, but they depend on whether Safi would be able to secure a position at one of the ad agencies in Moscow. They are always trying to recruit English-speaking staff. I have asked my contacts to put out feelers. We also use a large recruitment agency in Moscow, and I have spoken to them about a job for Safi.'

Leonard sat back, considering this option that he had not been expecting, impressed by Sasha's resourcefulness but still not satisfied, not even close.

Still, Sasha's reply allowed Leonard to see him in a new and more optimistic light. For the first time, Leonard admitted to himself that Sasha was not the egocentric oligarch playboy he had initially taken him for. Sasha sat back, watching Leonard digesting his answer, wondering what his next concern would be.

'I am marginally happier knowing that she will be continuing her career and not sitting about twiddling her thumbs, waiting for you to return home from a busy day at the office. If you cannot secure her a position, I will have to try helping her on my end. But I am still worried about Safi being in a totally alien environment, with no family to fall back on, if the need arose.'

'I understand your concerns, but, if we want to be together – and we do! – Safi and I have no options but to remain in Moscow for the foreseeable future. I have discussed us relocating to the States, to manage one of our restaurants here. We are busy negotiating premises to open a Rubicov in LA, and a second, smaller Rubicov in Manhattan. My father lives in London, where we have opened our flagship restaurant. Perhaps you have heard of it? For the time being, I need to oversee the Moscow and St Petersburg restaurants. My father needs me there as a stabilizing influence for now. My cousins may take over my position in the near future, at which point Safi and I can reconsider our options.'

Leonard was beginning to relax his initial impression of Sasha, changing it to one of respect. He was straightforward and honest; there seemed to be no hidden agendas. Leonard had to give the younger man his due; Sasha and Safi were in an awkward position, no one could choose who they fell in love with, and their relationship would not work if they remained apart. Leonard was not going to make it more difficult for his daughter than it already appeared to be; no one would benefit if he remained hostile to this new turn of events. And so Leonard decided he would reluctantly give it his support; there was no other way out. The relationship would have to run its natural course; Leonard was not sure it would last, they were from such different cultures, he hoped marriage was still a long way off.

He patted Sasha on the shoulder as he rose from his armchair.

'Breakfast? I think we have covered enough ground for today, and I need to make my way to the hospital to see Rupert.'

Sasha rose, relieved that the inquisition had not ended in a stalemate. He had the impression Leonard had resigned himself to Safi moving with him to Moscow.

They walked into the restaurant together. Safi's head shot up as she saw them entering, trying to see Sasha's expression as they reached their table. Leonard leaned forward and kissed Safi on the forehead. 'Well, my girl, I have given this young man of yours my blessing. He has promised to keep you safe. All there is left for us to do is celebrate your engagement, before we all leave for our different destinations.'

Safi, a bundle of nerves, jumped up, hugged her father tightly, then hugged Sasha, tears of happiness and relief streaming down her face.

'Oh Dad, I have been so wretched with worry. Thank you so much for seeing it our way. It has not been an easy relationship, with Sasha in Moscow and me here in New York. but it has lasted over six months and we want to be together. My moving to Moscow is the only way we can realistically manage it.'

They all fell into discussing how to celebrate their engagement, with Sasha suggesting they have it at Rubicov the day before he returned to Moscow. Safi passed on the good news Dan had told her that morning: Rupert would be out and about within twenty-four hours of his stent being fitted and with luck he would be able to attend the engagement party, too.

The brunch ended with Leonard leaving to see Rupert at the hospital. He knew Rupert would want to know all the latest news about Safi and Sasha; he had let it be known that he thought they made a swell couple. Dan was waiting for Leonard when he arrived at the hospital and had already had a call from Safi to fill him in on their exciting news.

Dax and Dan were both consumed by Rupert's condition and were insistent he convalesce in their loft apartment – but Rupert's doctor had other ideas. The stairs to the loft, the doctor said, were not a good idea until Rupert had regained his strength. Dan suggested he move in with Rupert, but Rupert made it very clear that he preferred female company when it came to caring for his needs, informing them that he had graciously accepted Samantha's offer to move in to his apartment. She was returning from Hong Kong and had decided to rent out her apartment before leaving; she now needed a place to stay while she prepared for her move back to Hong Kong.

Rupert, they all noticed, had a twinkle in his eye; he obviously had something up his sleeve where Samantha was concerned, as he seemed to be showing no signs of sadness about her departure from his life.

They all stared at him, waiting for him to explain his obvious delight at the situation he found himself in. But, for once, Rupert said nothing. Leonard pulled up a chair, regaling him with Safi's news, starting with their initial concerns about her being too young to be thinking of marriage and then her moving to foreign lands where she had no kith or kin. He warmed to his subject, finding relief in voicing his thoughts and worries aloud to Rupert, someone with whom he felt he could share his concerns. Rupert lay back against the pillows, closed his eyes, and concentrated on Leonard's clipped vowels, enjoying the sound of his British accent, and wondering whether his own transatlantic one sounded more American than British after all these years.

'Sasha is a nice-enough guy,' Rupert began after a long sip of water, 'but living in Moscow will be tough; even with no money worries, it is a hard city, not a romantic one for a young couple to forge a new relationship in. Safi would be the one who would have to compromise. Sasha has had an international education, more European than American. Most Russians in their social circle would speak English; most everyone spoke English in the business world.' Rupert thought for a moment then leaned over to Leonard. 'I give them six months. If Safi lasts through that bitter Moscow winter, they may, with luck, last the course, and we'll be celebrating their wedding together'

Hearing Rupert's thoughts gave Leonard no cause for optimism, but he put a brave face on it. Bidding Rupert farewell, he mentioned the engagement celebration for the Friday evening in the club at Rubicov, hoping to see him fit and hearty enough to join the celebrations before they returned to England.

Rupert drew Leonard close.

'I know you feel that Safi is moving far away, but let's make plans to visit Russia together; that will help us both come to terms with this new stage in her life. I was hoping she would settle here with us in Manhattan; I know Dan and Dax were, too. She has become a much loved member of our family. You know, we will all miss her terribly.'

Agreeing to visit Russia together they hugged, and Leonard left Rupert to the hospital staff, who were preparing him to have his last few tests before they discharged him into Dan's care, until Samantha moved into his apartment with him.

Deep in thought, Leonard found his way to the subway. He wanted to give them his blessing, but felt the loss more than he had imagined he would. Safi was his little girl – she would always be his little girl in some ways. He knew she had grown up a great deal since moving away in the last year. All the same, she was precious to him, he adored her. She had always been such a delight and never gave them a day's worry from the time she was born. She was the one who showed interest in his business and he had encouraged her, believing she had a flare for what he had hoped she would make her career.

The advertising agency had gone from strength to strength; they had joined with two other agencies and together they had built a worldwide business with connections to agencies on the West Coast and Manhattan. London and Brighton had given him the much-needed campaigns to take on work across the pond, now he wondered whether it was possible to open an agency in Moscow; it was something he would have to give serious thought to.

Greg McDonald, who he had sent to New York to head up the British project, if offered the challenge might find it hard to refuse and consider starting up a new agency in Moscow. Feeling pleased with his ideas, he became less negative about Safi moving so far away; with hard work and backing from his partners, Leonard thought, they might just pull it off. That way he could keep an eye on Safi and be sure that she did not become estranged from the family or the business he knew she showed a passion for.

Back at the Bowery Hotel he found his family enjoying afternoon tea. Instead of in the atmospheric dimly lit sitting room with its worn mismatched shabby-chic furniture, they were relaxing in the large Atrium warmed by a cold winter sun streaming in through the glass. They had all been out shopping for the engagement party and had the brown bags from Bloomingdale's piled around them. Everyone, he noticed, seemed in high spirits; it amazed him – an adman, no less – what shopping could achieve. Taking a seat beside them, he ordered vodka straight up. If he could not beat them, he might as well join them. Vodka, after all, was as Russian as he was going to feel.

Safi moved next to her father, wanting to draw him into their celebratory mood. She noticed almost immediately that he seemed to have lifted in spirit. They enquired after Rupert's condition and Safi was amused at his refusal to have anyone care for him but Samantha; Rupert would never disappoint, he loved women so much. How he had managed never to remarry was a mystery. Sasha had gone off to call his family with his news and to organise the party for the weekend. Safi let it be known that he had called to tell her his whole family would be flying over for the party. Leonard noticed that his daughter's eyes sparkled with happiness; he had to admit it was infectious. Fiona was swept up, too, enjoying all the excitement.

Leonard felt sure that meeting the Russians was going to be a vodka- and caviar-soaked affair, and he was averse to neither.

Sasha had left them after the tea to arrange the engagement party and to call his mother and then his father. He was not sure what reaction he would receive from either, but was confident his mother would support him. She had always encouraged him to follow his deeper instincts. She had briefly spoken with him about his relationship with the 'English girl,' as she called Safi, and had realised her son for the first time showed signs of being serious. There had been so many girls in the past, it was hard to imagine or believe his playboy lifestyle would end.

Yvetta, his sister had known of his love affair and had stood by him when he had periods of doubt after returning to Moscow. It was Yvetta who had encouraged Sasha to fly over when he thought he had lost Safi because of his stupid possessiveness. Now they were all dropping everything in their busy lives to be there to celebrate this moment with him. He felt overwhelmed at how quickly things had turned out for the best. Safi's father viewed him with more than a little doubt, but had shown he was prepared to give him the benefit of that doubt. True, he had not been easy to charm, but Sasha respected that. Leonard deeply loved his daughter – but then Sasha deeply loved her, too. He needed the older man to know that.

Sasha had been as honest with Leonard as possible, understanding his concerns, knowing his own father had already voiced doubts about a union with this young English rose, and of living a complicated life in Moscow. Moscow was not always the safest place for foreigners – or, for that matter, anyone with money. Sasha put everyone's negativity behind him when he called to pass on his happy news. Delighted, they showed their willingness to support him in his choice of wife. Sasha had no doubt they would all love Safi. It was hard not to love her, she was everything anyone could possibly ask for as a daughter to his mother, and most of all he felt his father secretly approved of his choice. He had noticed how his father had immediately chosen him to chaperone her at the Rubicov opening.

Chapter 13

Sasha did not believe in love at first sight, but after one night with Safi he had become smitten, surprising even himself and – for once – not being sure of his chances. He had known she favoured Niles, who he had managed to make short shrift of, especially after the nightclub fiasco, which had given him the ideal opportunity to show his concern for her wellbeing. The rest was history.

All he had to do was keep Safi safe and happy with him in Moscow. Sasha found his mind drifting in and out of thoughts about his relationship with Safi. His own family had doubts about his ability to remain faithful to one person. But so far, much to his own surprise, he had managed not to stray, even though he had had ample opportunity while they were apart. This alone made him believe Safi was the right person for him: he had lost interest in his usual wild parties and endless stream of sexual partners.

He felt wonderful in her company, she made him a better person, she calmed a side of him he had always found hard to control. Over the years his life had been about hard work – hard-partying, yes, that too, but hard work above all else. Like all his family, he was dedicated by obligation to the family business and by extension to the family's livelihood, to say nothing of duty to each other. Still, a part of him wanted a different lifestyle, to not be tied down by the burden of his bloodline, to be set free in some way. Perhaps with Safi he could break free from this, start a new life, a different city entirely – one that would liberate him from his Russianness, which often seemed a burden in itself. Like his father, he could live in another country, becoming less influenced by his heritage, by the weight of obligations to everyone he was related to. They had many loose ends to tie up before it became possible for the family to fully diversify, but it was starting to happen, and he would make it a priority, before the government of the day did.

Perhaps his carefree attitude with the opposite sex had run its course; he had grown tired of jumping in and out of bed, not having a vital connection with anyone special. Russian girls liked him for his status or his money; American girls fell for his looks and European manners; European girls, he found, were less impressed by anything he stood for, but he never felt they took him seriously. It was just a game to them.

With Safi he had found what he was looking for. She was beautiful and smart, strong-willed, fun in bed, without being needy or calculating. Mostly she was sincere. with a wonderful vulnerability that he loved. Having found her he was not allowing anyone or anything to stand in his way. After all, he had nearly lost her and that had taught him a valuable lesson. She was not to be taken for granted, and he had to remind himself that he would have to work hard at keeping her in love with him.

Sasha wanted to meet with Dan before the engagement party; he needed Dan's blessing, he still could not fathom why Dan and Dax were so important to Safi's life. Perhaps it was because Safi adored them so much. She held them both in the highest esteem. He needed to talk things through with them, too. They were, after all, Safi's family in New York and he owed them that. He knew, too, that both Dan and Dax were hoping she would remain in Manhattan, as part of their extended family. Thus, Sasha's gain in Moscow was their loss in New York.

Safi had brought so much happiness into all their lives, which she was completely unaware of. Sasha suddenly felt in awe of her ability to be special to everybody she met. Even Pete the barman thought the world of her; he almost felt guilty for taking her away from everyone she had made such close connections with over such a short period of time, but love was selfish and he wanted her with him and now he had achieved that, he was not letting her go for any reason.

Having the whole family at Rubicov was a huge undertaking. The staff at the restaurant went into full swing; orders from Sasha's father about what he expected had already been received. There were extra orders for caviar, truffles, quail's eggs, champagne and strawberries, with the best wines and Cuban cigars on the menu, not to mention the flowers Sasha's mother wanted adorning the tables. Yvetta had ordered a special cake to be delivered made of Russian liquor and covered with red ruby icing. The sous chef had been put on special duty to prepare a Napoleon cake. The head chef had his orders too for certain dishes to be on the menu. Caviar, for starters, served in silver ice-holding bowls. Stroganoff for mains plus beef wellington, followed by desserts like Eton Mess and Napoleon cake.

His father wanted it to be a celebration that suited both cultures of both the families and, Sasha was pleased to leave the organising and logistics of the engagement party to his parents, while he kept things running smoothly finding spare beds for those who were flying over at short notice from Russia for the celebration, having his family involved showed their commitment to his happiness.

The engagement party was going to be for the family only; close friends Safi had made while in Manhattan, like Lauren and Bianca were not invited to this celebration. Sasha and Safi decided over brunch what kind of evening they thought it should be, one where they had a chance to get acquainted with each other's families. Everyone was relieved that Rupert would make it, after his near-miss at the Christmas party; Samantha would bring him. Dan and Dax insisted on having Pete included: he was family as far as they were concerned. All thought Bruno should have the place of honour at the table, but Dax's paintings of him would have to suffice.

A feeling of melancholy settled over Safi as she left with Sasha; leaving her family at this moment seemed wrong, yet she wanted to stay with Sasha at his apartment. Dan and Dax were meeting Sasha for an early breakfast the following day. Safi was spending the rest of the day with her family. Time was flying by and she had to decide what her plans were going to be before she joined Sasha in Moscow. The engagement celebrations had taken precedence over other discussions.

Sasha encouraged Safi to remain with Dan and Dax until her visa expired, and then to fly to England to spend as much time as she wished with her own family before she joined him in Moscow.

Safi imagined flying to Moscow with Sasha after the engagement party; he had taken her by surprise with his suggestions. A part of her was disappointed, but she agreed with his thinking: it made sense but did she want to be sensible?

It felt silly to go through all the hoopla and then not to be together; they had been apart for long enough. She wanted to start her life with him straight away, not months down the line. Suddenly she felt exhausted; the emotions of the last few days seemed to have taken their toll. Closing her eyes, she curled up in a large wing chair, trying to slow down the chaos overtaking her every waking thought.

Sasha, just out of the shower, noticed Safi sitting with her legs pulled up under her chin, staring out at the night. He stood, drying himself while watching her closely. She normally did not let him shower alone, but he had given up waiting for her to join him. Now he wondered what she was feeling; neither had had much time to be alone with their thoughts.

He pulled on tracksuit bottoms, then busied himself in the kitchen pouring each of them a glass of wine. Sasha sat in the chair next to Safi, putting the wine down between them on a table. Noticing she had not reacted, he leant over to find she had fallen asleep. Smiling, he picked her up and carried her to bed, tucked her in and left her to sleep. Returning to his seat to contemplate on their last few days and what lay ahead while he finished both glasses of wine, he admired the Manhattan night stretching out in the distance a long way down.

Safi was obviously exhausted from the hectic emotional rollercoaster of the last few days(in fact, it seemed like weeks rather than days). Sasha realised his perseverance had paid off and it pleased him greatly. His engagement idea had worked out better than he imagined. While Safi remained behind to spend time with her family, it would be up to him to create a welcome environment for her when she arrived in Moscow. He knew she would love his apartment; that was the least of their problems. She could add whatever feminine touches she desired, but what bothered him most was how she would find something to keep her busy while he was away during the day. She needed something to get her teeth into, their winters were too long and unforgiving to sightsee.

If nothing else, Yvetta was a consummate professional when it came to work. She had offered to help, which he appreciated. He wasn't sure whether Safi would take to the art world, or to his sister's infamous moodiness. He was prepared to try and sell the idea to Safi to begin with; it was all he had come up with – if she hated it, they would have to try and find her something else. Of course he had the added problem of keeping her safe. Working for Yvetta would help; she would teach Safi the logistics of Moscow. She needed to acclimatise; Moscow was not Manhattan, where she could run around any time of the day or night without being concerned for her safety. Moscow was another story: one wrong turn and she could be lost, perhaps for ever, if she fell into the wrong hands. He was being neurotic, not without cause, their winters were notoriously brutal.

Sasha put these thoughts out of his mind – they were too frightening to contemplate. Feeling the need to be close, he turned off the lights and crawled into bed, folding his arms protectively about her. Moaning softly, he kissed her lightly, holding onto her for warmth and protecting himself from his own nightmarish thoughts. Here, now, it was easy to imagine Moscow a long way away, but he knew he had to prepare. Safi's move to Moscow would be many things, but it wouldn't be easy – he knew that much.

Waking with a start, Safi turned to shake Sasha awake; he was thrashing about in his sleep. She watched as he struggled with some unknown demons, his usually immaculate hair clammy and plastered to his forehead. Sasha stared at Safi with relief as he woke to find her safely in his bed. Grabbing her tightly, they melted into each other's arms. Sasha, urgent in his need, took her possessively. Breathing hard, he collapsed and rolled off; holding onto her hand, he kissed it softly. Regaining strength, he crawled under the covers and kissed her until she writhed with pleasure, begging him to stop. Laughing at their mad lovemaking, Safi lay contentedly in Sasha's arms, feeling his strong fingers massage her back and stroking her hair.

'What time are you meeting Dan and Dax for breakfast?' Safi asked. Sasha looked over at the clock on the bedside table. 'We have time, maybe I can have you for breakfast instead.' They stared at one another; neither wanting to allow the reality of their crazy few days to intrude on their time together.

Pulling the covers off, she sprang out of bed.

'Up, up, up,' she said with a renewed buoyancy. 'I could burst with happiness. Let's find a coffee shop before you go off and leave me for all your Russian family arriving soon.'

Sasha towel-dried Safi's hair as she sat on the end of the bed between his legs; neither wanted to waste time waiting for her hair to dry. She put it up into a high ponytail, allowing the rest to dry on its own. They grabbed their coats and boots, which they slipped on in the elevator as it descended to the pavement.

It was bitterly cold as they made their way to a favourite coffee shop they knew would be open at 6.30am. Sipping coffees, Safi, suddenly starving, ordered a banana muffin while Sasha tried to explain his nightmare without mentioning she was in it. He was lost in a landscape of endless white snow in freezing temperatures. She listened quietly, squeezing his hand reassuringly.

Winking with a naughty smile on her face, Safi teased, 'Don't worry so much, everything will work out when we are together in Moscow. I promise never to let you out of my sight, so there is no way you are going to get lost in some snow storm, unless it's with me.'

Feigning disbelief, he relaxed into the chair, picked up the Wall Street Journal and started to read, ignoring her purposefully. Safi sat staring at him for a second or two, grabbed the paper out of his hand, jumped onto his lap and kissed him hard on the mouth.

'You're not going to get away with that, young man, as my mother would say.'

'Oh my God, is that what I'm letting myself in for – turning into your mama already?'

They sat together chatting and laughing until Sasha left for his meeting with Dan and Dax, and Safi returned to the apartment to get ready for a day with her family. They had not yet been to the Met and no one wanted to miss the Alexander McQueen show Savage Beauty. It was supposed to be incredible. McQueen had died in such awful circumstances and was so young and brilliant; Safi wanted to pay her respects to such a powerful English designer. After the show they were going to make their way to Bergdorf's to lunch on the top floor, which overlooked Central Park: it was a vision when covered in snow, something she knew her folks would appreciate seeing.

Dan opened the door for Sasha; they had all decided to remain at the apartment for breakfast. Sasha turned up with bagels, lox and cream cheese. Dan had the coffee-machine brewing, while Dax had laid three places on the breakfast counter, with mugs, fruit juice, and a platter of fresh fruit, not to mention the bowl of mixed roses they so loved. The bagels were toasted and ready to eat by the time they settled to chat after indulging on the fruit and coffee.

New York got back to work pretty much straight away after Christmas, but Dan had decided to take time off to spend with Dax and his dad.

Dan started the conversation by filling Sasha in on Rupert's progress while Dax had them laughing, retelling and mimicking Rupert's idiosyncrasies, flirting with all the nursing staff, second-guessing all the doctors, and driving everyone insane. (No one more so than Dan, who was offended when Rupert refused to be cared for after he was discharged, until Samantha stepped up to save the day, cannily asking him to stay over at his place as a favour, as she did not have a flat to return to. She gave Rupert the perfect opportunity to accept help without losing face.)

A moment's silence descended on them, when all three spoke at once. Sasha put up his hand like a schoolboy, asking to be allowed to open the discussion, but, not being able to contain his thoughts for another second, Dax jumped in: 'Sasha, that was one hell of a move you pulled off at Christmas lunch. I have to take my hat off to you, for perfect timing. You certainly had us all eating out of your hand – apart from Safi's father, that is, who we thought was going to burst a blood vessel. Instead it was Rupert!'

Sasha, sighed, agreeing that he had no other course of action left open to him. Realising he was on a losing wicket with Leonard after experiencing his early and obvious disapproval, Sasha decided he needed a failsafe tactic to get them to allow Safi to return to Moscow with him, instead of her having to beg for their approval. Having limited time, he had rushed to Cartier, where he had stood in line waiting to be served in the Christmas crush. He recalled the long wait in that line, going for broke with that ring – 'not a wing and a prayer but a ring and a prayer,' as Sasha joked – praying Safi's answer would be a 'resounding yes' after his dramatic proposal.

Dan shook his hand and said,

'I have to hand it to you, Sasha, you had us all fooled. I am not sure what reception you would have had if my dad had not diverted everyone's attention.'

Dax, never one to mince his words, asked Sasha straight out, 'Are you sure you are doing the right thing by Safi, taking her away from everyone who cares for her to a pretty unfriendly place, where she probably only has you to depend on?'

Sasha took his time before answering a very relevant question, one he had gone over a million times.

'To be honest, it's not going to be easy. It's something I have been worried about, too, and wanted more than anything to speak to you about. She might like helping out in the galleries to begin with. I know she will love the apartment in our home. It's our Moscow home, and Anna, my mother, lives downstairs. We have staff so she won't be on her own ever, really.'

Dan looked doubtful; he and Dax were hoping that Safi would become a fixture in their lives and were finding it difficult to come to terms with her exiting so soon. Sasha was a decent-enough guy, but they were more than a little worried about Safi being sucked into something she might find difficult to deal with once the dust had settled. Especially living in such close proximity to Sasha's mother, Anna? Safi had never been on her own entirely, she was an independent spirit, but was she streetwise enough for Moscow? Manhattan was an entirely different story.

Dan thoughtfully took his time while Dax kept himself busy tidying up, nervously arranging the flowers Sasha had brought. He found it difficult to hide his disapproval. On the one hand, he was happy for them both; on the other, he adored Safi and did not want to see her flounder in a culture that was so alien to her.

'I almost feel responsible: if I had not introduced you both, maybe she would still be here with us. Maybe that's a selfish attitude on my part. No one can control who they fall in love with. Don't misunderstand me, we think you are a great guy, but, like you, we are worried for Safi, too.' He held up his hand, indicating that he wanted to continue before anyone interrupted his train of thought.

'It's no use going round in circles, though. I am going to suggest something to you and perhaps together we can try and make things as failsafe for Safi as possible.'

Both Dax and Sasha leant forward to hear what Dan was going to propose.

'Give Safi six months. If she is not happy and you are both still in love, leave Moscow and return to New York.'

Sasha, momentarily taken aback, was lost for words.

'Six months is not a long time. I have a duty to my family and the business.'

Sasha held up his hand. Now it was his turn to take control – of the conversation, but of his relationship with Safi, too.

'I fully accept your concerns for Safi's wellbeing and happiness – those are my concerns as well. If she is homesick, she can visit as often as she wishes. If she finds living in Moscow unendurable, for whatever reason, then of course I will have to consider leaving sooner than planned. More than that is not possible to plan for: there are too many variables at stake, for us both. Perhaps living together in Moscow will be a trial period for our relationship, but I am not putting a time limit on our relationship: that will have to be Safi's decision.'

Sasha seemed shaken. Dan and Dax looked at one another, both feeling that they might have overstepped the mark. Perhaps they were being selfish about their own sentiments, forgetting that this was a young couple in love.

Dax, being the more emotional one, came around to Sasha and took his hand in both of his.

'Listen, maybe we have overstepped. We have no claim on Safi, and if her folks are letting this go ahead, well, who are we to make ultimatums? You are in love, that should be enough for all of us. After all, neither of you are teenagers – well, scrap that, at least one of you isn't. Safi would be horrified with our meddling. She has become such a part of our lives and I suppose we are selfishly taking ownership. Seeing her go out of our lives has made us blind to her needs – and yours. I hope you will forgive us.'

Dan was not sure that he felt as benign about this whole affair; he, for one, did not believe Safi would last longer than three months in Moscow. But he was not going to say another word. Perhaps Dax had a point. Apart from Safi's parents (who seemed to have been won over by their desire to be together), it was none of anyone's business.

Dan offered his hand to Sasha, who willingly accepted it.

'I wanted your input, knowing how much you both adore Safi. So yes, I will accept your sentiments in this matter, but I believe Safi is stronger than you think. Whatever problems arise, we will muddle through together. I hope that you will stay in constant touch with Safi, too; there is no reason she cannot speak to you as often as she wishes, or you with her. I believe that will be her lifeline, having you all involved in our lives; that way she won't feel so distant and far away.'

Dan and Dax nodded their agreement, relieved to have been invited to be part of their lives.

Sasha had in one fell swoop gone up in their estimation; he was, Dan thought, a clever facilitator and knew how to bring everyone around to his corner. This was an admirable quality. Perhaps Safi had chosen the right guy after all.

They fell into chatting about the coming engagement party, with Sasha asking their advice about who to seat where and how to bring the two families together without too much fanfare. This was a subject the two D's could warm to, having had plenty of recent experience in it themselves.

Sasha's family were a diverse lot. Alexi was from the old school, staunch in his ways and traditions regarding family, his province to rule as he saw fit, having earned his position through age and hard work. His tastes had become more European during his years living in London, but that did not make him any less Russian. His second wife, Valentina, had grown up in St. Petersburg and had a far more progressive attitude to things foreign than most Muscovites. She had joined the Bolshoi Ballet from a very young age, but had become disillusioned with the way it was managed after Perestroika. After an injury she was demoted; not sure they would reemploy her in another position, she began to search for something new.

Sasha's mother, Anna, was Russian to the core. She had worked most of her life and had little understanding for those seeking an easier lifestyle. Most in the family turned to Anna when it came to matters of the heart; besides dispensing solid advice she loved nothing more than keeping up with their lives.

Anna had never married a second time and was content to oversee the formidable business empire she and Alexi had built, remaining the matriarch of the family. Over the years his parent's relationship had changed to one of mutual respect rather than one of husband and wife.

Yvetta considered herself an international businesswoman and loved and respected her Russian roots. She straddled comfortably between both worlds. She enjoyed mixing in the upper echelons of Russian society, yet doing as she pleased when abroad where she did not have to worry about prying eyes. In the art world she had quite a bit of clout, due to her family's investment.

Mika, their oldest brother, was born when Sasha's parents were very young and was considerably older than both himself and Yvetta; he was more like a father figure than an older brother. No one in their family liked to have to answer to Mika, who was revered for his connections and his ability as a trouble-shooter.

Mika kept his own council; they seldom saw him. He was known as the family loner and Alexi's right-hand man when things needed sorting out. Sasha was hoping Mika's presence would keep the rest of his extended family under control once the vodka started flowing.

Sasha had no concerns about Safi's family meeting his immediate family, but was apprehensive about them meeting his grassroots Russian family, who he knew could be boorish in their ways. Safi's family would have to get used to bearhugs and downing vodka after every course. They were fortunate it would only be for one evening, rather than at every family meal.

Like all Russians, starved for so long of consumer goods, his family dressed the way Russians enjoyed dressing: to impress – and this was never truer than for special occasions. No casual clothes for them; they would be in designer gear and accessorised in the best money could buy.

In a conversation with the maître d', Sasha had decided on mixed seating to allow the families to become acquainted. Four round tables of ten filled the large, ornate, red-carpeted room with its heavy brocade drapes. Each table had a profusion of red roses on white tablecloths laid over floor-length gold brocade fabric. It was a rich baroque scene fitting for a Russian dining room. The paintings adorning the high-gloss black walls were contemporary with art-deco chandeliers to lift the dramatic damask atmosphere.

Starters would be a casual affair of Russian delicacies: a table groaning with ice-filled tureens of caviar and every fish dish including herring in sour cream, borscht (the traditional beetroot soup) with sour cream, wonderful Blinis batter filled with caviar, Pelmeni, a pointed pasta-like dish filled with chicken and eaten with sour cream, small cabbage balls filled with savoury mince, and long aspic loaves filled with meat that one could slice like bread. French loaves with butter would be plentiful to smother the caviar on.

Champagne and vodka with cranberry juice would be flowing, a Russian version of kir, to prevent anyone from overdosing on all the vodka that would be consumed between each course.

The main meal would be a more American, continental affair, with seated name places that were considered most carefully. Who to seat next to his various family members gave Sasha a major headache; he was a bag of nerves for the evening's celebrations. Greeting his family on arrival as they gathered in the foyer of the Rubicov apartments, they bear-hugged and shed tears of joy, departing excitedly to ready themselves for the engagement party that evening, set to begin at seven sharp. Sasha had four of his cousins sleeping in his apartment, and Safi would arrive early with the two D's.

On entering the club dining room Safi with Dan and Dax all came to a mouth-dropping halt. The staff already in attendance, Sasha turned, noticing their reaction on entering the room. Dan gave a low whistle while Dax, who was never one to hide his unbridled enthusiasm for something he thought was worth a reaction, made it more than evident that he loved every last dramatic detail.

They examined the buffet table, marvelling over the delicacies displayed in a mixture of large beautifully decorated tureens, raised platters showing off whole curved pink salmons. While in rows along the table there were small, unique delicate, beautifully decorated, tiny tasting dishes. Exotic red flowers in tall vases added softness to a myriad of mouth-watering Russian fare.

Moving on to examine the stunningly dressed tables, a perfect setting against the rich drama of the club décor, Dan nodded his approval. The long Russian tasting table was a perfect foil with its sophisticated modern white tablecloth and white dishes offset by small rose-filled vases. Compared to the round tables groaning with crystal glasses, it was tastefully restrained by comparison. Sasha wanted to impress Safi's family, but he also liked to satisfy his own family's baroque tastes.

They had a few moments to change before the family arrived. Sasha dressed in a dark grey Armani suit and tie; his pointed black boots were his only eccentricity. He looked appraisingly at Safi's choice; they headed towards the elevator for their special evening, with their respective families.

She had on one of Lauren's mid-calf, tasteful-fitting Chanel black dresses. It was sleeveless, with a high-slash neckline and pearl straps to mid-back. Safi's long dark bob with drop-pearl earrings framed by her huge brown eyes and heavy lashes finished with lip-gloss made Sasha's heart swell with pride at the thought of his family meeting her. She was going to blow their socks off. He was beginning to understand why he had so willingly committed the rest of his life to this delicate, willowy English beauty. Slavic beauties relentlessly pursued him on his return to Moscow, women who would agree to marry him without a second thought; apart from Allana, a childhood friend, he had never felt this way for anyone before.

He knew his cousins would tease him about his playboy status and Safi would be learning about a side of him he never liked to reveal; he hoped she wouldn't get upset by their banter, there was no avoiding it.

Safi left to meet her parents in the foyer, wanting to arrive with them at the function. Sasha's family had a short ride down in the elevator and would arrive first. Sasha wanted to give them time to settle before meeting with their soon-to-be English relatives who, they would learn, were far more reserved than their soon-to-be Russian family.

The rumble of laughter emanating from the elevators could only be his family; no one else would be that noisy, always in high spirits and ready to party. Sasha knew they loved nothing better than a celebration.

His mother entered with Yvetta; following close behind was his father with the demurely elegant ballerina, Valentina Popov, now his wife. His uncles, aunts, and cousins swarmed in, greeting them warmly. Sasha waited for their reaction, but he had no need to worry; their nods of approval were enough for him.

Alexi greeted the two D's with genuine warmth; welcoming them to their family, he introduced each as the best there was in New York for anything to do with architecture, interiors, or the arts. Yvetta was drawn to them immediately, and cornered Dax to chat about the paintings he had done for Rubicov.

Safi had no need to worry how her family would react to Sasha's family. They were bear-hugged with cheeks kissed not twice but three times, and everyone wanted to speak with her folks. Jake was whisked away by one of Sasha's cousins to meet his Russian relatives. Safi found herself surrounded by Anna and Yvetta; they guided her towards the table groaning with Russian delicacies.

Alexi called for a toast to welcome Safi's family. There was no avoiding the endless supply of vodka and champagne being served. The jovial atmosphere relaxed Safi, and she was pleased to notice that her father had lost his stressed-out, anxious demeanour. The glass of vodka he was holding that Alexi kept filling was obviously helping.

Rupert immediately charmed everyone he met. Samantha, Pete, and the rest of Dax's family were chatting affably with Sasha's family. Everyone was gesticulating and nodding their approval at the Russian fare on offer.

The mothers, standing to one side, were chatting, trying to become a little more acquainted. Safi made her way towards them and Valentina joined them, too. Introducing Valentina to her mother nonchalantly as Alexi's wife, noticing her mother's obvious discomfort at the situation, Safi was relieved when Anna managed to dispel her fears, putting her at ease as she welcomed Alexi's wife warmly. The women seemed to enjoy one another's company, and Safi felt happy to leave her mother to become acquainted with both Sasha's mother and stepmother-in-law-to-be.

Sasha squeezed Safi's hand; they found themselves alone for the first time, feeling pleasantly surprised and a little relieved with their engagement party so far. Sasha pointed out his family's high spirits: they were showing off more than usual, which proved how important it was for them to be seen in the best light. Alexi obviously felt at home with his new English family, but the cousins were more flamboyantly exuberant.

Sasha's cousins were regaling Jake with anecdotes of their many conquests, meting out a fair bit of gossip in the process.

Being able to observe everyone from a solitary distance did not last more than a few minutes before guests were once more drawn into the celebrations by Alexi, inviting everyone to take their seats at the name-places provided. Safi was seated between the matriarchs of the family, Fiona on one side, with Anna on the other. Sasha, she noted, was seated between the patriarchs. It was obviously a Russian custom; no one but her English family seemed to notice the seating arrangements.

Each dish was toasted with thimbles of vodka. Each course consisted of at least two to three dishes, and was accompanied by a different wine. The silver tureens on each table were filled with mountains of caviar, adding to the exotic mix of European fusion dishes. Safi noted that Anna preferred to indulge in the caviar, spooning it onto French bread with lashings of butter. Feeling the need to join in, she followed Anna's example, hoping to develop a taste for the delicacy she knew was so loved in Sasha's mother-country.

The caviar piled on top of butter and French bread had a pleasant, popping, salty yet creamy sensation. Anna encouraged her to wash it down with vodka. Gamely obliging, Safi laughed with both her mother and Anna as she added a fair amount of cranberry juice to the alcohol. Feeling more relaxed, she sat back happily, watching others as they chatted away to their new relatives seated beside them, noting with amusement how the Brits among them were fast learning (as she was) how to indulge in the foreign fare, not to mention the endless supply of vodka.

The guests started to mingle, with some swapping seats; all seemed reluctant to end the evening, happily sipping the after-dessert liquors and wines, and adding to the already jovial inebriated atmosphere of raised voices around her.

Tapping a spoon for attention, Sasha rose to thank both families for their support and for the warm welcome. With a slight slur, pressing his hand to his heart, Sasha promised to hold Safi's family as close as he held his own family, and to cherish and love Safi with all his heart.

Everyone nodded with approval, toasting for the last time, she hoped as she did not have the stomach for another drop of alcohol. She was, in fact, beginning to feel unwell. The rich food did not help either, or the tension and excitement of the evening. Rising from the table before embarrassing herself in front of everyone, feeling warm and clammy, she made her way to the restroom just in time. Pressing a cold damp cloth to her forehead, she peered in the mirror, not wanting to show any evidence of having been sick. Thankfully, the awful dizziness and cold sweat had gone.

Satisfied, she reapplied lipstick and some blusher, and returned to the festivities just as everyone was saying their last farewells. No one seemed to have missed her as they grabbed her into a bearhug. She was secretly thankful she was able to tolerate all the hugging, after feeling so ill moments before – goodness knows how it would have panned out had she thrown up all over one of her new relatives?

The next morning Safi woke to a buzzing phone. Grabbing it from her bedside table, she knocked a glass of water over the cell. Rushing to the bathroom, she managed to dry her cell then put it down to relieve herself when it started to buzz again. This time her phone fell on the floor, clattering as it hit the tiles. She leant down to pick it up and felt her head swimming and the colour draining from her face. She was not sure how long she had been lying next to the toilet on the cold bathroom tiles, but woke to her cell and room phone ringing at the same time, plus urgent banging on her door.

Making for the door first, she opened it to a worried Sasha and her mother, gave the cell to Sasha and indicated to her mother to answer the ringing bedside phone.

Promising to call back, they both turned to stare at Safi, who was now lying flat out on the bed with blood trickling down her nose. Sasha and her mother both ran to the bathroom for a towel, and together they returned with a cold compress. Holding the compress to her nose, Safi tried to explain what she thought had happened.

'I think I fainted while on the toilet and must have banged my nose on the tiles as I hit them.'

'We were beside ourselves with worry,' Fiona said. 'No one could get hold of you. We were about to ask hotel security to open the door for us.'

It appeared she had passed out for almost an hour! Feeling ridiculous, she explained the fiasco with the cell and then how she fainted right after that. Her mother, along with everyone else, had been calling since early that morning; thinking she must have been exhausted, they left her to sleep, but then concern set in and they decided to check on her as it got closer to lunch.

Strangely, she now felt on top of the world; all energy had returned and she was rearing to go. Smiling apologetically, she assured everyone that she was okay. Feeling the need for some privacy, she shooed them all out so she could get herself ready, not wanting to miss saying goodbye to anyone. Reluctant to leave her alone, Sasha remained behind to make calls while she took a shower; he kept calling to see whether she was okay. Safi adored his attention, it gave her confidence that even a Russian winter would thaw in the wake of their union, bringing a bit of wet English weather instead.

Agreeing she should spend the last few days with her folks before they returned to England, she had returned to the Bowery Hotel with her parents on the night of their engagement. Together with her family, they stayed up late into the night, retelling stories, and laughing about their ignorance at Russian customs and intolerance for too much vodka, caviar, and rich food. They were all genuinely impressed with the evening. She was delighted both her parents approved of Sasha's immediate family, especially Anna, who they believed to be the backbone of the family.

Leonard enjoyed the Russian exuberance for life and embraced Alexi's warmth, feeling happier about Safi's chances of adjusting to life in Moscow. He was led to understand she would be encouraged to become part of their lives and no longer had fears for her safety. Safi was dying to know what Sasha's family thought of her uptight English family, not to mention her extended American family of Dan and Dax.

She was not surprised to learn from Sasha that his cousins frowned on homosexuality.

'Rubenovitch was our original name until we shortened it to Rubicov, which is much easier to pronounce. It suited our restaurant's to be called something everyone could get their tongue around.'

He stared at Safi, realising he would have to be very careful about answering her questions. He did not want her to feel she had to defend her family; Russians were quick to criticise, but equally quick to defend their kith and kin with their lives.

He lifted her chin, looking into her eyes and managing to wink before kissing her. Safi bit his lower lip lightly; feeling her passion rising, she pushed her hips against him, becoming aware of his excitement. She pulled him into the bathroom; he kicked the door shut. He locked it, in case someone decided to find them. There were now so many wanting their attention. They had hardly had time to sneeze since the engagement party the previous evening. Safi had never felt such heightened excitement, something inside her felt different, her whole body was on fire with desire. Cell phones continuously pinging, they returned their attention to family matters once more.

The family were downstairs in the reception area waiting for them, Sasha rushed down while Safi did a quick change, blow-drying only her fringe; the rest she left to dry in a high ponytail.

A car was waiting to take them to Rubicov to meet with Alexi and Valentina for a farewell dinner, which Alexi had insisted upon. Safi, elated and bright-eyed, looked particularly ravishing in a tailored dark-red satin trouser suit, her hair tied back, with ruby-red lipstick against her pale skin, the whole ensemble adding to her new-felt confidence.

Safi's family were dumbstruck by their daughter's transformation; she had blossomed into a stunning woman while living in Manhattan. Her mother admired her suit and loved her deep-purple clutch and sling-back heels, adding height to her already long legs. Alexi whistled softly as Sasha entered hand in hand with his English beauty, now realising why his son was so completely smitten with her. Beneath that English reserve Alexi saw something else: fire in her black eyes, which he interpreted as unmistakable raw sexuality.

They dined in the main restaurant, at a table reserved for them, away from a buzzing noisy frenetic scene where waiters in long black aprons carrying heavy trays served the hungry masses. Settling at the white linen-covered table, minimalist by the previous night's standards, they studied the menu with recommendations from everyone including the waiters. Safi advised her parents to stick to ordering only a main meal, as she remembered from past experience that starters and deserts arrived in abundance as if by magic.

All were flying home to their respective destinations the following morning. Safi had decided to stay with Dan and Dax until her visa expired. She would then fly back to London to visit with her family and friends for several days before leaving for Moscow. Sasha had arranged to meet with Safi in London so they could make the journey together to Moscow. They would stay with Alexi and Valentina in Mayfair for a few nights before her final goodbye to everyone.

Chapter 14

The excitement of her last few days were overwhelming; everything had crystallised into a dizzying reality after Sasha put that ring on her finger. It was a strange feeling finding herself back in her room at the loft, almost a different person to the one who had last lived with the two D's.

She had arrived a novice and was leaving, much to her delight, not too far from her original wish for a life less travelled. She had yearned to be independent, but the truth was that allowing others into her life had in the end freed her from conforming to everyone else's wishes. She may never have had the courage to venture out of her comfort zone if it were not for the two D's. She wanted to spend as much time with Dan and Dax before leaving. They had been her surrogate parents and she had immersed herself in their lives.

Christmas had been a milestone for Dan and Dax, too, and she felt guilty for having upstaged their festivities. More than anything, Safi wanted to keep her close connection with them. Life was going to be dull without their meddling and Dax's high drama; she was going to miss them awfully.

Dan and Dax were thrilled Safi had not left with Sasha for Moscow or returned to England with her parents. They were planning to make the most of having her all to themselves for the next four weeks, and did not waste any time, starting the moment Safi walked in the door after her tearful farewells. They made her settle in one of her favourite high-backed, leather-studded chairs to share all her gossip. Never one to waste an opportunity to mimic or replay any situation he found amusing, Dax launched straight into his rendition of Sasha's Russian family. Starting with the delectable Yvetta and moving on to Valentina, who they adored and found tres chic, with her dancer's physique and mannerisms.

To Safi's astonishment, Yvetta had confided in Dax that she was gay but dared not reveal this to her family, who were backward and old-school about such things. She indulged her romantic dalliances when travelling and free from the eyes (and judgement) of her family. Safi sat staring at Dax with her mouth open; she had never for one moment got the impression that Yvetta preferred women. After all, according to Sasha, she was madly flirtatious and had men lining up to marry her.

The two D's advised Safi to keep this information to herself and certainly not to share her newfound knowledge with Sasha; indeed, it might put her in an awkward position if it ever came to light. Agreeing, Safi thought it could be advantageous knowing this about Yvetta, who was, by all accounts, a very tough customer. Dax mentioned that Sasha's cousins were great fun, yet Russian to the core and dogmatically conservative.

Pete had problems dealing with their blatant dislike of black people. Their racism was of the antique kind, and most objectionable. They believed black people to be lazy apart from their talents in music. Pete tried to put a brave face on it – he had experienced more than his share of racism over the course of his life, he said – but the two D's could tell that he was insulted. Which he had every right to be, of course.

Pete kept his own council, comfortable in his own craggy skin, preferring to intellectually annihilate their ignorant statements, but in a judicious and sensitive manner. Safi was mortified that Pete had been subjected to such rudeness and ignorance. The vodka obviously loosened their tongues and obliterated their manners, parading their prejudices so openly to a much-loved guest. She did not believe Sasha, who adored Pete as much as she did, would have been happy had he been aware of their behaviour towards Pete. She resolved to speak with Pete about it and get his take on the whole ugly saga, and she was definitely going to mention it to Sasha.

The rest of the evening was spent laughing at Dax's Russian accent and crying 'Na Zdorovie!' every time they lifted their glasses at the table to down any drink.

Bruno was back on her bed, obviously sensing something unsettling. It was going to be sad not to have him around, he had been a comfort during her time in New York.

Safi got right back into her old walking routine with Bruno: her torn skinny jeans and old boots went back on, while Bruno wore his new butch fleece jacket to keep him warm on the freezing sidewalks. Safi and Bruno went to their favourite haunt for coffee; they chose to sit outdoors, where blankets were provided and the outdoor heaters kept them warm. Safi felt relaxed for the first time since her family arrived from England, not to mention her life suddenly moving in a whole new direction. She needed the space to adjust to her new status as Sasha's fiancé; remaining behind in Manhattan had been a clever decision, she needed closure before embarking on this new life in Moscow with Sasha.

She decided to organise her time left with the people she cared most about. Sasha pinged to say good night; it was almost dinnertime for him, a time difference of eight hours. He was obviously turning in early after his flight back. She ordered another coffee and another doggie biscuit for Bruno, then set about leaving messages for Lauren and Niles, who she wanted to catch up with.

Rupert answered on the first ring. 'I thought I went down well with the Russkies,' he said, 'so you should be okay as long as you remember to mention your uncle Rupert on occasion.'

She laughed and promising she would. They made arrangements to meet at his usual hangout in the park. Then he said, 'Let's all visit my winter Dacha for a weekend before you defect to the other side.'

'I think that's a fantastic idea. I would love to see your winter retreat in Connecticut.'

The two D's had to clear some of their work schedules, but thought it a great plan to visit Rupert's Dacha.

Neither Rupert nor Dax had yet come to terms with competing for Dan's attention.

By the time they got to Pete's Bar, Bruno was panting for breath and Safi wondered whether it a good idea to have him climb five flights to the loft. He had become less agile on his Victorian legs since she had been in Manhattan. Bruno gave Pete a short welcome then plonked his considerable weight heavily into his basket under the bar that held a bowl of water for him to drink.

They sat at the bar and Safi let Pete rumble on about everything in his usual gruff but comforting manner. She never tired listening to his gravelly voice, it had a mesmerising, relaxed tone. Bruno was snoring peacefully and she knew she was going to miss these moments terribly.

Looking up he noticed Safi's expression. 'What's up, girl, I can tell there is something on that mind of yours, spit it out.' She smiled at his lazy New Orleans drawl and decided to come clean. 'Pete, Dax mentioned what Sasha's cousins were saying at the party. I can't believe what I heard, it's just ghastly!'

Pete looked down at his beer bottle for a while, deciding how to play this. 'Well, I won't pretend I was happy, but they ignorant boys, that's all, take no mind.' Safi stared at Pete, wanting to hug him, but held back her emotions.

'I certainly do mind, Pete. I've never in my life been so insulted and hurt. How dare they speak that way to you, there's simply no excuse for such bad behaviour.'

'Well, the funny thing is, I don't think they considered me part of what they were talking about.'

'Oh! Tosh!'

Pete shook his head amusingly. 'No, I believe they did not see me as a black person – even as they were saying such disparaging things about my people. I guess they were pretty smashed from all that vodka.'

'It's still not excusable.'

'Safi, don't make a fuss. Let it be; you can't start your stay in Moscow on a war path with his relatives, or with Sasha. But, girl, stay on your toes out there, I hear it can get wild. If anything ain't right out there, you promise to let me know, you hear.'

Choking up, she leant over and hugged him; she knew he meant every word he ever uttered, that's why he always made her feel so safe.

Noticing the time, she left Bruno with Pete, jumped in a cab, and made her way to Dax's studio.

Safi had not seen any of Dax's new work. But now he was obviously ready for his first critique. Dax had all his canvasses leaning against a wall; there were a dozen or so portraits and landscape-sized paintings of large dimensions. She found herself completely lost as she wondered from one to the next. Taking a few steps back, she honed in on the work as she studied each in turn, marvelling at the depth of each work.

Dax had taken on a commission for a well-known French agent who had specified nature in the floral sense for a customer he had in mind. None of the paintings were naively illustrated: they had presence, at a glance they were exactly what had been asked for, but on closer inspection there was unmistakable drama. Safi was momentarily dumbstruck every time she was exposed anew to Dax's work. Knowing he expected her to be honest, she was more than a little surprised when she noticed how insecure he appeared.

'Well,' Dax said, his voice pitched somewhere between excited and ashamed, 'let's have it, don't spare me.'

'Oh my God, Dax, are you kidding! It's nothing but brilliant. You never fail to shock me – in a good way, I mean. Your work always draws me in and it's always a mystery to me how you manage to cultivate a kitsch subject into the realms of high art!' Turning away from the painting and towards the entrance she said, her voice suddenly lower, 'Has the Frenchman seen this work yet?'

'No, he is coming in an hour. That's why I wanted you here with me, for moral support. The work has taken me months to complete. I must say he has left me to get on with it, but I'm a quivering wreck.'

They decided to have a bite to eat at a small hummus bar where they could watch the studio in case the agent arrived early. Dax hardly touched his food, and at once she realised the importance of this commission for him. They lapsed into a comfortable silence while he concentrated on his presentation.

They noticed a bike pull up in front of the studio. The guy folded the bike into a small mechanical square, and lifted the bike in one hand while removing his helmet with the other. Dax jumped up, left Safi to pay the bill, and ran across the street. Safi guessed the Frenchman had arrived. Deciding to allow them some time, she sauntered across to the studio. Dax had taken a seat across from his work and she watched as the Frenchman made his observations. He looked at each in quick succession, then stood back to more closely observe them.

Suddenly, he turned to face them, acknowledging Safi for the first time. 'You will hear from me soon,' he said.

He had asked for no presentation; perhaps the work had spoken for itself. Not one to show his alarm, Dax shook hands and watched the Frenchman pick up his bicycle. Outside they watched the Frenchman fastidiously tuck his trousers into his boots, don his helmet, then he was gone. Safi saw the glint in Dax's eye and they both doubled over and shrieked with laughter.

'What was all that about?'

'I guess that's how he does what he does, I will hear in due course,' he said, mimicking a French accent as his cell rang (probably Dan to find out if the French agent liked his work). She noticed Dax turn towards her, his eyes shut, judging by his expression, he must have found out the guy hates his work. Safi saw him nodding away, then staring numbly at the cell as it went dead in his hand. Head down low he sunk onto his knees. Safi watched, not knowing whether it was good or bad news. God, it had to be bad, judging by Dax's body language. The cell rang again. Not saying a word, Dax dropped the cell and swung round.

'He loves them, he absolutely loves them. They are taking the whole lot, and the agent is keeping one for himself! DuPont is apparently one of the most respected agents, art critics, and auctioneers in the world! I think I might have arrived.'

Safi could not stand it any longer, the suspense had been nauseating. She threw herself at Dax and together they danced round the studio. 'Tonight we are celebrating at Pete's.'

Safi laughed and said, 'Nothing ever changes.'

For the first time, Dax would be earning major dollars and it thrilled and frightened him at the same time. DuPont had intimated he would introduce Dax's work to museums he was connected to; if they showed interest in his work it could be a major change for Dax career-wise. Dax was gaining respect in the art world; he was never short of work and had done major pieces for prestigious restaurants and for private collections; corporations had given him commissions. Galleries exhibited his art when he had major work, but he had never been approached by the top galleries and had not contemplated his work being hung in a major gallery: it would be like reaching a pinnacle he had never dreamed of.

Dax knew Dan would play a major role in keeping his feet firmly on the ground. He called his mother, who he knew would inform the rest of his family. She always sucked every last detail out of him. Like most mothers, Rachel adored hearing about any successes her son had, large or small and he loved indulging her; besides Dan, she was the centre of his life. Safi sat smiling at Dax's obvious pride; sharing his happiness with his family was something he never failed to do. As he explained to Safi, his family had endured years waiting for him to find himself, any happiness he could bring them was the least he could do. Without the love of his family and Dan, he would be just another flamboyant lost soul.

Dan was waiting for them at Pete's with Bruno, who had remained with Pete in the bar. The 2 D's excused themselves, having business to discuss. Safi settled with Pete and Bruno at the bar and filled them in about her day with Dax and the art critic DuPont. Nodding his head approvingly, concentrating on every word. he wondered loudly whether, 'The Dax hanging in my apartment, given to me during his early years when he was just starting out, may just turn out to be a good investment.'

Safi had her own ideas about exporting Dax's work to Moscow with Yvetta's know-how. She had not shared her thoughts with anyone yet, but it was something she could very easily get her hopes up about. The four of them eventually settled down to dinner and the conversation turned to Bruno. Pete thought he was getting a bit old for the stairs, perhaps they should consider him staying with Pete (who had an elevator he could ride up and down in) until they worked something out. He would bring him to work every day so they would see him. The suggestion came as a shock; they had never imagined Bruno not living with them. But they also knew that Pete had a point; sadly, Bruno was indeed getting old, but life would never be the same without him.

'Time to sell the apartment?'

This time everyone turned to stare at Dan.

Dax slumped his shoulders and plonked his head down on the table, mumbling, 'I can't take any more, it's enough for one day.'

Laughing, they all agreed with Pete's suggestion: Bruno loved Pete and it would be like a holiday for him. It would also get the two D's to consider selling the apartment and relocating, especially now that Dax was going to be the rich one amongst them. 'Don't jinx my success,' Dax said, laughing softly, 'it's never good to take anything for granted, especially not in the art world!'

They were getting on with their lives, Safi realised, with or without her. She listened to their conversation bouncing back and forth, suddenly feeling torn. Part of her wanting to remain with them in New York, another part excited to be with Sasha. The conversation moved to real estate – where would they move?

Pete already knew. 'Chelsea, of course, to a brownstone place for me to stay when you need a babysitter.'

This was greeted with shocked silence. Dax spoke first. 'Pete, when you're right, you're right.'

Dan was on a roll. 'Our lives will take on a whole new direction when we think of having a family.' He was now completely sold on the idea, and with his usual infectious excitement. As for Dax, the mention of babies had him delirious with excitement, he could hardly sit still. They had not given their plans for the future much thought since Christmas, he was delighted they were back on track.

Not one usually to enjoy upheaval or change, Dax was all for this new idea. 'I will get on to the realtors first thing tomorrow.'

They had tried to get Bruno to climb the stairs before giving in to Pete's suggestion; sadly, it was obvious to them all that Bruno could no longer make the five flights without great difficulty. Safi had run up the stairs to collect his belongings for Pete; together they all fussed around Bruno, tearfully saying goodnight. Bruno loped off happily, yet it did not seem right not having him around anymore: he had been a puppy when they brought him back to the loft. Dax was determined to find their new home in record time, so Bruno could come live with them again. It was bad enough losing Safi; they did not want to part with another member of their family. Letting Bruno live with Pete had turned out to be a necessity he hated.

Safi FaceTimed Sasha and gave him a blow-by-blow rundown on the day's excitement. They were back to their old way of communicating, but this time there was an end in sight, which was now only six weeks away. They had decided the separation was a price for which they were prepared to pay: not only for Safi to say her goodbyes, but also for Sasha to get his life in order before she arrived to be with him.

Their conversations now took on a more relaxed tone, both of them madly excited at the thought of living together permanently. Sasha regaled Safi with places, parties, and a Muscovite lifestyle she thought sounded extravagant and very Russian. She was happy to immerse herself in a new culture, and she was fast ticking off the boxes of things she wanted to try and taste, much to her delight. She would not be a mere tourist passing through – not in Manhattan and certainly not in Moscow, where she would live, taking the good along with the bad, as in any other city one chose to live in. She could not wait for every conversation with Sasha; she became more excited about living in another country. Having lived in New York, now she was going to live in Moscow – who would have believed it?

Something that would never have happened had she gone to university; it was what she had dreamt of, doing her own thing, marching through life to her own tune. She found her diary and hugged it to her chest; it had been more helpful than she could have imagined, actually seeing her ideas and ideals penned down on paper rather than remaining only a pipe dream in her mind.

Dax had arranged to meet various real estate agents, wasting little time getting it all off the ground before either (or both) of the two D's changed their minds about this new project. Dax wanted it all to fall into place, sooner rather than later.

Rupert had cajoled everyone into finding a long weekend in which to travel up to his winter hideout. Samantha had not yet fully shipped out to Hong Kong and they were working on how to manage their relationship between the two cities. Safi had not realised how important Samantha had become in Rupert's life; she found it amusing that Rupert at his stage of life should find himself in the same position she and Sasha had been in not so long ago. At least for her and Sasha there was an end in sight.

She was not sure Rupert and Samantha would be able to sustain their love life that easily if Rupert were not prepared to spend more time in Hong Kong. She looked forward to hearing his decision about living in Hong Kong three months of the year; so far he had not succumbed to the plan Samantha had tried to set in place for them.

Being Rupert, he wanted Samantha to do all the travelling between the two countries and she was having none of it, which is what attracted Rupert to Sam in the first place. She always gave him a hard time, which he seemed to relish. There was nothing Rupert loved more than a woman who was able to deal with his pig-headed stubbornness.

Dax's latest success had enabled him to take time off from his studio, and he set about finding a new home for them with a ferocious determination. He dragged Safi to see various unsuitable brownstones; some needed complete gutting before anyone could think of setting a foot inside them. Daniel had specified that he wanted a place they could make their own, but not completely from the ground up; it would eat into their budget on a huge scale and he was not prepared to go into debt finding endless problems once work began. So far everything they viewed was either a lost cause or unbelievably expensive.

Safi met with Lauren and Bianca to catch up on their news. She met with them in a small bistro near their apartment for lunch; when they stood up to greet her, Safi stared at Bianca in shock. Bianca was pregnant and showing. They were obviously delighted and bursting to share their news with Safi. For some reason they had lost touch with everyone in the months running up to Christmas. Neither Dan nor Dax had mentioned any of this to Safi. She listened to their news with astonished interest. Lauren had obviously decided to settle down with Bianca and they had visited Brazil together, returning to find that both wanted a life of domesticity, nodding she wanted to know how Bianca had become pregnant.

Bianca explained that she had always wanted to have a child, and having settled with Lauren they decided to find a donor. It was quite simple, really: they had investigated and found a donor bank they both felt comfortable with. They went ahead with having the sperm injected, and soon after that Bianca found herself pregnant. Her travelling to far-flung locations for work put on hold, her family in Brazil could now manage comfortably without her. Her mother had passed away and her sister and brothers had work and Bianca subsidised their living expenses. Her visit to Brasilia with Lauren had convinced her that she was now free to enjoy the fruits of her career and what she wanted was to be a mother.

Safi excitedly told them about her engagement to Sasha and her imminent move to Moscow. Enjoying their unbridled enthusiasm, she decided it a good opening to ask about Niles and Greg. Niles apparently had left for LA, having found a job on the West Coast with a small law firm that specialised in entertainment rights, something he had wanted to get into. They had not heard from Greg and, as far as they knew, he had never contacted Niles after their friendship had ended. Safi left the two women with an invitation to meet once more at Pete's Bar, before she flew to London.

Safi arrived at Dax's studio to find he had left to view a new brownstone that had suddenly come onto the market. She sat for a while chatting to Dax's assistants, who came in to help when he was busy. There was always at least one person to help him catalogue his work and number and date everything. Safi had met Rena on several occasions, an art student who she found had been helping Dax steadily for the last year. They all seemed to be excited with Dax's newfound success; everyone loved an artist on the cusp of fame, Rena said. Up until that moment, Safi had not thought of Dax being famous. Rena informed her that DuPont, the art dealer, was now often in touch with Dax and that they had become firm friends.

Dax was meeting people who, he believed, would promote his work in a new light, and receiving invitations to museum functions and parties. Some of these functions were held at private homes and others at prestigious art institutions. Private collections were priceless and Dax was more than a little overwhelmed by the vast amounts of money these collectors had to invest in favoured artists. He understood that DuPont wanted him to familiarise himself with these people; it was all part of becoming known. He was building Dax up in the eyes of investors; galleries and museums would take note. It was important to have a varied portfolio with a long list of buyers from around the globe.

Safi returned to the loft, relieved that her first week without Sasha was over; time would fly after a fortnight away at Rupert's winter get away. It would be only a matter of time before she was back in England with her family and friends before Sasha was back in her life.

Waking to raised voices floating in from the terrace, she made her way up to find the two D's in a heated discussion about a dilapidated brownstone they had just been to view. Dan was arguing his point about the building being a long-term project that would give them time to finance the renovation over a number of years once they agreed on a price, which he was hoping they could negotiate well below the asking price. But Dax said he couldn't come to terms with months turning into years while they lived in a building site before they could actually call it home.

They welcomed Safi's intrusion, both hoping she would have an outsider's objectivity to help them settle their concerns. She listened attentively as Dax gave her a creative view of the brownstone.

Dax always exaggerated when he needed her to like something he was not sure about, but this time, to Safi's surprise, he was low-key in his description of the four-storey building they were considering to be their new home.

Dan was in agreement with Dax's description of the dilapidated state of the building, but he could envisage that, with patience, hard work, and lots of dollars thrown at it for at least a year before they could comfortably live in it, it would become a wonderful home. In fact, Dan had not wanted to throw money at a dilapidated brownstone, but after the viewing and the location, he had changed his mind.

The three of them went to Pete's Bar, where the conversation continued, this time with Pete being asked for his advice. Pete put both his hands on the table and leaned forward.

'I say you go for this place, it sounds right.'

Conversation suspended, they stared at Pete; he wiped his hands on his buffer cloth and walked off to leave them to think about his suggestion. Dax, not convinced, watched Dan as he called the agent with an offer, winking at them.

'Don't worry it will take a while before we make any definite decision but at least we can hold on to it while we are negotiating.'

She fell into bed feeling a little more carefree since her engagement to Sasha, but also realising for the first time why her anxiety this last week had been so strong. She felt comfortable here and safe; she belonged. She had arrived a stranger, shy and introverted; now she was part of something she loved. And yet, she realised she was holding onto a pipe dream, everything was changing around her anyway. The lives of her loved ones in Manhattan were fluid and not fixed, and changing as rapidly as her own. How could she be such a wimp? She had always considered herself ready for new challenges. She sat down on her bed with a mug of tea and took out the diary she had not opened for a very long time. Pen in hand, as if no time had passed since her last entry, she started to write in it once more.

Allowing her thoughts to flow freely, she wrote for hours. Finally, exhausted, her eyes struggling to stay open, she let the diary fall out of her hands. Switching off the light, she hoped when she read her scribbles the following morning, something would make sense.

The sunrise was creeping over the buildings, water tanks splayed out on the roof tops with the various billboards advertising the latest drink or movie: it was a view she had grown used to. Down below, the traffic was just starting to hum with lines of yellow cabs starting their shifts. She was going to miss the frenetic pace that had somehow become part of her life. The crowded cafés and endless busy street life was something she adored and would miss.

Safi looked at the diary lying open on the floor and was reluctant to re-read her thoughts. She decided a mug of tea would help her concentrate before trying to make some sense out of her previous night's scribbling. Settling in the armchair facing the floor-to-ceiling windows, she opened her diary but kept her eyes focused at the scene below rather than on the open page. But the first words to engage her were not what she wanted to see.

Should she ignore her paranoia about Moscow?

Lonely was her first word. 'I am scared of being lonely, not having anyone like Pete or Dax to confide in when I need reassuring. Who am I going to talk to when things get tough? It won't be the same being so far away. I am going to miss the close connection I now have with them. A phone call or even FaceTime won't be the same as being here.'

These were her true feelings about leaving; no matter how much she wanted to be with Sasha, she had a bond here she was reluctant to break. Her folks were wonderful and England had been brilliant, but being in New York had been a growing experience she cherished: it had been the most fantastic time of her life so far.

'Commitment? Can I stay the course with all those disadvantages stacked against me, against us? I owe it to myself and to Sasha to give it a go and to get these doubts out of my system before I leave. I need to be more positive and in the right frame of mind for what lies ahead of me. The question is, how do I do that?'

She must have fallen asleep at that point. Pulling the blanket closer around her shoulders, she sat blankly staring out of the window, then back down at the page, rereading her words, trying her best to gain the upper hand before her fears did.

Her brain felt numb, she could not think of one uplifting thing. Exhausted, she crawled back under the covers, put her pillow over her eyes, and lay there until she fell asleep.

Her head, if not her heart, felt lighter. Perhaps a hot shower beating down would energise her into a more positive frame of mind.

Rinsing off the shampoo and applying conditioner kept her busy, but as she started soaping her body, carnal thoughts of her and Sasha in the shower together had her breathing hard. She satisfied her needs with the water pounding over her until she calmed. Finding strength, returning to her legs, she stood reaching for the towels, one wrapped around her hair and the other around her body. Returning to the room she lay flat out on her bed staring up at the ceiling. That was the most intense feeling of sexual desire she had had since Sasha's return to Moscow.

Slowly, she felt a smile spread across her face and, lying on the bed, allowed it to spread through her body. Suddenly she felt enormously excited for her future; all her former doubts about living with Sasha in Moscow melted away. Perhaps the physical distance between them had allowed her to develop anxieties that would solve themselves when she was beside him once again, for the first time living the life of a Muscovite, rather than wondering what it would be like from thousands of miles away.

Throwing on some blue skinny jeans, a ribbed black polo neck sweater, and her flat over-the-knee boots, she went to find Dax. She found him on the terrace, on the phone to Dan, trying to persuade him to meet for another reconnoitre about the brownstone before a decision was made, if their offer was accepted. Safi knew once Dax got hold of an idea or started a project it became all-consuming. Dax was, as always, getting himself worked up over making such a huge life changing decision and wanted to sound everyone out. Safi and Pete and Rupert were all viewing the brownstone later that day. She knew no one's opinion made the slightest difference to Dax's final decision, but it gave him time to come to terms with accepting Dan's certainty about the whole project.

Finishing his call, Dax looked at Safi with an unmistakable glint of excitement in his eyes. He swung Safi round to face him; giving her a hug he suddenly pulled away, and she saw that the excited glint had been replaced by tears. Safi stood back.

'Dax, what's the matter?'

'Oh, Safi, we are going to miss you. Dan and I have not stopped wondering what you are going to do with yourself in Moscow?'

Safi tried to interrupt but Dax kept going.

'The language barrier won't be easy to overcome, for one thing, and how are we going to know whether you are coping? You must promise us that you will reach out to us if you have any doubts about this move, once you get there? I promise, no matter what I am doing at the time, you will get my undivided attention.'

'I know,' Safi said, 'I have been experiencing the same doubts. I feel the same about leaving you and Dan and Pete and Bruno even Rupert and his nonsense. It's going to be such a wrench, but I do love Sasha, and if we want this to work I must give it my best shot. New York was the first step in my journey to independence, to becoming my own person. But Russia is going to be when I really make that break from everyone's apron strings. My dad still sees me as his little girl. I adore him, and a part of me loves him being so protective, but I have to prove that I can make it on my own. Especially if he wants me to be in the ad business. I want to work alongside him, not for him, if you understand what I mean.'

Dax understood exactly what Safi was trying to express and he was taken with her insightfulness; for someone so young she certainly was being analytical about her needs. He hoped she would be able to put her insights into practice as easily as she expressed them.

The weather was unseasonably mild and perfect for an outdoor lunch. Dax had arranged for them to visit all Safi's favourite haunts; they were going to visit galleries and stores and lunch in her favourite place under the trees at Bryant Park. There were always interesting fashion types to watch and bitch about. Safi had a wonderful witty edge, which made it all the more fun.

Dax passed Safi her helmet; she had become used to riding pillion on his new BMW motorbike round Manhattan, an easy way to wind in and out of traffic.

Settling for The Grill at Bryant Park, they rejected the outdoor seating as the morning sun had lost its warmth. The day had turned out to be just what the doctor ordered for Safi. Dax had taken her to a new gallery on Madison and she was thrilled to see they had given over the whole space to an exhibition of his work. Dax had only just found out about the gallery using his work as filler while they waited for a more well-known artist's work to arrive from abroad. DuPont had swung the deal with the gallery and Dax was more than happy with the arrangement. DuPont had not lost interest in Dax's work since his successful commission for a restaurant in Paris; the Frenchman was determined to have Dax's work recognised in the art world.

They shopped, having fun trying on madly expensive, extravagant clothes. Dax had persuaded Safi to buy a pair of red ankle boots with killer heels that she had been trying on He insisted that she did not look like a giraffe. 'All those Russian girls have legs up to their armpits,' he said, 'you will give them a run for their money and keep Sasha's eyes securely glued to your shapely legs instead.'

Safi worried about towering over Sasha, but hearing about the long Russian pins persuaded her to make the purchase, still nervous about fitting in to the new environment she would soon find herself part of.

They settled in a corner, where they could spy on everyone entering the restaurant. It was just before Fashion Week and they were lucky to find a table. The bus boy filled their water glasses as they relaxed into their seats to study the menu and eye anyone worth looking at making their way to the tables.

Dax kicked Safi under the table. Her head shot up from her menu to follow Dax signalling: coming towards them was the most beautiful group of girls Safi had ever set eyes on. They were collectively towering over the waiter who was showing them to their table. Safi noticed the

Birkin bags, killer heels and the Russian accents. She did not have trouble understanding the message Dax was trying to impress on her: these were the stunning Amazonian giants she would be up against. Safi sank further into her chair, pretending to study the menu but not being able to stop herself from ogling each and every aspect of these girls. Dax and Safi studied them openly, internalising their mannerisms; the waiter interrupted their concentration when he presented each with champagne flutes. Safi was about to object, when she saw someone waving from a few tables off. Holding up her glass to salute them was Polly.

Polly could not be avoided, she would not allow it, and was obviously letting them know she would be over to chat once she was finished with her interview.

'Well, what did I tell you,' Dax said, 'legs up to their armpits.'

'I know,' Safi said, 'but surely these are models and not ordinary mortals.'

'Polly will fill us in, but I doubt they are models, more likely hookers.'

Safi looked doubtful. 'They can't possibly be, their clothes ooze sophistication and expensive taste.'

'I have heard they demand $1000 just to be taken out to dinner.'

Dax's cynical vision of these beautiful women gave Safi's wounded ego unexplained confidence. Dax went on to explain he had read and heard about these women from many of his clients and friends: they were all business and tough as hobnails. There were obviously men out there, especially amongst the traders on Wall Street, who found it convenient to have uncomplicated sex, or a date for an evening, happy to see it as a business arrangement rather than an emotional involvement. She started thinking about Sasha with some of these women, but stopped herself just in time.

'Well, my idea of hookers is obviously outdated,' Safi said. 'I don't understand how anyone could use their body with such little emotion involved. Obviously, it pays well, by the looks of them.'

Left alone at the table while Dax went to the bathroom, she continued to watch the Russian women with interest and became aware of a queasy feeling in the pit of her stomach. Her mouth felt dry, and as she reached for the water her hand started to shake. Lightheaded and alienated from those around her, she was unable to react when Polly sat down opposite her in Dax's seat.

'Safi, Safi, oh dear … Dax, I am so pleased you are back.'

'Safi, can you hear us?'

Aware of Dax and Polly calling her name, the colour draining from her face, she fell forward, hitting her head on the table and fainting outright.

On opening her eyes, Safi found herself surrounded by worried faces; she managed a weak smile.

'You fainted,' Polly said. She was holding Safi's hand while Dax, the waiters, and others she did not recognise seemed to be agreeing with whoever spoke.

'Oh, but I feel absolutely fine now. Gosh, I am so sorry, how awfully embarrassing.'

'No need to feel sorry we were just beside ourselves with worry. Dax, I think we should call a cab and get Safi home.'

'Oh, please don't make a fuss, really, I am totally feeling okay now. In fact, I was about to order an expresso.'

Everyone seemed to be satisfied that she was okay, the waiter running off to fetch her coffee.

Apart from Dax and Polly who had found a chair to join them, her client having left demanded to know what had happened.

'Now what on earth happened? One moment I saw you sitting there, and the next you were out cold.'

Keeping quiet for a few moments to collect her thoughts, she started to confide the feelings of anxiety she had been experiencing since her engagement to Sasha and her fear of joining him in Moscow.

'I suppose it's the fear of the unknown,' Polly volunteered.

'That's just it. The challenge excites me, yet I'm petrified of leaving everyone. Being with Sasha is what I have been dreaming of for months, so none of it makes an iota of sense to me.

'Safi, do you think you are ready for marriage?' asked Polly.

Safi studied her hands, looking up.

'I love Sasha, what more do I need to know?'

Polly sat forward.

'Safi, now listen: Sasha is a tad older, worldly and sophisticated; you, on the other hand, are beautiful and sweet, an innocent. Whether you are ready for a life in Moscow remains to be seen.' Polly made it very plain that she had her doubts.

'Yes, I seem to be lacking confidence. I need to get a grip.'

'Ah well that is why I came to chat. I have a very dear friend starting as editor for a new fashion magazine in Moscow. I will let him know you are coming. He will find something for you and be delighted to take you under his wing.'

Dax had been very quiet since Safi's episode. He sat back and allowed Polly to take control, but he was not happy. Dan he knew would feel even more apprehensive about her leaving.

She promised to stay in touch with Polly. As they hugged goodbye, Polly put something into Safi's hand. She opened her hand in the cab and gasped. Lying in her palm was Polly's gold card with her private numbers. Dax whistled. 'Well, you have been invited into her golden circle, which is an honour, if I ever saw one.'

Chapter 15

The public holiday and weekend with Rupert in Upstate New York was only a few days away and they were all looking forward to being out of Manhattan. Safi and Sasha spoke every day, neither could wait for London and being together. Safi found herself checking Moscow time, to find out when Sasha would be awake and online. She knew he had been making plans for her arrival in Moscow, yet he was reluctant to share them, wanting everything to be a surprise for her. He was so proud of his city and wanted to share its magnificence and history with her. There wasn't much about London or the UK Safi was able show her fiancé. Like his father, Sasha loved London and all things British, had spent his school years at one of the top private schools in Scotland, then studied at Harvard, an Ivy League university in the States.

She realised that Polly was right; by comparison, she was lacking education and totally unsophisticated in the ways of the world. Russia suddenly became this huge looming brown bear in her mind, she was depending on Sasha to broaden her educations on so many levels, and hoped she was up to the task that lay ahead.

Safi could hear Sasha's longing; he was adamantly against FaceTime sex, though, because of its depressing after-effect on her. Safi tried to entice him, purring like a cat and whispering naughty things over the phone, but he would not succumb, much to her annoyance, as she was suddenly in the mood and therefore more than a little frustrated. She knew he wouldn't play along, though; nothing interfered with his workday. She would have to get used to that.

The Russian goddesses had put her off her stride, and Safi, acknowledged this was the reason for her sudden anxiety attack.

Behaving in this paranoid neurotic fashion was something she absolutely had to get control over, otherwise she was lost. Her feelings of inadequacy about being able to make it in a completely foreign environment (where she could not even read the signs, to say nothing of the language barrier or the chilling winters) were not helping.

Dan and Dax popped their heads round Safi's door, both behaving like small boys with a new toy. Safi leaped off the bed to see what the excitement was about; that was when she saw Bruno racing up the last flight of steps towards Dax and Dan, who were waiting at the top of the landing for him He was panting but looking fitter than he had in a long time and a much thinner version of himself.

Pete was not far behind and as proud as punch; he explained the new organic diet he had Bruno on. With regular exercise he seemed to have become a younger version of the old Bruno, much to everyone's joy. Wasting little time, Bruno jogged up to his favourite place on the terrace, scratched at his smelly blanket, and promptly went to sleep. Everyone stood round watching him when Pete announced he was off to New Orleans for a few days. 'He's all yours. I expect to see him in good shape on my return.'

Not wanting to leave Bruno they all opted for a home movie and ordering in. Safi loved their evenings at home. With the crazy changes and activity in all of their lives recently, having Bruno back for a while and staying put was a perfect solution. Dogs had a way of making everything seem okay. Pete had closed the bar for the holiday, giving his staff time away after a busy summer. They had arranged a farewell for Safi in the bar on his return. She had a number of people to invite, since she did not know when she would be back in her favourite city again. The bar would be closed for the farewell party. She was amazed at how many friends she had made in her short time away from the UK and wondered whether Muscovites would be as friendly.

Staying at Rupert's hideaway in Connecticut felt like a great way to spend time with everyone before she said her goodbyes. The two D's and Bruno and Safi were heading to a station where Rupert would pick them up in the SUV he kept at his home. Dan had recently encouraged his dad to spend a few weeks a year with Samantha in Hong Kong. At first Rupert was dead-set against the idea, but as Samantha's job became more demanding and her return trips less frequent, he realised what his life might be like without her. Rupert and Safi were booked to leave on the same date: Safi to London and Rupert to spend a few weeks with

Sam in Hong Kong. This made their time together a double farewell. Rupert wanted to bring the family together before their lives took them in different directions and was delighted when everyone accepted his invitation.

The train journey gave them time to daydream and Safi noticed D&D more relaxed than she had ever seen them. Fast asleep, Dax had his head on Dan's shoulder as they sped through the outskirts of New York, heading into scrubland that turned into undulating fields and farmlands; Safi was mesmerised by the beautiful scenery as they sped past hugging coastlines towards Boston. The Express Amtrak train took three and a half hours to reach their destination; with no traffic and no airport hassles, it was an ideal way to start their long weekend away.

Dax had packed a deli hamper as they had left on the earliest train out of NY. Finding themselves ravenous two hours into the journey, they tucked into lox, cream cheese and bagels, washing it all down with hot Starbucks lattes from a flask Dax had cleverly decanted it into. Dan pulled out a pack of cards. Not being able to play card games, they indulged Safi with snap rummy, soon moving on to their own game of Gin Rummy, something Safi remembered her parents playing. She decided it was an ideal time to work on her invites for her farewell at Pete's Bar.

As they pulled into Boston station, Safi found she had close to fifty people on her list. Many being casual acquaintances. Still, the party would be an opportunity to say goodbye to everyone, not just the major players in her life but even people she had met watching Rupert play chess and at the cafes and coffee bars she frequented with Bruno, including the fabulous Fashionistas she met through Lauren. She glanced over her list with a sigh, realising it was a list of people she would miss not chatting to. Their interest and casual chatter had helped her feel she belonged to the area she had never imagined she would grow to love.

Rupert was waiting at the station. It was a house Rupert had bought as an investment. Over the years he had reclaimed it for himself, staying for extended periods during the hot Manhattan summers. He had many friends in the area, largely from New York and Miami, all escaping the humidity.

They drove through forests, spotting homes of various sizes through the trees. Rupert chatted endlessly about the Berkshires and how it had grown over the years, pointing out homes of friends in the area. From the road they turned onto a gravel path which continued on for half a mile over what seemed a very bumpy ride. They came to a stop in front of a sprawling but still somehow charming white house with a black-tiled roof and grey shutters.

The house was filled with artefacts from Rupert's travels that were perched on pedestals and hung on walls. Shelves were filled with photos in silver frames. Rupert stood back and watched Dan as he picked up frame after frame. Dan remembered places and times shared with his parents and his dad when they were alone after his mother died.

Sam came over to stand beside him. 'Your dad has lovingly collected and preserved your memory for years. This is where he chose to come to feel close to you, during a lifetime apart from you.'

Dax never one to hide his thoughts said, 'Thank God that's all over with now.' They all shared the moment with Dan.

Rupert had conveniently disappeared, not being able to hide his emotions. Samantha called after him. They walked with her through the vast wood-beamed open-plan living area into a cosy kitchen and eating area stuffed with food and laid out on a black round wooden table that could easily accommodate them all.

Rupert entered as they were all piling their plates. Safi noticed that nothing needed to be said; the years in the wilderness had been and gone, and all noticed the unspoken love between father and son.

The conversation turned to the house and how they all loved every aspect of what they had so far seen. Rupert had chosen a warm cosy atmosphere instead of the pared-down one he favoured in his NY apartment. He indulged his passion for fabrics from his various travels to the far East and India, while working for the textile industry.

Feeling pride in his home and vast collection of imported ornate pieces of furniture from his travels, Rupert took them on a guided tour. As they walked through the covered, surround outdoor patio to the sleeping quarters, they all took turns to climb onto three wooden, ornate Indian carved beds filled with coloured silk cushions and striped puffed-up mattresses. They drew the brocade curtains.

'You will have plenty of time to try those,' Rupert said. 'Come on, I have so much more to show you.' The next level was down a few stairs into a wide passage lined with tall wooden amours from China in red lacquer with large round bronze inlaid handles. Hanging from both cupboards were red-fringed Chinese tassels. 'Those are storage for linens.'

Safi found herself repeating 'I love it' every few minutes, while Dan kept up with his dad, concentrating on every detail and asking many questions.

'This room is especially for Safi,' Dan exclaimed, examining the headboard which was upholstered in a heavy red-and-gold threaded fabric. Rupert had left the rest of the room's décor white with dark grey shutters on the windows. At the end of the bed, he had a long wooden seat with black-and-white cushions, while the shower room was tiled in small grey mosaic tiles, the only decoration being a tall mirror over a masculine square white basin standing on four black iron legs.

The mirror opened, revealing ample shelving and eliciting respectful, quiet approval from all as they continued down the passage, following Rupert into what could only be Dan's bedroom. It had become a shrine to his childhood. Being the first room before entering the bedroom, the bathroom could only be called mirrored glamour. The walls were covered in cracked antique mirror filled with black frames of all sizes. On closer inspection, every photo was of Dan at different stages of his childhood, from his baby years to college and beyond.

'Dad, this is amazing, thank you. I am lost for words.' Rupert, happier than they had ever seen him, none of his self-deprecating remarks on offer, seemed at home with his surroundings and more than eager to take all the credit, flying his way. 'Come, come, there is more to see.' Following him into the bedroom, they were confronted with an ornate double wooden bed. The bed was pure drama, each side had small steps to climb onto a bed covered in white linen and a mixture of long rolled grey and ochre pillows, and attached were heavy fringed tassels. Folded at the foot of the bed was a cerise silk duvet flanked by tall wooden carved pillars. The carved headboard was leaning against yellow faded silk fabric; it was stunning, fit for a Maharaja.

'That is some bed, Dad.'

'Crazy hey, a bit over the top but who cares.'

'It's magnificent, where did you find it?'

'It's from a store in Bombay where I used to spend many happy hours indulging my collector's eye.'

A shabby dresser and two antique chairs covered in the faded yellow fabric alongside a small round French table with a collection of Indian bowls was all there was to accompany the ornate carved wooden bed.

In the dressing area, Dax was delighted to see two of his paintings: one of Bruno and another of two Pugs staring out at them. The real Bruno had been following them from room to room, then noticed his doggie bed on the Persian rug in front of the tall bed, climbed in, curled up, and went to sleep.

Rupert threw open grey shutters to show off the view of the woods beyond. Next to the bathroom was another door covered with the faded rushed fabric. Safi, ever inquisitive, found it opened onto a balcony.

Dan wanted to know how long it had taken Rupert to decorate the house to such a high standard.

'Oh, I had the fabric and collectables in storage for quite some time, and when I purchased this place, it was time for me to do something meaningful with it all.'

An English interior designer from LA and Samantha had, over many visits and Rupert's approval, managed to turn the house into the home they now saw.

'Come and see the master bedroom. I think it's the most beautiful room in the whole house.'

Safi and Dan's room were opposite one another, but Rupert's bedroom was up a few stairs into another section of the house. They entered through old wooden double doors into a vast space with washed wooden floorboards, pale yellow Persian rugs, and, in the centre, an enormous carved silver four-poster bed. It was a magnificent piece that needed very little adornment. The bed itself was so imposing they hardly noticed the faded grey bedding with a profusion of taupe and grey pillows stacked against the head of the bed. To soften the pewter frame, pleated taupe linen fabric hung behind the head of the bed in folds, similar to Dan's bed. Large distressed wooden tables of different sizes were next to each side of the bed and filled with books, magazines, and a profusion of faded roses in clear glass vases.

Facing the bed against a wall was a huge linen-studded chesterfield with pale yellow and green and rose silk pillows. There were no photos paintings of any kind. They entered a passage lined with floor-to-ceiling cupboards; the doors covered in rushed grey linen fabric, leading into a bathroom with a bronze tub on claws and a sink on black legs with open basket storage and a window overlooking the woods.

A shower with two showerheads and an enclosed toilet behind smoked glass was hidden from view by a black painted Chinese screen.

A passage led out onto the surrounding patio, which was covered with photos from Rupert's childhood in England; all the family history was to be found on those walls.

'Dad, how could you have kept this place to yourself, never telling anyone what an amazing home you have up here in the Berkshires? I am speechless with admiration. The interior and the fabrics and collectables have all been used with such attention to detail about you and your life – it's mind-blowing'

'This was all for you, Dan,' Samantha said softly. 'He did it all with you in mind.'

'How so?'

'I wanted you to have it. It's still for you when I'm gone, but now that you are back in my life, we can enjoy it together. Enough with the sentimental stuff. Let's go pop a cork and have some champagne; it's not every day I have the pleasure of my family under my own roof.'

Samantha patted Dax on the arm and gave Dan a hug,

'Your dad loves you so much. Even when he was angry with you, he still held you very close. This was all done with you in mind. Let him share his joy, he has been waiting a very long time to get you here. The house was only completed three months ago and it's too cold in the winter months. As you can tell, even now it's pretty chilly up here, but he wanted everyone to enjoy it before we all scatter.'

Dan, thinking out loud, said, 'Maybe it's a place we can all gather in the summer months to enjoy together?'

Samantha, wanting to encourage Dan, added, 'What a wonderful idea. We will definitely plan to make that possible.'

The rest of the weekend was filled with guests popping in to meet Rupert's family and visiting his friends for brunches and dinners. Tanglewood still had the odd concert into the autumn season and most of Rupert's friends liked attending the Sunday lunch concerts on the lawn. Safi loved the casual picnic atmosphere; it reminded her of concerts in Hyde Park and Glyndebourne, but not as stuffy. People here did not bother to dress for Tanglewood. They sat on folded canvas chairs, blankets over knees, handing out hot dogs stuffed with mustard, pickles and ketchup. Safi found the chilly clear blue sky, carefree attitude and the classical music drifting towards them relaxing after the frenetic pace and intense atmosphere of Manhattan.

At night, when they all retired to their rooms, after a day full of laughter and more people than she could ever before remember meeting, crawling into bed was free of any troubling dreams and sleep came easily.

Mornings greeted them with chilly blue skies which were perfect for jogging. Safi joined Samantha and Dan on their early morning jog through the woods, while Rupert and Dax got the breakfast sorted. Returning to the smell of fresh bread, pancakes and muffins, coffee, scrambled eggs, fruit, and yogurt, Samantha had the kitchen well stocked with everything they could possibly want. Each morning was a repeat of the previous day, and each morning they sat for ages around the table, just chilling and chatting. She had never seen any of them so chilled and relaxed. It was turning out to be a great bonding exercise; Dax and Rupert seemed to have mellowed in their uptight attitude towards one another. No one mentioned Safi's anxiety attacks and she herself had forgotten they had even occurred.

Listening to her excited rundown about each day's events, Sasha had noticed her relaxed, light-hearted mood. She told him she could not wait for him to visit Rupert's amazing hideaway in the Berkshires, perhaps as soon as next summer, when the family was again planning to decamp out of New York.

Their train journey back to Manhattan was spent in quiet contemplation, each in their own thoughts. Staring out at the scenery and enjoying the mellow feeling, she noticed Dan and Dax were both fast asleep. She herself soon nodded off.

Dan at first was overwhelmed by Rupert's affection. Unaccustomed to living under the same roof as his father since his childhood, he found they were reverting to a long-forgotten, father-and-son dynamic. After so many years without a father, being under the same roof with his dad seemed have made all the difference.

Dax and Rupert's relationship had moved into a more comfortable phase; they had bonded in the kitchen preparing the breakfasts. Rupert found he could confide in Dax openly about his taste in art and passion for antiques and classic cars, to say nothing about his renewed interest in travel, and having Samantha in his life. The Berkshires allowed the two D's the space they needed after the intense negotiations over the run-down Brownstone they were hoping to purchase. Nothing had been finalised but the realtor had lined up a buyer for their loft, which had been viewed in their absence; she was confident that the buyer would meet with their approval if a price could be agreed on.

As for Safi's imminent move to Russia, though little was spoken about it, there seemed instead to be a silent consensus, judging by the expression on everyone's faces when Safi's cell rang and she ran off excitedly to speak with Sasha. No one was happy about the move.

Feeling equally impotent, they chose to keep their feelings of helplessness between themselves. Samantha was the only one to voice her thoughts on the matter when Safi was out of earshot, saying, 'Sometimes it's best to let people we love make their own mistakes.'

There seemed nothing left to say but to support Safi, which reluctantly they hoped they were doing by not discussing their doubts. They had now left behind Rupert and Sam – who Safi would not be seeing for a while – who would be staying in the Berkshires until winter set it, when they would be leaving for Hong Kong for the season.

The conversation chugged along, slowing down as they watched New York come into view. It was always exciting to see New York's skyline again, no matter how briefly one left it for.

Bruno managed the five flights to the loft like a puppy, while the humans panted and puffed up the stairs with the bags. They had not been long in the apartment when Pete rang the buzzer. They presumed he wanted to talk about the farewell party for Safi, which was to be hosted at his bar, but when they settled down at the breakfast bar it became apparent that he had other things on his mind. Rolling the beer bottle back and forth in his hands, never one to rush, Pete looked up and caught Dan's eye.

'You happy with that offer you got for the loft?'

Dan stared at him intently, trying to work out the significance of the question, while Dax and Safi waited for the conversation to unfurl itself for them.

'Well, yes and no. Why?'

A smile played round Pete's mouth. "Cause it's the best offer I have.'

'Pete, oh my God, that's fantastic. In that case, the offer is accepted, since it's staying in the family.'

'Pleased to hear it.' They clinked their bottles and Pete explained about his trip to New Orleans. He had sold his half ownership in the bar to his friend; the Big Easy was now picking up again and things were better than ever business-wise. Previously reluctant to give up his share, Pete was now more than ready to move on from his attachment to his old life. He had received a fair offer for his small apartment in Manhattan and thought living so close to the bar would be ideal – well, apart from the stairs, they all agreed laughing.

'I do not want to spoil everyone's mood,' Safi said, 'but what is happening with the negotiations for the dilapidated brownstone?'

Surprised they turned towards Safi.

'Haven't you left us for Moscow already,' Dan said, teasing.

'We are going ahead with the purchase. I will be signing all the documents tomorrow and then the trouble starts.'

'Well, now that you mention it,' Dax cut in, 'Pete has suggested moving into Safi's room until we are able to move into the brownstone.'

'I have plenty of storage room down in the bar cellar.'

Everything was changing: even if Pete would now be owning it, visiting the loft would never be the same. Change happened when one was least ready for it.

Her gran always said it was the one thing she could depend on; that change was the one thing that would never change, and the one thing no one ever got used to. Safi had thought her gran was being silly, but now she realised it was her way of sharing a very long and varied life.

Life seemed to be changing for everyone, the changes were coming up so fast, she wasn't ready for them yet. The day after the farewell party she would be flying to London. Her mom was getting excited to have her home for a while before Sasha arrived and whisked her away to London, then Moscow. Her mom's feelings on the subject of Moscow had not sorted themselves yet and, for the most part, she refused to talk about it, telling Safi not to push her, it would take time.

For the first time Safi understood how her mother felt, she had had the same sentiments leaving everyone in New York behind.

She needed to depend on her mother's support, fearing her dad would try his best to dissuade her from going to Russia.

He was trying to entice her to stay by offering her an amazing opportunity at the agency. Being given an account of her own, under different circumstances, Safi would have been over the moon, eager to show her ability. Greg had always given her the impression that she was capable of more than she thought.

The whole experience was emotionally draining, but leaving Manhattan seemed to be the most heart-breaking. Returning to Brighton to face her family's obvious unhappiness about her engagement to an older man, who she was following to a foreign land they believed would be a tough place for her to feel at home in, did not help her anxiety attacks, which her parents knew nothing of yet.

Pete had kept her buoyant, listening patiently whenever her thoughts happened to spill over into conversation, whenever she expressed self-doubt or even fear. He tried to keep her grounded.

She had invited just about everyone in Manhattan to her farewell.

'This is proving a good exercise in free advertising for the bar,' Pete said, teasing her. 'It will make up for closing over the holiday.'

Snacks were on the house, but all beverages would have to be bought by the punters at the bar, who came to bid her farewell. Safi went down to Pete's early to help him and the staff get ready for the evening. A small jazz band (invited by Pete) had set up in a corner; it was something he had long thought of introducing .

By nine the band was playing and the place was heaving. Everyone danced and swayed to the cool sounds, wine glasses or beer bottles in hand. Plied with drink, Safi found herself having an amazing time, promising to return and thrilled to see so many of the people she knew and liked.

The evening went on until past closing time, and she was far from sober hugging and crying as she said her farewells. The two D's persuaded her to come home with them before she disintegrated all together. Reluctantly agreeing, she hung onto Pete, thanking him and telling him how much she adored him and did not know how she was going to cope without him. He nodded to Dax and together they managed to get her to climb the stairs to the loft.

Her legs were like jelly; she fell into bed, just managing to wash her face and brush her teeth. She was fast asleep when Dan covered her. He sat a while looking at Safi, wondering how she was going to cope in such a different environment on her own. She had become part of all of their lives, it was going to be strange not having her around.

Waking with a massive headache, she lay looking out at the view she had grown to love. Finding a lump forming in her throat and tears welling in her eyes, she dragged herself into the shower. It was her last day with the two D's and Pete. Her flight from JFK was that evening, direct to Gatwick, where her parents would be waiting for her the following morning.

The day was planned: brunch at their favourite restaurant, and onto Dax's studio to view the work he had been busy with for a corporate commission. DuPont had introduced him to many new clients and he had received interest from several. He had accepted this commission for a large corporation which had a vast art collection, their headquarters were in Seattle. He was looking forward to viewing the art the company had collected for their sculpture park, paintings and installations. He felt honoured to be counted among the artists in their collection.

Dan and Pete had organised an early dinner for Safi at Rubicov at Sasha's insistence; he had organised for them to lay on all her favourite dishes. Pulling on her jeans and boots, she heard Bruno scratching at the door. Hopping over to open it, she realised she was going to miss him – he had become such a huge part of her life, too. Safi refused to spoil her day by being sad. Bruno loped in with a card attached to his collar. She giggled and bent down to untie the ribbon. She helped Bruno onto the bed and sat down to open the card. A photo dropped out as she opened it; picking it up she found herself staring at a baby wrapped in a blue blanket. Perplexed, she opened the card to find it was from Lauren and Bianca. She realised now that they had not been at her farewell party.

She read the card, then ran out with the photo to show Dan and Dax the baby. 'Laurence Brandon Shaffer Lombardi Rodriquez, phew, what a mouthful. I guess they have named him after Lauren and Bianca, and given him both their last names; not such a bad idea,' Safi said. The two D's had not mentioned Lauren and Bianca since the baby news; Safi guessed they had discussed it privately. Dax wondering aloud, 'Hopefully, an invite will arrive for the Bris or will it be a Christening?'

They all laughed at the complication of the whole thing.

'Maybe it will just be a baby-naming celebration,' Dax said.

'Whatever it will be, it will be fantastic,' agreed Safi. 'I'm sorry to be missing it; please take a gift from me, too.' She found their number in her phone and called to wish them and to say her farewell, promising to keep in touch, then she put Dax on the cell to the proud parents. The day flew by.

The early dinner at Rubicov had a table groaning with their specialities and the waiters had prepared a cake with 'Welcome to Moscow' in ruby red icing.

They all saw her off; not wanting to dissolve into tears, they huddled together in a joint hug. Safi bent down to kiss Bruno's snout, climbed into the cab, and waved as it sped off towards the airport.

Safi found she was visibly shaking; hugging her coat tighter, she leant her head back and fought back the tears. God she loved them all so much. The ride to JFK was a blur of texts and tears; by the time she checked in and found a seat in the lounge she was ready to face her new challenge. Sitting in business class for the very first time in her life, she started to feel a little more excited, grateful about Sasha's insistence to upgrade her ticket for the flight back home.

Chapter 16

Pushing the suitcase trolley though the doors, Safi was not sure who would be there to pick her up and was thrilled to see her brother waiting for her, looking beyond him to see if either of her parents had come.

'Only me,' Jake said, giving her a bear hug. It was lovely to see him, Christmas seemed aeons ago. Jake took over pushing the trolley as they turned up the tunnel that connected to the hotel on the south side of the airport. Safi suddenly woke up.

'Where are we going?' she asked.

'For coffee at the hotel before we head on home,' Jake said with a smile that was altogether too gentle.

'Is it that bad?'

'Let's get that coffee and some scones and cream,' Jake said, 'just what I fancy.'

Making themselves comfortable at a corner table, watching Jake put lashings of clotted cream on top of blueberry jam, Safi leaned over before he had a chance to stuff the lot into his mouth. 'Spit it out, Jake, what's going on?'

Nodding, he stuffed the scone in his mouth anyway. She sat back waiting for him to finish chewing, gulping some tea she barely tasted because of all the anticipation. 'They're not in a good place right now, probably my fault.'

'Why?'

'Well, besides you going behind the Iron Curtain, I am off down under next week. I got a really brill offer in Melbourne. They need computer geeks, so I'm off.'

'Mum and dad must be devastated, losing us both. Pity they never had that insurance child they always spoke about.'

'Maybe they tried and it never happened,' Jake said. He was no longer smiling.

They both sat in silence, staring at the planes as they taxied onto the runway.

'You never mentioned any of this to me,' Safi said. 'I knew you were thinking of going, but this seems sudden?' Jake was non-committal.

'It's done now. They will get used to being on their own, they have been anyhow since you left.'

'I know, but I am sure they never imagined we'd both be thousands of miles away.' Safi's cell buzzed she had new messages: one from Sasha she read quickly, then smiling she read the texts from her mother and two from her dad.

'Better get going, they are home waiting for us.'

She looked at Jake knowingly, her voice sounding so small, almost childlike; somehow being home took her back to her childhood. It was strange how being back home with her parents could do that.

As they turned into the driveway, it felt as if she had never left. Safi determined not to fight with her mother or her dad. She wanted this short stay in her home to be meaningful. She needed their love and approval: it would go a long way, she felt, to expunge her anxiety, to know they supported her, even if they were not one hundred percent behind her and Sasha's engagement, or Moscow, for that matter.

As she walked through the double doors into the entrance hall, she was thrilled to see they had hung a welcome home banner over the entrance to the kitchen. It was something they always did when she used to come home from camp during the summer breaks and Jake from varsity. It was great to be home even if it meant they hadn't let go, she was still their baby and maybe she never wanted them to fully let go, it made her feel safe and closely held.

Her mom came through to greet her with open arms and hugged her closely for what seemed forever. Safi surrendered to the hug, holding onto her emotions for dear life; all she needed was for her mom to guess how delicate she was feeling about leaving for Moscow.

They settled down in the kitchen while Jake took her bags to her room; returning, he found his mom in tears. 'Hey, this is a happy time,' he said, 'why the tears, Mom?'

She smiled weakly. 'Oh, you know, it's just wonderful to have you both home at the same time, even if just for a short while. Who knows when we will be together like this again, just the four of us.' She blew her nose and, thankfully, that was the end to it, as they settled into their usual gossip and chat about life in Brighton and old friends.

Safi called her dad and asked if she could visit with him at work before he came home; she wanted to reacquaint herself with everything and everyone she knew.

Borrowing her mom's Mini, she realised how much she had missed driving. It was a beautiful crisp day with a stunning blue sky. Safi drove along the beach road, the surf was up and people were jogging, mums were out in full force with their buggies, catching the last rays of autumn sun. She pulled into the building and parked in the allotted space, walked to the lift that went straight up to top floor of the building where her dad had his offices. The glass building had been altered to accommodate the different departments when his business amalgamated with one of the large ad agencies in London and Hong Kong, and now they were merging with a New York agency, too.

She was proud of her dad; he had built his business steadily over the years and was reaping the benefits. She knew he loved every angle of the business and was keen for one of his kids to share it with him. It had always fallen to Safi to undertake that job and she was letting him down. She felt sad thinking about it, realising she still felt the need to please him.

He had his back to her as she walked in, looking out of the tall glass windows of his office.

'Hi, Dad,' she said.

He turned and, to her relief, opened his arms. She ran for that hug, needing it more than he realised. They chatted about Rupert and his Berkshire home. Leonard listened to his daughter and watched her closely, realising that she had not mentioned Sasha or Moscow, but thought better of changing the subject. Instead they went on a tour of the offices, where she met old friends and work colleagues.

Hearing a familiar voice, Safi felt a jolt of recognition and popped her head into one of the boardrooms to make sure she was not mistaken. There was Greg, as large as life in his usual tight-fitting black jeans and black sweater offset by his usual love of bright shoes. He was delighted to see her, telling her about his life since their last meeting in NY. He freelanced for her father and was happy not to belong to any particular agency. He liked the troubleshooting life; it took him in all directions, overseeing projects and bringing together teams to work on whichever product needed his talents.

Safi crawled into her old bed, old friends staring down at her from the wall. Confronted with classmates and geeky boyfriends, she covered her face with her pillow, too tired to think about her past, falling into a trouble-free sleep, exhausted with jet lag and emotion.

The weekend was planned for quality time with her immediate family, but as Saturday rolled into Sunday the days were filled with friends and neighbours popping in for quick hellos often followed by brunches, lunches and suppers shared with whoever stayed for the meals on offer. She loved catching up, at least at the beginning; it seemed so much had changed since her time in New York.

Most of her friends had decamped to London; only Safi and Jake were deserting their parents for countries foreign. Her mum seemed to encourage the steady flow of friends popping in, while her dad and Jake stayed long enough to be polite, then disappeared to the TV room to watch endless sport.

Cricket brought yells of 'Yes,' while rugby brought shouts of 'Oh no!' Safi had never shared their love of sports, but Jake and her dad had had hours of bonding over sporting events they both loved. She knew her dad must be grieving Jake's decision to leave for Australia, and felt sad and guilty in the same measure; losing both children to faraway places could not be easy.

Her mother opted for a frenetic pace with Safi: they shopped, lunched, browsed the lanes, had facials and long walks on the beachfront, and visited the hairdresser together. During all of that time, not once did her mother allude to marriage plans or how Safi would keep herself occupied, make friends, or learn the language. She avoided any mention of Moscow or, for that matter, Sasha. Indeed, she, too, seemed purposely to be avoiding the subject altogether. Not wanting to upset their precious time together, Safi found the longer they avoided the subject, the less she was able to speak to her mother about any of it; it had become the big white elephant in the room.

Safi now wondered whether avoiding unwelcome topics had always been their problem, or was her mother waiting for her to open up before she said anything?

Sasha would be arriving to spend the last weekend with her in Brighton. Once he arrived, there would be no time to broach any of this with her mom. And questions abounded in Safi's mind. For example, where did they think Sasha would sleep? Surely not with her in her old room! She could not help but giggle at the thought of her and Sasha in her single bed, together with all those old photos hanging on the walls; it was too ridiculous to contemplate.

Back home after a brisk walk on the beach with her mom and Rosie their Labrador, they settled in the kitchen. She was bracing herself for an embarrassing question, when her mom surprised her.

'I guess you and Sasha will be using the guest room when he arrives,' Fiona said.

Relieved, Safi nodded, adding, 'Well, either that or us creeping around at night. I can't imagine him sleeping in my old bed, staring at my old school photos.'

Her mom had always had a good sense of humour. 'Yes, I can see that would be awkward. I will see that it's ready when he arrives.'

Safi caught her mom's eye and decided it was now or never, Fiona as she liked to think of her mom when, in a tight spot, was quintessentially English, in so many way's. She was blonde, pretty and liberal with a small c, if the topic was uncomfortable her mom would rather pretend it did not exist at all.

'Thanks, Mom, I appreciate it. Do you want to talk to me about anything before Sasha arrives? It's best to say it now.'

Safi noticed her mom tensing and was immediately sorry for bringing up the subject when she sat facing Safi straight on.

'I have avoided talking to you, Safi, not because of Sasha, but because I am losing you and now Jake as well. It's just too hard for your father and I to absorb right now – but don't you worry, we will have our mourning period when you have both left. Then we will bounce back, I am sure; won't we, Rosie?'

Safi watched her mom as she stroked Rosie and realised Rosie had become her mom's anchor, almost like Bruno had been hers when first in Manhattan on her own.

Safi borrowed her dad's BMW four-wheel drive to fetch Sasha from Gatwick; Leonard preferred her to drive a larger car on the motorway, even though Safi preferred her mom's Mini. Her tummy was in knots as she parked the car, taking note in case she forgot where she parked. The BA flight was early and Sasha only travelled with hand luggage, so she expected him to get through quickly.

As he pushed through the doors, she could not contain her excitement, rushing towards him and throwing her arms around his neck, almost knocking him over in the process. He steadied her as they hugged until Sasha pulled away. Grabbing her hand, they continued through the crowd, with only eyes for one another.

Safi suggesting they catch up over coffee at the airport hotel, before heading back to Brighton where they would have no privacy at all.

Sasha leaned over. 'Do you think we could rent a room for an hour or so'?

'That's not a bad idea,' Safi replied, giggling. As they entered the hotel, the idea got the better of her and she headed straight for the reception desk.

'Excuse me,' she said to the well-dressed receptionist, 'do you think it would be possible to hire a suite for an impromptu private meeting? I am flying out in a few hours and need to do some interviewing before I leave. It has to be a suite with a reception area – it's for a movie, you see.'

Sasha stood by, trying to look professional, pretending to be an assistant, checking his watch from time to time. Safi turned to Sasha and said crisply, 'Would you mind signing and giving them the credit card, please, and finish up the transaction, thank you.'

'If you could show me the suite now please,' she said, following the manager calling over her shoulder for Sasha to come up as soon as he was done.

Riding up in the lift, the manager said, 'If your company had booked ahead, we would have arranged for flowers and fruit to be in the suite.'

Safi, now in gear, had no trouble playing the parody out. 'Well, there is a casting at Heathrow today. The secretary was supposed to book Gatwick, too, but unfortunately she slipped up.' With an irritated sigh, she added, 'Heathrow have casting for the male star; we are only casting for a body double today. Our female lead refuses to do nude scenes.'

Stepping into the suite, Safi nodded her approval. 'I will send my assistant down to collect the girls; he can prep them on the way up. Could we please not be disturbed. I would like it to go as quickly as possible.'

He left Safi with the key and nodded to Sasha as he came through the door. 'Good luck with the casting.' Sasha casually closed the door behind him, they stood looking at one another for a few seconds, then howled with laughter, both with hands over their mouths.

Sasha picked her up and carried her through to the bedroom. 'Oh my God! I enjoyed that,' Safi said. Sasha, now lying on top of her on the bed and kissing her all over, stopped for breath. 'Where did that come from? You were so professional.'

Safi laughed a deep-throated laugh. 'I have no idea. I was quite good at amateur dramatics at school.'

'Amazing what the thought of some sex can do.'

Sasha and Safi smothered one another in a tight embrace, completely intoxicated by the feel of one another. Sasha's head was nuzzling her neck with soft kisses as he found the fastening to her jeans; she willingly helped, lifting her bottom for him to pull them down. She felt a thrill of desire and excitement as the jeans slid down her body together with her miniscule knickers. With Safi's dexterity, Sasha managed to free himself of his buckled belt. Smiling stupidly into each other's eyes, they freed themselves of all restraints as their clothing fell to the ground. All doubts she harboured totally dissipated as they clung to each other. The heat of the moment over, they were brought back to reality as their breathing returned to normal once more.

'God, I have no idea how I managed to live without you,' he said, 'thank goodness that is now over for both of us.'

Leaning on her hand, staring at Sasha tenderly with complete and utter love, Safi said, 'Me too. I have been having awful panic attacks; but now you are here, Sasha. I love you so much it hurts.'

Grabbing Safi in a tight embrace, he suddenly became aware of a cell phone ringing. Safi stared at the time, hardly believing three hours had passed since she had left for the airport. Sasha handed Safi the buzzing cell, grabbed his clothes off the floor and made his way to the bathroom.

'That was my mum wanting to know whether we were okay. They had expected us back hours ago. I am afraid your flight was held up, so don't forget that when they mention it.'

They both giggled away as they straightened themselves up and left the suite, happily chatting away until they reached the hotel lobby where Safi fell back into her acting role, thanking the staff for their assistance and turning around to wave at a complete stranger (possibly an actress auditioning for the role) as she exited through the swing doors with Sasha out the hotel.

The few days with her family in Brighton flew by. Safi could tell that her mother warmed to Sasha's old-fashioned manners and, charm offensive, while trying to put a brave face on her feelings about losing her daughter to a country she knew very little about.

Her father, on the other hand, was completely withdrawn. Leonard spoke when he was addressed, but seemed to make absolutely no effort to engage either Safi or Sasha in conversation. Safi found that he was pleasant enough to Sasha, but knowing her dad she realised that he was sending her a silent message of disappointment. Jake saved the day by being completely mad, keeping everyone howling with laughter at every opportunity with stories of Safi's childhood and his own craziness.

They explored Brighton, and Sasha was introduced to anyone who was anyone by the time they said their goodbyes to her family at the train station. Safi felt relaxed and ready for Sasha's London family; after all, nothing could be any worse than dealing with someone else's family. If

Sasha could do it, so could she. Fiona and Leonard would be in London to dine out with Valentina and Alexi before she left for Moscow.

She was not looking forward to her last farewell, knowing her folks were finding her departure harder than either of them was prepared to acknowledge, but she was determined not to have it spoil the mounting excitement she felt about being with Sasha on a daily basis at last. She decided that her parents would soon get used to the idea once they visited and saw for themselves how happy she was, which she was convinced of now.

The taxi drove through the gates of Alexi's Kensington home. Valentina and Alexi had a 5-bed- and six-reception-room home on four floors. They were welcomed warmly by one of the servants as they arrived. The luggage was whisked off to their suite on the top floor. Safi knew Alexi was mega-wealthy, of course; nonetheless she was gobsmacked by the opulence of the Chelsea house. The chandeliered entrance and chequered black-and-white tiled floor with winding black wrought-iron staircase was stunning.

Sasha took Safi on a tour, showing her the kitchen, where he claimed to have learnt to cook his favourite dishes. The kitchen resembled a sitting room one could cook in with chandeliers and comfortable sofas and a table large enough for twelve, with the cupboards in white oak. A large round glass table and chairs looked out onto a beautiful walled garden that could be reached through double patio doors.

She could not wait to see the reception rooms, and followed Sasha into a formal dining room with a walnut table that was large enough to seat twenty-plus people. The walls were covered in red fabric panels, set into high-gloss black wood frames. On the side wall a highly lacquered red console ran the length of one wall. On either side of the server were two beautiful Lalique standing lamps, with black shades. They walked through adjoining doors into a medium-sized living room decorated in soft blush rose and creams, which Safi loved, with heavy champagne silk curtains piling on either side of the bay windows, looking out onto a small courtyard, filled with pots of topiary and flowers. There was an office and TV room and well-stocked library, and two more interleading rooms used only occasionally for balls. They climbed down a short winding marble staircase to an underground cinema, gym and lap pool and three garages. Across the passage from the entrance hall was an impressive book-lined study furnished in old battered studded leather armchairs and a huge ornate antique desk.

Sasha opened a hidden door under the stairs that housed a lift to carry them up the stairs. She was beginning to realise where their luggage had disappeared too so quickly. 'Let's walk the marble staircase, it's so gorgeous.'

'Anything for you,' Sasha said, laughing as they climbed the stairs. At the top of the landing were three bedrooms: one was Alexi and Valentina's; and two adjoining rooms (a bathroom which had been for a nanny, Sasha explained, the floor originally containing the nursery).

They made their way up to the third floor that opened onto a small landing, entering the room through a small passage with a door that led into a grey marbled bathroom. The bedroom had a slanted ceiling with low slatted beams painted in a distressed off-white, a large king-size bed filled the room with an old French rattan headboard and a bed filled with pillows, which Safi could not stop herself from diving into. Sasha laughed and said, 'I know, don't they look inviting.'

'Just to lie in for the moment,' Safi said. 'I can't imagine how they find all this wonderful linen; it smells and looks so fresh and pristine. I love the mink throw hanging over the end of the bed, so cuddly.' Sasha pulled her up from the bed, hugged her, smacked her bottom, and pointed to the walk-in closets, where Safi found all her things had been neatly hung and folded away in the shelves, her shoes on the racks.

'Wow, I could get used to living like this,' Safi said. Smiling, Sasha said, 'Get dressed, we are meeting my father and Valentina for cocktails and dinner in half an hour. After that we are joining some of my chums at a club close by. I have not seen them for ages and can't wait to show you off.'

The evening with Alexi and Valentina at the London Rubicov passed in a haze of questions for Safi. The staff welcomed Sasha with approving nods and smiles, which Safi found a bit familiar, but Sasha did not seem to mind. Valentina had arranged an evening at their home to entertain Safi's family when they arrived from Brighton and had invited them to stay. Their little girl Marina was visiting with Valentina's mother in St Petersburg and would miss meeting Safi, but it was an ideal opportunity for the family to unite under one roof, before Valentina flew off to Russia. Safi found that Valentina was someone who one did not contradict; she was used to everyone following her lead when organising their lives. Sasha had mentioned Valentina enjoyed her day organised to the last hour. Ballet had trained her to be disciplined, and she had explained to Safi she found it hard to lie about and was far happier when busy.

Safi's thoughts strayed to the lazy comfortable brunches with the two D's and her lovely hours willing her hours away chatting to Pete, and wondered whether Valentina was ever able to chill; even her clothes were pristine, designer from head to toe. She went on to explain she kept up her ballet exercises in their gym every morning, after which her day was filled with meetings. Being involved in the arts she was fairly busy and her family took up the rest of her life and time.

Alexi and Sasha had left Safi and Valentina alone after dinner, excusing themselves to discuss work. Safi found Valentina's personality slightly intimidating; she appeared slight and feminine in appearance, but underneath she was obviously a force to be reckoned with.

Alexi, on the other hand, was warm and funny, he was easy to chat to. Sasha, when together with his father, seemed to have little time for anything but work. Safi was not used to revealing much about herself until comfortable with her companions, and Valentina was not companionable, not yet anyway. When Sasha returned, the tenseness in her shoulders visibly relaxed, with relief.

Sasha walked past the lines waiting to enter the club. As they entered the dark glamorous décor of the club, Safi felt herself being transported back to her last experience at a club in New York. A shiver ran down her spine as she recalled the spiked drink. His friends were waiting for them in a booth, they greeted Safi with warmth, and the evening developed into a madly fun time as they danced in a group with his friends and their partners; everyone seemed happy to let their hair down with wild abandonment.

Sasha disappeared to the bar, leaving Safi dancing with his friends. Natalie took Safi by the hand and led her off the dance floor. 'Let's do the loo,' she said, giggling, 'I am desperate.'

Safi thought Natalie was stunning: she was tall and slim, with wild blonde curls she allowed to do their own thing, She kicked open the door with one of those long legs, and sat on the toilet seat with her knickers round her ankles. Rummaging in her bag she brought out a small packet, closed her bag and lay it on top, spread the white powder neatly on the shiny surface of her black satin evening bag and sniffed up the powder through a straw. Safi watched fixated by her lack of caring and obvious confidence in her surroundings, ignoring the girls coming in and out of the toilets. Natalie looked up and said, 'Oh my God, do you want some, I have barely enough for one hit.'

Safi smiled no weakly and shot into one of the toilets, feeling ridiculously stupid and uncomfortable with the situation she found herself in. Should she wait for Natalie to leave or was it best to pretend she did not care? To her relief she recognised the voice of one of the other girls in their party and heard Natalie leave with her.

Making her way back to their party, she glanced over at the bar to see whether Sasha was still there. Stopping short she gasped as she saw some girl sitting on his lap, arms around his neck and with her lips close to his ear. Safi watched, not the girl but Sasha; she wanted to see his reaction and whether he was encouraging her.

'I would not worry about Ziggy,' someone said, 'she tries it on with everyone.'

Safi swung round to face Greg, not sure whether she was happy or not to see him. Seeing Safi's obvious discomfort and shock at seeing him, Greg took her hand and led her towards Sasha.

'Mate, I think you need to take better care of Safi,' Greg said. 'This place is obviously freaking her out, not to mention that Rock Aristo that just got off your lap,'

Sasha pulled her towards him, but she had not recovered and reluctantly gave way to his embrace. Greg pecked her on the cheek and disappeared into the crowd on the dance floor.

'Want to leave?' Sasha asked.

Safi nodded yes, not wanting to reveal her shaky angry voice. They made their way back to his friends, said goodnight to those they could find and left.

Outside the club Sasha hailed a black cab. Once Sasha closed the door, she slid across the seat, remaining in her corner. He found her hand and squeezed it; she could feel his eyes on her but dared not look at him, feeling close to tears. She had not figured out what had upset her so much, but she felt wretchedly insecure. Sasha took her chin in his hand and pulled her face round towards him. Safi tried to avoid his eyes by looking down. Sasha whispered, 'I love you,' and before she could stop herself, tears welled up in her eyes and started to roll down her cheeks. In spite of herself, her pride be damned, she was sobbing uncontrollably.

Sasha undid his seat belt and pulled her into him. Holding her closely and not saying a word he allowed her to cry until she slowly got herself under control. The cab parked outside the gates, Sasha paid and ran to catch up with Safi as she walked towards the house. Turning her around to face him, he said, 'Why are you so upset with me?'

Staring at him she was not sure herself, but realised that Natalie's coke habit had brought back her experience at the club in New York, followed by seeing Ziggy or whatever her name was all over Sasha, and then to top it off being confronted with Greg. Her trauma of what had happened in New York got the better of her, it all came flooding back, she lost her nerve, feeling like a complete fool for being so trusting of everyone. She was not sure whether it was Natalie's coke habit or Sasha or Greg she did not trust. It all became mingled, a confused mess in her mind. She sank down on the seat outside the entrance, knowing she would have to explain her feelings to Sasha.

'I am sorry,' she began, 'but for some reason the New York club experience unnerved me more than I realised.' She explained further, beginning with Natalie and the coke, and was still explaining when Sasha sucked in his breath and kneeled down in front of her, taking both of her hands in his.

'God, I am sorry,' he said, 'I had no idea.' Safi managed a weak smile. 'Please don't worry about Ziggy. I used to know her years ago – we all did. No one gets serious with Ziggy; she flits from person to person and obviously has not changed in all the years I have known her. As for Natalie, I had no idea about the coke. And Greg showing up, that was pretty weird.'

Safi suddenly felt exhausted. 'Sasha, can we go to bed? All I want to do is sleep. It's been a really long day and my folks will be here tomorrow for the weekend.'

Without speaking, they made their way up in the lift to the top floor. Sasha, she noticed, allowed her to get ready for bed alone. Lying in bed with her eyes almost closed, she noticed him coming into the room munching a sandwich. Safi sat bolt upright in bed, reached out and took the sandwich straight out of Sasha's hand, and bit into it hungrily. Her eyes did not leave his startled face as she swallowed the last bite, then giggled. They both cracked up hysterically, laughing until it hurt. The tension of the night gone, they made their way down the stairs and back to the kitchen to raid the fridge, ravenous for more.

Alone in the kitchen with no other distractions besides food opened up an opportunity for Safi to discuss her fears about living in a different culture she knew very little about. Sasha himself had mixed feelings about her being happy and promised Safi he would do everything in his power to help her settle in. They made their way back to bed in the early hours of the morning, happier than they'd felt in a long time, but not too tired to make love, slowly and meaningfully enjoying each other's bodies, feeling safe in their desire and love for each other.

The weekend with Safi's parents sped by. Leonard seemed to have accepted losing his daughter to Sasha's family, whom he genuinely seemed to like. Alexi was charm personified and it was hard not to warm to his personality. Fiona and Valentina found they had little in common, the gap in their ages did not help, but Valentina was, if not exactly warm, always the consummate hostess, and Safi admired her ability to keep them all busy and entertained at the same time.

Valentina was from a Jewish background; her father, she was proud to announce, was a Tartar from the Crimean strong people. Her mother was from an old and very cultured St. Petersburg Jewish community. She adored her mother's love of tradition; since the Iron Curtain collapsed, her mother had reignited the Friday night Jewish tradition of breaking the bread and having all the family round the table, but instead of the traditional chicken soup, they served Borscht, the creamy, rich, and hearty beetroot soup with potato. The rest of the meal was traditional roast chicken, vegetables and Lokshen pudding everyone loved and Safi could not have enough of. Valentina proudly announced that her recipe was Americanised version of the original over cooked traditional Jewish pudding.

The restaurant supplied the mille-feuille dessert with freshly cut fruit beautifully displayed on a bed of ice cubes; it was so stunning that everyone thought it a flower arrangement at first. Alexi went on to explain that 'Russians knew mille-feuille as a Napoleon cake made of many thin pastry layers that no one had time to bake any longer.' Instead, they settled for what he thought was an inferior version called mille-feuille; scandalous, he laughed, as he popped the small custard cakes into his mouth.

Eating together as a family made a difference; it relaxed everyone and they came together to laugh and even argue. Her family partook heartily in Valentina's Friday night Shabbat dinner, even the lighting of the candles, as Valentina explained saying a blessing and then a prayer over two platted loaves with vodka chasers, which Safi's father found amusing, since wine was usually shared rather than vodka. He had indulged in many a Friday night dinners with his partner in the firm, so he knew a thing or two about the Jewish traditions. Hugs all round. 'Good Shabbas to my new family. Na Zdorovie. Cheers, let the feast begin.'

Valentina explained that Russians were a mixed lot and they loved to celebrate most traditions, even Christmas was something they now loved, especially the children. They invited Safi's parents to spend

Christmas with them in Russia, to visit with their daughter, and to allow them to be their hosts over the festive period. Safi and Sasha thought it a brilliant idea, and by the time they all turned in for the night, Leonard had agreed.

Safi spent Saturday with her folks, assuring them she would call them often, knowing she had not done enough while in New York. Brunch on Sunday was in the kitchen where Alexi loved to show off his considerable cooking skills, but everyone was subdued, knowing it was Safi's final goodbye to her folks, who were leaving at noon back to Brighton, and out of her life once more until Christmas.

Waving goodbye to her folks, Safi leaned into Sasha, feeling sadder than she had in a while She knew her parents were going to be depressed returning to an empty nest, their lives were changing, Jake had left for Australia and she too would soon be gone. A deep feeling of guilt swept over her; swallowing hard, she resolved to be a better daughter to them in future.

Part II

Chapter 16

A fish out of water described exactly how Safi felt in Moscow. She loved the city but hated the icy cold weather. She should have listened when everyone warned her winter was not a good time to be anywhere in Russia. Particularly since it was to date the coldest winter for many years. Experiencing below zero temperatures was unimaginable. She now understood why people wore furs and did not argue when Sasha presented her with a floor-length mink, hat, and gloves, not to mention fur-lined boots. Even dressed for the cold did not prepare her for the icy winds that whipped in over the Moskva River; breathing in the cold air hurt her lungs, her face felt brittle to the touch. Sasha had warned her it was one of the coldest winters on record and was not to be taken lightly; braving the cold in Moscow could be life-threatening if one was not adequately prepared.

Kolya was in charge of all of her travelling needs. At first Safi disagreed vehemently with Sasha. 'I do not need a babysitter to take me whenever I venture out alone,' she had said.

'Don't argue with me, please, Safi, it will put my mind at rest, especially in this arctic winter that we are experiencing right now. If you get lost in this weather, you may just freeze to death out there.'

So Kolya became her shadow whenever she left the building and she became used to having him around. He was a giant who thankfully spoke textbook English. In the first few weeks, Safi appreciated his guidance and helpful translation to almost everything. Getting around Moscow by herself without knowing the ropes would have been a challenge she was happy not to have to deal with; everything sounded like gobbledegook to her ears. People hunkered down in their furs against the cold and snow blizzards.

The city looked beautiful covered in a blanket of white snow, Safi thought. Viewing it through the windows of the warm SUV as they drove through the traffic was, she admitted, comforting compared to fighting the icy winds on the streets. As they made their way around the ring roads towards Yvetta's gallery, Safi shivered involuntarily at the sight of an old woman shuffling across a bridge; below the river was a block of solid ice.

On their arrival the family made her feel wonderfully welcome, each member in turn had them over for dinner in their homes, and Safi soon became used to their warm teasing concern for her welfare and happiness. Between lapses from Russian into English they argued endlessly about what was best and appeared to disagree with each other on almost everything about how she should go about beginning her new life in Moscow.

For the first few weeks, Safi hardly had time to feel alone. Yvetta had her visit galleries and art fairs in Moscow; she was introduced to everyone who was anyone in Yvetta's arty world, and Safi loved their attitude to all things Russian, embracing the contemporary exhibitions many galleries were showing on the outskirts of the city. It was a world she knew very little about but immediately felt an affinity with, through Dax, who she mailed daily informing him about everything she had seen and learnt.

There was a tiny seed germinating in Safi's mind, she had not mentioned it yet but it kept growing the more she saw of the art world. She wanted to share it with Sasha, but found him preoccupied with catching up at work since their return; their evenings had been taken up with dinners and social engagements, so Safi decided to chat to Yvetta. Safi formulated how to present her ideas in a sensible light; not knowing how Yvetta ran her gallery, she did not want to appear brash.

She had tried to let Yvetta know she was coming. Kolya had no explanation for Yvetta's cell not picking up her calls, so Safi left her a message instead. On arrival they found the gallery closed. Safi felt deflated, she had been so excited and buoyed by her idea she had not planned for anything else that day.

Kolya suggested she try Yvetta again while he tried to find out why the gallery was shut. Listening to Yvetta's voicemail in Russian and then in English yet again, Kolya informed her that Yvetta's and most galleries shut on a Monday. He looked apologetic for not knowing. In his less-than-perfect English and Russian accent, he offered to take her home; but Safi was not in the mood to spend a day alone catching up on her mail. Instead, she asked Kolya to drive her to the Gum shopping mall in Red Square.

She had been keen to visit the 19th-century emporium and old Russian State department store that had become a shopping ground for the well-heeled. She had not yet ventured to any of the grand stores she had heard so much about.

Kolya wanted to accompany her in case she got lost, but Safi thought it ridiculous. They argued back and forth until Kolya reluctantly agreed to wait for her in an agreed place when she was ready to leave. With a worried expression, he dropped Safi at the main entrance of the mall near Red Sq. She felt sorry for him but was relieved to be on her own and ducked into the shopping centre, bumping straight into Nina, one of Sasha's relatives. They hugged and exchanged greetings. But after their initial greetings, they stared at one another, realising neither was able to make themselves properly understood in the other's language. Feeling embarrassed, Safi pointed to a dress in the window and breathed a sigh of relief as she stepped into the store.

Safi noticed Nina's bewilderment at her hasty retreat. Safi wondered round the store, not really taking much note of the merchandise apart from the smartly dressed sales assistants, waiting for her to choose something, realising her fur must have given them the impression she was loaded. In fact, at that moment, she felt very alone.

Dejected, she stumbled out of the store. She had never really been into shopping by herself. She thought fondly of her odd visits with Lauren and Dax to find something for her to wear; they were the expert shoppers. But now she felt homesick, or at least sick for New York, which had become her home.

Her hoped-for shopping adventure, she began to realise, had become a very lonely experience and not at all what she was hoping to fill her time with. She walked on aimlessly looking into the windows of the stores, one more exquisite than the next. Checking her English store map, she made her way to Bosco restaurant in the centre, from where she could relax and people-watch.

Suddenly hungry, she stood in line waiting to be seated, when she saw someone wave at her. Realising it was Nina again, a feeling of dread and relief passed through her. Making her way towards their table she prepared herself to be introduced to yet more people she could not converse with. To her relief, both women at the table mentioned Nina's name in perfect English, explaining that Nina had been concerned for Safi, not having been in Moscow long, and insisting she join them.

Safi visibly relaxed, thrilled to have company and to be able to speak to someone, anyone she knew even slightly. She was beginning to have an out-of-body experience, wondering around so aimlessly. To her relief, the menu was in both English and Russian and she ordered spaghetti bolognaise.

Nodding in agreement, the other women seemed to follow her choice. Then they chatted away in Russian, leaving her unable to fathom a single word, feeling alone all over again, her relief vanishing and her heart quickly becoming cold. Seeing her obvious pained expression and the way she was pretending to be distracted by her phone, they apologised, telling her that they thought her beautiful and wanted to know who her favourite English designers were. They loved VB and Burberry, Alice Temperley, Rocksanda, Alexander McQueen, not to mention Stella McCartney. And didn't she love Selfridges! And oh had she watched Made in Chelsea, they just loved it!

Safi could not help laughing, shook her head, and decided to be honest. 'I have no idea who half those designers are, to be honest. I have never been madly interested in fashion.'

But she did have a few designer items she had been given, mostly while in Manhattan. Declaring that she mostly dressed for comfort during the day, Safi quickly realised her response was not what they were hoping for and she spent the rest of the meal in polite but rather awkward conversation. They pointed to the black-and-white canopied passage opposite the restaurant and told her that if she wanted to find anything, the food emporium was a wonderful place to search. It was as well-stocked as Harrods' food hall, they said, and a must to walk through.

It gave her a great excuse and she left them chatting away while she took up their suggestion. Chandeliers ran the length of the store, with every delicacy one could possibly want, but all she wanted was to get hold of Kolya. Nina and her friends were waiting for her at the restaurant. Having settled the bill, they refused her offer to pay them back and invited her to go shopping. Relieved to have an excuse, they hugged her, promising to take her shopping to exquisite stores she had yet to visit. Safi nodded, waving as she casually made her way to meet Kolya.

Back in the safety of the car, they made their way to the Arbat Ostoztenka area, where Sasha's family had their family home, a purchase they were proud of. Today the area's classically styled mansions had been beautifully restored. It was known as the Golden Mile (Perchistenka St). Sasha lived in the mansion with his mother, Anna. They shared the same butler and servants, but the living quarters had been separated completely by a magnificent circular staircase, and recently a small lift had been added. The upper floors had been converted into a two-bedroom apartment. There was a spacious open-planned lounge with a high-gloss black kitchen. Tall high-backed overstuffed red upholstered chairs ran the length of the bar and were set off by a large contemporary gold-framed portrait of a clown, but on closer inspection was made up of thousands of religious iconoclastic memorabilia. The L-shaped dark grey suede sofa with oversized cushions to sink into was just what Safi yearned for as she headed up the staircase to make herself a much-needed cuppa and to watch her life-saving English channels on an obscenely oversized TV attached to the wall.

But first she had to master the sliding painting covering the TV and that moved into the side unit at a press of a button. Mastering the remote buttons was a learning curve she was only now getting the hang of, opening curtains when she meant to open the sliding TV, and vice versa. Getting it right was the one thing making her crack a smile when on her own, which was pretty much most of the day.

Entering the house, she found the tall marble pillars, high ceilings, low-hanging chandeliers, and many closed doors. It was a cold, intimidating experience. Leading off the hall and down a long circular passage was Anna's apartment. The sweeping black-and-gold wrought-iron staircase led to Sasha's apartment. Anna had welcomed Safi on her arrival with a party in her beautifully decorated apartment, which all led off the circular entrance. Once the doors were left open, the space transformed into a welcome, warmly furnished home leading off one beautifully furnished room after the next.

The kitchen was always staffed with either a cook or one of the servants. Safi loved Anna's country-styled kitchen. Everything was on display in glass-fronted cabinets with a long refectory table running almost the length of the room. Below the long wooden table piled high were casserole dishes and plates. The copper pots and pans hung above and the industrial lighting gave off the atmosphere of a welcoming space, unlike the rest of the house. Safi liked to visit here, where there was always someone to talk to, or a slice of cake to have with her cuppa.

Here was where everyone in the family congregated when Anna was home. Anna, who loved to cook up a storm on the huge agar against the wall. In an alcove off the main kitchen were faded floral sofas with a glass topped carved wooden coffee table. Everyone was welcome in this space and Safi found it her favourite place when alone. The staff welcomed her whenever she appeared, offering whatever the huge larder off the kitchen or the fridge had on offer, both always stocked to overflowing.

The formal living areas downstairs were Anna's, but the antique-filled rooms and formal dining room were seldom in use. Safi had noticed Anna's vast collection of Russian artefacts behind well-lit glass shelving. A small courtyard in the front of the mansion was for cars and Safi knew there was a garden but so far had not seen it without a blanket of snow. She felt incredibly spoilt and privileged living in such opulence, but was beginning to feel like a square peg in a round hole, both in or out of the house.

When entering the house, she felt she was in a hotel, hating all the double doors that hid the warmth of the interiors. Climbing the stairs to Sasha's apartment made her feel out of sorts; one mother and son living in their own apartment was strange. On one level, she understood, but it had a contrived feeling she was not used to.

On their arrival, Sasha had told her that she was welcome to the whole house whenever she felt like using it. But Safi had no intention of invading Anna's space. Sasha's apartment was wonderfully comfortable once she passed through the opulent entrance, and she was sure she would soon become accustomed to their way of living.

She had just settled on the sofa when her phone buzzed. Knowing it was Sasha calling as he did every day since their arrival, she answered straight away. She loved his teasing and sexual innuendo, which made her feel desired and always left her glowing. His calls lifted her spirits and made all her doubts disappear; the same thing happened when he arrived home: lightness, happiness, an embrace and affection and often a whole lot more. Since their arrival, they had not yet settled into a routine.

Sasha had come home, showered, changed, and they were out the door within 30 minutes. Socially Sasha had kept her entertained from the moment she had set foot in Moscow. Indeed, she had been to almost every restaurant, show, opera and ballet, always joined by his friends. Safi had met so many of Sasha's friends that she no longer remembered anyone's name; should she run into any of the women she would not be able to recall many of them. She found them friendly, beautiful and exquisitely dressed, often a bit too dramatic in their tastes, for Safi, everything a statement, glamour or opulence and groomed from head to toe. Polly came to mind the only other dramatic dresser she knew, but Polly's taste had a twist of humour. Moscow at night was stunning, the theatres were always full to capacity, and Safi loved the high culture most Muscovites enjoyed so proudly.

She found Sasha's friends wives' or girlfriends were career-oriented and worked long hours, some in family businesses while many others had forged out careers for themselves. She was relieved that they all made an effort to engage her in conversation, but inevitably the conversation always lapsed into Russian, a language so hard she had no idea how to master even a few words. Sasha had given Safi a list of things to occupy her day, suggesting she become familiar with Moscow before she ventured into anything permanent like a career.

She agreed readily, having followed the same principle in Manhattan. But somehow having Pete to chat to when it got lonely and Bruno to care for made it seem far less daunting – to say nothing of the fact that almost everyone spoke English (of one sort or another) in New York. The language was going to be a mountain to climb if she was going to be happy living in Moscow; she was trying hard not to give in to her doubts about never mastering any part of it.

Sasha had instructed Kolya to help her with elementary words to help make herself understood, and she had practiced with him as they drove through – or, rather, sat still in – the ceaseless traffic, but putting it into practice was easier said than done. Whenever she tried to speak Russian, everyone immediately answered in English.

On the way home, she wondered whether it would be a good idea to join a Russian language school. 'What do you think' she asked Sasha. 'Not sure if it's such a good idea right now,' he said. 'Perhaps you should wait until spring; it's not long now, then you can use the metro and get around easily.' Safi sat silently, not knowing how to respond; she knew deep down he may be right, but she needed something to do besides riding about with Kolya during the day. Sightseeing was becoming a bore. After all, how many churches could she see?

'Perhaps Kolya can take me into the countryside to see places outside Moscow too?' 'Well yes, he could, but it's a particularly cold winter, and I am not keen on you having to be out there in this weather. What if you became stranded?'

Safi stared at Sasha. She was at a loss for words. He looked so handsome, she was crazy about him, when he was with her nothing mattered, but she was starting to go crazy; she needed something to occupy her time. Sasha put his hand over hers, the pressure was slight but enough to let her know that he understood.

'I will call Yvetta tomorrow. She has been away in St. Petersburg on business, but we will come up with something. Please don't get upset, it will work out, and the winter will be over soon.'

'Well, I was on my way to Yvetta's gallery on Monday, but found it shut.'

'Yes, Mondays the galleries like in most places seem to close.'

'I wanted to present an idea to Yvetta. It's been on my mind for some time, but perhaps it's premature since I have only been here one month.' Safi noticed an expression of concern cross Sasha's face. 'Is it a bad idea to approach her with my idea?' she asked.

'No, not at all, just be careful with Yvetta, she can be hard to deal with. We all step on eggshells around her. She is brilliant at what she does, but challenging her in any way can be an uncomfortable experience. I have learnt how to deal with her over the years, but, even for me, it's still an ordeal when its misfires.'

They sat in silence for the rest of the ride home, each in their own thoughts. She wondered whether Sasha would bother asking her what the idea had been; she was dying to discuss it with him, but now she felt reluctant to pursue it any further. Turning off the purring Maserati in the underground garage, he leaned over and pulled her chin towards him, giving her a warm passionate kiss.

'I need some mad passionate love,' he said, 'then you can tell me all about this idea of yours.' Her emotions were all over the place, hitting the floor one moment and floating elated the next. She allowed Sasha to guide her towards the lift door instead of climbing the stairs. As the doors closed and the lift began to ascend, it suddenly came to a jolting halt.

'Let's make love right here in the lift.' Facing the walls of the small lift, he pulled her trousers down to her knees. She gasped as she felt his hardness plunge into her roughly from behind. It hurt like hell, she felt confused and not sure how to respond to his aggressive behaviour.

Sasha had a way of making her feel both ravaged and excited at the same time, and she gave in to her discomfort. He turned her around, lifted her against the elevator wall, folded her legs around him, and entered her from the front with heated passion. She felt faint as he crushed her mouth with his, finding her tongue. Pulling away he whispered, 'I want to consume every part of you. I never have enough of you. I want to own every part of you, I want you again on our bed – and everywhere else. I want to fuck you until we both collapse with exhaustion. I promise I will make you happy. I am crazy for you, all of you.'

He released her slowly as the lift rose to their floor, picked her up and carried her to bed. Bending over, Sasha started kissing her slowly from her toes up, then down again, until he started massaging her with his tongue and kissed her until she screamed with release. Pulling his hair towards her, they kissed. He mounted her again and this time slowly grinded into her with relentless determination that made her reel with love as she felt his release at last inside her. They clung together until she pushed him off, then crawled into bed, drew the covers up, and fell asleep holding hands.

Safi woke to find Sasha gone and wondering whether she had dreamed the most incredible night of passion she had ever experienced. She lifted her head slightly to punch the clock radio and could not believe that she had slept until noon. On the pillow beside her Sasha had left a note:

'You are going to be the sweet death of me, don't stop ever, you are magnificent.'

Dancing around under the shower, every part of her she touched felt tender. She had never experienced such aggressive lovemaking. She could not stop wondering whether Sasha had taken a drug to make him behave so out of character? Picking up her phone, she found a message from Sasha.

'Kolya will be waiting for you, when you are ready, he has orders to drop you off at my office, can't wait to see you, wear a dress!'

After her shower she opened the curtains to a clear blue sky. The winter sun was steaming brightly through the window, yet she shivered.

The music on the radio was some hip-hop number and Safi found herself bouncing to the music as she dried herself tenderly.

Safi went through her cupboard, one hanger after another, throwing each dress she thought might do onto the bed. She pulled on some tights and thigh-high coloured soft calfskin boots, discarded all the dresses, and opted for her soft camel cashmere ribbed dress with the turtleneck collar that lay folded on the shelf with her sweaters. She tied a soft LV pale pink silk shawl around her neck, stood back, and liked what she saw. She was getting back to her Manhattan style, her confidence was slowly returning, it had been ages since she had enjoyed dressing up, especially during the day. Safi pulled a brush though her black hair, which she watched sway as it dropped down her back in thick folds, her fringe was getting long enough to comb off her face, it was time to grow it out.

Making an effort with her makeup, she put some colour on her cheeks and smudged the shadow around her eyes. Drawing the shadow outwards to make her eyes seem large as they slanted upwards, adding mascara, her eyes looked sexily broody against her pale complexion and dark hair. She took Sasha's mink out of the coat cupboard and slung it over her shoulder theatrically, feeling like a femme fatal. Smiling, she decided to do the complete look, putting on the hat and gloves Sasha had bought for her. She was feeling confident and wanted it to show. The bright sun helped – not to mention Sasha's mad, passionate declarations of love – made her feel as warm as the mink enveloping her from head to toe, and she needed as much warmth as she could get right now.

Safi could tell Kolya approved; he had that secret smile playing around his lips and eyes as he held the door open for her and passed her the seatbelt. As they set off through the traffic, he put the radio onto a pop station and they both sat comfortably in silence, enjoying the music, Kolya tapping the rhythm out on the steering wheel. He always wore a phone headpiece to stay in touch. More often than not, Safi suspected, he did other business on the phone while he ferried her about. She did not mind in the least; she felt safe with Kolya, he was a pleasant guy to have around, in a bulky sort of way.

They reached Sasha's building. Kolya drove into the under-car parking, helped her out, and insisted on taking her all the way up to Sasha's office on the top floor. Kolya had obviously called ahead, as the lift doors opened onto Sasha's floor; his secretary was waiting for them. Safi followed the perfectly formed petite blonde in a tailored, tight-fitting, sharp dark grey suit and crisp white shirt to Sasha's office. She spoke a perfect English, introduced herself as Natasha, and Safi could not help noticing her wide mouth, perfect teeth, baby blue eyes, and pixie nose. She was, Safi thought, exquisite.

As she entered Sasha's floor-to-ceiling glass office, she stopped in her tracks as she saw Pete, Dan, and Dax waiting for her. All three gave a low whistle as they saw this luxurious version of Safi enter in her floor-length mink, hat, and gloves.

Rooted to the floor for less than a second, she threw herself at them, hugging each in turn and trying hard not to burst into tears.

'You look like a Russian Tsarina or whatever they call Russian royalty,' Dax said. It was so good to hear his voice again. Sasha, nodding in agreement, took Safi's coat as she shed her gloves and hat. But Dax, elated with approval – or jet lag, perhaps – wasn't finished yet. 'You look unbelievable love, that outfit too, perfection, don't you think, Dan?'

Unlike Dax, Dan didn't seem to have found his voice yet – perhaps he was confused by the sudden change of scenery, or the sudden change in Safi. Certainly, the long flight seemed to have taken its toll; rarely had she seen him look so tired. Safi laughed. 'I knew it was going to be a special day. I was feeling so happy. I just wanted to make a special effort today, and I'm so pleased that I did.' Like Dax, she found that once she started talking she could not easily stop. 'But what are you doing here?'

Sasha cleared his throat, and smiled at Safi. 'Let's not go into that now, we can talk about it over lunch. I have a table booked on the top floor of one of our best restaurants. We may as well make the most of such a clear beautiful day, the view will be spectacular.'

Walking into the restaurant, Safi saw Yvetta waiting for them. She jumped up to greet Dax and the others. Safi was not sure what was going on, but she felt there was something she was missing. Sasha was being very mysterious. Dax and Yvetta immediately fell into deep conversation, but Safi could not concentrate on their discussion: she was too excited about seeing Daniel and Pete. They fell into easy conversation and she tried to catch up on what was happening with their recent project, and if Pete was sick of them living with him, since he now owned the loft. 'Well, that is one of the reasons we decided to accompany Dax. It was time for a break from the stress of our building and Pete wanted to see where you lived; so here we are'

'Yes,' Dax said, speaking fast still, 'DuPont has been negotiating an exhibition for me in Yvetta's gallery for a one-man show to open early next year.' Safi was dumbstruck: her thoughts had materialised before she had a chance to put her ideas to Yvetta. She swept aside her fleeting disappointment, realising that Dax and Yvetta were the professionals. The project could be something she might work on in the future; her instincts were obviously good. Dax was thrilled to have his first one-man show opening up in Russia: it was a huge coup and his first step outside the US.

Dax turned his attention to Safi and changed places with Sasha, so that she was sitting between Daniel and Dax. They both took a hand, lifted it to their mouths and kissed each of her hands lightly. Such a gay thing to do, she thought, but it was the most natural thing in the world for them, it made it all the more real having them back in her life again, even if for a short while.

'Where are you staying?'

'We have opted for the magnificent Metropole on Red Square. After reading A Gentleman in Moscow, I have always wanted to stay there.' They laughed at Safi's expression of disapproval; she had hoped they would be staying at Sasha.

'We will be here over the weekend. Not long, a taster, but we will be ba—'

Sasha interrupted to save Safi further disappointment. 'I have persuaded them to visit with us for one night at the Dacha just outside Moscow, so you will have them under the same roof.' Safi looked at Sasha enquiringly. 'We have not been yet,' he said, 'we usually go in spring and summer, but it's going to be a particularly good weekend weather-wise, so we decided to go. My mum and Yvetta will be joining us, too. We set off early Sunday morning and return Monday evening in time for their flight back.'

Safi returned with the two D's and Pete to their hotel (she wanted to relax and have a proper natter with them), while Sasha and Yvetta went back to work.

Kolya dropped everyone off apart from Yvetta, who wanted to make her own way. Kolya was dispatched to ferry them around and to bring them back to the mansion in time for one of her special meals. Safi was aware of Kolya's body language when he saw Pete; then noticed his expression when he realised the two D's were in a relationship. He clearly did not approve, and she decided to tackle him for sure when they were alone. It was outrageous!

They asked to be dropped at Gum; Dan had read up on the architect and wanted to see the glass dome. He explained that Vladimir Shukhov was responsible for Constructivist architecture and had built the elongated shopping galleries during the Soviet era. For the first time since her arrival in Moscow, Safi enjoyed the opulence and what the stores had to offer. They had coffee in the beautiful Bosco restaurant and Safi insisted they visit the palatial subway stations.

Dax came out marvelling at the incredible opulence and luxury of it all. 'I had no idea the Russians could be so exhaustingly dramatic and camp with interiors. I love it.'

'Those interiors are left over from the communist era – can you believe the luxury they lived in while the ordinary people were lining up for a loaf of bread in the icy cold, while a privileged few enjoyed this opulence?' Safi said, suddenly realising how much she missed just chatting without thinking of offending; her thoughts came bubbling to the fore, she felt liberated for the first time in ages, carefree and damned if she was being politically incorrect. She needed to purge herself of pent-up feelings.

Kolya had warned them not to remain around Red Square. They looked too foreign and it may attract unwanted attention by the criminals that hang around to rip off unsuspecting visitors. Safi had been warned by Sasha to dress down when going out and about, but she looked and felt a million-dollars today, and was enjoying the attention and glances they received from shoppers; even the aloof shop assistants who had ignored her the other day could not do enough for them today.

As they walked through the lavish food emporium, the two D's priced and bought some interesting pieces for their new home, and were disappointed when a delivery service was not offered. Safi noticed that Kolya had been following them quietly from a distance and she decided to make use of his services. Kolya waited for the items to be packed while they continued shopping. Pete seemed to feel uncomfortable with being waited on, but had to admit that Kolya made one hell of a security guard; his size alone was formidable.

'No one's going to mess with that guy,' Pete said.

'He's quite nice really,' Safi felt the need to add.

'Hmmm, wouldn't like to meet him on a dark street, that's for sure. Have you noticed those bulging muscles, those dead eyes? No expression passes over his face; he's like a statue.'

Safi did not know why but she felt protective towards Kolya; she had noticed that underneath the tough exterior hid a soft heart, and, when he allowed himself to relax, she found him amusing.

'I have spent almost every day with him since I arrived,' Safi said. 'Sasha insists that he look after me until I get the hang of Moscow. It's been bitterly cold here and the snow has been hazardous this winter. Sasha thinks I may get lost and freeze to death.'

They entered Red Square and made their way to the Duma to view the buildings and palaces and take in Saint Basil's Cathedral, the architecture was stunning with the sun catching the gold and coloured domes shining in the bright light against the crisp icy blue sky, was nothing but spectacular.

Pete groaned. 'Man, New York is cold, but this wind in the open square is bone-chilling.'

Balaclavas pulled low, beanies, gloves, long wool coats, and thick scarves covering every inch did not seem to help. The cold seeped into their boots, their toes ached from the cold. Everyone agreed it was a day to remain indoors. They were not used to this weather. Kolya loomed up between them, bumping Safi out of the way as he confronted a small band of gypsies following closely behind them. None of them had noticed the stragglers Frisking them, Kolya pulled Daniel's wallet out of one of their pockets, and sent them running. ' I think time to take you back to hotel,' he said.

They stood stunned as Kolya handed Dan back his wallet. 'I did not see that coming,' Dan said. 'Da, this is Russia, you are easy pickings for gypsies, they are quick.'

They spent the late afternoon laughing and catching up with gossip, Dax making them ache with laughter as he tried to copy the Russian mannerisms, he had noticed displayed by some of the assistants helping them in the stores. 'God, they can be rude and dismissive,' Safi said with a sigh, 'but I guess I will get used to it.'

'Let it out, girl,' Pete said, 'we will be gone soon, so you better be getting it off your chest.'

She sat for a while trying to collect her thoughts – confused, mixed-up emotions she had not yet processed – not knowing quite what to say. She felt ambivalent about her loyalty to Sasha and his home. She felt it disloyal to moan, realising how fortunate she was to be living in such incredible luxury, wanting for nothing, yet. And yet, as Pete had said, it felt so good to let it out, especially in the company of people who really knew and understood her. God, it was good to see them again.

Looking up, she saw six pairs of eyes expectantly waiting for her to offload. Indeed, these three men knew her better than she knew herself. When they inquired about Sasha, Safi's eyes lit up and they knew that part of her life was good.

'Yeah, we can tell, it's good,' Pete said.

Safi shook her head. 'Not speaking the language is a huge problem. Not having anything to do is depressing. Sometimes I feel as if I am in a boat lost at sea, just bobbing about on waves that are tossing me every which way. Maybe that sounds stupid, but that's exactly what it feels like, to me, anyhow.'

Pete nodded and made his usual knowing sounds. Safi looked up, almost expecting him to be polishing a glass behind the bar. 'You're missing home, girl, you're missing ole Pete, D&D and Bruno to chat to. That's what's ailing you, you're lonesome, nothing worse than being lonesome' Finding a lump growing in her throat, she suddenly gulped, tears rolling down her face. Dax and Dan sat down beside her, putting a box of tissues on her lap. Feeling embarrassed, she smiled weakly at them. 'I'm such a wimp.'

'It's this fucking weather,' Dan said softly, 'bad time to be here. Come spring and summer, this will feel like a different city and you'll forget this even happened.'

The phone buzzed. Shaking into their winter gear they made their way to meet Kolya; he was fast becoming their only connection to the outside world. 'I know what you mean about Kolya,' Dan said. 'Love him or hate him, need him we definitely do.'

Safi laughed, that's exactly how she felt.

Chapter 18

Anna had opened all the doors and Safi felt the warmth she missed whenever entering the entrance hall they all led off. She had to question Sasha about why his mother kept her living quarters closed off; it seemed so out of character, his mom was such a warm person. The lounge had a fire burning in an oversized, black wrought-iron grate with the ornate deco marble surround. The room was stunning: low lighting gave it a warm glow with a lived-in feeling.

They sank down in the overstuffed cushions around the fire. Vodka snaps were handed round on a small silver tray. Safi knew it was just the beginning; by the time the meal was over, the shots would be followed by glass after glass, no objections heeded. The two D's and Pete were on a guided tour with Yvetta. 'Can we do your quarters, too?' Dan asked.

Sasha nodded as they left the room. He held Safi's hand tightly, not wanting her to join the posse, and said, 'Let's keep my mum company.'

'What a marvellous home. Pete said, I love that you have your own apartment upstairs, Sasha, great idea, means your mom need never feel alone in this huge house. We Americans should do that kind of thing more often.'

'Let's eat, should we; everyone hungry?' Anna enquired.

Safi wondered whether they were going to make use of the dining room; she hoped not, the kitchen would be where she knew they would be happiest, comfortable, and homey, surrounded by all that wood and cooking paraphernalia. To Safi's delight, that is indeed where the table was set for them. Dan walked round the room, marvelling at the oversized masculine space that worked beautifully as a gathering for friends and family.

The copper pots were too much of a temptation for Pete; picking up a spoon he played a tune on the pots hanging above the table, announcing, 'Dinner is served.' Obviously too much booze already, Safi thought, but Pete managed to set the right tone for the meal and the evening passed in a haze of alcohol, borscht, and sweet and sour cabbage, finished off with pancakes filled with sweet ricotta cheese and syrup laced with a liquor everyone guessed had to consist heavily of vodka. Laughing, they begged for some strong coffee, without a trace of vodka.

Pete sat next to Anna during the meal. Safi noticed that Anna laughed, smiled, and was animated in a way she had not seen her before. Dax and Yvetta discussed the vibrant growing art scene in Moscow; he was meeting her the next day for a tour of the galleries and museums. She found herself happily watching her family mingle with Sasha's, catching bits of conversation. She learnt more about Sasha's side of the business through Dan's questioning.

Doing business in Moscow was not as plain-sailing as one might think: it was politically complicated, there were many handouts involved. Alexi had removed himself to run the other businesses from the safety of London. Sasha joked with Dan that, if he remained having to battle his way through the bureaucratic underworld, he would be grey or maybe even dead before he had the chance to enjoy life.

Safi wondered if he ever had the intention of sharing any of this with her, or whether the vodka had played some part in his confidences to Dan.

Her antennae had been in overdrive since arriving. For example, she picked up nuances she did not yet understand between Anna and Yvetta. Sasha himself was different around Yvetta; they all seemed to be treading water when around her.

Yvetta had always been gracious to Safi, and in all of their dealings, Safi had noticed that Yvetta's professionalism and energy were boundless. Where her work was concerned, she seemed to toil all hours of the day. When Safi was around, Yvetta had endless patience, explaining artworks and meticulously writing down galleries for her to see. Yvetta made sure Kolya knew where to take her and when.

Dax was to spend Saturday with Yvetta. He wanted to familiarise himself with the gallery space. Sasha would take over from Kolya and ferry them about, showing Dan the architecture and giving Pete a tour of café life here, a taste of the hip side of Moscow that was fast developing. In the evening they would be treated to Russian high culture. Sasha had managed to book them much sought-after tickets for a special performance of Swan Lake at the Bolshoi Theatre.

The evening ended with yet more vodka snaps all round. Kolya was waiting to drive them back to their hotel. Sasha and Safi would pick them up at ten sharp; they had a lot see in a limited time. Moscow was joined by concentric ring roads, and getting around was not always easy in the traffic, but Sasha hoped that Saturday would be less frenetic.

Moscow at night was stunning. The New Yorkers sat back enjoying the view from the high-sided SUV, pointing to various landmarks with childish delight. The two D's had not travelled abroad together in a long time due to work commitments. Dax was making strides into the world of art and Moscow would be his first one-man show outside New York.

After visiting Art Basil in Miami, Dax felt Dan had a point: there were some artist's work that took up too much of one's time cerebrally, the connections were endlessly self-indulgent. He much preferred the crossover of craft and fine art; one could appreciate the quality of the work without having to understand the artist. The work stood alone. All the same, Dax thought that some artists – in particular Damien Hirst – did well to meld both high craft and individual quirkiness. Like Duchamp, Hirst brought shock, with the ability to engage almost everyone. The cycle of life laid out, with never-ending visual exploration, Hirst knew how to entertain the punters with his work. This trip to Moscow, he hoped, would bring elements of Russia into his work– but he hoped also that that work would stand on its own wherever they were in the world.

Safi was always an honest judge of his work; knowing she would be in Moscow when his show opened gave him a certain measure of comfort. Kolya dropped them in front of the Metropole Hotel. Dan noticed he stayed put behind the wheel, staring straight ahead as they got out of the car. He did not bid them good-night, and, as the door closed behind them, he shot off, wheels screeching. Pete shook his head and said, 'Maybe he doesn't like black people too much.'

'I think he doesn't like gays much, either,' Dan said, laughing, as they entered the hotel lobby.

Dax had a small breakfast in their room before leaving at nine by taxi to meet Yvetta at her gallery. It was a clear icy morning; wisps of white vapour escaped as he breathed the cold air into his lungs. Finding the gallery closed he walked along shuttered storefronts.

Spotting a Starbucks opposite the gallery he escaped inside, feeling the cold seeping through the soles of his boots. Seating himself near a window hoping to spot Yvetta, Dax settled with a steaming latte and croissant, relieved the serving staff spoke English perfectly. There was only a smattering of people hunkered down over their coffees, computers open on tables, not that much different from Manhattan, really, apart from the view outside, of course. Looking at his watch, not wanting to begin his day irritated by Yvetta's tardy time-keeping, Dax started to wonder whether he had misunderstood the time for their meeting. Perhaps it was a language issue? But no, impossible – Yvetta's English was impeccable. He had begun to text Yvetta when he felt a tap on the shoulder. Staring up, he met the smiling blue eyes of the most exquisitely dressed young man, tall, blond, and delicately handsome.

'Dax? Ah, good; sorry we are late. Yvetta is in the gallery. Come, we have much to show you today. I am Fritzi, ja.' They shook hands. It was only as Dax followed him out, when Fritzi turned to chat, that Dax realised that he was a she, and German not Russian.

Yvetta and Fritzi had quite a day planned for Dax: he visited major galleries, was shown traditional Kandinskys and Malevichs at the Tereshkova Gallery, to say nothing of the more experimental galleries exhibiting avant-garde and performance art. They stopped off at the Garage, a contemporary art collection and café in Gorky Park. A modern low building mostly filled with conceptual art, the café was trendy and busy with kids skateboarding outdoors in the park, not unlike a scene in Manhattan.

Yvetta was brusque and lacking any sense of humour; Dax found her hard going. Fritzi, on the other hand, was charming and charismatic. Dax was impressed by how quickly Moscow was catching up with the rest of the contemporary art world. He hoped he would see some private collections: Moscow had more billionaires per square mile than any other capital city. DuPont informed him they loved spending on art, amongst other collectables. DuPont had arranged for him to see an impressive collection.

Fritzi was driving, with Dax in the front passenger seat, and Yvetta, mostly on calls, in the back seat. Fritzi dropped them off in front of an impressive office building. In the glass lift Dax marvelled at the incredible view of the Moscow River snaking its way around the city. Yvetta displayed a distinct irritation at his enthusiasm for her city; he was starting not to like this woman.

Stepping out they were met by a guide, offered refreshment, then led down a corridor into an open space to view a collection of sculptures. Lynn Chadwick, Henry Moore, Giacometti, Noam Gabo. Leaning over the banisters, Dax noted a Richard Sera in the lobby far below.

They passed through a dark passage lined with artefacts housed in specially lit walled cases. Dax stopped to examine and read where some of the intricately made pieces were from: excavations in Egypt, Israel, Syria, and even Iraq dating back to Byzantine times. He knew of people in America having secret collections, but he found such incredible wealth uncomfortable; there was something intimidating about priceless art not housed in a museum.

The central domed roof was hung with a floor-to-ceiling, lime-green Chihuly chandelier, of which the tip of the last piece of glass skimmed the floor. Walls were covered with Picassos, Matisse, Lichtensteins, and many Andy Warhols. A huge tapestry by Miro hung alongside installations of delicate butterflies and video art throwing amazing images across the floor and walls. Dax was dumbfounded, he had never imagined viewing a museum collection of privately owned priceless art. Turning to face the obnoxious Yvetta and the charming flamboyant Fritzi, he said,

'Thank you for the most interesting day.' Feigning a throbbing head, he asked if they minded dropping him at the hotel; he needed rest before attending the Bolshoi Ballet that evening. With obvious irritation, Yvetta made their excuses to their guide and ushered them out of the building and back into the SUV. She did all of this without uttering one word to Dax. But as the car dropped him off she caught his hand and said,

'You need to learn Russian protocol.' Dax politely took her hand off his. 'Thank you for the advice, and for today.' He closed the car door and passed through into the lobby, where he immediately went to the bar, ordered himself a gin and tonic, and fell into one of the plush armchairs. He threw his head back and closed his eyes, trying to calm down.

DuPont would have to deal with Yvetta; Dax found her insufferably rude, arrogant, and quite clearly a narcissist. She was all business, but definitely a difficult bitch: someone he feared would make Safi's life very uncomfortable if she got on the wrong side of her. He had no idea what he had done to annoy her so much, probably something to do with conversing with Fritzi most of the time.

Pete and Dan were at breakfast when Sasha and Safi arrived at the hotel earlier than planned. Later, as the passenger next to Sasha, they were in a world of their own, enjoying each other's company. Sasha enjoying having a chance to share his city with someone who could appreciate the history and significance of the architecture.

Pete and Safi watched and viewed the buildings and tried to take in some of the information; not wanting to interrupt the flow of conversation, they opted for gossip and spent a wonderful two hours catching up. By all accounts, Pete was happier than he had been in a long time. Buying the loft was the second-best decision he had made since buying the bar.

Their conversation ended when Sasha announced the architectural tour was over and they were going to ditch the car; the next leg of their tour would be on the underground. They travelled to five or six stations, marvelling at the opulence of each station. The trains rolled in every few seconds; spotless trains and spotless stations. Everyone in their own world, no different to the subway in Manhattan, apart from being politer.

Sasha rounded off the tour with a stop at the rooftop bar of a skyscraper, the winter sun warming them as they watched a white frozen world far below. They wound their way back through the traffic towards the hotel. It had been a relaxing day and Safi loved that Sasha could do this for them Safi hoped Dax's day with Yvetta had been successful; she wanted them to love her new family.

Safi was the first to break the silence. 'You have been so lucky with the weather. I was able to see more of Moscow today, since arriving.'

'Kidding, right?' Pete said. 'I can't feel my toes; they haven't caught up with the rest of my body yet.'

'It's been a particularly severe wint–' Sasha began apologetically.

'Those warm rays we caught at the sky pub is what I've been looking for,' Pete interrupted.

Outside the hotel, Sasha gave instructions to meet at the Bolshoi by 7.30, dress code formal. Seeing their shocked expressions, Sasha laughed. 'Just joking,' he said. 'Smart casual will do.'

They found Dax in the bar, chatting to some Americans. On seeing them he excused himself. It was hard for Dax to hide his feelings; after hearing about their day, he shook his head.

'I had a tough day. I can't say Yvetta and I are going to be best pals.' He described the incredible art – and described Fritzi, too, Yvetta's assistant and, possibly, girlfriend. He gave a less than favourable description of Yvetta's behaviour towards him. Dan and Safi understood that without DuPont handling the whole project, Dax could not go ahead with the commission or the exhibition.

Tchaikovsky's traditional Swan Lake was a ballet Pete had not been to before, apart from some modern ballet in New York and it completely blew him away. They all listened as Sasha gave a synopsis of the story. They all wanted to hear a real Russian's take on one of the world's most famous ballets.

The original had four acts and was based on folk tales, telling the story of Odette, a princess turned into a swan by a wicked sorcerer. The swan then turns into a beautiful princess and the dashing Prince Siegfried falls madly in love with Odette the Swan Queen. The sorcerer wants the prince to marry his daughter, Odile, the Black swan, but Siegfried finds out the truth and chases after his true love, Odette, rather than marry Odile. 'The rest you have to watch,' Sasha explained. 'The last act is the most beautiful, a pure act of love for the swan princess, Odette.'

Through Valentina's contacts with the Bolshoi, Sasha had managed to acquire five seats, almost unheard of at such short notice. Valentina had been the principal dancer in the Mariinsky Ballet in St Petersburg (known as the Kirov Ballet). Then she joined the Bolshoi for a short spell before retiring to marry Alexi. Sasha confided the Bolshoi wanted Valentina to be a mentor for one of their principal dancers after her injury, but she had refused, not wanting to become embroiled in the virulent infighting the Kirov Ballet was experiencing.

Sasha surprised them with an invitation to visit backstage; the immense organisation to put on the performance left them enormously impressed. Yuri, the director, showed them around with great pride and introduced them to the principal dancers.

The evening was a resounding success and Safi was glowing with pride at Sasha's effort to entertain her New York family.

As they returned to the house, they both realised all was not well. The doors leading to Anna's apartment were wide open. They could hear someone shouting, then the sound of banging and broken glass. Sasha immediately begged her to go upstairs, he would explain later, but he needed to deal with this now and preferred her not to be there.

Frightened and at a loss, she hesitantly made for the stairs, while he ran down the passage towards his mother. Safi stood on the first landing, rooted to the spot as she saw Sasha manhandling Yvetta into the kitchen. He closed the door, but Safi remained rooted, waiting to see what had happened. That was when Yvetta stormed out of the kitchen, hands waving above her head, a wild look on her face, and ran out the front door.

Suddenly all was quiet, until she saw Sasha walk slowly back down the passage towards his mom's apartment. Not long after she watched as mother and son walked towards the kitchen together, Anna with her head against Sasha's shoulder as he held her close comforting her.

Not wanting them to see her eavesdropping, she could not hang around and, shaken, made her way up to their apartment. She would have to wait until Sasha explained the disturbing scene she had just witnessed. She hoped he would confide honestly in her; she was, after all, part of the family now.

Safi was already in bed by the time she heard Sasha coming in. She did not pretend to be asleep, but sat up as he entered the room. He sat in the armchair next to her side of the bed, his face pale and angry. She could tell he was exhausted, and saw that he was struggling for words to explain what had happened.

'The reason all the doors are shut leading to my mother's apartment is a boundary we have set,' he said slowly. 'Tonight my mother had guests, and she had given the staff the night off, so left the doors open.

Yvetta has rages; it has been under control for a long time, but when she explodes she usually takes it out on either myself or my mother.

At work she is professional and capable. These rages have been going on since she was a teenager; no one ever understood the reason for them. She has been under therapy for many years. It's tough for all of us to deal with her abusive behaviour, especially when she is challenged. Once in a while, someone or something sets her off and she blows her fuse. This time I am sad to say it was Dax.'

'Oh my God, what did Dax do?'

Sighing, Sasha said, 'Probably nothing that he is aware of, but she blamed mom. I know it does not make sense, but this is how Yvetta perceives the situation, that we are indirectly to blame for inviting him here to embarrass her.'

'Not very rational, is she.'

'Yes, that's the problem. She strikes out like an angry child attacking anyone who she thinks is to blame.'

'What are we going to tell Dax?'

'Best to not to say a thing. He will be gone tomorrow, no point upsetting him. It will all be forgotten soon, especially if it suits Yvetta's needs. His agent can deal with her. She has never allowed her rages to interfere with her work. I would prefer to keep this quiet; no need for anyone else to know.'

'But what about tomorrow? Won't Yvetta be at the Dacha?'

'No, she was not invited. And, in any case, she spends her weekends with Fritzi, who is not welcome.'

She patted the bed next to her. It was after two pm and they had an early start. 'Let's leave the explanation about Fritzi, or whatever her name is, for another time.'

At least Safi now knew why the doors downstairs remain closed; such a shame. They fell asleep, Safi curled into his back, her arms protectively around him, hugging him close. As she dropped off, her own mother came to mind: she had not spoken with her for two weeks. And this was after promising her mom she would call her more often than she had in Manhattan. Jake was now gone, and she was gone; whatever happened she would call her mom later that day.

Sasha was dressed shortly after dawn and headed down the stairs to help his mother in the kitchen. Safi had been instructed again to ignore last night's debacle with Yvetta, and not to mention it to anyone.

Wondering into the kitchen some hours later, she found Anna and Sasha deep in conversation, which abruptly stopped as they saw her. Safi felt that Anna showed relief at the interruption. Hot coffee and pastries were on offer while they busied themselves filling baskets with hams, fruit and bread for the day.

Braving the crisp cold morning they filled Anna's SUV with food; she was to go on ahead to open and prepare the Dacha. Kissing Anna on both cheeks, they set off to pick up her New York family with an empty trunk for their baggage. They drove in silence as they headed onto the ring road that led to Red Square. Sasha did not seem in the mood to talk; Safi was not sure whether she felt excluded or whether she understood his reluctance to open up a dialogue about the previous night: it was bound to spoil the day. He turned up the radio; the sun was now streaming in though the car window and they both enjoyed the warmth and the music washing over them.

Pete was the first to arrive, the two D's not far behind with the hotel porter. The trunk full, they settled for a comfortable journey though the countryside, to the much spoken about Dacha that Safi was dying to see.

She imagined that it would be a few hours' drive, but to her surprise the roads were relatively quiet that time of the day and they made it to the outskirts by nine. They noticed fields and forests flying past. The scenery had changed dramatically as they headed out of Moscow, the houses became fewer and the land seemed to stretch endlessly into the distance.

Sasha made a sharp turn into what seemed a private forest with roads leading off in all directions. They continued along a tree-lined road with the sun filtering in and out of the trees preventing them from seeing much detail. A structure became apparent between the trees, and Sasha drove down a slope into a hidden excavated garage. They heard the doors close behind them and the sun was suddenly blocked out.

'Well, we have arrived, grab your overnights and let's start the day,' Sasha said.

Squashed into a small steel lift with the three overnights, they rode the short distance up in collective suspense. The doors opened to a lobby. Following Sasha they entered through an archway to a view of endless forest, a grey lake covered with floating ice, with a winter sun fast melting the ice as it cracked and floated like broken glass on the lake. It was a spectacular winter scene that left them standing at the window in silence, until Anna broke the spell, offering snaps all round to warm them.

Dax and Pete could not pull their eyes away from the frozen winter scene outside. Dan turned to take the snaps, his eyes appreciating the warm wooden flooring below his feet, covered with thick Persian rugs. Folk art adorned the wall above an open fire place now roaring away, with surround cushioned seating. The room was furnished for comfort with different coloured sofas, much like a family room in any large American house: the star attraction being the view through the bank of windows running along the side of the house.

Pete couldn't tear his eyes off the frozen lake and the faint sound of cracking ice as it melted.

'Wow! That's what I call a view. It's spectacular, must look a whole lot different in the spring and summer.'

'The house is on two levels,' Anna said. 'The rooms are below with doors onto the woods and a path leading to the lake, but that is all closed now for the winter. The kitchen is the hub of this house. Come, we have lunch now.'

Anna led them into a kitchen, not unlike the one she had in Moscow: the oven stood in its own alcove with coloured patterned tiles making it a homely space. The island was a replica of her one at home, apart from its warm country feel and coloured tiling.

The dining area was part of the kitchen and brought surprised delight from everyone; a massive oval wooden table was painted in scenes of old folklore in bright colours, and each wooden chair was painted a different colour. The central lights were low Tiffany lights running the length of the table. A large window at one end had two large chesterfield sofas in bright red linen, a low rough wooden table covered in books, and pots filled with herbs. At the other end, doors opened up to a wraparound balcony which was shut, but allowed a view of the forest outside. The painted dining table was filled with the food Anna had brought from home, but she obviously kept preserves and dried meat hanging in a larder off the kitchen. It all smelt heavenly and no one needed a second invitation to tuck in.

'This place is quite something,' Sasha said, 'it's completely hidden from view. Only from the lake can one see the boxlike design, as it's cantilevered over the garages to give it height to enjoy the views. The family share it. My father bought it several years ago from a Russian-American, who had apparently built it to resemble his Hudson River house in Upstate New York.'

Dan appreciated the likeness, while Dax thought it reminded him of homes on long Island. Still, it had a distinct Russian flavour: the scenery made that obvious, but the interiors were distinctly folksy Russian, too. They all agreed that the paintings, rugs, and the table were pure Russian fantasy. Anna and Safi and Dax opted to stay in the warm house, while the others donned walking gear. Pete was all for exploring; he wanted pictures of the ice on the lake. Safi and Dax helped Anna clear up while she laid the table for tea, for when the others returned. Bundling them in her truck to drive around the area, Dax wanted to see the other homes. Some were ridiculously palatial, but most seemed shuttered and closed for the winter, which was a depressing sight, since they were so beautiful in the bright sunshine.

Frozen and almost frostbitten from their walk, they returned to warm themselves at the fire. Anna had warned about the below-zero temperatures, the sunshine was deceiving. One needed special gear to brave the unusually bitter Moscow winter.

Sasha showed them to their rooms, all with fires roaring, luckily turned on by a switch even though they resembled old-fashioned fire places. The rooms were basic and featured huge double beds with heavy fur covers, and a bathroom with a walk-in shower. Sasha explained that, since Anna loved to bath, Anna's room alone had been fitted with a bath. Below the top floor were several bedrooms all running the length of the house, facing the woods and lake. It was one of the few homes used on a regular basis throughout the year; most of the owners of the surrounding houses lived abroad.

Safi loved their room, with the fire blazing in the grate it felt a safe haven from the arctic weather. She told Sasha that Anna had made the house incredibly welcoming for them, she must have gone to so much trouble to get it ready before they arrived.

'This weekend has been a welcome distraction for her,' Sasha said. 'She welcomes any distraction from Yvetta when she becomes irrational and abusive.'

This was his first mention of the previous night and she wasn't sure how to respond. Sitting down on the bed, she pulled her fingers through the soft fur cover. Sasha was not aware that she had watched it all from the landing, so she responded with an understanding nod, not wanting to give away what she had seen and heard.

Sasha kicked the door shut with sudden and unexpected force. He came over to the bed, pushed her down with one hand, and with the other pulled off her leggings and undid his jeans, allowing them to drop round his ankles. He dropped his head between her legs and kissed her until her back arched. Gasping as her body was still shaking with release, Sasha took her with such urgency, she could feel the tension release as he shuddered, whispering in her ear, 'God, I needed that, I love you.' Both giggled as they tidied themselves and rushed up the stairs for tea.

Pete and Anna were deep in conversation when they joined them, while the two D's were nowhere to be seen. Just as Safi was about to give up looking for them, Dan and Dax arrived carrying a gift for Anna tied with a stars and stripes ribbon. The tin was covered in a scene of Abraham Lincoln pointing his finger. 'Your country needs you' was written across the tin, while stars and stripes adorned the rest of it.

Anna was bemused as she opened the tin, letting out a giggle as she offered everyone a marshmallow. Sasha took a fork and held it above the flames in the sitting room, and they all followed suit, dripping melted marshmallow down their chins. Dax brought out a wooden box filled with packs of cards. Everyone but Safi, who retired to bed, huddled on the couches, learning how to play Canaster, gin rummy from Anna, and poker from Pete. The evening ended with leftover's and yet more vodka.

Anna got Pete and the two D's up for a quick breakfast as they gathered in the kitchen to say goodbye to Safi and Sasha. Kolya was nursing his coffee, waiting to take them to the airport. Safi clung to each in turn and tried not to shed a tear but could not help herself. She gave Kolya a knowing look as they huddled in the lift to descend down to the garage. She hoped he had picked up her vibe; the last thing she wanted was for them to be treated like undesirables by Kolya. She meant to have a word with Sasha about his attitude; she had noticed how he had managed to squeeze his considerable bulk into a small corner of the lift as the doors closed on them.

Chapter 19

Monday was a holiday for Anna and Sasha. Without the others and Pete around everything felt a bit flat. Anna suggested dropping Safi off while Sasha went to check on his sister. Safi felt herself stiffen, wondering whether she would broach the subject of Yvetta with her.

Slowly, almost reluctantly, Safi got in the car with Anna. She was nervous about being alone with Anna for an extended amount of time. As the car started up, and the beautiful landscape unfolded around them once again, Safi found herself nattering away about her mom, not knowing why she felt so on edge alone with Anna: they had not spent any time together, perhaps that was why. Thoughts were flying through Safi's mind as she found herself talking ten to the dozen, noticing that she had not given Anna an opportunity to say a word.

'Oh, Anna, I am so sorry, I have no idea why I am so nervous being with you on my own.' She felt it was best to come clean; Anna was not anyone's fool, and must have picked up her vibes by now.

Anna put her hand over Safi's. 'I think you are good for Sasha, he smiles and is happy, yes?' Safi nodded and waited for her to continue.

'Sasha has not mentioned leaving Moscow – that is good for me, you understand? You make me happy, I make you happy.'

Safi nodded again, not sure that something Anna had said wasn't lost in translation. Safi had not looked at Anna with a critical eye. She accepted Anna as Sasha's mum; she supposed she did the same with Fiona her own mother. Anna, she had noted, had an air of authority, but not in appearance. She was of average height in her heels, well rounded and dressed sensibly without fanfare, yet Safi could tell Anna must have been quite a beauty she had elegant features, like Sasha, but her severe short grey hair made her appear much older.

'Um, well,' Safi mumbled, 'I think he is still planning to leave at some stage.'

She looked at Safi then, to Safi's surprise, changed tact completely. 'I think you come to work with me tomorrow, yes.' Safi sat very quietly for a few moments trying to work out what Anna had just suggested.

'You understand?'

'Anna did you mean that I should come into work with you tomorrow?'

'Da, exactly, not tomorrow, today'

'What would I do?'

Anna laughed. 'You see.' Patting Safi's hand, she smiled, pleased with herself.

Safi wondered what Anna had in mind for her. After all, she could not speak the language, and she knew zero about business. She felt a small seed of excitement in the pit of her tummy. She had something to do at last, why should she care what it was. Just getting up each day and being productive would be bloody marvellous.

Anna tooted as they drove into the driveway and one of their servants came out to help with the baggage and left-over containers from Sunday's feast.

Anna told Safi to meet her downstairs at two and to wear something 'like skirt, maybe jacket.' Safi stood in front of her cupboard at a loss, then decided to wear her New York City work wardrobe, thankful that she had kept most of the clothes. Pulling on a black pencil skirt and grey jacket with a light pale grey turtleneck sweater and tan boots, she filled a tan Coach shopper with whatever, and was happy with the result. On second thought, perhaps the turtleneck made the outfit too casual. She decided on a crisp white shirt instead, adding a narrow tan belt, and headed down to meet Anna.

Anna was waiting for Safi at the bottom of the stairs, nodding her approval as Safi reached the bottom step. 'You need warm coat.' Safi grabbed her long puffer coat she had worn to the Dacha and they headed out the door. Back in the car, Anna spent the entire drive talking to people on her hands-free. She smiled at Safi and said, 'They wait for you, all good.' Anna drove into a parking space that was reserved for her; they rode up in a lift from the garage under a building Safi had only got a glimpse of as they entered through a side entrance. She patted Safi on the shoulder. 'You be fine, not worry.'

Safi and Anna were met by an elderly gentleman and a younger one. They had barely introduced Safi before whisking her away with them, sitting her down at a long table with a bank of phones in front of her. Waiting to find out what they had in mind she found herself alone for the first time in ages. Just as she was about to call Sasha, the younger of the two came to collect her; they passed cubicles where everyone seemed to be on phones and computer screens.

The floor above had a more relaxed vibe: people were milling about, some in groups. She could see through glass partitions that reminded her of her father's advertising agency. She felt a stab of sadness, realising she missed work and mental stimulation more than she was prepared to admit. Still, whatever she was going to end up doing here, it had to be better than spending her time with Kolya. After he had displayed his prejudice over the weekend, she didn't much want to spend any time with Kolya at all.

Ringo introduced himself, the name made her laugh, but he assured her it was his name. Everyone thought he looked like the Beatle and the name had stuck. Safi had to agree he did have a large nose, but the closely shaved head did not remind her of Ringo Starr, even if he chose to wear round wire-rimmed glasses, like John Lennon.

She liked Ringo, who had a wicked sense of humour, and hoped she would be working with him. He sat her down at one of the computer terminals and brought up various images that he wanted her to label in English. She gave it a go and found that she only stumbled twice out of a dozen images. Ringo was impressed and started her off right away. She did not have a chance to ask what it was for, but got stuck in, completing dozens of images before Ringo returned to take her to the canteen for a break. They did not allow anyone to work for longer than an hour at a time on the images: it was he told her, bad for the old grey matter, not to mention the eyes.

'Ringo, maybe you can fill me in on what I am doing this for?'

'Ah, I give you three guesses. Go on, try and tell me what you think.'

Safi sipped her tea and stared at him over the rim of her cup. 'Honestly, I haven't a clue.' Laughing, Ringo banged his hand on the table. 'You're not far off. That's very funny.' Safi looked blankly at him. 'How is that funny?'

'Well, we own a TV station and we make programs. This one is for a game show, mostly about food. We have to know the names of food images in English, for the contestants to guess, and that's what you are doing.'

Ringo explained how the show worked, and told her which channel it appeared on and what time.

'But they could find the English words on any of the search engines,' Safi said, 'why do you need me to find words for them?'

'Ah, well, we need to have the words there long before the show goes out, so that the quizmaster can have them in front of him. Then the viewer gets to choose between many different English words to get the right one to win a prize! The Rubicov's own an entertainment channel, it takes a huge amount of work and many people to keep the ideas fresh. We also buy in programs from the UK and the States. For instance, we do our own version of MasterChef. We need to attract sponsors.'

Safi sat in thought, she had no idea that the family owned such a wide range of interests. Sasha had not told her; she wondered why not?

Ringo sat with Safi, showing her how to separate the groups and the colours before naming the products. It all had something to do with making choices, so the host of the show found it easier to access. After a few hours of work, Anna's secretary called down for her. Safi took a lift to the top floor of the building, which opened to a reception desk manned by smartly dressed girls. Safi followed Anna's secretary down a long corridor, where she found Anna on a call to Sasha.

'Ah, she just walked in,' Anna said, switching to English for Safi's benefit, smiling and handing her the phone.

'Well how did it go?' Sasha asked.

Safi tried to catch up with discussions about working for Anna that had obviously preceded her knowledge about the job.

'Nice of you to enlighten me,' she replied.

Sasha laughed. 'No time for that. It was best to throw you in at the deep end.' Perhaps he was right, she thought; she did not want to sound disapproving of them trying to help her, certainly not in Anna's presence, but there was an irritating element all the same. She noticed Anna watching her closely.

'Actually,' Safi said, 'I found the process interesting and would love to visit the show, see how it all works.'

'You will have to talk to Anna about that. I am sure she can arrange it.' Anna was smiling. 'Time to go home, we can speak about the rest on our way.'

Was she being manipulated? She knew she was being paranoid, not to mention neurotic, a hangover from her childhood. Her parents had always organised her life; she had fought hard to be her own person. She was miles from England, yet here she was being organised once again by others. She wanted to forge her own way without others helping her. Russia was making her feel insecure. Anna was on calls during their drive home, which gave Safi time to reflect on her feelings, sort herself out before she saw Sasha or spoke to Anna.

She was being an ungrateful bitch, she thought – she could hardly blame Sasha and his family for her lingering childhood issues. Where was the emotional intelligence she always prided herself on?

The problem was, she realised, she had no one to talk to, no one to sound out her feelings or her doubts. Her diary had been her salvation when she felt confused. Did she honestly still need a comfort blanket? It seemed that way. God, she was still so bloody childish; what did Sasha ever see in her?

Anna turned to Safi, looked at her for a moment. 'Safi, I speak English not so well. You young girl, very young, I think Moscow hard. You must take time, everything be okay, you see.'

She felt grateful for Anna's encouragement, at least. Anna must have a sixth sense, or was Safi totally transparent?

Nodding her agreement, trying to smile, instead she became choked up and tears started to roll down her face. Anna looked startled.

'What's matter, Safi? Sasha make you unhappy?'

Shaking her head, she said, 'No, not Sasha, it's me. I feel sort of lost. Sorry just being stupid.' She drove the car into the drive and turned off the engine.

'We talk in kitchen, come.'

She followed Anna into the kitchen, where they sat at the kitchen table, coffee in hand, with a cheeseboard, homemade bread, delicious chutney, and grapes. Before beginning their conversation, Anna insisted they both eat first.

'My English not good,' Anna said, smiling and pointing to Safi, 'you Russian not good. We manage, yes?'

Safi could not help laughing: here she was in this magnificent house with this amazing female business mogul, living with the debonair, handsome, kind Sasha, what the hell was the matter with her? She definitely needed a kick up the backside, that was for sure. Anna noticed that she had recovered her sense of humour and took advantage. She leaned over and put her hand over Safi's.

'I not your mother. I need daughter like you, kind, sweet, loving. You wait, give time, you see, all be okay. Sasha right, we need not Russian in family, we need beautiful English lady like you, better; too much Russian in family not good.'

Safi felt overwhelmed by Anna's warmth and honesty. Safi felt sure Anna was referring indirectly to Yvetta, but Safi had sworn to Sasha never to mention that episode to Anna. Looking down at her coffee, feeling slightly unworthy of Anna's warmth, all Safi could find to say was, 'Thank you for believing in me.'

She felt so incredibly stupid for doubting this family, she totally did not deserve them. Here she was again being a doubting Thomas, not only about them but about her own abilities to make the most of what she was being given. Safi resolved to man up. After all, being her own person meant taking the opportunities that were so obviously staring her in the face and grabbing them with both hands. It was up to her what she made of the breaks that came her way.

Some English stiff upper lip would not go amiss. Had she outgrown her journaling? Perhaps she ought to start it up again,; her emotions were obviously out of whack and needed sorting out.

Sasha came home to find his mother and Safi in conversation. He decided that it had been a good move on his part suggesting his mother take Safi with her to work. Anna had agreed readily with Sasha that it was not in fact a good idea for Safi to work with Yvetta. He also wanted his mother and Safi to bond. She could do with a daughter like Safi. It had been far too long that he alone had the task of being the good child, it put untold pressure on him to please his mother.

After realising Safi was just about holding her head above water in her new alien environment, Sasha had engineered a visit under false pretences from the two D's and Pete, hoping it would end as an opportunity for Dax to exhibit his work. After listening to Sasha's idea about Dax's work, Yvetta had informed Sasha that only if Dax's agent was involved would she give him a show. DuPont had thought it a wonderful opportunity for Dax to have a one-man show in Moscow. They set a date for the following year. Their meeting had gone well until

Dax unwittingly upset Yvetta. Now it was up to DuPont to sort it out. Sasha was sure the professionalism Yvetta was so well known for would override her other issues.

While out on their walk at the Dacha, Daniel and Pete had taken the opportunity to speak with Sasha about their concern for Safi's feelings of alienation and loneliness.

On their return, Sasha found time to corner his mother about Safi not working with Yvetta and the rest had fallen into place. Now here they were, to his delight, getting on just as he had hoped. He felt sure that Safi was going to make an ideal daughter-in-law for Anna, and, if she became involved on some level with one of their companies, that would be ideal, too. He would not have to leave Moscow just yet.

Anna suggested that they dine together and got busy putting some supper together. Safi was relieved Sasha had not made any arrangements for them to dine out, or meet up with his friends. She knew he was doing it to keep her stimulated, but she much preferred a cosy family setting. To her surprise, being at home with Sasha's family was what she needed to feel she belonged in some way.

The evening had a transforming effect as they all worked together to prepare the meal. Sasha opened a bottle of white wine to complement Anna's homemade gnocchi, scallops, and salad, and they finished with Safi's platter of fresh fruit. Time passed with light conversation, and laughter at Safi's description of Ringo Starr. She had to admit she had had a fun-filled day and loved having a job, any job.

'I hope this is not forward of me, since I only started yesterday, but would it be possible to see a show at the TV studio? I have never had the opportunity to watch a show being produced with a live studio audience.'

Anna nodded. 'Not a problem. I get "Ringo Starr" take you when show go out.'

Safi was up and dressed early for work the next morning, waiting downstairs in the kitchen for Anna, so they could have a coffee together before they left for work. Anna gladly accepted the coffee handed to her by Safi, showing no surprise to see her ready for the day.

Kolya entered the kitchen to let them know he was ready to drive them, his job now changed since he was no longer needed to ferry Safi about. After a lengthy conversation with Kolya, Anna explained that he would be dropping her off at another location for a meeting, and then would take Safi on to work.

Sitting in the front seat with Kolya, relieved he was no longer her only contact with the outside world, she joked that he was now free of ferrying her around town. 'I enjoy, not problem. Speaking English good practice.'

She wondered whether it was worth mentioning his attitude. She had felt slightly less comfortable in his company since he had showed his homophobic side so blatantly, not to mention his racist behaviour towards Pete.

Pete had taken it well. She sadly recalled how he had experienced racism with Sasha's family at their engagement. He had heard some Russians were still very suspicious of foreigners, especially those with ethnic backgrounds.

Sitting deep in thought, she became aware of Kolya speaking to her. 'American family, yes?'

'Daniel is my cousin, and Dax is his partner and soon-to-be husband.' Watching his reaction she waited for a response, but Kolya was the epitome of discretion; not a flicker passed his expression. 'Pete is like family to all of us, he is the kindest, most dependable person one could wish to meet.'

Kolya sat in silence until they reached the building, when he jumped out to open the door for Safi.

'Man like man, I not like. I think about American family, they love you very much.'

Safi smiled. 'The world is different now, Kolya, lots of lifestyles are more acceptable.'

'Da,' Kolya said, shaking his head.' I old-fashioned, sorry.'

Ringo met her at the entrance, looking very pleased with himself.

'Come we have a new job, no more fruit.' She followed him to the lift, noticing that he had a clipboard in his hand with Russian writing on it. The Cyrillic alphabet was something she still had not fathomed out although it was everywhere it, just looked so different to anything she was used to.

They got off on a lower floor and headed towards the reception, where Ringo handed the clipboard over the counter to an efficient-looking blonde, who scanned it, made some calls on her headphone and printed out two identity tags for them to wear. She gave Ringo what sounded like very precise instructions in a clipped and none-too-friendly voice.

He led her to a seating area with their identity tags hanging from their necks. She waited for Ringo to explain, but before he could, they were met by a harassed-looking girl, who spoke perfect American English.

'I will take you up to the production floor. Someone else will guide you around the studio. Then you can watch the show.'

They walked down a long corridor with red lights on above each door and a sign in Russian which she guessed meant no entry. The girl (who had not bothered to introduce herself) guided them into what looked like a small reception room, where they could help themselves to refreshments.

Coffee in hand, Ringo and Safi made themselves comfortable on some swing chairs. They watched some show that was on the huge TV monitor on the wall.

Ringo seemed to know the show and started explaining who the celebrities were on the panel. After some minutes, Safi found that she was beginning to get a handle on the show, but had no idea what anyone was saying. All she had to go on were the guests' expressions. Ringo found the remote and changed the channel, showing Safi that the screen split into individual shows, allowing them to watch each show as it was being filmed. It was a lifestyle channel like they had in most countries, many of the shows were the same only in Russian. There was Project Runway and America's Top Model, only hosted by Russian models. Some of the shows were game shows, but most were spin-offs of popular shows she had seen in the States and back home.

Another clipboard came to collect them, this time introducing herself as Irina. She showed them how the production team worked, so that the show ran smoothly.

Giant pieces of fruit were on the stage, each had a chair built into one side where the contestant sat: one side vegetables, the other fruit. The stage had a fully equipped kitchen with a workbench. Irina explained that the contestants who sat on the chairs represented competing teams. The chefs would prepare dishes with either fruit or vegetables, and the teams had to guess what the dishes contained. The items of fruit or vegetables would pop up on a screen for the contestant to choose from. The audience participation was to give the contestants a clue by holding up placards for a right or wrong answer. The contestant who won would be invited to join the chef in the kitchen as an assistant for the next dish. The losing team would have to guess as many of the ingredients in the next dish as they could. This resulted in a winning team, who would be invited to dine at the chef's table to enjoy the spoils of the day's cooking.

Safi and Ringo thought it a mad game but were looking forward to watching from the audience.

The show started with the celebrity chefs in their opposing apron colours running onto the stage to welcome the contestants to guess their dishes. There were two hosts, one in the kitchen with the chefs and the other to direct the contestants. The chefs would show the audience their fruit or vegetable, while the contestants remained ignorant. The audience would watch the chefs prepare their dishes. The hosts would speak to both chef and audience while the dishes were being made. The contestants would be teased by images of cakes, pies, quiches, stuffed vegetables, and an array of deserts and meals. Once the meal or cake had been prepared, one previously made would be taken out for the contestants to guess. The fruits and vegetables would pop up on a screen and the winning contestant would accumulate points. A clue would pop up intermittently in English under the food item; if the contestant understood the item in English, they would receive extra points for guessing the item in a foreign language.

The audience were animated and completely participatory. Safi found herself enjoying the game along with the audience; even though she could not understand what was being said. it was so visual it was easy for her to follow.

The contestant was shown a cake the items whizzed across the screen with both contestants pressing their buzzers. After numerous tries an English name popped up under a carrot, and one of the contestants immediately pressed the buzzer and was awarded five points. The game continued when a pineapple popped up on the screen. The other contestant buzzed; each now had five points.

The cake was obviously a carrot and pineapple cake. The chef would make another dish and the whole game would be repeated once the dish had been prepared.

It was a mad show but the two hours went by in no time. Ringo had taken a shine to Safi; her unspoilt, friendly manner with no airs and graces was a breath of fresh air, certainly compared to the rich girls he came into contact with. Those girls were either tough, hard-edged business-minded girls, determined to step on anyone who got in their way as they climbed the corporate ladder. Or they were looking for Mr Moneybags. He had met Sasha on occasion and had, of course, heard about his playboy reputation. Ringo could not figure out why someone so young and inexperienced had managed to capture Sasha's attention. Now that he had met Safi, it was not hard to understand; she was beautiful and nice, not an easy combination to find, certainly not in Moscow.

Ringo dated girls, but he fancied boys; in Russia, someone from his background could not afford to give into those leanings. He was Anna's right-hand man, coping with whatever she requested from him. She had chosen him to help out on a project when her English-speaking team needed a dogsbody to help them out. A year in an American school as an exchange student had been his ticket into the corporate world, and now he was happier than he'd ever been in his life.

He understood the family's need to keep her occupied until they found something else for her; he knew his time with her would not be long. Anna had questioned him closely about the different projects he had done with her. She was struggling with a decision about what the right path for Safi would be. Ringo had come up with an idea for Safi that he had not yet been able to voice and was looking for the right moment to suggest it to Anna.

Sasha had found that Safi's spark had returned and he was encouraged by his mother's interest in her wellbeing. Anna put great store in Safi staying in Russia and had impressed on Sasha that it was up to them to help her find what made her feel most settled. Safi had made it clear that she was interested in the production side of the TV programs, and he had taken it up with his mother. They decided to put Ringo in charge of her options, and to find her a runner's job if she was up to doing something that meant being bossed about.

Sasha did not want Safi to be unhappy, but he felt that her being a runner was as demeaning as naming fruit for a game show. He needed to find Safi something that enabled her to hold her head high when she met with friends and family. People were easy to judge, and he did not want them to undermine Safi's abilities. She was good at her job and that was working in an ad Agency, having the opportunity to one day take over her father's. Sasha had thought this through from seemingly every angle.

Alexi had thought it ridiculous to expect Safi to do all these stupid demeaning jobs, she was young yes, but she was now part of their family, and he would speak to Anna and to Valentina, too. Between them, he felt, they could come up with something that could benefit everybody, especially Safi.

Alexi had a point, Sasha thought. Anna meant well, but Sasha realised his mother thought it was part of life to start at the bottom if one wanted to succeed, especially when young with opportunities at hand. But this was an older philosophy from an older generation. Still, Sasha saw her point and understood it from a grounded and generational viewpoint. Safi was different, he felt, she deserved more. He thought that his father and Valentina were right to feel that she could not be expected to start working from the ground up, especially when he and his family had connections. He had yanked her out of New York and dropped her into an alien environment. It was up to him to find Safi something of value to stimulate her – but what?

Safi wasn't worried about appearances, but she also did not understand Russian pride about losing face or snobbishness about one's position in society.

He would discuss the dilemma with his mother and hoped she would see it his way. Safi just could not go on doing such menial jobs, they had to put their heads together to find her something more in keeping with her station in life; after all, she was his fiancé. He knew his family and friends would not take Safi seriously for accepting any job handed to her; she was, after all, now part of one of the richest Russian families, according to Forbes magazine, anyhow.

Safi had been at a loss after her contact through Polly with Vogue had not worked out. Soon after arriving in Moscow, she had called to acquaint herself with the editor of Russian Vogue, only to learn he had suffered a breakdown and had returned to New York.

Finding this avenue now closed to her, they decided it might be wise to acclimatise Safi to Moscow, waiting for the weather to change to warmer climes before rushing about to find an ad agency.

Sasha was desperate to see her settled and happy. He did not want to lose her through lack of compassion, or for their relationship to dissolve into a battle about her unhappiness. Moving to the States was not yet on the cards; he had to remain in Moscow for several more years. Safi had become distant in bed, too; no longer the teasing sex kitten she had not so long ago loved to be, always happy to take the lead in their sex games and try something new. Indeed, at first and for a long time afterwards, she had satisfied him more than he thought possible, especially considering the freedom he enjoyed in the single world before meeting her.

Hearing Sasha out, Anna sat for some time staring out of her window. Should they create a position for Safi, or should they use their contacts to find her a position in one of the ad agencies they used. It was not the Russian way to mix family and business; it never worked out as far as she was concerned, and she did not like it. Anna had Safi's welfare at heart; she genuinely cared for the girl. She knew that Yvetta would never change her ways; her irrational behaviour was an illness. God knows Anna had tried everything, regardless of her daughter's abusive behaviour, but Yvetta's illness prevented her from having any meaningful, loving relationship with Anna and she had suffered enough of her abuse. It wasn't just Anna who had suffered over the years: Yvetta's behaviour was heart-breaking for both Alexi and Sasha. Mika lived in St Petersburg and was thus removed from her meltdowns.

Alexi had another daughter now with Valentina: Marina was the sweetest addition to their family, and Anna even accepted her as such. Alexi and his family visited Russia only in the summer months. Even though Anna was on the best of terms with her ex-husband and his wife, occasional glimpses and embraces of Marina would not fill the hole she felt more with each passing day.

Her dream was for Sasha to marry someone she could relate to, and to give her the grandchildren she yearned for. Yvetta had chosen an alternative lifestyle frowned on by most in Russia. Anna worried for Yvetta's safety; she flouted convention though her name protected her. And that flamboyant friend of hers did not help matters. Fritzi loved nothing better than the bohemian, decadent alternative lifestyle; even the way she dressed was asking for trouble were they to find themselves in the wrong neighbourhood. She brushed her thoughts of Yvetta aside and turned to face Sasha.

Ringo knocked on the door with urgent messages; he was Anna's right-hand man and she felt his absence sorely when she asked him to help Safi for a while. She valued his sharp mind and easy manner. He had a way of turning problems into challenges, so perhaps he would be the perfect person to sort out Safi's career dilemma.

Ringo greeted Sasha as he dropped the papers onto Anna's desk. As he was about to leave, Sasha called out to him, 'How was your week with Safi?'

He stood at the door for a moment, and then went back into the room. 'I do not know how you would like me to answer that question. Forgive me, but I understand that you are hoping to find her something of interest to do. If I may be so bold, I have a suggestion.'

Anna immediately encouraged Ringo to go ahead.

'Well, I was wondering whether Safi could work with me, be my right-hand man, so to speak. She could help sort out problems, travel with me to the various offices and cities, and if it's possible, sometimes accompany me to London or the US when Anna hasn't the time to go.'

He was about to apologise, when Anna banged her hand on the desk.

'That is a brilliant idea, what do you think Sasha?'

'Can we find her a suitable title?' Anna looked at Ringo for a suggestion, when Sasha suddenly came up with one. 'Executive administrator.'

Ringo and Anna smiled.

'That is perfect,' Anna said.

'I can now see why my mother depends on you,' Sasha said to Ringo. 'I am impressed with your problem-solving ability. We will have to find a suitable title for you, too, one that appreciates your position here.'

Fully aware of this opportunity, indeed having waited for it for some time now, Ringo said, 'Perhaps Personal Chief Executive for Rubicov Enterprises.'

Anna stared at him for a moment, noticing his discomfort. 'Yes, that's perfect, but perhaps your salary does not reflect that title. We will have to discuss that tomorrow.'

Ringo closed the door behind him and closed his tear-filled eyes. Safi had brought luck into his life, he would never forget that.

'I don't think we should say anything to Safi for now,' Anna said when they were alone again.

Sasha agreed; he wanted Anna to propose the plan to Safi: he knew she would make it sound like a job offer, rather than a position that had been created especially for her.

Safi had a strong work ethic and being independent was important to her. She needed to feel confident in her ability to take this position on.

He left the office to collect Safi from the production studios.

They met in the reception area. As Safi walked towards him, she noticed how the girls at the reception desk were flirting with him. She stayed back to watch, feeling her heart beat ten to the dozen seeing him in a whole new light. She suddenly realised how handsome he was. Running her fingers through her hair, she fiddled in her bag to find some gloss for her lips, then stepped from behind the pillar and walked nonchalantly towards Sasha. Sasha turned to greet her with the most amazing warm smile, hugged her and waved goodbye to the flirting blondes behind the desk. She could tell the girls were taken aback, her heart suddenly flip-flopping the way it did when they first met.

Chatting to Sasha about what she had witnessed at the studios, she noticed he seemed pleased. Rarely was he ever so light-hearted or fun, responding to her chit-chat with hilarious observations.

Her feelings of jealousy evaporated as he dismissed the receptionists' flirting with disdain, laughing at their obvious social-climbing efforts, all because of his family name. He held Safi's hand, brought it to his mouth, and kissed her palm with such passionate feeling that she felt a flutter in the pit of her tummy.

His look told her that he was thankful he had met her, thankful that he had left behind the tiring world of flitting from one girl to the other, never finding any warmth or sincerity in any of them. She took his hand and put it on her heart and let it slide between her thighs. Safi found herself madly excited, and before she knew it, she was convulsing with the most delicious climax. She gasped and giggled. My God, Sasha just needed to touch her at times and she climbed the walls of ecstasy. Now it was his turn to take her hand and put it between his legs, Safi undid his zip, bent over and found him erect, and plunged her mouth around him, enjoying his sounds of pleasure as he gave in to her giving him head. Thank goodness they were stuck in traffic, or else he would probably smash the car.

She felt him stiffen as he released himself into her mouth; never had she enjoyed swallowing as much as she did at that moment. She just totally and absolutely loved this man. The traffic started to speed up and they sat in blissful silence with knowing grins on their faces, shocked but pleased at their impromptu lovemaking, and oblivious of the world around them. It was exhilarating and exciting, Safi was shocked she found their hedonistic behaviour an aphrodisiac, an unexpected insight into desire she never knew she had. Doing it when and where it was so easy to be caught. Danger obviously turned her on. She was starting to feel like herself again; it seemed to be such a long time since she felt so wonderfully naughty, and ready for fun.

'I'm starving. Let's get out of this traffic and go for dinner, just the two of us. What do you think?'

Safi nodded and allowed Sasha to take her wherever he pleased. She was just happy to be with him in this mood, free of tension; the longer it lasted, the happier she would be. Feeling insecure and miserable was a total put-off and she had been behaving that way for long enough. Sasha would have tired of her whining and sulking, and gone right off her. She was feeling lightheaded and madly happy and wanted it to last for ever.

Something had changed, she felt it, and wanted to hold onto her feelings of love and, yes, happiness for as long as it lasted.

They drove into a parking garage and took a lift up to a skyline restaurant in a five-star hotel Sasha knew well. Here they could find a secluded table without a booking. The maître d' chatted to Sasha, while Safi noticed a cocktail crowd overflowing at the bar, many sharing large platters of sushi, now a must-have all over the world. Finding a place at the bar amongst the crowd, Safi sat watching those around her in animated conversation: these were the beautiful people, somehow they had a way of finding each other, not only here, but in every major capital city in the world, and it seemed sushi was the most popular dish everywhere. She was not that partial but understood the craze: it looked stunning and the low calories were obviously a bonus. Sasha had gone to the bathroom, leaving her with a glass of champagne and a bowl of olives she needed to take the taste of her recent sexual flutter away.

On his return, she followed suit and went to check she looked okay. She felt as though she had just got out of his bed. She realised she was being overly self-conscious, but she felt this self-consciousness slowing her down.

Returning to the bar, Sasha was in conversation with what could only be described as a high priestess of style. Or perhaps a high priest, for at first Safi wasn't sure whether it was a very feminine man or a very masculine girl, dressed androgynously. Black skin-tight trousers, thigh-high suede boots and a brocade dark maroon double-breasted smoking jacket plunged low enough to show a sign of breasts with a necktie and a diamante brooch of a spider. Her hair was white and shaved at the back; the rest hanging in a sharp angular bob, long on one side and short on the other.

As Safi approached, she half bowed, perching on the end of the barstool she offered a ring-adorned, long-fingered, delicate handshake, almost flirtatious.

Safi stared up at red lips and startling blue eyes, deciding instantly that she knew at once who this person had to be, the accent was most definitely Americanised English German. Fritzi introduced herself with Germanic charm, managing to draw Safi into her aura completely. She'd never met anyone quite like her: this woman was charismatically fascinating (and not only to Safi but to everyone else as well, it appeared), she carried herself with arrogant confidence. She noticed that Fritzi held a fascination for those around her, aware of holding them all in her aura, they could not take their eyes off her, and she loved it.

A short conversation followed when the waiter called them to their table. Fritzi stood at least a foot taller than Sasha. She brushed a hand over Safi's cheek, then winked at Sasha and walked off, with full knowledge that every eye in the room was following her as she left the bar.

'Wow and wow again,' Safi said, more to herself than to Sasha, 'so that is Yvetta's girlfriend. She is unbelievable.'

Sasha nodded in agreement.

'And does not suffer fools gladly, either. She is the only one who can keep Yvetta under some kind of control. I, for one, am grateful to her, but let's not talk about my sister, please.'

Safi did not want to spoil the evening, or the closeness they were both feeling. Smiling, she picked up the menu. 'It's in English, it must be my lucky day.' They spent the evening in a flirtatious mood, chatting and laughing intermittently about their sexual tryst in the traffic.

Sasha felt in complete agreement with Safi about it being her lucky day, but he did not want to elaborate why he felt it was the beginning of something good for them both. With Safi busy and stimulated at work it could only be good – or, at least, better. right now. Things had been getting too intense, he felt as if he was losing the Safi he loved so much, but today their exciting lovemaking had returned, and hopefully other aspects would improve, too. The Safi he knew and loved, sensual and so very spontaneous to the moment in an uncomplicated fun-loving way, was returning to him. Sasha had never had problems attracting the opposite sex; they loved him at kindergarten and they never stopped. He was someone who was not afraid of their feminine side. Someone who appeared vulnerable but had a firm edge. This is what he was told by Polly, and he hoped she was right, because he wanted nothing more than to have Safi see him that way.

Sasha loved women and he loved their company. Most of all he loved sex and had no qualms about experimenting, as long as his partner was willing. Safi, he knew, was sexually adventurous, but he was holding back. There was so much more he wanted to share and introduce her to, but with her – and perhaps her alone – he had the patience to wait. She had the innocence of youth. It excited his Machiavellian side to have her follow his lead, without the need for control.

She could not hide her curiosity; now that she had seen and met the wildly interesting Fritzi she wanted to know more about her.

'Can we talk about Fritzi? I find her fascinating – like everyone else, it seems. Did you notice every eye in the bar followed her as she walked out?'

Sasha nodded and said, 'Yes, that's our Fritzi. She likes nothing more than shock and awe to make an impression, good or bad.'

'Do you know how they met?' Safi thought better of mentioning Yvetta's name, somehow this anonymity took the sting out of talking about Sasha's sister. In a matter of fact tone Sasha went on to reply to Safi's fascination with Fritzi and his sister, not wanting to rebuff her there were enough family complications about the issue, although the subject was an irritant he'd rather sweep under the carpet for now.

'Here in Moscow. I believe she was on a modelling assignment and walked into Yvetta's gallery.' This time, he did not seem at all displeased to mention Yvetta's name.

'She introduced Yvetta to the Berlin gay scene, the turning point in her coming out. Before meeting Fritzi, I do not think she was leaning that way. But Fritzi pursued and eventually seduced her. That was it for Yvetta; she and Fritzi have been inseparable since. My father had her investigated, of course. He was not happy with Yvetta's choice of partner, to say nothing of the same-sex scene.'

Safi looked down at her hands. 'But your dad seems quite at home with Dan, and even Dax, who have both worked for him.'

'Well, they are not family, and he has become slightly more sophisticated in his opinions. 'I can imagine it must have been really hard for Yvetta?'

'Oh yes, you have no idea. We had monumental upheaval and raging, when both my parents would not accept Fritzi into the family.'

'And they haven't changed their minds?'

'My mother's mind never changed. My mother sees Fritzi as the devil incarnate. Anna has strong feelings about East Germans. The fact that Fritzi is, of course, from the new united Germany, doesn't matter to my mother at all. She won't let political reality interfere in her view of the old Berlin or the united Berlin's decadent lifestyle.

Safi nodded, showing she wanted to hear more.

'My father, on the other hand, realised that Yvetta was much calmer once Fritzi installed herself against everyone's wishes into Yvetta's apartment and life. Valentina had her part to play in helping my father with his prejudices, she after all is from the ballet world where it was not frowned upon at all.'

Safi found the acceptance of alternative lifestyles hard to deal with in Russia. 'But most Russians are not comfortable with gays, I have seen that first-hand with Kolya's attitude to Dan and Dax once he realised, they were gay.'

Sasha agreed. 'It will take time.'

That is one of the reasons Yvetta has turned her irrational toxic behaviour on my mother, because of Anna's disapproving of Fritzi. Yvetta has shown a side that we have never before witnessed: it is so irrational and at times quite frightening, that we had to bar her from the house, unless invited.'

'Oh God, I am sorry, Sasha. I did not want to get onto Yvetta, I know how you hate talking about it, let's change the subject.'

What are you going to do to me when we get home? I hope not go to sleep. I am feeling madly erotic.' Taking Sasha's hand she opened her legs and let him feel her throbbing wetness under the table. She clamped his hand between her legs and picked up his other hand, putting each finger into her mouth and slowly sucking them. Not wanting her mood to change, he called for the bill and they made a quick exit to the car park. But he was too excited by her teasing. Pushing Safi against a wall behind a pillar, he lifted her up against the car. With her legs around him he thrust himself deep inside her.

Gasping, she clung onto him, taking his thrusts as he climaxed. She lay back on the hood of the car as Sasha slid down and kissed her until she yelped with pleasure. They ignored the cars as they roared out of the garage, not caring whether or not they had been seen. Suddenly, Sasha straightened her skirt and removed his keys from his pocket. Leaning over, he said something in Russian, picked up her handbag from the ground and handed it to her, and greeted two men casually getting into their car. He opened the door for Safi to climb into the passenger side. As he closed the door she could tell that he was furiously adjusting his trousers before walking around to the driver's side, where the two men had just got into their car. Once in the car, Safi stared at him as he let out his breath slowly.

'Phew, that was a close call. Those were cops; they would have arrested us had they suspected. It's a crime to make love in public.'

As they backed out of the park, Safi started laughing and could not stop; tears ran down her face before she managed to get her words out. 'God, I am mad for you. I love our illicit lovemaking. I am so hot I could do that all over again.'

Sasha turned to look at her, she could tell he was dumbfounded.

'Am I terrible?'

He took her hand and kissed it. ' Oh, no not terrible; but definitely terribly, incredibly, sexily bad, bad, bad. Just feel what it does to me.' And he moved her hand to his hard-on. 'This is what you do to me, you mad, bad girl. I am going to teach you things that are going to make our lovemaking even more delicious.'

'Mm, please, sir, do tell, I can't wait. Even better, show me,' Safi said. But privately she wondered how on earth their lovemaking could be better than it already was.

'Oh, believe me, I will, sooner than you think.' As they settled into the traffic the phone rang: Sasha's attention was diverted to business and reality crashed back into their lives. Safi felt all the recent stress evaporate from her body, it had been replaced by a sweet feeling of happiness and a release so huge she felt light-headed. All of a sudden, she was utterly and deliciously exhausted. Leaning her head back against the headrest, she closed her eyes and drifted off. Sasha woke her gently as he pulled into the driveway, leaning over to apologise for having to leave her: something had come up at the restaurant that he had to deal with straight away.

She let herself in as he powered the Maserati out of the driveway. The lights were all on in the hallway and she found Anna in the kitchen, she was about to say goodnight when Anna pointed to a chair and held up her hand to indicate that she was just finishing a call and wanted Safi to stay. Feeling unkempt and slightly embarrassed, Safi indicated that she needed the bathroom. She most definitely did not want Anna to suspect what her and Sasha had been up to: she would never again be able to look her in the face. Anna was sipping some wine when she returned. 'Maybe wine?' Anna asked, swishing the red wine around in her Lalique crystal glass.

Safi nodded and sipped her wine. Not trusting her voice to sound at all normal, she waited for Anna to open the conversation. The moment was intimate and embarrassing, and felt unnecessarily elongated. She hoped she looked normal, too, having just reapplied her makeup, washed quickly and brushed her hair. She hoped Anna had not noticed her dishevelled appearance when on her call – but, then again, Anna was the kind of woman who appeared to notice everything, while rarely making her opinions known. But tonight, Anna showed no sign of having noticed – indeed, Anna, too, seemed unusually distracted. She launched into a proposal she wanted Safi to listen to.

Safi sat in stunned silence, wondering whether she was dreaming. After her earlier, erotically-inspired, light-headed euphoria, she may be hallucinating. But no, Anna, glass refilled and sitting attentively forward, was waiting patiently for Safi to respond. When she eventually found her tongue and her mind felt clear, Safi said, 'Anna, I am not sure if I understood correctly.'

'Well, tell me what you heard.'

'That Ringo needs someone to help him and has suggested me.'

'That is right, and I agree. He works all hours, time he became important man and important man need help, what you say?'

'Yes, oh yes, but what would I do?'

'Not worry, Ringo in charge, soon you learn, yes.'

Feeling lightheaded all over again, Safi jumped up and ran round to Anna, hugged her tightly. 'I am so happy, Anna. Suddenly all that sadness I was feeling before has lifted.' She kissed Anna on the cheek. 'Thank you so much for believing in me. I won't let you down.'

Anna stared at Safi. 'I think you wonderful, girl. We lucky to have you here; Sasha lucky man.' Safi smiled and laughed softly. 'Well, he is everything I want, too. I love him.' Anna wiped a tear from her cheek. 'You bring softness to family, this is good thing. Tomorrow is weekend, we speak more. I go to bed.' With that, she picked up her glass of wine and swept out of the kitchen waving Safi goodnight.

She wanted to phone New York, where it was late afternoon, and give the two D's her news, while hearing all of theirs; but she suddenly felt exhausted all over again. Too tired even to focus properly on Anna's news, but feeling an increasingly warm and reassuring buzz of contentment, Safi showered and curled up in bed. She left the night-light on for Sasha, closed her eyes, and felt herself drifting off under the feather duvet, free of her usual apprehension for what the next day would bring, knowing she would at last have something challenging to look forward to in the mornings, instead of her day stretching out ahead of her, endless and impossibly slow, with Sasha's return from work at the end of each day her only reward and salvation. She had been pretty close to sinking into total depression, and as she lay suspended in semi-consciousness between wakefulness and sleep, she could finally acknowledge how close she had been to giving up, that her days in Moscow and with Sasha had been numbered.

Safi woke to find Sasha's side of the bed empty, not sure whether he had slept in the bed or not, finding herself lying halfway across both sides. Both her cell and the bedside clock informed her that it was 6.53 in the morning. She blinked, closed her eyes, examined the time again, as though it would miraculously return to a more normal time, or Sasha would suddenly be lying beside her, safe and warm. No such luck. 6.54 blinked brightly, almost cruelly. She thought about her earlier sense that she was hallucinating; no, she knew now that this was real. Not wanting to panic but a queasy feeling settling in her stomach, she splashed her face, pulled on her sweatshirt and pants and headed downstairs.

There was evidence of leftover breakfast in the kitchen; feeling a little calmer she walked down the passage towards Anna's suite. The door and passage leading into Anna's suite was open. Safi knocked softly. Getting no reply, she walked towards the lounge area, finding the door shut and hearing muffled voices, she leaned in to listen for Sasha's voice.

Anna was definitely angry or upset – Safi could not tell which. God, was it Yvetta again? Safi hoped not. Yes, that was Sasha trying to calm his mother down; then a third voice she did not recognise started speaking, and Safi could tell that it was in anger. There was a thud and Safi jumped; a sound escaped from her throat. Holding her hand over her mouth, she leaned against the wall. What to do, had they heard?

Not knowing whether to stay or leave, she remained where she was, the voices now quiet. It was so silent now. Leaning against the door, she was relieved to hear movement, then footsteps. She scampered as fast as to could to the safety of the passage, not wanting them to think she was eavesdropping. She could tell anger when she heard it, even in Russian.

Making her way to the kitchen, she poured herself a cup of coffee from the machine, bit into an apple but stopped chewing as she heard animated voices heading down the passage, then the front door slamming. She recognised the roar of Sasha's engine as it sped off. She felt panic stricken but frozen in place, wishing that Sasha had taken her with him even as she wondered where he was headed. Feeling dislocated and alone, all the positive feelings from last night suddenly extinguished and replaced only by confusion, she swallowed and stood there for what seemed like ages. But no one appeared to be around. Slowly, summoning up her courage, she headed back down the passage to find Anna. She wanted to know whether everything was all right, had there been a fight, that thud was pretty loud. Safi reminded herself that, for all intents and purposes, she too was part of this family, no matter how complex and confusing this family appeared to be.

This time her knock was greeted with an unfamiliar male voice. On hearing the 'Da' she pushed open the door to find Anna surrounded by several people she did not recognise.

'Oh, sorry, I did not realise that you had visitors. I was just wondering where Sasha had gone.' Safi could see that Anna was trying her best to be normal when she answered. 'Sasha have problem. We have problem but not explain now, not worry.' How different this Anna was to the relaxed and charming and confident Anna of last night, offering Safi a glass of wine and a job, almost at the same time. This Anna seemed broken, brittle, distracted, biting her lower lip as she turned away from Safi. Anna tried to smile encouragingly, but Safi could tell it was for her benefit. One of the men who appeared to be there in a professional capacity, yet friend, turned to speak with her, perhaps he was their lawyer, he resembled one, dressed in a pinstriped suit with little wire rimmed glasses.

'Please do not be concerned. It's best if you return to your quarters for now. Sasha will be back in a while.' He spoke to Safi as if he knew her, but she had never seen him before – of this she was certain.

He spoke perfect English in an American accent. She looked at Anna for confirmation, but Anna was already signing papers and had someone leaning over her, pointing where she should put her signature. Anna seemed impossibly busy, it seemed to pain her to look at Safi right now. Indeed, she seemed to be doing anything but making eye contact with Safi.

Having no choice, Safi returned to her room. She picked up her cell phone, wondering whether it was wise to call Sasha, or to wait for him to return. Something that did not concern her was obviously going on. It was clear, too, that no one – certainly not Anna – wanted Safi to make this her business. Deciding that whatever it was was business and nothing more, she switched on the TV. Her mind was still running wild with scenarios: it was as if all the television studios she had visited that week were running shows concurrently in her brain. The men with Anna did look pretty heavy, especially the one leaning over her as she was about to sign. Sasha had sounded angrier than she had ever heard him.

She tried to put the pieces of his absence together: he had left at about ten last night, and for all she knew had not returned all night. Certainly, his side of the bed had not been slept in. To hell with it, she thought, she would call him anyway – whatever the truth of the situation was, it had to be better than what was playing out so vividly and nonsensically in her head. Suddenly she felt terribly alone. She unlocked her phone with a shaking hand.

A feeling of dread descended over her and images of violence flashed across her mind. Brutal scenes she had seen in movies about Russian mafia, crooked politicians, and ruthless businessmen. 'God, I am being so melodramatic,' she told herself, reflecting on the fact that most of these Russian villains were featured in American movies. As Sasha had once told her, the real Russia was very different from anything one saw in American movies. (He had gone on to say that the real America was different from what you saw in American movies, too.) Sasha's phone went immediately to voicemail. 'It's me,' she told the uncomfortable silence, 'can you call me, where are you?' She tried to keep her voice light, soft, sweet. It was best if he did not know she was aware things were not right.

Hours had now passed, it was now noon and she had heard nothing from Sasha, not even a text had come through. Anna had not called either. She threw on a pair of jeans, lots of layers and a baggy sweater, found her fur-lined boots, and grabbed her warmest fur-lined puffer coat. Reaching the bottom step, she stood for a while deciding whether to tell Anna she was leaving. She was still unsure of whether or not to go. After a moment, steeling herself against the cold and so much else, she decided to take the initiative: it was about time that she did; after all, the house was not exactly in the middle of nowhere, she had been cocooned long enough, it was time for independence of spirit, and she felt claustrophobic being stuck up in that apartment not knowing what was going on and no one respecting her enough to fill her in.

Safi left a note on the kitchen table, stood for a while longer trying to hear something, anything; it was deadly quiet, eerily so; shivering she ran for the door. Pulling her fur hood up as the snowflakes started falling, hurrying along the pavement, snow crunching under her feet, she followed the railings stretching along the houses she recognised from driving past with Kolya. She hoped they led to an area with cafés and shops that she remembered browsing around with Sasha when she first arrived but had never been to on her own.

The distance was much further than she remembered. Doubt was creeping into her mind, she no longer remembered landmarks – everything looked different, or, worse, exactly the same. Perhaps she had walked the wrong way. People were about, at least: they must be heading somewhere. Deciding to continue, she headed towards a set of traffic lights at a crossroads. Fresh snow was falling heavily, the landscape looked very different covered in a blanket of snow the landmarks she usually recognised were now blurred and the streets were no longer as easy to navigate.

Safi stopped at the crossroads to check her cell. No message from Sasha yet, surely, he would contact her soon. Crossing over the street, she noticed people leaving and entering what she hoped was a restaurant or café. The street signs were now completely covered with snow. Safi pushed the door open to find the place buzzing; people were lined alongside a counter ordering coffee. She joined the line, checking her cell for the app for Russian translations; it was easier to show them her cell phone than to struggle to be understood. Finding an empty table, she settled down with a mug of hot chocolate and what resembled a baguette filled with cheese and pickle.

Checking her watch, she realised it was well past lunch; no wonder she was starving. Her mind temporarily taken up with satisfying the hollow pit of her stomach from hunger and shock, she started to relax, her shivering lessened. The snow was piling high against the side of the windows; unlike New York she had not seen any snow ploughs clearing the roads. The café was now busier than when she arrived, the mostly young crowd were filling up the tables around her. No one took much notice of her; some gave her a cursory glance, but no more, guessing she was foreign, she supposed.

Safi stared out of the window: there were fewer people out, all with heads down against the falling snow. White cars were moving slowly past, windscreen wipers splashing white spray off the sides, just traces of colour showing through. She did not know where she was, or what was going on, but she knew for sure that things were not right. She flashed through her last moments in the house. That man leaning over Anna was pretty menacing, and Anna had been so dismissive, as if she had not recognised her. Perhaps Anna had been sending her a message. The men were surprised when she entered after knocking, almost at a loss how to handle the situation. She recalled that Anna had said something to the man leaning over her in Russian, who had told Safi to stay in her quarters. How would he know that she was living there? The more Safi thought about the whole scenario, the more she felt she had made the right decision to get out of the house.

The light outside was fading; how much longer could she sit in this café. She had not heard a word from Sasha, or Anna for that matter. She started going through the call-list on her phone. She lifted her head as someone pushed the door open. At first it did not register, everyone wore hats, hoods, and glasses to protect themselves from the falling snow, but this person was clearly looking for someone, oh my God it was Sasha.

Their eyes locked as Safi shut down her cell. Overcome with relief, she watched as Sasha made his way over. He grabbed her in his arms and held her tightly.

'Let's get out of here, come.' Suddenly, Safi started to shake, tears rolling down her cheeks, she buried her face on his shoulder. She was sobbing now, immobilised, her whole body wracked with relief at seeing him. Sasha put her hat on, lifted her out of the seat to fasten her coat, then led her towards the door.

Kolya jumped out of the car to help them into the back. The car obviously had snow chains on, as he joined the traffic it seemed to gain speed once past the traffic lights. Noticing suitcases in the back she looked at Sasha questioningly. Squeezing her hand, he made it clear that explanations would come later, not now. Safi was not sure whether it was appropriate under the circumstances, after all she had seen and felt, not to get any explanation. Still, she decided to keep quiet, at least for the moment, not sure how she would deal with anything more dreadful than her already out-of-control imagination.

The snowfall had stopped and the major roads had been cleared. They were heading out of the city, that much she could tell. The car was warm, shaking out of their coats and gloves, they relaxed into the seats. Sasha held her hand tightly, kissing the back from time to time. She felt exhausted now that her fear had abated. She felt limp and loose and wrung-out, as though there was nothing left inside her. Closing her eyes, she drifted off, not caring where they were heading. Sasha was safe, that was all that mattered right now.

She woke to find the car dark and stationery, and the noise of Kolya removing the luggage from the back. Safi sat up with a start, looking around for Sasha with wild eyes. She felt the tenseness in the back of her neck relax when she saw him standing just outside on his cell. Noticing that she was awake, he ended the call and came over to help her out of the car. 'You slept all the way. I did not want to wake you, but we have arrived at the Dacha. I will explain everything when we have settled.'

The Dacha had been made ready for their arrival, and they were greeted with fresh flowers, a very Russian thing that Safi had come to love. A fabulous fire was roaring in the grate. The kitchen counter had an array of comforting food. Safi noticed a whole honey-glazed ham, a basket full of different breads and another with fruit. A cheese board had been laid out too.

'Is your mom here, too?' Safi asked.

'No, she has quite a bit to sort out.'

'All this food for only two of us. I am ravenous.'

Sasha laughed, and he seemed more relaxed all of a sudden, and she felt a surge of reassurance, as though everything would be back to normal very soon. 'How about some cheese and bread to start with, and then we can tuck into the rest this evening.'

'Great, a really hot cup of tea?'

'Coming up, your ladyship.'

She watched Sasha make her tea and set out the bread and cheese as she settled at one of the bar stools at the kitchen counter. She could tell that Sasha was making light of his mood, delaying having to explain what had taken place earlier that day. Safi thought again of Anna, looking almost frail, even helpless, with those men looming over her. Anna had always seemed strong; she was shocked to see her so vulnerable and disorientated. It was as though everything, in that moment, had been turned upside down. No wonder Safi, knowing nothing but sensing something awry, had run.

Kolya entered with two musclebound men. A woman had entered and stood waiting for Sasha. He excused himself, and she could hear him talking in a serious voice, giving what sounded like instructions. Returning, he smiled apologetically. 'They are staying until we leave.'

'But who are they?'

'A security precaution. I am afraid that after last night we are taking no chances, either here or at the house in Moscow.'

She stared at him, then back at the security precaution. They carried guns in holsters under their arms. Who knew what other ammunition they had?

He turned Safi to face him, but he too looked different now. His face wore a strained expression, his usually full lips were now a thin line, his brows were creased, and he had an intense almost aggressive expression in his eyes, she supposed it was anger. She touched his arm, wanting to touch the suddenly changed face but thinking better of it., afraid all over again, she said, 'Sasha, I need to know what's going on.'

'When I left after dropping you off last night, you do remember the call that came in just as we arrived home?' He was talking too fast, but his tone soon slowed, became even, his face softening somewhat. She nodded, not wanting to interrupt. That call was from the police. Men had made a booking at the restaurant after playing poker all night at one of our clubs. Theirs was the last booking of the night. After the meal, they questioned the bill, but in an unusually aggressive manner. Then one of the men asked to see the maître d'. My cousin alerted our security, who were manning the exit doors. By this point, the men had ordered our staff to line up at the front of the bar, and threatened to shoot them one by one if the business did not hand over protection money.

'Protection money?'

'Yes, this can and does happen in Russia, but our family have had an agreement for many years with certain people, and this has never happened before, not like this. Business of this kind is done quietly behind closed doors.'

'My God, what happened?'

'We did not know these men. They were not from Moscow. My cousin realised that he had to find out who they were working for. At this stage our security became involved. Some names were mentioned and it became obvious that they were unfamiliar with our protection contacts, police who we pay handsomely, to avoid this kind of thing from happening.

'Threats were made, guns were drawn; unfortunately, there were deaths on the side, of these extortionists. Our police contacts were called. It took all night, but there was a more serious element to this; while we were busy at the restaurant, men had turned up at our home. Someone had given them the entrance code and my mother was confronted by young men she did not know.

'They did not touch her, thank God, but they tied her to a chair and, left a message and, damaged priceless objects on the way out, to let us know that what had just happened was serious. And it was – these people were not playing games, they meant business, this might be a warning coming from elements in either the government or the police, we do not yet know, it's all an unknown development, at the moment. We will find out more soon, Mika will as always get to the bottom of this, he will send his bloodhounds in undercover. This is Russia, so we have to find out who is behind this before it escalates and becomes serious, not only to the business but also to our own safety.'

Safi stared at Sasha with disbelief; it sounded more like a movie than reality. 'I know, you were in the house, but they were not interested in anything besides threatening us. Giving us a strong warning. The strange thing is there was nothing stolen. They wanted us to know we were vulnerable, that they could hurt us if they wanted, which is even more worrying, we need to find out what they want?

'The police were in the house when you interrupted my mother in her sitting room earlier today.'

'What about your mother? Is she staying in the house? And what about us?'

Sasha wanted to assure her that their next move would be less invasive, but who was he to make such assurances? Yes, Safi was obviously afraid, but a part of him was afraid as well. He was still visibly shaken and he knew it. This was obviously a message sent to warn them, the next move would be the one they had to be ready for, it could be either political or someone would be arrested for angering – who, exactly, they did not as yet know, either in the police department, in which case Mika would be able to unruffle feathers, but they would not cause wanton destruction to precious Russian relics, so they have been counted out of the equation.

Was it political or gang-related, this they would know soon enough, Mika would make sure of that he still had powerful friends in both the police and government agencies. .And not knowing was, of course, the worst punishment of all. The family was now in limbo, and would remain so until it became clear what exactly their unknown enemies had in mind. All would become clear with time, Sasha knew, but that was exactly what scared him – how long would this go on for, this uncertainty, this doubt, this fear, his mother was attacked even if not hurt, she was a target, why?

'Anna was convinced she knew what this was. She was positive she had recognised one of the boys, the ring leader, orchestrating everything. But we have to wait until we know for sure before we can do anything. My father's name was mentioned – this has convinced us that it may still be political. One of the messages told to my mother warned my father and his family not to return to Russia, if he wanted us to remain alive.'

Sasha's attempts to placate Safi had had the opposite effect. She was more alarmed than ever. Her mind started spinning. Did she want to be involved in this? Was she already involved? Maybe she should leave Russia. Did she want to leave Russia? Leaving Russia meant leaving Sasha, leaving Sasha meant leaving everything she had come to love. The conversation in her head went around in a circle and she felt suddenly dizzy. Her thoughts were speeding ahead like a race car. Racecar, a palindrome, a puzzle, the same word backwards and forwards, around and around. Well, now she really had to sit down, she felt positively ill.

Sasha could tell she was struggling to be calm. He did not blame her for being scared. Safi needed to trust him, she had to make up her mind whether she could remain with him. Ultimately, it was not for him to convince her either way – it was for her to convince herself, through a conversation with her heart and her head. If her life was with him, she needed to come to terms with what could happen, it was unavoidable. Extortion, kidnapping and even murder were the weights attached to a solid-gold life, to extreme wealth and influence. He prayed that she loved him enough not to run.

'But why would they threaten Valentina?' Safi asked. 'Or, for that matter, Marina? They have not done a thing?'

Sasha looked frustrated; she could see that he was finding the whole affair far from easy to fathom himself, some of it did not make any sense it was much too personal. For some reason that she could not explain, she had a flashback to her last visit to Brighton, to that walk along the beachfront with her mother, to the welcome warmth of the sun and her mother's smile. She seemed a very long way away from home all of a sudden, and in a very distant place.

She longed to hear her mother's voice, but she knew that if she spoke to Fiona now, she would tell her everything, and that her mother would be scared for her daughter's life, and that it would be very quickly and strongly suggested that Safi return home. Was that what Safi wanted? Perhaps. But she wanted to be with Sasha too. She wanted to feel safe and loved, she was, and yet she wasn't ? Now it's a waiting game, Mika I am sure will uncover who we are dealing with there is not much we can do at this stage, apart from wait until more information comes to light.'

'What about the men your security killed? Surely that will mean these people may retaliate.'

'I know this is hard to take in: here in Russia security are police; they carry guns and use them if the need arises. In this case the need did arise, to protect innocent people. That aside, the people who sent them will see them as collateral damage, they were more than likely hired help from some mercenary underground armed group, that way a finger cannot be pointed at the culprits.

'How long do these things take before we can feel safe?'

Sasha felt his heart soar. Safi, he realised, was prepared to hang in with his family, she was not bailing out. He looked at Safi for a long time without giving his feelings away – a peculiarly Russian form of inscrutability. It touched him unexpectedly that she had used the word 'we': it may have been her showing a form of loyalty to his family.

Safi held Sasha's gaze without flinching. She wanted him to understand her loyalty and that Brits did not let down those they held dear; on the contrary, they supported them through thick and thin, unless it was no longer possible to do so. Loyalty and support were part of her stiff-upper-lip upbringing, her parents had always stood by their family and friends through sticky patches, and that was what Safi wanted to do.

Running for cover seemed cowardly, even though she felt spooked beyond belief.

Before Sasha could answer a security staff member appeared. Sasha excused himself, Safi could hear them talking softly, she wished she could understand even a small amount. She heard Sasha on the phone with someone; she could not see his expression but she could tell from his tone that something was afoot.

She decided that doubt and fear were futile until she had a more solid understanding of what was going on. There was nothing to do but trust Sasha and his security detail to keep them safe. Feeling exhausted from the stress, she moved to the lounge where a fire was roaring in the grate. She lay back in one of the huge armchairs and tried to relax. Her thoughts were all over the place. Should she tell her parents what was going on? Definitely not, they would be besides themselves with worry and fear for her safety.

When Sasha returned, she looked up expectantly, trying to read his expression, but he was barely looking at her now. It was as if she wasn't in the room. He sat down heavily opposite in a twin armchair facing the flames. She watched his expression closely; all she could see was frustration – or was it exhaustion? Either way, she felt she could relate with his feelings. But right now, it felt like he did not want to connect on any level, that he was cutting her – and everyone – off. She hadn't seen him this way before.

He threw his head back, resting it on the back of the chair. His lean, muscular legs stretched out in front of him, Safi pushed the Ottoman towards him, stood to lift his legs, but Sasha caught her and lifted her off her feet onto his lap, holding her close and surprising her with sudden intimacy, an aloofness turned to unexpected warmth. She felt relief and childish pleasure as she nuzzled her face into his neck and they stayed that way for a while.

She could hear his shallow breathing become calmer; lying in his arms she marvelled at how safe she felt. It was hard to imagine that, in reality, none of them were at all safe, until whatever had occurred was resolved.

She lifted her head to look at Sasha. He was breathing softly now, asleep. Smiling, Safi lifted herself gently. She covered him and left him to doze. She fell back into her armchair where she could observe him from a distance. She examined his face, as peaceful as a child's, the taut, muscular jaw, curly black hair and the fine line between his brows, were quite Slavic, his face was a masculine version, of those Russian supermodels, elegantly handsome.

Being at a distance gave her space to ponder and gather her emotions. She wanted to show a united front with his family: it was the least she could do under the circumstances; she could only imagine how much they were suffering. Anna, such a strong woman, looked defeated with those burly policemen leaning over her. How frightening it must be to be confronted by aggressive, threatening strangers in one's own home. One would think that money could buy security, but having money invited all sorts of problems of its own, she could see that now. Safi shivered, realising that she had been fast asleep while the whole thing happened. It was a shocking thought.

Looking up, Safi noticed Sasha had been watching her. She smiled weakly, wondering whether he would be able to tell how nervous she really was.

He sat forward. 'God, I feel much better. How long did I sleep for?'

'Forty minutes, at least.'

'Good, my brother is on his way. He will arrive well after midnight. I will wait up for him. We have much to decide and I'm hoping Mika has some news that will throw some light on this mess" Not feeling great about having to turn in on her own, but not wanting to further burden him with this information and reveal the extent of her insecurity, she put a brave face on it. 'Okay, but promise you will wake me if something comes up.'

The house had been searched from top to bottom, Sasha had the security search the premises once more before Safi turned in, reluctantly leaving, she hugged Sasha, trying to reassure him that she was fine as long as he was around.

Chapter 20

Sasha met with his security, briefing them about Mika's late arrival. The female security guard was to remain in the house, while the men remained out doors to keep watch for any unusual activity. Sasha sat at the dining table with three cell phones and his computer. He contacted his mother for an update. Anna had moved to one of the Rubicov apartments with security in place. The insurance assessors were investigating the damage to her apartment at their home, while police were taking samples from the break-in.

Anna would remain at the Rubicov apartment until a completely new security system was installed with outdoor cameras and indoor security screens to monitor anyone on the premises. Sasha now insisted his mother have electric gates installed. In the past she no longer felt it necessary, but now he took the opportunity to mention it once more. He was saddened by the turn of events after having lived on the premises for over twenty years. None of their properties had ever been compromised before, and now she readily agreed to whatever needed to be done to keep them safe.

Anna picked up on the first ring early the following morning, hoping for an update from Sasha. She had not slept since her home had been invaded. Apart from dealing with some immediate practicalities, they had not had a chance to go over events. Anna had some worrying thoughts she wanted to share. The more she thought, the less sense she was able to make of the break-in. Before she mentioned anything to Alexi, they had to have more proof, of the alarming consequences it brought with such a painful realisation. The repercussion for the family would be too devastating to contemplate. She prayed she was wrong but nothing else made sense, even by Russian standards. There were many factions all working for different masters, that was todays Russia, one needed to be alert at all times, but they had many sources and none had any inkling that anything was afoot.

The extended family rallied round She had a mammoth task persuading them that she would be okay at the Rubicov family apartment, the last thing she needed was to be fussed over. She listened to Sasha's news about Mika's arrival and insisted on seeing him at the Dacha rather than discussing anything he had to say on the phone, but time was of the essence and Mika wanted to get to the bottom of certain inconsistencies before they told Alexi their suspicions. She found the news of her eldest son's arrival in Moscow a sign of how serious the situation was. Mika usually had his men in the field iron things out, He was the lone wolf in their family. The only one to live in St Petersburg, and the only one who operated under a cloak of secrecy, the family respected and depended on Mika, for their safety.

Mika understood rumour from fact and supplied it when it was needed. He had studied law at Oxford, but unlike Sasha and Yvetta he had only spent a few years away. On his return he had joined the family business and moved to St Petersburg. No one asked what Mika did for the businesses; they understood Alexi valued his input more than any other member of the family. Mika had his ear to the ground.

They discussed what Sasha found on arriving at the restaurant, after the call from the police. The bodies had been removed and thankfully none of his staff had been injured. Their own security detail had been carted off to the police for questioning. Mika had arranged for lawyers to secure their release without charge. According to Mika, the police felt that the damage at their home was unconnected with the disturbance at the Rubicov restaurant. More surprisingly, the chief of police believed the threats to be a ruse to throw everyone off their scent. After all, the Rubicov name was well-known, and criminal threats dogged the oligarchs, especially in Moscow.

How they had so quickly come to such a conclusion was obviously to divert suspicion away from any police involvement, they wanted as little to do with it as possible. Believing the break-in at their private residence on the same night was not connected suited Mika, who went along, insisting the police findings were correct; he did not want the two to be interlinked. The less he had to deal with the police the better.

Alexi, had been informed of both incidents and had accepted Mika's council. Mika faxed Alexi documents in the middle of the night. As details of both break-ins came in from his men, Mika had related the extent of the damage at their home on a conference call to Anna and Alexi. Anna was almost too scared to voice her thoughts, less they became a reality. She calmly replayed the scenes in her mind. Something did not quite compute; the longer she went over the scenario, the more she believed her judgment correct.

They had run through the break–in at the house and what had been damaged and destroyed. Priceless Russian antiquities had been smashed, Russian masters had been damaged, the canvasses had been slashed with knives. Glass cabinets had been broken damaging smaller collections housed inside. The intruders must have known the entrance code, surprising Anna in her bedroom. They had sent two women in to detain Anna in her suite, while the men dressed in black with balaclavas went about damaging artworks. They departed without fuss once their job had been accomplished. The two intruders bound and gagged Anna, while they went about damaging the art, they deemed valuable in her suite of rooms. Anna remained bewildered by their actions: besides a note left on her antique desk, no threats had been made. And what did the note say? It was a poem she did not recognise. An educated guess had found that the poem might be by a German philosopher. Even more bewildering, but they needed an expert in old German to translate it for them, maybe Goethe but no one had found the time to verify anything yet.

Sasha had returned to find the damage and his mother bound and gagged. He was relieved to find her unhurt, apart from shock. They left the rest for Mika to deal with, while Sasha went to check on Safi, relieved to find her safe and asleep.

Alone at the apartment she had moved to in the Rubicov building, getting her bearings once more having breathing space to make her own deductions of the horrific event. Anna recovered her equilibrium. She now began to wonder who and why someone had done this awful thing to her and Alexi. Why would anyone in their right mind do such wanton damage without stealing anything? It was almost like watching a performance. What was it all about? A performance, she thought, as if this was in itself a clue. The idea nagged at her, the way a young child nags at its mother. A child, she thought. A performance.

The police and the insurance people were intrigued; never before had they visited the site of a break-in with nothing stolen, and so much pointless damage done. Priceless crystal and Fabergé eggs tossed out of display cabinets like toys out of a pram. It was sacrilege. They noticed how angry the art expert had been, thumping his fist at the senseless destruction of such valuable, precious Russian objects and art.

The mystery of the whole ugly episode was so intriguing, she had lost hours of sleep going over it in her mind. What did the German poem mean? Why the wanton destruction of precious art works and antiquities? It was revenge done by someone with a score to settle – or was it more than that? She feared it was. Perhaps Mika's men had come to the same conclusion.

'I must be present with you and Mika before you speak with Alexi on a conference call,' she told Sasha. 'I do believe we might yet come to the same awful conclusion.'

'May I ask what that might be?'

'Let's hear what Mika has to say before I voice to my fears.' Anna rang off. Shivering, she realised how wretched, abused, and alone she felt. Was there nothing in this whole world to fix what was obviously so very broken? It was almost dawn; she would be ready when Kolya arrived to drive her to the Dacha. But could they wait Alexi needed to know if their findings about the break-in was found to be correct.

Mika's men had not taken long to deal with the trouble at the club and restaurant. Gambling debts often wreaked havoc, especially with punters who thought they had a special relationship with the owner, socially or politically. In this instance, the police were correct about the two break-ins being unconnected: the threats made against the staff and his father were more than likely from a disgruntled gambling syndicate.

Mika had no concerns about dealing with an unruly element or thugs, be they political or gang-related. He would have the Rubicov business cleaned up before the police had a chance to distort or turn anything to their advantage, gaining leverage in their affairs with underhanded financial bribes. He needed to get the problem solved and closed down quickly.

His people were trained to deal with difficult situations, and negotiations were preferred, but if needed they were not averse to using strong-arm persuasion. Negotiations had already moved forward, in this case to bring the unfortunate misunderstanding to a conclusion. Neither side wanting the police to become involved, they understood each other's needs and, therefore, were unusually receptive to a quick negotiation and settlement.

The break-in at the house was a more delicate and complicated issue; it would take enormous will and determination from all of them to deal with. The insurance assessors would not fall for anything less than a complete investigation and, they needed to be ahead of events before they knew what was to come.

Mika had flown to Moscow to smooth out some final details about the Rubicov situation and to make sure his mother was well, after the break-in, he had much to do, before arriving at the Dacha to iron out and discuss all scenarios in the event of unknown surprises, with Alexi.

He had been saddened and shocked at the leads his men had uncovered about the break-in at the house, they had tracked down art students, who were only too happy to spill all when threatened with violence. There was no longer any doubt who was responsible. The leads had uncovered a devastating reality, now he had to brief Sasha, and together they would have to break the news to their parents.

At forty-two, Mika was the eldest of his siblings. Sasha was thirty-six, the middle child and loved by everyone. Despite being educated overseas, Sasha had a Russian soul. Family came first. One could take a man away from his roots but never out of his soul, that was Sasha through and through. His education was foreign but his heart was Russian.

Sasha met Mika as he entered with the security men. They hugged briefly; no pleasantries were exchanged on this occasion. Mika helped himself to coffee, it was going to be a long, stressful night.

Sasha led the way to where he had set himself up: the dining room table cleared apart from his papers, phones, and computers. The usual view from the long expanse of floor-to-ceiling windows were now black. Only the security lights were on, illuminating the ice floating down the lake eerily.

Mika stood in front of the windows, sipping his coffee, watching the black floating ice as it travelled across a forbidding, inky lake. Turning slowly he spoke softly, 'Sasha we have a problem that cannot be swept under the carpet any longer. A problem we have all ignored for far too long. It pains me to say this, but Yvetta and her cohort and conspirator, Fritzi are behind this horrific attack on our mother and wanton destruction at our family home.'

Sasha stared at Mika in disbelief, momentarily lost for words. 'No, that's not possible. How on earth have you come to that conclusion, you must be mistaken. Why would she do such a terrible thing, and to her own family?'

Mika understood Sasha's reaction; he had always protected her, tried to understand her actions in the past, even covered for her on occasion.

Yvetta had become more abusive to her family over the years. Alexi had indulged her entitled behaviour; in his eyes she could never do wrong: she was his champion, successful in her own right. The money they poured into the art collection she had built up over the years had brought in a comfortable profit and, more importantly, prestige. Profit and prestige were the bottom line by which their father judged success, but when Fritzi came into Yvetta's life, his attitude slowly began to change. Yvetta's and her mother had never had a close relationship; Anna tried but Yvetta spurned her at every turn.

Both of Yvetta's parents had immediately disapproved of her lover, and this manifested a smouldering hatred in Yvetta (although Anna suspected that this hatred for them had long been present before Fritzi's arrival in their lives; Fritzi had just been a much-needed outlet and perhaps excuse, a justification for unjustifiable rage). No amount of discussion or argument made the slightest difference to Yvetta's constant, abusive, toxic behaviour towards her family. Her reality became unrealistic: the more the family tried to shower her with love, the more Yvetta pushed them away. In the end most left her to her own devices, hoping that with time she would change her attitudes; instead those attitudes had become more entrenched.

'Yvetta viewed her family as the enemy to be expunged from her life,' Mika told Sasha, 'In her eyes, they judged her and, had abandoned her and now her lover, too.'

Sasha sat in shock. How were they going to break this news to Anna? She would be heartbroken. Indeed, the whole affair was heart-breaking and hard to understand. Yvetta had everything any girl could ever want or need in life: love, opportunity, kindness. Why had she turned into this unlovable, angry person? It was beyond comprehension. They all came from the same environment, had the same loving parents, and yet here was Yvetta behaving so unlike Mika and himself. Both sons adored their parents and were empowered by their love and guidance; how could she feel differently? It had to be some kind of illness, there was no other explanation for it.

Anna woke to the TV blaring and her phone buzzing on the bedside table beside her. She found the remote to turn the TV off, then with shaking hands picked up the phone.

Mika asked her to turn on her computer. They needed to talk face to face. Both boys wanted to see their mother, they feared she would crumble, the news of their suspicion too much for her.

Anna was strong, but her family were her bedrock, and to be attacked by her own child, even indirectly, was more than most parents could handle.

Anna could tell from their demeanour: Sasha, ashen, exhausted, slunk lifeless in the chair, while Mika had a granite expression on his face.

She had feared this moment. It was not for her children, even though adults, to have to break such devastating news to their mother. Before they could speak, she put up her hand to stop them.

'I know,' she said. 'I know. I knew long before the police came that it was Yvetta who let them in. Besides us, she was the only other person to know the code. At first, I would not, could not, admit to this. But when I was tied up and gagged, I recognised the willowy form of the women in black with the hood over her face. It was definitely Fritzi. And then she left that German philosopher's poem on my desk. Who else could it have been?'

They sat in silence, allowing the reality of the situation to sink in. If they knew, would the police know, would the insurance know, what would happen to Yvetta? No one had alerted Alexi to this part of the findings as yet, but it had to be done and decisions had to be made, there was no room for hysteria or emotion. Yvetta had to be saved from going to prison, a deal had to be struck with the Insurance Police; the rest was of no consequence. After that, they would have to decide as a family what steps to take, a decision none yet wanted to consider.

Anna was the first to break the silence. 'Sasha, I do not want you to misunderstand what I am about to suggest. You know I adore Safi, but right now I have to concentrate on our immediate family. Perhaps this is a good time for her to visit with her own family, until the dust has settled here.' Mika agreed this was family business and Safi was not yet considered family.

'This stays in the immediate family,' Mika said, 'no one need know, it's safer all round.'

Sasha nodded, wishing he could curl up to Safi right this moment and wake up finding it had been a nightmare. But the nightmare would not go away – it was something they would all have to learn to live with. The family would have to solve the problem one way or another, though how that would be Sasha was not yet sure. First would come the fall-out, which, Sasha thought, would be considerable. Safi needed to be protected from the ugliness of it all. He hated the thought of misleading, her but it was a necessary evil, for all of their sakes, Yvetta's most of all. He had to get his head together before Safi woke up; she would have to leave for the airport today, Kolya would take her.

Anna needed some quiet time and her sons wanted to catch some sleep before they spoke with Alexi later in the day. Everyone needed a clear head and some space to collect their feelings and thoughts. Exhausted, Sasha retired to their room, relieved to find Safi asleep. Her hand felt warm and comforting as he placed it on his chest, covering it with his own, shut his eyes falling into a restless sleep.

Sasha woke to find Safi dressed and ready for the day, drinking her much-loved mug of tea, while watching Mika toss pancakes like an expert in the kitchen. He could tell from Safi's expression that she was enjoying his brother's company. Though not blessed with Sasha's beauty (he was more conventionally handsome, with a rounder, softer face), Mika had charisma in spades. He had always been a lady's man, and was charming and good-looking even in his late-forties.

Enjoying their banter, Sasha poured himself a cup of fresh coffee, kissed Safi, then sat down to enjoy the stack of pancakes piling up, surprised to find he was ravenous. Fresh fruit, maple syrup a pot of coffee downed by everyone. Deciding it was time to start the conversation with Safi he so dreaded, not wanting her to leave Moscow, not even for a moment, their lives were just falling into place since her arrival almost three months ago.

Sasha cleared his throat. 'Safi, Kolya is going to take you to the airport today. It's not what I want, but after last night we have all come to the conclusion that it would be safer for you not to be here, or involved.'

Safi sat quietly for some moments, her confusion quickly replaced with relief and then – to her surprise – something resembling happiness. 'Yes,' she said, 'I agree. It would be an excellent time to visit my folks now that Jake is in Australia. And then perhaps the two D's. I can't wait to see their new brownstone.'

Sasha smiled. He knew Safi well by now, and how skilled she was at covering up her emotions when it was called for. The stiff upper lip, never let the side down, keep calm and carry on. And, in this instance, to his immense joy, Sasha was on side.

He hugged her tightly. 'Thank you for seeing it our way. I will be much happier knowing you are safe.'

But now she was worried for Sasha's safety all over again – what would happen to him during her absence? Still, she smiled and brushed a tear away, before jumping up with a renewed and unexpected energy and saying, 'Well, come on let's get the show on the road. Time to let everyone know I'll be seeing them all soon.'

Kolya was waiting at the car. Sasha held onto her tightly, whispered in her ear. Giggling, she waved to Mika, and the car sped off, leaving Sasha feeling bereft, as though his relationship with Safi had somehow also been damaged along with all the other valuables ruined in the house. What was a valuable when it was no longer valuable, he wondered. What did it become? Nothing? A piece of the past? A relic? An antiquity but no longer an antique? A fragment of something larger, something special? Then he followed Mika into the house, to get ready for their conference call.

As they entered the house, Mika turned and looked at Sasha intently, as though Sasha, rather than Yvetta, was the secretly guilty party. It was Mika's familiar but nevertheless unwelcome, interrogative stare – a stare perfected over years doing hard work with hard people. The kind of stare you encountered with special forces and the most longstanding members of the police force.

It was a long way away from the Mika casually and charmingly flipping pancakes a mere hour ago. And at that moment Sasha was tired of Mika, tired of his stare, tired of everything. He knew he was going to have to put up with Mika's thoughts on his relationship with Safi and readied himself as he threw himself back in his chair in front of the bank of computers and phones. How much questioning could one person take? he thought. How on earth had their lives suddenly taken on this chaotic downward spiral, without any doing on their part? It was beyond comprehension, a cosmic joke that was not remotely funny.

'She is not only delightful,' Mika said, and Sasha had to repress the desire to punch him, but for once Mika was being complimentary. For one thing, Mika would (and always had) won any fight between them. 'I know the age difference, of course, but nonetheless, Safi seems to have beauty and brains and, a sensible head on her shoulders, and if you do marry, she would be a wonderful daughter in law and daughter to Anna.'

'Do you think it's fair though for her to take on our family, with all its varied complications here in Russia, besides this awful business with Yvetta?'

'Well, no, she doesn't know Mika but she is nothing but loyal and happy to learn. And I need her, she is the best thing that's happened to me. I am tired of fooling around like you. I want some sense of stability in my life.'

Sasha sighed, he had given so much thought to what Mika was reiterating; right now he did not have the stomach for reality or the issue. 'Mika, I know you mean well, and when this is out of the way, we can sit and discuss Safi and me. But not right now, please.'

Mika nodded. 'Yes, you are right, but I am always ready to listen if you need to talk. Well it's almost time to have our call with Alexi. I have sent father all the details about the damage at the house, as well as the restaurant affair. it's going to be an awful shock for him, but we have to break this news about Yvetta to him now, sadly. He and mother are going to have to make tough decisions.'

Kolya picked up Anna on his way back from the airport. She wanted to be with her sons. The house was crawling with police and other professionals, and although the apartment was luxurious it was not ideal, nor her home.

Hearing both his sons on the conference call, Alexi knew something unusual had occurred. If nothing else his sons had been well trained and each had their part to play, in their many concerns worldwide. The property portfolios were for Alexi to deal with; the restaurant empire had always been his love, the food business had kept their family afloat and fed during the worst of times in Russia, starting with that small market stall.

Mika got straight to the point, explaining exactly what had occurred at the house and how they had received information about Yvetta and Fritzi's involvement. Alexi was quiet for a while he had read the reports Mika had sent through and the senseless damage to priceless art, but this new information was too monstrous to comprehend. He fell back in his chair, what about Anna how on earth does a mother deal with such an awful realisation about her child, their child. Anna would be devastated and as heartbroken as he was.

Alexi came back into view. 'How is Anna coping with this?'

Sasha told his father: 'Mother had worked it out before we received the information, from Mika's men.'

Mika continued, 'We are all shocked at this sudden aggressive unstable turn in Yvetta's behaviour, nothing this bad has happened before, her rages had subsided since her affair with Fritzi.'

Alexi held his head in his hands, tears were streaming down his cheeks. 'This has to come to an end, where is Yvetta now, she should be in London soon for Frieze, she has a stand at the exhibition every year.'

Sasha filled them in on Yvetta's movements since the break-in. 'As far as we know, both Fritzi and Yvetta are in Berlin at the moment. Then they will be at Frieze in London, where both Yvetta and Fritzi have a stand. One at Frieze Masters and one at Frieze. I am sure she will be sending you tickets to the opening as usual.'

'Well, that is a good thing,' Alexi said. 'She must have left the same night for Berlin, after the break-in.'

'I suspect so,' Mika said, in his quiet, but controlled manner 'There was no answer when I called to let her know what had happened at the house. She obviously planned it very well, so nothing could be traced back to her. Fritzi is the flamboyant, theatrical one; fortunately for us, Anna recognised her straight away.'

Alexi knew what had to be done; he outlined a rough plan, which they had to finesse before it could be put into action.

If they did not adhere to the family's instructions, Yvetta and Fritzi would be told in no uncertain terms that they would both go to prison.

Yvetta would not return to Russia. Instead, she would be sent to a well-known psychiatric institution in a remote area of Colorado that dealt with therapies to help people like her, with borderline, aggressive, and sociopathic personalities.

As for Fritzi, she would not be allowed back in Russia. If she put one foot on Russian soil she would be charged and put into prison. The finer details would be worked out by Mika, who had contacts both in London and the Colorado Mountains.

Alexi was always a quick thinker and supremely pragmatic – he had not become one of Russia's richest men for nothing. There was absolutely no chance they could allow Yvetta to go to prison; it would be more than their family could endure. The media (the media that they did not own, at least) would have a field day, as would all their rivals in commerce. If the family was seen as momentarily weak and off their guard, others might find it an opportune time to hit them hard. Yvetta would not be allowed to bring the Rubicov name into disrepute, or to bring disgrace on the rest of their family. Alexi would not stand for it. At that moment, he felt he had had about as much of that girl as he could take. Her mere name seemed a prelude to one sort of trouble or another, and hearing it introduced in conversations often gave him a headache in anticipation of what was to follow.

She would have to remain in that institute her whole life, if it meant the story did not become public. The insurance company would not let the matter drop easily; they would want to pursue the perpetrators and it would not take them long to trace who was responsible. After all, if Anna could figure it out in a few minutes, trained professionals would have the truth in their sights in a matter of days if not hours. The family would have to pick up the cost, but would the insurance company bring their own charges? The police were easy to deal with; if the family did not press charges, they would have no choice but to drop the enquiry.

Alexi wanted to speak with Anna. He knew that it was doubly hard for a mother when it came to the misdeeds of her child. The sadness Yvetta had brought down on her family was a disgrace that he would never allow to happen again. He had been blind to her illness, had concentrated on her – and his own – success only.

She had always been a manipulative child but he had overlooked her treatment of Anna. Indeed, he had overlooked so much of his children's lives in pursuit of his own success – something that he regretted more and more with each passing year. He was trying now to be present, and not to repeat his mistakes, with Marina, his youngest (and, in some ways, most beloved) child.

It was now at an end forever, she would not be pulling the wool over his eyes again. The years of therapy had obviously done very little to help her with her multitude of issues – different diagnoses from different doctors had confused, rather than clarified, the issue – it was time to have her committed. He hoped to God that they would be able to mend her mind so she could live amongst them in peace, be a part of the family once again rather than an increasingly embittered and insane antagonist.

Anna and Alexi cried together on the call. Yvetta had been such a precious child, they loved her dearly. Had they loved her too much, they wondered now? Spoiled her too extensively, neglected her in crucial ways, always eager to overlook negative aspects, unable or unwilling to point out or address her temper tantrums and antisocial behaviour?

But all of that was in the past. It was impossible to ignore Yvetta now, to keep feigning ignorance over her insults and attacks, or to see the good in someone who was so obviously mostly bad? She had overstepped all bounds of normality. Her campaigns against Anna had to come to an end before she destroyed her mother (a good, kind, wholesome woman; in so many ways the opposite of Yvetta), which was obviously her intent. It was beginning to seem that Yvetta would not stop until she destroyed the whole family – and so the family must stop Yvetta, must save her (and them) from herself. It would not be easy, but what choice did they have? As Alexi saw it, it was either them or her.

How Anna would recover from this he did not know. She was a strong woman but this had obviously knocked her sideways, years of Yvetta's misdeeds and insults had taken its toll – on all of them, but especially on Anna. He could tell from her voice and demeanour that she was in shock and he could not blame her. How on earth could a child who had all the comforts and opportunities in the world turn out to be so crazy? It was almost impossible for a parent to describe his child as evil, but, Alexi was increasingly beginning to think that was precisely what Yvetta was. It was a tough one to crack, and he for one was not going to try. He'd leave it to the experts. The sooner he rid his mind of the poison that was Yvetta, the better.

But he knew Anna would find it more difficult; the boys would have to keep a close eye on her. He was saddened that they had to send Safi back home. He hoped that she would return. Anna might, he hoped, find some salvation in nurturing her, teaching was her forte, he himself had never had the patience for it.

Chapter 21

Safi sat on the flight to London, feeling drained and bewildered with the speed of events. She had no time to take stock of her emotions. She was pleased to have a seat in first-class. She did not want to be sitting next to some stranger, feeling so wretched. The hostess came around with champagne. Not normally one to drink so early in the day, Safi gulped two glassed down, hoping to stop the chaotic thoughts buzzing through her mind. There were so many unanswered questions. She hated running out on Sasha, it was not her nature, but even she could tell that staying was not an option, she would only be a hindrance, complicating everything with concerns for her safety.

Her mother would collect her from the airport. She knew they would be delighted to have her home, but what on earth was she going to tell them? They had been afraid enough of her living in Moscow, and what had just happened would confirm their worst fears. Indeed, Safi worried they wouldn't want to let her go back. Certainly, she reminded herself, she was an adult now, but she sure as hell didn't feel like it right now, the glass of champagne and first-class ticket notwithstanding.

Fiona was waiting at Gatwick with open arms and Safi fell into them, happy to be hugged by her mom; it felt so wonderfully good. Indeed, all of it felt good: being back home, the air over here, the relaxed atmosphere, all of it. On the drive home, Safi told them about the break-in at the restaurant and then the house. Her parents were shocked and relieved that he had thought about her safety and sent her home, until it was safe for her to return. they seemed to be taking all of this a lot better than she had expected them to – and a lot better than she herself was processing it.

As they walked through the front door, Safi felt as if she had never left. It amazed her that one could feel that way after being away for so long. They fell right back into a routine of shopping, lunching, visiting friends, and catching up with everyone's lives – Safi found herself loving every minute. Her father said she was welcome to spend time at the agency: they were busy with a project he thought she would enjoy.

Taking him up on the offer, she spent hours with Greg and others she knew well, sharpening her brain again after months of disuse in Moscow, flexing her creative muscles and pleasantly surprised that they did still exist. She had worried that the creative part of her brain had atrophied; but, if anything, ideas now came to her immediately and abundantly, as though there was an overflow from her time away from the agency. She realised she had missed the creative life. Greg was fun to be with again, and it took her no time to feel comfortable in his company; he had the ability to make her feel capable and needed.

Sasha called daily and they would chat about what she was up to he wanted her to enjoy herself not to worry about returning just yet, things would be sorted, out soon enough. He missed her and would try to join her in a week or two, he said. Safi took him at his word and busied herself in her home life, enjoying it for the first time in years. She had fallen into a routine, going into work with her father in the mornings and spending time with her mother and friends in the afternoon.

Alexi, Valentina, and Marina, who had grown into a tall, lanky girl since Safi last saw her, had driven down to spend a day enjoying the seaside in Brighton. Alexi took Safi aside, apologising to her for what had happened, He was, he said, mortified that her safety may have been jeopardised in their private home. He let Safi know that he thought of her as a valued member of their family,

Sasha had told him of her upcoming job with Anna. Alexi kept his thoughts about this development to himself, having other ideas for Safi. The demographics at home had changed dramatically: he wanted Safi to run Yvetta's gallery; she seemed the perfect person to continue the business, in Yvetta's absence.

The two families passed the day comfortably in one another's company, lunching in the lanes then walking off their indulgence along the beachfront. Like all children, Marina loved being near the sea, the fresh air, the other children in a similar state of ecstasy, the open-air stalls and festive atmosphere of a warm afternoon. Leonard gave Alexi a tour of his agency, confiding that he often wondered what he may have done differently to encourage his children to follow in his footsteps. He envied Alexi having his family involved in the family's business interests. Safi spent a wonderful fortnight with her family and friends; it did wonders for her psyche; she felt rejuvenated. The greatest gift of these two weeks were how Safi had managed to bond with her mother in a way neither of them had managed in her years growing up. Somehow the separation and Safi's engagement to Sasha had changed the mother-daughter dynamic, and she had noticed that her father had been less patriarchal, too.

Her mother seemed to sense she needed to talk and she encouraged Safi to speak of her feelings, without comment. Fiona understood her daughter needed space to formulate her thoughts and feelings. Safi's confidence in her as a mum had developed into an adult relationship, and Fiona's own feelings towards her daughter's need of her was something she needed and valued. It stopped her from being judgemental, bonding with Safi now seemed what was important for both of them. Safi had noticed that her dad had bonded with Alexi over their visit and, he saw Safi's relationship with Sasha in a new light, he surprised himself, he liked the family a great deal.

One side of her accepted these changes and was happy about them; and yet another part felt sad. The childish bond was no longer there, which meant that she herself was no longer a child – but in a moment that, for the first time in a long while, she wanted to be sheltered and cared for, kept warm and safe. Everything in Russia seemed so overwhelming, and she was aware that – both inside of that house in Moscow, and outside of it, with Kolya – she was placated and babysat like a child.

Her parents, on the other hand, were standing back, allowing her to make her own choices, no longer expecting her to follow their plans for her future. But were Safi's choices the right ones? she wondered. Now that it was a reality, she felt her former wishes for a life out there in the big wide world, making choices for herself, no longer quite as exciting. She had not expected adulthood would be quite as frightening, and this trip allowed her a welcome respite from all of that.

She was finished with introspection for the time being; it gave her a headache. She made herself comfortable in her business-class seat, grabbed the latest Vanity Fair, Vogue, and Tattler she had bought at the airport, to hungrily reacquaint herself with the fashions and latest gossip. She was going to shop in Manhattan with Dax and, she hoped, Lauren.

Pete had insisted that she take up her old room while visiting; the two D's brownstone was not yet set up for visitors. Sasha had to put off joining her in New York, not sure if he'd make it. She declined to stay in the flat at Rubicov on her own until he arrived. She preferred to be close to Pete and the two D's.

She was still clinging onto her younger self. Well, she could not let go of all her childish bonds all at once. She needed to be mollycoddled by the two D's; they adored looking out for her and she adored their ownership for her wellbeing. Safi was all for growing up, but to grow up all at once, and to leave the child-side behind for ever, well, that was too much, too fast, she decided. Baby steps.

Being on holiday, she decided, was like being a child again, free of choices and chores, an opportunity to feel special, spoiled, and surrounded by people you loved. Cherished, that was the word, and what a wonderful word it was, too. She looked forward to being cherished. Sasha had cherished her, at the beginning and long afterwards, lavished attention on her, made her feel special and safe. That was one reason why she loved him – one of many. And he continued to cherish her, wouldn't – or couldn't – stop.

Her parents had let go, she had made choices, whatever happened in her life, Safi knew would be her own doing, to a point. She had exerted her independence, against their will, and, with love and no small amount of respect, they had let her know they trusted her to make the most out of those choices. She knew she came from a good, loving home, that her parents had given her everything in their power, and rewarded her with self-respect and a strong sense of who she was and what she wanted out of life. God, life was complicated, people were complicated, everything had seemed so cut-and-dried when she knew exactly what she wanted. Now that black-and-white world seemed as grey and unclear as a Moscow winter – did she still know what she wanted?

Being away from Sasha seemed always to unsettle her. Life had so much to offer, had she fallen into early domesticity, like a throwback to some 1950s woman? So much for her mother's hippie ideals, so much for flower power and flights of freedom. So much for being footloose and fancy free. Was she missing out on experience again? Was she making a mistake? And how would she know for sure? Her friends would find it amusing, they always thought she was the adventurous one.

True, she had stepped away from her familiar world – but stepped away to what? She had settled for love and domesticity after all. Suddenly she felt distraught at the realisation that her life wasn't actually all that unconventional or adventurous, she was just bloody immature. Still, her last night in Russia had had more than enough adventure for her. She needed her family and friends here to feel grounded again, to feel normal, whatever that word meant exactly (and no one seemed to know for sure).

What was it about flights that invited the luxury of such excessive introspection? And business-class made everything that much more excessive. She called for the hostess and ordered another bottle of wine to drink with her meal. Introspection was overrated, she decided, enjoying that buoyant, pleasantly dizzying, up-in-the-air feeling that flight afforded one.

Luck would be on her side, she felt sure of it. She tasted optimism like champagne bubbles, and her problems seemed as distant as the shapes of clouds below. After all, she had Sasha in her life, her constant, her guiding star, the love of her life. Just the thought of him made her heart thump – or was that the sudden bout of turbulence. Everything – luggage, laptops, tray-tables – was suddenly, momentarily alive. The FASTEN SEATBELT sign was switched on. Flight attendants floated across the aisles, talking reassuringly in soft voices, telling everyone to buckle up. Safi lay back and smiled. Whatever happened, she thought, she would be okay.

The taxi into Manhattan was very different from the first time she had made the trip. Then, the sights and smells seemed wildly exotic, the frenetic pace scary, alien, unlike anything she had ever known: all those people knowing where they were going, apart from her. Now she felt the same excitement, only she was one of those people who knew where she was going, who belonged in this city. Not only that, she felt at home, and wonderfully so. The familiarity made her jump with a feeling of elated joy. New York made her feel liberated and free; she realised that she loved this town , it was alive with opportunity and chutzpah, a word she had become familiar with while here.

Even though it was apparently Yiddish, chutzpah, to Safi, was quintessentially New York: the word explained being a bold, confident, no-nonsense person in such a perfect way. New Yorkers had chutzpah in buckets full. She had learnt to feel at home with people interfering in your business when not asked (it made one feel noticed, rather than ignored, and that was a great feeling after living in Moscow), or, for that matter, being able to blend in on a busy street, be anyone or no one (and in Moscow she always felt foreign, always felt strange), knowing only that she belonged here, that this was home.

Pete was exactly where he always was: in the bar with Bruno. Safi had a happy feeling of déjà vu and a familiarity she missed. They settled right back into their patter – but something was different this time. She described to Pete what she had witnessed in the house in Moscow that night. She noticed that Pete listened without his usual understanding grunts; instead, he stared at Safi with open incredulity. Rather than buffing the glasses in his usual laid-back way, she now had his full attention. 'You living in the Wild West, girl. It ain't safe to my mind, my, my, it ain't, for sure, Safi! Girl, you need to come home.'

'I am home, Pete.'

'Exactly, and now you got to stay home. Don't go back there, to God knows what.' He shivered. 'I get cold just thinking about my time over there.'

Laughing off his reaction, she made light of the whole experience; but she felt and appreciated his genuine concern for her safety. Realising she wasn't able to answer all of his questions about the robbery, and not wanting to disturb her further, Pete reluctantly changed the subject. She was thrilled to find that he had met someone, although all she could get out of him was that it was a woman named Rene; his life was changing, too.

Safi climbed the steps to the loft. On opening the door, she noticed the difference immediately: it had Pete's stamp on it now. Pete liked order with very little clutter. The space seemed larger; the piles of books lying on every surface had been replaced by fresh flowers and the sophisticated neutrals had been replaced by a profusion of colour. A large L-shaped emerald green suede sofa replaced the grey linen one, the wing-studded armchairs were now tan Barcelona chairs. Pete liked the old classics, even down to the huge glass coffee table placed on a thick grey rug, the only neutral in the room.

Safi picked up one of the coffee table books, sinking back into the comfortable sofa as she paged though it. They were all familiar pictures of places and faces she recognised in the neighbourhood. Turning back to the cover, shocked to notice the book and photos were by Pete. She had never known his surname and she just loved and accepted him as Pete, had never somehow thought to ask, and of course Peter never volunteered up the information. He was just Pete, from Pete's Bar.

But it had to be the same Pete whose name was on the book: the bar was on the front cover, too. His full name was so unlike the Pete she had come to love and know. Peter Juke Ormond. It was lyrical, lovely actually, she never thought of Pete as a Peter, it was so formal, Pete was who she knew him to be, laidback and dependable. She had to have a copy and signed by Pete. The memories these photos brought back, of a time that felt lost and yet was here to be found, right outside the window, now. As she paged through the book, she was delighted to see a photo of herself and Bruno, but taken at an angle that was only recognisable to those who knew her well.

Safi now had an insight into Pete's happiness. He had consolidated all of his options, letting go of his old ties with New Orleans, and perhaps feeling a sense of liberation in the process. He was all New York now, which of course had been true of him for many years.

She wandered down the passage to find her old room, now a colourful profusion of fabrics, blue patterns, navy checks with yellow and green cushions. Pete had a real eye for colour, as evidenced from his bar (and its colourful clientele), her room felt fresh, happy, and the sheer blinds on the huge windows softened the whole space. The room was beautiful, and so, she realised, not for the first time, was Pete.

Walking around, getting used to the new look in the loft, she wandered up the stairs to the roof garden. She was happy to find everything as it was, apart from the hammock, which was now replaced by a stone trough filled with tulips about to burst into bloom. All this domesticity had to be the work of the new love in Pete's life. Safi suddenly felt insecure. Pete had always been there for her without question, she hoped one day she would be able to return the favour.

And this new woman in his life? She better measure up, otherwise Safi would have something to say about it. Sasha texted to say that he and Mika would be arriving in New York from Colorado after they finished up some business there. This meant Safi's time with the two D's and Pete was limited. The two D's, both of who had been in meetings all afternoon, had arranged to meet Safi at Pete's Bar as soon as they were done. As it happened, Dax was done first, and he held Safi at arm's length as she opened the door. He looked her over with approval, then pulled her close, hugging her warmly. He was the only person in the whole world Safi would tolerate being so overtly critical of her looks, but today he had only praise for her.

They collapsed onto the L-shaped sofa with Pete's newly published coffee table book, between them, no one had received a copy of yet. Safi could not contain her interest about Pete's book, the loft, and the décor, but mostly she wanted to know all about the new love in his life. She was amused to learn that Pete had met his lady friend in his own bar, and not too long ago, either. She had sauntered in one morning, having just moved into the area, found Pete behind the bar a great listener, and quickly became a regular. But she only liked to stop by when the bar was quiet and she had Pete's attention all to herself.

'She must be lovely if Pete likes her.'

'Dan and I had our reservations at first. But she seems to make Pete really happy. And as you can tell she has had quite an influence round here.'

'I knew something was up. I just could not believe Pete would go for such bright, happy colours.'

'Pete has his own ideas, but Rene has softened the place with fresh flowers; she owns a florist on the Upper East Side.'

'Has she been married before? What's the story?'

'As you know, Pete is not one for sharing.' Dax smiled shrewdly, and Safi knew there was something more. 'But Daniel dropped in to Rene's florist and took her for coffee recently and got the whole story. She moved to Manhattan several years ago after her mother passed on. Apparently, she had Parkinson's, and Rene being the only child remained at home in Sedona not far from Phoenix until she passed on. Then she decided to have a whole new start, moved here and bought the Flower store and met Pete.'

'Sad, but also kind of lovely. I am happy for them both. I hope it works out.'

'I am sure you will meet her this evening?'

Safi did not want to repeat the whole story about the robbery and evaded Dax's questions, using the family's business in Colorado as the reason for visiting. She knew Dax's reaction would unnerve her. Having witnessed Pete's reaction to the story, she could only imagine what Dax would say. Still, she had a feeling that Dax knew something was up. Dax always knew. Dax was sensitive and intuitive and knew Safi well enough to know when something was off. Safi told herself that she would wait until Daniel arrived and then tell them both at once, finding a moment to drop the story in nonchalantly, almost as an afterthought, making as light of it as best she could, as if there was nothing extraordinary about the incident. If only!

They ventured into the bar to wait for Dan to arrive and found Pete in animated conversation with a lady. Safi could tell by Pete's body language that this lady must be Rene. Pete seemed totally taken with her; Safi hadn't seen Pete as energised with anyone; he was hanging on her every word. As she turned, Safi found herself staring into an open, angelic face. Rene had a wide smile with perfect teeth, wide-set green eyes and short blonde curly hair. One could not help but find her engaging she was a very beautiful curvaceous Latina. She had an easy, somewhat world-weary way about her, much like Pete.

In fact, they were so alike that Safi marvelled at the similarity in their demeanour and personality; they were meant for one another. Pete had, she thought, found his soulmate. It was hard to tell Rene's age, but Safi thought late-thirties at the most, perfect for Pete. Dan arrived during their conversation and everything changed. Dan's expression of genuine concern as he hugged Safi protectively, looking over her shoulder, shaking his head, conveying the alarm that he shared for her safety with Pete. They had obviously spoken.

Dax picked up the vibes immediately. 'What on earth is going on?'

Safi tried to brush the whole robbery off as just one of the things that happens in Moscow to people in the business world. But that wasn't going to be enough, she realised soon enough. They wanted to hear every detail. And once Safi began she could not stop; it all just came tumbling out. Safi had their full attention and she felt their disbelief. Everyone stared at her she could feel their shock, their warm, communal sense of concern for her wellbeing.

'My God!' Dan said. 'No one would believe any of this.'

The more she repeated her experience of the break-in, the less real it sounded, even to her own ears – but there was no denying it had happened.

'So, they decided to send you to safety,' Dax said finally. 'What happens now?'

'I will hear when Sasha arrives in a few days.' Safi realised how that sounded, that she didn't have a say in the matter one way or another, that everything was up to Sasha, that her own life was perhaps out of her control.

'I believe the two robberies were not connected. The Rubicov robbery has been resolved, but the robbery at the house has left everyone mystified.

No one can figure out how they managed to get past the security code. No one knows the code besides the immediate family. Nothing was taken, only destroyed.

'It must be an inside job,' Dan volunteered. A disgruntled staff member, perhaps. They will find them, I am sure.'

'Well, the security has been beefed up now. When I get back I can look forward to high gates with sharper spikes, more cameras and TV monitors, even a twenty-four-hour guard.'

The two D's were meeting Safi for breakfast for a tour of the brownstone and Dax's studio. Exhausted, Safi did not wait for Pete to lock up the bar and retraced familiar steps up to the loft and her redecorated old room. Finding a call from Sasha on her cell, nostalgia set in and she wondered whether she had moved on in her life at all.

Bruno greeted her with his usual doggie exuberance: snorting and nuzzling himself against her legs as she joined the two D's for breakfast. She enjoyed walking the five blocks to their new brownstone, there was no mistaking which it was by the scaffolding outside.

Dan insisted on showing Safi his architectural drawings pasted across one of the walls, explaining in detail what had been done and what was left to do. Then Dan demanded they don a hard-hat as they moved about the different floors. It was easy to tell the house would be stunning on completion, what amused her the most was that D&D were living in a tiny room on the ground floor while the building work commenced around them. It was so unlike Dax to live in such discomfort.

Dax made light of Safi's teasing. 'Well, it's not that bad, really. It's cosy and we have everything we need.'

Dan smiled at Safi, winking. 'He will do anything to walk me down that aisle.'

Laughing, they made their way out of the building site and onto the pavement. Deciding it was a gorgeous day out and walked the twelve blocks to Dax's studio.

One of Dax's assistants opened the door for them and continued cataloguing, while Dax pulled out drawing after drawing, prints and masses of preparatory work he had been busy with since Safi had left. He was absorbed and, in his element, taking them both through his thoughts and ideas for various projects and the commissions that had come in that still had to be completed. It was easy to understand why DuPont was so taken with him, he was no lightweight, fly-by-night artist, but a master of his craft.

Leaving Dax's studio, they made their way Uptown to meet with Lauren, who Dax had invited to lunch, knowing Safi loved catching up. They met in Seraphina, delicious pizzas and spaghetti on the menu (something Safi missed – her last experience with Italian food being her first venture to Gum), and close enough for some serious retail therapy.

Lauren, Safi noted, had not lost her style, even now that she was a mother. Bianca, Safi learnt, modelled only in New York; she worked much less but was content to look after their child. Lauren confided that her life had become far less social. Bianca had only recently agreed to hire a nanny, so she hoped they would be stepping out a bit more.

The three days with her New York family passed in a haze, Safi was not sure she was ready to move to the Rubicov Moscow apartment with Sasha. She needed more time. The recent events had shaken her more than she liked to admit, perhaps he would understand her staying until things at home had been resolved?

Chapter 21

Sasha and his parents arrived at the clinic in the Colorado Mountains to meet with the director and resident psychiatrist. It had been an emotional two days spent arranging for Yvetta to be admitted and then sectioned if necessary.

The questions asked had put both his parents into an emotional tailspin, they were not ready to delve into their past as parents, or to be introspective. Their lives were consumed with surviving through communism and perestroika and, they were used to doing what had to be done without too much fuss. Interrogating their relationship with Yvetta and even their lives before her, resulted in a recommendation for his mother to visit with a colleague in Moscow. Everyone, including Anna herself, agreed that she needed to have someone professional to share her thoughts and feelings with.

Both parents were advised not to blame themselves for Yvetta. Genetics played a part as well as environment; it would take years of therapy to change Yvetta's way of perceiving the world. They were given a reading list to familiarise themselves with personality disorders. Yvetta would arrive at the clinic with Mika, who she respected and feared in equal measure. Alexi tried to make it clear to the director that his daughter was not to be allowed to leave – this was for her benefit and the safety of others. If she left, he would find her, have her brought back to Moscow, and arrested. The director tried to put their minds at rest: Yvetta would be assessed; if she was deemed a danger to herself or others, they would detain her indefinitely. If not, the director would contact Alexi to make new arrangements.

Anna was a concern to both Sasha and his father: she had taken personally the meeting with the psychiatrist, whose questions had offended her sense of fairness and integrity. She knew herself to be a good mother, but all mothers doubted their parenting skills from time to time. With Yvetta, Anna's belief in her parenting skills had fluctuated wildly – her feelings about her daughter were almost as erratic (and, at times, irrational) as her daughter's behaviour itself. She blamed herself in many ways for her daughter's dreadful behaviour. Anna found it difficult to reconcile her intellect with her emotions. They had sent Yvetta away to boarding school at a very young age, perhaps that was a mistake, but they wanted her to have the best education money could buy and, not be influenced by the old ways. The West would enable her and Sasha to experience free speech and, a free press altogether different to growing up in Russia.

Alexi was far more resilient; he had closed off his feelings and was not prepared to be introspective. He was done blaming himself; second-guessing Yvetta or her childhood or her condition was a waste of time, as far as he was concerned. He was, after all, a proud pragmatist, which meant that he lived in the present and dealt with all challenges practically and directly. Nor was he fond of all of this psychological gobbledygook, self-help books, and euphemisms for Yvetta's condition. As Alexi was fond of saying, in heavily accented English, 'It is what it is.' A circular, self-contained, self-satisfied formulation that pleased him no end. Yvetta's condition was what it was, and they were dealing with the fall-out the best way possible for Yvetta and the family.

Dealing with his daughter on his return to London was yet to happen. Alexi was, Sasha believed, preparing himself mentally, for the show down he knew would follow once Yvetta was faced with the consequences of her actions.

Yvetta would fly accompanied by Mika to the Colorado Clinic.

Fritzi would leave for Berlin the same day, hopefully never to be seen or heard of again. She would be escorted onto the plane. All contact with Yvetta would be severed once they were separated. Fritzi would have no way of contacting Yvetta, or finding out where she was: cell phones and computers were not allowed at the Clinic, and all contact with the outside world was forbidden. The clinic had come highly recommended as the best in its field.

Alexi knew his heart had closed to his daughter, who had received all the love and support any other child would thrive on. She had chosen her destructive path. Instead of sharing her problems with the family, she had attacked them, which, in Alexi's view, was unforgivable. If this clinic could not help (and he doubted that it could), he would have her locked away forever. From now on, he would share his thoughts with

Sasha and Mika, but not with Anna. Anna was not to be hurt anymore, he would see to that.

Sasha arrived in Manhattan emotionally drained; his parents had returned home: his father to London, and his mother to Moscow. His mother needed space to heal. He hoped Mika would be able to protect her from having to deal with the inevitable investigations that was still on going. They had managed to persuade Anna to remain in the apartment until Sasha returned home to check the security at their home had been satisfactorily installed.

Arriving at Rubicov late that evening a day earlier than planned, he decided not to contact Safi until the following day. He needed to catch up on sleep – and to clear his head. Seeing Safi would be stressful (everything – even things he had once enjoyed – seemed suddenly to be stressful); he was not sure how what had occurred in the house that night had affected her, or whether her feelings about remaining in Moscow with him had undergone a change of heart. Right now, he did not want to deal with negative thoughts, and he drowned them out in the shower. He would deal with everything when rested.

His sister invaded his thoughts – that was Yvetta for you, she liked to take up space in your head, to command attention, to take control. She liked to be the centre of things, for better and worse. Mostly worse; at least of late, she had been the centre of some very bad things. And that was just what the family was aware of – Sasha shuddered to think what she had been involved in that had not yet come to light.

They had been so close as children growing up, supporting one another through school in England. She had been a familiar presence in an initially unfamiliar place. She had always been the more complicated one. It was hard to fathom her thought processes and moods, most of them negative, the glass was always half empty as she struggled against the tide. The easier her life it seemed the more complicated she would make it appear. Her conception of every situation (herself the centre of them all), her peculiar sense of reality, was very different from his own, to the point where it was a wonder they were from the same family, let alone brother and sister. He had never understood her mindset. Perhaps when she reached her teens the intervention should have taken place, none of them had realised that Yvetta needed help. Teenagers were known to be irrational from time to time but Sasha would watch her lurch from one relationship to another, blaming others for her emotional fallout after each breakup, never able to face any consequences for her behaviour to others.

One day she would be happy, the next a black cloud descended as if somewhere between yesterday and the following day she had flipped, in to a totally different person. Dissuading her from a vindictive action towards those she perceived as the enemy was useless, once it had been set as a reality in her mind. When one tried to reason with her, it only provoked her rages no wonder he had given up years ago. Yvetta could not bear to be disapproved of, a look could send you into prolonged coventry, purposely ostracising family or friend. It was a tedious, thankless relationship to endure as, it was always one sided, Yvetta gave nothing in return and, expected it to be her way or no way. Dealing with Yvetta was stressful and a thankless task for his mother.

Sasha had always felt sad for his mother, who had bent over backwards to accommodate his sister, only to receive in return torrents of toxic abuse. His father was removed from her raging behaviour: Yvetta needed him on side, having exhausted the goodwill of the rest of her family. Alexi enabled her to build her business – that was one thing she was good at, her gallery had gone from strength to strength, and it kept Alexi happy, until recently. She had lost Alexi's trust entirely now, with her jealous vindictive attack on their family. Sasha could not imagine the pain it caused both his parents, confronting his sister was going to be a very tough call for his father, and Sasha was pleased that Mika would be there to support him.

Sasha woke to a distant ringing, fumbling for his cell phone, confused by the time on the clock (was it six a.m. or p.m.? he had no idea). With his phone finally firmly in hand, he realised it was p.m. Smiling, he listened to the most recent voicemail from Safi: 'Where are you? When are you arriving? I am so confused. I am at Pete's Bar.' It was wonderful to hear Safi's lovely, soft, cultured, English accent; she had a way of making everything she said sound slightly breathless and sexy.

Sasha had barely set foot in Pete's Bar when Safi flew into his arms, hugging him close and covering his face with kisses,

'God, I'd forgotten how much I adore you,' Safi said, in that beautiful, breathless voice. 'Lucky you arrived in time to remind me.'

Sasha laughed good-naturedly, but felt an unexpected pang of concern: being back in Manhattan with a network of friends and loved one's around her, it would be easy enough for her to move on. Moscow had not been easy, he knew that. And she had stuck beside him all that time, as resilient as she was beautiful. Devastated at the thought of losing her, he grabbed Safi by the hand and pulled her close and lifted her chin, kissing her softly on the nose and mouth, whispering in her ear, 'Give me a chance to remind you again.'

They laughed, but Safi could feel the heat rising all the way up from her toes. She leaned into Sasha. 'I can't wait.'

The two D's walked in with Rupert and Rene, it was like old times, apart from Rene and change of address.

'Like old times.' Rene introduced herself to Sasha. 'Apart from me, right,' she said, smiling knowingly to Pete. Coming around to put his arm round her shoulder.

'Yep, things sure moved on.'

Sasha had forgotten how great it was to be in company that accepted him for who he was without question. He wished he could be in this kind of company all the time, but knew that it would be a long time before he moved to the States. The evening passed with banter and serious conversation about the break-in, but Sasha found he was able to set their minds at rest, ending with Rupert inviting Sasha and his family to spend Christmas at his Connecticut home. He wanted all three families under one roof, insisting Moscow was far too cold for him to visit in winter. Sasha could tell that Safi wanted it to happen, and he would see that it did: keeping her happy was a priority. Having only two nights left before returning to Moscow, he was happy to indulge everyone with arrangements for the time left. He would be indulging Safi's every whim until he left with her next to him on that plane to Moscow. He told himself that he would never take her for granted – he knew her true worth.

Sharing the ride up to Sasha's apartment in the elevator was agony, both were fired up with desire. As the elevator doors closed behind another couple who were exiting, Sasha slammed the button to stop it from ascending any further. Gasping with excitement as he pulled down the tights under her short leather skirt, he grabbed her from behind, pushing his face between her legs until she yelped. He felt her legs weaken and something surge within them, a mutual and momentarily insatiable desire. Sasha picked her up, threw her over his shoulder, punched the button to start the elevator, smacked her bottom, and carried her into his apartment, lowering her onto the bed.

They were completely lost in enjoying each other in every way. 'I love you, love you, love you' Rolling off, he lay beside her, stroking her hair, waiting for her to turn. He needed to look into her eyes, that is where he would find how she felt. Safi turned slowly, swung her leg over him until she sat straddling him. She pushed his hands above his head, and untied her hair, letting it fall over her face. Using her ribbon, she tied his hands to the headboard.

'Now you're mine, my slave,' she said, and began to make love to him slowly and meaningfully yet teasing him when he became excited, wanting it to last as long as possible. Safi felt strong, she felt in control and she loved that feeling; she felt as if she could carry on all night. She wanted him again and again; she had never felt this way before, it was almost as if she was high on sex, totally mad for him. She leaned her breasts into his face as she untied him, then brought his hands down as she stretched her back the length of his body, bringing his hands round to bring her to a climax.

Safi lay exhausted until he rolled her off. She looked up into his eyes. Could Sasha not see that she was more than just in love? She was so totally his – did he not feel that? There was absolutely nothing she would not let him do to her, anytime, anywhere, she could not get enough of him. So, she wondered suddenly, who was whose slave? Who was really in control? Finding her voice hoarse with sex, she said, 'I will never leave you. I want you to stay inside me for ever, anywhere, anytime, anyhow, I am all yours, for ever.' Sasha pulled her close and held onto her until they both passed out. His mind had gone numb. All he could feel was his love for this girl. She surprised him in bed and out, and that was more than any man could ask for. He suddenly knew how happy he was – and how lucky.

Valentina had recently taken on a position at the Royal Ballet to host young Russian dancers who had moved over from the Bolshoi and the Kirov schools to dance in London. They depended on her to mentor them until they had settled into their new home. Valentina was intensely disciplined about everything she took on. Being involved with her first love once more came as a wonderful gift and she wanted to nurture her new-found connection with dance and the Royal Ballet.

She treated her charges with kindness and a firm hand; she found them lodging, introduced them to the right Russian crowd, but most of all she was there to smooth their path into a new dance company, helping with any problems they encountered. She sat in on their hours of exercise at the Royal Ballet and watched as they practiced for shows, always on hand when they needed encouragement.

Alexi supported her in every endeavour. He held her hand, guided her through her fall -out with the Kirov, helped when at a loss after leaving a life of dance away from a country she loved. It had been tough, but with Alexi's love and confidence she found her independence once more. Then they had Marina and life took on a new meaning for both. Alexi needed her now, when she was just finding her way back to her first love; even if she was only mentoring talented young dancers, it put her back in touch with a world she thrived on.

He needed her to be strong for them both right now. How could a child behave so wickedly to her mother? Valentina wondered with a shudder.

Marina was such a sweet child, she thanked God that Alexi had her in his life. Valentina hoped that Marina would heal his sadness about Yvetta. Valentina was shocked when Alexi returned from the Colorado Clinic It was the first time she had ever seen him close to a breakdown. He was like a completely different person. Alexi was a fair man and liked nothing more than supporting his family, but this daughter had squeezed his open heart to a tight fist, he was like a prize fighter ready to do maximum damage.

Anna had taken it out of him, and he felt wretched about her having to return to Moscow on her own. Anna was a strong woman, but no one could survive a child's attack on her own mother without crumbling.

'Everyone blames the mother,' Anna had said. 'What did I do?'

Alexi told Valentina that Anna kept repeating 'What did I do to make her so wicked, so sick? I cannot understand it. The doctor told her it was not her fault, it was not our fault, we were not to blame ourselves, but Anna kept on and on; eventually he had to give her medication to keep her calm. She just could not come to terms with what had taken place. Like me she was sickened, then sad, then angry. All the emotions they brought out; it was soul-destroying to watch Anna crumble.'

Valentina knew she would have to be there when Alexi and Mika confronted Yvetta; she was scared Alexi might kill her, she knew his temper once he was provoked, she had seen it with his staff, but never with his family.

Yvetta had plunged a dagger in his heart and he would never open it to her again. He was a Russian: once hurt there was little one could do to lift the darkness. He would never forgive. He needed Valentina's strength and she would be there for him as long as he needed.

It was the week before Frieze. Yvetta had not called, but they knew that she had arrived to oversee the installation of her shows. There was no point in antagonising her before the show was over. Their VIP tickets had arrived for the first night for both the Masters and for Frieze.

Alexi could not bring himself to face Yvetta before the showdown at their home. Valentina suggested that she attend with a friend; Alexi, she would say, was away on business, only returning on the last day of the show. Once their duties were completed, papers signed, and the artwork had been shipped to Florida for storage, until the opening of Art Basil in the summer, Yvetta had been invited to dine with them at their home with Fritzi. It was the same every year, and they knew that she would accept their invitation; each year she came to show her respects to her father and to make sure that he continued to bankroll her investments in the art world; without his rubbles she would not be able to attend all the major shows or invest in the artists.

Yvetta pulled off her woollen balaclava as she exited the house into a waiting black-windowed Range Rover. Heart pumping with adrenalin and excitement, she removed her gloves, stuffed them into her travel bag, pulled on her knee-high boots, and asked the driver to drop her off at the airport. She had two hours to kill in the business lounge before her flight headed for Berlin, then on to London for the beginning of the main art fair of the season.

Everything had been planned to the last second. She loved the planning leading up to this moment: the destruction of Mother Russia's private art collection, her priceless antiquities, smashed into a million pieces. Oh yes, Anna would pay. Anna was Mother Russia, who had abandoned and ignored and abused her one and only daughter for an interloper. They would pay, all of them, for the wilful hurt they caused her and Fritzi. How dare they! She would teach them all a lesson. Fritzi belonged to her; no one was going to lord it over them, no one. She alone would teach them all who was in control.

Fritzi loved her, she would never leave her, never. This was their finest moment together. Together they had planned the whole break-in – no, she would not call it that; it was their 'performance piece,' their own anti-establishment, highly experimental, innovative, and boundary-pushing performance artwork.

Fritzi would leave with the students, their hired hands, young artists waiting to be recognised. They would do anything for money and she had more than enough to satisfy them. Each art student had been carefully selected. Fritzi had trained them herself; two of the students had cameras on their black motorbike helmets to record the performance. It would be screened at a special evening in one of the many galleries, and titled 'The Destruction of Mother Russia's Decadent Future.'

No one involved would know the personal nature of the break-in; to the students it was destroying a random oligarch's private plunder of Russia's antiquities. A payback for raping all the wealth for themselves and leaving the rest of them to rot, poor and defenceless against this new and corrupt motherland.

Fritzi had flown on a Lufthansa flight to Berlin the following day; they would visit Fritzi's extended family and fly to London for Frieze, no one any the wiser.

Sasha had been called away to a threat at Rubicov, Fritzi's contact had passed on the information, perfectly timed for them to carry out their performance piece; leaving Moscow the same day would add to the plan's perfection.

Fritzi hung out with gamblers. She loved the whole nightlife scene, crawling the bars and clubs where she met people Yvetta had little time for. But she indulged Fritzi, keeping her in Moscow was her objective. Fritzi liked to gamble, she loved putting on the Ritz, dressing up, being noticed. That whole drag scene was not Yvetta's idea of fun, it was, in fact, dangerous in Moscow. Fritzi knew how to play a character, that was her whole raison d'être, to be noticed, wherever she went, especially in circles that could advance her image as a femme fatale, a good cover for her real love: woman. Men were for other uses, she would say.

Fritzi was tall enough to dress in high fashion, sexy and masculine at the same time; finding that both men and women were attracted to her, she played the role well.

Yvetta, on the other hand, loved to be feminine; she loved fashion and she wore it well on her small lithe body. Fritzi had seduced her one evening in a hotel bar in Berlin, and Yvetta had never looked back. Fritzi was her alter ego, she made Yvetta feel strong. Underneath, of course, Yvetta suffered in silence, searching for a fixed identity, any identity at all, not knowing who she really was.

Every day was a struggle, no one ever understood her, people could be unforgivably insensitive to her needs, selfish, even cruel. Those who wronged her deserved to be punished, indeed to suffer – how else would they learn that they were out of line? Fritzi understood, too, that Yvetta's family needed to be punished for their behaviour towards them. After all, they always wanted to control Yvetta, who was a grown-up. Yvetta loved this about Fritzi – how understanding she was of their importance as a couple – and of the insignificance of Yvetta's larger family unit – and how she shared her love of organised chaos, creative anarchy, and sense of elaborate revenge. She would not let anyone control her, least of all her mother, who never understood how she was replacing her own daughter with Sasha's bit on the side, that shiny Limey slut, how dare she help that girl and not her own daughter's lover.

The truth was that Anna had never accepted Fritzi, and that was because, on a deep level, she had never accepted Yvetta. Why should she have to ask for what she wanted, and at her age and status in Europe's creative community? It was insulting, humiliating, a crime that deserved to be addressed – no, redressed, appropriately punished. She refused to be treated like a child. Everyone needed to know who Yvetta really was, and to admire her formidable intellect, her stature, her style.

As Yvetta regurgitated her grievances, over and over again in her mind, her reasons for punishing Anna became clearer and she felt vindicated, revitalised and refreshed. Her mother deserved nothing less, Yvetta would not stand for any half measures. Anna had to be taught a lesson, no one was going to tell her what to do or how to live her life ever again. As for Anna, Yvetta intended to distance her from her life; she had to protect herself from their anger towards her and Fritzi. She could feel their disgust and disapproval. It was in their eyes, it was always there making her feel bad about herself. They were weak and she was strong.

Berlin had passed without incident. From there they flew to London, ready for the week's gruelling schedule, running from one show to the next, promoting their chosen artists at the Masters and at Frieze. Her father would want to see value for his patronage. She resented his hold over her business, but what choice did she have? She could not exactly go it alone at this point. As her father himself would say, it was what it was. He owed her; after all, he was her father, why should she need to show him that she was successful for him to bankroll her? it was ridiculous the way her parents treated her, because she was a daughter and not a son.

She always had to kowtow by attending a dinner at the end of Frieze each year with that opinionated, ignorant bitch Valentina and her father. Exhausted, it was the last thing Yvetta needed in her life, but there was no getting out of it. Yvetta had to sit there, a virtual prisoner, as they lorded it over her and Fritzi. They pretended to be progressive, but they were thoroughly conservative, old-fashioned, full of hatred and possibly envy as well. They never rewarded her choices, and instead were always critical of her actions. Before Valentina came onto the scene, Alexi was hers – and she, in turn, was his little girl – now, he only had eyes for that cow-wife of his and runt of a child. God, she loathed that child, another interloper who took her father's love away from her. But she would show them, she did not need any of them in her life: the less she saw of them, the better off she was.

On arrival at the house, Yvetta noticed that the dining room door was closed. Valentina was nowhere to be seen. The butler greeted them at the front door, taking their coats and showing them through to the study, quietly closing the door behind him.

Fritzi and Yvetta stared at one another, saying nothing but thinking the same thing. This was strange, they were always greeted by Alexi and Valentina. Sitting quietly as they waited (and how she hated to wait – on anyone!), Yvetta's anger mounted at being treated like a stranger in her father's home. How dare he!

Fritzi moved around uncomfortably in her chair as the minutes ticked by with no sign of anyone else around. Something was not right, she wondered, was someone ill?

Looking up as the door opened, Yvetta was shocked to see Mika, accompanied by two strange men. Mika greeted them coldly, taking a seat next to Fritzi as Mika's hired hoods stood on either side of the door. Alexi walked in, looked straight ahead, past Yvetta and Fritzi and seated himself behind his desk.

Alexi sat looking at his daughter for what seemed a long time. Increasingly unnerved, Yvetta asked, 'Is everything okay, Papa?'

'Neet, Yvetta, everything is not okay. I want you to watch this video. I do not want to hear one word, do you understand?'

Yvetta shook her shoulders as if to say, Okay, if that's what you want, suddenly compliant, Daddy's little girl again, sitting back in her chair to watch whatever was so important for her to see, probably Marina, their little princess, doing some charity thing with her mother. Alexi always wanted Yvetta to get involved with their charities, it was so boring.

Alexi pushed the control on the computer and an image flashed up on the TV screen. At first she did not recognise anything, the image was so dark. Then she saw figures dressed in black with balaclavas pulled over their faces – six of them. Yes, that was Fritzi, and, oh God, that was her, breaking the antiquities, throwing them on the floor, laughing as they smashed to smithereens, their precious Fabergé eggs, priceless crystal being swiped off the display shelves, the cabinet crashing to the floor, paintings slashed, sculptures decapitated, disabled, broken beyond recognition. Then Fritzi in Anna's quarters, the students tying her mother to the chair, Fritzi sweeping everything on her desk to the floor with a flourish. Only Fritzi could be that dramatic – Yvetta felt a momentary flash of pride – then brandishing a knife in her mother's face. Anna was petrified, the strong, always invulnerable Anna now scared, afraid at last, as though broken down to her rawest elements, like the sculptures, good. The artistry wiped out and the crudest emotions on display: fear, hatred, awful anticipation.

Yvetta sat fascinated as she watched the scene of destruction in her mother's home. An expression of vindication on her face, she looked up to see her father watching her. He had noticed, good, let him see how she despised them.

Alexi stood, walked over to his daughter, and slapped her hard across the face. Yvetta reeled backwards in her chair. Fritzi, now shaking with fear, did not make a sound to protect her, but sat rooted in her chair. Holding her cheek, Yvetta started to scream, then cry. She was, in that moment, a torrent of sound rolling across the room. She lashed out at her father, but he was too strong for her. Shoving her back into the chair, he walked round to his desk in disgust, shaking with uncontrolled anger, he had struck Yvetta much like she had mindlessly with out as much a care in the world, struck out destroying priceless art.

Falling into his chair, he switched off the film having seen enough.

'This is what's going to happen. I see you do not deny this is your work and Fritzi's. You are proud of what you have done? Well, it sickens me how you have turned out. Let me tell you, Yvetta, you are no longer a valued member of this family.' He held up his hand. 'I do not want to hear one word from you, not one. Mika and the nurse that has arrived from the clinic where you will be placed for your own safety indefinitely will be escorting you onto a plane this evening. If you as much as set one foot outside the boundaries of this institution, you will be brought back to Moscow, where you will be incarcerated in a Russian jail for the break-in and wilful destructions of valuable, priceless antiquities of the Russian Empire, going as far back as the Romanoffs.

'Your gallery will be either shut and all works auctioned, or I will hand it over to be run by whoever Mika and the family choose. It will no longer belong to you. You will be taken out of my will and you will never ever be supported by anyone in the family again. Your apartment will be sold, everything you own will be sold or confiscated. You will be penniless apart from the support at the clinic that the family will bankroll.'

Yvetta crumbled to the floor, started screaming, thrashing about, rolling into a ball, rocking back and forth, howling like an animal in a rage. The nurse, one of the burly men at the door, managed to sedate her and Yvetta lay motionless behind Fritzi's chair.

Fritzi sat staring straight ahead, frozen with fear, perhaps for the first time in her life. What would they do to her? She knew of people in Moscow disappearing never to be heard of again. Or, worse, would they make her the scapegoat and offer her up to the Russian authorities? She looked up to see Alexi leave the room, only to re-enter, and sit down at his desk. He looked exhausted, pale, sick even; maybe he would have a heart attack, that was good, the bastard. She hated these Russian oligarchs, the bastards had raped Russia, how dare they have so much power and use it so crudely? The Germans should have won that war, the Russians were corrupt animals. She stared at Alexi, willing him to confront her. After all, she was a German citizen in England, what could he do?

Mika stepped forward and said something to his father, but Alexi shook his head, drank some water, and picked up a printed sheet of paper.

'This is your ticket back to Germany. If you put one foot on Russian soil you will be arrested. You will never contact anyone in this family again. Yvetta will be out of contact. In fact, take a good look at her now, because this is the last time you two will ever see each other. You will not be able to contact her where she is, or vice versa. It will be years before she is free, if ever. I do not care whether you have possessions in Moscow or money. You will not receive one rouble's compensation from this family. Kolya will be accompanying you until you disembark in Munich, to find your own way to Berlin. All Yvetta's credit cards have been cancelled, so, if you have been using any, they will be null and void. Kolya will inform us when you arrive back on German soil. They are welcome to you. Now get out of my sight. I never want to set eyes on you again, and if we do hear from you in any form or manner, you may not live to tell the tale. By the way, the movie you so cleverly had the students use at an underground art show has been confiscated and kept as evidence. So do not even think of denying any involvement. Once confronted by our security, the students all sang like little birds.'

Fritzi knew she had lost everything. She had no fight left; she was free, the main thing was to start again. Best to keep her head down and follow orders, until she was no longer in their clutches.

Kolya escorted her out of the house by the arm, the butler waiting with her coat at the door. A black taxi pulled up and Kolya all but threw her in. He made it clear that he was carrying a firearm and was not shy of using it. Indeed, she could feel the firearm in her ribs as they sat in the taxi. He had made her use the toilet before leaving; obviously he was not going to let her out of his sight. They waited in the first-class lounge.

'Don't think this is a treat for you,' he informed her, 'it's easier to control you in a small space. There's no room for you to escape, or try any funny business. I will follow you everywhere, even to the ladies' toilet. So relax until we get to Munich, because this will be your last taste of luxury paid for by the Rubicovs.'

Fritzi knew charming Kolya would be a waste of time. She needed her wits about her; who knows what this Russian would do to her if she bolted. She would be free of them all, once she stepped onto German soil. It would be good to start fresh. She loved Yvetta, but there would be other lovers (all of them drawn to her formidable beauty and flamboyance); they had reached the end of the line, she had to look after Fritzi now, re-invent herself, something she was exceptionally good at, play another part. Lying back in her seat, she closed her eyes, planning her new persona and name. She felt excited to begin again and she found herself smiling broadly, something which no doubt annoyed Kolya no end. They had three hours together, and she intended to annoy him as much as possible during that time.

Mika and the nurse from the clinic escorted a mildly sedated Yvetta through immigration. Everything went to plan. He left her in the care of the institution, with videos for the director and the medical staff to watch; they needed to see what Yvetta was capable of. Mika had brought the video with to London once the students had been questioned, it was handed over. The nurse had filmed Yvetta's behaviour at the house without her knowledge; this was handed over to the director, too. It was an indelible spot on her character, one that would live with her forever. They would have enough to work with until such time as Yvetta herself started co-operating.

He would have the clinic thoroughly investigated when he returned, one could not be too careful. Mika did not like leaving anything to chance; the Russian doctor had to be trusted under the circumstances, discretion was a priority. So far they had cooperated with all their wishes. Yvetta had been admitted without fuss, he had no reason to doubt their integrity and medical professionalism. Mika had one of his security men remain at the institution indefinitely. He had no doubt Yvetta would try to escape; he was not prepared to take that chance. His man would report back to him if any problems arose.

Sasha and Safi returned to Moscow. The house not yet ready for them to move back into, they stayed at the Rubicov apartments with Anna. Safi found Anna distant, so different from the warm, affectionate, sharing and caring Anna who had taken Safi under her wing after her arrival in Moscow. Not knowing how to respond to her melancholy, Safi decided not to refer to the break-in until Anna spoke of it.

Her English reserve kicked in. Sasha asked Safi to be patient. Alexi arrived with Valentina, and Mika flew over from St. Petersburg. His cousins, who ran various enterprises (including the restaurants), would hold the fort while they were locked down in meetings with the insurance company and the various authorities.

She was content to spend a fun time with Sasha's cousin, Natasha, newly arrived from London and Paris. Not yet settled, Natasha was happy to indulge in what Moscow had to offer and Safi tagged along for the experience. Natasha set about reacquainting herself with Russian high society, introducing Safi to 'Russian royalty' in the process. Safi found the whole experience fascinating; the closest she had come to royalty was in gossip magazines.

Natasha was fun to be with and fashion-mad, and reminded Safi oddly of Nicky Ray, who she had not thought about for so long. Though less stylish or complicated than Nicky Ray, Natasha had a unique optimism Safi admired. Little tended to quash her natural exuberance for all thing's lowbrow or highbrow, she seemed to enjoy both with equal indulgence.

She accepted an invitation to a Russian tea party held in private, ornate, gold-mirrored rooms. Natasha's mother took great pride explaining the cultural indulgences of a bygone era. Mothers and daughters sat around beautifully laid tables covered in fine-bone china, starched, embroidered tablecloths with flowered centrepieces on each table, indulging in tiny pastries, while having polite conversation about the coming ball going back to a baroque time of Catherine the Great. Women wore priceless gowns, some dressed in costumes of the era, dancing in formation to a chamber string quartet. Dancers were hired from ballet companies to perform court dancing, leaving the audience to appreciate their skill and beauty, indulging in their rich historical past. Safi wondered whether Sasha would agree to attend at least one ball; it was like stepping back into history, the tea party gave her a bird's-eye view into a small group of very privileged women.

The only balls she had read about or seen in magazines were the Crillon coming-out ball in Paris, for the offspring of the rich and famous, and the Metropolitan ball she had learnt about in New York, attended by the celebrity world and organised by the editor of American Vogue.

She found Natasha's personality ironic in its contradictions, going from one extreme to the other, introducing Safi not only to the cream of the crop of Russian high society, but to underground, politically-oriented, anti-Putin student cafés and galleries, where a mixture of adults and students hung out. In England these would be thought of as leftist socialist groups, but here it was hard to know what they would qualify as. Conversation was hard to follow, though many spoke English; their chosen subject: democracy and corruption.

She admired Natasha's ability to spend equal time amongst both groups of people, wondering how she was able to reconcile one with the other, indulging herself in both without being disapproving of either. Natasha encouraged Safi to chill out. 'Enjoy all,' she advocated, adding that 'politics crazy, yes, ideologies today, gone tomorrow.' Using broken English to emphasize her point.

Spring had arrived and the weather had improved – it was amazing how some brightness and warmth could do wonders for the human soul. She felt changed, charged, invigorated. Moscow was not yet anything like her home (and she wondered if it would ever be), but it was, all of a sudden, a much nicer place to live. There was no Kolya following behind. She felt liberated at last, able to explore without fear of getting lost. Having a girlfriend helped fill her days, while Sasha and his family regrouped and life returned to normal. Natasha introduced her to an English and American gym, with classes she was happy to sign up for. Suddenly her days were filled with routine, and getting up and out of bed in the morning no longer seemed so heavy an activity. Natasha insisted on speaking to her in Russian, giggling when she used incorrect words, helping with phrases she found helpful for communicating with Russians when out on her own.

The Cyrillic alphabet was beyond her understanding (and, she sometimes suspected, she would never fully get the hang of it), but she was determined to enrol in classes, or encourage Sasha to help her find a teacher with enough patience, teaching her a few hours a week. How long would it take her to fully adjust to Moscow? How long was a piece of string? Could a foreigner ever really feel at home here? Well, Safi was keen to find out. Apps were her bible for words she needed in a hurry, like street signs, to help get around the city. Feeling less of a stranger she was beginning to enjoy what Moscow had to offer. Sasha's lovemaking had taken on a more aggressive turn; he needed a release, she supposed, from the tensions he was experiencing. She did not mind the urgency of his needs, but he spoke little in the evenings when he fell into bed, devouring her with an intensity she had not experienced before.

Sasha's usual playful, fun manner seemed to have flown out of the window. He had little patience for light-hearted conversation. She knew he was struggling with the authorities, but his evasive – or, at least, isolated – attitude was bugging her. She believed they should not keep anything from each other if this relationship was to succeed, but there were things he did not want to talk about – the aftermath of the break-in, for instance. If it continued, she knew they would have a showdown, and she wanted to avoid stressing him out even more. She had no intention of discussing her concerns with Natasha; she liked to keep her private life separate, especially if the person you were confiding to was a close relative of your fiancé.

She still had no one to share her deeper concerns with. She was not sure which was worse feeling alienated from life or love. Living abroad had its advantages, it made you appreciate what you had always taken for granted. 'Grow up, Safi,' she told herself, 'it's time to face your demons, before they win this battle with your inner voice!'

Safi sat on the rowing machine, her thoughts racing in every direction. Working out at the gym was helping to bring order to her chaotic feelings. 'I will tackle Sasha about his mood. He will just have to communicate with me openly if he wants our relationship to last.' Safi knew she could not continue as they were – something had to give. Life was like a ridiculous paradigm: as soon as one side improved, another bothered her more. Could she ever be completely happy? What did complete happiness look like anyway? Perhaps it was human nature to always be frustrated about something, to want something better, something more – to seek, to strive, to hold yourself to an ever - higher standard.

She missed going in to work with Anna, who had not returned to the office since their return, but had instead squirreled herself away at the Dacha, where she did not want to be disturbed. Illness had been given as the reason for Anna's absence. Ringo with Sasha and Anna's other staff were now trying to run that side of their Rubicov enterprises.

Nights were spent in the company of Mika, Alexi and Valentina, who had not returned to St. Petersburg or London, respectively. They ate in silence, having spent the day in business meetings, after which Mika returned to the club (where he had taken up residence) and Alexi and Valentina to their Rubicov apartment. Valentina would soon be returning to London to be with Marina and to continue her work with the Royal Ballet students. She alone had brought light relief to Safi's evenings with Sasha's family. It was not difficult to pick up nuances in their body language, Safi thought. It was obvious that Sasha did not want to confide in her, there was something more going on – but what? She wondered whether Yvetta had been told about the break-ins. Safi knew that she had left the previous day for the art fairs in Europe and the States. Safi had noticed that her name had not been mentioned at any of their recent family dinners. Safi thought this was odd; even though Yvetta had problems with her mother, she would surely be informed of the break-ins, especially at their personal residence. Safi had tried to broach Yvetta in relation to Anna and the break-in but noticed that Valentina had deflected her question. 'Ah, well, Yvetta is away for quite a while on business, and I believe she is having troubles with Fritzi.' Still, Safi felt it odd that Yvetta had not been round to their family home to comfort her mother, or to see the damage for herself even if they never saw eye to eye; it was her mother who had been attacked, after all. Maybe she had and Sasha had not told her in passing conversation and, she might be jumping to conclusions, from past expectations, where Yvetta was concerned.

Safi was undressing when Sasha joined her in the apartment after dinner. He stood at the window in the bedroom, looking out at the night with a drink in his hand. Safi noticed he had started drinking vodka quite a bit since their return. She had never known him to drink so often and so heavily. Walking over, she put her arms around him to comfort him. They stood like that for some time, looking out at the night lights, when he turned and picked her up.

He carried her through to the bathroom and unceremoniously dumped her in the bath. Leaning over, he pulled her flimsy night top over her head as he turned on the faucets. Picking up the soap, he lathered her all over, indicating for her to stand as he soaped her private parts, his fingers lingering inside her, then pushed her down and under the water as he wet her hair. She came up for air gulping, staring at him enquiringly. He had not said a word through the whole process, and even now he ignored her gaze; it was as though she was simultaneously the focus of his attention and not in the room at all.

He continued to lather her hair with the shampoo, massaging her scalp. Safi began to enjoy the process. When he pushed her head back into the water to rinse her hair with the shower, she felt her back arch and her nipples protrude from the water as she leaned back, almost entirely pliant, deliciously subservient. She relished her passivity almost as much as the hot water rushing over her. Then she felt his lips on her nipples, sucking her until it hurt, everything changing slowly and then quickly, a not unpleasant feeling of confusion washing over her, too. She opened her eyes and watched him, not knowing what he would do next. The uncertainty was electric. Sasha shed his clothes in a pile on the floor and climbed into the bath. Facing her, he pulled Safi on top of his erection and allowed her to ride him. But Safi could tell that it was not enough; he wanted something else.

As she lifted herself off him, he pushed her out of the bath onto the tiled marble floor. Climbing out of the bath, he pulled her hair back with one hand as he mounted her. She bit his lip until she was sure it bled. Sasha rode her hard, pulling her legs up over his shoulders from the front, then, to her surprise, entering her from behind. He rammed himself into her until she yelped with pain. But he did not seem to be aware of her at all. He just kept pumping until Safi struck him, pleading him to stop. Sasha had a wild look in his eyes. Safi stiffened when she felt his release in shudders. He collapsed on top of her, pinning her under his weight. Tears ran down her face. In the sudden silence, she became aware that she was sobbing, but Sasha had not moved or responded. Safi struggled to roll him off enough to scramble out from under him. Crying uncontrollably, shivering, nose running, she knelt over Sasha. He was completely out. She pushed and pulled, but Sasha did not move. He began to breathe heavily, unpleasantly, a drunken snore. He had passed out on top of her.

Wet hair hanging in strings around her face, she grabbed the towelling robe to pull around her as she rose from the marble floor. Noticing blood between her thighs, she thought her menstrual cycle had started. As she sat on the toilet, she realised she was burning and that the blood had come from behind. Still shivering, Safi cleaned herself up. Had she just been raped? She did not know, but knew it had been the most awful experience of her entire life, being manhandled by the man she loved. She felt devastated inside and scared. Hearing Sasha groan, she tiptoed back into the bathroom but found he had left. Frightened to face him, she sat on the edge of the bath, wondering what to do next. But her mind was blank, her head in her hands, everything still spinning. She could not move. Eventually, cold and confused, she walked into the bedroom to find him spread out on the centre of the bed fast asleep.

She sat for a long time in the sitting room, staring out at the night sky again but seeing nothing now. She heaved herself off the sofa and gulped down two glasses of water, then went back into the bathroom to dry her hair. The dryer warmed the rest of her body and her mind eventually began to clear enough for her to think. But thought was painful, too, as she revisited Sasha's violent attack, feeling violated once again, this time by the memory.

She was sure it would be considered an attack on her person, no one could possibly call that lovemaking, since there was no love involved. He had not even acknowledged her. Feeling a little stronger, she walked back into the bedroom, sat on the edge of the bed and stared at Sasha, this person she no longer knew. Her emotions ran from hate to pity, then back to hate and anger at his treatment of her. How dare he manhandle her in that manner. Who did he think he was, to treat her with such little respect? There was nothing for it, she had to leave now. She could not face him, she just couldn't.

Running into the closet, she started throwing clothes into her bag. She pulled on her thick leggings and boots, sweatshirt and fur-lined hoody, grabbed her coat, and let herself out of the apartment. Once on the street, Safi felt the chill both inside and out as an icy wind hit her face. The twenty-four-hour doorman was shocked to see her, but he could not speak English and Safi tried to indicate that she needed a taxi to take her to the airport, straight away. Waiting in the entrance for the car to arrive, she checked her cell phone for the time, pleased to find that it was not yet midnight, not too late to find a flight to New York.

The black Range Rover pulled up and Safi ran for the back door, hardly giving the doorman a chance to help her. As he shut the door, she heard him giving instructions to take her to the airport. Lying back as the car sped off into the night, tears began welling up in her eyes and she held her hand in front of her mouth to quiet her sobs. She lifted her eyes to meet Kolya's staring at her in the rear-view mirror. She tried to collect herself, avoiding his questioning eyes. He was quietly talking in his ear piece. It could not be Sasha he was talking to, he had passed out. So who was Kolya speaking with?

Now alert (the crisp air and cold wind had seen to that), Safi stared out of the window. Having made multiple trips to the airport, she knew the route, and this was not it. Where was he taking her? God, she needed to be alone, to get away from this family. But now she was trapped – trapped in a house, trapped in a car, trapped in a strange city. The sense of imprisonment was endless. Desperate, she started to feel for the door handle. But it was pointless, the doors were locked, of course. Kolya stared at her in disbelief, realising that she was trying to escape while the car was moving. They drove for half an hour in silence. Kolya turned into a drive, shut off the engine, finished his conversation on his earpiece, and turned around to speak to Safi.

'Come we get out, Da.'

Safi sat glued to the back of the seat. 'Where are we?'

'Nadia Gluckman, a good friend. You stay here. Da, tomorrow we go airport.'

Safi liked Kolya, but she knew that he had worked for Sasha's family for many years. His loyalty did not lie with her. Sasha's family was very powerful, which meant it would be in Kolya's interest to obey them – what choice did he have? She sat staring at him. After the initial adrenalin rush of running away, she felt exhaustion taking hold of her.

The realisation of her situation struck her, the nakedness of her helplessness. She was not sure what to do, or whether she could trust Kolya. She saw him take in her hesitation, see the hurt in her face as she avoided his gaze again. Nadia came over to the back window, she had black curly hair and an open face Safi felt less intimidated staring in to the soft brown eyes, of the young woman. Nadia put her hand through the window and touched Safi lightly on the shoulder, speaking an accented American English: 'Hi! my name is Nadia I am an old friend of Kolya's, he called me to say you needed somewhere to stay for the night and, did not want to drop you off at a hotel.'

'But I want to leave,' Safi said. 'I must leave tonight.'

Nadia realised that Safi was desperate and for some reason in a state of shock. Being a trauma nurse at a clinic in Israel, she was accustomed to handling people in shock. She was home for a while to visit her grandparents, who had not immigrated and, had the use of her aunts apartment. She held out her hand to Safi, gently coaxing her out of the car. 'Tomorrow you can book the first flight out. Nothing flies until the morning anyway. It's dangerous to wander around an empty airport this time of night on your own. Please come inside. I am sure a hot mug of tea would go down well.'

Smiling kindly, Nadia helped her out of the car and into a small, ground-floor terraced townhouse, simply but nicely furnished in comfortable warm tones with rugs and throws casually thrown over the floral sofas.

'Kolya is very concerned for you and, knew I was here for a while before I return to Israel, I am visiting my grandparents' Nadia knew it was best to talk, put Safi at ease, perhaps encourage her to open up to her, sometimes talking to a stranger was easier.

Sasha woke confused to find Kolya sitting in a chair at the side of his bed. He had no idea why Kolya would be there. He slowly turned to see whether Safi was around.

'She is not here,' Kolya said. Sasha did not like the tone of his voice, as though Kolya was, in that moment, his superior, as though their roles were reversed. Sasha stared at Kolya, then pulled the pillow over his head. Flashes of the night coming back to him in sharp focus. What had he done? He had lost Safi, the one person he never wanted to lose. What had possessed him to behave like an animal? He felt wretched, sick. Leaning over the bed, he started to wretch. Kolya raced into the bathroom for the waste basket and held it under Sasha's mouth until he stopped heaving. Then he helped Sasha into the shower, leaving him when he felt he was strong enough to stand.

He went into the kitchen, found some tomato juice, and doctored it with whatever he could find. He made a hot pot of coffee and waited for his boss's son to show himself. He had to find out what had happened. He had never seen Sasha in this state. Safi was obviously frightened out of her mind. The family had been through crises before – outside pressures and threats – and Kolya had helped see them through. But this time was different, the enemy came from within, it was family.

Kolya had lost his father and older brother in the Afghan war and was the only sibling left to look after his mother and his younger sister. He had done well working for the Rubicovs; they looked after him and he would look after them in return. He was sure they would come through even this shameful episode in time.

The shower had not been running for a while. When helping Sasha into the shower, he had noticed the blood-stained towels on the bathroom floor. Sasha was in the bedroom, sitting on the carpeted floor, holding the blood-stained towels in his hands. Clutching them to his chest, he said in a soft voice, 'Dear God, what did I do, is she okay, Kolya?'

Kolya nodded to intimate that Safi was okay, then relieved Sasha of the blood-stained towels, which he threw into the wash basket. He helped Sasha up, handed him a tracksuit and watched as he struggled to put it on. Kolya led him through to the kitchen, where he insisted Sasha drink the tomato concoction and the coffee from his fancy Nespresso machine, while he popped some toast into the toaster. Kolya watched him carefully, trying to assess his state of mind. Handing him the butter and jam for the toast, he sat next to Sasha as he ate, waiting for the colour to return to his face.

'Where is she, Kolya?'

'I think perhaps you need to tell me first what happened here.'

There was no fight in Sasha as he shook his head. 'To be honest I can't remember much, but I must have hurt her, Kolya. Did you see that blood?' Before Kolya could say anything, Sasha was up and over the toilet bowl, wrenching again.

They sat quietly for a while. Kolya kept his gaze on Sasha; he could see that his memory of events the previous evening was slowly returning. He was visibly shaking. Suddenly, he started hitting his head with his hand. Kolya grabbed the hand and held it, gently but firmly almost like one holds a child's hand when crossing a busy street. When he let it go, Sasha said, 'I mixed some strong anti-depressants with vodka, Kolya. I think I treated her very badly. I remember her crying for me to stop, but I was a brute. I think I hurt her badly, took her against her will.' His voice became lower. 'She will never forgive me, never.'

Kolya stared at him then at the floor. He was not sure how to deal with this; it was out of his comfort zone, that was for sure. As a boy, Kolya had stopped his father from hurting his mother many times when he came home drunk. Vodka was a curse, that is why Kolya never touched the stuff. He had seen first-hand what it could do to perfectly good men; it made them behave in ways alien to their nature when sober.

'Safi was running away to the airport. I took her to a friend for the night instead, but now I have to return to take her to the airport.'

Sasha nodded. He understood there was nothing he could do to stop her. She would never agree to see him, not now – and nor could he blame her after his behaviour. Maybe later with time she would speak to him. Until then, he had to let her leave.

'Okay, book her a first-class ticket to wherever she wants to go. Take care of it please, Kolya. Take care of her.'

Kolya nodded again. 'What are you going to do?'

'I am good for nothing today. It's Saturday. I will go back to bed, sleep this off, and go and see my mother at the Dacha.'

He followed Kolya to the door, thanked him, and fell back into bed. Still shaking with grief, he buried his face in his pillow and sobbed. He could not believe Safi was out of his life, it was his own fault. They were all depending on him, especially Anna, and he had let them all down.

The following day, Sasha woke with a clear head No messages from Safi – or Kolya, for that matter. He called Kolya to find out whether Safi had left, and where she had flown to, but he knew before Kolya answered that she had gone to New York. The two D's would kill him, and he deserved nothing less. He would have to deal with the repercussions like a man: there was nothing for it, no amount of excuses would bring Safi back into his life. He had to deal with his demons once and for all. Perhaps madness ran in his family.

He kept berating himself, it made him feel oddly better. He was not a religious person, but whatever it took he would fix this, atone for the wrong he had done to Safi. None of this was her fault, yet he had diverted and transferred his own suffering and anger towards her. He had inflicted awful punishment on her. How could she forgive him when he was struggling to forgive himself? It was unforgivable behaviour and he needed salvation. In his own way, he was perhaps no better than Yvetta – hateful, arrogant, destructive to himself and to others close to him. He had turned into a Russian Bolshevik pig, something he detested.

Sasha shaved and dressed. It was Sunday. His mother was suffering more than any of them; she had taken herself off to the Dacha to lick her wounds, leaving them to hold the fort. This was the only time he had ever known his mother to hand over her work to anyone. Thank goodness for Ringo, who knew everything there was to know, and had stepped up to the job with little fanfare. Ringo had everything running like clockwork in less than a week, reorganised the workload and took most of Anna's calls, met with her clients and smoothed over all of their concerns. He impressed Sasha with his abilities. Sasha had initially underrated Ringo, but now he deserved to be rewarded. Ringo had given him folders for Anna to check and had written a report to keep her up to speed with day-to-day affairs. Sasha organised with the lawyers and the bank to have him sign for anything that needed Anna's signature if immediate attention was called for and the family were not available. Sasha could put Anna's mind to rest and she could remain at the Dacha until she felt strong enough to cope once more. He was told she was not taking calls from the office, or, for that matter, from anyone.

Arriving at the Dacha he found Anna deeply engrossed in a book. Looking up through her half-moon glasses, she managed a weak smile as he came over to give her a kiss. Sasha looked down at the pile of books, wondering what was keeping her so caught up, and noticed that she had been making notes. He picked up one of the books to read the title: Stop Walking on Eggshells. His mother was reading in English.

'What are you reading about?' Sasha asked, surprised.

'It's all about Yvetta's condition. It was recommended by the doctor at the clinic in Colorado.'

'And is it helping?'

Looking sadly at Sasha, Anna gave a resigned shake of her shoulders. 'I am slowly starting to understand her condition. Very few have a turnaround – very few and – some even take their own lives. It's all very sad.' Wiping a tear from her eye, she leaned her head back and closed her eyes. 'I still find it hard to accept her behaviour, all her evil campaigns, the lies and tantrums we have all put up with over the years. It will never stop, at this point we need to be honest about it and not placate ourselves with false optimism. I can't see her ever being well.'

Sasha sat down opposite his mother and took her hands in his.

'I am so very sorry, Mum. I wish I could change things, but it has gone way beyond any capability I may have had. I don't think any of us could have stopped her from self-destructing. Her mindset became fixated, it was just a matter of time before she became abusive or destructive, but I could never tell when she was going to blow. If I could, I would have prevented this awful thing from happening.'

'Sasha, darling, please stop; it won't help anyone, least of all you. There is very little any of us could have done, she had her own warped reality.'

He handed over the folders and papers for her to sign. Sitting, quietly watching his mother, shame washed over him. He wanted to tell her what he had done to Safi – to pour out everything, and be punished, and absolved – but could not find the words. His mother would never forgive him, she cared for Safi so much. It would kill his mother to know that he was capable of such brutish behaviour. After all, Safi was the daughter she never had, and now Sasha had ruined her, too. Sasha reflected that perhaps he was as evil as Yvetta, only that evil manifested itself in a different way, more quietly and cruelly, less deliberately, more occasionally. He hated lying about Safi, but lie he had to, telling Anna she was in New York to catch up with the two D's and help them out with the brownstone.

'Please tell Safi when she returns that I still would love her to come and work for me,' Anna said, and Sasha felt a further flash of guilt that she had so readily believed his lies. She trusts me, Sasha thought. Safi had trusted me, too. And what did I do with that trust? It was premature discussing what Safi would do on her return to Moscow, when she may she never return to Moscow at all. With renewed anxiety, Sasha turned away from his mother. 'Alexi has other ideas in the pipeline,' Sasha said, eager to change the subject. 'He wants Safi to run Yvetta's gallery. What do you think?'

Anna looked up in surprise. 'Actually, I think it's an excellent idea. If Safi is willing to learn the ropes, why should we not continue with the art investments? So far the gallery has been keeping its head well above water. Yvetta was a good businesswoman, I will give her that.'

They settled down at the kitchen bar for a light lunch prepared by the staff who had remained to look after Anna's needs, while she remained at the Dasha, instead of returning twice a week to maintain the place, while empty. Anna seemed content to stay where she was until she felt strong enough to cope. She wanted to move directly into the house once the art works had been restored and new cabinets had been installed with the few valuable pieces that had survived the attack, until she had the energy to find others she thought she might love to own, it had taken her years to collect those now destroyed, a great loss.

Sasha left his mother to her afternoon nap, and returned to Moscow. Stress had a strange way of affecting people and Sasha tried to deal with his tension headaches and anxious feelings by doctoring himself with alcohol and over-the-counter medication. He knew he could not blame his brutish behaviour only on his pill-popping and vodka, nor on the stress induced by Yvetta's behaviour. After all, he obviously had some ugly, animal instinct within him that only he could account for. It was too easy to blame someone else for one's own behaviour, to invent fake criminals and fake crimes to cover everything up. This was what Yvetta always did, incapable of taking responsibility for her own actions, lashing out at everyone else. He felt ashamed to the core; no amount of apologising would be enough to make up for what he had done to Safi. Picking up the phone he dialled the only number he knew would be able to help him with this problem.

Mika answered on the first ring.

Chapter 23

Safi arrived at JFK after a sleepless flight, the events leading up to Sasha's physical attack turning around and around in her mind. She knew Sasha was a good person; how could she be so mistaken about someone she loved? Since the attack on Anna, she had noticed a marked change in his mood. He had become anxious and intense, the fun side of his personality had vanished and he had little patience for small talk, dismissing her efforts to lift his dark moods with idle chatter. She had empathy for Sasha and the family, it was an awful thing to have happened, but she was not to blame and he had no right to take his unhappiness out on her. She was not a dog to be kicked by its owner at the end of a miserable day at work. She would not stand for it. She felt her resolve strengthen, and by the time she disembarked at JFK, she no longer felt her departure was hasty or overly dramatic.

Trembling, with a lump forming in her throat, she dialled Daniel's number, trying to collect herself before he picked up.

'Safi!' he said on hearing her voice. But the happiness in his voice compounded her own sense of isolation.

'Yes, it's me, I've just arrived in New York.'

'What a lovely surprise.' But he recognised from her voice something wasn't right. 'Are you okay?'

Safi tried to catch the sob building up, but it was useless.

'What's going on, Safi'?

Wiping her nose, she managed to talk. 'I had to leave. I can't really talk now. Can I go to the house?'

Dan gave her the address, and she, in turn, gave it to the cab driver. She pondered how to tell the two D's what had happened. It had been rape, she was sure of that. Sasha had attacked her. No one in their right mind could call what happened normal sex. Or could they? She felt so miserable, not knowing what precisely in their dynamic had changed. Up until that point they were playful but always loving. Perhaps she had changed? Confused by her thoughts, she closed her eyes and tried to shut her mind down. Easier said than done. It was good to be back in New York, at least.

Waking to the sounds of their voices, Safi felt relieved to see the two D's. She clambered out of the cab with her rucksack, which was all she had managed to grab from the apartment in her frightened state. She fell into their arms as the cab sped off, relieved to be with her own family and in a city, she thought of as home. In that moment, there was no doubt in her mind that she had made the right decision coming here. She was in a safe space with those who cared about her.

Anxious and concerned, Dax found her hand and led Safi into their new home. Now almost complete, the brownstone was a magnificent transformation. Daniel was ahead to open the door, leading Safi gently into a vast kitchen, so different from the one in their loft. Sitting her down in the great room leading off the kitchen, they sat on either side of her on the sofa, surrounding her with support, keeping her safe and warm and making sure she knew she was loved and could share anything with them. This was a safe space, free of judgement, full of love. She leaned her head on Daniel's shoulder, while Dax held both of her hands, softly stroking and patting them, gently trying to calm her as she sobbed.

'Would you like a cup of tea, sweetie?' Dax asked. Usually, when he said these words, he imitated (and not very well, either) a British accent, but not this time. His voice was low and soft. Safi nodded, trying to collect her emotions. 'Does anyone else know you are in New York?'

'Only Sasha and Kolya.' Holding the mug in her hands, relieved for the warmth and the company and the undeniable affection these men had in her, she looked at them, not sure she was able to recount what had happened out loud. The incident had only replayed in her mind, albeit over and over, in a series of violent and increasingly lurid and disturbing images, but finding the words to explain Sasha's brutish behaviour was another challenge altogether?

'I am struggling to find the words, it's hard, so hard to come to terms with Sasha's behaviour. I ran away, I was so frightened and hurt. He attacked me.'

'What! What do you mean he attacked you?'

Suddenly the words came pouring out. 'Everything changed. He changed after the attack on Anna. I tried so hard to understand, but he became moody, started drinking, had no patience. I mean, he always drank alcohol, but I'd never seen him drink so often and so much. The only thing that seemed to help him was making love – and then two nights ago he attacked me.' She started crying. 'I think he raped me.' They stared, lost for words. Safi described what had happened in the apartment, described every little detail of his desperate, brutish lovemaking. How he dumped her in the bath, dragged her out by her hair, took her from behind against her will until she begged him to stop; how he collapsed on top of her pinning her under him, how she found blood running down her legs from his attack, how she found him passed out on their bed. How, in shock, she cleaned herself up and ran out of the apartment late at night. The doorman had called Kolya, who had been wonderfully kind to her. She looked down at her hands shaking in her lap, then looked up at their shocked expressions, a feeling of both shame and relief flooding through her. She waited calmly for them to say something.

Dax began to cry; Dan put his arms around him. 'They came over to Safi, sat down next to her again, both putting their arms around her, holding her close, crying together softly. Daniel stroked her hair, while Dax held her hand. They sat together for a long time, saying nothing. Words were not necessary; there would be plenty of time for words later, now all they wanted was to give her comfort. She knew only Dan and Dax would be able to console her, understand her, give her the unconditional love she needed; they would not judge her or make her feel guilty or dirty. She felt anger at the feelings of shame that intersected and invaded her thoughts. He was the one who needed to feel shameful, not her.

'I feel so ashamed, why do I feel like this?'

Dax was the first to speak. 'I think it's a natural emotion. You are angry, blaming yourself for allowing it to happen. Sometimes things happen that we cannot control. I am sure you will experience many more emotions, mostly anger, sadness, perhaps even pity for Sasha. I think you might have to talk this through with a therapist. It might not be enough to share it with us. You will need guidance to process all of your feelings.'

Daniel started pacing the room, visibly angry. Dax and Safi sat watching his anger build as he punched his fist into his hand.

'God, I could kill him. He is going to come crawling back for forgiveness. We cannot allow you to return, Safi. Who knows what he might do next time. You have to break it off.'

'I don't know, maybe Sasha's ill.'

Daniel turned, quietly fuming at Safi. Dax jumped up; he knew Dan was going to say something Safi did not need to hear yet. She needed time to process her feelings; they had to be patient with her.

'The most important thing is that she is safe,' Dax said, 'she is here with us, Dan, she made the right call. That's all that matters right now.'

'He is right, Safi.' Dan's voice was softer now. He sat back down. 'That is all that matters for the moment. We will figure the rest out, but you will have to let your folks know that you are here, they will worry. I understand that you can't tell them the real reason, but you will have to think of something?' Safi nodded. 'Maybe tomorrow. I just can't talk to them – or to anyone, really – right now. Do you think that would be okay?'

'I will call your dad,' Dan said, 'say you are here and that you will call tomorrow. I do not want them to worry. How's that?'

It was only midday but she felt exhausted. Dax showed her to the spare room; while she showered, he prepared hot chocolate with a dash of brandy, fussed over her, and refused to leave her side until she had fallen asleep. Pulling the covers over her, he tiptoed out and down the stairs to Dan.

He could hear Dan on the phone to Leonard. It was early morning in England. Dan was struggling to keep the conversation light, not to give them any cause for alarm. Dan looked up as Dax approached. Dax put his head on Dan's shoulder to comfort him; they stood for a while consoling each other, both desperately sad for Safi, neither quite knowing what to do. Dax wondered why Dan did not want Safi to tell her folks, surely, they should know? 'Dan, do you think it's right for Safi not to tell her folks, this is beyond normal behaviour, they should be told, in my opinion.'

Dan looked doubtful, 'Safi can do what feels right for her, but in the state she was in I just did not want her to go through the whole thing with Fiona and Leonard, parents are not always the first port of call in this situation to my mind, but who am I to talk, Rupert wasn't exactly the present dad, so maybe you are right?'

Daniel's cell rang, displaying an unknown number. He stiffened and answered tentatively. It had to be Sasha, Dax thought, watching the dark expressions passing over Dan's face as he listened to the caller on the other end.

Sasha had made no excuses for his behaviour, he admitted to everything Safi had told them. Apart from the vodka, they learnt he had taken anti-depressants. He understood no forgiveness could be expected and that he would never be able to atone for his brutish behaviour. He loved Safi and would do anything to gain her forgiveness. Even if she no longer wanted him, he needed to see her and ask for her forgiveness. He wanted to know whether she had arrived safely and what state she was in. Sasha would arrive late that night, would they help prepare Safi to see him?

Initially, Dan answered calmly, but when his emotions got the better of him, he could not keep the anger from his voice. Before he knew it, he was screaming at Sasha.

'How dare you ask for our help? You disgust me. Absolutely no, no way in hell am I going to allow Safi to see you.'

After a pause, Sasha said, 'I know you are angry, but don't you think that is up to Safi?'

'Maybe, but I am her guardian while she is under my roof. You asked me if she has arrived safely. The answer is that she is a lot safer here, without you, than she would be with you. Why would I let her see you and put her life in danger all over again? God knows what you intend to do to her next.'

'I will be there tomorrow morning, Daniel; you can knock my block off then, if you still have the need. I love Safi and I will fight for her. Whatever it takes I will do.' Daniel slowly put his cell down; there was little he could do if she wanted to see him. They felt protective towards Safi, but in the end, it was her call and not theirs.

Momentarily not knowing where she was, Safi woke with a pounding headache. She lay staring at the ceiling for what felt like ages, her body aching in places she had not noticed before. A desolate feeling passed through her. She closed her eyes, hoping it would lessen; instead, she found herself softly crying, tears pooling in her throat, a deep sadness enveloping her. She did not know or care what time it was, all she wanted to do was to hide, not face the world. She did not have the strength to talk to her parents, who would know immediately something was wrong. She could never tell them ever.

She heard footsteps on the stairs. Oh God, who was it? She could not face anyone, not even Dan or Dax. She needed space to collect herself. Turning to face the wall, she pulled the covers over her head as far as they would go and pretended to be asleep. She felt someone sit on the bed, then a hand lightly on her side. Suddenly aware of her own sobs, she recoiled further under the covers. Perhaps whoever it was would leave her alone if she refused to turn around. The toughest thing she had to admit to herself was that she still loved Sasha.

She became aware of a familiar smell. Cologne, yes, it smelled just like Sasha's, but it couldn't be. She was being ridiculous, her brain was frazzled, maybe she was still asleep and in the midst of a nightmare. The hand had not moved, she could feel it shaking slightly; there was no sound, but now the presence sitting on her bed became overwhelming. Safi suddenly turned and screamed, her hand flew to her mouth and she sat cringing up against the headboard, her knees up at her chest, staring wide eyed with fear at Sasha. It wasn't possible, she must be hallucinating; the two D's would never allow him in the house.

He looked at her frightened reaction and recoiled, downtrodden, broken, she could tell he was crying. She had never seen him cry before. Then she became aware of a swelling under his eye. My God, someone had hit him. Still, he said nothing. She had never experienced such loud silence. What was he doing here? Safi felt her heart melting; he looked so frightened and so sad. Then a crazed feeling of anger consumed her how dare he invade her private space, how dare he.

Sasha could see that she was experiencing different emotions and recognised her anger; he knew he deserved it – and more. Suddenly, Safi swung out and hit him full across the face. 'Get out, get out, I never want to set eyes on you again. I hate you! You, you brutalised me in the most horrific way. I loved you, how dare you invade my space, how dare you?'

'Please, please, Safi, can we talk. I know this is hard for you to believe, but I love you more than life itself. I would never knowingly hurt you, never.'

She stared at him, wondering if he was mad. 'But you did just that!' He shook his head. 'I know and I wish I could reverse what happened, but I can't. There is no excuse for what I did – none. Please believe me when I tell you that I was not myself.'

'What do you mean? It was you, wasn't it?'

'I stopped off at a friend's pharmacist and he gave me some drug to lift my depression. What he did not tell me was that it had hallucinatory, mind-bending chemicals, and when mixed with alcohol it could alter one's behaviour.'

She stared at him; he had not been himself these last few days, she saw it in his eyes, but had thought he was drunk.

'I am so sorry, Safi, believe me. I knew what I was doing, but I had no control. When I came around, Kolya was sitting on my bed. I started retching nonstop. He put me in the shower and fed me coffee and some concoction of tomato juice and dry toast, until I was able to comprehend what had taken place.'

He sat quietly for a moment then shuddered at the memory. He had an image of the bloody towels again, as fresh and frightening as when he had seen them for real. 'When I saw the bloody towels and that you were gone, I died inside. Kolya told me he had fetched you, thank God! I told him to take you wherever you wanted to go. Then I spoke to Mika – I told him everything, he told me to pull myself together, that he would not be surprised if I lost you for ever. He said to take the company plane and explain myself to you, whatever the outcome. I wanted you to know, it was never my intension to harm you. I love you, Safi, I truly love you.'

'Why have you got a black eye?'

'Oh, never mind. I deserve it, it does not hurt'

'If we are going to be honest with each other, I think you better tell me.'

Touching his eye, he smiled weakly. 'Daniel.'

She stared at him. 'Really, Dan hit you?'

'Yes, as he opened the door to me, he slugged me in the eye.'

Putting her hand over her mouth, she could not suppress a small smile Sasha was dying to reach out, to take her in his arms, hold her, but he knew it had to come from Safi; he dare not go near her. This was his punishment – he had her trust and he had ruined it, blown it, destroyed what they had carefully and intimately built together. They sat on the bed silently for some time, each in their own thoughts. 'I think you need to tell me why you have been in such a foul mood since returning to Moscow. I tried to empathise, but you were cold, distant, even nasty and short-tempered with me. She faltered but continued. 'All you seemed to want was sex, not lovemaking. Only animal sex seemed to satisfy you, and then the attack happened.' I have no excuse apart from the drugs I was popping to cope with not being there for my mother when she needed me most, I let my family down, that's how I felt and my mother's sadness has seeped into my soul.

Sasha knew he had problems after Yvetta's attack on his mother. He felt uncontrollable anger towards his sister after seeing his mother disintegrate at the Colorado Clinic. He was not able to share Yvetta's attack on his mother with Safi; it had to remain in the family, only. He did not want to lie to Safi – to hold anything further from her, ever, especially now – she deserved an explanation of some sort, he knew but Yvetta, had to remain their problem to solve.

'For police and insurance reasons I have not been allowed to share any information about the attack on my mother. It's highly confidential, it has to remain in the family for reasons I cannot explain. Please understand it would destroy our family if it became public. All I can say is Yvetta will never be returning to Moscow; she has left for good, and so has Fritzi. They have become a problem that cannot be ignored.'

Safi sat quietly trying to digest what Sasha had just told her. She knew it must have been difficult to keep his emotions intact. Did Yvetta have something to do with the attack on her own mother? It was beyond comprehension, but she could not delve any further. He had already divulged more information than he was allowed; she would have to accept what he had just shared with her, and leave it at that.

She sat quietly nodding, letting him know that she appreciated him trying to help her understand the predicament they found themselves in with the Russian authorities.

'I now realise that this whole business with my mother has affected me more than I was aware of. She has been a recluse since the incident and we have been sick with worry about her. Anna blames herself for everything. We are trying to give her the space to come to terms with the attack, hoping she will in time realise that it had nothing to do with her.'

'Yes, I realised that your mother was depressed and withdrawn. I am so sorry, but Sasha, you are blaming yourself, too, perhaps you should realise that it is not your fault either?'

'I feel responsible. It's hard to explain but I have always felt responsible for my mother's wellbeing and Yvetta's. It's just the way it's always been in our family.' Safi wanted to comfort him, but she could not bring herself to touch him, she was not ready, she would be soon but not yet.

'The break-in brought things to a head for my mother. My mother wants what all mothers want: to have love from their children, and Yvetta shows neither empathy nor love.'

'Perhaps it's time to let go,' Safi suggested. But did this mean she had to let go of the anger she still felt towards Sasha; her confusion and pain were still as fresh as the bruise on his face. They sat quietly together. Sasha's presence felt stronger than ever, she could feel the thumping of her heart in her ears. She did love him, she knew that, and yes, he loved her, of that there was no doubt. It was ridiculous, really, what people do to each other's emotions. The electricity between them was palpable; she could tell he felt the same. The tension was almost visible.

There was movement outside the door. Had the two D's been eavesdropping? Probably. She could not blame them for feeling nervous about their meeting; she had been in an awful state yesterday. Safi looked at the clock next to the bed. It was noon; she had slept right through the night. She suddenly felt ravenous.

'I am starving, are you?'

He looked up at Safi. 'I think you have a posse of bodyguards outside the door.' Smiling nervously, he extended his hand. Hesitating for a second, she allowed him to take her hand gently into his. With superhuman control, Sasha helped her off the bed. His body avoiding touching any part of her; he knew if he as much as brushed against her skin he would envelope her into his arms. Safi stood for a while, unsure of her own feelings, only that what she felt she felt strongly, and that nothing was as simple as it had first appeared. She nervously struggled with her flats, pulling them onto her feet, dashed into the bathroom to have a quick wash, pulled her hair back into a ponytail, and was back out within five minutes. The black tracksuit she had slept in would have to do.

They found the two D's missing, but to their credit, a brunch of bagels, cream cheese, and lox was laid out on the breakfast bar, not to mention fresh coffee from Starbucks. Not waiting for Sasha, she smeared cream cheese on a bagel and stuffed it in her mouth. Gulping down the wonderful hot coffee, she began to feel almost human; now all she needed was a hot shower to begin the day she had only moments ago dreaded.

Sasha watched with amused relief as the colour began to reappear in that beautiful face he loved. His heart almost burst to see her happy again. He felt suddenly happier than he had been since before the break-in. He knew she was angered and hurt but she would he knew, forgive his unforgivable brutish act on her body, he felt humbled by her ability to see him in a good light to have empathy when he had hurt her so deeply. Safi was stronger than him her ability to overcome and to move forward was astounding. No Russian could do that, he was sure of that, he found he admired her strength to forgive those she loved. He would have to earn her trust, but he wasn't going to push it, there had to be no doubt in her mind when they were united once again.

'I am going upstairs for a shower,' she said. 'I still have my travel clothes on. I must have passed out on the bed. I can't believe I slept until noon today. I have to call my folks, they are waiting to hear from me.'

Sasha made himself comfortable with the Sunday papers, content to wait as long as it took for her to join him; he wasn't going anywhere without her. Daniel and Dax sat on the top step of the landing, close enough to Safi's door to bust in if they needed to. Safi had obviously not realised Sasha's presence immediately. The two D's had almost burst into the room when they heard her gasp with shock at seeing Sasha; then they heard her outburst of anger and the sound of a smack: They knew it was Safi, Sasha would have let her do anything to him, he was a complete mess, he was certainly getting what he deserved. She was being strong, even aggressive which was hard for Safi, after last night they had not expected her to fight her corner so quickly, she hardly had time to recover but she was facing Sasha, letting him know, he was not forgiven, that was a good thing, instead of letting the anger fester, she was confronting him, getting it out and that's what Safi needed, and Sasha wanted, to show he was prepared to take anything she meted out.

Daniel had not been able to contain his anger at seeing Sasha at the door, and had hit him full-on on the jaw. Sasha had reeled back, shocked, but managed to find his balance.

'I deserved that. I see you are a man of your word. May I come in, please? I am not going anywhere until I have spoken with Safi.'

Shaking, Dan said, 'Why the hell should I let you in or near Safi? For that matter, explain that to me after your disgusting brutish behaviour, you don't deserve Safi.'

'Yes you are absolutely right, I don't deserve to come in or to see Safi, but please Dan and Dax I have to face my demons and I have to tell Safi that I wasn't myself, I was out of my skull, and she needs to know that, it wasn't her I was seeing at the time, I can't explain because I don't know myself why the hallucinations affected my behaviour. All I know is I have to explain and say I'm a monster, but that I love her and, need her to know I would never in my right mind harm her purposely. I know people who do these things say this, I can't fathom out myself what happened but that was not me, it can't be me, I've never in my life done anything like that ever or hurt a woman, least of all Safi.'

Sasha was pale, sad, and crying, something the two D's were a sucker for and they acquiesced with reluctance, both following him up the stairs to her door and only backing off when Sasha held his hand out beseeching them, not to alert Safi of his arrival. Feeling helpless they sank down together on the top step of the landing to listen. ' Dan held Dax hand his head hung low, 'Are we doing the right thing, I'm not sure, God I will kill him if he goes anywhere near her, I might live to regret this.'

What they heard changed their minds; he had not raped her intentionally, he had abused her in way's no person should be treated, especially someone they love, that was for sure, but they forgave him, too, and hoped Safi would in time, they believed Sasha was not in his right mind at the time. Obviously, the guy had been under tremendous pressure by the sound of it. The vodka and drugs did not help matters, either, but they agreed that he was a good guy, even brave, and with a heart. Together they tried to tiptoe down the stairs and out of the house to fetch bagels and lox. Daniel arranged the food on the counter, leaving the coffee in the Starbucks containers for warmth. They retired to their study one floor up.

Daniel had met Safi on his way up to the study. She nipped into their study to give them all the details, her eyes almost bright now; they agreed Sasha was a good guy, she needed to forgive him, in time, not all at once. He needed to sweat a bit more, that's if she could stop herself from falling into his arms. This was the worst thing that had ever happened to her, yet she felt she could overcome it, why she did not understand, yet. She hugged Dan and Dax and dashed down the stairs. Relieved at the turn of events, the two D's did a little jig, hugged, and settled down to read the Sunday papers, they hated to see their Safi hurt and seeing her spirit strong again was wonderful.

Safi changed out of her tracksuit and ventured down with the two D's to find Sasha fast asleep. He had collapsed on one of the armchairs, his legs stretched out on the ottoman, mouth wide open, with one arm hanging loosely over the chair. She stood and watched him for a while, feeling more tender towards him than she had in a long while (asleep, every man is as innocent as a child), and was about to suggest they let him be, when Sasha opened his eyes and extended his hand, pulling her towards him gently. Needing little encouragement, she allowed herself to fall into his lap and hugged him tightly, almost as if she felt sorry for him, rather than herself.

Sasha tried to appear strong warding her off playfully, then enfolded her in his arms and held her close to him. Dan and Dax both choked up as they saw Sasha's eyes well up with tears and his head droop over her shoulder in the embrace.

'Well, I think this occasion calls for some whiskey,' Dan said. 'I for one need a stiff drink to calm my nerves.'

But the conversation was stilted.

'Well,' Dax ventured, 'we thought that was it between the two of you. I must say, Sasha, you are a lucky man. You certainly behaved like a brute.'

No one wanted to make light of what had happened, but Dax could be funny, in the most awkward times, defusing a situation most would find impossible to defuse and the whiskey had relaxed them enough to see his stab at humour as an attempt to lighten everyone's mood. Safi tried not to smile at Dax's ability to be funny at a non-funny time. Daniel then Dax smiled with relief. Sasha wasn't sure what was to come next, but the tension had broken something had to give and, before they knew it they were all in floods of tears, after quiet enveloped the room.

Sasha was the first to break the heavy silence; taking Safi's hand, he looked into her eyes, and said, 'That will never happen again. From now on, we will share our personal needs good and bad. I need your strength, Safi, without you I am nothing. You mean everything to me. My family are my strength and, so are you.

Sasha wasn't into sweet talk; this was hard for him. Safi said nothing. Overwhelmed, she held his hand. It was obvious that he had suffered a great deal. She believed him and she knew Daniel and Dax believed him too.

Chapter 24

Moscow in spring was beautiful: the trees were heavy with blossoms, the parks busy with joggers, mothers pushing strollers, and walkers with their dogs enjoying the warmer temperatures after a particularly bitter winter. Anna had moved back into the family home and returned to work with renewed energy. Ringo had kept her closely informed of all decisions, giving her little cause for worry. Anna, more than anyone, valued loyalty, and Ringo had taken on the mantle of responsibility with little fuss, showing he was more than capable of leadership. The family rewarded those they trusted and Ringo had more than proved himself.

Mika and Alexi had remained in Moscow, upgrading the family's security apparatus. Moscow had become a battleground for criminal elements. Now more than ever, the right palms had to be greased (in the police service and other government departments; to say nothing of criminal elements in the gambling syndicates), and Mika made sure they were.

Anna and Sasha together cajoled and encouraged Safi, persuading her to work with the Rubicov gallery staff. They convinced her she would find her feet, learning the business through experience. And, of course, when she needed them, they would guide her with their knowledge and expertise. What thrilled Safi most was that her first experience with an exhibition was to be with Dax. She knew that DuPont preferred working with Safi than Yvetta. She would rely on his expertise.

He promised them a blockbuster show, benefitting both Dax and Safi, their first major art exhibition under his tutelage and guidance. DuPont was convinced Safi would be an asset to the gallery's success. With his encouragement she gained confidence; everyone who worked for the gallery were more than accommodating. For Dax to be successful internationally, the opening show would have to be a sell-out. Those little red dots next to his paintings were what they were aiming for.

Safi took to the art world like a duck to water: the staff were indispensable, every day was a learning curve, but she was not afraid of hard work. Her main obstacle was not speaking Russian; most people she dealt with spoke a perfectly good English, but on a daily basis the buyers who came to the gallery were Russians. Safi found the staff referring to her for guidance in price reductions when an offer was made for a particular work. The artists often rejected a sale if more than a twenty percent reduction was offered; it was her job to guide the artists professionally. For the first few months, she lived on conference calls to DuPont, who spoke several languages. Without his guidance she would have floundered. His training allowed her to shore up confidence in her ability. After her first major sale she felt elated.

Staff introduced her to the everyday running of a gallery: packers, shippers, dealing with custom forms, and tax reductions. This was to say nothing of framers (customers often changed the frame the painting was exhibited in). Running a gallery was no different from running a business. Work had to be turned over and clientele enticed into the gallery. Some needed expert advice, others were searching for a special artist's work. Safi found the work stimulating; she had no idea there was so much to learn. Major shows were chosen and arranged a year or two in advance. Exhibition spaces costing a fortune had to be furnished to high standards, work hung, sculptures mounted onto plinths, decorative furnishings used for enhancement.

Beside their homegrown talent, Rubicov Gallery represented renowned artists. The important shows for Rubicov were in London, Miami, and New York. They attended two international shows a year; it became a constant battle to balance their diary throughout the year.

Germany was no longer an option as the Rubicov family declined to deal with the Berlin connection. The German artists previously represented by the gallery were removed from the list; works had been crated and shipped back to them. The reason given was that 'The Rubicov gallery is under new management.' All previous works represented by Yvetta and Fritzi were terminated.

DuPont guided the gallery to show at major exhibitions, including the Biennale in Venice. If successful, Dax could be represented by Rubicov, although a homegrown artist would have to be their leading choice. The gallery's side brochures for artists had to be printed; books were published on major artists' work and sold at the gallery. Invitations were sent out on a regular basis for hosted charity venues. Safi found the staff more than competent. Ilona had worked for Yvetta and, ran the gallery Safi found her in put invaluable, the other members of the team, followed her lead and she had no issues to deal with as the new person in charge at the gallery. They found her glamorous presence lent a cache to the gallery, something more lucrative than having immediate knowledge, and with Ilona's help and DuPont's guidance her days flew by soaking up new facts faster than she thought she was capable of doing.

Yvetta had not encouraged the family to attend her soiree evenings, preferring an artier alternative clientele. But DuPont had different ideas, encouraging a mixed clientele; movers and shakers from Russian society were now sent invitations.

Together with the Rubicov family, Safi hosted the odd event, encouraged celebrities and well-known artists to attend from other mediums such as the opera and ballet. The gallery became a new sophisticated spot to be seen, and buying pricy works of art became a competitive sport. Anna and Alexi were thrilled with the new direction the gallery had taken under DuPont's guidance – an improvement even over Yvetta's considerable success with the gallery, and without the headache, daily demands and extreme diva behaviour of Yvetta herself. Safi, happier than she had been in months, found her life had taken a turn she would never have been able to predict.

They had moved back into their apartment on the top floor of the family home. Sasha needed to be sure his mother's anxieties about living in the house did not return. As the weeks passed, Anna continued to amaze them; she now sported a more youthful blonde hairstyle. Her wardrobe had undergone a transformation, too, favouring off-white or black Chanel accompanied by their signature pearls, while her battered leather briefcases were replaced by designer bags. The image was completed by black-framed Prada glasses, a perfect foil for her soft blonde bob. The old dowdy Anna was replaced by a sharply dressed contemporary woman, still very much the matriarch of her family but with a more up-to-date look.

After a few glasses of wine over a casual dinner in her handsome kitchen (the only room in the house that had not been refurbished after the break-in), Anna confided to Sasha and Safi her change of image and newfound interest in life outside of work. She had met someone, much to Sasha's shocked delight. She told them how her attitude transformed after the long hiatus at the Dacha. How she buried her melancholia in books that were recommended by her therapist, who she no longer saw professionally but socially. How sharing her feelings had freed her from her lonely and increasingly agitated state of mind. This had enabled her to move on, and now she felt reborn, young even and most of all happy. She discovered to her shock that it had been so long since she had been really happy that it came to her as an altogether new feeling. She no longer carried that heavy burden; her children were adults and responsible for their own choices. She had learnt to let go: of anger, of guilt, of recriminations, and regret. She had given herself permission to get on with her life, while she had the energy to do so. After all, how many years did she have left on this earth? Was it worth wasting them on depression and crippling self-doubt? Living well, as they say, was the best revenge.

Anna had come to terms with how things were ('It is what it is,' as Alexi would say), not how she wanted them to be. She loved her daughter, was saddened by her behaviour, but what she felt now was acceptance rather than guilt.

From Safi's point of view, Yvetta had left for one of London's major art shows, and never returned to Moscow. It was hard to comprehend her reasons for leaving her whole world behind, a world she loved and was an important player in. On some level, Safi felt guilty for taking over the gallery. She empathised with Anna, who had suffered so many years from Yvetta's erratic behaviour. Something huge must have persuaded her to cut all ties with her family and her business, yet by all accounts it had turned out in Safi's favour. Some would even think the odd coincidence – Yvetta more or less disappearing and Safi suddenly taking her place – strangely fortuitous?

'Thank goodness my cousin Yvetta ran off with her eccentric friend, probably to Berlin, a very decadent place. It's certainly turned out okay for you, even the art world here in Moscow couldn't handle such an obvious gay coupling, much too decadent even for the new Russia'. Safi had laughed at Natasha's summing up of her interpretation of Yvetta's reason for leaving. Still, the fortuitous bit worried Safi, who did not relish courting trouble with either Yvetta or Fritzi down the line. When Safi repeated Natasha's explanation to Sasha, she noticed that he listened intently, before laughing it off with 'Natasha has a fertile imagination, but she might have hit the nail on the head where my sister and Fritzi are concerned. I do not think you have to worry at this stage about either of them, they won't be returning to Moscow – or, for that matter, Russia – in a hurry.' With that, Sasha terminated the conversation, no longer wanting to dwell on his sister. He never spoke about Yvetta for more than a minute at a time, and even then, with an unusual awkwardness and sense of discomfort.

Sasha had moved to Rubicov Enterprises, which had had many of its company positions restructured. Anna had made it clear it was time for her to move aside; she wanted less responsibility and to start enjoying her life once again. Sasha was appointed to take over control of Rubicov Enterprises, and his cousin appointed to run Rubicov's restaurants and club in Moscow.

Mika was the trouble-shooter in the family, he was their own private version of the KGB: Nothing escaped his attention in any of the companies. Mika dealt with all government departments; he had colleagues and friends in both high and low echelons of society. He kept a close watch on political developments, keeping ahead of any political changes in the new Russia. Russia was indeed rapidly changing – too fast for many people's liking –nothing was what it seemed at face value.

The recent attack on the family and restaurant had caught him off guard, resulting in immediate action. As a result, Mika had installed a new security team for the family in Moscow.

Safi's life had now become – delightfully, sometimes dizzyingly – hectic. The bored, anxious girl who had arrived in Moscow in the middle of the worst winter for years was forgotten. In her place was a happy, stimulated, very much in-love Safi. The only downside was the security guard she had to contend with on a daily basis; Mika's new directive for the family had affected her as well.

Anna enjoyed mentoring Sasha; it gave her a chance to work closely with him, something she would never be able to do with Yvetta. The Rubicovs believed in strong family ties and their business empire was strengthened by their philosophy of synergy, to encompass all new enterprises under the family umbrella. Even those family members with professional degrees worked for the family business. The family was run more like an autocratic meritocracy. 'The young had not yet rebelled,' Natasha had joked over lunch one day with Safi. Natasha had been idle for quite some time after her return to Moscow – hopping around between nightclubs and trendy restaurants, and amusing and impressing everyone with her anecdotes about the high life in Manhattan and London – but she knew it would not be long before she was drafted by the family to enter into one of their enterprises. Strangely enough, she found this comforting rather than irritating. No one was ever forced to do something they did not enjoy. Besides – and perhaps best of all – the family was open to young blood and fresh ideas; if it was a viable business being created, the family would support it, without question.

'Our generation has not yet forgotten our Bolshevik past,' Natasha continued, flashing Safi the smile that would have bankrupted a less affluent Russian family. 'We cherish success more than anything, we love the power of choice it gives us. Especially me, I love buying power.' Safi could not argue with her sentiments. In fact, she valued Natasha's honesty and forthright attitude to life – her endearing bluntness. Natasha was truly one of the new generation of Russians, unapologetically ambitious and eager to be further elevated in society. She had completed a degree in media studies and English literature at Bristol University, followed by a stint at the Sorbonne in Paris.

'I am taking my time. I am not in such a hurry to tie myself down until I find my true passion.' Laughing at herself (and how refreshing to find a young person – not least from a prominent family – unafraid of laughing at herself), she added. 'I'm either a romantic, or just running scared.'

Safi laughed. Nothing could curtail Natasha once she got going; it was entertaining, if nothing else.

'Maybe I am leaning towards starting up my own fashion and media blog, commenting on scandal here and out there in the world of hip culture. What do you think'?

'I think it sounds intriguing. How do you get started with something like that?'

'I have been messing around with this, but it's time to get serious. I have an interview tomorrow with Mika and also the film studio. Let's see what happens.' Through the youngest members of the family, the Rubicov businesses stayed connected with the latest and hippest trends. This gave the new generation opportunities to realise their potential; as long as they put in the hours they were encouraged to develop their ideas, which in turn kept the company up to date with groundswell opinion and in touch with the wider world. Their diligence, discipline, ambition, endurance, and innovation were always amply rewarded.

Sasha was being groomed to manage their multinational enterprises. Safi had so many questions she needed answered, yet she felt paralysed to do so. Their sex life had taken on a boring pattern, of late, maybe her needs had changed? Perhaps, in an odd way, insecurity heightened her sex drive: before she had wanted to devour him, own him physically, now she was exhausted and content with regular lovemaking. She no

longer felt that passionate excitement, that wild feeling brewing inside her; somehow they needed to get some of that excitement back.
But how?

Safi had a rare moment to reflect on their relationship as a couple and her, reliance on DuPont who was always professional but always with a flirtatious undercurrent, a perfect French gentleman some would say, no beautiful woman escaped a Frenchman's attention. Perhaps it was time to move into a place of their own. Anna had obviously regained her life back. She was often away over weekends, and her relationship with Dr Maurice Rheingold had become all consuming. Anna, Safi thought was enjoying her life, safe from the threat of Yvetta's raging and unwelcome intrusions into Anna's suite of rooms, she had witnessed not long after arriving.

Sasha protecting his mother at their family home was no longer a necessity, or even especially desirable: not for Anna, and certainly not for Sasha and her. The new security at the house was now in full working order; it was impossible to get in without rigorous scrutiny any time of the day or night. Yet she was reluctant to voice her opinions, their relationship had become strained, and Safi convinced herself that it had to do with her success at the gallery. Perhaps her close working relationship with DuPont might be ruffling Sasha's feathers, she was always talking about how flirtatiously French he was and, on and on praising his input, to the success of the gallery. There was not a day they did not communicate either by cell or FaceTime to talk about the gallery. DuPont had become indispensable to her success at the Rubicov Gallery, and Sasha had shown great restraint, knowing how important he was to Safi, Dax, and the Gallery.

Despite his eccentricities (or perhaps because of them), DuPont was certainly an attractive older man. She was in awe of his knowledge, and his professional interest in her was flattering, he was imparting valuable knowledge and had become her tutor, and she his willing student. She could not deny any of that. DuPont was indispensable to the success of Dax's show and the gallery itself, creating an atmosphere between DuPont and Sasha would not be advantageous to the Rubicov gallery, not to mention Safi's ability to run things alone without DuPont More than anything, she needed to get things back on track between herself and Sasha. Moving into their own place might go a long way in helping and, having a project of their own to talk about.

Everything leading up to the galleries first show with Dax as their major artist was moving forward; there were hitches but it was slowly coming together.

Dax and Safi spoke daily on conference calls with DuPont; he had visited Moscow a number of times, wining and dining her was his way of making sure everything was being organised to his liking.

Proofreading of the brochures had to be finalised before printing. These included invitations, including a short biography on Dax and the philosophy behind his work. A coffee-table book was being printed in New York; the timing of the shipment had to coincide with the show. Crating, shipping, and documents had to be in order and insured. Dax was understandably anxious; his nerves and excitement were at fever pitch. Safi relied on DuPont and Daniel to calm him down. Privately, she entertained multiple worries. Russia was not supportive to gays, Dax was so obviously gay. It was hard not to wonder how he would be received by the public. And the success of this key exhibit would be a reflection of her own success with the gallery. Indeed, this exhibition was as key to her as it was to Dax.

DuPont suggested interviews on Russian TV but Dax refused. He was happy to have exposure in magazines and newspaper art columns, nothing more, he remembered his last visit, exposure in their media made him feel uncomfortable about being a gay man in a homophobic society.

Fortunately for Dax, Polly had reconnected with Russian Vogue, and she had organised a photo shoot and interview in New York. DuPont wanted as much exposure for Dax's show in Moscow as possible, especially in the right circles.

Fritzi had previously been the gallery's point-person for the press, arranging interviews and organising exposure for artists.

Yvetta had been respected in the art community; some galleries loyal to the old management had on occasion declined to buy or handle work from the new regime at Rubicov. Their success under DuPont's guidance had ruffled feathers in the art community, too, some having to change their own style of management to compete with a more modern approach, but other reasons were coming to light as well.

DuPont was highly respected as a New York Museum curator, dealer, and auctioneer. His contacts with other Russian art experts had warned him to tread carefully, there were many who could cause trouble if they wished, if the stolen artefacts rumour was true.

Safi voiced her concerns of the possibility of Dax's sexuality affecting the success of his show to Sasha one evening over dinner.

'How do they know that Dax is gay?' Sasha asked.

Safi thought for a moment. 'You know I have never thought about that. I have no idea.' He squeezed her hand comfortingly. 'I am pleased you have come to me with this problem. DuPont, with all his contacts, cannot sort this out, but it will be sorted out, I promise you that.' He stood up. 'I will be back. I need to make a few calls.'

Safi was not sure whether Dax's sexuality was their only problem. She had heard rumbles about the galleries' dubious dealings before their management changed.

'Well, there are some other concerns as well that have come to light.'

He hovered over his chair, deciding whether or not to sit back down. 'Explain.'

'There are rumours that the Rubicov Galleries are dealing in stolen antiquities. Sasha did not speak, did not sit, but leaned forward with a hard look in his eyes. 'DuPont will not want to be involved with us if this spreads – the art world is a small one. This may be another reason some of the galleries are not dealing with our gallery any longer.'

Sasha looked alarmed. Still not saying a word, he flipped open his cell and walked into another room, where he engaged in lengthy conversations with a number of people.

Still not able to understand Russian, Safi could now follow snippets of rudimentary conversation, wanting to know who Sasha had called and if it had anything to do with the gallery. He returned asking for DuPont's contact number; he had a proposal that might put an end to their problem.

She stared at him for a moment, a feeling of resentment building up inside her. She was not quite sure why she felt this way, but she did not like being side lined, especially in such a clandestine and exclusionary manner. Once again, she felt shut out of the country, and the language. Once again, and after all this time, she felt hindered by her outsiderness. She felt angry at herself, angry at Sasha, angry at Russia (how could one be angry at a country? absurd – but then anger was itself absurd), angry at everyone and everything. She would have to handle this very carefully, not wanting it to turn into something she may regret. Fumbling for her cell phone while stalling, trying to gather her thoughts before speaking as she handed him her cell for Dupont's contact details, she blurted out,

'Sasha, don't you think you should fill me in first, before speaking to DuPont?'

They stared at each other for a long time, then Sasha nodded.

'I am so used to taking control. Sorry, you have a point.'

'I mean, this is my job,' she said, feeling energised and self-confident now, sensing her victory and relishing his quick and quiet concession.

'I know, I know,' he said, unwilling to concede again, with that Russian stubbornness that she both envied and abhorred. Still, she knew she had a point. She wasn't just a pretty face, she was working her ass off for the gallery and here he was treating her like some underling. Going above her head and shutting her out – it was the opposite of intimacy and equality. DuPont never made her feel inadequate, why should Sasha? She was going to marry this guy, for God's sake, how dare he! Safi felt anger rise like bile in her throat.

She had never experienced this before – or had she, perhaps in another form, a physical one. Sasha could see hurt and anger in her eyes. Shocked at her reaction, he sat down, closed the cell and waited for her to speak again.

'Well?' she said glaring at him,

In the, I am waiting attitude, pissed Sasha off. He was not use to being spoken to in this way, especially by Safi. What was happening to them?

'Let's start over, shall we before this turns into something we might both regret?' Sasha said. They were both in unchartered waters:, Safi emboldened by her newfound independence and Sasha with unresolved feelings towards DuPont, who had too much influence over Safi for his liking; Safi tired of being quietly controlled, even in her own job, of being subservient at home and – now, presumably – at work, too. Their sex life was as dull as ditch-water lately; Sasha blamed her new-found adoration for all things DuPont for this.

Safi could tell Sasha was upset. He might want to start over, but how was she going to handle him? Control, she thought, is a paradox: he has too much and, too often, I don't have enough. She realised she was petrified in case his reaction was something she was not prepared to live with., would he voice his disapproval of DuPont's control over the gallery, she needed DuPont she was feeding off his vast knowledge of the art world and, loving it, and it was something she was not prepared to negotiate. Oh my God, this might all come crashing down around me, just when everything's going well. Sasha and I may be coming to an end! Her feelings overwhelmed her, she jumped up and ran to the bathroom, shutting the door while trying to control her tears. For the first time in her life she had found something she was passionate about and, she was so reliant on those around her, it made her feel vulnerable, she wanted this passion to be her life, would Sasha support her, she wasn't sure? But she wanted this Gallery to succeed and Dax's show was the beginning of other foreign shows, to lift the profile of the gallery here abroad and, her own success depended on it too.

Shocked at her reaction and not quite understanding, Sasha hung back, not sure what to do. He waited for Safi to return sipping his glass of wine, hoping she would have calmed down. Safi feeling unprofessional and stupid for jumping to conclusions, this was so important to her, but had she over stepped, never having been in a position of control she was eager to show she was capable of making decisions, after all they had put her in this position, suddenly regretting everything, she straightened her skirt, freshened her makeup (trying in that moment to affect the attitude of a new and better person, refreshed and relaxed), and walked into the room. Seeing Sasha calmly sipping his wine as if nothing had happened, she blew her cool, walked over, picked up her wine glass, and poured it over him.

There was a momentary pause as the wine trickled down his face, staining his pink shirt. She heard him draw in his breath. It was as though everything was happening in slow-motion. Before she could step back, Sasha grabbed her arm, pulled her over his knee, and spanked her bottom playfully. Struggling helplessly, tired of deciding how to feel, tired of feeling aggrieved, her anger evaporated into giggles. Relieved and madly hot, Sasha kissed her passionately, yelped as Safi bit his lip, took off his necktie, and tied her hands together. Safi lay helpless in his lap as he spanked her for biting him. He carried her to. the bedroom, where she flung her tied wrists around his neck, and felt wild with passion. This was happiness, this feeling of wild passion was what connected them, regardless of anything that happened in the moments before. Safi found his lips, his tongue. Biting down hard she tasted wine mixed with blood, as they kissed passionately, neither wanting the moment to end. They collapsed onto the bed drenched in sweat and exhaustion after the best lovemaking for a long time.

Lying in bed, watching Sasha sleeping, the sun rays filtered through the shutters. They had so much personal stuff to sort out in their relationship, she realised; the distance between them had grown with each passing day since their return. Thinking back to the beginning of their relationship, she realised it had never been plain-sailing, but they had managed to move forward after each battle.

Their fallouts were spectacularly dramatic, always ending up with them in the sack, bringing them closer together, if only for a moment. But did those moments of passion actually fix the underlying problem? Sasha was, she now realised, an alpha male. He had to feel in charge, even if he wasn't in control. She lay back and wondered whether it was a purely Russian trait, or were all men inclined to be that way? Experience in men was not yet her strong suit, but he was certainly testing her resilience to bounce back, not to mention her emotions, which fluctuated like a yo-yo. Would things improve after marriage? Did she want to take that chance?

Safi lay back, staring at the ceiling. She had invested so much of herself in this relationship, it was ridiculous to throw in the towel now; anyhow, she absolutely adored Sasha. God, she wished she could confide her feelings to someone, anyone, just to get it off her chest. But she knew it was ultimately her decision whether to stay or leave. Sasha stirred and Safi knew she would see this relationship through, all the way to the altar. Just lying next to him stirred up a hornet's nest of emotions; his masculinity was so overpowering even when asleep. It gave her a thrill. She would just have to learn how to manipulate his controlling instincts to suit her. Smiling at her own astuteness, she leaned over. She knew how to make his morning a happy one. It had been a long time since they enjoyed a lazy day making love till noon, without Sasha fretting over his new position at the helm of Rubicov Enterprises.

Realising the gallery had kept her totally occupied, they were both anxious and suffering with similar feelings of inadequacy, aware of their burden to succeed in their new positions, their new and manifold responsibilities. Their problems were not at all dissimilar, and they were united in love. Hopefully, now that they were aware of this, things would lighten up between them.

Anna now spent almost every weekend over at her lover, which allowed Safi and Sasha to relax over leisurely brunches in the magnificent kitchen they both loved. Feeling reenergised once more and comfortable with each other, they fell into an easy conversation about their relationship. Marriage was a reality, a tangible event and a topic they were both happy to discuss. Where and when was another matter. Each came up with obstacles, but the excitement of it occurring (whether imminently or eventually – and they discussed all possibilities) dominated their conversations. Safi thought they should wait until Dax's show was out of the way; Sasha thought they should marry in secret and only let the cat out of the bag when at Rupert's country home with the family over Christmas in Connecticut.

'It would disappoint so many people not to mention my mum,' Safi said. 'I can't do that to them. My dad would never forgive me for not allowing him to walk his only daughter down the aisle.'

Exhibiting his competitive flair, Sasha noted that 'Dax and Dan may actually beat us to it. When do you think it will happen for them?'

'I think that subject is on the backburner until their brownstone has been completed and Dax's show here is behind him. God, I hope his show will be a success – for both of us.'

It wasn't just her days at work that were busy for Safi, but her nights as well. The gallery's popularity had deposited numerous invitations on their doorstep. Safi had sifted through them, and discussed those of particular interest to Dax's show with Sasha and DuPont, who encouraged them to keep up their high profile on the social scene until after the show.

Through DuPont she had learnt about some disturbing stories circulating. Safi felt it her duty to alert Sasha that these crazy stories that were out there; they had to be quashed before the gallery became tainted by the wild rumours.

'DuPont has heard through the grapevine abroad that Yvetta and Fritzi have been ousted by the Rubicov family, because of their connections with the Russian mafia and their dealing in stolen antiquities,'

There was no evidence that either Yvetta or Fritzi had been dealing in stolen antiquities, but they could not afford to have the gallery associated with these accusations. If the stolen antiquities had passed through the gallery, it could mean an internal investigation of the gallery's finances and result in the gallery being blacklisted and closed by the government.

The family certainly did not want DuPont to pull out of his dealings with the gallery because of baseless rumours. DuPont would want to protect his reputation and they needed him to remain involved until the gallery, with Safi in charge, had managed to secure a respected presence in the market. Rumours were bad business for the Rubicov name. A rumour was akin to a slow-release poison. Once a rumour took hold, it was almost impossible for it to be eradicated.

Mika together with Alexi and Sasha discussed late into the night how to deal with this dilemma that now faced one of their international enterprises. The real reasons for Yvetta and Fritzi's departure had to be kept secret. A way had to be found for the rumours currently circulating – which showed no signs of abating – to be manipulated in the family's favour. It was widely assumed that Fritzi was responsible for fanning the smoke of the fake rumours. Mika and Kolya left for Berlin to have a face-to-face meeting with Fritzi. She had to be persuaded in terms she understood, even if she was in Germany they could and, would deal with her, if she was the source of circulating the rumours about the stolen antiquities, in the art world. The gallery could not be connected with any underhand dealings in the art market; it would ruin their reputation.

No one had heard from Fritzi since she had been escorted onto the plane at Heathrow and deposited in Germany by Kolya. Mika's contacts had monitored her movements but only for eight months. The clinic had not reported any contact with Yvetta by anyone outside of the family. It would not take them long to track down Fritzi, who was, even in Berlin, a memorable persona. Mika had many contacts in Berlin; the Iron Curtain may have come down, but many from East Berlin still spoke a good Russian and they remained in close contact with a surveillance team who worked for the Rubicov Company on occasion.

Kolya, together with one of the agency surveillance teams in Berlin, took less than twenty-four hours to track Fritzi down. She had changed her image considerably and it was, Mika noted, a great improvement. Fritzi now sported long blonde hair swept off her face. Her tall figure was now clothed in high-end designer classics. She managed to carry her new wardrobe with as much panache as she did her androgynous look.

Mika found her waiting for them at a corner table in a fashionable restaurant. She still succumbed to her smoking habit, but now instead of a cigarette holder she sported a fashionable gold electronic cigarette. She nonchalantly blew out puffs of grey smoke while watching them approach her table.

Mika ordered an espresso. Not a word was spoken until Mika had finished his coffee. They both watched as Kolya entered the restaurant. Taking a table nearby, walking in a light and almost elegant manner for such a large man, he spoke to the waiter in a perfect German.

Mika studied Fritzi for a long while; her reinvention was nothing but spectacular. In spite of himself, he was impressed. She was a stunning woman, not a single scrap of the old bohemian Fritzi was apparent any longer, only this model-like creature sitting before him, with her long legs crossed demurely over the side of the chair, one foot calmly swinging, showing off expensive snakeskin sling-back heels. Mika was familiar with fashion; the new breed of women in Russia loved all things designer. He recognised Fritzi's DFV wrap dress: it suited her small breasts, showing only a hint of cleavage as the cross-over plunged in the front. She met his stare and his critical summing up of her new persona confidently, without a hint of disdain.

'My new image, you approve?'

Mika moved closer, signifying – against his better instincts, perhaps – a tacit and undeniable approval. Still, he would not be distracted in his mission. Nothing less than the future of the business was at stake. The business and the family – that was the thing about Rubicov Enterprises, the two were for ever and impossibly intertwined. He smiled seductively – he could be charming, too – and, leaning over the table, removed the electronic cigarette out of her hand. Putting down the cigarette, which was the size and shape of a pen, he took her hand in his, as though they were lovers all of a sudden. Showing off her manicured, painted nails, as her slender fingers lay in the palm of his hand, he brought his other hand down over her hand. He held it there for a moment, then she felt the pressure as he tightened his grip. She smiled, too, enjoying this. She was kinky, all right, but everyone had their limit, the point at which they screamed out stop. He kept tightening and she stopped smiling. Her elegant face changed. He kept his eyes on hers as she flinched. He relaxed his grip, allowing her hand to slip onto the table, slightly pink from the pressure of his grip.

'Fritzi still your name, I presume? Good. I am not here to compliment you on your change of image. I am here to warn you not to mention the Rubicov name in any manner, whatsoever! This is what we are going to do. You are going to go into one of the major galleries here in Berlin with me that dealt with the Rubicov gallery in Moscow, and you are going to introduce me as the owner of the Rubicov gallery. You are going to speak glowingly of your connections with my gallery and how you worked with my niece Yvetta to build the reputation of the gallery. Kolya will accompany us and you will introduce Kolya as an expert in Russian antiquities. He once worked for the Russian government and insurance companies, and now works for the Rubicov family, tracking down priceless antiquities stolen from our collection.'

Fritzi stared at Mika. Her eyes dropped, all hints of self-confidence and seductiveness gone, her pallor now as grey as the smoke from her electronic cigarette, still beside her on the table (she did not dare reach for it again). She nodded.

'If we hear any derogatory rumours circulating that could damage the gallery or the Rubicov name in any way, our connections here in Berlin will extinguish the source of those rumours, as quickly as I have turned off this cigarette you so elegantly smoke. Do we understand each other, Fritzi?'

She met his eyes again; there was no mistaking what he meant. Mika was someone no one played with, and she wanted to live now more than ever. Her life had changed for the better, her new contacts in the European underworld were profitable and had a long reach. She knew she had been stupid to start those rumours but she had done it for Yvetta, her old lover; now she knew it had been a mistake, one that could end her life. She felt fear, real fear, and it startled and aroused her. It was something real, alive, and that was precisely what she was looking for in her life: the heat of the moment, the edge of the knife.

DuPont, Safi reported to Sasha, had learnt through contacts that the Rubicov family were searching for priceless missing antiquities due to a break-in at their family home. Furthermore, the family had promised to alert the art market to watch out for any suspicious items that surfaced.

In any case, Mika's visit had been a success. Safi suddenly found the Moscow galleries that had previously been reluctant to deal with them now welcomed interaction. They were able to offload prints and in return buy other works, freeing up a lucrative part of their market. DuPont had arranged the crating and shipping for Dax's work. Documents had to be in order before customs would release the work. DuPont was to fly to Moscow a month ahead of the show to work with Safi and her staff.

Dax was content to have the final say before the show opened to a celebrity-filled gallery.

'I like viewing my work after it has been mounted for the show,' he told Safi over the phone. 'It will give me a fresh perspective and enable me to make changes for the right reasons.'

Safi knew Dax, like most artists, experienced many doubts, only appreciating the paintings with fresh eyes once he saw them situ.

'DuPont is known to be the best curator in the business,' Safi said excitedly and not for the first time. 'The gallery will be transformed by your work. I am so excited for you, Dax. Hopefully, it will be a success for both of us.'

Dax had been calling daily, neurotic about customs releasing his work and any damage done during shipping. Every little thing worried him. Relieved to see his work at the gallery professionally crated and in perfect condition, Safi messaged Dax immediately and showed him the crated works leaning on the walls. She persuaded Dax to relax and try and concentrate on other things now that his work had arrived safely.

Keeping Dax calm had been a major strain for everyone. The brochures had been printed and proofread, a few minor errors had been corrected, Dax's philosophy and personal history had been honed by DuPont, and a few hundred coffee-table books by a famous photographer were already for sale in major stores and museums throughout Moscow. More could not be done to advertise his show.

DuPont moved into the Savoy, an old favourite of his which provided him with everything he needed for the duration of his stay in Moscow. Safi and the staff found him a pleasure to work with. He had them eating out of his hand, running in circles to please his every whim. Everyone liked him, apart from Sasha, who found his natural flirtatious French manners an irritant, especially when he turned on that charm to wine and dine Safi at every opportunity. Safi laughed off Sasha's possessive jealousy.

'He is old enough to be my dad, Sasha, don't be such an ogre to him.' Sasha tried to see the humorous side to the situation, but could not help the unease he felt whenever he experienced DuPont's sophistication and knowledge, which was sucked up in bucket loads by Safi, who was obviously in awe of his position and power in the art world.

Before Dax's arrival for the opening show, DuPont had the work un crated and moved about by the hanging staff until satisfied, allowing each painting the space and power of place it deserved to breathe. The lighting above each painting had been adjusted sympathetically and to perfection.

The most dramatic of the paintings had pride of place in the entrance, which could be viewed from outside, and brought many on the sidewalk to a stop. Dax's work was obviously attracting the attention they hoped it would. Some knocked on the closed gallery doors to ask whether they could view the rest of the exhibition; all were given brochures and encouraged to return on the opening date. Safi was amazed at the public attention the work was drawing. She could not wait to tell Dax how his work was being received before the doors had even opened.

Daniel and Dax were arriving a day before the opening of the exhibition, both staying at the Savoy with DuPont. They met in the opulent gold-ceilinged breakfast room before setting out to view his work. To their amusement they were entertained by a piano player at eight in the morning, while feasting on a delicious breakfast in the most opulent surroundings he had ever breakfasted in. The hotel had a long history before and during the communist era and was once more popular with its original décor untouched by time.

Safi's nerves were on edge, she was beginning to fret, and – for the first time in weeks – the exhibition had become the least of her immediate concerns. She had not breathed a word to anyone yet; she wanted to be sure of her facts before setting off any alarm bells.

If they were who she thought they were, surely the team would have alerted Safi to the couple walking past the gallery every day for the past week. She was too fearful to give her thoughts even the slightest confirmation or justification. Yvetta was a jealous person and how would she react towards Safi, and yes she did have doubts about taking over her gallery. Still, if she saw the women again, she would alert Ilona, her right-hand at the gallery. She knew the staff at the gallery would set her mind at ease. There would be ample security at the gallery on the opening evening, they had their own security detail on a daily basis, as did most of the stores and galleries in the area. She was being nervous and neurotic, allowing her guilty feelings get the better of her and, told herself that Dax was being nervous and neurotic enough for the both of them, and her nervousness could only be unhelpful. It was Dax's show, so no one could blame her if it failed to impress (although judging by the advance excitement, that was extremely unlikely to happen). It was her first major exhibition at the gallery; if successful, she knew DuPont would want to work with her again. And the Rubicov family would trust her to run the gallery as she saw fit in the future. In short, what happened over the next few days had the potential to make her name and secure her future. She was aware of this potential, and this made her nervousness sharper still.

In the run-up to the exhibition, Safi and Sasha hardly had time to chat, but they had scheduled tonight to dine alone.

She had just settled on the sofa when she recognised faltering disbelief in his voice as he spoke on the cell phone. As he came through the door, she could tell it was something serious. He was talking very rapidly now. There goes our night alone, she thought., looking at him expectantly as he closed his cell and steeling herself for disappointment. and sank down next to her on the sofa.

'I have just received a call from Mika,' he said, sinking down next to her on the sofa. 'Someone has spotted Fritzi and Yvetta in Moscow.'

Safi's hand flew to her mouth. 'Oh, my God! I thought I was seeing things. But no, it must have been them!' She was becoming increasingly excited. 'I thought I recognised Fritzi's elegant walk, but I had no idea that it might be Yvetta with her.'

'Safi, what are you talking about?'

'Well, you know so many people have shown interest in Dax's work since it has gone up. For the last few days I have noticed these two attractive women walking past the gallery. I thought I was imagining it, because they did not look like the old Fritzi or Yvetta – although I still had this weird feeling. I can't explain it. And now that you say they are here, I am convinced it was indeed them that I saw.'

Sasha made her tell him exactly what she had observed: the dark glasses on the tall blonde, and the fashionable felt hat on the smaller one, with visible strands of long red hair flowing down her back. They had both stopped brazenly to view the work in the window. Safi had not noticed a sense of nervousness in either woman's demeanour.

'That's why I thought it a stupid thought, and the assistants certainly did not recognise either of them. Surely Ilona would have?'

They sat for what seemed ages, Sasha obviously undecided about the two women being either Yvetta or Fritzi; surely the Colorado Clinic would have contacted them if Yvetta had gone AWOL.

'I will call Mika and tell him what you saw. He can then take it from there. Thank goodness my mother is staying at Maurice Rheingold's Dacha for a holiday. She need never know.'

'But she will surely be here for the opening in two days' time?'

Safi left to put the last touches to their intimate dinner in the kitchen, while Sasha and Mika got to the bottom of the never-ending shadow Yvetta cast over her family.

Mika had spoken to the clinic in Colorado; there was no longer any doubt that Yvetta had gone missing. They had discovered Yvetta had bribed one of their staff, resulting in outside contact without their knowledge for a number of months. Mika was livid; the clinic was being paid a fortune to keep them informed and Yvetta safely within their property.

'So far it has been ascertained that she had been in touch with someone on the outside who had arranged for a false passport and a car to take her to the airport,' Mika informed Sasha. 'There is no doubt in my mind that it is Fritzi who was able to organise this escape. But why are they in Moscow? Are they crazy? Well, yes, of course they are, but they are not suicidal, are they? Both know how dangerous it will be for them if caught.'

Sasha did not have any answers to Mika's question, but he knew how cunning his sister could be. Cunning and confusing – he often thought Yvetta's machinations made no sense, even to herself. But then what did he know? He had tried most of his life to figure her out, and had ultimately resigned himself to the fact that he did not have a clue.

'I wonder whether the two women Safi saw outside the gallery were decoys to throw us off the scent,' Sasha suggested. 'Yvetta knew that once she was missed we would be informed.'

Mika was quiet for some time.

'We will have to find out before she has the opportunity to cause us any problems,' he finally said. 'Keep your phone close, and I will keep you informed. I have to call Alexi and contact our agents in Berlin. Kolya will have his people in Moscow on the lookout.'

Security was beefed up at the gallery, an armed guard was assigned to Safi once more. Unknown to DuPont, they had security follow him at a discreet distance. Mika did not intend to take chances.

Yvetta had her own unsavoury underground friends in Moscow, some of whom were capable of unspeakable behaviour. Young thugs who did anything for money. There was no moral code any longer; the mighty rubble had replaced Communism as the country's new religion.

Safi took all the security in her stride, but was worried about Dax and Dan.

'What are we to do when Dax and Dan arrive at the gallery with DuPont tomorrow?' she asked Sasha.

'They will have security assigned, and I will see that they have a car ferry them wherever they need to be.'

'Sasha, do you mind if they do not know the reasons for this security? I do not want them to worry – especially Dax, who is beyond neurotic about the opening evening as it is.'

'There is no need for them to know about Yvetta,' Sasha said. 'In fact, we would prefer it if nothing was said at the gallery. Best to keep this in the family.'

'That's why you kept it from me for so long,' Safi said.

'Well, yes,' Sasha said, but she did not want to add to his already enormous discomfort, so she left it at that.

Relieved that they were both in agreement, Safi left early the next day for the gallery to await the arrival of DuPont and Dax. Her nerves were shot; what if Dax was disappointed with how his paintings were displayed? Would she be able to handle two huge egos at loggerheads? She loved Dax, but she needed DuPont; it would not bode well if they had a bad atmosphere at the opening evening. No amount of damage control could help an unhappy Dax. Now, with something resembling stage fright, Safi scrutinised everything that could possibly go wrong, and struggled to regain, even for a moment, the optimism of her old self. She tried to talk sense to herself. Dax was bound to be bowled over – after all, everyone else was. The glass isn't half empty, she told herself, it's positively overflowing – and with champagne, no less. This is my big night; enjoy it!

She felt a need to offload her concerns but Sasha was pre-occupied with work, and no doubt with Yvetta's secret return to Moscow.

She felt passionate about this show but a part of her still felt guilty, was Yvetta coming to ruin her opening night, she hoped not. Replacing her at her gallery must surely bruise that fragile ego. On some level, she didn't blame Yvetta, if she felt aggrieved, but, Sasha had told her they left Moscow because they could not live in a homophobic society.

Sitting in the back of the car as the driver negotiated the traffic, she noticed her cell had been turned off. Safi switched it on to find a dozen messages. Thankful for the distraction, she listened to Dax's excited hello on arrival, and another from Dan. There was a message from Ilona, who was awaiting her arrival to greet DuPont, Dax, and Daniel. It would be their final day's work, with the gallery closed for the private viewing the following evening. She just hoped to God Dax would approve of the hanging.

Safi and Ilona stood on the pavement ready to open the door for Dax, Dan, and DuPont. DuPont escorted Dax into the gallery; following silently at a distance the two young women watched Dax work the room. He stopped at each painting and read the signs in Russian and English next to each. All eyes were riveted on Dax, waiting for his reaction; but Dax remained completely absorbed. He then walked right out of the gallery. Eight eyes followed him onto the pavement and watched as he stood looking at the work they had chosen as an introduction to his oeuvre. Safi felt the tension as they waited for him to indicate in any way what he was thinking or feeling. Walking back into the gallery, he stood in front of them, shook his head, then threw up his arms in animated delight, 'I am speechless. It's fantastic! I wouldn't change a thing, not a thing. It's brilliantly hung and the lighting is perfection.'

Safi could hear everyone sigh with relief (perhaps none as loud as her) as they all spoke at once. Dax shook DuPont's hand and hugged him, then everyone else in turn.

'Now I'm going back to the hotel to sleep. The tension has been exhausting.'

Everyone laughed but Dan who, Safi noticed, looked the most relieved – even more so than Safi. He had probably put up with more than any of them. All they needed were lots of red dots and it would all have been worthwhile.

DuPont did not want to tell anyone his news until he knew Dax approved of his show.

'Well, already we have a sale and, that's before anyone has even seen the show,' DuPont said in his romantic Metropolitan Parian accent.

All eyes swivelled in his direction.

'Who?'

'Ah, well, we were keeping it a secret, but Ilona and I have had six offers for the painting in the window.'

'Safi was delighted, That's fantastic, why didn't anyone tell me?'

'We wanted to surprise both you, Safi, and Dax. I have no doubt the buyers who did not get that painting will be offering for others.'

Dax was presented with a coffee table book of his work and asked to sign it for DuPont. Safi did the same, as did Ilona. After that the two D's left for the Savoy. The plan was to meet at the gallery the following evening to prepare for the cocktail party and the opening. Everyone was happy to have their own space until then.

Safi notified gallery security to organise for a car to be brought round, feeling safe in the knowledge that the security had been discreetly beefed up.

No one seemed to have noticed that there were now a half a dozen tough-looking guards roaming about inside the gallery and manning the entrance. The car was checked by one of the guards. Frowning (he even did that in an elegant manner), DuPont ducked into his seat alongside Dax and Dan. Safi just raised her shoulders in resigned ignorance, but once back inside the gallery she checked her cell phone to see whether Sasha had any news on Yvetta and Fritzi.

Nothing incriminating or unusual had been found in Moscow, and all underground contacts had come up with nothing extraordinary to report.

The Berlin security had not been able to track Fritzi down; she had been out of the country for more than six months, no one had a lead. She was last seen flying to an island in the Caribbean, and there the lead had gone dead.

At Safi's suggestion, Dax had donated one of his smaller paintings to be auctioned at the opening evening by DuPont. The painting was mounted on a tripod, together with a signed special edition coffee-table book in a holographic gold and red cover. All proceeds were for a disabled children's charity, one of many supported by the Rubicov family.

The family had turned out in full force to support their opening evening. Dax, Dan, and DuPont arrived to be met by a gallery so full they could hardly move amongst the beautifully attired clientele. Celebrities from film, theatre, dance, and opera were well represented, as were those from the banking world, plus a scattering of oligarchs. Alexi and Anna had made sure everyone they deemed important was on their guest list.

To Safi's relief, Dan had persuaded Dax to adopt a subdued European style of dress, rather than his usual flamboyant attire. He now sported a dashing, dark, navy fitted suit, purple-and-tan-striped waistcoat, and tan cowboy boots. There was no mistaking who the artist was. Safi was starving and grabbed a canapé and glass of champagne from one of the waitresses. As she put the glass to her lips, her eyes followed the waitress around until she descended the staircase to refill her tray.

Safi found Sasha and whispered in his ear that the waitress resembled one of the women she had noticed returning to view the painting in the window on numerous occasions, and once even requesting to be allowed in. It was strange that she should be working as a waitress on their opening night. Sasha obviously did not think Safi was being overly suspicious.

Relieved, she noticed Kolya descend the staircase; no doubt he would find out who she was. There was little time to dwell on the matter; she worked her way around the gallery, introducing herself to the clientele. Sasha, she noticed, was nowhere to be found. Safi found Dax standing in front of one of his paintings, explaining the philosophy behind his work to a large group. She had never really listened to Dax give a comprehensive answer from a personal perspective; he preferred to explore the impact his work had on the viewer, rather than his own artistic process.

'I live in an urban jungle. New York is where I was born. There are many layers of sophistication and insouciance that run through everything we build, eat, drink, and think. Although my subjects appear carefree, my work is above all highly charged and sensually emotive: that is what I hope to relate through the layers of paint and imagery.' Everyone seemed to be in total agreement with Dax's explanation. He had caught the mood of the room, had managed to connect his work with Russian emotion and poetry of the soul.

DuPont was listening to Dax from the side lines and nodded his approval. Art had become minimalist, sculpture replaced by installation, some morbidly macabre, others unforgivably narcissistic. Painters were getting a raw deal, lagging behind. Dax was refreshingly honest both in and about his work.

Not only was his work appreciated, the work was a sell-out; every single painting had a red dot next to it. No one had been expecting this level of success, least of all Safi. This was beyond their wildest dreams. DuPont felt vindicated: Dax had been a worthwhile investment, he was determined to take him all the way. These works would go up and up in value in no time at all, he was sure of that.

It was time for the auction and DuPont took centre stage, his true profession coming to the fore. By the end of the auction, the donated painting and special-edition coffee-table book had pulled in over two million for the charity.

Safi had no idea what had happened to Sasha. She had lost sight of him early in the evening. Now, scouring the room as guests were leaving, wanting to share her success with him and hear his take on the night, she still could not see him anywhere. Anna had left with most of the Rubicov family members, leaving behind only DuPont, Dax, Dan (now the three D's), and herself.

'Has anyone seen Sasha?' she asked the three D's. But her question fell on deaf ears. They were high on the evening and Dax's success.

Descending the stairs, she heard a commotion coming from one of the rooms. The catering staff had packed up long ago, so who on earth could possibly be down there? She pushed open the door, but the room was totally dark. Feeling along the wall she flipped some switches, blinking as the fluorescent lights turned on. She was in the archives where they stored many of the works still to be re-catalogued since they had taken over the management of the gallery. Safi made her way down the aisles. Finding a vault-like door at the end, she managed to push it open a fraction with her shoulder.

Sitting in the middle of the room tied to a chair was the waitress she had told Sasha about. Standing over her was Kolya, Mika, and Sasha. The girl was screaming at them through a blood-stained mouth. Her hands and feet were tied to the chair. Safi noticed she had a fat lip and swollen eye.

Sasha was sporting a black eye, too, while Kolya was pointing a firearm at her temple. Mika was leaning up against the wall, watching the proceedings calmly. No one looked especially surprised to see Safi.

'My God, what's going on?' she asked. She felt suddenly dizzy. 'Who is she?'

No one had a chance to fill her in about the waitress. The girl took her chance on seeing Safi. 'Ah, here comes the real thief,' the girl said in her Russian accent filled with bile and arrogance, 'the one who stole Yvetta's gallery right from under her nose.'

Safi stood her ground. Who was this girl? She did not recognise her.

'This is one of Yvetta's student thugs,' Sasha said. 'She was in our home, destroying our property. She was here tonight to do damage to Dax's work. If it had not been for your suspicions, Safi, she would have succeeded. Not only that, she was going to use that pistol, too,' Safi put her hand to her mouth,

'Against me?'

'Anyone in your disgusting, thieving family would have done,' the girl said.

Kolya, now beyond all patience, smacked the girl's face so hard Safi heard her nose crack; blood was now spattering everywhere.

'Please stop that, Kolya,' Safi stuttered, shaken, 'it's not helping, surely?'

'I think you should leave this to us,' Kolya said in a voice sharp enough to shut Safi up. She had never seen Kolya enraged – or in action – quite like this. She saw now his considerable worth to the family. 'We have not yet found out what she was after. She was found down here in the vault, searching for something. She has been sent by Yvetta or Fritzi to collect something, and she is not going anywhere until we find out what it is.'

'Okay,' Safi said softly, trying not to look at the girl on the chair but unable to focus on anything else, 'they will wonder where I have got to.' She was trying hard to remain calm. Meanwhile, her head was spinning and she wanted to be sick. 'I don't want to arise suspicions, so I will go upstairs and leave with Dax and the others. Please be careful, I think she can't take much more physical punishment.' She looked at Sasha. 'Are you okay?' He nodded but turned away.

As Safi was about to head upstairs again, she found the lights in the storage room out. Feeling along the wall, she flipped a switch; the light was obviously on a timer. Walking along the stored works on railings reaching almost to the ceiling, she noticed a sack of rolled-up rags shoved in one of empty spaces at the back. Not having time to investigate, she ran back into the room to call Sasha. The girl was now whimpering but she was also talking; Kolya was holding a bottle of water against her swollen lips. She beckoned for Sasha to follow her, pointing to the rolled-up sack. She was dying to see what it could be but left it to Sasha, and made her way back into the gallery.

Everyone was still in animated discussion about the show. Dax was on top form while Dan made calls telling everyone he could at home about Dax's sell-out success. Safi thought it best to get them out of the gallery before they became aware of the ugly scene downstairs. There were just too many questions she did not have any answers to, and this business with Yvetta and Fritzi – which Safi herself felt she was only now learning about – was far too complicated for her to explain.

The hours ticked by as she waited to hear from Sasha. Overwrought and exhausted, she threw on her tracksuit, hanging the beautiful dull gold brocade D&G trouser suit back in its zip bag, made sure her cell was fully charged, and lay on the bed to rest. It was dawn when she woke, relieved to find Sasha beside her; the sun was catching something lying on the mirror dressing table. Staring at it for some time, as it danced and shimmered in the sunlight, her eyes were now focused on more objects. Without disturbing Sasha, she crawled over to inspect. Safi's mouth dropped open; not one or two but a dozen or more magnificent figurines and Fabergé eggs were lined up the length of the desk.

'Oh God! These were the antiquities they were stealing and illegally dealing through the gallery. It wasn't a rumour at all.'

Shifting, half-awake now, Sasha said, 'Yep, Fritzi's cover has been blown wide open. They will be searching for her; there won't be a place for her to hide. They are determined to find her.'

Safi sat on the edge of the bed. 'What happened last night? I stayed awake as long as I could.'

'Well, once she started to talk, there was no stopping her. She used Yvetta and the gallery as a cover. We are convinced Yvetta had no knowledge of Fritzi's side line in stolen antiquities. Frieda, the girl in the gallery, was another of Fritzi's lovers; unknown to Yvetta, she had quite a few.

Frieda was sent to rescue Fritzi's haul before it was discovered. Being one of the catering staff at the opening was a perfect cover. If you had not spotted her, Safi, she would have walked off scot-free without us knowing a thing about the whole ugly business.

'Who was she going to shoot with that pistol?'

'I think that was just bravado and playing for time. The pistol had blanks in it. It was purely cosmetic. She probably carried it as protection if caught, but it wasn't meant to be used. We called the insurance police and they collected her. I think, her delinquent petty thief record is behind her, she has now, joined the big time and, she will be spending many years behind bars. The Russians don't take very well to foreigners stealing from them.'

'She wasn't Russian?

'No, Eastern European. That's why she spoke perfect Russian.'

Sasha informed Safi what had taken place last night. Sasha had followed Kolya down the stairs, but the girl had disappeared. None of the catering staff appeared to know where she had vanished to. Sasha followed Kolya into the storage room. Kolya continued into the vault, while Sasha stayed behind in the storage room. The amount of artwork stored below was mind-blowing. As he walked along the aisles, pulling out and examining paintings, he became aware of movement coming from one of the aisles. Sasha tiptoed towards the noise. As he peeped around a corner, Frieda struck him hard in the face. Reeling he fell backwards. Hearing the thud, Kolya rushed in as Frieda was legging it towards the stairs. Kolya grabbed hold of one of her legs as she tried to escape and dragged her back down, resulting in her split lip. Not one to give in, Frieda began to scream. Kolya immediately put his hand over her mouth to shut her up. The last thing they needed was to alert someone. Sasha remained with their assailant while Kolya made his way up the stairs to find Mika; they needed to know what he wanted done.

Frieda was not co-operating; they tried to persuade her it was in her best interest to tell them everything she knew. Kolya noticed the handgun protruding from her trouser leg, it had been hidden in the back of her boot and had obviously dropped out. Kolya was holding the handgun to her head when Safi had walked in on their interrogation. Obviously recognising Safi, Frieda started to rant: this had given them more insight into her state of mind.

Frieda sang like a songbird once she found out that Fritzi had been double-crossing her with Yvetta, who she had imagined was only her business partner. Job done, they called their contact in the insurance police, deciding to keep part of the haul found in the storage room. They turned in only part of the stolen antiquities. Mika wanted to find out the value of the haul on the open market before any decisions were made. The police were happy enough with the break in their case and the items found. Mika realised that the stolen items found were part of a larger haul. The police were convinced the Italian mafia would factor in Fritzi's contacts: Rome was their best bet; the bustling city was well-known for handling stolen antiquities. Yvetta would more than likely be in Italy awaiting the arrival of the items Frieda had been sent to the Rubicov gallery to retrieve.

Mika needed to find Yvetta before she became embroiled in Frieda's dealings with the Italian mafia. Yvetta was foolhardy, arrogant, imperious, and reckless enough to jump into such dealings with abandon, believing herself superior to everyone else and feeling sure she would never be caught. Frieda had been offered a deal she could not refuse: years in a Russian jail, or to work with the authorities. Apparently, there had been no contest.

Now, Frieda was prepared to be their decoy. They were sending her to Italy to meet Fritzi with some of the antiquities. Taking no chances, Mika had arranged for their private jet to be ready to fly himself and Kolya out to Italy in search of Yvetta; they had to find her before the police became involved.

As before, Yvetta's involvement with the break-in needed to be hidden from anyone outside of their immediate family. The Russian police were not aware of Yvetta's involvement and disappearance from the clinic. Something would have to be done to keep her safe, not only from herself, but from harming their family in any way whatsoever.

Anna had to be protected from finding out Yvetta had escaped; she was in a delicate frame of mind as it was, in the early processes of making a recovery, and they could not risk any kind of relapse.

Alexi wanted her shielded from their daughter's unpredictable, dangerous behaviour. Outside matters were a whole lot easier to control; they could be ruthless when it came to damage control within the business, but dealing with family was proving to be their toughest challenge.

Mika and Sasha had conference calls with Alexi most of the next day before they set off for Italy; strategies had to be worked out for Yvetta before they left Russian soil.

A consensus was reached to have Yvetta treated at a new clinic in Switzerland. They had been investigating alternative treatment options since Yvetta was taken to the Colorado clinic.

Chapter 25

Mika had spoken to the Russian insurance police and had learnt that Frieda was cooperating with their every request. They had her in a secure lock-up, all her calls to Fritzi had been monitored under their instructions. Frieda was given the option of spending many years in a Russian prison, known for their cruelty, or being transferred to a German prison.

Fritzi had given Frieda documents to fill out for shipping and contacts for crating the artworks allocated for an exhibition in Berlin out of Russia. They allowed the process to go ahead, contacting the underground authorities in Berlin to hold the artworks and only releasing the shipment when assured of where it was headed.

The insurance company were positive that the shipment once released from customs in Berlin would find its way to Italy; if wrong they would notify Mika immediately. Word on the ground was that Fritzi was spotted in Rome; she had met up with someone well-known to the authorities, but also an informant to the police in Rome.

The contact came from Italian nobility and worked for the Italian police. No one knew of his work for the police's 'art department,' but he would be able to point them in the direction the shipment was heading, if in fact Italy was not the final destination.

Mika and Kolya flew to Rome; Mika had his own contacts in the city, and the two men stayed with a friend of the Rubicov family in a villa just outside of Rome. He was hoping to be able to apprehend Yvetta before the police became involved.

The problem was not tipping off Fritzi before the shipment arrived. He knew they wanted to apprehend Fritzi, but the police needed a lead. This was a major case: many antiquities and precious old paintings had been lost through theft.

If they managed through Fritzi to arrest some of the dealers handling these stolen artworks, it could help them crack the network right open. Mika doubted they would find the people who organised these intricate operations – they rarely did. Such criminals were disciplined professionals, with many layers of secrecy and underlings built up to protect them.

Mika was only interested in Yvetta; he was happy to assist the police in any other way, as long as Yvetta was not directly implicated or involved. If the family caught sight of Yvetta with Fritzi in Rome, they could lure her away. That was the tricky part, finding them together; luck had to be on their side. Transporting her to the clinic in Switzerland would be easy.

With the help from his contacts in Rome, Mika recruited a few people to help him on the ground. Photos of Fritzi and Yvetta were given to their foot-soldiers, who were only to contact them if a sighting was made.

Mika did not have long to wait before he received a photo on his cell phone to verify the sighting. Transferring the photo to his iPad, Mika and Kolya studied the likeness to the old Yvetta. There was no mistaking, it was his sister, her hair was now short in a boyish cut and died pure white, a drastic change in appearance for his sister, she looked elfin but still stunningly beautiful with her aristocratic bone structure. They had previously been sent photos of Fritzi but none of Yvetta. Mika was starting to wonder if Yvetta had not accompanied Fritzi to Europe after all. Three days had passed before a sighting of her had been made in a side-street café with Fritzi.

Mika was aware that Fritzi had made sure it was a safe place for them to be together, having made it her regular before Yvetta felt safe enough to accompany her.

Kolya met one of the foot-soldiers to instruct him of a plan they had concocted that Mika hoped would lure Yvetta away from the café. One of the foot-soldiers, a very attractive woman, had been instructed to flirt with Fritzi in a familiar way. Having a decidedly Russian temperament, being more emotional and jealous by nature than most, Yvetta might just walk off in a huff rather than make a scene.

If this did not work they would have to revise their plan. The authorities had let Mika know that the shipment in Berlin had been redirected to Marseilles. This information momentarily upset their plan, until they realised Fritzi was staying put until her shipment had arrived.

Sitting outside a café close by, Kolya wondered whether their plan had fallen flat. He ordered espresso after espresso, until his earpiece sprang to life, letting him know there was action. The male foot-soldier was speaking excitedly into his earpiece. Kolya bent over to concentrate on the delivery, his Polish was sketchy at best.

'Fritzi has taken the bait,' the man said, in a low, even, practised voice, but one not without a modicum of controlled excitement. 'She is flirting back with their decoy. Yvetta had not yet reacted.'

'Tell the female foot soldier to spice things up,' Kolya said. 'Speak to Fritzi in English, rather than Italian, so Yvetta cottons on to what is going down.'

Kolya stationed someone outside in case Yvetta suddenly bolted; they needed someone to follow her.

Kolya had a syringe in his pocket ready to inject Yvetta once they had her close enough. It would put her out for several hours. He had a car waiting; all she had to do was co-operate.

By the time Fritzi realised that Yvetta had disappeared, it would be too late; she would never know whether Yvetta had gone off on her own or not. Kolya was about to order another espresso when his earpiece jumped into life again.

'Now Yvetta has taken the bait,' the male foot-soldier said. 'She has walked out in a huff. Fritzi followed her out. They are now arguing loudly on the pavement.'

The male decoy was on hand, trying to placate Yvetta; he was now following her down the narrow street. He was telling Fritzi not to worry, he would bring Yvetta back, she was just upset.

'Fritzi has gone back into the café,' the voice informed Kolya. 'She was used to Yvetta's tantrums. Where could she go?' The female decoy had apologised, said she had not realised that they were a couple, and made her excuses. Once outside, the female decoy ran after Yvetta and the male decoy.

Yvetta was now waving her hands up in the air, shouting at the male decoy, telling him to leave her alone. But he continued to smooth-talk her, first in Italian, then English. Yvetta noticed the woman who had been flirting with Fritzi trying to placate her, too, that was when Yvetta – short-tempered, petulant – had had enough and struck out. The female decoy grabbed Yvetta's arm as it came towards her and plunged the needle Kolya had told her to use into it. Both decoys caught her as she collapsed between them.

The car in which Kolya travelled with the driver came to a screeching halt beside the two decoys, who were holding Yvetta up between them. The door flew open and they unceremoniously threw the sedated Yvetta onto the backseat, speeding off once again.

Kolya was impressed with their work; they had done a good job. He had not been sure the woman would correctly use the syringe he had given her – but she had, and he now had enough left in case she came around before they managed to get her safely onto the plane.

Mika had been kept abreast of developments. Pleased everything had gone according to plan, he left for the private airport, where the plane was ready for take-off.

The clinic in Switzerland had been notified of her arrival.

They would be able to land at an airstrip near Ilandz, not far from a village called Disentis, where Yvetta would be collected by the clinic.

It is a Swiss canton called Graubünden, which was also a popular ski resort in the winter months. Here, they spoke a version of Latin Italian called Romanish, and Swiss-German. Amongst his other talents, Kolya spoke a decent-enough German.

The clinic, Mika was told, could only be reached via cable-car up to a point, after which a train would take them the rest of the way up to a mountain plateau. There was no way Yvetta would be able to escape from this place; tourists were not welcomed and all visitors to the clinic were accompanied on their journey up or down the mountain. In winter the whole place was at times unreachable through bad weather, like St Bernard's Pass; it would be closed off to all access. The operation had gone smoothly. Luck and patience and good planning had paid off so far. Still, Mika would not breathe easily until Yvetta was ensconced at the clinic, properly isolated at last, cosseted safely by the Alps on either side.

It saddened him to remember what a beautiful lovely little girl she had been. Who knows what had gone wrong or why she had become a threat to her own family, one Mika held dear. She would have to be kept safe until cured of whatever demons had possessed her to threaten her own mother.

Yvetta woke on the flight, shocked to be surrounded by her brother, Mika, on the one side, and Kolya on the other. Groggy from the drug, her mouth felt dry, her body heavy. Mika passed her a bottle of water, but continued to watch her like a hawk. He knew that unpredictable behaviour was to be expected. He could see confusion and anger in her eyes. For her part, even in her doped-up state, she felt his hard gaze and it angered her greatly. Even when she was sedated, she was not fully subdued.

'How did you find me?' Her speech was slurred, but her mind was obviously trying to fit together the pieces leading to her abduction. She, who liked to feel that she could outsmart everyone, had been outsmarted. She could feel the resentment coiled within her, wanting desperately to be released. But not now. She would bide her time, and then she would strike. She knew she was superior to everyone around her, and soon everyone around her would know it, too. 'Did Fritzi contact you? Her speech was slurred but her mind was obviously trying to fit the pieces together leading to her abduction.

'She has been such a cow since my escape from the Colorado clinic. God knows why she went to all that trouble to help me escape if she was going to let you know where to find me.'

Mika decided to allow Yvetta to believe her own deduction; it played perfectly into their hands. Fritzi would soon be captured, the less the police knew about Yvetta's involvement the better; they did not want the family to become involved with the stolen antiquities. By all accounts, Fritzi had been using Yvetta and the Rubicov gallery as a cover for the legitimate shipment of the stolen art; the family would have to plead ignorance when questioned.

Mika shook his head sadly in agreement, but the hard look remained in his eyes. 'She has abandoned you, Yvetta, played you for a fool, using you for her own ends. She used you and then dropped you as soon as you were no longer of use to her. It was obvious to all of us – except you. You didn't see it because you did not want to see it.' He could tell the truth had hit her in the solar plexus; she appeared to be in pain, her mouth twisted and her eyes blazed. Tears streaming down her cheeks, she doubled over, holding herself in a foetal position. The woman who always had to have the last word, put everyone in their place, was speechless for once.

Mika and Kolya stared at each other; Yvetta was in a far worse mental state than anyone imagined. Mika hoped that this Swiss clinic would be able to help her. The Swiss were supposed to be synonymous with the likes of Jung and a plethora of other doctors who delved deeply into the psyche.

Yvetta remained curled up in the foetal position for the rest of the flight. Kolya wanted to sedate her again for her own sake, but Mika understood that she should be fully aware of her faculties when they handed her over to the orderlies in Disentis.

She would have to sign documents before she could be admitted for treatment. He had no doubt she would be willing; her world had imploded, she had no one left on the outside for support. This was her only chance to become rehabilitated, her only way out of complete alienation from the outside world.

Fritzi remained at the café, comfortable in the knowledge that Yvetta would return when she had calmed down. After all, they had been through many similar situations. The light was fading when Fritzi headed back to their small hotel in a cobbled side street in the old Jewish quarter of Rome. Hopefully, Fritzi thought, Yvetta had returned to their hotel.

Rome at night was frenetic with tourists. One never knew with Yvetta. Fritzi sometimes joked that Yvetta elevated sulking to an art form. If, indeed, sulking was an art, Yvetta would be a grand master, a Picasso of petulance, pouting, and the pantomime of pain. She was probably staying away in spite. Fritzi visited their favourite haunts, but no one had seen her. Days went by and still she had not returned.

Fritzi checked out of the hotel; it was time to pick up the shipment. She could no longer wait for Yvetta. She was confidant Yvetta would turn up eventually; if not, she would track her down once this job was over. After all, it was difficult to imagine a life without her. True, their life together was crazy, but it was their life, and they loved each other, and that was that. She was aware that a lot of people suspected that she was using Yvetta, but anyone who truly knew Fritzi and the extent of her feelings for her lover, knew this was not true. Some people suspected that Fritzi was incapable of real love, that she was performing at all times, that her life was about artifice and superficiality and little else. This was not true – Fritzi's love for Yvetta was real. With Yvetta, she both was and wasn't performing.

A nagging thought played on her mind, but she dismissed it out of hand. There were many islands in the Caribbean, that was the false trail she left for them to search. It would lead them around in circles – scenic circles, but circles nonetheless. She had gone to ridiculous lengths to protect Yvetta from being found; she was a silly bitch to run off like that.

Fritzi concentrated her thoughts on Marseilles; her shipment was safe and all had gone to plan. Frieda had been a good girl (Fritzi could imagine grooming her to be another Fritzi – although God knows, one Fritzi in the world was more than enough), following her instructions to the letter. No problems had been encountered securing the items left behind at the gallery. After the deal was done, all they had to do was keep their heads down and enjoy a comfortable lifestyle on the dollars earned from this last transaction.

Yvetta had signed the documents and was resigned to her fate, not exactly humbled but frighteningly close to it. Mika and Kolya watched her disappear into the cable car with the orderlies. Saddened by her loss of will to fight, Mika turned to Kolya, shaking his head: how did it come to this? He never thought that seeing his once invulnerable sister seem so vulnerable and broken would hurt like this. Indeed, Mika thought it would feel empowering to see her get the justice she so richly deserved.

But this did not feel like justice, far from it. His sister seemed so helpless and so small. Mika felt protective of her again, for the first time in many years. He felt the sting of the irony and turned away from it, and away from Kolya. Both lost for words, they returned to the plane for the flight back to Moscow. No doubt the police were waiting in Marseilles for the shipment to be picked up by Fritzi;, she would soon be locked up in a Russian jail, hopefully they would throw away the key. Even if she was eventually released, she would be an old woman by that time. He felt his old anger toward Yvetta transferred solely to Fritzi; filled with a renewed rage, as though Fritzi alone was to blame for years of Yvetta's behaviour – behaviour that long preceded Fritzi's arrival in her life – he felt oddly refreshed, not as guilty or heavy-hearted as he had moments before. Fritzi was the source of much of this, he assured himself. With her out of his sister's life, Yvetta, who would never be normal or stable in a strict sense of the term, would perhaps be rehabilitated – there was hope for her yet. There was always hope, Mika thought, putting aside his pragmatic attitude (inherited from his father), trying out optimism instead. The temperament of a Russian was hard-headed realism tempered by a gilded romanticism, he liked to think. And the flighty Fritzi would have to become pragmatic fast – he was sure she would rather see the inside of a Russian jail than have her throat cut if the mafia felt compromised after the shipment was seized.

It took a week before the Russian Police notified him. They had allowed the shipment to be picked up by Fritzi, whose papers had proved to be authentic. The Russian authorities did not want to step on the toes of the French police. They wanted Fritzi to be free and did not want further complications Otherwise, the antiquities and Fritzi would be out of their reach, locked up in a French prison.

The authorities had apprehended her before she had time to offload her precious haul unknowingly to the Russians. This avoided any contact with both the Marseilles underworld and the French authorities.

Confused by whom she was dealing with, Fritzi spoke French, then German; eventually the penny (or, in this case, kopek) dropped and she changed to Russian. By the time she had time to gather her wits, they had bundled her up with her precious shipment before the authorities in Marseille realised anything untoward had gone down.

Fritzi, the authorities informed Mika, had blamed Yvetta for turning her in. Yvetta was called every name imaginable, but they wanted to assure Mika that Yvetta would be left out of their enquiries. They had what they wanted; under interrogation, Fritzi would give them her contacts. The Russian antiquities were back in the mother country where they belonged, and for that they were grateful.

Mika felt vindicated. There was no reason for Yvetta to continue her love affair with Fritzi; they had helped expunge her hold, her evil influence, over his sister. As for Fritzi, she got what she deserved; he hoped it would be the last of her contact with any of his family. What Yvetta needed was distance from Fritzi – and, indeed, distance from the family.

Alexi, ever grateful for Mika's ability to clean up any mess the family managed to find themselves in, was saddened by the news of Yvetta's state of mind. He would have to make a journey to the clinic when the time was right and the doctors thought his daughter had made sufficient progress to have visitors. He wondered whether Anna would accompany him; she had suffered more than anyone in the family from Yvetta's erratic, dangerous behaviour. He doubted it was advisable; the less contact Anna had with Yvetta for the foreseeable future, the better for them both. Sasha would have to hold his father's hand; Alexi had never experienced the emotional vulnerability he was now feeling. This business with his daughter had taken its toll. She was now safe and the reputation of this Swiss clinic was reassuring. The family had now found the best possible help; more they could not do.

To everyone's delight, Anna announced her engagement to Maurice. It was to be a small, intimate wedding by Russian standards. Sasha and Alexi were thrilled for Anna, who needed to be looked after; it released Sasha from a job he no longer felt able to do, and released Alexi from guilt.

Anna and Maurice would move into the Rubicov family home. This gave Safi and Sasha the opportunity to move into their own place, which was long overdue. Between work and travel commitments, they spent their time viewing homes. Some were on a massively grand scale, others were apartments that were overly ornate or in areas neither wanted to live. Sasha suggested that until they found what they were looking for they move into the Rubicov building near the restaurant and club: it was central to everything and the apartments were beautiful.

DuPont had been true to his word, guiding Safi and Ilona through major shows and introducing Safi to artists and punters alike. Ilona and Safi were grateful for his input ; he became an increasingly invaluable part of their team - much to Sasha's chagrin. He could not figure out DuPont's charitable interest in their gallery, apart from Safi, that was. For her part, Safi just laughed off his suggestion as 'ridiculous. Please don't frighten him off; we would never manage without his guidance. He's done a huge amount to assist your family gallery – I'm sure you wouldn't want to interfere with that.'

Indulging her, he kept a close eye on DuPont and Safi's friendship, aware that no harm could come of it while DuPont remained in Manhattan.

With DuPont's guidance they attended the important shows throughout the year, rather than waste valuable time and money on shows and trips that were unlikely to yield returns, where it was not in their interest to buy exhibition space for the gallery.

The summer had flown past. Anna's wedding had come and gone; the Rubicov family had been in full attendance with a smattering of friends, and Safi's parents who had flown over for the occasion. Jake, meanwhile, was having a grand time down under, was loving all the extreme sports, had a lovely Aussie girlfriend, and a lucrative job with Google. The lifestyle suited him in Melbourne, and neither Safi nor her parents expected him to return. Sad for her folks, but Safi felt they had come to terms with the choices both their children had made, and she knew they were proud of her success at the gallery.

Her father, nowhere near retirement, surprised her with the news that Greg had become the go between with their overseas agencies and had proved himself invaluable. This was the job he had hoped she would do, Safi noted with mixed emotions: glad someone competent had taken her place, but still feeling a slight sting at what could have been. Greg was a brilliant team leader, Safi was pleased he had settled down, it took some of the stress off her dad and enabled him to relax and play more golf. Her mum had immersed herself in charity work, and, much to Safi's amusement, was now playing competitive bridge, which she adored.

Her cell buzzed in the early hours one morning: never a good sign. She had to read the message a few times before it hit her. Rupert had suffered a massive stroke and was completely paralysed down his right side. Dan was beside himself with grief; they did not think he would recover. Safi woke Sasha to tell him the news. deciding she should fly over. Her father informed her that he would be at Rupert's bedside with the rest of the family.

Rupert sadly passed away while Safi was in the air. The funeral had been arranged to his precise wishes. His lawyer was in possession of Rupert's revised will; everything was up to date, according to Dax. After his reunion with Dan and, especially, his Christmas scare, Rupert had made sure to get his will in order.

The two D's brownstone was now a sombre place. Dan had requested his family to stay there: Safi, Leonard, and Samantha (still in a state of shock) were welcome under his roof; he wanted them close. The house, now completed, had turned out to be spectacular; it gave Dan strength that his family could enjoy the comfort of their new home at such a sad time.

Dax was relieved to have them close for Dan, neither forgetting the role Safi played in bringing Dan together with his father. She was asked to say a few words at the funeral service. Samantha was happy to organise the food at the house for those who wanted to return after the funeral. Dan resembled a ghost on the morning of the funeral. His father's passing had come as a complete shock and, like Samantha, he was unprepared for the sudden separation. This brought him and Samantha together in mourning, though most of the time they said little as they sat together, gathering their thoughts and arranging the funeral. How cruel, Dan thought, to be reunited with his father only to lose him so soon after. No, he decided, how fortunate, to be reunited with his father, and to have spent all those wonderful days together in recent months, to have shared so much, and cared so much. Now that his father was gone for ever, their years in the wilderness seemed such a waste. Although Rupert didn't approve of Dan marrying, he would have adored having a grandchild.

Safi listened to the honesty of his words as Dan stood up in front of everyone reminiscing about Rupert. Saddened, but also realising how lucky she was having her father alive and beside her, she reached for Leonard's hand. He was tearing up. It was difficult to see her father, usually so strong, in such a broken state, but refreshing also to see how vulnerable and human he could be. They all loved uncle Rupert, each for their own reasons; he was a force to be reckoned with and they would miss him terribly.

Safi looked over at Samantha. Not related, she would probably fade out of everyone's life now that Rupert was gone; she hoped Dan, at least, would keep in touch with her. Her father followed Dan to the lectern to speak about his cousin; his few chosen words gave an insight into Rupert's life growing up in England. Few knew about this chapter of Rupert's life.

Then it was Safi's turn. She had fretted about what to say, discussed it with Sasha, Dax, and her dad. In the end, she had opted for a poem she had written the night before, which she hoped would express their love for uncle Rupert. Looking up, she stared down at her family, and then cleared her throat nervously and started reading the poem.

'Dear Uncle Rupert. I did not get to say goodbye.
I did though get to say hello.
I did get to know you.
I did get to share your love for chess in the park.
I did get to see you rekindle your love for family.
I did get to share your love of travel.
I did get to share your love of beauty.
I did get to enjoy that twinkle in your eye.
I did get to know your kindness of spirit.
I did get to know your love of loyalty.
I did get to know you Uncle Rupert as a dear friend.
And now I do get to hold your memory close to my heart.'

Safi looked up to see Dan and Dax both crying, and Sam, too. Oh God, she did not want to make things worse. Perhaps the poem had been a bad idea – but it felt right, though. Her dad bent over as she sat down and said in a soft voice,

'That was beautiful, Safi, truly from the heart.'

She felt somewhat better. Rupert was all the things she had mentioned and more. It was so hard to convey one's thoughts and feelings when someone had lived a lifetime and then suddenly were gone, just like that. Moving closer to her dad, suddenly feeling like a child again, wanting nothing more than a parent's comforting words and touch, she gave a little shiver. She missed having her parents around. It was awful being so far away from her family when reminded of their frailty, but isn't that what she had wanted?

After the funeral, her dad took the opportunity to speak to Safi before flying home to England.

'Safi, where does DuPont fit into the picture? I have noticed that he has a particular interest in you.'

Safi smiled. 'He's Dax's agent.'

'I know that, but have you noticed, darling, that he adores you?'

'Dad, for goodness sake he is old enough to be my father'

'Yes, but has he realised that, do you think?'

'Our relationship is strictly business. His input has been invaluable to the gallery, and he's been like a mentor to me in the artworld.'

'Well, I am not sure it's strictly business, as far as you are concerned, so be on your toes.'

She looked at her dad, but dismissed his concern about DuPont out of hand: it was in a father's nature to be overprotective and suspicious to a fault. But her father also wasn't aware of the degree that DuPont had assisted her in her new line of work, helping the gallery (and thus Safi at its helm) achieve great things. Besides, she had enough of Sasha being suspicious of DuPont's intentions. As far as Safi was concerned, it was an honour to have the exceptionally well connected and experienced DuPont to assist them. And he was always professional and a perfect gentleman. Safi could see him now, who was standing against a bookcase, glass in hand, watching her intently. Their eyes met for a millisecond, sending a shiver down her spine. Oh my God, she wondered, do I have feelings for DuPont? At this, the most inappropriate of moments, she felt indisputably: attraction.

Safi smiled weakly and made her way towards him. They had not spoken since the funeral. As she crossed the room, she took in the figure he cut.

DuPont was a tall, elegant, devastatingly attractive man. But she had always known this, only now she felt uncomfortable for some reason.

'Those were words from the heart so poignant, really beautiful,' he said, kissing her lightly on both cheeks. This time there was no mistaking the shiver down her spine and lightness in her chest. Really beautiful. Maybe he was talking about her in a coded way. Christ, why did her dad have to bring it to her attention? Everything had been okay before! Moving away slightly, feeling a little dizzy, she fiddled with her scarf. His closeness felt unsettling and her dad was watching

'Are you okay, Cherie?'

'Just a bag of nerves, and sad.' They discussed Dax's show and the interest it had generated from galleries in New York.

'We must meet this week, let's say at my office, before you return. We need to choose which of Dax's numbered prints you need shipped to your gallery.' Safi nodded; she knew they had agreed to screen prints to add to Dax sales.

'Okay I will meet you Tuesday if that's not too late?'

She noticed DuPont exchanging a few words with her father before he left. She hoped Leonard had not said anything rude to DuPont – she would cringe if he did – but DuPont waved farewell with no sign of discomfort.

Safi adored being with Dan and Dax again. In contrast to Dan's sudden sadness, Dax was still on a high from the success at the Rubicov gallery. She also made time to see Pete, of course, and Lauren, Bianca, and their baby (now a toddler). She felt so completely at home. The two D's enveloped her, making her feel needed and loved, took an interest in everything she said and did. It was a change from her normal everyday life. Not that she could complain – her life in Moscow now was a hundred times better than when she first arrived in that frozen (in more ways than one), inscrutable city. Even so, Moscow never quite rivalled her love for New York – or, for that matter, London.

Dax was still on a high from his show at the Rubicov gallery, he was keen on running off numbered prints from one or two of his paintings, had chosen them with DuPont but wanted Safi's input. If the original paintings went up in value the signed numbered prints would be in demand too.

Daniel returned to work determined not to mope around, he was busy and felt it the best way to deal with the loss of his father.

Pete had called Dan daily encouraging him to come over with Safi, trying to draw him out a week after Rupert's funeral. Pete wanted to get him back to everyday life.

Pete had been there during his father's absence from his life, and he was showing Dan that he was still there, even though life had changed.

Dax and Pete were the closest thing to family Dan had left in New York, the realization made him feel vulnerable, 'We'll see you at the bar Tuesday night, thanks Pete.'

She arrived at DuPont's Madison Avenue offices to be met by an immaculately dressed assistant apprehensively paging through an art magazine. Safi had barely got a sense of the space, when another assistant arrived to escort her into DuPont's inner sanctum. His offices were nothing but spectacular: windows facing the Park, walls covered in priceless art, sculptures on plinths, and African artefacts placed on a Philip Stark elongated console. The eclectic furnishings, modern and classic, mixed with odd pieces of French antiques, gave the room a spacious yet comfortable appearance.

DuPont walked Safi round his office, pointing out his favourite collector pieces while regaling her of their history. Leading her over to the white Barcelona daybed, he took a seat facing her on one of a pair of tan Barcelona chairs. The petite curvaceous assistant arrived to work the computer on the massive glass coffee table separating them. The assistant fiddled a while until large images of Dax's work were brought up on a flat screen attached to the wall. After the three of them had discussed which images would suitably serve as screen-prints and limited signed edition prints for the Rubicov gallery *the choices were immediately forwarded to Dax for his approval), DuPont, leaning forward and smiling softly, said,

'Now it's time to go for lunch. I have booked at my favourite little Italian across the road. It's very popular and it would be rude to be late.'

Safi noticed the humour playing around his mouth and the twinkle in his eye, She felt relaxed in his company. The old familiarity returned and she admonished herself for being so stupid. What was she thinking?

DuPont had secured his favourite corner table, allowing a marvellous view of the beautifully groomed people in the restaurant: obviously businessmen – mostly middle-aged, confident and relaxed in their surroundings – with a scattering of groomed NYC women amongst them. Safi was by far the youngest person in the room. Noticing heads turn in their direction, she wondered what the other diners were thinking; Some stopped to greet DuPont and she was introduced. As one of his valued colleagues, heading up one of the top Moscow galleries.

'I feel so young here,' Safi said.

'I would not worry about that: you are well on your way. You have accomplished a successful show in a foreign country.'

Again, that twinkle in his eye; he made everyone feel good about themselves that was his secret and his charm – and he was so damn attractive. One of the men who had been introduced passed their table on his way out, asking Safi for her business card. DuPont watched Safi hand over the business card, reflecting on her confidence, she had come a long way. The Rubicov gallery he thought was lucky to have her.

'Well, that is another learning curve for me, I surprised myself having the presence of mind to have these with me at all times at your insistence.

'What would I do without your guidance? Really, I would be totally lost.'

'Maybe Safi, but I think you have good instincts. Instincts counts for more than experience in our business.'

She became silent and DuPont noticed her staring at him unguardedly.

'May I ask what you are thinking?'

'I was wondering what my father said to you.'

DuPont, uncharacteristically silent for a moment, either searched for the right way to answer, or had no idea what she was referring to.

'When exactly, do you mean?'

Before she made a fool of herself, she said, 'Oh, never mind, I just noticed him chatting to you as you were leaving after Rupert's funeral.'

'Well, to be honest, I thought his comment rather odd, now that you mention it.'

Safi stared at him. 'What did he say?'

'He told me that he thought all the men in your life were far too mature for you.'

Safi looked dumbfounded and embarrassed.

'Really! What a thing to say I am so sorry.'

'Do you think he suspects something, Safi?'

Unprepared for this question, she felt the same excited flutter in her chest. Not knowing how to respond, she took DuPont's hand softly and held it for a while. Then she looked him straight in the eye, shook her head ever so slightly up and down, and whispered,

'I think I have feelings for you, yes.'

DuPont was now shocked at her honesty. 'You do realise I am almost as old as your father?'

'I do, but you are so much more attractive than my dad.' DuPont laughed. 'And way sexier, too.'

'I am not going to lie: I adore you, Safi, and I am so happy that you feel the same way. What about Sasha, though? Are you not getting married soon?'

'It could be our secret, couldn't it?'

'Before we start anything, are you sure you are going into this with your eyes open?'

Safi tightened her grip on his hand.

'Yes.'

DuPont became very serious and called for the bill. Out on the pavement he hailed a cab. From the time they entered the cab to the moment they entered DuPont's apartment on Park Avenue, no words passed between them.

He greeted the doorman as they entered the lift, ascending to the top floor, which opened straight into his apartment, DuPont did not take his eyes off of her.

DuPont held her face in his hands, looking for any signal of doubt in her eyes; but all he saw was excitement and desire. He found her respond to his touch, allowing him to take complete control. She felt that familiar yet distant-seeming electricity.

They kissed passionately while he slowly undressed her, leaving Safi in her underwear. Taking her hand, he led her through to his bedroom.

Not taking his eyes off her, he undressed as she watched, then lay down next to her. Safi noticed that he was pretty fit; there was not an ounce of excess fat on his body, the grey fluffiness on his chest thinned towards what could only be described as a huge bulge in his black boxers.

Safi became excited by his unhurried foreplay. He was embracing the whole of her, in no mad rush. Erotic frenzy had been replaced by an almost agonising slowness, yet it was passionately exciting in a different way.

Starting at the top, DuPont worked his way down her body. She felt his hand cupped over her, the pressure he exerted had her wild with desire; his finger finding her spot, she felt her senses reel as her back arched, building slowly until she exploded and climaxed to his strokes. Allowing her to finish, he kissed her lightly, then mounted her in the missionary position. In the same unhurried manner in which he had initially seduced her, he pushed hard inside her, lifting her legs around him as she enveloped him, feeling him deep inside, lifting her lips to meet his as he exploded inside her. Clinging onto him, Safi whispered, 'I loved you making love to me.'

He held Safi close and buried his face between her small breasts. 'You are beautiful, magnifique.'

'This can be our special place when I come to Manhattan,' she said. 'Our secret place. No one need ever know.'

DuPont looked at Safi, pulled her back into an embrace, and they started all over again,

'I am going to find it hard to share you. I have experience on my side.'

'I feel so wonderful, so excited about having you, all of you. I have always wanted to live my life to the full, now I feel I am. I need both of you in my life. I feel so loved. Can you understand?'

Laughing DuPont smacked her bottom. 'You are greedy, young lady, but I love it. It will make our stolen moments more meaningful.'

They dressed and DuPont put her in a cab.

'I will spend my last hours before my flight in your arms. Can I?'

'I will text you,' he said, and he blew a kiss as the cab drove off. She felt glowing and sensual, exhilarated and excited. She realised only now what Sasha and her father had perhaps suspected all along – she had always been attracted to DuPont. He was so masculine yet sensitive. She adored him; he made love rather than possessed her. He was a divine man, she could smell his delicious smell on her clothes; putting her hands under her nose, she inhaled his expensive soap and aftershave. Now not only his most dedicated pupil, she would also enjoy being his secret lover, too.

Safi punched the numbered code into the brownstone's keypad, hoping to find the apartment empty and to have some time alone at last. She wanted to avoid any suspicious looks or inquiring minds. When you were in love – or even in lust – one loaded look could give the game away, especially with people who knew you intimately, like the two D's. She felt a little guilty, a little sneaky, but mostly deliriously happy.

She made her way to her room and languished in a hot bath, trying to sort through her feelings. It was too early to make sense of what had happened, to turn something magical into something regrettable, to overcomplicate the most honest of emotions. She did not want to think about it at all yet – ignorance being as blissful as a hot bath – she wasn't ready to start second-guessing her actions, to let her conscience (wherever in her suddenly splendidly relaxed body that was situated) beat her like a drum.

She would be speaking to Sasha soon, but first she had to deal with this crazy euphoric happiness. She wondered how she would feel when she heard Sasha's voice on the other end of the line.

Thank God she was alone, because she had a permanent smile on her face. She couldn't shake it off. She tried to make a serious face but failed miserably. Giggling, with wet hair hanging down her back, she knew it was time to call Sasha: the euphoria was turning into dread. The sound of her phone ringing made her jump. She was sitting listlessly on her bed, staring into space. She answered tentatively, butterflies in her stomach.

'Hello? Oh, hi, Dax.'

'Are you okay? What happened at DuPont?' Dax's voice was warm and firm, but not unusually so.

'What do you mean, what happened?' she said, perhaps a little too quickly. Then, changing the subject, 'Did you not receive the forwarded pictures of the prints we chose for the gallery?'

Safi could hear someone trying to get through.

'I have to take this call, I will call you back, okay.'

She answered, knowing it would be Sasha on the other end.

'Hey, how you?' she said. 'Sorry I was on the phone to Dax about his prints for the gallery.'

'I'm missing you terribly. Can't you fly home earlier?'

Safi silent for a while, trying to stop her hand from shaking.

'I really don't think so. Dan is pretty miserable. I need to be here for him for a while. I will be home Saturday.'

'I can't wait!' he said, and suddenly she was thinking about DuPont all over again. She wanted to calm her nerves, and feelings of guilt. It was happening already – reality, which up to now had been two steps behind her, quietly catching up to her. She closed her eyes and remembered how DuPont had touched her – all over and for what seemed like the longest time. Thinking back on it elongated the moment further still. No, she was not ready for reality to catch up to her yet.

She flipped open her cell, eager for a message from DuPont, but found nothing. Disappointed, she wondered whether he had had second thoughts about their relationship. They were always in touch, the gallery was a perfect foil, why hadn't he contacted her yet?

She agonised about her next move. Would texting him make her appear more eager? She was behaving like a complete idiot – or, worse, a lovesick teenager. She was waiting for life to happen, when she should be taking the initiative herself. Well, that could be easily remedied.

It was a gorgeous, warm day so she decided to walk down Broadway, stopping off at some of her favourite stores Although Moscow would never be Manhattan for her, she and Sasha had settled into a pattern together, both of them loving their new challenges. Since Dax's successful show, the Rubicov family had given her carte blanche. She was following DuPont's investment advice, buying valuable collections for the gallery. Their next show would be to shift works Yvetta had invested in. Safi wanted to put her own stamp on the gallery. They were hoping to attract a different clientele: those who built up collections, investment buyers. With Sasha's encouragement and major investment from the Rubicov family, the gallery, DuPont had assured her, would grow in reputation and flourish even further.

DuPont was a genius – a madly attractive one. Their relationship had shifted onto another level, a risky one. It was difficult sometimes just to keep her head, but she knew that the professional part of their relationship would benefit everyone. She just had to become adept, a kind of acrobat, like Philippe Petit, the Frenchman who walked between the Twin Towers on a tightrope.

DuPont did call, but only on her last day in New York. He had left an address and time to meet at the studio of an artist he was keen for Safi to represent.

She wore her travelling clothes, packed her roll-on, and jumped into a cab to meet him. Having said her goodbyes to everyone over breakfast, she would head straight to the airport after being with DuPont.

Safi sat in the back of the cab, her excitement building. She couldn't wait to see him. It was like having a new dangerous toy she wanted to play with constantly. Their intimacy was so new, so strong; she was not sure whether she could keep her hands off him. Her heart was beating wildly as the cab drew up along the street, and there DuPont stood, as stylish as ever and incredibly handsome like a grey fox, in his elegant, relaxed way. DuPont leaned in and paid the cab while Safi struggled out with her luggage. He kissed her lightly on both cheeks, their eyes met momentarily, and Safi knew in that fleeting glance that he still felt the same. Her heart lurched. It took restraint and more discipline than she gave herself credit for not to jump into his arms.

The artist was right for the Russian market: a first-generation Russian-American, she used materials dating back to Imperial Russia, through the communist era and up to the present. Her sculptures were organic in form and textural in their complexity. Bowled over by the intricacy of the artwork, Safi immediately agreed to represent her. There was a flurry of shared and infectious excitement between the two women. Safi promised to arrange a show at their gallery in Moscow and left all details for DuPont to organise.

Safi and Dupont headed Uptown for a lunch date with a colleague he wanted her to meet; suddenly their conversation was strictly business. Safi wondered whether he was testing her, giving her the opportunity to step back from something she might regret with hindsight.

He was conducting a business call in French, had not even touched her hand, or kissed her even on the cheek. Her mind was racing, had she misread the signals? Not wanting to make a fool of herself, she kept to her side of the spacious black limo. They walked out of the car and into a minimalist Japanese restaurant that was below his office building.

The others were already seated at a table for six; amongst them, Safi was surprised to note, sat Polly. Safi went over to hug her (how long had it been since they last saw each other?) and Polly insisted on being seated beside Safi, with DuPont seated three away at the large round table.

Excited by Dax's show in Russia (which, Safi discovered, had been featured in the New York Times) and impressed by Safi's new career sang the praises of DuPont, who she declared was the Deon of the art world, a promotor and critic extraordinaire who preserved art's mystic.

'The Rubicov gallery is very fortunate to have DuPont as your mentor,' Polly said in her charming but cheeky, urbane, ingratiating, old New York tone that Safi found she had missed all of these months. 'Under his tutelage we will all be investing with you, one of these days.'

Safi laughed nervously: she had not only fallen under his tutelage, she had literally fallen under him and for him. Perhaps Polly, with her years of experience, had intuited this. Safi reminded herself to be very, very careful of what she said and didn't say in Polly's presence. Polly wasn't an ace gossip columnist and keen reader of the lives and loves of the who's-who of the Big Apple for nothing. As if to confirm this, Polly gave her a knowing smile, which she appeared to extend across the table to DuPont. Her new-found career had given her the confidence to seduce him, but perhaps it was going to be short lived. DuPont, it appeared, had already lost interest? Did Polly intuit this, too? Was that sultry smile, keen and knowing and full of ironic self-amusement, perhaps slightly pitying, too? Safi suddenly felt unsure of herself – and of everyone else as well.

The business lunch continued well past noon. Polly was the first to leave, with all of Safi's details (but hopefully no other information). The New York Armory show had just started, and the other diners were keen to discuss business with DuPont. Conversation now switched to French. Safi sat politely – her French good enough to understand most of the discussion, but not good enough to join in; nor was she invited to. She felt her exclusion keenly. For the first time in months, she felt very, very small, and a large amount of anger was welling up inside of her. She felt humiliated, angry mostly at herself. So she was important enough to be paraded around New York, but not important enough to be included in the situation? Was she so disposable and irrelevant that she could, without apology, be left out of the conversation entirely? Was she merely a child in very expensive grown-up clothes (clothes DuPont had no qualms about removing from her body – but not today, evidently; today she was nothing special). The French conversation continued as did her loneliness – for what seemed an endless amount of time. Safi wasn't used to feeling left out. It wasn't that she wanted to dominate the conversation. In fact, she regarded herself as a team player – but what if your team wanted nothing to do with you and didn't value your opinion? What then?

She thought about her time with Greg at the advertising agency in New York, and how valuable that time had been. It had been valuable because her opinion was valued, and because she learned from others who learned from her, in turn. This lunch was the opposite of that. What was the point of having a voice if you couldn't get a word in edgewise, and no one was listening in any case? The whole situation was now becoming fraught with embarrassment; having next to no experience how to deal with her predicament, she played with her wine glass, trying very hard not to appear upset. Insecurity and anger whirled within her. DuPont had not shown the slightest interest in her today. It was becoming obvious their tryst had been a one-off as far as he was concerned, something to be enjoyed, but not to be taken too seriously. She had imagined herself unforgettable, but perhaps she was disposable, just another pretty face in high society, inexperienced and indistinct, one of thousands.

Feeling a complete fool, she excused herself from the table and conversation she had so rudely been excluded from, and spent an inordinate amount of time in the bathroom (which was so polished and enormous, like the restaurant itself – and empty, too; the perfect place to loiter in), hating herself and everyone else.

She returned to the restaurant, but opted to sit on one of the couches near the entrance facing their table, pretending to read her phone. She was ready to bid DuPont a ladylike farewell, thank him for the introduction and lunch, and be on her way to the airport. Hopefully never to be seen again. Bonjour! But what she really wanted was to cry and fume and make a scene at his wilful neglect of her feelings. Checking the time, she noticed she had one hour before she had to leave for JFK if she was to avoid rush-hour traffic. There was no mistaking DuPont's intent any longer. She wished she had someone to confide in about DuPont, but of course she could tell no one – not even the two D's. She was about to get up when DuPont, accompanied by his dining companions, approached her, walking over to the sofa, arms outstretched and smiling broadly.

'Ah, môn Cherie,' one of his tablemates murmured, 'we are so apologetic, please forgive our tardiness. Business discussions should never take the place when such a beautiful woman is in our company, but our time is limited.' Each kissed her three times on the cheek as they bid them farewell. Safi stood dumbfounded smiling politely. DuPont, for his part, seemed earnestly apologetic, looking at her in that steady, soft-eyed, intimate way again. He took her by the elbow leading her back to their table, and ordered another bottle of sparkling wine before he sat down.

Taking her hand in his, he held her gaze, taking his time, allowing the waiter to pour the wine before he spoke.

'I adore you, Safi, and yesterday was wonderful.' He paused, as though what he was about to say would pain him – and possibly her as well. 'You are a beautiful, adventurous young woman. What man of my age would not be flattered. But I am not ready for a clandestine affair, that in all probability will end badly for us both. Surely you can see that, no?'

She was lost for words but knew he was right, even though it was, not what she wanted to hear. Sitting back, her hand still in his, she allowed her eyes to do the talking. DuPont noticed her resigned expression of understanding. His soft eyes looked sad.

'The Rubicov family are a powerful force in Moscow and abroad, they have huge assets and one should never dirty one's own doorstep, if you get my meaning? We would both be playing with fire, you do see, that?'

Acknowledging he was right she shook her head in agreement. She had always considered the urbane DuPont a romantic, but now she saw that he was at heart pragmatic – or perhaps, like Sasha and Alexi, he had within him a bit of both.

'I have feelings for you I can't explain,' she said and put her hand on his leg. She noticed him freeze, then gently replaced her hand on the table where he could see it. How everything had changed, she thought sadly, and in just a few short hours. From elation to sadness to – what would come next? Safi, a true romantic through and through, was not one to give up easily. She felt suddenly empowered. Leaning in closely she whispered in his ear. 'I'll be leaving shortly for JFK. You don't want to send me away unhappy.'

She sat back and smiled, waiting for his response. She did not have to wait long. DuPont's eyes were half closed as he looked at her; taking her hand, he let it fall into his lap. She could feel his excitement.

'Look what you are doing to me.'

Safi gave a throaty laugh. 'Let's go somewhere private, just this once, then it's the end. I promise.'

They made their way up to his floor of offices. He asked not to be disturbed. Once in his private rooms with the door locked, he undressed Safi, leaving her completely naked in the light of the windows. She felt totally exposed to the outside world, but loved the excitement and the danger of their liaison. Her heart beating wildly, she waited for his next move, allowing him to take the lead.

With DuPont it felt like a slow tango; he savoured every moment. She watched him as he walked towards her, shedding his clothes along the way. They stood facing each other his lips found her mouth, his tongue exploring her sensuously as his hand drifted down her body. Reaching her hips, he lifted her onto the window ledge, her back arching and hips thrust towards him. With her legs around his waist, he took her unceremoniously, before lifting Safi onto the Barcelona bed. It did not take long before she felt her body jerk as they both collapsed onto the leather bed, panting.

'You are going to kill me, but I will die a happy man.'

Safi turned around, engulfing him in her arms. 'Aren't you happy I seduced you again?'

They dressed and sat quietly for a while.

'Safi, no more, do you understand me? This is not good for business and not good for you. It's a dangerous game you are embarking on. Please listen to me. We can't go back, but we can move forward from here, to a new understanding? Keep it, as you say, our illicit secret, one we take to our graves – but it's the last time!'

'I have to go,' Safi said, 'but I agree. I wanted to part the way we started. I could not bear having to leave without having loved you one last time.'

'Safi, call me when you are in the gallery. We will do wonderful business together, like the professionals we are. We will make money instead of love – lots and lots of money. I will teach you everything I know, and you must behave when we next meet or our working relationship will have to end.'

'Seriously?' She searched for that mischievous glint in his eyes. Smiling, DuPont kissed her on both cheeks and watched the lift doors close.

She had loved seducing him; he made her feel invincible, all-powerful, a seductress of men, bending them to her will. Such a feeling was a powerful aphrodisiac – too powerful, perhaps. After all, one person's aphrodisiac was another person's poison. She adored DuPont, his age, innate charm, and confidence attracted her. What attracted her most was the masterful way he handled her, mentoring her, mesmerising her, never revealing too much about himself, never demanding anything or spoiling everything by falling for her in that puppy-dog way that turned men into boys and boys into fools. Instead, it was her who fell, who became – if only for a moment – wonderfully, deliciously foolish. DuPont was better than all of that, as patient as he was elegant and experienced, imparting knowledge she was hungry to learn, yet keeping her at a distance, keeping her at bay.

She slept like a baby all the way back to Moscow, waking in time to freshen up as the plane started it's descent. A car had been sent to pick her up. She was surprised at how disappointed she was not to see Kolya behind the wheel. But he was now in charge of Rubicov's security. She missed his humour and always felt safe when he was around.

DuPont was right, she would never want to be on the wrong side of their trust in her. She loved Sasha, her dalliance with DuPont was an aberration and a mistake: it would never happen again. She was stupid to put her happiness with Sasha – her future, her everything – in jeopardy.

Perhaps it was the death of Rupert that had made her so reckless – but no, she thought, she had been attracted to DuPont long before. Being thousands of miles from Russia (she was still reluctant to think of it as home) gave her the license, distance, space, and safety to act a little crazy.

Of course, both Russia and America – large landmasses with their own strange codes – were so unlike the UK. She had grown up with the National Health Service and a largely tolerant society that had benefited from the heady, revolutionary 1960s and '70s, the long arm of which had bestowed a sense of freedom, independence, and creativity to her own generation.

Now she was living in a society straddling between freedom of thought and totalitarian conservatism from the top-down. Russia was a paradox, doomed perhaps to endlessly repeat its own mistakes, a robust country in which true democracy seemed always out of reach. Instead, entrenched authoritarianism and autocracy, ancient and insidious, often appeared the country's default mode. She recalled a quote she had read from the German philosopher Hegel: 'History teaches us that man learns nothing from history.' And yet there were signs of progress everywhere in modern Russia – just not enough, and, crucially, not in the right places. She was living in a hybrid-model country that was in many ways still working itself out – a contradiction in terms, terms she rarely understood. Russia was a capitalist dictatorship, one that was clawing its way out of a communist mindset. She had never been interested in politics, but living in Moscow made her aware of the liberties one took for granted in the West.

Maybe all these differences had in some ways unsettled her personally. By liberating herself sexually in New York she felt liberated psychically, too, pushing forward a future too often dictated to her and by others; the true owner of her body and her destiny, taking back control. Did she feel controlled by the Rubicovs and her life in Russia? Did she like always being coddled and cared for and controlled? Not always, no. Sometimes she wanted to break out, act out, go crazy, be naughty, throw caution to the icy Russian wind. Well, she had done so in New York.

She was looking for excuses, justifying her behaviour. She thought about Yvetta and Fritzi running away from a society that excluded them because they were gay. Dax and Dan were lucky their sexual orientation had escaped notice during his show. This was modern Russia at its worst. Yet the Russia that Safi lived in could also be hospitable, heady, hedonistic, frenzied, fun.

The only upside in Moscow was Sasha and the gallery, which she had taken to immediately. Yet without DuPont and Ilona she would be lost. Still, she was learning and very quickly, she had to admit. She was impressed at how quickly she picked up skills that, mere moments before, she did not even know she needed to have.

She suddenly became aware of her status in the business and it did not please her. She needed to rise above being just a front for the Rubicov gallery. She needed to learn the business inside out; that was the only way she would be able to prove her worth, solidify her independence and herself. Be her own person once again and for ever. She would open more galleries, perhaps in New York and London. Make Rubicov's artistic endeavours truly international, and herself the lynchpin of it, indispensable, a success in her own right. Her spirits lifted as she thought of the challenges that lay ahead.

Chapter 26

Sasha had listened to Safi recount Rupert's funeral in dribs and drabs over the week she had been back. She told him also of a visit to the studio of an artist she was happy to represent. He could tell that she was animated, keen to share her experiences and make him feel included in her time away. Yet something was different about her since her return, something he could not put his finger on. She appeared nervous, distant, preoccupied with work, immersing herself in the art world. It was as if he had said goodbye to one Safi as she flew to New York for Rupert's funeral, and said hello to an entirely different Safi on her return home.

Life had taken on a hectic schedule. They both welcomed time together over the odd free weekend, lazing around in tracksuits, using the gym facilities at the Rubicov club, having food sent up from the restaurant. Living in the apartment had turned out to suit them; neither felt the need to move. Sasha watched Safi as she caught up with news in the foreign papers, something she loved doing on Sundays, a habit inherited from her parents and long, lazy weekend mornings in Brighton. Safi, he knew, had a habit of internalising her thoughts until she could no longer contain her feelings. With a little help, he was sure she would open up.

'Hey,' Sasha said, leaning over the kitchen counter, feeling energetic all of a sudden, even confrontational, 'you have been pretty distant since New York. Anything you want to share?'

She was sitting on the sofa, across the room, but she may as well be in a different country – in New York City still.

'Well, yes, actually there is.' She looked up from the International Herald Tribune, brushed back her hair, smoothed down a page. She smiled at him but that, too, he thought, was oddly removed. Like the facsimile of a smile. Faded, like newspaper print.

'Thought so. Want me to come sit on the sofa with you?'

'Please, but you will have to indulge me.' Sensing his buoyance, his boyish, almost animal, enthusiasm, she felt suddenly shy. 'I have been chewing this over for a while.'

'I'm all ears,' he said, and, as if for emphasis, pulled the lobe of his left one. 'You're not leaving me, are you?'

'Be serious. Being in Manhattan gave me time to reflect on my role at the gallery.'

Sasha looked at her expectantly, even nervously.

'To put it bluntly I feel bad about taking Yvetta's place at the gallery.' She put her hand out for him not to interrupt. 'I feel sad that she and Fritzi had to run off to make decent lives for themselves because of Moscow's intolerance about homosexuality. I appreciate the confidence everyone has in my ability to learn the ropes, but really I am not happy just being a front for the gallery.'

'But Safi, you are hardly a front.'

'Let me finish,' she said, and they were both surprised by the unexpected sharpness of her tone. She was not 'a front,' but she did appear affronted. Perhaps her last visit to New York really had changed her. 'Without Ilona and DuPont, I would have failed miserably.'

DuPont. Sasha's least favourite word at the moment, and there she was mentioning it again. It had been a whole ten minutes, he thought sardonically, since she had last mentioned it. DuPont, that smooth, smug, self-satisfied bastard. A poseur, a social climber and starfucker, a faux-sophisticate. Yes, Sasha had his own opinion on the fabulous Mr DuPont. But he said nothing, not wanting to tip the conversation – already so unsteady and unpredictable, this new Safi so unlike the old, more restrained Safi – into an argument both of them would later regret. He was suddenly so uncertain about everything, and his uncertainty bothered him. He liked to think of himself as resolute, as determined and decisive. But he was none of that now. Worst still, he couldn't put his finger on what was different about her. He stared at her, smiled passive aggressively, intent on conveying his quiet annoyance.

'I tried to help, too,' he said, in a tone needier than he had intended.

She gave him a cold, almost pitiful look. No woman respected a needy man. Women were biologically wired to attend to needy babies – needy men, not so much. 'Oh, yes, you helped a lot, of course. Your family have been amazing. But that's not the point.'

'What is the point?' he said, gazing at her newspaper and feeling as though they were both struggling to arrive at a simple but suddenly out of reach answer to a crossword puzzle clue. He watched her close the paper and fold it in half, as if to indicate the seriousness of the new turn in their conversation. Six letters. Across. A man you would be foolish to leave your fiancée alone with. But of course Sasha already knew the answer – how could he not? Not out of reach at all, but staring him in the face. DuPont.

'The point is, I need more. I need to feel that I can make a difference. Learning the ropes is fine, but I have to become independent, be able to run the show on my own. But what's the point if it belongs to Yvetta? Please don't misunderstand me, I realise that your family have been incredibly generous to me and I know you have assured me that what's yours is mine – but I need to be my own person, earn my way. That's the way I was raised. If Yvetta decides to return all the work I have put in, it would have been for nothing.'

Sasha stared at the floor for a while. So much for an idle Sunday, he thought, before feeling fortunate to be in love with such an ambitious and self-willed young woman.

'I can't discuss Yvetta with you, unfortunately, but I will take what you said up at our next board meeting. Perhaps you can sit in on one of our meetings and tell the board what you have in mind for the gallery? I am sure the lawyers will be able to draw up documents to name you as a director of Rubicov Galleries.'

Safi stared at Sasha.

'Just like that?'

'I can't see why not,' he said, eager now to put this conversation behind them and go back to their lazy Sunday ritual which hopefully included lovemaking. 'I totally agree with you.' He made eye contact once again, put his face near hers, placed a hand on her knee. He wanted desperately to rekindle the intimacy that seemed to have lost them around the time Safi left for New York. 'We will have to work out some legalities, but that's what our lawyers are for. We don't pay them a fortune for nothing.'

Safi put her hand over her mouth, her eyes misting over, feeling dizzy all over again, for the first time in days – but brilliantly so. She put her hand over Sasha's, tightened her grip. ' 'If they agree that will mean no more playing around. I will be solely responsible for the gallery's success. Maybe I am getting a bit ahead of myself.'

He saw the gleam in her eyes, unmistakable – unbridled ambition, pure as lust. He saw her pull back from it, but only slightly, prudent for a moment. Then he saw her smile. Filled again with wonder and love for this woman, he pulled her towards him.

'That's why I love you: one moment you are so serious, and the next you become like a helpless child. But I have complete confidence in you, it's obvious you love the art world. I have no doubt the gallery will flourish under your guidance.'

'And of course, at least initially, I'll still have the help of Ilona and DuPont.'

'Oh, it won't be long before you know more about the art world than even DuPont,' he said in the even voice he used when intent on not betraying his emotions. His father had taught him never to exhibit any weakness. Don't show your hand too early – or, if possible, at all. The point, he thought now, the real point, was to keep Safi as far away from DuPont as possible. How he would do this, exactly, while giving her more control over the Rubicov Galleries, he had yet to figure out.

'What about Yvetta?' she said.

'Don't worry, all that will be handled by our lawyers.'

'You work them hard, these lawyers,' she said coquettishly.

'They bill us hard, we work them hard,' he said, suddenly relaxed again, feeling confident in their relationship once more. 'It's the way of the world.'

Safi curled up on the couch next to Sasha, now feeling a complete bitch and such an idiot to have jeopardised their relationship. She did not deserve this fantastic man and his loving family, but she was determined to fix that. She playfully pushed him down on the couch and began to kiss and undress him. He put his arms around her and she felt ensconced in love – and this, too, was the way of the world.

Alexi had flown to Switzerland to visit the clinic Yvetta had been secreted away to by Mika and Kolya. This was a place his resilient and often ingenious daughter would have a hard time escaping from. It was practically impenetrable. You had to travel to the top of the mountain by cable car, then take a train for a short distance on a steep gradient uphill track to reach this fortress-like clinic.

He was met at the reception desk by an attractive older woman. The scenery from the fortress was stunning: the sheer drop through the mountains to forests way below held him spellbound.

Alexi turned to follow her into an office.

'Beautiful,' he said. 'The seasonal changes must be awe-inspiring.' She nodded her head in agreement as she took a seat behind her desk, somehow silently conveying that she was not one for small talk. Alexi noted encyclopaedic volumes, he supposed on the mind, filled the shelves almost suffocating the small, neat office. On the wall facing them were four small, square, closed-circuit television screens capturing the action (or, more accurately, lack thereof) in four different rooms. The rooms all looked the same, the screens grainy, illuminated by occasional flickers of motion. For the most part, the screens were static with inactivity, and controlled sterility. Indeed, looking at the screens even for a moment had a sedative effect. Individually, the screens must mean something, but cumulatively they meant nothing, the one cancelling the other out, like falling dominoes. He tried to refocus and met her gaze, which was alert and unusually stern. He could not help but think she was silently analysing him. And what was her analysis? That he had failed his daughter? That his daughter had failed him? Poised and ever-upright, with an air of silent professionalism. Frau professor Lundt's posture was as precise as her Swiss-German, lilting dialect in English. She waited for him to finish his coffee and small shortbread cookie. Then, when he had consumed the last bite and neatly wiped his hands with a napkin, she pointed to the screen on the wall. He tried to make sense of an image that, a moment before, he had barely been cognisant of.

Leaning forward, straining his eyes, he recognised Yvetta sitting in a circle with others. They were animated, each speaking in turn, with the exception of Yvetta, who he noticed was thinner than he had seen her in a long time. She looked pale, morose, and withdrawn. Concerned, he looked at her for context, but she drew his attention to the date on the top right-hand corner of the screen. She switched to another screen, a later date – yesterday morning, in fact. He now viewed an Yvetta fully animated, looking healthy, even happy, taking part in a life-drawing class. Relieved, he realised she was showing him his daughter's progress since she had been admitted. 'Ja, she is now greatly improved. This is our art therapy class – her favourite. That first video I showed you, that was your daughter's first week here. That was five months ago, as you will have noticed from the date. You can see she has turned a corner. When she arrived, she was a very depressed, angry young woman. We still have much work to do to change her mindset; there are many different treatment options. We are still working on which Yvetta will respond best to.'

'Do you believe she can fully recover?' Alexi said. It was not the first time he had asked this question to a doctor.

'I cannot give you a definitive answer.' Not the first time he had heard this answer, either. 'It could take years of treatment. But we do believe a change of mindset is possible, yes. There are a number of structured programmes and different treatments'

'Why do you think our daughter has developed this destructive, angry illness of the mind?'

She hesitated before she formulated her answer. Her posture remained upright, her words even, exact. She was the kind of woman who lived her life in a premeditated manner, planning and processing her every thought and movement, leaving nothing to chance. A clockwork woman, mechanical, methodical, she gave him her stern but sincere expression.

'I will recommend some reading material, it may better help you understand. It's both biological and environmental but mostly its inconclusive. Family members should not blame themselves. She has accepted treatment, which is very important and should give you hope for an eventual change in her behaviour. We will keep you informed of her progress, it's best that she does not see you this visit. Maybe at a later stage, but not yet.'

Alexi's eyes were still on the screen but his words were directed at the doctor.

'I need to know my daughter is safe here. Is it at all possible for her to escape? She can be very manipulative, persuasive and charming.'

'We are aware of her behaviour patterns, and are learning from her every day. The doctors and staff are trained to deal with highly intelligent, extremely manipulative patients. She will never find a way off this mountain by herself: it's not possible, you can be assured of that. The sheer drop and the mountains remind our patients every day how impossible escape will be.'

Travelling down the mountain in the cable car Alexi felt reassured; they may finally have found the right institution to help his daughter. Perhaps there was cause for optimism – Yvetta looked happy enough certainly happier than she had looked in many months. In Yvetta's absence, Alexi was thrilled by Safi's influence and commitment to the gallery; the gallery was breaking even with a more than reasonable margin of profit, which was more than it had when Yvetta was running it.

Now Saffron wanted a secure stake in the gallery. She was an astute and clever young woman, he respected that, he would organise for his lawyers to draw up a contract that allowed her complete control, with a caveat.

The director of the Swiss clinic had put his mind at rest; his anger over Yvetta's attack on the family had softened. But Yvetta's actions would never be forgotten – never. Russians did not forget or forgive. All the same she was his daughter. The family were not dealing with a normal situation, he had to remind himself of that, she was ill. He did not understand these things, but he was trying to come to terms with her condition.

The lawyers would work out how to add the caveat into the contract for future possibilities. Saffron was not a member of their family, marriage was not a failsafe, who knew what the future held; the business would always remain in the family only. How else to maintain security, loyalty, dynasty, and family unity?

It was up to Sasha and Saffron: only once they were married would the contract come into force with her signature, and not before. Until then the Rubicov gallery would remain in Yvetta's name, with Safi as the chief operating officer.

Safi had been back in Moscow for six months, organising for upcoming shows and charity events. On DuPont's advice, Ilona had travelled to important art fairs in Europe. Many of the Russian works had not been shown for years. Russian art was back in demand and the Rubicov gallery owned a great deal of Russian art. Yvetta had neglected these valuable works, opting for Banksy's street art and lesser known contemporary Russian artists.

Her dealings with DuPont had been few and far between since arriving back in Moscow. Safi knew he would continue to guide and advise them, but for now he opted to work with Ilona. At first she felt a pang of jealously at the obvious way he chose to cool their relationship. She felt the sting of neglect, even if she understood the reasons behind it. Perhaps it was time for her, too, to become pragmatic. After all, she was aware that she needed both Ilona and DuPont to make a success of the gallery if she was to succeed in her plan for expansion in the future. Perhaps she should take DuPont's decision to cool things off not as a slight but instead as a kind of compliment, a sign that DuPont viewed her as an emerging player in the art world that he could not afford to get emotionally entangled with. She began to appreciate the distance between them. he was a smart man, doing her a favour by cutting off their affair at the knees before it consumed them in a dangerous liaison that could only end badly.

Daniel wanted her to return for the reading of Rupert's will. Their wedding would be a week later and it would allow her to see DuPont in person. Safi felt they needed to break the ice to move forward as friends.

She would need Sasha with her if she was to face DuPont with any modicum of dignity or confidence, having him with her would be a stark reminder of DuPont's reason for breaking off their dalliance, before it had time to blossom into a full affair. Sasha would have to find the time to stay on after the union of Dan and Dax. Without his presence she was not sure whether she would be able to resist the temptation; her liaison with DuPont was still very fresh in her mind. Using Sasha to give her moral strength would not be her best moment, but in the end it would, she hoped, provide all three of them with the best outcome.

Flying into Manhattan, sitting beside Sasha in first-class, vividly brought back images of her affair with DuPont. Safi could not help feeling hot with excitement. She tried to suppress her desire to seduce DuPont until he begged for forgiveness. She imagined him at her mercy, begging her to take him back. She was being wicked, yet it felt
really good.

Feeling both ashamed of and excited by her thoughts, she made her way to the toilet before they landed. Safi stared at herself in the mirror. Why was she being so bloody stupid? But she felt so incredibly hot. Did she want him so badly because he was the only man to push her away (even if it was for valid reasons), to tell her no.

She touched herself and gasped. The thought of seducing DuPont sent her into a frenzy of sexual desire. There was nothing for it, she had to satisfy her needs before she landed. She bent over as the waves engulfed her. She bit down hard as she tried to stop any sound escaping. As the waves continued, she found the need to satisfy herself all over again. How on earth was she going to stay away from him? She needed something hard inside her. Oh my God, she was beyond control.

Looking in the mirror she bent forward and blew a kiss at her own image. Wow, she felt incredible; she felt madly sexy. She needed Sasha, she wanted more. Would he be up for joining the mile-high club? Safi pulled down her skirt, stuffed her knickers into her bag, and made her way down the passage to their first-class seat. She pushed past Sasha, lost her footing, and sat down on his hand with her bare bum. She had left open the zip that went all the way down. As she slid off onto her seat, she felt his hand feel her bum. Good, he had realised what she had done. Turning around to face him, she saw that Sasha shared her thoughts.

He leaned over and whispered. 'Let me go first. I will be on the right, it's the larger of the two.'

She gave him her hand as he kissed her fingers lightly – the same fingers she had used on herself moments before. Their eyes met; she felt her stomach lurch with excitement. She slowly took her hand back as he left his seat, following him with her eyes. How long did she have to wait?

Everyone was asleep. The cabin was dark, not even the crew were around. She found the toilet and pushed the toilet door she had recently vacated, open, squeezing in. Sasha locked the door behind her.

Sasha was ready. As he pulled her skirt up, she positioned herself on his lap and undid the top buttons of her shirt as he smothered his face between her breasts. This time she knew it would take longer to reach a climax but she did not care, she needed to be satisfied again. The thought of Sasha inside her and the illicit sex they were having (two bathrooms, two men, one plane, one girl) brought on the strongest climax she had ever experienced. Safi thought she would faint. She stuffed both hands into her mouth so as not to scream. She had never felt so on fire, her entire body, every nerve end, was alive.

He took her face into his hands, kissing her passionately. 'Safi, never leave me. I absolutely adore and love you to distraction.' Safi leaned into Sasha, tears running down her cheeks.

'I don't intend to. We better get out of here before they arrest us.'

Sasha let himself out; no one was around. He stuck his head back in. 'You're safe. It's quiet out here, take your time.'

The forthcoming celebrations were going to be madly exciting; Dan and Dax had planned their nuptials down to finest detail. They wanted nothing left to chance, particularly not the inclement weather.

The reading of Rupert's will was planned for a week ahead of the wedding, it was not only convenient, but it was their way of including Rupert in their plans. The family were to meet at the lawyer's office for a formal reading.

She arrived at Bancroft, Croxley and Ginsberg on Madison Avenue to be greeted by a group of diverse people standing around chatting. Dan was as surprised as anyone by the crowd, having no idea who would be a recipient in his father's will. Mr Ginsberg had sent out a formal letter asking her to attend the reading; it was the first postal letter she had received while in Moscow.

Samantha had received two embossed invitations: one for the reading of Rupert's will and another for the wedding. Pete was there and Rupert's old chess buddy, Jack Levy. There were two women standing alone that Safi did not recognise; she noticed that they introduced themselves to Dan. One was a groomed woman of advanced years (Safi guessed late sixties), with short grey hair with a shock of white running through the quiff in the front. The other woman was much younger, but they had similar facial expressions. Safi wondered if they were mother and daughter.

Mr Ginsberg's secretary called them into a conference room, asking them to be seated at a long and highly polished maple table. There were eight cut-glass tumblers filled with iced water, one at each seat. The walls were covered in large black-and-white nondescript prints comprising mostly of lines and squiggles; some only a dot in the centre of a large frame.

They all waited expectantly for Mr Ginsberg to join them for the reading of the will. All eyes turned to watch a portly, bespectacled, smartly dressed older man in a dark navy pinstripe suit take his place at the head of the table.

He stood looking at each in turn, nodded, smiled, and introduced himself. Consulting a leather-bound folder in front of him, he explained that he would start with the non-family members, and asked each to leave once he had completed their portion of the will. Mr Ginsburg turned to speak to Daniel.

'I did not know your father well; in fact, we only met twice.' Mr Ginsburg was English. Although he had a transatlantic accent, his mannerisms and facial expressions were definitely British, he managed to look apologetic and arrogant at the same time, she was sure of that. 'His previous lawyer recommended our firm to him when he retired. We only recently before his passing revised his wishes for the will.'

Mr Ginsburg turned away from Daniel and indicated that he was talking to the room again. 'Now could you please answer when I read out your names, so I know who I am speaking to.' He began to read. 'Mrs Rosa Danziger.'

The older of the two women, tentatively put up her hand.

'Good, thank you. Miss Gina Danziger.' He looked over his glasses at the younger of the two women, who shifted uncomfortably in her chair to acknowledge her name.

'Now if I may refer to your father as Rupert?'

Dan shook his head in agreement. Safi felt relieved; she had had to remind herself they were talking about Rupert. This whole reading was so strange, so alien, so freakishly formal, so un-Rupert, really, in every way. Safi looked around her at the familiar faces in the room. No one, it seemed, had the foggiest idea who Rosa and Gina were. The proceeding was like watching a drama unfold, an out-of-body experience that they were all part of. It was like a dream that, in its slow, static nature and numbing formality, felt real in all the wrong ways.

The lawyer continued a roll call round the table to familiarise himself with the faces that matched the names.

'Let's begin should we'?

Ginsburg looked up once more. 'Should we continue?'

Too shocked to comment, everyone acquiesced to the lawyer's suggestion. Safi felt her body stiffen, sensing that her name would soon be called. She had always felt so at home around Rupert, but now she felt decidedly uneasy.

'To our wonderful Saffron who came into our lives and changed everything in it for the better, thank you for 'being you and never ever change inside or out. You are perfect. To Safi I leave my favourite British artists. A small original painting by the surrealist Francis Bacon. One original op art painting by Bridget Riley. Two paintings by David Hockney. A small Frank Auerbach drawing. One Leon Kossoff drawing. Two drawings by Lucian Freud. And a collection of erotic drawings by Audrey Beardsley. Enjoy them. Love, Uncle Rupert.'

All eyes were on Daniel now.

'Daniel, I left you until last. You were my reason for living when your darling mother, Sofie, passed away. I cherished every moment that I had you to myself. And then we entered the wilderness years: what a waste of precious time those were. I am a stupid old man and I thank God every day that I came to my senses. I like to think we made up for some of that wasted time. You have been a model son and a friend. I am proud of your many achievements. I know this is a sad time, but I am proud to be able to leave you what I have worked so hard for during my lifetime. I pass it on to you with love: enjoy and cherish all that I have loved. Your loving father, Rupert.

'To Daniel, my son, I leave the rest of my estate. This includes the real estate. The house in the Berkshires. Three apartments in Brooklyn. The beach house in Fort Lauderdale, including all original artworks within it. All outstanding loans have been taken care of. I have tried to leave my life in order, with as little as possible for you to deal with on my behalf. I am pleased to say your old dad did okay. I love you, be happy and live a life full of love. We will continue this precious bond when we meet again.'

Daniel sat in a fog of emotion and shock. The lawyer finished off the reading and excused himself.

'Daniel.'

It was Dax who softly prodded Dan back to reality. Everyone was still in shock by Rupert's generosity, barely wanting to move lest it had been a dream, not knowing what to say.

'I need space and time to digest my father's will,' Dan said finally, still not looking up. 'I know his generosity has shocked us all. Rupert was an enigma; not even I knew he had accumulated this much wealth over the years.'

Daniel got up to leave, then thought better of it and turned around to acknowledge Rosa and Gina.

'Rosa, I am sure Gina and I both need to digest what has just come to light; please can we meet tomorrow?' Rosa nodded. 'I will call you in the morning. Perhaps we can meet for brunch.'

Pete took charge as the two D's went off. The rest of them headed to Pete's Bar to make sense of everything. Pete had invited Rosa and Gina to join.

'You are now family,' Pete had said, and Safi could see that they, too, were won over by his unprepossessing nature and natural charm. 'We can drink to Rupert's memory and his generosity.'

The bar was a welcome shelter from the stark opulence of the lawyer's offices and after a few beers they had enough Dutch courage to begin a discussion none had known. how to start. On her third beer already, Rosa added some Aussie logic to the tangible atmosphere.

'I guess Daniel has gone walkabout. The poor bugger has a lot to digest.'

In perfect Aussie-speak, Rosa had managed to convey everyone's thoughts. Safi learnt that Lisa had died of breast cancer last year.

Checking her phone, Safi found a voice message from Sasha. 'We have a date with DuPont this evening. He is taking us to the opera at the Met.' Just when she thought this day could not get any more unreal, now this. Safi felt her stomach turn over; she had not spoken or seen DuPont since arriving in New York, but they had found the invitation waiting for them on their arrival. Sasha had apparently accepted on Safi's behalf, knowing how important he was to her career and it would have been rude to refuse, his gesture of tickets during the opera season, while she was at the reading of the will.

Safi was a bag of nerves in the cab; she had experienced enough drama for one day. She marvelled at how handsome Sasha looked in his tux. She had chosen to wear her favourite pale pink Prada with high neck and plunging back, accompanied by her beaded Judith Lieber evening clutch. Sasha had approved of her choice; it set off her dark hair, which she swept up into a side knot.

Looking demurely elegant was the idea, but she felt ridiculously dirty and she could not deny it; she felt a smidgen of excitement. Please don't let Sasha notice anything untoward. Sasha helped her out of the cab. As she followed him up the steps, she noticed that her palms were sweating. Apparently, she wasn't the only one who noticed.

'Your hands are clammy, are you feeling, okay?'

She smiled weakly. 'I think I'm a bit shaky after the day's drama.' But she had no chance to dwell on her duplicity, spotting DuPont, looking as elegant as ever, waiting in the lobby, with two women. Two women! That was DuPont for you. 'Ah, there you are,' he leaned over to kiss Safi thrice on her cheeks, and then Sasha. She was having that out-of-body experience again, floating above, watching herself go through the motions.

'This is my ex-wife Monique and my daughter, Chantal, from Paris. They come every year for the opera season.'

The five of them exchanged greetings and chatted easily. DuPont behaved so normally, no one would ever guess their secret. She felt her terror abating, wiped the clamminess off her hands and onto her dress as they settled into their seats. She was happy to find herself between Sasha and Chantal, with Monique on the other side of Sasha.

She was surprised that Chantal, though beautifully turned out, was quite ordinary, while Monique was a petite, feisty, well-preserved and self-assured Parisian.

The evening went without incident; Puccini's La bohème was stunning she had expected to hate it and was pleasantly surprised to be drawn in by the drama of it all, the music was divine, enabling her to relax. She found herself removed once again, but this time deliciously so, forgetting where (and with whom) she was.

They were to spend the intermission at the Grand Tier Restaurant, where DuPont had booked a table. Safi was dreading the conversation, but found DuPont a completely different person around his family. DuPont was always unflappable, of course, but now he seemed especially at ease, even proud of his family, who he allowed to dominate the conversation. Monique was a force to be reckoned with, and kept the conversation going, mostly about the opera. Safi felt relieved that Sasha held his own with her insatiable knowledge.

Returning to the table from the bathroom, she bumped into DuPont on his way to the men's room. They stopped momentarily, both at a loss for words. Safi smiled weakly as she passed him, then felt his hand on her elbow, leading her behind a huge potted plant.

'I find it very difficult to behave around you, but we must, Cherie, we must.'

'I thought you were ending our tryst.' Safi had meant to sound firm but her voice betrayed her – she sounded flighty, silly, very much in lust, even to herself.

His eyes hooded, he leaned in close to her ear. 'Maybe just once more. You never know, I might be dead tomorrow. To deny each other this pleasure would be a crime, no?'

Staring in disbelief at him, she felt a buzzing in her head, but her heart felt icy cold. 'Never, not while Sasha is here, we can't; it's much too dangerous.'

DuPont was adamant – he thrived on danger, she realised that. And perhaps she did, too.

'Meet me tomorrow,' he said. 'I will text you the address of an artist's studio.'

Safi found her way back to the table. She smiled at Chantal, who leaned over and whispered in her ear.

'Be careful of my father, he loves beautiful women.'

Safi hoped that Sasha had not overheard the remark – but of course he had (nothing, it often seemed, escaped his eyes or ears), and he caught Safi's eyes. It was as though his eyes were daring her to respond in some way, to look away from him guiltily, or meet his steady gaze. Instead, she made light of it.

'Oh, your dad is not only charming, Chantel, but invaluable. Without his help I would be lost at the gallery.' Safi addressed this to Chantel, but the words were meant to reassure Sasha as well.

Monique cut in sharply. 'My husband has taken on quite a few protégés in his time; under his tutelage they have all blossomed, but I must say you are the most beautiful. How fortunate – for me – that you live in Moscow and have a handsome beau.'

'Fiancé, Cherie,' DuPont said, 'and stop teasing my Russian friend, you are both wicked.'

Monique threw her head back, laughing, showing perfect white teeth.

'Well, we all know your reputation, darling – I mean in the art world, of course.'

In the cab back to their apartment, Safi felt the need to say something, if only to break the uncomfortable silence; but afraid to give her feelings about DuPont away, she opted to remain quiet. Did this in itself give the game away? No, now she was overthinking everything. She looked out of the window, watched cars and buildings flash by in the illuminated darkness.

Sasha took her hand, playing with her engagement ring. Then he took her chin in his hand, turned her face towards him, and kissed her softly on the lips

'Don't worry about DuPont. He won't live long if, I catch him making a pass at you.'

Safi found herself giggling; if only Sasha knew?

'You're not serious, are you? We really need him business-wise – you know that.' As the buildings flashed by, she felt they were having the same conversations over and over, only in different cities and continents. 'I would hate to break up our business relationship because of his flirtatious nature.'

Sasha was quiet for a moment.

'Only because I trust you, not DuPont.'

A chill ran down her spine: she was playing with fire, yet she loved having sex with DuPont, he was so different to Sasha. One she wanted to marry, she loved Sasha but sexually she felt Sasha was in control, his lovemaking was urgent, DuPont allowed her to be in control, because he enjoyed the foreplay and, dragging out the moment of pleasure. Isn't grabbing life by the coat tails what she had so badly wanted, once? And yet that Safi seemed far removed from this Safi now, worlds away.

Now that she had the choice to follow those desires through, she had her doubts about wanting to indulge herself further. Both these men played an important role in her life. Didn't men do this kind of thing all the time, was this one of society's many double standards, or was she just trying to rationalise cheating on Sasha?

'DuPont is harmless,' she said.

'Everyone is harmless,' Sasha said, 'until they're not.'

Their eyes met. They both understood what he was referring to – himself, of course. That one incident had been an aberration. She could feel him shudder at the thought. It had taken them a long time to become relaxed with one another after Sasha's drug-induced attack on her, and he had been trying to atone for his brutish behaviour ever since. It was a relief to be back on par.

Putting her thoughts to one side, she answered the only way she knew would satisfy Sasha: by putting her hand on the top of his thigh, and letting it rest there momentarily before she increased the pressure. Sasha put his hand over hers and squeezed it. She turned to face him, they stared into each other's eyes, both needing to escape the confines of the cab.

Sasha kicked the door of their apartment closed behind him, pulled Safi over to the table, and lifted her up so she was lying full out on the table. Lifting her legs around him, holding her tight, he carried her to the bedroom, where he dropped his tux trousers to the floor. She pulled the dress away from her face and took one look at Sasha – now collapsed on top of her, in full tux jacket, white shirt and bow tie, without his trousers but still wearing his socks and shoes; a sight for sore eyes – and collapsed with laughter.

Later in bed, Sasha fast asleep next to her, she lay staring up at the ceiling. To hell with following her sexual desires: who was she kidding? She would tell DuPont no, she did not want to hurt Sasha.

He was such a wonderful man. They were both her senior by many years and both gave her the confidence to succeed, but she did not love DuPont; she loved Sasha. Love might not last for ever, but she hoped theirs would. She needed to become the master of her immature, insatiable sexual appetite. Men would not find her attractive for ever; her mum always told her that women go downhill after forty and men get better with age. DuPont certainly proved that point, Safi lay awake until the early hours of the morning, rationalising her feelings. She wondered whether Monique and her husband lived apart because of his many affairs; or whether theirs had been a marriage of convenience. Monique appeared to be so laissez-faire about his lifestyle, yet at the opera they seemed to be the best of friends. Safi wondered whether she would end up as sophisticated one day.

Sasha had a day of meetings. Safi wished she could persuade him to accompany her to the appointment with DuPont; but she needn't have worried. Daniel was to meet with his half-sister Rosa for brunch, which left Dax free to accompany Safi.

Dax was beyond excited about his upcoming nuptials, and had been running himself ragged making sure every last detail was organised with Daniel's approval. Safi could only imagine the process up until now, the back-and-forth bickering before they settled on any of Dax's ideas. Not being in New York City did have its advantages, she thought. She felt for Dan, imagining him trying to dampen Dax's enthusiasm and flair for going over the top. She was tremendously excited about their union, wanting to be part of the preparations, but feeling a little removed from it all while staying with Sasha at the Rubicov apartments.

Sitting in the cab with Dax would change all that; she would catch up on everything once they got DuPont's meeting out of the way. DuPont was waiting for her on the pavement as the cab pulled up to the curb. Opening the door, expecting to see Safi by herself, he put on a great show when greeted by Dax crawling out of the cab after her. Entering the narrow alleyway into the studio, she was not sure what they would find: a love nest or a genuine artist's studio.

She felt DuPont's breath on her neck as they squashed into the old elevator that pulled them up to a loft studio. Dax was facing the lift gates while DuPont had positioned himself close behind her, humming one of the tunes from La bohème; shit, he could be annoying, she could not wait to get out of this cage.

Inside the whitewashed studio space, they were greeted by an elderly African artist, his long white hair tied at the nape of his neck. Dax knew him by name only, and was blown away to meet someone he had admired for years.

'Jim is an old friend,' DuPont began. 'He has, as it happens, always had a thing about showing his work in Russia. So, I have brought you here by invitation. His work needs no introduction of course. I think the Moscow market might appreciate his portrayal of Americana, so vividly pronounced in his photographs. They were both in awe of his work, many of which lined the walls, and paid lip service to his genius. She left it to DuPont to work out the details for a show with Ilona. She was preparing to leave when DuPont asked her to follow him up the stairs to a platform above the studio.

Hesitating, her legs weak with nerves, she followed him up the spiral staircase, waiting for an angry telling-off, and was surprised when he gently sat her down.

'Look, I am sorry about yesterday. I was a stupid oaf. It won't happen again'

Relieved, she searched for the words that would put an end to this dangerous attraction she felt. He was so dashingly elegant, even when he was apologetic. Lowering her eyes to avoid him, seeing her weakness, she shook her head to intimate that it was fine, then turned and dashed down the spiral stairs, tripping down the last few steps.

Jim tried to break her fall, 'Careful, sweetie, those stairs are treacherous even for young pretty legs like yours.' Another flirting old charmer. Laughing nervously at her clumsiness, she smiled up as DuPont made his way down, just in time to prevent her fall. Saved by DuPont – and not for the first time, either. But what happened, she wondered, if the person who saved you from trouble was the person who got you into the trouble to begin with?

Out on the pavement Dax whistled. 'Those two are wolves. I would not trust them with my grandmother.'

Laughing, he stuck out his hand to hail a cab that would take them Uptown; they were going to spend a day together, with Dax introducing her to his wedding planner. The two D's intended to show her every last detail for their big day, including cake-tasting, which she had heard about but never experienced.

They spent the day in a wonderland of opulent and oh-so-tasteful wedding bliss.

'So boringly tasteful Dax where is that usual show-off flamboyance we love.'

Laughing, he confessed he had something up his sleeve, but she dare not tell Daniel who had already reined him in, with the help of Lisa their planner.

'I want it to be a surprise for everyone, so I'm not sharing.'

The cake-tasting ended with a choice of two: a colourful macaroon tower mixed with edible roses or a three-tier white cake with Dax, Dan, and Bruno on top. There was no contest, of course.

The evening was spent at their brownstone. Daniel was cooking, while Sasha, Safi, and Dax set the table and prepared salads. They chatted all the while about the wedding and opera and DuPont's wife and daughter – just about everything, apart from Rosa, that is, who appeared to be off limits.

Desert arrived with Safi and Sasha, compliments of the Rubicov restaurant. While Dax was cutting slices of Napoleon cake, Safi plucked up her courage, her inquisitive nature getting the better of her.

'Are you inviting Rosa and Gina to the wedding?'

'Well I did, actually, but they return to Perth tomorrow. It's not too far from LA, so maybe one day, who knows, we'll connect again.'

'Do you think you'll keep in touch?' Safi asked.

Dan shook his shoulders.

'We have nothing in common, really – no shared memories, and now Rupert is gone. I guess maybe I'll send a card at Christmas.'

The subject was closed. Dan left to make coffee. Relieved he had responded to the questions, Dax gave everyone a conspiratorial smile. Obviously he had not yet been able to draw Dan out, now that the subject had been broached it would make it easier for them to discuss Rosa and Gina in everyday conversation.

The wedding preparations were heading to a close. All Dan and Dax had to do was shop for their wedding suits. He turned to Safi. By the way, Safi, I spoke to DuPont to thank him for the opera and dinner the other night.' Safi noticed that Sasha had a wicked smile on his face.

'And?'

Nothing really. I just told him to read Pushkin's Eugene Onegin, or to see the opera. It's a fine Russian work and may give him an insight into Russian romantic spirit: unlike the French, we don't share.'

Dax howled with laughter. 'You tell him, Sasha, all Frenchmen think they are irresistible to women – and some to men as well. I speak from experience.'

'What on earth 'did he say?' Safi said, suddenly flustered, awkward all of a sudden, hoping she was doing a good job of concealing her hot-and-bothered look.

'That he would look it up.'

'He didn't seem insulted or anything, did he?' She realised as she said it that perhaps she was revealing her hand – after all, why did she care so much? why couldn't she take a joke? – but it was too late. 'That was quite threatening.' She felt her annoyance at Sasha and her dislike of being caught unawares being internalised until it became something else altogether, something awkward and unflattering.

'Don't underestimate him, Safi,' Sasha said, his voice even but uncomfortably alert. He is a very experienced and clever man who will understand a subtle hint. Relax, his sophistication will appreciate my warning.'

'Oh well, I am not worried. She felt exposed. Relax – she could do anything but. Worst of all, her behaviour would not be unobserved by the others at the table, who, each in their own way, were keenly attuned to her moods and manners. 'He probably fancies Ilona anyway, since they work so closely together.' But she felt how unconvincing this was even as she said it. Ilona was too awkward and unpolished to ever appeal to DuPont, Safi thought, weighing in the sentiment of her own sense of envy, competitiveness, and possessiveness over DuPont, who gleamed in her mind as though he himself was a prized object in a flashy gallery.

'Good,' Sasha said, 'I can relax then.'

Perhaps everyone needed to relax, but relaxing was easier said than done. Still, if you were going to pretend to relax, you could do a lot worse than to go shopping in Manhattan with a charge card. Safi was thrilled to have Sasha join them: he had a wonderful eye without ever being boring. Massimo, the Italian salesman, had the two D's sorted in a couple of hours. He was devastatingly good-looking in a suave, groomed, wavy long-hair European way. He was also straight. This didn't bother the two D's, who teased Massimo about his impeccable taste. Safi had brought a dress, but after watching the three men walk out with complete wardrobes for the wedding, she wondered whether hers was a boring choice.

Dax insisted Safi shop for a dress, too, and they swept her into Blue Marine, Dior, and Ralph Lauren, all of which had been recommended by Massimo. It had been a long time since she'd had so much fun trying on clothes, her favourite men making her feel wonderfully important, giving her all their attention as she modelled each outfit for them.

Along with Safi, Dax's brothers were in the retinue. Dan and Dax had given very little direction, apart from ordering everyone to look divine.

She fell in love with a pair of silver Ralph Lauren palazzo pants with a spectacular jewelled buckle, worn with silk satin off shoulder high neck rushed teddy. A sharply tailored short round neck jacket allowing the silk bow from the teddy to finish off the look.

'That is perfect for the wedding,' Dax said, 'it makes a change from a long dress.'

Sasha liked it, too, but wanted Safi to buy the high-neck, low-back electric-blue lace evening gown she had tried on at Dior. She knew she looked incredible in it as it was fish-tailed at the hem.

Both cost the earth and she ummed and ahhed

'They are unbelievably expensive,' she said, 'buying both seems extravagant.'

'Not at all,' Dax said. 'Pack them up, we'll be taking the heels and clutch evening bag; that way you have a choice and the perfect bag and shoes to wear with either.'

'A gift from Dax and I,' Dan added.

Safi was about to object when she saw Dan's face warning her to be gracious.

'Thank you, what an amazing gift. I'll adore wearing them.'

She noticed Sasha about to intervene, but even he got the message: this was something they wanted to do for Safi.

They managed to hail two cabs back to the brownstone, dropped off the shopping, and made their way to Pete's Bar for a closed party. Pete had arranged for the two D's the first of three pre-wedding celebrations.

Sasha had arranged another pre-wedding family dinner at Rubicov for the out-of-towners.

Safi's parents were arriving two days before the wedding from Brighton, as were Alexi, Valentina, and Marina from London.

Dax's parents, his three brothers, and their wives would, Dax informed Safi, be embarrassing everyone with the usual not so funny speeches at his family home on Long Island at a luncheon over the weekend. But, Dax promised, the wedding would be short on speeches: one from his oldest brother and another from Daniel, and that was it.

'Wow, this is turning out to be like an Indian wedding with all the pre-parties.'

Daniel tried to hide his despair, but failed miserably as he looked heavenward, catching Safi's eye. But Dax was far too happy to care.

The two D's had hired an unconventional venue for their wedding – Safi had never imagined a rooftop venue. They rode up in a central glass lift exiting onto a pillared, open-spaced concrete floor with terraces leading into a mature garden, where they were planning to have the ceremony. Dan guided her around the glassed indoor space, explaining how it would be set out with tables and a dance floor, all overlooking the Hudson River and its bridges.

'Once dark the view should be magical,' he said.

'This is an enormous space,' Safi said. 'How many people are you having at the wedding?'

'So far 250. As you can see, this space will allow for that and more. Once the space has been transformed by Lisa, the wedding planner, I know it will be spectacular. She has become a friend and knows exactly what we are after.'

Another friend, Safi reflected. No wonder they kept adding to the guest list.

'By the way, isn't it time you and Sasha tied the knot? Your engagement is dragging on a bit, what's the story?'

Safi was speechless for once. Her and Sasha had broached the subject, of course, but with all the recent drama and Sasha's new position in the family business their plans had taken a back seat.

'Honestly haven't a clue,' Safi mumbled awkwardly. 'Too much has been going on of late. Maybe your wedding will spur us on.'

Dan gave her an odd look, but decided not to pursue this line of inquiry any further. Walking back to their apartment, deep in thought, all the excitement about the two D's wedding made her wonder whether Sasha had had second thoughts about marrying her. If he had, she wouldn't blame him. Something was definitely bothering him; she could not put her finger on it. She knew there had been tremendous upheaval in Sasha's family life since the break-in at their home.

Her own position in the family had changed. She had signed the first legal documents the lawyers had drawn up. She now had carte blanche to do as she wished, buying and selling works, deciding which exhibitions to attend and which artists to promote for the gallery. Safi had been given the legal clout to spend how and where she wished on the gallery's behalf. Her parents were initially sad and disappointed she had given up her place at Oxford.

Now she knew it had been the right decision: carving out a profession though experience could not compare to a degree in English Lit, which would have left her not knowing what to do next. It would have taken years to find her passion, and perhaps she would not find it at all. Many – perhaps most – weren't as lucky as Safi had been, toiling away, day after day, year after year, behind some desk, in some windowless room or cubicle, answering the telephone or arranging stacks of numbers or doing the thankless work a robot would sooner or later be tasked with. Safi had to admit that she loved everything she had learnt about the art world. She had enrolled in a course of Art History at the American school in Moscow and had loved every minute of her course, even if mostly by correspondence, it had kept her busy through all the upheavals and during the cold Autumn months.

The advertising world she thought might still be in the offing, had fallen away after relocating to Moscow with Sasha. Her life was falling into place, yet, she had courted danger like a gambler throwing his last dice into the ring. No prizes could possibly replace what she already had, so why was she bent on such dangerous stakes?

She felt miserable about her moment of madness with Du Pont; it had been delicious but now she wanted to distance herself from this attraction when in his company. Besides, she still suspected that Sasha was on to something – not only to DuPont's flirtatiousness, but also to Safi's openness to that side of the man she so wanted to consider a mentor, and – sometimes, secretly – a lover once again.

Somehow she had to show him she was in control and was calling an end to it. He had sensibly pushed her away; now he was playing with her knowingly, jeopardising her relationship with Sasha. It may all be a game to the playful DuPont, but Safi wanted no part of it. Or did she? She had to find a way to show him that she no longer needed him professionally; it was time to stand on her own two feet.

With Du Pont's help they had rid the Rubicov gallery of the collection built up by Fritzi and Yvetta. The gallery was now ready to invest that money and she was going to do it without Du Pont, she was going to bid against him at the auctions at Sotheby's in London coming up after the wedding. Sasha and Alexi would be accompanying her and she would solicit the help of one of London's youngest art experts, and show DuPont that she meant business.

Feeling better about her decisiveness and her DuPont dilemma, she strode into the Rubicov apartments with renewed zeal to live up to her determination to beat DuPont at his own game, and to throw herself wholeheartedly into her chosen life with Sasha.

Her sexual drive had to be tamed; she was achieving more than she could ever have imagined, and she wanted to be free of the guilt she felt building up inside.

The following week was taken up with pre-wedding celebrations at various venues, leading up to the two D's big day. Putting her self-doubts aside, Safi allowed herself to be immersed in their happiness and the party atmosphere. After all, the two D's had made everything possible for her. If it was not for them, she would never have had this life, this job, to say nothing of the man in her life.

She happily gave in to Sasha's choice for the wedding and wore the long, electric-blue lace Dior with the fish-tail. Once in the dress, the moment upon her, standing round the canopy with t rest of the family retinue, she knew without a doubt that it had been the right choice. Indeed, everything about the day appeared exactly right. Well, it did for a short while, at least. Dan and Dax were already in place and the rabbi and priest were about to begin the ceremony when one of Dax's brother's children, a beautifully dressed flower girl started a coughing fit, having swallowed a decoration on the posy she was nervously chewing. At first everyone thought it amusing, but then she started turning blue. It was no longer a joke. She was rushed out by her father. Everyone stood in shocked silence, not sure how to proceed, when someone waved from the exit to alert everyone all was okay.

Dax (who liked to plan for all contingencies, but certainly hadn't envisioned this one) looked as if he was about to faint. Dan, Safi noticed, pulled Dax round by putting pressure on the hand he was holding. She noticed their eyes meeting and knew the wedding would proceed as normal, the drama of the day she hoped had passed. She thought of the expression my better half and suddenly understood it. Dan and Dax completed one another.

The ceremony over, everyone threw candy and surged forward to wish the two D's a wonderful future together. Safi found herself being hugged, kissed, and wished by faces she hardly recognised or not at all. Then she found herself face to face with DuPont as he leaned in close to whisper in her ear. Her father was making his way towards her – he always seemed to know just when to appear. She recalled when she was a teenager, alone in her room with her boyfriend Graham. Sometimes then Leonard had known when not to appear, and appeared all the same. But still, right now, she was grateful for his presence. She swung round to hug her dad and then found herself safe amongst her own family, as they joined the rest of the crowd making their way into the reception area. She looked back but DuPont had disappeared from view; no doubt he would find some other distraction to amuse himself with. That was what he did, after all, moved from one shiny object to another, satisfied with everything and nothing, the fluid beauty of art corrupted always by the hard currency of money.

The wedding venue was a magnificent, magical affair – artistic in its own right. The whole space had been transformed by glass candleholders leading up the aisle and a theme of silver and gold threaded though long-stemmed white lilies in standing glass cylinders that led to the unadorned, ceremonial white silk canopy.

As dusk settled on the scene, the fairy lights in the tall potted trees sparkled, adding a sophisticated glamorous edge to the party. Guests were milling around being served canapés and champagne, a European flavour the well-travelled Dan had insisted on.

Safi picked up her place-card and was happy to be sitting at a table of eight, which included her family and Sasha's. The two D's had chosen a table on their own, decorated romantically with candles, glass bowls of flowers and candles and a chandelier of pale peach gladioli hanging over the table. Safi found it quite magical and clever for them not to have seated themselves with their extended families. After all, they would hardly be seated.

During the speeches it was hilarious to watch their expressions as Dax's brother had them crying tears of laughter at Dax's journey though confused adolescence to adulthood and success as a renowned artist in his own right. This last part brought tears of happiness to her eyes. She hadn't quite realised how fantastic Dax's trajectory truly was. He deserved to be happy, and she was incredibly happy for them both.

The band opened to a number the two D's had chosen, Etta James At Last, after which everyone bombarded the dance floor, partying late into the night. Safi made sure that Sasha stayed close to her side as she danced the night away, surrounded by her family and enjoying the uninhibited antics her dad and Sasha's family got up to on the dance floor. There was a drum roll and everyone stood back as the wedding cake was rolled onto the dance floor. No doubt Dax's surprise for Dan, a tall skyscraper built up in layers of his latest project was magnificently formed into a spectacular wedding cake, with one of Dax's Rubenesque woman reclining with a hand languidly stroking Bruno, too old to be part of their happy day but never forgotten.

Dan was blown away by the ingenuity of the cake, as was everyone who crowded round to get a better look at it.

'What a shame to cut into it.'

'Ah, but you must, it's bad luck not to' called Alexi. This was a typical Russian sentiment. But Dax had another surprise for Dan: another drum roll sounded, and a replica of the original cake was rolled in, but this time it was a sculpture by Dax. It was truly a magnificent piece lovingly worked, every detail had been fashioned and finished in marble. Overwhelmed by the gift and Dax's talent, Dan lovingly hugged his partner and now husband, took hold of the cake-cutter, lopped off the top half of the skyscraper, and sent it away to be cut up for, and distributed to, their guests.

The party continued late into the night and Safi was relieved when she noticed DuPont's charm being put to good use on a girl half his age, and perhaps even younger than Safi herself, who lapped up all the attention lavished on her by this elegant, handsome Frenchman, who she had no doubt would have her in his bed before she could count to 10. She was relieved to find that not an ounce of jealousy coursed through her veins; perhaps she was over her moment of madness and sexual attraction for him. Admiration – of art, of beauty – came easily to DuPont, Safi realised, but love not so much. She wondered if he was incapable of love, viewing it as just another transaction or acquisition, another object to be purchased – and then discarded when its shine wore away.

Thrilled by this realisation she partied the rest of the night away, letting her natural English reserve fall away and enjoying the freedom to kick off her heels, let her hair down, and have a fun time with everyone, including and especially the two D's, who were great dancers.

Exhausted she accompanied her mother and one of Dax's sister-in-laws to the bathroom to refresh her makeup. Leaving before the others. Safi's heart stopped as she felt a cold hand on her bare back. She swung round hoping it would be Sasha. Instead she came face to face with a tipsy, lecherous DuPont.

'Cherie, you owe me a dance, no?'

For a moment her resolve crumbled. God, he was handsome in that tux and so incredibly hot.

'Not a chance, Du Pont,' she said, steadying herself, trying to look away from his chiselled face and penetrating eyes. 'We are business associates, remember? That's what you wanted and that's what I now want, too. So, Cherie, let's leave it that way, oui?'

She was rambling but she could tell his eyes were undressing her.

'You are so right to stay away from me. I would love to devour your sweet smell and bury my tongue deep into your hot, beautiful pussy.'

God, he was incorrigible, and could be quite disgusting, but he had managed to arouse her with his dirty talk all the same. It's that French accent, she thought. No, it's those chiselled features. No, it's those eyes. No, it's everything. Yes. No. Oui. She felt deliciously confused and thoroughly turned on.

Safi mustered all her strength to turn away from him. Her legs felt like jelly. Shit, he knew how to seduce her. He really was a master at his craft – an evil genius, maybe. He was playing with her emotions. She deserved it, she knew that, having been the one to have initiated the affair; now she had to deal with her own mistakes. She searched for Sasha but instead found DuPont claiming that dance he was after – and something more. Safi tried to ignore him as he pulled her close, grinding himself into her as he held her. She couldn't move, his mouth close to her ear.

'Can you feel that's what you have done to me? I will risk anything to have you back in my bed. Anything,' he said again, lingering at her earlobe, pressing into her further, deeper, his words somewhere between whispered and slurred.

Safi caught Sasha's eye. He was staring at them. She rolled her eyes; the next thing she knew DuPont was no longer holding her captive. Sasha had intervened. She collapsed into his arms – grateful for his presence, his touch, his everything – as she watched DuPont slink away into the crowd of dancers.

'Thanks for saving me. He is drunk and embarrassingly lecherous.'

Sasha pushed her away from him.

'What did he say?'

Thinking on her feet for once, she said, 'He was speaking in French but it sure wasn't business.'

'Bastard.' And suddenly she found Sasha's mouth and kissed him hungrily. If he realised the true context of her deflection – or her arousal – he did not let on.

'Custer's last stand,' he said, when he could talk again, like all old men, who can blame him? You look incredible in that dress.' Sasha was clearly relishing his victory now, the fact that he alone possessed her.

'Well, you are the only one who's going to be removing it.'

Sasha pulled her close and she folded into him as the last slow number for the evening played itself out.

If he ever found out … No, she couldn't go there, it was much too scary to contemplate.

The two D's were flying off to the South of France and the Amalfi Coast for a romantic honeymoon. Safi had managed to grab them before the evening was over; hugging them each, she wished them a special happiness. She did not know why but, overcome by emotion, she struggled for the right words. Now she regretted not saying more – saying, for example, how much the two D's meant to her. But how on earth could she even begin to express that? At least they were thrilled with their special day.

Now she had London and the Sotheby's auction to deal with. Determined to beat DuPont at his own game, bidding against him was going to be fun. Knowing she had not asked him to bid for the Rubicov gallery would send a message in itself.

Chapter 27

Alexi had invited her parents to fly back to London in their private jet, which gave Safi extra time to spend with her folks. It was a new experience for her parents to be whisked through airport control in a different section, and onto a plane waiting on the runway, she knew her mother would have a comment.

'How the other half live, ay, not complaining though,' Fiona said.

After champagne and a late lunch, the flight touched down in London – to another chapter, Safi thought, and a new mentor.

Laughing they both settled down to champers and a light lunch served by a Russian air hostess with the longest legs Safi had ever seen. Judging by the conversation Valentina was having with her about the Mariinsky Kirov ballet, she had too had been a former dancer At every opportunity they gossiped about the troubles at the Bolshoi Ballet company.

Safi admired Valentina: she had forged a successful business in her own right She had mentored many dancers who had joined the various ballet companies in London and worked hard to bring them across to dance for the Royal Ballet.

Back in London, Safi confided in Sasha her wish to bid against DuPont for art works they were hoping to secure for the Rubicov Gallery.

Sasha did not quite follow her need to bid against DuPont, but promised that he would support her if it came down to a battle of wills. After all, if anyone distrusted DuPont as much as Safi now did, it was Sasha.

The young curator and art expert that Safi had hired to do their bidding met with her at a preview of the artworks to be auctioned, pointing out pieces she had not previously considered. She found him a breath of fresh air. Zackary Van Zyl was a seriously cool guy, and a minefield of knowledge about global trends. Everyone who was anyone wanted to tap into his visionary ideas, but to his credit Safi found that once his services were secured he discreetly extricated himself from the other punters at the preview and concentrated on guiding her round. By the time they sat down for tea at Sotheby's restaurant, Safi had a list of works and estimated values. She gave him carte blanche, with a ceiling price she shared only with him, at his suggestion.

The week leading up to the auction, Safi kept busy on conference calls to the gallery in Moscow, preparing for new works to be catalogued and securing dates in the diary for shows and private viewings to maximise the exposure and artwork the Rubicov gallery was now promoting.

Yvetta's collection of minimalist works by obscure artists had been sold off, the German paintings secured by Fritzi had been returned to the artists, and the valuable Russian collections that had been put in storage had been dusted off and put on exhibition throughout Moscow and were sent to other capital cities for viewing before returning to the gallery and offered for sale to a few selective buyers.

Rubicov Gallery was slowly building up a formidable reputation in the art community and Safi hoped that reputation would serve as a springboard to their success – she had plans to open galleries in New York and London. She had studied the art market closely, and with DuPont's help and tutelage, had found her feet, while building up a close working relationship with a number of experts and museums, including respected galleries in Moscow and St. Petersburg. The Rubicov gallery was becoming a noted player in the international art market.

Safi believed it was time they be noted as a major player when it came to securing major contemporary works, as well as past masters.

Securing museum-quality artists who gave them a niche in an otherwise bloated populist art market would be their primary aim. With Van Zyl's expertise she believed they would succeed.

She was pouring every ounce of energy into elevating the gallery and ensuring it became a leader in its field. She had at last found a vehicle to fulfil her need for exciting challenges. Building something of value on her own hopefully would put an end to her need for dangerous liaisons.

Challenging her parents' wishes for her future had, in some respects, freed her from blindly following the path they had set for her. She was proving she could take responsibility for her own choices, and she knew her parents were beginning to respect those choices. DuPont's behaviour at the wedding angered her. She had never expected him to lose his sophisticated veneer, putting them both in danger. She stood to lose everything, and God knows what the Rubicov family would do to him. The stories Sasha had told her about other family members who had strayed made her blood run cold.

She had dropped her desire to bid against him, it was a childish reaction, he had been drunk after all, and they were both professionals. Besides, he had taught her so much and schooled her about the business – she could not forget it.

Safi walked into the auction house accompanied by Alexi and Sasha. Van Zyl was already waiting with a marked catalogue and paddles he had secured. They followed him into the row of seats he had chosen for them. The works they had agreed on during the preview were nowhere to be seen; they would be brought out as the lots were called.

The excitement in the room was palpable. She realised that it was her first auction and told herself to take it easy and to steel herself. Nevertheless, it was a heart-palpitating experience;, her palms were damp with nerves. It was dizzying and dreamlike. She tried to concentrate as Zachary pointed out various big hitters in the field who were there to bid on behalf of anonymous buyers. She knew that museums, if interested, would be bidding by phone. hoping Gerhard Richter's painting were not out of their reach, but when the lot exceeded its price and sold for millions, exceeding all expectations, the other lots would automatically exceed their reserve price. She hoped their lots would come up before the Picassos Rothko's and Giacometti's.

The auctioneer welcomed everyone and without preamble began the auction. Safi had caught sight of DuPont in the front row, surrounded by a bevy of beautiful young women hanging on his every word.

She relaxed as the first lots were brought out. She was getting into the swing of things. Some paintings she noticed did not make the reserve price, while others had paddles flying up as the bidding reached a ceiling no one was prepared to exceed. The process was expertly handled by the auctioneer, who never relaxed until the last paddle remained and the hammer came down. Van Zyl had marked the lots they were to bid for and Safi found these lots were fast approaching. The first lot was one of the latest works of Kazimir Malevich, a colourful Supremacist minimalist piece highly sought after by many private buyers. She noticed that van Zyl watched closely, not bidding until the price was reaching its ceiling. Then, just as the hammer was about to come down, he put up his paddle. They could tell the other bidder was hesitating. The hammer came down and Safi jumped in her seat with joy; they won that bid at a competitive price. This was exciting, she could hardly breathe, every nerve in her body was on edge, and the feeling of elation as they won the bid was orgasmic. Zackary had nerves of steel. She could tell Alexi and Sasha were as impressed with him as she was.

The next few lots were bought by Alexi; a collection of drawings by an artist Safi had only vaguely heard about. Alexi had obviously discussed the purchase with Zack (as she now thought of him – his Christian name was far easier to pronounce than van Zyl).

In all the excitement, Safi had forgotten about DuPont. She soon noticed, however, that he was turning around to stare at them every time his bid failed. Then she realised they were not bidding for the same works; she noticed he was becoming agitated at losing each bid he made.

Zack pointed out a woman he had noticed on a cell phone; every time DuPont's paddle was raised, his bid would be beaten by someone seated next to the auctioneer, who took the silent bids. She could not help wondering whether the person bidding against DuPont thought that he was working for the Rubicov gallery, but who on earth could that person be?

She leaned over to point this out to Sasha and Alexi. They were now riveted on the woman, and as mystified as Safi. After six lost bids by DuPont, they were convinced that the woman was bidding against him.

Alexi, who respected DuPont and valued his work for the Rubicov gallery, scribbled a note and asked for it to be given to DuPont. They all waited to see his reaction. He turned to thank Alexi with a nod. He was obviously waiting for his next lot to come up and moved to the back of the room, not wanting to alert the woman they had noticed. They had no idea what his next lot would be. Noticing DuPont leave, the woman rose from her seat. Safi turned around to watch what DuPont's next move would be as he passed the woman, but it was impossible to see beyond all the standing punters at the back of the room, what she looked like, they could only see her paddle going up each time.

Bewildered and confused, Alexi had only one thought: it had to be Fritzi. But how? According to Mika, she was locked up in a Russian prison. He wondered whether Sasha had the same thought. But it was such an improbable deduction that he let it go. DuPont would find out, Alexi was sure; it wasn't his concern. Safi was sure that if Sasha found out who was bidding against DuPont he would tell her, but she was not going to make it her business to find out. Fortunately, he was not bidding for the Rubicov galleries, she hated to think they had enemies.

Sasha bent over to whisper in her ear. 'I thought you were going to bid against DuPont through Zack.'

She smiled. 'I thought better of it. Besides, Zack would never have agreed, not fair play and all that stuff.'

She winked and they watched as Zack successfully put up his paddle for the last three paintings they had agreed on; by all accounts, he had saved them money with his last-minute strategy.

They left for the Arts Club for an early dinner to discuss the auction and the direction the Rubicov should take with Zack, who was now Safi's new mentor and art advisor. As they walked through the foyer, DuPont stopped Alexi. Safi watched the exchange closely with a smidgen of discomfort; Alexi soon returned to fill them in. DuPont had tried to confront the woman but did not catch sight of her again amongst the crowds filing down the staircase.

He found it extremely mystifying, not only had this woman thwarted every bid, she had managed to vanish even though he was only a few people behind her. DuPont believed the woman must have been in disguise and had removed whatever it was that threw him off; she probably passed right by him and he had not realised who she was, which made the whole episode even more mystifying. Alexi could not shake his original suspicion about Fritzi. He needed to wait Safi must never find out about Yvetta and, the criminal activities she had carried out with Fritzi at their home. They had made her aware of Fritzi's theft of antiquities and she had accepted their story about Yvetta.

Alexi was ushered right past the crowds waiting to be seated; like Zack, he was a well-known member. Settling into their seats, she became aware of the celebrities around them. Seated in front of her, wasn't that Gwyneth Paltrow? Safi thought her prettier in reality than all the photos she had seen in various magazines. The conversation immediately turned to business. Concentrating her mind on what was being said, Safi soon lost interest in who was around her. Zack was without a shadow of a doubt the right choice for Rubicov. Being gay helped her relax completely in his company. She wanted to introduce him to Dax's work, too. DuPont had taken Dax as far as he could, and that was considerable, but she thought with Zack he would find a different market, one that might suit him more.

Sasha left with Alexi while Zack and Safi finalised their business and remained on to chat over coffee. Zack was, it seemed, a celebrity in his own right. People stopped to chat at their table, and by the time they got up to leave, Safi had met well-known faces from screen and TV, and a number of politicians who found it necessary to pay him homage.

'Wow,' Safi said, 'I had no idea you were such a celebrity.'

Zack smiled shyly.

'Well, not really. Most of the people you met have used my services, so not so different from you.'

'Gosh, with all these clients, are you going to have time to work with me expanding the Rubicov Gallery into Europe and the New York?'

'Safi, I am looking forward to the challenge. Usually, I am busy pleasing clients and scouting around for what they desire. Working with you will be a breath of fresh air for me, especially as you are giving me carte blanche handling the art for both galleries. It's a huge undertaking, and I am honoured that you trust me.

Walking out of the Arts Club, someone brushed past Safi, almost throwing her off balance. As they came face to face, Safi was sure it was the woman who bid against DuPont. Zack turned to find Safi rooted to the spot.

'What's wrong? You look as if you've seen a ghost.'

But Safi did not respond. Waving goodbye she hopped into a cab, settled back in the seat, and decided she could wait no longer. She had to let Sasha know; he would know what had to be done.

She found Sasha still in conference with Alexi; not wanting to disturb them she decided it could wait, and retired, changing into a tracksuit, and settled into a deep corner sofa with a pile of fashion magazines, something she had loved doing when staying with the two D's in NY. She had barely begun to scroll through the first magazine when the phone buzzed. Alexi had summoned her to join them in his office. Safi's eyebrow shot up – this in itself was unusual, but it might give her the opportunity to sound them out about what she felt about the woman who brushed past her at the Art's Club.

On entering the study, Safi immediately knew her premonition had been correct; both Sasha and Alexi looked grim. Alexi waved Safi to a chair. She watched his face as he finished his call. Whatever had been said was obviously not good.

'Fritzi has bought her way out of prison,' Alexi said. 'Mika is still collecting the information, but it had come to his attention a few days ago.'

Sasha said, 'Why has he only told us now?'

Alexi shook his head. 'Mika is furious, as are the insurance police. They are working together to find out what's going on. Mika is convinced that the woman at the auction was Fritzi. Apparently, she is a master at disguise. We know she speaks Russian fluently without a trace of a German accent. and Mika wanted more solid information before confirming that Fritzi had escaped a Russian open prison, unheard of until now.

'How on earth did she manage to get out of Russia?'

'Those facts remain unknown at this stage, but Mika believes she is determined to get her revenge on our family. Fritzi is a sophisticated criminal, with many contacts. He suggests that we have a personal security guard with us at all times until she is apprehended.'

Safi tried her best to remember every detail about the woman who brushed past her. She now realised that it had not been an accident: she had meant for Safi to notice her. 'Well,' Safi said, 'she did not appear to be the same woman we saw at the auction, but I definitely recognised her – quite why I am not sure, but there was something very familiar about her. But what that is has not come to me yet.'

They stared at her, waiting for her to elaborate.

'What did she look like, this woman who brushed past you?'

'The woman we saw at the auction was middle-aged. The woman who brushed past me was very young and lanky with long blonde hair. The woman at Sotheby's had flat shoes on, I remember noticing that as she left her seat to stand at the back. The other woman had stilettos and a very clingy, short wrap dress barely covering her behind.'

'Was it her height that drew your attention to her?' asked Alexi.

Safi shook her head. 'No, it was the way she moved. I think – in fact, I am sure – it's the way she carries herself. Remember when we met Fritzi in that restaurant in Moscow? She had that arrogant walk and way of holding her head up. This woman does the same.' For a moment, no one spoke, all feeling suddenly sure that the unidentified woman was in fact Fritzi.

Alexi continued, 'I can't believe she has the nerve to behave in such an open, brazen manner, flaunting herself in front of us. It's almost as if she wants us to recognise her, but why?'

They sat discussing her motives, going around in circles, when the maître d' from Rubicov in London called to speak to Alexi. They watched Alexi's expression change from one of anger to one of dismay. As he put down the phone he looked at them, then slammed his hands down on his desk.

'Strange and very disturbing.' Shaking his head, he told them a group of young men with one woman had caused mayhem at the Rubicov bar in London. 'We are used to upper-class twits being drunk, but not this kind of behaviour. Apparently, this group started a fight, guns were drawn, the woman knifed the barman, and before anyone knew what was happening, one of the men smashed a vodka bottle over the security guard's head, causing him to be taken to hospital. Everyone was taken by surprise. The fight flared up before anyone knew what caused it.'

'Did the security get them?' Sasha asked.

'That's what I do not understand. This group were so aggressive, muscle-bound, and strong and quick enough to walk out before anyone could stop them. Once outside they vanished into thin air.'

'It was staged. That's why no one reacted sooner. They engineered the whole scene for maximum effect. But why? Alexi observed, the security and bar staff are convinced it was staged too.'

'Do you think it is Fritzi again?' Sasha said. 'It must be. It's too much of a coincidence if it's not her. No, that would be almost impossible, don't you think?'

They left the study for the kitchen, where Alexi and Sasha rustled up a quick meal, while continuing to discuss the situation.

Safi found it strange that they had not mentioned Yvetta once. According to Sasha, Yvetta often booked herself into a retreat, the family kept abreast of her movements; she was safe from this mad woman for now. But Safi wondered if any of them were truly safe from Fritzi. She was startled when Alexi voiced her thoughts, and understood there would be some things about the Rubicov family she would never know, especially where Yvetta was concerned, so much of what she knew of Yvetta and Fritzi did not tally.

'I am going to check that Yvetta is safe one never knows,' he announced, his voice lower since they had entered the safe space of the kitchen. 'Heaven forbid this mad woman might have found out where Yvetta is.'

Sasha knew his father would not elaborate in front of Safi. Nodding in agreement, Safi noticed the look that passed between father and son. It was a sadness for them all that Yvetta was so unpredictable; they would always have to watch out for her wellbeing. This was evidently a family burden, something they all shared and a responsibility they carried within them.

Alexi knew his daughter had to be safe high up in the Swiss fortress, but to satisfy himself he would call the clinic first thing in the morning. He would warn them to watch out for any unusual visitors and generally continue to heavily monitor Yvetta and her movements. So far none of the family had permission to visit with her yet; the doctors were not advising any personal contact until they were sure of a marked improvement.

Yvetta's treatment could take anything up to five years. That was a very long time, and thank God the family could afford the treatment – many others were not so lucky. Getting well was all that mattered; Yvetta was happy as far as the reports he received showed. Yvetta's health was in the clinic's hands now. Alexi thought her admission would give him license to relax – but apparently Fritzi had other ideas. Alexi was relieved they had found a place with a high success rate, he was convinced his daughter would be able to overcome this affliction and join society once more: that was his heart speaking, his hidden emotional side, one he seldom even admitted to himself. The alternative he did not want to contemplate; Yvetta spending her whole young life shut away would be too horrendous.

Alexi woke them late that night, well after midnight. He himself had woken to find Valentina had not returned. Beside himself with worry, he had called one of the dancers she was hosting. Valentina had left the rest of the ballerinas just after twelve; they had all dined at a restaurant after the show. Sasha had never seen his father (usually controlled, even in moments of anger and upset) so lost and agitated: he was up and down, walking around in circles. His breath suddenly became shallow. Gasping for air, he collapsed in a chair in their bedroom.

Sasha was kneeling by his father, while Safi ran to the bathroom to fetch him some water, anything to help him breathe. Turning around, she ran to the bedside table: a better idea had entered her mind. She grabbed a brown paper bag from Sasha's bedside table, emptied out his favourite candy onto the bed, and gave it to Sasha, insisting Alexi blow into the bag. This was the best way to calm someone in shock – she had seen it work before. Alexi slowly regained his composure, but now he was like a bull in a china-shop, marching back and forth, clutching his cell into which he shouted orders, none of which made the slightest sense. Short of calling 999, there was nothing else they could do at this hour.

They heard voices and footsteps on the stairs; the housekeeper knocked and burst into the room. Though she spoke in Russian, Safi managed to decipher a few words. In fact, the woman's anxious, scared demeanour and panicked gestures would have made it clear to anyone that she wanted Alexi to follow her downstairs. She was struggling to speak, sobbing. Madam was in a terrible state, she said. Alexi almost threw himself down the stairs, with Sasha and Safi following closely behind.

There were three policemen inside waiting for Alexi. One of them was obviously an inspector who, due to Alexi's status, had been woken to deal with the situation Valentina was slumped on a sofa in the hall, covered with a blanket. The housekeeper was kneeling at her side, smoothing her hair away from her bruised face and holding her hand. No one could believe what they were seeing. Valentina's eyes were swollen shut and her mouth was bleeding, her knees were scraped and her hands were bleeding. She appeared to be drunk, her words slurred and incoherent. Alexi kneeled beside her, tears flowing down his cheeks.

Sasha took the policemen into his father's study; they seemed visibly embarrassed by Alexi's reaction. 'What has happened, Officer, do you know? Has my stepmother been in an accident?'

'Well, sir, everyone is mystified as to what precisely happened, according to the restaurateur who identified her immediately. She had left the establishment at 12.30 with the Russian group. One of the restauranteur's staff, on his way home, had found her lying in a pool of blood at the back of the restaurant.'

'We wanted to call the ambulance but the lady made it clear that she had to be brought back here,' the officer explained. 'The restaurant staff helped clean her up before we brought her back here. But she has not been able to explain yet. what happened. She seems to be drugged, sir. We learnt from the waiters the lady does not touch alcohol, so the only explanation is that someone slipped something into her water. She must have passed out and fallen in the alley near the dustbins.'

Sasha thanked the officers and explained that his father would not be able to speak with them until later that morning. As the officers left, the family doctor arrived to tend to Valentina. It was obvious that nothing would become clear until she was able to speak; she seemed to be unharmed, apart from her cuts and bruises.

Everyone retreated into the kitchen. Valentina had been carried by Alexi to her bedroom, where he remained until the doctor took his leave an hour later.

Shaken but now in control of his emotions, Alexi poured a stiff drink, sat down at the kitchen table, and stared into his glass for what seemed for ever. Gathering around him, they all waited, to hear what he had found out. Was Valentina going to be okay?

He lifted his head, still in a daze. 'When I find the people who did this to Valentina, they will pay. No one does this to my family, no one. Sasha call Mika. I need to speak to him immediately.'

Sasha stared at Alexi. She could see he was struggling to find the right tone to address his father in. She knew them all so well, she thought – their gestures and postures and movements and moods – but there was so much she did not know as well. So much heartache and pain seemed to have gone into securing this unbreakable family bond.

'Papa,' Sasha started, but Safi could see Alexi was not listening. He lifted his eyes to Sasha's, the look was one of intense anger no amount of reasoning was going to calm his father.

Sasha left for the study to make the call, then returned to fetch his father, who got to his feet with obvious exhaustion, and turned to look at Safi and the housekeeper.

'There is nothing more we can do tonight. Please go to bed. I will speak with you tomorrow.'

It was a long night. News had not been good since Fritzi's escape, things were happening that did not tally, coincidental or not, it was his job to find out. One thing was for sure, she had to be stopped; this time she would not be going back to jail.

Sasha felt it his duty to remain with his father. Saturday morning was slowly coming into focus through the window. Periodically, during the course of many cups of coffee, Alexi would run up the stairs to check on Valentina. The doctor had given her a sedative which had knocked her out through the night. Alexi recalled recent incidents over and over until there were very few avenues left to analyse; they both came to the conclusion that it had to be Fritzi causing this new bout of chaos. They believed her motive was revenge, but what did she have to gain with her brazen attacks?

They would have to wait until Valentina was well enough to discuss her awful experience. The police would want to question her, too. Alexi wanted her story before the police had a chance to question her – something she said might lead to Kolya and Mika finding Fritzi before the authorities did. Always, with the Rubicovs, keeping it within the family was the first and most pressing concern. The more people from outside knew of their situation, the more exposed they would be. This was why the family operation was so successful, because outsiders were implicitly untrustworthy, because the family cared for and fended for itself.

Alexi wanted Fritzi dealt with. The West was much too soft on criminals, he thought, and Fritzi had been given far too many opportunities for redemption. He was done with the lenience and undue tolerance of the liberal west – done with it absolutely. If anything, it encouraged criminality: young people who disrespected their elders, an absence where tradition and religion and morality used to be. A world run amuck. Fritzi was the worst kind of slime, trying to take the family on, trying to ruin them. Who the hell did she think she was? She hadn't reckoned with their full force yet, had no idea what she was dealing with. Up until then, they had been kind. No longer. Things were about to change. No, her time had run out. She would not have another opportunity to repeat her mistakes. Due process was no longer a viable option for him, nor did he have the patience. It was time to solve the matter once and for all, and by himself.

Alexi was called away to tend to Valentina. The housekeeper, Mrs Richie, from a Russian mother with an English father, had taken up her favourite morning vegetable smoothie earlier than usual. It seemed that no one in the household had had much sleep during the night. Even the cook, Mrs Kaminski, and Mrs Richie started their day two hours earlier than usual, all upset about Valentina. The only person not waiting down in the kitchen for news about Valentina's condition was Sasha, who had passed out on his bed with exhaustion. Safi pulled the covers over him, kissed him softly, and made her way quietly down to the kitchen to join the rest of the household staff hovering about the kitchen for news. Andre, the driver, sat around the kitchen pretending to read the paper while Mrs Kaminski prepared breakfast. The maids kept their routine, but it was obvious they were waiting to hear how the mistress was doing. The doctor had made an early morning call and left after half an hour, but Alexi had not come down from the suite he shared with Valentina.

Without Valentina or Alexi around, the staff were at a loss, their usual routine out of kilter. Safi recalled how life could suddenly be turned upside down in the Rubicov household – how often, during her year in Moscow had there been some sudden crisis that was, almost always, swiftly and efficiently dealt with, life returning to normal (or what passed for normal here) once again. And how impressed she always was with everyone's resolve, their Russian sense of pragmatism and onward progression against even the toughest odds, the solutions employed to fix even the direst problems, the tenacity, the youthful optimism of even the oldest members of the family. But this time something was different. She could feel it, too, a sense of strain and exhaustion in the air, the look of severe anxiety in the faces of even the most menial staff members, to say nothing of immediate family. The way the housekeeper (usually so calm and implacable) was pacing, or Sasha, removed from everything and everyone, appeared to be doing nothing at all – she felt his weird absence echo in the room. She suddenly longed for his sleek and always comforting presence. Without him she felt like an outsider once again. And in her own country this time. He, who always knew what to do, had no plans now, she thought. She tried to steady herself, to deaden her anxiety with some British-Russian blend of stiff-upper-lip pragmatism. In the sudden quiet, she remembered another moment of panic in the Rubicov household, but this time thousands of miles away. She had experienced a similar level of anxiety during one of Moscow's worst winters, and wondered whether it could have been Fritzi who caused mayhem that fateful day, too? For a moment, everything appeared to link up in her mind, make a certain fractured sort of sense, or symmetry, only to break up and beg more questions than it answered. She felt that this incident was part of a pattern, but the larger picture was agonisingly out of reach. A piece of a puzzle revealing what? Or, rather, who? Perhaps that was a better question.

Sasha woke at midday, in time to persuade the officers, who were waiting in his father's study to question Valentina to return the following day. The family doctor had recommended complete rest before she attempted to recall her dreadful experience. She was still suffering from shock.

Safi joined Sasha for brunch. Mrs Kaminski was thrilled to have someone to tend to. She had sent the maid to collect the tray from Valentina's suite. When the maid returned, they all looked up for any scrap of news. She shook her head, nothing. It seemed the tray had been left for her in the sitting room for collection.

Mika was out of communication, busy tracking Fritzi down. Sasha supposed all they could do was wait for news on that front, too. The London Rubicov restaurant had no further news on the disturbance the previous evening; the culprits had vanished into thin air.

They sat around working on their laptops for a while after lunch, separating only to make calls. Safi remained in the family room while Sasha made his way up to Alexi and Valentina's suite. The journey was familiar, but it felt strange this time. He felt the slowness of his own steps, his hesitation as he paused at the door. He felt fatigue, too, though he had slept much of the day: a general sense of exhaustion at this unwelcome turn of events. It wasn't always easy being part of an influential family, he reflected. Perhaps the family's coat of arms could be a double-edged sword. He turned the handle slowly. On entering, hushed voices could be heard through the bedroom doors. He tentatively pushed the door open, poking his head round. Alexi waved him over.

Sasha pulled up a chair next to his father, where they both sat in stunned silence as his stepmother's hoarse whisper recalled the attack, in graphic detail.

Valentina had left the restaurant with the young ballet dancers. After their usual prolonged farewell on the pavement, she was about to wave a cab down when she noticed a young woman running towards her. Thinking it might be one of her charges from the Royal Ballet she let the cab go by. As the girl passed her, Valentina realised she might have been running for the same cab and not waving to her. She stepped forward to look for another cab. The girl turned and made her way back towards Valentina, dropping her handbag as she reached her. The two women bent down simultaneously to retrieve the bag. As Valentina straightened up, something hit her head. Dazed, at first she thought they had bumped heads. At that point things became muddled and very strange.

Valentina took a deep breath and cleared her throat as she tried to visualise what happened next. 'I felt a scratch on my arm. My legs started to buckle, and the girl put her arm around my waist as if to help me. Thinking she was going to take me back into the restaurant, I remember protesting as she half-walked, half-dragged me into the alleyway. I could feel my tongue slurring strangely as I tried to make myself understood. Then a hand struck me across the face again and again. I must have lost consciousness after that. I have no idea how long I lay in that alleyway before one of the restaurant staff found me. Everyone thought a mugger had attacked me for my possessions, but my jewellery was still in place. They found my bag lying in the alleyway and helped me empty the contents onto the restaurant table. Only my cell phone was missing. One of the staff returned to the alley to see if it had fallen out, returning with a cell that wasn't mine.'

Alexi now focused on every detail, asked whether she had brought the cell back with her. Valentina shook her head. 'I have no idea, you will have to search my bag.'

Alexi riffled though his wife's possessions and returned with the cell. They sat down to figure out if there were any clues on the cell phone that could help solve why Valentina had been singled out.

Alexi's fingers shook as he scrolled through the phone, cursing as he realised it had a code. When the cell pinged he dropped the phone with fright. Father and son scrambled to pick it up, each wanting to read the message before it pinged again or was lost as it popped up on the front of the cell.

'Schadenfreude' was all they could read. 'Try that as the code to open the cell,' Alexi suggested. Nothing, the phone was still locked.

Valentina sat up from her reclining pillows. 'It means malicious joy, I think, from others' discomfort.'

'A German word,' Sasha said.

Alexi jumped up in agitation. 'How on earth has this woman managed to form a network so successful that it enables her to infiltrate our business and private lives with brazen attacks, without being caught?' He was thinking aloud. Sasha and Valentina watched as his mind raced from one possibility to another. Neither interjected but they all came to the same conclusion. It was Fritzi for sure.

She had obviously paid and recruited a tight circle of various degenerates to help her carry out her vengeance on the family.

She had to be caught before she caused any further harm.

'We can't allow the police to become involved with this attack on our family or business,' Sasha said. It would open a whole can of worms that we might not easily be able to close. And we have to keep Yvetta out of this at all costs. No one needs to know of her involvement with Fritzi or the attack on Anna on our family home in Moscow.'

They discussed strategies, what to tell the authorities and what to leave out. Alexi left with Sasha to speak with Mika in the privacy of his study, leaving Valentina to rest.

Alexi had insisted on blood tests to determine what Fritzi had given Valentina to render her helpless. He had initially been nervous that it might have been a lethal poison, but he now doubted this due to Valentina's obvious recovery. He himself felt enormous relief. Apart from the emotional exhaustion and bruising, Valentina now appeared well, considering what might have happened in that dark alleyway. Many had fallen foul of Russian poisoning over the years too, many to mention and it was still a method they used to get rid of political opponents, the latest here in London at a Japanese restaurant, Alexander Litvinenko of polonium poisoning.

This was another warning shot across their bows. He hoped to stop Fritzi and her band of criminals before she had the chance to kill anyone with her unhinged behaviour. She was playing with fire, terrorising his family. He would make sure she turned into ash before she had another opportunity to dream up any more hare-brained schemes.

Chapter 28

She was her parents' youngest, a freethinker despite a narrow-minded upbringing and schooling that followed a communist philosophy. She learnt to speak both German and Russian fluently. After the two Germanys united, her family remained in East Berlin. The changes happened around them, but unification with the West robbed her father of his status, and with it his pride.

Her once controlling, dominant father became an embittered, lonely figure. Gone was his former status as an officer of the old communist system. He was no longer in the Stasi, a hated and now disbanded Russian arm of the KGB. Instead he now sat day after day watching those he spied on requisition secret files on their past, having to endure their anger and disrespectful stares as they demanded to see the evidence that had ruined so many innocent lives. All because of the secret police. Now not so secret at all, and not powerful anymore either.

He imagined they took great pleasure at his apparent fall from grace. He was left without power and a low salary, bereft of his former livelihood, while they prospered in the new Germany.

Fritzi's older sister Greta had attended the free university in East Berlin during the communist era, but now her parents had to scrimp and save, the state no longer provided. Her sister had taken up with an African from Cameroon, who like many other Africans took advantage of the free education the communists offered at the East Berlin University. With her Cameroonian boyfriend, Greta escaped the narrow confines of her family home for a taste of a more Western way of life. East Berliner's were not allowed across into West Berlin, but those studying from other countries could come and go as they wished. They brought with them many products and luxuries sought after by those trapped on the other side of the wall. Greta thought like many women at that time, if they married a man from another country they would be allowed to leave with him once he completed his studies, sadly it was never allowed. Greta's mother was horrified by her favourite daughters chosen lifestyle, Greta was never rebellious like Fritzi while they were growing up, and, Greta unlike Fritzi adored her father, until of course she changed too.

Floundering in the new Berlin without the support of the State, her parents lost track of their daughter's wild, hedonistic Western lifestyle.

Fritzi hated her father, he was a monster. Her mother was a typical German hausfrau who seldom criticised her husband's wishes. Her father had forbidden her to play with or visit her childhood friend's home. Erika's parents were musicians and free-spirited degenerates and frowned on by those in a position of power, such as her father. Erika was too outspoken for her own good, deemed a bad influence for his younger daughter. Fritzi loved Erika, they had been friends from a very young age. But when Erika suddenly vanished, Fritzi's trust and ideals changed forever.

The soldiers guarding Checkpoint Charlie vanished, as millions spilled over the wall into West Berlin. They were no longer shooting East Berliner's escaping over the wall; the wall was being hammered down, the country – indeed, the world – was changing. They were on the brink of something new: a new decade, a new world.

Checkpoint Charlie collapsing could not have happened at a better time for the young Fritzi as she joined the throng of East Berliners crossing over to the West. She made her way to friends who were fortunate to have escaped to the West, where she was able to survive, without her own family. The Communist East had never suited her. Fritzi loved the freedoms of the eighties; becoming financially independent was her mantra, being free to do as she wished at last was her aphrodisiac.

At first she floundered. The government gave those from the East money to get started, but Fritzi was far too young to apply. She had not yet finished school, had no proper education to fall back on. Her one asset was her tall lanky athletic frame and she quickly learnt how to put it to use.

Only sixteen, Fritzi's new family helped her find a modelling agency with a good reputation. They valued her potential and provided a secure environment for her to learn the craft. She soon flourished in her new career, becoming much sought by the high fashion houses, walking the catwalks in Paris, Milan, London, and New York.

She impressed everyone and found that high society was not as far away or as unobtainable as she had at first imagined. Indeed, it was surprisingly easy to access, if one had the right tools at one's disposal. She got to see the world and, with her attractiveness, intelligence, and allure, felt sure that she could conquer it. Best of all, she was shrewd, intuitive, and given easily to improvisation and grand gestures of performance. She found she could become different people at different moments – or become no one at all. She became expert at concealing the vacuum within her, a vacuum that could only be filled by affirmation and acquisitions, expensive things, and expensive people, too. Anything, she discovered, could be bought for the right price – even (or especially) human beings. And she herself was an object of great beauty, and thus worth a great deal. Wealthy people spoke their own kind of language, she quickly learnt, and with her significant skills of mimicry she was quickly able to speak it, too. The language was centred around money but pretended to be about everything else. What she wanted, most of all, was more – more of everything. What she loved was control, moulding people, and breaking them, too.

Aware of the attraction her charismatic personality and looks had on both men and woman, Fritzi indulged in seducing both with equal ardour, becoming expert at ferreting out the powerful and the rich, who showered her with gifts, not only to have her in their company, but to accompany them when they needed someone attractive on business trips. She loved making people fall in love with her, and then using those people for her own ends. Seduction was her primary currency, and in this sense she was a billionaire many times over. She holidayed on luxury yachts, often privy to business deals that were more about making vast sums of money than about adhering to the law. In this sense, she got an education far greater than she would ever have received at East Berlin University.

When she met Yvetta at one the many art exhibitions, she was invited to she was immediately drawn to her petite, feminine beauty; it helped that they could chat comfortably in Yvetta's mother tongue. Best of all, Yvetta had a fathomless amount of money, which meant that Fritzi became rich by association. Fritzi's world opened up for her yet again. Like Fritzi, Yvetta had grown up feeling like an outsider, alienated from her wealthy but tight-knit family, feeling that she was rarely appreciated or understood.

Like Fritzi, Yvetta had a wild and untamed side, wanted often to push the boundaries, and even to break the law. Like Fritzi, she had artistic inclinations and identified with anarchists and nihilists throughout history. Like Fritzi, she wanted to upend society, even if she was not always sure how to do this. And, like Fritzi, she had a vengeful streak, wanting to seek revenge on those she believed had wronged her, and full of a wild and all-consuming, passionate anger. The two women had much in common. Fritzi had no idea why she wanted to impress Yvetta with her limited knowledge in the arts, but she had managed to gain Yvetta's interest and with it an invitation to visit her in Moscow.

Yvetta adored Fritzi; she was everything her stuffy Russian family wasn't. She loved having close contact with the German art scene, Berlin was a hedonistic city and encouraged artists to develop their talents, especially since the creation of Kunstacademie in Dusseldorf where artists like Joseph Beuys studied and influenced the German artists with his social philosophy. Fritzi did not know about art, but she knew many artists and gallerists. Yvetta needed to branch out on her own, away from her family's reach, as an independent woman, patron, and businessperson, Yvetta viewed Fritzi as an asset. After all, Fritzi had contacts across a broad social and political spectrum (or so she led everyone to believe), even if she wasn't an expert in art. Yvetta felt safe with Fritzi, and, she satisfied her in bed, she was exciting in all the way's Russians were not.

Fritzi made sure Yvetta enjoyed the cat and mouse games they played when in each other's company. It heightened her desire for the inevitable seduction, trapping her in a sexual web of all things Fritzi. Yvetta would watch Fritzi work a room entice people into her seductive orb mesmerise them, but never felt jealous, Fritzi made it clear that she was not seducing her captive audience, but was using them to seduce her alone, it was a performance to excite her, and it did, it made her feel part of some crazy performance art, yet it was their intimate game, no one else was aware of. Their relationship became everything to Yvetta, who felt the only way to keep Fritzi in Moscow was to offer her a lucrative position. With Yvetta's tutelage, Fritzi's confidence about the art world grew, helping her establish powerful contacts in the independent art scene.

She learnt how to buy and sell to dealers and over time made contacts throughout the art world, becoming well connected. She forged contacts with the underworld in Russia and abroad and took advantage of the underhand deals she was offered. She found opening up lucrative avenues exhilarating. Using the Rubicov gallery as her front, she was free to deal in stolen artefacts around the world and, in turn, built up a flourishing bank account in a tax-free haven that asked no questions.

Fritzi had learnt her craft well. Her former career as a sort of shape-shifter, living amongst the rich and famous, had made her independently wealthy, but she was becoming bored with that side of her life. She felt the need to settle down, from her nomadic life since her cross over to the West as a teenager. Yvetta reminded her of her childhood friend Erika. and she recognised her initial attraction to Yvetta was that connection. Where for the first time with Erika's family she experienced a different family environment from her strict Germanic one. Erika's parents were musicians who were allowed to travel outside Germany and, brought with them the lightness Fritzi craved. Erika was outspoken a dangerous thing in East Berlin and, always in trouble with the school authorities. Her father never, approved of her friendship with Erika and, when Erika and her family vanished without trace, she was afraid to delve into her memories of that time fearful of what she might remember and, her powerlessness to save her friend. Fritzi became Yvetta's protector from her family. That, was what Yvetta wanted and, that is what Fritzi needed and couldn't give Erika all those years ago, when Erika needed, her. She loved Yvetta's delicate frame and her feisty Russian personality; she was difficult to handle but Fritzi relished the challenge, not too dissimilar to Erika's character.

Yvetta's family treated her like a child and Fritzi was not accepted into their midst, but treated like an outsider, which embarrassed and angered Yvetta. As Fritzi saw it, Yvetta was clearly the most innovative, artistic and brilliant member of the family, so why was she treated like the black sleep, why was she the least loved? What did her parents have against her? Or were they afraid of their daughter's brilliance and independent thinking? Perhaps what they hated most about her was that she refused to conform.

Anna showered affection on Yvetta's older sibling, Sasha, who was everything a parent could wish for. (Fritzi could relate to this, too. Fritzi's own mother clearly favoured Fritzi's older sister over her.) Sasha was handsome, obedient, intelligent, dutiful, and above all a loyal Russian son. Yvetta was troublesome and abusive to her mother and she had an alternative lifestyle, frowned upon by her family.

The Rubicov family did not approve of their daughter's chosen life style. Since Fritzi entered Yvetta's life, Yvetta had abandoned what little respect she had for her family's wishes and their conservative attitudes. (And here, Fritzi had much in common with Yvetta, too.) Yvetta unlike Sasha resented being sent to a cold English boarding school away from her family, where she was teased and, no one understood her Russian culture.

More often than she liked to remember, Yvetta returned from visits to her family home in a state of total hysteria. Fritzi hated the Rubicov family for torturing Yvetta into near madness. The very mention of the Rubicov family made Fritzi visibly angry, and this anger only encouraged Yvetta's own bitterness and rage. It was becoming almost impossible to calm Yvetta down. The hatred for her family and her mother grew over the years to fever pitch.

Safi, her brother's fiancé, an interloper as far as Yvetta was concerned, had added another layer of jealously to Yvetta's feelings of inadequacy.

Fritzi saw no alternative but to help Yvetta. In her mad, hare-brained scheme to ransack their family home, to punish Anna for allowing Safi into the family circle and not her own lover, Fritzi.

Destroying and pocketing some of their priceless family treasures would be easy pickings. Fritzi would know how to dispose of those she pocketed, in a very lucrative way. It would enhance her position in the smuggling ring, and would benefit Yvetta financially.

Planning the break-in was an aphrodisiac for Yvetta: it heightened her need for Fritzi in and out of bed. Yvetta was on a permanent high from morning to those endless, long hours of sexual release at night. Her body was keenly attuned to sensual pleasure, always wanting more.

She found it exhausting to please Yvetta's monstrous demands on her, and hoped the actual break-in would release her stress, and her building paranoia towards her family. She wondered whether Yvetta would actually go through with it when the day finally arrived. The truth was, Fritzi realised, Yvetta had little empathy for her mother, and next to no feelings for her family: hurting them seemed to be giving her the release she needed.

They planned to be out of the country before anyone had time to connect any involvement of the robbery to either of them. It seemed a sound plan at the time.

Yvetta took great pleasure in witnessing her mother helpless, this once powerful woman brought down to her knees, the archetypical matriarchal bitch begging Fritzi not to destroy their precious Russian collection. Anna, Yvetta decided, preferred objects to people – and, indeed, preferred other people to Yvetta. Well, they would show her who had the upper hand. The thought of it gave Yvetta a surge of delicious power. Lying in Fritzi's arms late at night – or even being in her company in a crowded venue or club – had made her feel this surge, too. She loved Fritzi for believing in her.

Everyone else in her family disapproved of her, especially her mother, who had abandoned her from a young age to a lonely life far from home, at an expensive boarding school in England.

Her mother had abandoned her father, Alexi, too. Anna's life was work, work, work. Everyone else came second, to the precious empire she had helped build.

Why Anna was revered by the rest of the family Yvetta could never understand. To them, Anna was God! But when Yvetta was with Fritzi she often felt a sense of immortality, a sense that they existed above mere mortals, certainly above the flawed, coarse, money-grubbing Rubicov clan. Without Fritzi, she felt she was missing a piece of herself, she felt jagged, disfigured, and through the holes in her brain the madness climbed in and took over. She fell to earth from great heights, and each time more damaged than the last. How many more times could she undergo such pain? How many more times could she allow her family to attempt to destroy her and the life she had so artfully orchestrated for herself? And at the core of the family, just like at the core of most families, was the mother, Anna, the root of all that evil, the rotten, irredeemable heart. Well, she would show her who was in control, she did not need her family. Fritzi was her family now!

The robbery and threatening Anna had been one of the most exciting experiences of Fritzi's life. Yvetta had reaped untold pleasure from destroying her mother's possessions, but once they were safely out of the country the euphoria of their success had made them careless – and was, sadly, short lived. They wanted more – more damage, more disruption, more ruin, more revenge. They wanted greater spectacle, more devastation even. They knew they were more intelligent than the rest of the family, but they needed the rest of the family to know this as well. They were artists and anarchists, unique, revolutionary. Unfortunately, it had not taken Mika long to track down who had been in charge and involved. Fritzi was lucky they had not had her killed, and had escaped going to prison.

Yvetta had not been as fortunate. They had locked her up in a loony bin and probably would have thrown away the key if Fritzi had not helped her to escape – but then it had gone terribly wrong. Yvetta had turned against her. Fritzi would never forgive her for that, never. She still wondered whether Yvetta had not been forced to abandon her.

She would see to it that the Rubicov family suffered, the way she had in that Russian prison. The family had set a trap and given her up to the Russian authorities, but they did not know who they were dealing with. After all, her father was a Stasi; he had taught her to use what you have to get what you want. It had been relatively easy to seduce her captors, pay them off, while ingratiating herself into one of Moscow's most feared criminal gangs.

Through her Russian contacts she was able to move money and stolen artefacts around the globe. It was to their benefit to secretly remove her out of the country, into Scandinavia and freedom. She would have some fun reaping her vengeance on the Rubicov family, while enhancing her own finances way beyond their imagination. She was already one of the most stylish people in the world, soon she would be one of the richest as well.

She would hurt and destroy that family. She knew that one way or another the opportunity would present itself – and it had. With the help of her contacts, she had managed to terrorise the family, but it was only the beginning. This was more fun than she had had in a long time. No one put one over Fritzi; she was in this fight to win. And she had a far more important prize in her sights.

So far Fritzi's expert chameleon antics had paid off handsomely. She had managed to foil all of DuPont's feeble attempts to bid against her for the artwork she was sure he was securing for the Rubicov gallery in Moscow. Then she had created a scene in the restaurant, drawing everyone's attention away from Valentina. She had brushed past the stuck-up Safi at the Art Club, almost knocking her off her feet. In a matter of hours, she had managed to fluster, then annoy, the key members of the family. The best part of all was their anxiety after she drugged and had that ballerina, the love of Alexi's life, roughed up. Now Alexi knew she was serious, but the family had no idea what would come next – how she loved to toy with them! She was sure of this because that smart-ass (and yet not nearly as smart as he thought he was) Mika would be on her tail by now, but she had set her decoys in place. Besides, Mika was always a day late and a dollar short. An oligarch lover she had cultivated in prison had seen to it that their plan was well executed; he disliked Alexi for his own reasons. so far everything had gone exactly as planned, her revenge would be sweet.

Mika had already learnt from bitter experience just how cunning Fritzi could be, but never imagined her ingenuity would outsmart even corrupt oligarchs and hardened criminals, quite as quickly after her arrest, they would have to be more alert, in future. She had seduced and bribed a few of the wardens with sexual favours, allowing her to gain more freedom. She then formed an alliance with known criminals and money launderers. They believed she even had a well-known oligarch and politician, who had been incarcerated at the same prison, under her spell. Mika knew this oligarch from previous, crooked, business dealings, which had backfired and landed him in Putin's bad books, he was to be avoided at all costs, Fritzi would learn this at her cost.

Gaining the warden's confidence, she was allowed to purchase provisions in the small village with other prisoners who had paid for the same freedoms and privileges. Fritzi was seen as a model prisoner and it took the authorities a few days before they realised, she had vanished from the compound.

An alert was put out for her recapture in Russia. A Red Notice had been put out for her capture across the continent. It was just a matter of time before she slipped up and they had her back in prison.

Mika listened with interest at the confidence with which the authorities brushed over their obvious embarrassment at her escape. The corrupt prison system was notorious. He would keep up with their progress reports of any sightings of Fritzi determined to apprehend her long before the authorities did. Fritzi was the Rubicov's gift to avoid further investigation by the Russian Insurance police into the stolen artefacts from their home. The family needed to keep them happy.

They were able to retrieve and return many of the stolen artefacts, before and, after Fritzi was arrested in Marseilles. It did not surprise Mika Fritzi was able to use her contacts to escape from a corrupt, prison system even so, she had given him the slip once too often and, they had given her a fair chance to begin with, now that she had showed her hand once again, he was determined not to allow her to play anymore games with their family.

He kept in constant communication with everyone he knew in the field in Russia and Europe, but so far it appeared Fritzi had vanished once more into thin air. The cell phone Fritzi had planted on Valentina was, they hoped, a lead to her whereabouts, but it was a one-off message. It was obvious she was diligent enough not to be tracked down by any electronic device she may use. Mika had to remind himself of an uncomfortable truth: that it was Fritzi who had outsmarted them, and not, alas, the other way around. All leads had run cold after the attack on Valentina, all had gone quiet, it was as if Fritzi had disappeared into the ether once more. But Mika was certain she would turn up, like a bad penny.

The police had got no further in their investigations in London, and the authorities in Moscow and Europe had picked up no leads. But Fritzi had to be somewhere, no doubt pulling the same old tricks, possibly using disguises and false passports.

He was playing a waiting game, seeing who would pick up the scent first. It would have to be the Rubicov family if they were going to deal with her before the authorities found her. Mika had his best intelligence networks working night and day, yet not a single lead had passed his desk in over a month. The whole thing was becoming tiresome and Alexi had become understandably paranoid, wanting Fritzi found under any circumstances, before she was able to strike once more.

The family had to be one step ahead of the authorities. For the police, the matter of finding Fritzi was becoming less and less urgent.

She would, he was sure, fall into their net at some stage, but Mika wanted her off the authority's radar long before she tripped herself up, and was caught by the Russians.

Chapter 29

Sasha and Safi returned to Moscow later than planned. Sasha tried to support Alexi after the scare with Valentina. He believed Alexi needed his presence, rather than any support Sasha could provide in any official capacity. Mika had always taken care of that side of things the less Sasha was involved the better.

Valentina had made a quick recovery and, to everyone's surprise, she put the whole ugly incident behind her. She continued with her everyday life, but with the addition of a security detail she had following her almost everywhere, a minor irritation she would soon dispense of. No further incidents had occurred and it appeared the culprits had vanished.

Alexi, on the other hand, could not let it go; it was taking over every free moment of his daily life. He sequestered himself in his study, constantly on calls to Mika, making sure they did not forget to keep up the search for this mad German girl who had once been Yvetta's partner. Alexi believed she would turn up again, causing further mayhem in their lives.

Sasha kept Safi updated, but she found herself totally immersed in the gallery. Working with Zack had brought many new avenues and opportunities for the gallery to go down.

She wanted to present an impressive spreadsheet at her next board meeting with the Rubicov family. They had entrusted her with running the gallery in Yvetta's absence, and she was going to prove she was worthy of their trust, even though not a bona fide Rubicov yet.

The only bone of contention was with her mother constantly nagging about wedding plans and reminding Safi that having a ring on her finger did not automatically mean that she was part of Sasha's family; her mom wanted to see her settled and secure.

Her parents were proud of what she was achieving, but not taking up her place at university attributed to their insecurity about prospects if she never married Sasha.

Safi knew Sasha was of the same mind; neither was willing to address the subject of the wedding just yet, not while his family was so unsettled. It was the wrong atmosphere for wedding plans; they needed everyone enthusiastically on board, especially Alexi, the head of the Rubicov family.

During Safi's last conversation with her mother, Fiona had informed her that Leonard had turned to Greg and was now grooming him to take over from his errant children.

Safi thought it a perfect solution. Greg was brilliant at his job; he had certainly been wonderful to work with when they were in New York together. She hoped her father would be able to relax his hold on the company, having Greg shore up his side of the partnership.

Her folks wanted to spend time in Melbourne near Jake. Jake had met his ideal match; both worked for Google and both loved extreme sports. Safi knew that more than anything her mother wanted to see both her children married and settled. She wondered whether her brother would be the one to walk down the aisle first, and found the idea just a little irritating, realising the pressure it put on her to get on with it.

Her parents would panic if she took them into her confidence about the recent attacks on the Rubicov family, yet she needed their understanding when it came to holding off their wedding arrangements. If Jake walked down the aisle first, it would probably take the pressure off.

Her sex life had taken on a boring, distracted phase. Sasha was never back before midnight during the week, exhausted from a gruelling day. They caught up on weekends, sometimes. They were virtually strangers; spontaneity and excitement had vanished. Making love in exciting places was a memory of the distant past.

More than that, she yearned to get back the element of danger and the heightened excitement it brought to their sex life. Hoping to approach the topic in a light-hearted way, she decided to order an array of sex toys to spice up their lovemaking. Valentine's Day was around the corner: an ideal time to seduce him. She had the packages delivered to the gallery. Taking advantage of his calls to apologise for another late night at the office, she secreted the packages at home, hiding her contraband in the underwear drawer.

As the packages arrived, Safi would open them alone at home with excited trepidation, the familiar but nonetheless fantastic tingle that she used to feel being seduced by Sasha. She had never had any experience with sex toys.

The toys arrived with an instruction CD. She examined the crotchless playful bra-less black lace naughty girl outfit with mesh tights and suspender belt. She tried on the outfit. Throwing her head forward to bush out her hair, she straightened up, catching her image in the full-length mirror. 'Ouch, hot, hot, hot!' God, she was turning herself on. Grabbing the CD, she pushed it into the machine and waited for the sex-manual instructions to start.

Fast-forward past the adverts, she settled down on the sofa to learn how to use her new toys. For the first time in ages, Safi felt the feeling she was missing, the unmistakable pulse and ache of excited pleasure between her legs. Watching the two people using the toys pushed her over the edge and she felt herself grinding with pleasure. Turning on the rubber toy, she plunged it into herself, yelping with pleasure as the vibrations shuddered inside her. With the other hand, she pushed down between her legs, massaging with an expert pressured intensity that made her body shiver with pure pleasure as she climaxed. Spent and lying back on the sofa she dozed off. Waking to a sound of movement, she grabbed the toys, ran for the bathroom, and slammed the door. She pulled off her outfit and threw both outfit and sex toys into the wash basket as Sasha walked into the apartment.

Managing to compose herself, she sauntered out a few moments later in her PJs to greet him.

'You look flushed,' he said. 'Not getting the flu, are you?' He sounded genuinely worried. 'I thought I heard you coughing.'

Smiling inwardly, Safi sauntered over and threw her arms around Sasha.

'Actually, I feel better than I have in ages. What's happening at work? You have been home so late almost every evening this week.'

Sitting down on the sofa, Sasha turned on the news channel and patted the seat beside him. Curling up against him, Safi stared in disbelief as she watched the scene of arrests unfold on the screen. Only understanding fleeting Russian comments, it was not difficult to recognise the important businessmen she had met when out with Sasha at charity galas. Here they were now, being pushed into police cars. They were arresting them all over the city. She recognised an important executive at the Rubicov television network as one of the faces flashed on the TV screen.

'God, isn't that one of your company executives they are carting off? And that's Mika, too, what's he doing there?'

'Safi, things in Russia are becoming more complicated every day. Businesses are being investigated for fraud against the State. It's close to the election and those in control do not want those with influence making trouble for them, hence the arrests. They will be warned, harassed, and threatened with confiscation of their assets and jail.'

Safi sat in stunned silence for a few moments, staring at the screen. 'But are you not worried that one of your TV company's top executives has been arrested? And why is Mika involved?'

'To be honest, most of what's happening is way beyond my comprehension. Mika will feel less threatened; he has powerful contacts inside the Kremlin and will smooth things over. I am sure we will all be briefed tomorrow. More than likely, this month will be fraught with meetings and new guidelines to follow, meaning I won't be home early for quite some time.'

None of this made much sense to her; she was not familiar with the intricacies of Russian politics. All she knew of Russian politics was from the derogatory comments she had heard while in the States, and her dad had often waxed lyrical about the corruption in the 'New Russia', and about rich gas and oil oligarchs, holding parts of Eastern Europe to ransom.

She knew that Mika had influence, of course. He had friends everywhere and she hoped he was able to solve whatever was going on. If he was sent to prison his family would be lost without him; everything in the Rubicov empire fell on Mika's broad shoulders.

'Let's go to bed,' Sasha said. 'I need to get rid of all this stress.'

She loved Sasha and wanted to please him, but their lovemaking was boring her to tears. It was all about getting rid of his pent-up stress; all she wanted was to rekindle the fun side of their sex life. Well, he had another thing coming if he thought she was going to miss out on Valentine's Day. She was prepared to kidnap him, if necessary, tie him to the bed while seducing him with her sex toys.

Blimey, she hoped married life wasn't going to be like this. She would stray for sure if that was the case. Maybe she wasn't cut out for marriage. Falling into a troubled sleep she tried to ignore the doubts welling up in her mind.

Safi woke to find Sasha had already left. She missed being at their family home, somehow it wasn't quite as solitary once Sasha was gone. The staff, she now realised, had kept her company with their chatter and Kolya had been a pleasant distraction in her early Moscow days. Not so long ago she had felt alien and lost living through her first sub-zero winter, a lost solitary child in a blizzard fighting her way through the storm, searching for familiarity in endless virgin snow.

She had found her way through that lonely beginning to be fêted by the rich and famous, a success story by most standards.

She was encouraging a new young Russian artist, brilliant worked canvasses dripping in paint. On the canvas, he interpreted his poverty and Russia's vast landscape and history with an incredible energy, using aged natural materials of rust mixed with the grasses and husks of wheat from the farmlands, dried and withered in the thick impasto and leaving a memory of failed harvests as they dried on the canvas. Since working with DuPont and Zack, Safi felt that she had learnt to trust her instinct; she did not care about the theory, as Dax so eloquently put it. 'I don't give a rat's ass about the reasons behind the work,' Dax was fond of saying, 'only about the process; if it works, it works.' Dax thought only the critics and the Art Historians cared about what the paintings were about; most artists were in love with the process and the challenge each canvas presented in its virgin state until that first mark was made. The painting took the artist on a perilous inner journey, working through a struggle only the painter (and sometimes not even the painter!) knew how to end.

Though not an artist herself, she had come to agree with Dax: a sculpture or painting had to engage her on some level at first sight, like Dax's work had. Right now, for example, she was waiting to hear from Zack about a project they were planning together. The telephone rang. She picked it up, expecting Zack's voice, but instead heard the familiar flirtatious French accent of DuPont.

Warily she listened as DuPont launched into his reason for seeking her out, and Safi had to admit it was something they both needed to discuss. He had almost lost the clients he was bidding for at the auction; he had not impressed them and this pained him more than anything. Not only was his reputation damaged, but his ego was more than a little bruised. The affront of rejection was new to him; it had never happened to him before. Was he losing his lustre, or was he just momentarily off his game? He had no time for self-doubt, which would only slow him down further. He believed that the aroma of insecurity was the most toxic fragrance of them all – it repelled others.

Two months had passed since and he had not been able to let it go. DuPont had tried to follow certain leads to figure out why and by whom he had been targeted that day. Nothing conclusive had come to light until today, when out of the blue a woman turned up at his office on Madison Avenue. There was a pause on the line and Safi, unable to contain herself, said, 'Well, don't keep me guessing. Who was she?'

'That Safi, môn dui, is the problem. I have absolutely no idea.'

'What did she want? She must have a name, surely?'

'She wanted to pick my brain, apparently. She brought out a Russian artefact she had been sold. She said she needed to know what it was worth, who she should approach to put it on the market without much fuss. The problem is, I am almost positive it's from Anna's collection.'

'Why haven't you spoken to Alexi? Surely, he would be the one to alert?'

'Well, you are correct, but I need to know if Ilona has a catalogue of the artefacts stolen from the gallery before I bother Alexi. Ilona worked for Fritzi and Yvetta, so it would be helpful. I am going to send a photo of the object, and if you could get back to me today, I would appreciate it.'

'How are you, Safi? It's been a while.'

She could detect an edge in his voice and felt a slight flutter in the pit of her stomach. 'Gallery is doing wonderfully, thank you. I will always be grateful for your guidance. Ilona has just come in with the copy of the artefact so I am going to put her on the conference line. It seems she has made a positive identification.'

'Ilona,' DuPont began, 'are you sure it's from the collection and was sold after the theft or is this a missing artwork?'

She looked at Safi then pointed to a small section of works that had never been retrieved after the theft; the likeness was identical.

'This is on our list as one of the few pieces never retrieved after the theft.'

There was a pause on the line as DuPont tried to figure out why he had been sought out as a dealer.

'Well, this is becoming more suspicious by the minute. Why on earth would anyone with a stolen artefact come to me, knowing my connection with the gallery? If they did not want to send a message to the Rubicovs, or take the chance of being caught with an invaluable illegal Russian objet d'art, I am the last person in New York to approach.'

'You need to speak to Alexi,' Safi said.

Ilona and Safi sat for some time going over how this valuable piece had suddenly come to light. There had been no further incidents since the attacks in London; all leads had gone cold. The woman who had wreaked such havoc seemed to have vanished into thin air. Everyone remained convinced that it had been Fritzi, who was ingenious at landing on her feet. Anyone who managed to engineer an escape from a Russian prison proved she had a talent for survival at any cost.

Sasha had been right: the arrests had been a shot across their bough, a warning from those in power: wealth would not protect them from prosecution. It was a loaded warning, to anyone who rocked the boat during the coming elections. Support for the recent protests by the public would not be smiled on benevolently, nor would those who sided against Putin. Things were changing, and not for the better.

Up until now Mika was able to smooth out run-ins with the authorities, but recent developments had not gone as smoothly for the Rubicov companies.

Meetings went on late into the night, and trips abroad kept Sasha busier than ever. She hated coming home to an empty apartment. Spending weekends at the Dacha with Anna helped and, it was good to get to know Maurice Anna's husband, who Safi found a comforting distraction from the Art world. Maurice was a professional man he had little interest in politics or business and they enjoyed his endless entertaining antidotes of his earlier life as a student doctor. A side of Moscow Safi did not know about.

Like Fiona, Anna was keen for them to tie the knot, but the recent upheavals kept pushing opportunities for a wedding further into the future. Anna tried to encourage them to have a quiet civil ceremony, to do the big number when it suited them with a fairy-tale Russian ball. Safi was taken in by Anna's description of the ball; she could imagine inviting her friends from England and the States, and using it as a PR exercise, too: sending out official invitations to all her important contacts in the art world, bringing artists, clients, and dealers together socially.

Sasha had not taken Safi into his confidence about increasing concerns over their business enterprises in Russia. Over the years they had diversified into the United States and England; and more recently they had opened two further Rubicovs in the Far East – one in Shanghai and the other in Beijing. He had taken over the reins of their Russian-based enterprises from Anna. It had taken Sasha quite some time to learn (with the help of his cousins) the extent of their farming, technical, and mining businesses in Russia. Together they had been working to consolidate the companies into smaller holdings, selling off chunks to rivals who had petitioned for larger stakes of the Russian Gas and Oil holdings after perestroika; now the stakes were higher and the geopolitical games were far more dangerous.

The Rubicov family had found the stakes too dangerous and far too high to remain in the game; they preferred to spread their capital around the globe, rather than keep it in one place. The rouble was sure to drop once the gas prices were replaced by some other energy that was less fraught with political pitfalls.

Sasha and Mika had been given the job of selling off their holdings in a quiet and satisfactory way. The remaining enterprises would be pared down, allowing for growth and modernisation in a fast-changing country.

Ringo, who Safi had worked with briefly, had become like Kolya, an extended and indispensable member of the family's inner sanctum. They were both given highly sensitive positions in the new scaled-down companies. Day in and day out, Sasha spent his life in endless conferences and meetings. He had little time for his private life. Whenever he returned to a frustrated Safi, he pushed back his nagging doubts about their relationship, he was not giving her the attention she deserved, and he knew she was bored with their sex life, Safi enjoyed foreplay and excitement and he wasn't performing, by a long shot, and felt she was getting to the end of her tether, playing for time before she blew a gasket.

The gallery had turned out to be their saving grace. Safi had taken to Yvetta's business with eagerness, imagination, and aplomb, and by all accounts had turned it from a successful enterprise to a winning one.

Alexi had taken an interest in the art business with the same genuine energy he took in Valentina's ballet interests. His father's attitude helped Sasha understand that he needed to be encouraging without being condescending about Safi's interests. It would help her grow, not only as a person in her own right but also in confidence. Enabling Safi to grow the business by giving her free rein and financial support would pay dividends as it became a viable money-making enterprise.

Sasha felt guilty about neglecting Safi so often, but there was nothing he could do until the business side of things had settled down.

He had been thankful for her closeness to Anna; his mother, like Safi's, had dropped hints to encourage them to marry sooner rather than later, but he had no intention of embroiling himself in any wedding arrangements for the foreseeable future. Luckily, Safi seemed to feel the same; he had not figured out why, but for some reason this endless postponement suited her. Though why she felt this way – indecisive or insecure or just eager to keep marriage at bay – did niggle at him. He would have to discover why at a more convenient and less onerous time.

Sasha felt he did not have a single ounce of spare energy and prayed that the trust his father and Mika had put in his abilities to streamline their affairs would prove to be correct. So far, with Anna's guidance and with the help of his cousins, hitches were being ironed out. High-level meetings were progressing smoothly, and everything they had worked for together was coming to a head. Once the companies were sold off he would take Safi away for a much-needed holiday.

But first signatures had to be put on the dotted line; if the lawyers did their job it should happen within the next three months. In the back of his mind, Sasha remembered that Safi had mentioned Valentine's Day: she had planned something special for them. Having neither the heart to disappoint her nor the energy for the argument that would probably follow, he had promised he would not miss it for anything. But he knew if something came up at the last moment, he would have to disappoint her yet again. Hating the fast pace both their lives had taken since returning from the two D's wedding, and not wanting to have Safi constantly hanging around waiting for him to come home, Sasha decided to have Ilona see him at his office. He hoped between them they would find a gap in Safi's schedule to allow her to visit Manhattan; if anything could help them both, it was her love for Dan and Dax and NYC. It would allow Sasha to work round the clock the last few weeks without distraction.

Ilona, he found, was ingenious at finding reasons for Safi to visit NYC. She had contacted Zack, who would be there with introductions to a number of artists they were hoping to represent. One of these artists, Ilona knew, Safi would fly anywhere in the world to meet. So far, he had been very elusive.

Safi jumped at the opportunity to meet with the artist they had recently heard so much about, and having Zack in NYC made her confident he would meet with them. Showing his work in their gallery would put them into another stratosphere.

Arriving in NYC always seemed to lift her spirits. This time, she realised, was no different from her very first trip in a yellow cab to the Big Apple.

Her life had taken many turns since then. It struck her that she still had no idea where life was heading, but for some reason she felt happy, even carefree. Something felt right. She had followed her own path and it had led her to this point.

She had learnt the ins and outs of the art world, she had expertise in a field she enjoyed and loved being part of. Hopefully her stewardship of the gallery would bring her independence. She would be her own person if she so wished – and she did indeed wish for that day. She was determined to become an expert in her field. Everyone was interdependent, no one did it all on their own, and she had the common-sense to take on all the help she was given and was determined to continue learning from the best. Perhaps she had learnt this sense of collaboration and mentorship from her father and his experience at the agency. One day she would own her own gallery, she was sure of that.

With this in mind, she joined Zack on a journey to a cabin in the woods near the Hudson River, to meet the elusive artist they had heard so much about, who had so far only shown in one gallery in NYC. Everyone wanted to give him another show, but he had vanished from the art scene … and here she was with Zack tracking him down to view his new work.

The forests dressed in their fall colours along the way was stunning, orange and yellow leaves brushed their window as Zack switched on the wipers to dust them aside. Zack was good company and relaxed behind the wheel of the hired BMW SUV. His dress sense pleased Safi she admired his sartorial taste in clothes with its gritty edge. His trousers were fitting showing his muscular thighs which ended above his designer trainers. His jackets tailored Saville Row tweed, and he always sported a kerchief in his top pocket. Today a casually tied camel scarf, finished off his super cool look. He was regaling her with stories of his childhood growing up on a game reserve in Southern Africa.

Eventually they found the gravel path leading through the trees to his hideaway studio. She had no idea what to expect. The guy could be Rambo or an axe murderer for all she knew. The studio was a huge wooden structure tucked away between the trees, revealing itself as they drove into a clearing to be greeted by two beautiful golden retrievers. Standing under a wooden archway was a six-foot blond Adonis bare to his waist. His plaid shirt was hanging over his hips, still tucked into the belt holding up cargo pants tucked into cowboy boots. He cut a pretty impressive figure. Safi could tell Zack's blood pressure rising, his usual forthright manner ebbing away as they got out of the car to greet the movie star staring them down. So far, he had not moved a muscle. His leaf blower had obviously done its job; there wasn't a single leaf to be seen in his front yard, even though it was fall.

The retrievers were now yapping and bounding all over the place with happiness at their arrival. They were obviously not guard dogs; Safi was grateful that at least someone was happy to see them. They made their way towards the master of the yapping hounds, waiting for him to welcome them. So far he had not uttered a word or moved a muscle. When they were about fifty yards from him, he suddenly turned heel and disappeared with his dogs into the house, leaving Zack and Safi wondering what to do.

Zack shook his shoulders and followed but as he reached the door, it swung closed in his face, the lock clicking as it made contact with the frame.

'Shit, this guy obviously has a communication problem,' Zack said softly. 'His assistant made the appointment with us at his say-so. I can't understand why he is now pissed off at our arrival.'

The door opened slightly and, in the doorway, stood a small slim Chinese girl. 'I am so sorry,' the girl said. 'He was expecting you this afternoon. Now he is working. He won't see anyone until the appointed time.'

Zack looked at his watch. 'What time would that be? It's now noon: almost afternoon, in my book.'

'Ah, not until four pm, that is when he comes into the kitchen for tea. So sorry, you please go into town and come back for tea four pm.'

Sitting in the car they had to decide whether to return or wait to see 'this egomaniac' as Zack none too affectionately referred to him. As it turned out, the wait was worthwhile. Janus was a dedicated, disciplined, thoughtful artist and man, disarmingly quiet for his size, a gentle giant whose work was mind-blowing. The materials he used for his sculptures were natural wood mixed with glass and combined clay. His paintings were minimalist yet captured exactly what he was about, showing nature at its most creative when it was at the beginning of its journey or at the end. It made one feel alive and aware that life was lived in the space between the two.

Janus had a stillness about him – it was effective, there was a toughness in his manner which was hard to penetrate. Safi allowed Zack to do the talking. Ying showed them out.

'I have your contact details,' she said. 'Thank you for coming. We hope you enjoyed the work.'

They returned to Manhattan in near silence, only coming to grips with the work and the artist as they were close to Dan's brownstone. They sat in the car for a few moments; his work had an effect, yet they were at a loss for words. Janus – and even Ying, his assistant – was hard to crack. They would wait and see whether Ying contacted them and go from there; it would, they both agreed, be an important show. There was no way Janus would agree to be at any show himself, he had made that clear without saying a word: one of the reasons he had shied away from the art world was his reluctance to engage with anyone.

She found the two D's relaxing in the family room with a guest they introduced as Lisa. Safi had not met her before but she immediately realised that Lisa was to be the surrogate mother for their baby.

Lisa was gay and Safi liked her immediately. Lisa was keen to help the two D's have a baby but did not want children herself, which was an ideal way for them to go. They would never know whose sperm had fertilised the egg, and had come to an arrangement with Lisa to give them two babies if things worked out the way they hoped. She had gone through all the medical tests and, according to the clinician, there was no reason for her not to have a healthy baby. Safi had never met Lisa before but she had apparently worked with Dan for many years as a colour technician, and, had grown into a trusted friend over the years. She was excited for them and wished Lisa a happy pregnancy, hoping to meet with her while she was carrying the two D's baby.

Safi wanted to ask her a million questions, but felt that may be intrusive, and possibly even insulting to the two D's It must be a nerve-wracking road for them all to go down, so many emotions and variables were involved; it made her shiver at the thought of things going badly. Instead, she told them about Janus. Being an open, gregarious person who loved the limelight, Dax found it hard to understand why Janus was so standoffish about promoting his work.

Safi suggested that Janus' attitude might come from financial stability, not needing to pander to the critics or the media.

'But don't all artists want their work validated in some way?' Dax said. 'I believe everyone likes to be validated, so I think your artist Janus the Adonis will contact you when he has left you guessing long enough. It's his game, making you wait, it adds some a kind of aura, don't you think, about him and his work?'

'I think you have something there,' Safi said, nodding. 'I'm surprised Zack had not worked that out, too. After all, he is an expert. We were pretty mesmerised after our meeting with him, to be honest. He had us both enthralled, something I have never seen Zack be.'

She had a meeting with DuPont the following day and had asked Dax to be there, not wanting to meet with him on her own. Dax had not worked out why Safi and DuPont had become uncomfortable in each other's company but he had a pretty good idea. DuPont was widely known to be a lady's man. Although Safi had never said anything, Dax was sure DuPont had hit on Safi. This was the most likely explanation.

His own relationship with DuPont had gone from strength to strength. DuPont had come through for him on many levels. He had sold work to some major galleries and had an exhibition coming up at the Guggenheim in Brooklyn, which he was thrilled about. DuPont could not do anything wrong in his eyes. Dax guessed from a straight man's point of view Safi was a stunner. Dax felt she was old enough to cope with DuPont's teasing and French charm. Still, he would watch them closely to see if his suspicion was right. He might even tease DuPont about being too long in the tooth for their beautiful Saffron, not to mention messing with a Russian.

Safi went to bed wondering why she had not yet heard from Sasha. She knew he had more than he knew how to handle with the family's different businesses coming under government scrutiny. She missed their light-hearted conversations and his attentiveness. Most of all, she missed the wild sex he used to initiate when she least expected it. There was a time when she thought he was going to introduce her to some exotic sexual games, but it had never happened. She still wondered what it would have been like.

His phone kept ringing. She had tried his office and his cell, but only his voicemail answered. Frustrated and tired, she left messages and hoped to hear from him before the weekend. It was so unlike him.

Hailing a cab to meet DuPont, she felt less than confident; nothing had come through from Sasha yet. Dax had promised to join her meeting with DuPont: a part of her wanted him to be there, another part longed for the attention DuPont was so good at lavishing on her. She desperately needed something more than that: she needed some hot sex. For precisely this reason, this was not a time to be alone with a past lover who she still found charismatic and madly attractive. She had been down that road with DuPont. She had initiated sex, then he had called it off, and she had begged to continue, then he begged to continue. Now she was in control again, but if she submitted to his charms the tables would turn and they would be back on dangerous ground. She did not need any more drama in her life. Indeed, life was getting much too complicated and having DuPont in her life again may not help her flagging relationship with Sasha.

There was no sign of Dax as she entered the building. Travelling up in the elevator, she became aware of a knot in her stomach. As she considered pressing the down button, the lift doors opened and there was Dax.

'Hey, why the glum face?' he said with a smile. 'Were you hoping I wouldn't show, leaving you all alone with Casanova?'

His joke was uncannily close to the truth. 'No, silly,' she said. 'I still have not heard from Sasha. It's been over forty-eight hours since we last spoke and I am just a little concerned, that's all.'

DuPont jumped up from behind his desk to meet them. Greetings over, he launched into his bizarre experience with the stolen artefact.

Safi wanted to know every detail about the woman who had brought the antique objet d'art to his office for valuation.

'Was she tall? Was she slim? Was she German? Was she young?'

'Oui, oui, but what has that got to do with anything?'

'Everything,' Safi said quickly. 'It could be Fritzi. She has been sabotaging the Rubicov family and involved with so much that's been happening recently, all of it bad. Alexi and Sasha believe she might have attacked Valentina. There is a chance it was her that sabotaged you at the auction.'

He sat staring at Safi. 'Okay, but what has all this got to do with me?'

'I am not sure. Did you talk to Alexi?'

'Oui, he has intimated the same as you. But what could Fritzi gain from sabotaging me, or seeking me out for an evaluation?'

They sat staring at one another. The hot property was sitting on DuPont's desk for all to see.

'Is this the infamous artefact?' Dax said. Safi shook her head. 'Ah, but it's not genuine at all. It's a fake to be sure. I have had it appraised by experts in the field and they assure me this artefact is an excellent copy of the real thing.'

'So what does Alexi think?' Safi asked.

'We have discussed it: unless this woman reappears in my office to collect her stolen Russian artefact, there isn't much anyone can do.'

Dax wanted to get on with his own agenda and tried to steer the conversation to the prints they were releasing for sale to the galleries.

DuPont instructed him as to how many of each to sign and release. No one wanted to flood the market, even though many of his paintings were highly sought after, the originals were in private collections or owned by various museums. DuPont already had buyers for the prints waiting in line.

'Safi, I have to leave you and DuPont to discuss your stolen objet d'art. Dan is expecting me; we are, as you know, in the process of making a baby, and Lisa our surrogate is ready for insemination. Both Dan and I want to be present. We want to experience as much of this as possible with Lisa until she delivers our baby into our arms.'

Dax had barely been gone a minute when the cell phone on DuPont's desk buzzed. Safi could tell that he was taken aback by the call. Pointing to the cell, he beckoned Safi over to listen with him to the person on the other end of the line. Putting her ear close to his cheek, for a moment intimate again, they stared in shock at one another as the disembodied voice made its demands.

The muffled tones were impossible to recognise, but Safi was sure she could make out a slight German intonation as they listened to the instructions being given to DuPont. 'I want you to sell the artefact in your possession as genuine. Yes, I know it's a fake, but no one but you, me, and the appraiser you used know this.'

'This is not possible in today's market,' DuPont said and his voice cracked. For the first time he appeared flustered. 'Everyone would know in a matter of time, and my reputation would be in ruins.'

'Ah yes, your reputation. Don't worry, DuPont, I have a client I will be sending to you soon. All you have to do is show them the objet d'art. The rest will happen once they are told it's the genuine article. This is the price I want you to quote.'

They both drew in their breath when hearing the 000 on the value

'This is not possible,' DuPont protested, 'only an auction could demand that number.'

'Ah yes,' the voice said again, 'but you will let them know they are being offered a rare opportunity to purchase this artefact before it goes to auction. The owner who is releasing it wants top dollars. His only stipulation is for it to be bought before it goes to the highest bidder.'

DuPont swallowed. 'You seem to have this all worked out. But what makes you think I will comply with your wishes?'

'I will send you an account number that I want you to wire the money to after the sale.

It has to be paid without any delay. If the transaction is to go ahead, the client will have to do the transaction on the spot. If you do not make the sale, or you warn the client, be aware you will lose more than you could possibly imagine: not only your reputation but also your integrity with the Rubicov family.'

DuPont rolled his eyes. 'Really?'

'Should we just say your secret love tryst with your little Shatzie is safe for now.'

DuPont recognised the Middle High German/Swiss reference to treasure as in love or romance and stared at Safi in shock.

Realising the word had given DuPont a shock, Safi lifted her hands in question. 'Who are you referring to? I have no idea what you are talking about.'

'Don't be a fool, DuPont, I have concrete evidence of your tryst with that English whore. I would hate to see your handsome face rearranged, not to mention your reputation in the art world. I will call back tomorrow. I take it we have a deal.'

The cell went dead. Safi now realised she was the little English whore, and that DuPont understood the stakes, not only for himself but for her as well. Colour draining from her face, Safi sunk down onto the chair at DuPont's desk. He stood staring at the dead cell in his hand, hardly believing the conversation they had just heard. It was too much to comprehend, or, for that matter, deal with in a calm, sensible manner. He felt his legs buckle and had to hold onto his desk to steady himself. He made his way over to the chair facing Safi, who was now sitting behind his desk. They sat in silence trying to work out the consequences independently for themselves.

'Safi, I am so sorry. I have absolutely no idea how we can avoid dealing with this threat. I believe you and Alexi are right: this can only be Fritzi. No one else would have the hubris to make such demands.'

Safi started to cry. She suddenly felt her whole world crashing in on her. Everything felt unreal, even the simplest movements seemed a strain. And yet she knew that this was indeed real, and that, as far as she could tell, there was no way out of this. She closed her eyes, but in the darkness she felt dizzy too. It amplified the throbbing in her head. She opened her eyes to see DuPont's usual charismatic charm evaporate, so that he became, in an instant, a different person: beaten, downtrodden, unattractive even. He sat dejected, shoulders drooping, head hanging into his chest. Safi for the first time noticed his age. DuPont looked old, tired, done-in. Was he ill, she wondered?

The image frightened her. She needed someone to take charge, someone she could rely on to solve this nightmare about to unfold. She knew she was not capable of fixing this – indeed, she barely had the strength to comprehend it. She had always looked to DuPont as a mentor, someone who could fix anything – but he couldn't fix this. It was as if, through their game of catch, her flirtation and seduction, the thrill of it all, they had taken turns digging a pit for themselves and each other, and now they had no choice but to lie down in it. Not a bed, a grave. Her head felt ready to explode with anxiety. She tried to steel herself, discover once again the optimistic Safi that had always served her well, that saw the positive side to every situation. Not now though. That Safi was long gone. There had to be a way forward, but if DuPont was not capable of dealing with the situation, they found themselves in, who could?

Someone had to be notified before the transaction went ahead, she knew this, but how could they hoodwink Fritzi? She seemed on top of every detail, way ahead of them in her planning.

The phone on DuPont's desk brought them out of their fog. Safi watched in dread as he lifted the receiver off its cradle. She watched him nodding gravely and emit reluctant grunts of acknowledgement. God, it must be worse than she could have imagined, he had lost his power of speech, replaced by zombielike movements.

Putting the receiver down slowly he eventually found his tongue.

'Safi,' he finally said when he put the phone down. 'I do not know how to break this news, but Alexi has asked me to do so. He has booked you on the ten pm BA flight to London. LHR. A car will be waiting to pick you up. He held out his hand for Safi to listen before she had a chance to interrupt.

'The Russian authorities arrested Sasha as his private jet was about to fly out of the country.'

Safi's hand flew up to her mouth. 'Oh my God, why?'

'I guess Alexi will fill you in when you get to London. That's if he knows anything. It seems the Rubicov family have more than enough on their plate. In the meantime, I will have to work out what I am going to do about this Fritzi problem.'

'It's our Fritzi problem,' Safi said, as though she needed to be reminded. 'All you can do is wait for her next call, fly by the seat of your pants, and call her bluff.'

'How do you propose I do that?'

Safi dug deep she had to be strong not only for DuPont, who seemed to be out of his depth but for herself too, it was self-preservation she wasn't about to let Fritzi ruin her life or her relationship with Sasha. She had no idea how Fritzi could possibly know about her tryst with DuPont and, believed she was going on DuPont's previous reputation with women, trying to alarm them with threats, to keep them as her puppets to play with at will, for her own mad reasons. Safi needed to compartmentalize that was what her brain now told her, stiff upper lip, deal with the facts each in turn, else her emotions would take over and, she would fall apart. If she tried to think what was happening to Sasha she wouldn't be able to cope. She pushed her thoughts of Sasha out of her mind and, forced herself to be in control, even if her hair brained scheme did not make sense she had to wake DuPont out of his near mental paralysis, help him, help them.

'Well, I have dealt with Fritzi in the past. She is cunning for sure, but she is also on the run. That means she is vulnerable, which means she is liable to make mistakes. And she must be in hiding. I honestly don't believe anyone would take whatever she had to say about our tryst seriously. She has done some questionable things in the past which discredit anything she has to say or do in the eyes of the Rubicov family.'

She noticed a glint of hope in DuPont's eyes as he held her gaze. For the first time, as she returned the intensity of his stare, she felt she was on the right track.

'Safi, I realise you are trying to help me deal with this situation before you leave, but imagining Sasha in the hands of the Russian authorities must be more than anyone can deal with right now. How do you suggest I play this with Fritzi? We have no idea who she is working with.'

'True, but: more likely Russian criminals here in the States. Or the Italian Mafia – she was working with them when she was apprehended by the Russians.'

'I still do not see how this can help us.'

'The expert Russian appraiser you used, do you know him well?' Safi remembered how they had caught that student working for Fritzi at the gallery during Dax's show. DuPont nodded.

'Could you get him on side? That way he will realise what is happening when the artefact is back on the market for sale as a fake. Then he can pass the information on to the authorities. Then you will save your reputation, as well as helping the Russians retrieve that replica and hopefully prevent something like this from happening again.'

'Have you forgotten the money the buyer would have spent on this fake?' DuPont said. 'The money would have been wired into an account by then and the fake be in the buyer's possession.'

'A small problem for the authorities, I am sure,' Safi said. 'They will be able to track down the owners of the fake, enlighten them and return their money when they have caught Fritzi, who will be able to give them information about the whole sordid criminal art world she is involved with. The buyers of the fake will then work with the authorities to put the fake back on the market, in order to lure the gang back into play. They will do this by making you the sole agent. I am sure they will contact you once again with various threats for a percentage of the sale.'

DuPont sat for a long moment, staring at Safi. 'How on earth have you managed to work all that out in such a short space of time?'

Safi shook her shoulders. 'I have no idea, but it seems the most likely course of action at such short notice, and when up against it, one has to think on one's feet'

DuPont reached out for his cell. They stared at one another as he waited for the other person to pick up.

'Dieter, hello, this is DuPont. Do you think you could meet me at my apartment later on this evening?' DuPont gave instructions for him to take the elevator to the roof garden, rather than to his apartment.

'Is that the Russian appraiser?' Safi asked. 'He must be German with a name like Dieter.'

'Sure, but he is East German. He lived through the communist era. He knows all things Russian, from the Caucuses to Berlin.'

'What are you going to do about your flight to London? It's after four. You do not have much time.'

Safi slowly got herself up, collected her things, and made her way down to the street. She stood for a moment, as though she had forgotten where or who she was, then hailed a cab and asked to be dropped at Pete's Bar. She needed to talk to someone she could trust and Pete was the only person she knew who would listen calmly. He had in the past given her invaluable advice and she depended on his ability to get to the crux of a problem, giving her his most pragmatic solution. If ever she needed help, it was now.

Four o'clock, well past lunch and, not yet the end of the working day. Pete was never busy at this time in the bar. Safi walked in to find Pete exactly where she hoped he would be, buffing glasses behind the bar. He lifted his head in acknowledgement with that old familiar warmth in his smile. She hoisted herself up onto her usual bar stool, leaning over to give him a peck on the cheek he offered. No words were necessary as he slowly prepared and placed her usual drink on the bar. Then, getting on with shining the glasses, he looked up expectantly, waiting for her to begin.

Her shandy was replaced by one coffee after another as the year leading up to this moment spilled from her lips. Apart from a grunt now and then, Pete, to his credit, did not flinch. He listened without any interruptions, which allowed her to get the whole damn mess (as he put it later) off her chest.

'You have no idea why they have arrested him, right?'

'None, not yet anyway.'

'It has nothing to do with this antiquity business you been on about?'

'No, that is a completely different problem between Fritzi, Yvetta, and the Rubicov family.'

'You run Yvetta's gallery now, right?'

Safi nodded in agreement.

'Let me get this straight: Sasha's sister is in an institution somewhere in Europe, this Fritzi was apprehended and put in a Russian jail that she escaped from. She sure is playing for high stakes. She's plenty mad at everyone – and with good reason, from what you've told me. The girl has nothing to lose: she lost her lady, and the gallery she used as a cover – to you!' Safi nodded again. 'From where I'm sitting, this ain't looking good. You gonna have to be watching out, that's for sure.'

'Pete, how do you see it, what should I be doing? I am terribly confused.'

'Don't say that I blame you. Best thing is, they catch this German woman. Mean time you have to hear what the story is down in London before you can make any decisions one way or the other. You are going to have to sit tight and hope it all blows over. Then I suggest your Russian family scoot outta there with their assets, and put up shop elsewhere, like other rich folk do.'

Pete never disappointed. He always said his piece straight to the point when asked. She hoped he was right, that it would all blow over.

She telephoned the two D's from the first-class lounge while waiting for her flight to be called. Not wanting to tell Dan or Dax more than she needed to, they were more than a little confused at her sudden departure, but they were happily preoccupied with their new venture into parenthood. They seemed to have no conversation left for anything else besides babies and work. Bringing them down to earth with her own problematic life was pointless. They had carved out their own little corner of heaven, no one deserved it more, and she felt genuine happiness for them. Yet a part of her felt some loss. She loved the attention they lavished on her; a baby would no doubt fill up all the love they had left to give.

DuPont called to fill her in on his meeting with the antiquity's appraiser. It had gone to plan. Dieter was happy to help the authorities; the Russian mafia had done him out of many deals in the past: he had bad experiences with both.

On this occasion he was happy to assist DuPont and keep him informed of any movement once the piece had been sold. Dieter thought DuPont brave to call their bluff, but he understood that DuPont had no option until a trap was set, and hopefully feed into the gang's newfound confidence and greed. The authorities would not be pleased at initially being kept out of the loop, but both DuPont and Safi were confident that catching the bigger fish was justification enough. Safi just prayed that Fritzi's gang would fall for the rouse, returning for more now that they had a sitting patsy like DuPont.

Chapter 30

Kolya was waiting for Safi at T5. He now worked exclusively for Alexi, having proved his worth on numerous occasions. Kolya was worried for Sasha, that was obvious from his conversation, but she could tell he had no intention of telling her more than she needed to know. Safi suddenly wondered whether they had any intention of telling her anything at all.

On arriving she was immediately shown into Alexi's office. He waved for her to sit in the chair opposite his desk, signalling for her to help herself to coffee and fruit. He always had breakfast sent up to his office on a trolley. She was pleased to share his feast, having eaten very little on the late flight out of JFK.

She sat back in the comfortable armchair. The coffee managed to help her feel a little more alert. She wondered how much Alexi would share with her. Surely the police had nothing to pin on Sasha. She hoped that Sasha, like his brother Mika, would be released in the dead of night to find his own way home. Sasha thought she did not know about Yvetta, or for that matter their previous problems with Fritzi but she had managed to piece together some of the facts after the break-in at their home for herself and, now those facts were helping her make some sense of how Fritzi operated.

She became aware of Alexi's intonation and raised voice. Her Russian wasn't good enough to follow the conversation, but obviously it was not going well.

Alexi put down the receiver and leaned back in his chair, allowing it to fall all the way back on its hinge. Safi watched him as he allowed the chair to bring itself back to its forward position.

He stared at her blankly; for a moment she wondered whether he'd forgotten she was there. He stood painfully, walked round, and took a seat in the chair next to hers. He, too, looked much older all of a sudden. He held out his hand for her to take. Holding onto her hand, he sighed, held Safi's gaze, and began to relate the disastrous nightmare facing Sasha since her departure from Moscow.

By the time Alexi had finished speaking, every nerve in her body felt as if it was being stretched to the limit. They had no idea when Sasha would be released while the present dictatorial, plutocratic government was in power. The government had taken control of their media business and had clamped down on the Rubicov gas and oil exports to Eastern European countries that were not in their favour.

The government held Sasha responsible for transferring the family's companies' assets abroad. The State did not approve of being left out of the loop, and so had arrested Sasha, no doubt to gain access to their gas and oil pipeline. Safi found her mind spinning. She had no idea whether they had the right to confiscate businesses or imprison anyone, but obviously the Russian tax laws were an issue and Sasha had fallen prey to Rubicov business practices in Russia. For this, Safi held Alexi responsible, not Sasha.

While Alexi continued to draw a picture of their present situation, Safi found it hard to concentrate on what he was telling her. All their businesses had been targeted apart from the restaurant.

The Rubicov gallery had valuable antiquities and works confiscated, taken as collateral. The only artists left to the gallery were minor Russian painters.

'Now Safi, this is what we would like you to do, if you are agreeable to my suggestion.' His tone remained even, calm, kindly even. 'We would like you to re-open the gallery here or in NYC. I will see to it that you receive funds to purchase works that will keep the Rubicov gallery at the forefront of the art world. With DuPont and Zak's help you will continue to build our name in the arts.'

'What will happen to Ilona, Ringo, all the people who work for you?' Safi asked. 'And will the authorities harm Anna and the rest of your family?'

Alexi smiled. 'You are a good person, Safi. This is why Sasha loves you, and this is why I trust you. As far as we know, their jobs are secure for now. Ilona will have to run the gallery in Moscow as best she can until she is able to persuade the authorities to return the priceless Russian works. This is an excellent opportunity for you to open another gallery, there will be limitless funds. The restaurants have not been touched and we have managed to use them to help us deplete our business in Russia. The gallery will do the same.'

Not being able to digest everything Alexi had told her about the businesses, she was not able to understand the finer points, or the complications the family were involved with. But she needed to know that Sasha would be free to join her where ever she was, she didn't think she could realistically cope without him in her life indefinitely.

'Surely the Russian authorities can't keep him prisoner without proof, I know they can, but please tell me Mika will be able to use his influence to have Sasha released, please Alexi I, don't think I can cope without Sasha beside me.'

'Mika has left Russia, he is now in Europe. Anna has managed to leave with Bernard, too. This is a very dangerous time in our country, not safe for rich people. They find all ways to take our money and livelihood, especially if they do not get a share. The Rubicov's look after all family and extended family. It was a big mistake not to include the government in our deals. Sasha will pay for this, now.'

'Alexi, please don't tell me Sasha won't be released. I cannot bear this. What will I do! Oh God, please. I don't think it will be possible for me to continue as if he does not exist. I can't see how it will work without Sasha by my side. I am not a Rubicov yet. It's not fair to Yvetta for me to run the gallery, she is family, I am not.' She knew she should stop talking, but she couldn't help herself, the Rubicov's did not realise she had some idea of the Yvetta problem.

Alexi understood how shaken Safi was. What he needed Safi to understand was that the family, in turn, needed her. Yvetta was not able to run Rubicov galleries, and there was no one else they could trust. Alexi needed to keep Safi close, not only for the benefit of the Rubicov Gallery (which she had done so much to improve), but for Sasha, who loved her more than Alexi had seen him love anyone. It would be too much for Sasha if she vanished from his life now. Alexi was afraid that this would break Sasha, who, despite his outward demeanour of strength, was more fragile than anyone cared to admit. 'You are exhausted, Safi. I think it's best if we continue this discussion later, when you have rested.'

Safi lay on her bed, her mind racing. Her parents were in Australia; it made no sense involving them at this stage. She would have to explain Sasha's absence at some point. Now she understood why he had not called. But she needed to hear his voice, to ask was he okay, was he hurt, was he hungry? He must feel desperate. Grabbing her pillow, she put it over her face as she felt tears stinging the corner of her eyes. It dawned on her that it might be years before he was free. She felt an ache in her chest and a searing pain. God, was she suffering a heart attack? Who could she talk to? She needed to yell, cry, do something to help her deal with what was happening. Alexi was all business, so calm and composed, but she knew he was suffering, he hid it well, for her sake. Where was Valentina? Surely she had not left him alone at such a terrible time. Her mind raced from one thought to another, until exhaustion set in. Her body felt like a stone, heavy with fatigue as she drifted off into a fitful sleep.

Sasha had managed to get Safi out of Moscow before all hell broke loose. Mika had warned him that the government had started to clamp down on various companies in Moscow and they had heard through Mika's contacts in the government that the Rubicov family were a target in their sights.

Warnings had come down the line to take TV stations off the air. Other stations that the government disproved of had finished their run, thanks in large part to government pressure. This had not pleased the media and political establishment just before an election. Chat show hosts had become increasingly brave and outspoken, angry their programs were coming to an end.

The gas and oil industry were in the process of being broken up and sold off. The deal had not pleased the government and Sasha had been apprehended and warned to involve government officials before the deal was sealed and signed. But Sasha knew this would not work. The family would be at a disadvantage, the deal would not be closed in time for them to get top dollar, to suit the government, the gas lines would be disrupted, frustrating the deal.

He had gone ahead and closed the deal. His family came first – this was the Rubicov philosophy, their animating principle, what held them together and elevated them high above the competition. They had worked hard and been loyal to each other and their employees and customers. He was not going to allow their profits to be siphoned off by the government; making a bad deal was not in their blood.

Sasha found himself deep underground stuck in a tiny cell, somewhere in a building he had no knowledge of. Days had gone by. He was no longer sure what day of the week it was. He refused to sign papers without a lawyer present. But a lawyer was not forthcoming. He found himself imprisoned within a contradiction that was itself a lose-lose proposition. Without his signature he would lose, the deal he had set up selling off part of the gas pipeline near the Ukraine border to an oligarch from the Ukraine, which was in itself a dangerous enterprise. The former Russian satellite was at logger heads with Russia for keeping the gas prices too high. If he did sign a deal with Russia, the Ukrainian deal would fall apart and the pipeline would be diverted. This meant that his freedom would hang in the balance – with or without the Ukrainian deal. He would be brought to trial and sentenced. It could take months or years; it was up to him, unless he could work out a deal that suited the Rubicov family with the Russians, that satisfied Putin.

Mika had left, but not before warning Anna and his cousins, who had all taken trips at a convenient time and would not be returning. Sasha felt helpless. All he could do was hope things would improve with time, and he would hopefully be allowed to plead his case, unless they worked out a deal with Mika and, Putin accepted his signature as proof, of their loyalty to Russia. If not he would have to find something to satisfy Putin and his plutocratic henchmen, his father and the family would be using all their political clout, calling anyone in positions of power that they had any degree of influence with, but the final deal would be Sasha's to make.

Sasha knew Safi would be desperate to find him. He hoped Alexi would do all he could to keep her involved with the family until he could join her, but how long would she wait? He could not expect her to wait forever. If only he could speak to her hear her voice, reassure her, comfort her, he truly loved Safi with all his heart, even if he had on occasion been less then faithful, his heart belonged to Safi and always would

DuPont had not been able to speak with Alexi or Safi; both of them were out of reach. He had laid the groundwork to apprehend Fritzi, but he needed Alexi's advice before the deal went ahead, and the fake artefact entered the marketplace. Only known to a select group of people, a red flag would signal should the item appear on the market for sale. A data base at the international level would flag up a work painting or artefact.

More than 50,000 were on the data base and countries sent notification or pictures of the art work in question. If the art work is of priceless value to that particular country Interpol would be involved, most stolen artworks crossed borders. Some were stolen to order for unknown buyers and destinations, never to see the light of day again, others were passed on through criminal operatives to buyers. It was a lucrative market, stolen works were uncovered in lofts, even caves where wars had been fought and ancient works looted.

The buyers had made contact. The authorities had been notified through Dieter the appraiser. The sting had been set in motion to catch Fritzi and the criminals she was working for.

DuPont's office had been rigged with listening devices. Nothing had been left to chance. The money would be tracked down after the sale. The buyers were encouraged to put the artefact back on the market if they wanted to make a killing.

They were initially kept in the dark about the fake sale, but their money would be going into an account set up by the authorities to appear genuine to Fritzi and her people. When Fritzi tracked the money, it would appear to be in her account. The authorities had to hope the money would remain in the fake account until the sting had gone through. This depended on Fritzi's gang's greed, and whether they introduced another buyer, making a double killing when the fake was back on the market.

Seeing a call-back from Alexi, DuPont lifted his receiver with relief. Exchanging their usual greeting, Alexi was keen to get to the crux of the call. He had little time for much else in his life. He slept little and, for the first time, stress was taking its toll on his health. His sole reason for being right now was to work on a plan to free Sasha from being incarcerated indefinitely in a Russian prison. It was not Sasha, but the Rubicov family, being punished Alexi felt as though he had aged twenty years over the last week – and he could not even imagine how Sasha must feel. He shuddered thinking about his son and heir.

DuPont filled Alexi in on the plan they had concocted with Safi's help. Alexi could not help smiling to himself – and how long it had been since last he smiled! indeed, he had forgotten how it felt to smile; it felt good! – she was becoming more of an asset to his family every moment of every day. In Safi, Sasha had displayed his typical, shrewd, solid good taste – now if only Sasha kept his head down and got out of prison in one piece. Never had he been more pleased to have this English, non-Russian in his family, she had brought them sanity, where madness so often reigned freely. She may even prove the key to locking up the awful Fritzi chapter of their lives. Alexi viewed Safi as goodness and light, where Fritzi to him was darkness and evil.

Alexi desperately wanted Fritzi caught, even though he had other, more pressing, matters to resolve. Fritzi had been a pain in the neck for long enough. After his conversation with DuPont, he called Mika to fill him in. Mika was living in Florida, only a few hours' flight away, from DuPont in New York and he wanted Mika and Kolya in on the Fritzi arrest.

No longer living in Russia, Mika was only able to follow news of Sasha's incarceration in dribs and drabs. He had exhausted all avenues he had called on for political favours. He had promised he would free Sasha at any cost. Alexi was frustrated, angry with himself and, Mika for leaving the final signing to Sasha and Mika agreed, he should have remained with his brother. Now his father needed him in Manhattan to make sure Fritzi was, apprehended either by the Rubicov's which he preferred, or by the authorities. His plan to rid them of Fritzi would have to wait, if Interpol was involved. Either way both problems were pressing. His father would never agree to walk away from their deal with the Russian's. The Ukrainian oligarch involved, in the deal was a problem, but the Russian oligarch had brought him in, for his own needs, to complete the sale.

If Fritzi's criminal syndicate could be handed to the Russian authorities on a plate, it may help Sasha's case, The Prison system would save face for allowing her to escape. Mika eased his father's concerns and frazzled nerves with this scenario. Mika hoped they were not shooting in the dark; they had few cards left to play. He could not bear the thought of Fritzi outsmarting them again; at this point, there was not much left of their pride for her to take. Money and prestige was one thing, but pride was something else altogether. Right now, Mika felt exhausted of all of these assets. Every moment that Sasha was held captive in a country where the leader was more like Caesar, and Russia was becoming more corrupt than Rome before it went up in flames, was a chance worth taking.

Yvonne Spektor was born in South Africa but moved to the UK in the 1970s. The Royal Academy of Arts named her Woman Artist of the Year in 2002. She lives in London with her husband Ken and cockapoo Shandy.

Printed in Great Britain
by Amazon